GORKY
PARK
AND
NIGHT WING

Also by Martin Cruz Smith

Martin Cruz Smith lives in California with his wife and three children.

MARTIN CRUZ SMITH

GORKY PARK

AND

NIGHT WING

PAN BOOKS

Gorky Park first published in Great Britain 1981 by Collins.
First published by Pan Books 1982
Night Wing first published 1985 by Andre Deutsch Limited.
First published by Pan Books 1987

This omnibus edition published 2003 by Pan Books
an imprint of Pan Macmillan Ltd
Pan Macmillan, 20 New Wharf Road, London N1 9RR
Basingstoke and Oxford
Associated companies throughout the world
www.macmillan.com

ISBN 0 330 42099 2

1 3 5 7 9 8 6 4 2

A CIP catalogue record for this book is available from
the British Library.

Printed and bound in Great Britain by
Mackays of Chatham plc, Chatham, Kent

GORKY PARK

For Em

Acknowledgements

I thank Anthony Astrachan, Dr Michael Baden, Anthony Bouza, Knox Burger, William Caunitz, Nancy Forbes, Dr Paul Kagansky, Anatol Milstein, John Romano, Kitty Sprague and Richard Woodley for their generous aid and encouragement during the writing of this book.

Especially, I am beholden to Alex Levin, Yuri and Ala Gendler and Anatoly Davydov. Without them Gorky Park would be a place without people.

Part One

MOSCOW

Chapter One

All nights should be so dark, all winters so warm, all headlights so dazzling.

The van jacked, stalled and quit on a drift, and the homicide team got out, militia officers cut from a pattern of short arms and low brows, wrapped in sheepskin greatcoats. The one not in uniform was a lean, pale man, the chief investigator. He listened sympathetically to the tale of the officer who had found the bodies in the snow: the man had only strayed so far from the park footpath in the middle of the night to relieve himself, then he saw them, himself half undone, as it were, and just about froze, too. The team followed the beam of the van's spotlight.

The investigator suspected the poor dead bastards were just a vodka troika that had cheerily frozen to death. Vodka was liquid taxation, and the price was always rising. It was accepted that three was the lucky number on a bottle in terms of economic prudence and desired effect. It was a perfect example of primitive communism.

Lights appeared from the opposite side of the clearing, shadow trees sweeping the snow until two black Volgas appeared. A squad of KGB agents in plainclothes were led from the cars by a squat, vigorous major called Pribluda. Together, militia and KGB stamped their feet for warmth, exhaling drafts of steam. Ice crystals spark-led on caps and collars.

The militia – the police arm of the MVD – directed traffic, chased drunks and picked up everyday corpses. The Committee for State Security – the KGB – was charged with grander, subtler responsibilities, combating foreign and domestic intriguers, smugglers, malcontents, and while the agents had uniforms, they preferred anonymous plainclothes. Major Pribluda was full of rough early-morning humor, pleased to reduce the pro-fessional animosity that strained cordial relations between the People's Militia and the Committee for State Security, all smiles until he recognized the investigator.

'Renko!'

'Exactly.' Arkady Renko started immediately for the bodies and left Pribluda to follow.

The tracks of the militiaman who had found the bodies led halfway through the snow to the telltale humps in the center of the clearing. A chief investigator should have smoked a fine brand of cigarette; Arkady lit a cheap Prima and filled his mouth with the powerful taste of it – his habit whenever he dealt with the dead. There were three bodies, as the militiaman said. They lay peacefully, even artfully, under their thawing crust of ice, the center one on its back, hands folded as if for a religious funeral, the other two turned, arms out under the ice like flanking emblems on embossed writing paper. They were wearing ice skates.

Pribluda shouldered Arkady aside. 'When I am satis-fied questions of state security are not involved, then you begin.'

4

'Security? Major, we've got three drunks in a public park—'

The major was already waving in one of his agents with a camera. With each picture the snow flashed blue and the bodies levitated. The camera was foreign and developed the pictures almost instantaneously. Proudly the photographer showed a photo to Arkady. The three bodies were lost in the flash's reflection from the snow.

'What do you think?'

'Very fast.' Arkady handed the photo back. The snow was being tramped down all around the corpses. Exasperated, he smoked. He ran his long fingers through lank black hair. He noticed that neither the major nor his photographer had thought to wear boots. Maybe wet feet would send the KGB on its way. As for the bodies, he expected to find an empty bottle or two nearby under the snow. Over his shoulder, beyond the Donskoy Monastery, the night was fading. He saw Levin, the militia pathologist, watching contemptuously from the edge of the clearing.

'The bodies look like they've been here a long time,' Arkady said. 'In another half hour our specialists can uncover them and examine them in the light.'

'Someday this will be you.' Pribluda pointed to the nearest body.

Arkady wasn't sure he'd heard the man correctly. Bits of ice glimmered in the air. He couldn't have said that, he decided. Pribluda's face turned in and out of the light of the headlights, a card half up a sleeve, eyes small and dark as pips. Suddenly he was discarding his gloves.

'We're not here to be taught by you.' Pribluda straddled the bodies and began scooping away dog-fashion, throwing snow left and right.

A man thinks he is hardened to death; he has walked into hot kitchens covered from floor to ceiling in blood, is an expert, knows that in the summer people seem ready to explode with blood; he even prefers winter's stiffs. Then a new death mask pops out of the snow. The chief investigator had never seen a head like this before; he thought he would never forget the sight. He didn't know yet that it was the central moment of his life.

'It's murder,' Arkady said.

Pribluda was unperturbed. At once he was brushing snow from the other heads. They were the same as the first. Then he straddled the middle body and pounded its frozen overcoat until it cracked and he peeled it open, and he cracked and peeled open the dress underneath.

'No matter.' He laughed. 'You can still tell she's a woman.'

'She was shot,' Arkady said. Between her breasts, which were dead-white, nipples and all, was a black entry wound. 'You're destroying evidence, Major.'

Pribluda cracked open the coats of the other two bodies. 'Shot, all shot!' He exulted like a grave robber.

Pribluda's photographer illuminated his progress in flashes of Pribluda's hands lifting stiff hair, digging a lead slug out of a mouth. Arkady noticed that besides the mutilation of the heads, the three victims also all missed the last joints of their fingers, their fingerprints.

'The men shot through the skull as well,' Pribluda washed his hands in the snow. 'Three bodies, that's a lucky number, Investigator. Now that I've done the dirty work for you we're even. Enough,' he ordered the photographer. 'We're going.'

'You always do the dirty work, Major,' Arkady said when the photographer had trudged away.

'What do you mean?'

'Three people shot and carved up in the snow? That's your kind of work, Major. You don't want me to investigate this. Who knows where it could lead?'

'Where it could lead?'

'Things get out of hand, Major. Remember? Why don't you and your men take over the investigation now, and I and my men go home?'

'There's no evidence I can see of a crime against the state. So you have a case a little more complicated than usual, that's all.'

'Complicated by someone tearing the evidence apart.'

'My report and photographs will go to your office' – Pribluda delicately tugged on his gloves – 'so you will have the benefit of my labor.' He raised his voice so that everyone around the clearing would hear him. 'Of course, if you do uncover anything relating to a possible offense concerning the Committee for State Security, you will have the prosecutor inform me immediately. You understand, Investigator Renko? Whether you spend a year or ten years, the minute you learn something you'll call.'

'I understand perfectly,' Arkady answered as loudly. 'You have our complete cooperation.'

Hyenas, crows, blowflies, worms, the investigator thought as he watched Pribluda's cars back away from the clearing. Night creatures. Dawn was coming up; he could almost feel an acceleration in the roll of the earth to the rising sun. He lit another cigarette to get the taste of Pribluda out of his mouth. Filthy habit – like drinking, another state industry. Everything was a state industry, himself included. Even the snow flowers were starting to show at the least prompting of morning. At the edge of the clearing, the militiamen still gawked. They'd seen those masks popping out of the snow.

'It's our case,' Arkady announced to his men. 'Don't you think we should do something about it?'

He got them moving at least to cordon off the area, and had the sergeant radio from the van for more men, shovels and metal detectors. A little sham of organization never failed to hearten the troops, he felt.

'So we're—'

'We're carrying on, Sergeant. Until further notice.'

'Lovely morning,' Levin sneered.

The pathologist was older than the rest, a caricature Jew in the disguise of a militia captain. He had no sympathy for Tanya, the team's *in situ* specialist, who couldn't take her eyes from the faces. Arkady took her aside and suggested she start a base-line sketch of the clearing, then attempt a sketch of the position of the bodies.

'Before or after they were assaulted by the good major?' Levin asked.

'Before,' Arkady said. 'As if the major were never here.'

The team biologist, a doctor, began searching for blood samples in the snow around the corpses. It was going to be a lovely day, Arkady thought. On the far embankment across the Moskva River he saw the first stroke of light on the Defense Ministry buildings, the only moment of the day when those endless, dun-colored walls had a touch of life. All around the clearing the trees emerged into the dawn as wary as deer. Now snow flowers started to show red and blue, bright as ribbons. A day when all winter seemed ready to melt.

'Fuck.' He looked at the bodies again.

The team photographer asked whether the KGB hadn't already taken pictures.

'Yes, and they were fine for souvenirs, I'm sure,' Arkady said, 'but not for police work.'

The photographer, flattered, laughed.

Good, Arkady thought, laugh louder.

A plainclothes detective named Pasha Pavlovich showed up in the investigator's office car, a five-year-old Moskvich, not a sleek Volga like Pribluda's. Pasha was half Tartar, a muscular romantic sporting a dark bowsprit pompadour.

'Three bodies, two male, one female.' Arkady got into the car. 'Frozen. Maybe a week old, maybe a month, five months. No papers, no effects, nothing. All shot through the heart and two through the head as well. Go take a look at the faces.'

Arkady waited in the car. It was hard to believe that winter was over in the middle of April; usually it hung on grimly into June. It could have hung on to these horrors a little longer. Except for yesterday's thaw, a militiaman's full bladder and the way the moonlight hit the snow, Arkady could be in his bed, his eyes closed.

Pasha returned pumped up with outrage. 'What kind of madman could do that?'

Arkady motioned for him to get back in the car.

'Pribluda was here,' he said when Pasha was inside.

Saying the words, he watched the subtle change in the detective, the little shrinking created by a few words, the glance out to the clearing and back to Arkady. The three dead souls out there were not so much a terrible crime as they were a sticky problem. Or both, because Pasha was one of the good ones, and he already seemed more conscience-stricken than anyone else would be.

'It's not our kind of case,' Arkady added. 'We do some work here and they'll take it away from us, don't worry.'

'In Gorky Park, though.' Pasha was upset.

'Very strange. Just do what I tell you and we'll be fine. Drive over to the park militia station and get maps of the skating paths. Get lists of all the militiamen and food vendors who operated in this part of the park this winter, also of any public-order volunteers who could have been snooping around. The main thing is to make a big production.' Arkady got out of the car and leaned in the window. 'By the way, is there another detective assigned to me?'

'Fet.'

'I don't know him.'

Pasha spat on the snow and said, 'There was a little bird, who repeated what he heard—'

'Okay.' There was bound to be an informer in this kind of case; not only did the investigator bow to the fact, he welcomed it. 'We'll be pulled off this mess that much sooner, with everyone's cooperation.'

When Pasha had gone two trucks rolled in bearing

militia trainees and shovels. Tanya had the clearing marked in grids so that the snow could be shoveled meter by meter without losing sight of where evidence was found, though Arkady hardly expected any this long after the murders. Appearance was his goal. With a grand enough farce, Pribluda might call before the day was out. At any rate, the activity bolstered the militiamen. They were basically traffic cops and were happy even if the traffic consisted of themselves. Otherwise, they were not generally happy. The militia enlisted farm boys right out of the Army, seducing them with the incredible promise of living in Moscow, that residence denied even to nuclear scientists. Fantastic! As a result, Muscovites regarded the militia as some sort of occupying army of shitkickers and brutes. Militiamen came to see their co-citizens as decadent, depraved and probably Jewish. Still, no one ever returned to the farm.

The sun was really up now, alive, not the ghost disk that had haunted winter. The trainees dawdled in the warm breath of the wind, eyes averted from the center of the clearing.

Why Gorky Park? The city had bigger parks to leave bodies in – Izmailovo, Dzerzhinsky, Sokolniki. Gorky Park was only two kilometers long and less than a kilometer across at its widest point. It was the first park of the Revolution, though, the favorite park. South, its narrow end nearly reached the university. North, only a bend of the river cut off a view of the Kremlin. It was the place everyone came to: clerks to eat lunch, grandmothers with babies, boys with girls. There were a Ferris wheel, fountains, children's theaters, walks and club pavilions hidden all through the grounds. In winter there were four skating rinks and skating paths.

Detective Fet arrived. He was nearly as young as the trainees, with steel-rimmed glasses and blue ball-bearing eyes.

'You are in charge of the snow.' Arkady gestured to the growing piles. 'Melt it and search it.'

'In which laboratory would the senior investigator want this process carried out?' Fet asked.

'Oh, I think some hot water right where they are would do the job.' Because this might not sound impressive enough, Arkady added, 'I want no snowflake unturned.'

Arkady took Fet's buff-and-red militia car and drove off, crossing the Krimsky Bridge to the north side of the city. The frozen river ached, ready to break. It was nine o'clock, two hours since he'd been roused from bed, no breakfast yet, just cigarettes. Coming off the bridge, he waved his red ID at the militiaman directing traffic, and sped through stopped cars. A privilege of rank.

Arkady had few illusions about his work. He was senior homicide investigator, a specialist in murder in a country that had little well-organized crime and no talent for finesse. The usual victim of the ordinary Russian was the woman he slept with, and then when he was drunk and hit her over the head with an ax – probably ten times before he got it right. To be blunt, the criminals Arkady arrested were ordinarily drunks first and murderers second, and far better drunks than murderers. There were few more dangerous positions, he had distilled from experience, than to be the best friend of or married to a drunk, and the entire country was drunk half the time.

Icicles hung wet from gutters. The investigator's car scattered pedestrians. But it was better than two days before, when traffic and people were shades lumbering through a hive of steam. He looped around the Kremlin on Marx Prospekt and turned up Petrovka Street three blocks to the yellow six-story complex that was Moscow Militia Headquarters, where he parked in the basement garage and rode an elevator to the third floor.

The Militia Operation Room was regularly described by the newspapers as 'the very brain center of Moscow, ready to respond within seconds to reports of accidents or crimes in the safest city in the world.' One wall was an enormous map of Moscow divided into thirty borough divisions and studded with lights for one hundred thirty-five precinct stations. Ranks of radio switches surrounded a communications desk where officers contacted patrol cars ('This is Volga calling fifty-nine') or, by code name, precincts ('This is Volga calling Omsk'). There was no other room in Moscow so ordered and restful, so planned, the creation of electronics and an elaborate winnowing process. There were quotas. A militiaman on the beat was expected to report officially only so many crimes; otherwise he would put his fellow militiamen on their beats in the ludicrous position of reporting no crimes at all. (Everyone recognized there had to be *some* crime.) Then the precincts one by one trimmed their statistics to achieve the proper downturn in homicide, assault and rape. It was an efficiently optimistic system that demanded tranquillity and got it. On the great map only one precinct light blinked, indicating that the capital city of seven million inhabitants had passed twenty-four hours with but a single significant act of violence reported. The light was in Gorky Park. Watching this light from the center of the Operating Room was the commissioner of militia, a massive, flat-faced man with a chest of service ribbons on his general's gold-braided gray uniform. With him were a pair of colonels, deputy commissioners. In his street clothes Arkady was slovenly.

'Comrade General, Chief Investigator Renko reporting,' Arkady said, according to ritual. Had he shaved? he asked himself. He resisted the temptation to run his hand over his chin.

The general gave the faintest of nods. A colonel said, 'The general knows you are a specialist in homicides. He believes in specialization and modernization.'

'The general wants to know your initial reaction to this matter,' the other colonel said. 'What are the chances of an early resolution?'

'With the world's finest militia and the support of the people, I feel confident we will succeed in identifying and apprehending the guilty parties,' Arkady answered forcefully.

'Then why,' the first colonel asked, 'has there not even been a bulletin to all precincts for information about the victims?'

'The bodies had no papers, and being frozen, it's difficult to say when they died. Also there was some mutilation. There will be no identification of the usual order.'

14

After a glance at the general, the other colonel asked, 'There was a representative of State Security at the scene?'

'Yes.'

The general finally spoke: 'In Gorky Park. That I don't understand.'

In the commissary, Arkady breakfasted on a sweet roll and coffee, then fed a two-kopek piece into a public phone and called. 'Is Comrade Teacher Renko there?'

'Comrade Renko is occupied in a conference with a committee from the district party.'

'We were going to have lunch. Tell Comrade Renko . . . tell her that her husband will see her tonight.'

For the next hour, he pulled the records on young Detective Fet, satisfying himself that the man had only worked on cases of special interest to the KGB. Arkady left headquarters through the courtyard fronting on Petrovka Street. Militia clerks and women returning from long shopping breaks picked their way around the limousines that filled the circular driveway. He waved at the guard box and walked to the forensic labs.

At the autopsy-room door Arkady stopped to light a cigarette.

'You going to puke?' Levin looked up when he heard the match strike.

'Not if it will interfere with your work. Keep in mind, I'm not getting extra like some people.' Arkady was reminding Levin that pathologists were paid 25 percent more than ordinary doctors who worked on the living. It was 'hazard pay' because nothing was so dangerously alive with toxic flora as a corpse.

'There's always a chance of infection,' Levin said. 'Just one slip of a knife—'

'They're frozen. The only thing they can give you is a cold. Besides, you never slip. For you, death's just a bonus.' Arkady inhaled until his nose and lungs were thoroughly corrupted with smoke.

Ready, he entered an atmosphere of formaldehyde. The three victims may have been wildly dissimilar as personalities; as cadavers they were uniquely three of a kind. Albino-white, just a tinge of lividity around the buttocks and shoulders, skin raised in fat goose bumps, a hole above each heart, fingers without tips and heads without faces. From scalp line to chin, and from ear to ear, all flesh was cut and removed, leaving masks of bone and black blood. The eyes had also been dug out. That was how they had come out of the snow. Levin's assistant, an Uzbek with a runny nose, was adding new embellishments, cutting into the chest cavities with a rotary saw. The Uzbek kept putting the saw down to warm his hands. A good-sized body could stay like ice for a week.

'How do you solve murders if you can't stand the sight of dead people?' Levin asked Arkady.

'I arrest live people.'

'That's something to be proud of?'

Arkady collected the preliminary charts from the tables and read:

Male. Europoid. Hair brown. Eyes unknown. Age app. 20–25. Time of death from 2 wks. to 6 mos. Frozen before any significant decomposition could occur. Cause of death, gunshot wounds. Soft facial tissue and third phalanges of both hands missing due to mutilation. 2 possible fatal wounds. Wound 'A' fired at contact at mouth fracturing from upper jaw, bullet traveling at 45 degrees through brain and exiting high in posterior of skull. Wound 'B' fired 2 cms. left of sternum into heart, rupturing aorta. Bullet marked GP1–B recovered loose in chest cavity.

Male. Europoid. Hair brown. Eyes unknown. Age app. 20–30. Time of death app. 2 wks. to 6 mos. Soft facial tissue and third phalanges lost to mutilation. 2 possible fatal wounds. Wound 'A' fired at contact at mouth, fracturing upper jaw and breaking off incisors, bullet traveling at diverted angle through brain scoring inside posterior of skull starting 5 cms. above meningeal groove. Bullet marked GP2–A recovered loose in skull cavity. [GP2–A was the slug Pribluda had dug out.] Second wound 3 cms. left of sternum through heart region. Bullet marked GP2–B recovered from inside left shoulder blade.

Female. Europoid. Hair brown. Eyes unknown. Age app. 20–23. Time of death app. 2 wks. to 6 mos. Cause of death gunshot wound 3 cms. left of sternum into heart, rupturing right ventricle and superior vena cava, exiting from back between third and fourth ribs 2 cms. left of spine. Heads and hands mutilated as males GP1 and GP2. Bullet marked GP3 found inside dress behind exit wound. No signs of pregnancy.

Arkady leaned against a wall, smoking until he was almost dizzy, concentrating on the papers in his hands.

'How did you get the ages?' he asked.

'Lack of wear on the teeth.'

'Then you've done a dental chart.'

'Done, but it won't help much. One steel boiler-plate molar in the second male.' Levin shrugged.

The Uzbek handed over odontology charts, along with a box of broken incisors notated as the bullets had been.

'One's missing,' Arkady counted the teeth.

'Pulverized. What's left is in another container. But there are some items of real interest that are not on the preliminary report, if you'd care to have a look.'

Clam-gray cement walls, stains around the floor drains, aching fluorescent lights, white flesh and pubic ruffs came into focus. The investigator's trick was to see and not see, but – Three dead people. Look at us, the masks said. Who killed us?

'As you see,' Levin said, 'the first male shows a heavy bone structure with well-developed musculature. The second male shows a slight physique and an old compound fracture of the left shin. Most interesting.' Levin produced a feathery tuft between his fingers. 'The second male dyed his hair. Its natural color is red. It will all be in the complete report.'

'That I'll look forward to.' Arkady left.

Levin caught up at the elevator and slipped into the car with Arkady. He had been a chief surgeon in Moscow until Stalin shook Jewish doctors out of the trees. He held his emotions like gold in a fist; a sympathetic expression on him was out of place, a tic.

'There must be another investigator to handle this,' he told Arkady. 'Anyone else. Whoever cut those faces

18

and hands knew what he was doing. He'd done it before. This is the Kliazma River all over again.'

'If you're right, the major will take over the case by tomorrow. They won't let it get so far this time, that's all. Why are you so worried?'

'Why aren't you?' Levin opened the doors. Before they shut, he repeated, 'The Kliazma River all over again.'

Ballistics was a room with most of its space occupied by a four-meter-long water tank. Arkady left the bullets and went on to the Central Forensic Laboratory, a hall room of parquet floors, marble-topped tables, green chalkboards and knee-high ashtrays embraced by lead nymphs. Separate tables were set aside for each victim's clothes, and different teams worked over the damp remains. In charge was a militia colonel with slick hair and plump hands called Lyudin.

'Not much but blood so far.' Lyudin beamed.

Other technicians looked up at the investigator's arrival. One of Lyudin's men was vacuuming pockets; another brushed crust from ice skates. Behind them was a pharmacopoeia colorful as candy in glass jars – reagents, iodine crystals, silver nitrate solutions, agar gels.

'What about the origin of the clothes?' Arkady asked. He wanted to see good-quality foreign merchandise, signs that the dead trio were criminals involved in the kind of black-market smuggling the KGB has to investigate.

'Look.' Lyudin directed Arkady's attention to a label inside one of the jackets. The word on the label was 'jeans'. 'Domestic thread. All of it junk, what you could buy in any store here. Look at the bra.' He gestured to another table. 'Not French, not even German.'

Lyudin, Arkady saw, wore a wide, hand-painted tie inside his open lab smock. He noticed it because wide ties were not available to the general public. The colonel was pleased with Arkady's frustration over the victim's clothes; forensic technicians became important in direct ratio to an investigator's frustration.

'Of course, we have yet to employ the gas chromatograph, spectrometer, neutron-activation sampling, but that kind of testing is very expensive for three separate sets of clothing.' Lyudin raised his hands helplessly. 'Not to mention the computer time.'

A big production, Arkady reminded himself. 'Colonel, there is no budget on justice,' he said.

'True, true, but if I could have something signed, authorization to conduct a full gamut of tests, you see.'

Arkady ended up signing a blank authorization. Colonel Lyudin would fill it with unnecessary tests he wouldn't conduct and then sell the unused chemicals privately. He was an expert technician, though. Arkady had no right to complain.

The technician in the ballistics room was shuttling bullets through a comparison microscope when Arkady returned.

'See?'

Arkady leaned over. One slug from Gorky Park was under the left eyepiece, a second under the right, the two fields of vision abutting. One slug was heavily damaged from its transit through bone, but both had the same left-hand rifling, and as Arkady rotated them he picked out a dozen points of similarity in lands and grooves.

'The same gun.'

'All the same gun,' the technician agreed. 'All five. The 7.65 caliber is strange to me.'

Arkady had brought only four slugs from Levin. He removed the two slugs from the microscope. The one in his right hand was unlabeled.

'Just came in from the park,' the technician said. 'Metal detectors found it.'

Three people killed in an open area at close range from the front with a single gun. Shot and then cut open.

Pribluda. The Kliazma River.

The Moscow town prosecutor's office was south of the river on Novokuznetskaya Street in a section of nineteenth-century shops. The office building itself was divided down the middle into a yellow two-story side and a gray three-story side. The investigators in the yellow half looked out onto a sad and tiny park where citizens called for interrogation could sit and despair. In the park were a flower bed the size of a grave and empty flower urns on swivel bases. From the other side of the building, the larger side, the prosecutor looked down on a playground.

Arkady entered the investigators' door and took the stairs two at a time to the second floor. Chief Investigators Chuchin (Special Cases) and Belov (Industry) were in the hall.

'Iamskoy wants to see you,' Chuchin warned.

Arkady ignored him and went on to his office at the back. Belov followed. Belov was the oldest investigator and owned what he called 'an indefatigable affection' for Arkady. The office was three meters by four, brown walls around pine furniture and one double-cased window, embellished by street and transport maps and an unusual photograph of Lenin in a lawn chair.

'You're hard on Chuchin,' Belov said.

'He's a pig.'

'He does necessary work.' Belov scratched a balding crew cut. 'We all specialize.'

'I never said pigs weren't necessary.'

'My very point. He deals with social garbage.'

Vsevolod Belov of infinite baggy suits. A mind scored by the Great Patriotic War like a wall once raked by machine-gun fire. Fingers webbed with age. Great-hearted and an instinctive reactionary. When Belov muttered about 'Chinese bandits', Arkady knew there was a mobilization at the border. When Belov mentioned 'kikes', synagogues were shut. When in doubt on any social issue, he could go to Belov.

'Uncle Seva, who dyes his hair and wears a sports jacket with a false foreign label?'

'Bad luck,' Belov commiserated. 'That sounds like musicians or hooligans. Punk rock. Jazz. That sort. You won't get any cooperation from them.'

'Amazing. Hooligans, then, is your opinion.'

'You'd know better than I with your intelligence. But, yes, such a masquerade as dyeing the hair and the false label indicates hooligans or someone with strong musical or hooliganistic tendencies.'

'Three of them shot with the same gun. Sliced up with a knife: no papers. With Pribluda first to sniff over the bodies. Does that remind you of anything?'

Belov pulled his chin in and his face wrinkled like a fan.

'Personal differences between the organs of justice should not interfere with the greater work,' he said.

'You remember?'

'I think' – Belov's voice strayed – 'that with hooligans there was probably a gang war involved.'

'What gang wars? Do you know of any such gang wars in Moscow? Siberia or Armenia, perhaps, but here?'

'I know,' Belov insisted, 'that an investigator who avoids speculation and keeps his eyes on the facts is never misled.'

Arkady let his hands fall flat on his desk and smiled. 'Thank you, Uncle. You know I always value your opinion.'

'That's better.' Relief carried Belov to the door. 'Have you spoken to your father lately?'

'No.' Arkady spread the preliminary autopsy reports over his desk and pulled his typewriter stand close.

'Give him my regards when you do. Don't forget.'

'I won't.'

Alone, Arkady typed his preliminary investigation report:

Moscow Town Prosecutor's Office, Moscow, RSFSR.
  Crime – Homicide. Victims – 2 Unidentified Men,

1 Unidentified Woman. Location – Gorky Cultural and Recreational Park, Octobryskaya region. Reporting Party – Militia.

At 0630, a militiaman making his rounds of the southwest corner of Gorky Park found what appeared to be three bodies in a clearing app. 40 meters north of the footpath on a line with Donskoy Street and the river. At 0730, militia officers, officers of State Security and this investigator examined three frozen bodies.

Because of their frozen state it is possible now only to state that the victims were killed sometime this winter. All three were shot through the heart. The two men were also shot through the head.

5 bullets recovered all came from the same 7.65-mm. weapon. No cartridges were recovered.

All the victims wore ice skates. No papers, change or other items were found in their clothes. Identification will be hampered by mutilation that removed the flesh of the face and fingertips. Reports – serology, odontology, ballistics, chromatography, autopsy and further on-site examination – are forthcoming, and a search of persons with possible knowledge of victims or the park site has begun.

It may be assumed to be a premeditated crime. Three people were killed quickly by a single weapon, all personal effects removed in the middle of the city's most crowded park, extreme measures carried out to hinder physical identification.

Note: One of the dead men dyed his hair and

another wore a jacket with a false foreign label, possible indications of antisocial activity.

Renko, A. V.

Chief Investigator

While Arkady read this flimsy familiarization report through, Detectives Pavlovich and Fet knocked and entered, Pasha carrying a briefcase.

'I'll be back in a minute.' Arkady put his jacket back on. 'You know what to do, Pasha.'

Arkady had to go down to the street to enter the prosecutor's side of the building. A prosecutor was a figure of unusual authority. He oversaw all criminal investigations, representing both state and defendant. Arrests had to meet the prosecutor's approval, court sentences came under his review and appeals came from his initiation. A prosecutor entered civil suits at his pleasure, determined the legality of local-government directives and, at the same time, decided the million-ruble suits and countersuits when one factory delivered nuts rather than bolts to another factory. No matter how great or small the case, criminals, judges, mayors and industrial managers all answered to him. He answered only to the prosecutor general.

Prosecutor Andrei Iamskoy was at his desk. His skull was shaved pink, a startling contrast to his uniform, dark blue with a general's gold star, especially tailored for his oversized chest and arms. Flesh had accumulated over the bridge of his nose and cheekbones, and his lips were thick and chalky.

'Wait.' He went on reading a paper on his desk.

Arkady stood on a green carpet three meters from the desk. On the paneled walls were photographs of Iamskoy heading a delegation of prosecutors at a ceremonial meeting with General Secretary Brezhnev, shaking hands with the General Secretary, speaking to an international conference of prosecutors in Paris, swimming at Silver Grove, and – absolutely unique – the remarkable *Pravda* portrait of him arguing an appeal before the Collegium of the Supreme Court for a worker wrongly convicted of murder. Behind the live prosecutor was a window guarded by maroon curtains of Italian velvet. Large brown freckles mottled Iamskoy's shining cranium, though sunlight was already fading, tucked behind the curtains.

'Yes?' Iamskoy turned the paper over and looked up. His eyes were pale, like watery diamonds. As always, his voice was so soft that a listener had to concentrate. Concentration, Arkady had decided long ago, was the key to Iamskoy.

Arkady took one long step forward to deposit his report on the desk and retreated. Concentrate: exactly who are you and what do you have to say? Define precisely what benefit you perform for society.

'Major Pribluda was there. You don't mention his name.'

'He did everything but piss on the bodies and then took off. Did he call to have me dismissed from the case?'

Iamskoy rested his eyes on Arkady. 'You are chief homicide investigator, Arkady Vasilevich. Why would he want you dismissed?'

'We had a problem with the major a short time ago.'

'What problem? The KGB stated their jurisdiction, so the matter was successfully concluded.'

'Excuse me, but today we found three young people who were executed in a public park by a skilled gunman using a 7.65-mm. pistol. The only guns Muscovites can get are Army issue, 7.62-mm. or 9-mm., nothing like the murder weapon. Also, the victims suffered mutilation. So far, my report draws no inferences.'

'Inferences of what?' Iamskoy raised his eyebrows.

'Of anything,' Arkady answered after a pause.

'Thank you,' Iamskoy said. It was his form of dismissal.

Arkady was at the door when the prosecutor spoke again as an afterthought. 'All legalities will be observed. You must overlook the exceptions, which really only prove the rule.'

Arkady bowed his head and left.

Fet and Pasha had taped up a map of Gorky Park, Levin's sketch of the death site, death photos and autopsy reports. Arkady slumped into his chair and opened a fresh pack of cigarettes. Three matches snapped before he got one to light. He put the three broken matches and the burnt one in the middle of his desk. Fet watched, frowning. Arkady got up to pull down the death photos and place them in a drawer. He didn't need to look at those faces. He returned to his chair and played with the matches.

'Do any interviews yet?'

Pasha opened a notebook. 'Ten militia officers who

don't know anything. If it comes to that, I probably skated by that clearing fifty times this winter.'

'Well, try the food vendors. Those old women notice a lot of things the militia don't.'

Fet plainly didn't agree. Arkady looked at him. With his hat off, Fet's ears stuck out at what Arkady guessed was just the right architectural angle to support the steel-rimmed glasses.

'You were there when the last bullet was found?' Arkady asked him.

'Yes, sir. GP1–A was recovered from the ground directly below where the skull of GP1, the first male, had been.'

'Fuck your mother, I'll be happy when we have some names for these corpses instead of One, Two and Three.'

Pasha bummed a cigarette from Arkady. 'Like what?' Arkady asked.

'Match?' Pasha asked.

'Gorky Park One, Gorky Park Two—' Fet began.

'Ah, come on.' Pasha shook his head. 'Thanks,' he told Arkady and exhaled. 'Gorky Park One? He's the big guy? Call him "Muscles".'

'Not literary enough,' Arkady said. ' "Beast". "Beauty" for the woman, "Beast" for the big guy, "Skinny" for the little one.'

'He really had red hair,' Pasha said. 'Red.'

' "Beauty", "Beast" and "Red". Our first major decision, Detective Fet,' Arkady said. 'Has anyone heard how Forensics is doing on those ice skates?'

'The skates could be a ruse,' Fet suggested. 'It seems very hard to believe that three people could be shot in

Gorky Park without other people hearing. The victims could have been shot elsewhere, then skates could have been put on them and they could have been carried to the park at night.'

'It is very hard to believe three people could be shot in Gorky Park without other people hearing, I agree,' Arkady said. 'But it's impossible to get ice skates on dead feet. Try it sometime. Also, the one place you wouldn't want to try to sneak three dead bodies into at *any* time is Gorky Park.'

'I only wanted to have your thoughts on that possibility,' Fet said.

'Excellent work,' Arkady assured him. 'Now let's find out what Lyudin's come up with.'

He dialed the Kiselny Street lab. On the twentieth ring, the switchboard answered and put him through to Lyudin.

'Colonel, I—' he got to say before he was disconnected. He dialed again. There was no answer at Kiselny Street. He looked at his watch. Four-twenty: time for the operators to shut down the board in preparation for leaving work at five. The detectives would want to go soon, too. Pasha to lift weights. Fet? Home to mother, or Pribluda first?

'Maybe they were shot elsewhere and carried to the park at night.' The investigator swept the matches aside.

Fet sat up. 'You just said they weren't. Also, I remember, we found the last bullet in the ground, proving they were shot there.'

'Proving the victim, dead or alive, was shot through the head there.' Arkady put one match back in the center of the desk. 'No cartridges were found. If an automatic pistol were used, the shells would have been ejected onto the ground.'

'He could have picked them up,' Fet protested.

'Why? Bullets identify a firearm as well as shells.'

'He could have fired from a distance.'

'He didn't,' Arkady said.

'Maybe he thought to pick them up because if anyone found them they'd look for a body.'

'He's carrying the gun in his coat, not waving it around.' Arkady looked aside. 'The gun and the shells in its clip are warm to begin with. The ejected shells, heated more by the ejecting gases, would melt into the snow long before the bodies were covered by snow. I'm curious, though.' He looked at Fet. 'Why do you think it was a single gunman?'

'There was a single gun.'

'There was only one gun fired so far as we know. Can you imagine how difficult it would be for a single killer to make three victims stand still at close range while he fired – unless there were other gunmen with him? Why did the victims feel their situation was so hopeless they didn't even run for help? Well, we'll catch this murderer. We've only begun, and so many things always turn up. We'll catch the fat son of a bitch.'

Fet didn't ask, Why fat?

'Anyway,' Arkady concluded, 'it's been a long day. Your shifts are up.'

Fet was first out.

'There goes our little birdie,' Pasha said as he followed.

'I hope he's a parrot.'

Alone, Arkady called headquarters on Petrovka to send a republic-wide west-of-the-Urals bulletin for information on crimes by firearm, just to keep the militia commissioner content. Then he tried calling the school again. Comrade Teacher Renko, he was told, was leading a criticism session for parents and couldn't come to the phone.

The other investigators were leaving, putting on their home-bound expressions and pulling on their coats. Their earnest coats, Arkady thought as he watched from the top of the stairs. Their better-than-a-worker's Soviet cloth. He wasn't hungry, but the activity of eating appealed to him. He felt like a walk. He got his coat and went out.

He walked south all the way to the Paveletsky train station before his legs took him into a cafeteria where there was a buffet of whitefish and potatoes awash in vinegar. Arkady moved on to the bar and ordered a beer. The other stools were occupied by railroad workers and young soldiers quietly drunk on champagne: sullen faces between malachite bottles.

A slice of bread with butter and sticky gray caviar came with Arkady's beer. 'What's this?'

'From heaven,' the manager said.

'There is no heaven.'

'But we're there now.' The manager smiled with a full set of steel teeth. His hand darted out to push the caviar closer to Arkady.

'Well, I haven't read today's paper,' Arkady conceded.

The manager's wife, a gnome in a white uniform, came out of the kitchen. When she saw Arkady, she

31

broke into a smile so powerful – it filled out her cheeks and drew attention to her lively eyes – that she seemed almost beautiful. Her husband stood proudly by her.

They were Viskov, F. N., and Viskova, I. L. In 1946 they constituted a 'center of anti-Soviet activity' by operating a rare-book store that harbored the scribblers Montaigne, Apollinaire and Hemingway. 'Interrogation with prejudice' left Viskov crippled and his wife mute (a suicide attempt with lye), and they were given what was jokingly called at the time 25-ruble notes: twenty-five years' hard labor in the camps (a humor of the time when Security and the Militia were one and the same institution). In 1956 the Viskovs were released and even offered the chance to operate another bookstore, though they declined.

'You were in charge of a cafeteria by the circus, I thought,' Arkady said.

'They found out my wife and I were both working there against regulations. She only comes in here to help on her own time.' Viskov winked. 'Sometimes the boy comes in to help as well.'

'Thanks to you,' Comrade Viskova mouthed.

God, Arkady thought, an apparatus accuses two innocent people, abducts them to slave camps, tortures them, rips out the heart of their adult lives, and then when one man from the apparatus treats them with the rudiments of decency, they are fountains of joy. What right did he have to a kind word from them? He ate his caviar, drank his beer and got out of the cafeteria as quickly as politeness allowed.

Gratitude was a dog at his heel. After a few blocks he

slowed because the hour was one of his favorites, the evening a maternal black, windows small and bright, the faces on the street bright as windows. At this time of day he felt he could have been in any Moscow of the past five centuries, and he wouldn't have been surprised by the sound of hooves in mud. In a store window shabby dolls were small, perfect Pioneers; a battery-driven Sputnik circled a moon-shaped lamp that urged 'Look to the Future!'

Back at his office, Arkady sat in front of his cabinet and went through his files. He began with crimes by firearm.

Murder. A lathe operator returns home to find his wife screwing a naval officer, and in the ensuing struggle the worker uses the officer's gun on its owner. The court took into consideration that the officer should not have been carrying a gun, that the defendant was attested by his union to be a diligent laborer, and that he repented his act. Sentence: ten years' deprivation of freedom.

Aggravated murder. Two black marketeers fall out over a division of profits and both are amazed, one fatally, when a rusty Nagurin pistol works. Profit is the aggravating circumstance. Sentence: death.

Armed assault. (Some assault.) A boy with a wooden replica of a gun removes two rubles from a drunk. Sentence: five years.

Arkady went through his straight homicide files searching for crimes he might have forgotten, murders that displayed careful planning and cool boldness. In knives, hatchets, bludgeons and manual strangulation, however, there was little care or coolness. In three years as a deputy investigator and two as chief investigator, he'd encountered fewer than five homicides that rose above childlike stupidity, or following which the murderer hadn't presented himself or herself to the militia drunkenly boastful or rueful. The Russian murderer had great faith in the inevitability of his capture, all he wanted was his moment onstage. Russians won wars because they threw themselves before tanks, which was not the right mentality for a master criminal.

Arkady gave up and shut the file.

'Boychik.' Nikitin opened the door without knocking and inserted his head, followed with his body, and sat on Arkady's desk. The chief investigator for government liaison had a round face and thinning hair, and when he was drunk his smile screwed his eyes into Oriental slits. 'Working late?'

Did Nikitin mean Arkady was working hard, too hard, futilely, successfully, that Arkady was smart, a fool? Nikitin conveyed it all.

'Like you,' Arkady said.

'I'm not working – I'm checking on you. Sometimes I think you never learned anything from me.'

Ilya Nikitin was chief homicide investigator before Arkady and, when sober, the best investigator Arkady had ever known. Except for the vodka, he would have been a prosecutor long ago, but saying 'except for the vodka' in Nikitin's case was like saying 'except for food and water'. Once a year, yellow with jaundice, he was sent to a spa in Sochi.

'You know, I always know what you're up to, Vasilev-ich. I'm always looking out for you and Zoya.'

One weekend when Arkady was away, Nikitin had tried to get Zoya into bed. On Arkady's return, Nikitin immediately got himself shipped to Sochi, from which he had daily sent long penitent letters.

'Want some coffee, Ilya?'

'Someone has to protect you from yourself. Excuse me, Vasilevich' – Nikitin insisted on using the patro-nymic in a condescending fashion – 'but I am, just maybe – I know you disagree – just a little more intelli-gent or experienced, or at least closer to some high sources than you. This is not a criticism of your record, because your record is well known and could hardly be improved.' Nikitin's head tilted to one side, grinning, a strand of wet hair sticking to his cheek, exuding hypo-crisy like an animal smell. 'It's just that you don't see the larger picture.'

'Good night, Ilya.' Arkady put on his overcoat.

'I'm only saying there are wiser heads than yours. Our purpose is to reconcile. Every day I reconcile government policy with socialist legality. A directive goes out to raze workers' houses to construct cooperative apartments that workers can't afford, a seeming breach of workers' rights. Iamskoy consults me, the Party consults me, Mayor Promislov consults me, because I know how to reconcile this seeming contradiction.'

'There is no contradiction?' Arkady led Nikitin into the hall.

'Between workers and state? This is the workers' state.

What benefits the state benefits them. By tearing down their houses we protect their rights. See? Reconciled.'

'I don't see.' Arkady locked up.

'From the correct point of view there are no contradictions,' Nikitin whispered hoarsely down the stairs. 'That's what you'll never understand.'

Arkady took an office car to the Inner Circle Highway and headed north. The Moskvich was a sluggish, underpowered car, though he wouldn't have minded owning one himself. By now the traffic was almost all taxis. His mind was on Major Pribluda, who hadn't called off the investigation yet. Ice fell out of the wheel wells ahead and exploded before his headlights.

The taxis turned toward Komsomol Square's railroad stations. Arkady continued on to Kalanchevskaya Street, No. 43, Moscow City Court, an old courthouse that, in the trick of streetlamps on brick, seemed to be actively moldering. There were seventeen People's Courts throughout the city, but serious crimes were tried in the City Court, so it had the distinction of being guarded by the Red Army. Arkady showed his ID to two teenaged soldiers on the steps. In the basement he startled a corporal asleep on a table.

'I'm going into the cage.'

'Now?' The corporal jumped up and buttoned his greatcoat.

'At your convenience.' Arkady handed over the key ring and automatic pistol the corporal had left on the table.

The cage was a metal grille enclosing the records area of the courthouse basement. Arkady pulled drawers for

December and January while the corporal watched at attention from outside the gate because a chief investigator held the equivalent rank of captain.

'Why don't you make some tea on the hot plate for both of us?' Arkady suggested.

He was looking for a stick to put up Pribluda's ass. It was one thing to have three corpses and suspect the major; it was another to find three convicts who had been remanded from the City Court to KGB custody. He went from card to card, rejecting those persons too young or too old, checking work histories and marital status. No one had missed these bodies – not union, factory or family – for months.

With a hot cup of tea he went on to February. One problem was that while major crimes – murder, assault and robbery – were all tried in City Court, certain cases the KGB had just as much interest in – those of political dissidence and social parasitism – were sometimes heard in the People's Court, where public attendance was more easily controlled. The basement walls shone with condensation. The city was laced with rivers, the Moskva, Setun, Kamenka, Sosenka, Yauza and, skirting the northern edge of the city limits, the Kliazma.

Six weeks before, two bodies had been found on a bank of the Kliazma two hundred kilometers east of Moscow near Bugolubovo, a village of potato farmers. The nearest town was Vladimir, but no one on the Vladimir prosecutor's staff would undertake the investigation; they were all 'sick'. The prosecutor general had assigned the chief homicide investigator from Moscow.

It was cold. The victims were two young men with

white faces and frosted lashes, fists stiff on the rime of a bank. Their mouths were strangely agape and their coats and chests cut open, terrible wounds that had barely bled. Levin's autopsy determined that the murderer had dug out the bullets that actually killed the victims. Levin also found flecks of rubber and red paint on the dead men's teeth, and sodium aminate in their blood, at which point Arkady understood the delicate illness which prostrated local investigators. Outside the village of Bugolubovo, invisible on maps though containing more occupants than the village, was the Vladimir Isolator, a prison for political convicts whose ideas were too infectious even for work camps, and sodium aminate was an Isolator narcotic used to calm these dangerous souls.

Arkady had reached the premise that the victims were inmates who, upon being released from the Isolator, were murdered by fellow gang members. When prison officials refused to accept his phone calls, he could have marked the case 'Pending' under Vladimir jurisdiction. His record wouldn't have been affected, and everyone knew he wanted to go home. Instead, he dressed in his chief investigator's uniform, presented himself at the prison, demanded and read the release log and found that while no inmates had been recently released, the day before the bodies were found two men had been placed in the custody of a Major Pribluda for interrogation by the KGB. Arkady phoned Pribluda, who bluntly denied receipt of the prisoners.

Again the investigation could have come to a halt. Instead Arkady returned to Moscow, went to Pribluda's office in the KGB's shabby Petrovka Street branch and found on the major's desk two red rubber balls bearing elliptical scars. Arkady left a chit for the balls and took them to the forensic lab, where their marks matched point by point the victims' teeth.

Pribluda must have taken the two drugged inmates directly to the river's edge, stuffed the rubber balls into their mouths to stifle any outcry, shot them, picked up the spent shells and, with a long-bladed knife, removed the evidence of the slugs. Maybe he thought it would look as if they'd been stabbed to death. Dead, they'd hardly bled. The torn bodies froze quickly.

Arrests had to be approved by the prosecutor. Arkady went to Iamskoy with the homicide charge against Pribluda and a request for a warrant to search Pribluda's office and home for firearms and a knife. Arkady was with the prosecutor when the call came that, for reasons of security, the KGB was taking over the investigation of the bodies found by the Kliazma. All reports and evidence were to be forwarded to Major Pribluda.

The walls wept. Besides surface rivers, ancient underground rivers burrowed through the city, blind and unseen currents with lost directions. Sometimes in winter half the basements in Moscow cried.

Arkady replaced the files.

'Did you find what you wanted?' The corporal stirred.

'No.'

The corporal saluted encouragingly. 'Things always look better in the morning, they say.'

By regulations, Arkady should have returned the car to the office lot. He drove home. It was after midnight when he rolled into a courtyard off Taganskaya on the east side of town. Rough wooden balconies stood out from the second floor. His apartment was dark. Arkady let himself in the communal entrance, climbed the stairs and unlocked his door as quietly as he could.

He undressed in the bathroom, brushed his teeth and carried his clothes out with him. The bedroom was the largest room of the apartment. A stereo was on the desk. He lifted the record from the turntable and read its label in the shadowy light from the window. 'Aznavour à l'Olympia.' Beside the record player were two water glasses and an empty wine bottle.

Zoya was asleep, her long golden hair over her shoulder in a single braid. The perfume Moscow Night scented the sheets. As Arkady slid into bed her eyes opened.

''S late.'

'Sorry. There was a murder. Three murders.'

He watched the thought finally register behind her eyes.

'Hooligans,' she murmured. 'That's why I tell the children not to chew gum. First it's gum, then rock music, then marijuana and . . .'

'And?' He expected her to say sex.

'And murder.' Her voice trailed away, her eyes closed, the brain barely roused enough to enunciate its cardinal rule and now safely unconscious again. The enigma he slept with.

In a minute, fatigue overcame the investigator and he was asleep too. Asleep, he was swimming through black water, downward toward blacker water in smooth, powerful strokes. Just as he thought of turning toward the surface, he was joined by a beautiful woman with long dark hair and a pale face. In her white dress she seemed to be flying downward. As always she took his hand. The enigma he dreamed.

Chapter Two

Naked, Zoya peeled an orange. She had a broad, child's face, innocent blue eyes, a narrow waist and small breasts with nipples as tiny as vaccination marks. Her pubic hair was shaved to a narrow blond stripe for gymnastics. Her legs were muscular and her voice was high and strong.

'Experts tell us that individuality and originality will be the keynotes of the Soviet science of the future. Parents must accept the new curriculum and the new math, both of which are progressive strides in the building of an even greater society.' She stopped to watch Arkady looking at her and drinking his coffee on the windowsill. 'You could at least exercise.'

Although he was tall and thin, a roll of fat showed through his undershirt when he slouched. His uncombed hair drooped. It malingered, he thought, like its owner.

'I am preserving myself for comparison with yet greater societies,' he said.

She leaned over the table to scan underlined passages in the *Teachers Gazette*, collecting orange pits in her hand along with the peels, her lips moving all the while.

'But individuality must not lead to egoism or careerism.' She broke off to glance at Arkady. 'Does that sound good to you?'

'Leave out careerists. Too many careerists in a Moscow audience.'

As she frowned and turned away, Arkady ran his hand down the deep furrow of her spine.

'Don't. I have to get this speech ready.'

'When is it?' he asked.

'Tonight. The District Party Committee is choosing one member to speak at the city-wide meeting next week. Anyway, you're hardly one to criticize careerists.'

'Like Schmidt?'

'Yes,' she answered after a moment's thought. 'Like Schmidt.'

She retired to the bathroom, and through the open door he watched her brushing her teeth, patting her flat belly, applying lipstick to her mouth. She addressed the mirror.

'Parents! Your responsibilities do not end when your working day is done. Is egoism tainting the character of the student in your home? Have you read lately the statistics concerning egoism and the only child?'

Arkady slid off the sill to see the article she'd underlined. The title was 'A Need for Larger Families.' In the bathroom, Zoya thumbed a disk of birth control pills. Polish pills. She refused to use the coil.

Russians, procreate! the article demanded. Fertilize a glorious roe of young Greater Russians lest all the inferior nationalities, the swarthy Turks and Armenians, sly Georgians and Jews, traitorous Estonians and Latvians, swarming hordes of ignorant yellow Kazaks, Tartars and Mongols, backward and ungrateful Uzbeks, Ossetians, Circassians, Kalmuks and Chuckchis tip with their upraised organs the necessary population ratio between white, educated Russians and dark . . . 'So it is shown that childless or one-child families, superficially suitable to working parents in the urban centers of European Russia, are not in the greater interest of society if we starve the future of Russian leaders.' A future starved of Russians! Incredible, Arkady thought as Zoya stretched on her exercise bar.

'—the student who has been introduced to originality must be all the more rigorously trained ideologically.' She lifted her right leg level with the bar. 'Rigorously. Vigorously.'

He thought of mobs of forlorn Asians stumbling through the streets of the Pioneer Palace, arms out, crying, 'We are starved of Russians.' 'Sorry,' a figure calls from the empty Palace, 'we are all out of Russians.'

'—four, one, two, three, four.' Zoya's forehead touched her knee.

On the wall behind the bed was an oft-repaired poster of three children – African, Russian and Chinese – with the slogan 'A Pioneer is a Friend to Children of All Nations!' Zoya had posed for the Russian child, and as the poster became famous so had her bluntly pretty Russian face. The first time Zoya was pointed out to Arkady at the university it was as 'the girl in the Pioneer poster.' She still looked like that child.

'Out of conflict comes synthesis.' She took deep breaths. 'Originality combined with ideology.'

'Why do you want to make a speech?'

'One of us has to think of his career.'

'This is so bad?' Arkady approached her.

'You make a hundred and eighty rubles a month and I make a hundred and twenty. A factory foreman makes twice as much. A repairman makes three times that on the side. We don't have a television, a washing machine, even new clothes I can wear. We could have had one of the used cars from the KGB – it could have been arranged.'

'I didn't like the model.'

'You could be an investigator for the Central Committee right now if you were a more active Party member.'

As he touched her hip, the flesh there contracted, imitating marble. Her breasts were white and hard, their ends stiffened pink. This very combination of sex and party was the graphic illustration of their marriage.

'Why do you bother taking those pills? We haven't screwed in months.'

Zoya grabbed his wrist and pushed it away, squeezing as hard as she could. 'In case of rape,' she said.

Children around the courtyard's wooden giraffe peeked out of snowsuits and caps as Arkady and Zoya got into the car. On Arkady's third try, the ignition turned over and he backed onto Taganskaya.

'Natasha asked us to go to the country tomorrow.' Zoya stared at the windshield. 'I told her we would.'

'I told you about that invitation a week ago and you didn't want to,' Arkady said.

Zoya pulled her muffler over her mouth. The car was colder inside than out, but she hated open windows. She sat armored in her heavy coat, rabbit-fur hat, muffler, boots and silence. At a red light he wiped condensation from the windshield. 'I'm sorry about lunch yesterday,' he said. 'Today?'

Her eyes narrowed sideways at him. There'd been a time, he remembered, when they'd spent hours under warm sheets, a cozy frost on the window. What they'd talked about, he admitted, he couldn't recall. He'd changed? She'd changed? Whom could you believe?

'We have a meeting,' she answered at last.

'All the teachers, all day?'

'Dr Schmidt and I, to plan the gymnastic club's part of the parade.'

Ah, Schmidt. Well, they had so much in common. He was, after all, secretary of the Party District Committee. Adviser to Zoya's Komsomol council. Gymnast. Mutual labor was bound to engender mutual affection. Arkady fought the impulse for a cigarette because it would have made the picture of a jealous husband too complete.

Students were filing in when Arkady reached School 457. Though the kids were supposed to be uniformed, most wore their red Pioneer bandannas with neat hand-me-downs.

'I'll be late.' Zoya hopped quickly out of the car.

'All right.'

She clung to the car door a moment longer. 'Schmidt says I should divorce you while I can,' she added, and shut the door.

At the school entrance the students shouted her name. Zoya looked back once to the car and Arkady, who was lighting a cigarette.

Clearly a reversal of Soviet theory, he thought. From synthesis to conflict.

The investigator turned his mind to the three murders in Gorky Park. He approached them from the point of Soviet justice. Justice, as much as any school, was educational.

For example. Usually drunks were merely held overnight in a drying-out station and then shoved toward home. When the number of drunks in the gutters – despite the rising cost of vodka – simply got to be too much, an educational campaign about the horrors of alcohol was launched, that is, drunks were thrown in jail. Pilferage in factories was constant and enormous; it was the private enterprise side of Soviet industry. Ordinarily a factory manager so clumsy as to be caught was quietly given five years, but during a campaign against pilferage, he was loudly ordered shot.

The KGB was no different in its fashion. The Vladimir Isolator served as an educational function for hardcore dissidents, 'but only the grave can correct the hunchback,' and so for the worst enemies of the state there was an ultimate lesson. Arkady had finally learned that the two bodies found by the Kliazma River were a pair of recidivist agitators, fanatics of the most dangerous sort: Jehovah's Witnesses.

There was something about religion that turned the state into the frothing maw of a rabid dog. God wept, God wept, Arkady said to himself, although he didn't know where he'd picked up the expression. The whole upsurge in religiosity, the market in ikons, the restoration of churches had the government whirling like a paranoid. Putting missionaries into prison was simply feeding them converts. Better a stern lesson, a red rubber ball to stifle them, the sort of anonymous end that best generated ominous rumors, even the frozen river bent to an educational purpose.

Gorky Park, though, was no far-off river bank; it was the purest heart of the city. Even Pribluda must have visited Gorky Park as a fat child, a gross picnicker, a grunting suitor. Even Pribluda should know that Gorky Park was for recreation, not education. Also, the bodies were months, not days, old. The lesson was cold, too old, pointless. It wasn't justice as Arkady had come to expect and detest.

Lyudin was waiting behind a desk covered with the apparatus of specimen slides and photographs, smug as a magician surrounded by hoops and scarves.

'The forensic department has gone all out for you, Chief Investigator. The details are fascinating.'

Lucrative, too, Arkady assumed. Lyudin had requisitioned enough chemicals to stock a private warehouse, and probably had.

'I can't wait.'

'You know the principle of gas chromatography, the effect of a moving gas and a stationary solvent material—'

'I mean it,' Arkady said. 'I can't wait.'

'Well' – the lab director sighed – 'to be quick about it, the chromatograph found in the clothes of all three victims very fine grains of gesso and sawdust, and on the pants of GP-2 a minute trace of gold. We sprayed the clothes with luminol, removed them to a darkroom and observed fluorescence, indicating blood. Most of the blood was, as expected, that of the victims. The smallest spots, however, were not human but of chicken and fish blood. We also found a very interesting pattern on the clothes.' Lyudin held up a drawing of the clothed bodies in the positions they had been found. There was a shaded area on the front of the supine female, and along the upper arms and legs of the flanking males. 'In the dark area, and only in the dark area, we found traces of carbon, animal fats and tannic acid. In other words, after the bodies were partially covered by snow, probably within forty-eight hours, they were also lightly covered with ash from a nearby fire.'

'The Gorky Tannery fire,' Arkady said.

'It's obvious.' Lyudin couldn't suppress a smile. 'On February three, a fire at the Gorky Tannery covered a large area on the Octobryskaya District with ash. Thirty centimeters of snow fell from February one and two. Twenty centimeters fell from February three to five. If we had been able to maintain the snow in the clearing intact, we might even have been able to detect an undisturbed layer of the ash. Anyway, that would seem to date the crime for you.'

'Excellent work,' Arkady said. 'I doubt we need to analyze the snow now.'

'We also analyzed the bullets. Embedded in all the bullets were varying amounts of the victims' clothes and tissue. The bullet marked GP1–B also yielded bits of tanned leather unrelated to the victim's clothes.'

'Gunpowder?'

'None on the clothes of GP1, but faint traces on the

coats of GP2 and GP3, indicating they were shot at a closer range,' Lyudin added.

'No, indicating they were shot after GP1,' Arkady said. 'Anything on the skates?'

'No blood, gesso or sawdust. Not very high quality skates.'

'I meant identification. People put their names in their skates, Colonel. Have you cleaned the skates and looked?'

At his own office on Novokuznetskaya, Arkady said, 'This is the clearing in Gorky Park. You,' he told Pasha, 'are Beast. Detective Fet, you are Red, the skinny guy. This' – he set a chair between them – 'is Beauty. I'm the killer.'

'You said there could be more than one killer,' Fet said.

'Yes, but just this once we're going to try this front to back instead of trying to fit facts to a theory.'

'Good. I'm a little weak on theory,' Pasha said.

'It's winter. We've been skating together. We're friends, or at least acquaintances. We've left the skating path for the clearing, close by but shielded from the path by trees. Why?'

'To talk,' Fet suggested.

'To eat!' Pash exclaimed. 'That's why anyone skates, so you can stop and have a meat pie, some cheese, bread and jam, certainly pass around some vodka or brandy.'

'I am the host,' Arkady continued. 'I picked this

place. I brought the food. We're relaxing, some vodka under our belts and we're feeling good.'

'Then you kill us? Shoot a gun from your coat pocket?' Fet asked.

'Probably shoot your own foot if you try that,' Pasha answered. 'You're thinking about that leather on the bullet, Arkady. Look, you brought the food. You couldn't bring that much food in your pockets. In a leather bag.'

'I'm handing out the food from the bag.'

'And I don't suspect a thing when you lift the bag close to my chest. Me first because I'm the biggest and roughest.' Pasha nodded – his habit when he was forced to think. 'Bang!'

'Right. That's why there's leather on the first bullet, but no gunpowder on Beast's coat. Gunpowder does escape through the hole in the bag with the next shots.'

'The noise,' Fet objected, and was waved down.

'Red and Beauty don't see any gun.' Pasha was excited, his head nodding furiously. 'They don't know what's happening.'

'Especially if we're supposed to be friends. I swing the bag to Red.' Arkady's finger pointed at Fet. 'Bang!' He aimed at the chair. 'By now, Beauty has time to scream. Somehow I know she won't, I know she won't even try to run.' He remembered the girl's body between the two men. 'I kill her. Then I shoot the two of you through the head.'

'Coup de grace. Very neat.' Pasha approved.

'More noise,' Fet flushed. 'I don't care what you say, that's a lot of noise. Anyway, shooting someone in the mouth is no coup de grace.'

'Detective' – Arkady swung his finger back – 'you're right. So I'm shooting you for another reason, a good reason to take the chance of firing two more times.'

'What is it?' Pasha asked.

'I wish I knew. Now I take out my knife and cut off your faces. Probably used shears on your fingers. Put everything back in the bag.'

'You used an automatic.' Pasha was inspired. 'Less noise than a revolver, and the shells are ejected right into the bag. That's why we didn't find any in the snow.'

'Time of day?' Arkady urged.

'Late,' Pasha said. 'So there's less chance of other skaters stopping at the clearing. Maybe snowing – that would muffle the shots even more. When wasn't it snowing this winter? So it's dark and snowing when you come out of the park.'

'And less likely anyone sees me toss the bag in the river.'

'Right!' Pasha clapped.

Fet sat on the chair. 'The river was frozen,' he said.

'Fuck!' Pasha's hands fell.

'Let's go eat,' Arkady said. For the first time in two days he had an appetite.

The cafeteria at the metro stop across the street kept a table available for investigators. Arkady had whitefish, cucumber in sour cream, potato salad, bread and beer. Old Belov joined the group and started on war stories about Arkady's father.

'This was early on, before we'd regrouped.' Belov gave a rheumy wink. 'I was the general's driver in a BA-20.'

Arkady remembered the story. The BA-20 was an

antique armored car consisting of a mosque-shaped machine-gun turret on a Ford chassis. His father's command of three BA-20s were trapped one hundred kilometers behind German lines during the first month of the war and escaped with the ears and epaulets of an SS group commander.

It was funny about the ears. Russians accepted rape and slaughter as the normal sideshows of war. They happily believed Americans took scalps and Germans ate children. What made a nation of worldshaking revolutionaries recoil in horror was the idea of a human trophy taken by a Russian. It was worse than horrible; to the invincible yet slightly anxious proletariat it showed the one stain darker than all others: lack of culture. The rumor about the ears dogged the general's career after the war.

'The rumor about the ears is untrue,' Belov assured the table.

Arkady remembered the ears. They used to hang like shriveled pastries on the wall of his father's study.

'You really want me to talk to all those vendors?' Pasha rolled a cold cut on his fork. 'All they say is they want us to chase the Gypsies from the park.'

'Talk to the Gypsies, too. We have a time now, the beginning of February,' Arkady said. 'And find out about the skating music they play over the loudspeakers.'

'Do you see your father the general often?' Fet broke in to ask.

'Not often.'

'I think about those poor bastards at the militia station in the park,' Pasha said. 'Nice little station –

53

regular log cabin, warm stove, everything. No wonder they didn't know the woods were full of bodies. They'll see lots of woods at their next station, and polar bears and Eskimos too.'

Belov and Fet caught Arkady's attention. To his surprise, these soulmates were vigorously disparaging the Cult of Personality.

'You mean Comrade Stalin?' he asked.

Fet blanched. 'We mean Olga Korbut.'

Chuchin arrived. The chief investigator for Special Cases was a composite of the most ordinary features, a stencil of a man. He told Arkady that Lyudin had called with a name from the skates.

Above the drabness of Moscow, on the brow of Lenin Hills, was Mosfilm studio. There were other studios in the country: Lenfilm, Tadjifilm, Uzbekfilm. None was as large as Mosfilm or as prestigious. A visiting dignitary would be carried by limousine along the compound's pastel orange wall, through the gatehouse, left toward a garden and a sharp right to the main door of the central film pavilion, where administrators, famous directors (always with heavy glasses and cigarettes) and amenable actresses with flowers lined up to greet him. He would be surrounded by many more huge pavilions, each housing sets, screening buildings, writers' buildings, administrators' buildings, set-design hangars, developing labs and warehouses and prop lots of Tartar wagons, panzer tanks and spaceships. It was a city in itself, with its own burgeoning population of technicians, artists, censors and extras – an extraordinary number of extras because of a penchant of Soviet films for crowd scenes, because no hard budget Soviet films could afford crowds, and because for many young people gaining an actor's pass to Mosfilm even as an extra was to be born again.

No dignitary and uninvited, Arkady found his own way between the central pavilion and the piles of snow dumped in front of the administration building. A glowering girl held up a chalkboard sign that demanded 'Quiet!' He found he had arrived at an outdoor set, a garden of potted apple trees sunk into sod and lit by filtered floodlights with the warm glow of an autumn sunset. A man in foppish, nineteenth-century clothes perused a book at a white wrought-iron table in the garden. Behind him was a false wall with an open window that revealed a gas lamp on a piano. A second man in rough clothes and a cap tiptoed along the wall, drew a long-barreled revolver and aimed.

'My God!' The reader jumped up.

Something was wrong, something always seemed to be wrong, and they kept reshooting the scene. The director and cameramen, in foul moods and stylish leather jackets, swore at the production assistants, who were pretty girls in Afghan coats. They all displayed a mixture of boredom and tension. The crowd was interested. Anyone in the immediate vicinity with nothing better to do – electricians, chauffeurs, Mongols in bodypaint, little ballerinas as timid as overbred dogs – watched in rapt silence at the drama of filming, so much more interesting than the drama that was being filmed.

'My God! You frightened me!' the reader tried again.

Standing as inconspicuously as possible by the generator truck that powered the lights, Arkady had ample time to find the wardrobe assistant. She was tall, had dark eyes, fair skin and brown hair drawn back in a bun. Her Afghan coat was shabbier than the other girls' and short, revealing her wrists. Standing motionless, holding a script, she had the stillness of a photograph. As if she felt Arkady's eyes, she looked toward him, and her gaze gave him the sense of being momentarily illuminated. She turned her attention back to the scene in the garden, but not before he'd seen the mark on her right cheek. In the militia picture the mark was gray. He saw now that it was a blue discoloration, small but striking because she was beautiful.

'My God! You frightened me!' The reader blinked at the leveled revolver. 'I'm nervous enough as it is, and you pull a stupid trick like that!'

'Lunch!' the director called, and walked off the set. This scene, too, had been played before, for the cast and crew decamped almost as quickly, leaving the onlookers to disperse. Arkady watched the wardrobe assistant place dustcloths over the garden table and chairs, pull up a wilting flower and turn down the gas lamp on the piano. Her coat was worse than shabby; patches had turned Afghan embroidery into a crazy quilt. A cheap orange scarf was tied loosely at her neck. Her boots were red vinyl. A remarkable ensemble, yet she carried it off with such self-possession that another female seeing her might say, Yes, that's how I should dress, right out of a trash can. Without floodlights the garden was overcast. She wore a smile.

'Irina Asanova?' Arkady asked.

'And you?' She had a low voice rounded by a Siberian accent. 'I know all my friends, and I'm sure I don't know you.'

'You seem to know you're the one I came to talk to.'

'You aren't the first one to bother me when I'm at work.' All this was said with her smile, as if no offense could be taken. 'I'll miss lunch,' she sighed, 'so I'll diet. Do you have a smoke?'

A few curls of hair had escaped from the discipline of her bun. Irina Asanova was twenty-one, Arkady remembered from the militia file. When he lit the cigarette for her, she cupped the flame in his hand with her long, cool fingers. The sexual touch was such a ploy that he was disappointed, until he saw in her eyes she was laughing at him. They were such expressive eyes, they would have made the homeliest girl interesting.

'Men from Special Cases usually have better cigarettes, I must inform you of that,' she said, and inhaled greedily. 'Is this part of a campaign to get me fired? If you chase me from here, I'll just get another job.'

'I'm not from Special Cases or the KGB. Here.' Arkady showed his ID.

'Different, but not very different.' She handed it back. 'What does Chief Investigator Renko want with me?'

'We found your ice skates.'

It took her a moment to understand. 'My skates!' She laughed. 'You actually found them? I lost them months ago.'

'We found them on a dead person.'

'Good! Serves them right. There *is* justice, after all. I

hope they froze to death. Please, don't be shocked. Do you know how long it took me to save for those skates? Look at my boots. Go ahead, look at them.'

He saw that her red boots were splitting from the zippers. Suddenly Irina Asanova was leaning on his shoulder and pulling one boot off. She had long, graceful legs.

'Not even an insole.' She rubbed her bare toes. 'You saw the director of this film? He promised me a pair of fur-lined Italian boots if I slept with him. Do you think I should?'

It seemed a real question. 'Winter's almost over,' he said.

'Exactly.' She slipped her boot back on.

What impressed Arkady, besides her legs, was how she managed her whole performance with such indifference, as if she didn't care what she said or did.

'Dead,' she said. 'I feel better already. I reported the skates stolen, you know, at the rink and to the militia.'

'Actually, you reported them missing on February fourth, though you said you'd lost them on January thirty-first. You didn't know you'd lost them for four days?'

'Isn't that generally when you find out you've lost something, when you want to use it again? Even you, Investigator? It took me a while to figure out where I'd lost them – then I ran back to the rink. Too late.'

'Maybe in the meantime you've remembered something or someone at the rink that you didn't mention to the militia when you reported the skates stolen. Do you have any idea who could have taken your skates?'

'I suspect' – she paused for comic effect – 'everyone.'

'So do I,' Arkady said seriously.

'We have something in common.' She laughed with delight. 'Imagine!'

But as soon as he began to laugh with her she cut him dead. 'A chief investigator doesn't come to tell me about skates,' she said. 'I told the militia everything I knew back then. What do you want?'

'The girl wearing your skates was killed. Two others were found with her.'

'What has that to do with me?'

'I thought you might be able to help.'

'If they're dead, I can't help them. Believe me, there's nothing I'll do for you. I've been a law student. If you're going to arrest me, you have to have a militiaman with you. Are you going to arrest me?'

'No—'

'Then unless you want to lose me my job, you'll leave. People here are afraid of you, they don't want to see you around. You won't come again, will you?'

Arkady was astonished at himself for letting this ridiculous girl act up. On the other hand, he understood how it was with students who got thrown out of the university and then hung on to any job they could get so they wouldn't lose their Moscow permit and be shipped home. All the way to Siberia for this one.

'No,' he agreed.

'Thank you.' Her solemn gaze turned practical. 'Before you go, could you give me another smoke?'

'Have the pack.'

The film crew drifted back to the set. The actor with

the revolver was drunk, and aimed it at Arkady. Irina
Asanova called after the departing investigator, 'By the
way, what did you think of the scene?'

'Like Chekhov,' he answered over his shoulder, 'but
bad.'

'It *is* Chekhov,' she said, 'and it stinks. You're not
missing a thing.'

Levin was studying a chessboard when Arkady entered
the pathologist's office.

'I will give you a concise history of our Revolution.'
Levin didn't look up from the black and white pieces.
'Once a man indulges himself in murder, in time he
thinks nothing of robbing, and from robbing he comes
next to foul language and atheism, and from these to
opening doors without knocking. Black's move.'

'Do you mind?' Arkady asked.

'Go ahead.'

Arkady swept the center of the board clean and placed
three black pawns there on their sides. 'Beauty and Beast
and Red.'

'What are you doing?' Levin viewed the havoc of his
game.

'I think you missed something.'

'How would you know?'

'Just let me go through this. Three victims, all killed
with one shot through the chest.'

'Two shot through the head as well, so how do you
know which shots came first?'

'The killer has planned carefully,' Arkady plunged on.

'He removes identification papers, cleans the pockets of his victims, actually flays their faces and cuts off the ends of their fingers to eliminate points of identification. However, he takes the added chance of firing two more bullets into the faces of the male victims.'

'To make sure they're dead.'

'He knows they're dead. No, on one man there is another point of identification to erase.'

'Maybe he shot them in the head first, then the heart.'

'Then why not the girl as well? No, he shoots one dead man in the face, then realizes he is only announcing what he's up to, and so shoots the second dead man as well.'

'Then I ask you' – Levin stood – 'why not the girl as well?'

'I don't know.'

'And I tell you as an expert, which you are not, that a bullet of that caliber won't create so much disfigurement that the men couldn't be identified. Besides, this butcher had already taken their faces off.'

'Tell me as an expert, what did the bullets achieve?'

'If the two men were already dead' – Levin folded his arms – 'local destruction mainly. The teeth, which we've already gone over.'

Arkady said nothing. Levin jerked open a drawer and brought out boxes marked GP1 and GP2. From box GP1, he poured two nearly whole incisors into his hand.

'Good teeth,' Levin said. 'You could crack nuts with these.'

The teeth in box GP2 hadn't fared as well. One shattered incisor and a separate packet of shards and powder.

'Most of one tooth was lost in the snow. However, what we analyzed shows enamel, dentin, cementum, dehydrated pulp, tobacco stain and lead traces.'

'A filling?' Arkady asked.

' "Nine grams." ' Levin used slang for a bullet. 'Satisfied?'

'This was Red, the boy who dyed his hair, wasn't it?'

'GP2 for God's sake!'

Red was downstairs in a cool metal drawer. They wheeled the body into the autopsy room, Arkady puffing on a cigarette.

'Give me some light.' Levin elbowed him back. 'I thought you hated this work.'

The center of the upper jaw was a hole framed by brown secondary incisors. With a pick, Levin prodded bits of the jaw onto a damp glass slide. When deposits covered the slide, he marched to a microscope on a worktable.

'Do you ever know what you're looking for, or do you simply guess?' he asked Arkady.

'I guess, but nobody robs an empty safe.'

'Whatever that means.' The pathologist applied an eye to the microscope while he stirred the broken bone. Starting with an eye-piece of 10X, he rotated the objective lenses. Arkady pulled up a chair and sat with his back to the corpse while Levin removed from the slide one granule of bone at a time.

'I sent a report to your office that you probably haven't seen,' Levin said. 'The fingertips were clipped off with shears. There is distinct and opposite grooving of the wounds. The facial tissue was not removed with a scalpel, the cuts aren't that fine – in fact, there's a heavy scoring of the bone. I'd say a big knife, maybe a hunting knife, and extraordinarily sharp.' A fine dust remained on the slide. 'Here, take a look.'

Magnified two hundred times, the dust was an ivory rubble interspersed with pink timber.

'What is it?'

'Gutta-percha. The tooth broke up the way it did because it was dead and brittle. He had root-canal work, and the gutta-percha was inserted in place of the root.'

'I didn't know that was done.'

'It isn't here. Dentists in Europe don't use gutta-percha, only the Americans.' Levin sneered at Arkady's grin. 'Luck is nothing to be proud of.'

'I'm not proud.'

Back at Novokuznetskaya, still in his overcoat, Arkady typed:

Report on Gorky Park Homicides.

Pathological analysis of Victim GP2 ascertains remnants of a gutta-percha pin in the upper middle right incisor root canal. The pathologist states this is a technique not characteristic of Soviet or European dentistry. It is usual in the U.S.A.

GP2 is also the victim who disguised himself by dyeing his red hair to brown.

He added his signature and the time, rolled the report out, separated his carbon and carried the original next door as tenderly as a commutation of sentence. Iamskoy was out. Arkady laid the report in the middle of the prosecutor's desk.

When Pasha returned in the afternoon, the investigator was in his shirt sleeves leafing through a magazine. The detective set down his tape machine and slumped into a chair.

'What's this, early retirement?'

'Not retirement, Pasha. A balloon, a bubble drifting heavenward, an eagle soaring free – in short, a man who has successfully evaded responsibility.'

'What are you talking about? I just broke the case.'

'There is no case for us anymore.'

Arkady described the dead man's teeth.

'An American spy?'

'Who cares, Pasha? Any dead American will do. Pribluda will have to take jurisdiction now.'

'And the credit!'

'Let's name a day for him. This affair should have been his from the start. A triple execution isn't our kind of case.'

'I know the KGB. Those prick-twisters. After we do all the work.'

'What work? We don't know who the victims are, let alone who killed them.'

'They get twice the pay of detectives, their own special shops, fancy sports clubs.' Pasha rolled along on his own track. 'Can you tell me how they're better than I am, why I was never recruited? There's something wrong with me because my grandfather happened to be a prince? No, you have to have a pedigree, sweat and dirt for ten generations, or speak ten languages.'

'Pribluda definitely has you beat on the sweat and dirt. I don't think he speaks more than one language.'

'I could speak French or Chinese if I'd had the chance,' Pasha rolled on.

'You speak German.'

'Everyone speaks German. No, it's typical, the story of my life. Now they'll take the credit when we've unmasked what, some, some—'

'Tooth.'

'Fuck your mother.' It was the national expression of exasperation, not an insult.

Arkady left Pasha in his funk and went to Nikitin's office. The chief investigator for Governmental Directives wasn't in. With a key from Nikitin's desk, Arkady unlocked a wooden safe, which contained a city telephone directory and four bottles of vodka. He took only one.

'So you'd rather be a snotnosed prick-twister than a good detective,' he told Pasha as he returned. Inconsolable, the detective stared at the floor. Arkady poured out two glasses of the vodka. 'Drink up.'

'To what?' Pasha muttered.

'To your grandfather, the prince!' Arkady offered.

Pasha flushed with embarrassment. He stared through the open door at the hall.

'To the Czar!' Arkady added.

'Please!' Pasha shut the door.

'Then drink.'

After a few drinks, Pasha wasn't so forlorn. They

saluted the forensic detection of Captain Levin, the inevitable triumph of Soviet justice, and the opening of the sea lanes to Vladivostok.

'To the only honest man in Moscow,' Pasha suggested.

'Who?' Arkady asked, expecting a joke.

'You,' Pasha said and drank.

'Actually' – Arkady looked at his own glass – 'what we've been doing the past two days hasn't been too honest.' Looking up, he saw the detective's newly revived spirits start to sag. 'Anyway, you said you "broke the case" today. Tell me how.'

Pasha shrugged, but Arkady insisted, as he knew the detective wished him to. A day spent talking to old babushkas should have some reward.

'It occurred to me' – Pasha tried to be matter-of-fact – 'that maybe something besides snow covered the sound of the gunshots. After wasting most of the day with the food vendors, I go and talk to the little old woman who plays the records over the loudspeakers for the skating in the park during the winter. She has a little room in the building at the Krimsky Val entrance. I ask, "Do you play any loud records?" She says, "Only quiet records for skating." I ask, "Do you have a program of music you follow every day?" She says, "Programs are for television, I only play records for skating, quiet records played by a simple laborer, the same as I have since the war when I was in the artillery. I earned my job honestly," she says, "for my disability." I say, "That's not my concern, I just want to know the order of the records you play." "The right order," she says. "I start at the top of the pile and work my way down, and when there are no

more records I know it's time to go home." "Show me,"
I say. The old woman brings out a stack of fifteen records.
They're even numbered one to fifteen. I was thinking
the shootings probably took place toward the end of the
day, and so I work from the back. Number fifteen, sure
enough, is from *Swan Lake*. Number fourteen, you want
to guess? The "1812 Overture". Cannons, bells, the
works. Finally, I'm getting smart. Why should the records
have to be numbered? I hold the record in front of my
mouth and ask her, "How loud do you play the records?"
She just looks; she hasn't heard a thing. The old woman
is deaf, that's her disability, and that's who they have
playing the records in Gorky Park!'

Chapter Three

A weekend in the country with the last snow of winter. Windshield wipers swatting flakes as thick as goose down. A bottle of spiced vodka to compensate for the car's inadequate heater. The enthusiastic hiss of tires. Fifes, drums, horns, the galloping bells of a sled. Forward!

Zoya sat in back with Natalya Mikoyan, Arkady in front with Mikhail Mikoyan, his oldest friend. Together the men had gone through Komsomol, the Army, Moscow University and the Law Faculty. They'd shared the same ambitions, the same binges, the same poets, some of the same girls, even. Slight and baby-faced under a mop of dark curls, Misha had gone directly from the Law Faculty to the Moscow City Collegium of Advocates. Officially, defense lawyers received no more than judges – say, 200 rubles a month. Unofficially, clients paid double or more, which was why Misha could afford good suits, a ruby ring on his little finger, furs for Natasha, a house in the country and a two-door Zhiguli in which to get there.

Natasha, dark and so delicate that she could wear children's clothes, contributed her pay as a Novosti press agency writer and one abortion a year; she couldn't use the pill, though she supplied her friends. Not too much baggage on this sled. Forward!

The dacha was thirty kilometers east of Moscow. As usual, Misha had invited eight or so friends to share the house. When the host's carload entered, stomping snow off their boots, arms laden with bread, jars of herring and bottles of liquor, they were greeted by a young couple waxing skis and a fat man in a tight sweater trying to light the fireplace. More guests followed: a director of educational films and his mistress; a ballet dancer trailed ducklike by his wife. Skis fell, it seemed continuously, from the sofa. Men in one room, women in another, the late arrivals changed into outdoor gear.

'A white morning.' Misha waved expansively. 'Snow more precious than rubles.'

Zoya said she would stay with Natasha, who was still recovering from her last abortion. Outside, the snow ceased falling and lay deep on the ground.

Misha found glory in blazing his own path through the woods. Arkady was content to follow and stop from time to time to admire the low mountains; he had a long, easy stride, and gaining on Misha's fevered plunging was no problem. After an hour, they rested so Misha could clean the ice compacted between his shoes and skis. Arkady slipped out of his skis and sat.

White breath, white trees, white snow, white sky. 'Slim as women,' birches were invariably called. Crutches for poets, too, Arkady thought.

Misha worked at the ice the way he worked in court: with a fury, dramatically. As a small boy he'd had the biggest voice, like a tiny craft with an enormous sail. He *hammered* at his skis.

'Arkasha, I have a problem.' He let the skis drop.

'Who is she this time?'

'A new clerk, probably no more than nineteen. I think Natasha suspects. Well, I don't play chess or sports, what else is there? The most ridiculous thing is that this child may be the most ignorant person I've ever met, and I live or die by her opinion. Romance is not a pretty matter, when you get right down to it. Or cheap. Well' – he opened his jacket and pulled out a bottle of wine – 'a little French Sauternes here, smuggled home by that dancer you saw flouncing around the house. The finest dessert wine in the world. I don't have any dessert. Want some?'

Misha unwrapped the tinsel from the top and handed the bottle to Arkady, who slapped its bottom and shot the cork out. He took a swig. The wine was amber and sugary.

'Sweet?' Misha caught Arkady's grimace.

'Not as sweet as some Russian wines,' Arkady said patriotically.

They took turns drinking. Snow fell from boughs, sometimes with one heavy thud, sometimes as lightly and rapidly as the steps of a hare. Arkady enjoyed being with Misha, and the best times of all were when Misha shut up.

'Is Zoya still on you about the Party?' Misha asked.

'I'm a Party member, I have a card.'

'Hardly. What does it take to be more active? A meeting once a month where you can read the newspaper if you want. Once a year you get out the vote, a couple of times a year you circulate a petition against China or Chile. You don't even do that. The only reason you have a card is that if you didn't you wouldn't be chief investigator. Everyone knows, so you might as well get the benefits out of it, get down to the District Committee a little and make some contacts.'

'I always have a good reason for missing a meeting.'

'Sure. No wonder Zoya's furious. You should think of her a little bit. With your record you'd be a cinch to be a Central Committee inspector. You could travel all over checking on law-enforcement performance, whipping up campaigns, making the local-militia generals shit in their pants.'

'That doesn't sound very appealing.'

'That's unimportant. The main thing is, you'd have access to Central Committee shops, you'd be high on the list for foreign travel, and you'd get close to the men on the Central Committee who make all the major appointments. You'd be on your way up the ladder.'

There was a solid, porcelain quality to the sky. It would squeak if you rubbed your thumb on it, Arkady thought.

'I'm wasting my breath,' Misha said. 'You ought to talk to Iamskoy, he likes you.'

'He does?'

'What made him such a celebrity, Arkasha? The Viskov appeal. Before the Supreme Court, Iamskoy denounces the authorities who wrongly arrested and sentenced the young worker Viskov to fifteen years for murder. Moscow Town Prosecutor Iamskoy, of all people, suddenly a protector of individual rights. Practically Gandhi, if you read *Pravda*. And who reopened the investigation? You did. Who forced Iamskoy into action by threatening to protest alone to the law journals? You did. So Iamskoy, seeing you won't be moved, takes the completely opposite course and becomes the bold hero of the tale. He owes you a lot. He might also want to see the last of you.'

'Since when do you talk to Iamskoy?' Arkady was interested.

'Oh, well, lately. There was a little problem of a client who claimed he'd overpaid me. He didn't overpay me – I got the son of a bitch off. Anyway, the prosecutor has been surprisingly understanding. Your name came up. The episode was touch and go, let's leave it at that.'

Misha overcharged so much that an acquitted man complained? Arkady had never put the word 'venal' by his friend before. Misha himself seemed depressed by his confession.

'I actually got the son of a bitch off. Do you know how rarely that happens? You know what you're doing when you engage a defense lawyer? You're paying a man to come before the court and disassociate himself from you. True! That's what almost always happens. After all, you wouldn't be on trial if you weren't guilty, and I don't want any guilt by association, I have my own much better name to worry about. Before the prosecutor even has a chance to point a finger, I publicly deplore this criminal's acts. I am not only outraged, I'm nauseated. If my client's lucky I might mention he never farted on Red Army Day.'

'That's not true.'

'A little true. Except this one time – I don't know why – I did everything. My client was not a thief, he was a father of small children, he was the son and support of the crippled woman sobbing in the first row, he was a modest veteran of famous battles, he was a faithful friend and an unstinting worker who was not a thief but only *weak*. Soviet justice, that narcoleptic judge and two ignorant arbiters, is harsh, yes, harsh as a feudal lord and human in the same way. Try to be smart and you'll lose your head. But throw yourself on their breasts, say it was the vodka, it was this woman, it was a moment of madness and who knows what might happen? Naturally, everybody tries it, so you have to be an artist to rise above the general pathos. I did, Arkasha. I even cried myself.' Misha paused. 'Why did I ask for so much money?'

Arkady tried to think of something to say. 'I ran into Viskov's parents two days ago,' he offered. 'His father manages a cafeteria near Paveletsky Station. What a story their lives have been.'

'I truly despair!' Misha exploded. 'You'll never know who to cultivate. Two days ago, I was lunching at the Writers Union with the eminent historian Tomashevski.' The small craft that was Misha was off on a new tack with a fresh wind. 'That's the sort of man you should know. Respected, charming, hasn't produced a piece of work in ten years. He has a system, which he explained to me. First, he submits an outline for a biography to the Academy to be absolutely sure his approach is consistent with Party policy. A crucial first step, as you'll see later. Now, the person he studies is always an important figure – that is, someone from Moscow – hence Tomashevski must do his Russian research close to home for two years. But this historical character also traveled, yes, lived for some years in Paris or London; hence Tomashevski must do the same, apply for and receive permission for foreign residence. Four years have passed. The Academy and the Party are rubbing their hands in anticipation of this seminal study of the important figure by the eminent Tomashevski. And now Tomashevski must retire to the solitude of a dacha outside Moscow to tend his garden and creatively brood over his cartons of research. Two more years pass in seminal thought. And just as Tomashevski is about to commit himself to paper, he checks with the Academy again only to learn that Party policy has totally about-faced; his hero is a traitor, and with regrets all around, Tomashevski must sacrifice his years of labor for the greater good. Naturally, they are only too happy to urge Tomashevski to start a new project, to plow under his grief with fresh labor. Tomashevski is now studying a very important historical figure who lived for some time in the South of France. He says there is always a bright future for Soviet historians, and I believe him.'

Abruptly Misha changed the subject again, and his voice dropped. 'I heard about those bodies in Gorky Park, that you had another run-in with Major Pribluda. Are you crazy?'

When they returned, everyone but Natasha was gone.

'Zoya left with some people from the dacha down the road,' she told Arkady. 'Someone with a German name.'

'She means Schmidt.' Misha sat by the fire to work on the ice in his boots. 'You must know Schmidt, Arkasha. From Moscow. He just took over the place down the road. Maybe he's Zoya's new lover.'

Reading Arkady's face, Misha saw the truth. His mouth open, his face red, he held his dripping boot.

'Do that in the kitchen, Misha,' Natasha said, and pushed Arkady down on the couch and poured glasses of vodka for herself and him while her husband stumbled out.

'He's a silly man.' She nodded toward the kitchen.

'He didn't know what he was saying.' Arkady took the vodka in two swallows.

'That's his method – he never knows what he's saying. He says everything, so he has to be right some of the time.'

'You know what you're saying, though?' Arkady asked.

Natasha had a quietly arch sense of humor. The softest dark shadows around her eyes made them appear brighter by contrast. Her neck was so thin that she put him in mind of a starving child, an odd thing to become for a woman in her thirties.

'I'm Zoya's friend. I'm your friend. Actually, I'm more Zoya's friend. Actually, I've been telling her to leave you for years.'

'Why?'

'You don't love her. The fact is, if you loved her you would make her happy. If you loved her, you'd do what Schmidt does. They were meant for each other.' She poured more for Arkady and herself. 'If you care for her at all, let her be happy. Let her be finally happy.' Natasha started to giggle. She tried to keep a straight face, but her pretty lips kept curling. She'd been as much of a clown as Misha when they'd all been at school. 'Because, the fact is, you find her very boring. She had two or three good years when you made her interesting all by yourself. Now, even I admit it, she's boring. And you're not.' She ran the back of a finger along his wrist. 'You're the only man I know anymore who's not.'

Natasha poured herself one more before going off to the kitchen very carefully and quite drunk, leaving Arkady alone in the living room. The room was hot, so was the vodka. Misha and Natasha had touched up the place with ikons and quaint figurines, and in the gold leaf of the ikons were reflections of the fire. Do for Zoya what Schmidt did for her? Arkady opened his wallet and took out a small red booklet with a profile of Lenin on the cover. On the left were his name, photograph and Party district. On the right, his dues stamps – he noticed that he was two months behind. On the last page a selection of inspirational precepts. The famous Party card. 'There is only one way to succeed, there is only one thing, there is nothing else,' Zoya had said. She was naked when she'd said it; the contrast between her card and her skin was something he remembered. He looked at an ikon. It was of a Madonna, a Virgin. The Byzantine face, especially the eyes gazing back, reminded him not of Zoya, not of Natasha, but of the girl he'd met at Mosfilm.

'To Irina.' He raised his glass.

By midnight, everyone had returned and everyone was drunk. There was a buffet of cold pork and sausages, fish, blini, cheeses and breads, pickled mushrooms, even pressed caviar. Someone was shouting poetry. At the other end of the room couples hopped to a Hungarian version of the Bee Gees. Misha was stricken with guilt and couldn't keep his eyes off Zoya sitting close to Schmidt.

'I thought we were going to spend this weekend together,' Arkady said the one time he got Zoya alone in the kitchen. 'How did Schmidt get into it?'

'I invited him.' She carried out a bottle of wine.

'To Zoya Renko' – Schmidt raised his glass at her return – 'selected yesterday by her District Committee to speak on new challenges in education before the entire City Committee, making us all very proud – especially, I'm sure, her husband.'

Arkady came out of the kitchen to find everyone looking at him except Schmidt, who was winking at Zoya. Natasha saved Arkady from more confusion by handing him a drink. A sentimental Georgian crooner slipped down on the turntable, and Schmidt and Zoya rose to dance.

They'd danced before, Arkady could tell. Balding, but trim, Schmidt was very smooth on his feet, with a muscular wedge-shaped jaw accustomed to leading. He had the thick neck of a gymnast and the black-rimmed glasses of a Party thinker. His hand almost covered Zoya's back as she leaned into him.

'To Comrade Schmidt.' Misha hoisted a bottle as the song ended. 'To Comrade Schmidt we drink a toast not because he's gained a sinecure at a District Committee doing crossword puzzles and selling office supplies on the side, because I can remember once taking home a paper clip myself.'

Misha spilled some vodka and nodded happily at everyone, only getting started. 'We drink to him not because he attends Party conferences at beach resorts on the Black Sea, because last year I was allowed to fly to Murmansk. We drink not because the District Committee buys him cases of fine wine, because we all get to stand in line for a warm beer from time to time. We drink not because he wants our wives, because the rest of us can always masturbate if need be. Nor because he can drive over pedestrians in his Chaika limousine, because we have the advantage of the world's greatest subway system. Not even because his sexual habits include necrophilia, sadism and homosexuality because – please, comrades – we are no longer living in the Dark Ages. No,' Misha concluded, 'we drink to Comrade Dr Schmidt for none of these reasons. The reason we drink to him is because he is such a good Communist.'

Schmidt showed a smile as hard as a car grille.

Dancing, talking, sitting became increasingly drunken. Arkady was in the kitchen making coffee for five minutes before he realized that the film maker was lying with the dancer's wife in a corner. He backed out and left his cup. In the living room Misha sleepily danced with his head on Natasha's shoulder. Arkady climbed the steps to his bedroom, and was about to open the door when Schmidt came out and shut it.

'I drink to you,' Schmidt whispered, 'because your wife is a great screw.'

Arkady hit him in the stomach. As Schmidt, surprised,

bounced off the door he hit him in the mouth. Schmidt landed on both knees and rolled all the way down the steps. At the bottom his glasses fell off and he threw up.

'What happened?' Zoya stood at the bedroom door.

'You know,' Arkady said.

He saw loathing and fear in her face; what he hadn't expected to see shine so brightly was relief.

'Bastard, you,' she said and ran down the stairs to Schmidt.

'I only said hello to him.' Schmidt groped for his glasses. Zoya found them, wiped them on her sweater and helped the District Party leader to his feet. 'He's an investigator?' Schmidt asked through split lips. 'He's crazy.'

'Liar!' Arkady shouted.

No one heard. Arkady realized, his heart pounding at great speed, that Schmidt had lied at the bedroom door. This once, no, they hadn't quite worked up to fucking – not under her friend's roof, not while her husband was there. Arkady had believed the lie because it was truer than his marriage, and there was no way to explain that. Everything was backwards. Zoya was militantly outraged; Arkady, the cuckold, was ashamed.

From the front of the dacha he watched Schmidt and Zoya drive off. Her lover's car was an old two-seater Zaporozhets, not a limousine. There was a full moon over the birches.

'I'm sorry,' Misha said as Natasha thoughtfully wiped the rug in the living room.

Chapter Four

Iamskoy said, 'Your work is, as always, a model. The discovery of this victim's dental work, coming as quickly as it did, was a bombshell. I immediately ordered a thorough investigation by the organs of State Security. This investigation went on throughout the weekend – while you were away from the city – and involved a computerized review of thousands of foreign residents and known foreign agents dating back five years. The sum result was that not one individual close to the description of the victim cannot be accounted for. It is the opinion of the analysts that we are still dealing with a Soviet citizen who had this particular dental work performed on him while visiting the United States, or by a European dentist trained there. Because all possible aliens have been accounted for, I am forced to concur in this opinion.'

The prosecutor spoke with great earnestness and sincerity. Brezhnev had the same gift that set the style: a direct, low-keyed reasonableness that had taken so much into account that its authority was self-evident and there was no sense in argument; argument, in fact, would be a betrayal of the air of reasonableness so generously set.

'I'm in the position, Arkady Vasilevich, of determining whether I as prosecutor now insist that the KGB assume responsibility of this investigation or allow you to continue your fine work. The merest chance that there might be foreign involvement is disturbing. Clearly, there is the possibility of your investigation being cut short. That being the case, why not have them initiate their inquiry now?'

Iamskoy paused as if he were considering the question.

'There is more involved, though. At one time there would have been no question; the MVD would have investigated Russian or foreigner alike, in the same basket without discrimination, without public trial, arrested them and sentenced them without the slightest regard for socialist legality. You know what I'm talking about – Beria and his clique. These were excesses carried out by a handful of men, but we cannot turn our faces. The Twentieth Party Congress dragged these excesses into the daylight and instituted the reforms under which we now operate. The MVD militia now is strictly limited to interior criminal matters. The KGB, likewise, is strictly limited to matters of national security. The role of prosecutors in overseeing and protecting the rights of citizens has been reinforced, and the independence of investigators has been articulated. Socialist legality is built upon this division of powers so that no Soviet citizen can ever again be deprived of his full rights in open court. So what happens if I take the case away from an investigator and hand it to the KGB? It's a step backward. This particular victim probably was Russian. Didn't he have other dental work, a steel molar, that was distinctly Russian? There's no doubt the other two victims were Russian. The perpetrators of this crime and the wide variety of people touched by this inquiry are Russian. Yet here I would be – on no real evidence – muddying the waters of reform, and bringing into confusion the separate powers of our two arms of the law. What does my duty to protect civil rights mean if I do that? What does your independence signify if at the first moment of indecision you abdicate it? Avoiding our responsibilities would be easy, but, I am convinced, wrong.'

'What exactly would convince you the other way?' Arkady asked.

'If you proved the victim or killer was not Russian.'

'I can't. But I do feel that one victim was not Russian,' Arkady said.

'That's not enough.' The prosecutor sighed, as an adult sighs to a child.

'It occurred to me this weekend,' Arkady said quickly before he was dismissed, 'what the victims were doing.'

'Yes?'

'Gesso and sawdust and gold dust were found in the victims' clothes. Those items are all material used in the restoration of ikons. Ikons are a very popular item on the black market, even more to foreign tourists than to Russians.'

'Go on.'

'There is a chance this one victim was foreign, and from the evidence on his clothes, that he was engaged in black-market activity, where foreigners are heavily involved. To be absolutely certain that we are not dealing with a foreigner, that we are operating within our limits, I want Major Pribluda to deliver tapes and transcripts of all aliens who were in Moscow in January and February. The KGB will never do it, but I want my request and his answer recorded.'

Iamskoy smiled. Both men understood the pressure that such an official request and answer would bring on Pribluda to assume jurisdiction of the case now rather than later.

'Are you serious? That is a provocative – some would say outrageous – action.'

'Yes,' Arkady said.

Iamskoy was taking more time to turn him down than Arkady had expected. Something in the proposal seemed to intrigue the prosecutor.

'I must say I am always amazed by your intuitive mind. You've never been wrong yet, have you? And you are the senior investigator in Moscow. If you really are set on this, would you consider all non-diplomatic aliens?'

For a moment Arkady was too stunned to reply.

'Yes.'

'That can be arranged.' Iamskoy made a note on a piece of paper. 'Anything else?'

'And current tapes,' Arkady added quickly. Who knew when the prosecutor would ever be so agreeable again? 'The investigation will also be expanded to other areas.'

'I know you to be an investigator of infinite resources and zeal. The day is early.'

Beauty lay on the autopsy table.

'Andreev will want the neck, too,' Levin said.

The pathologist put a wooden block under the neck, making it bow up, and pulled back the hair. With a rotary saw he sliced through the bones. The smell of burning calcium spread. Arkady had no cigarettes; he held his breath.

Levin cut under the seventh cervical vertebra along the angle of the vertebra's spur. As bone separated, head and neck rolled off the table. Arkady reflexively caught the head, and as quickly put it back. Levin switched off the saw.

'No, Investigator, she's all yours now.'

Arkady wiped his hands. The head was thawed. 'I'll need a box.'

What were the dead, anyway, but witnesses of man's evolution from primate indolence to civilized industry? And each witness, every bundle of bones hacked out of peat moss or tundra, was itself a new clue to add to that mosaic called prehistory. A femur here, a brainpan there, perhaps a necklace of elk teeth, all were dragged out of their ancient graves, packed in newspapers and dispatched to the Soviet Academy's Institute of Ethnology overlooking Gorky Park, there to be cleaned, wired together and scientifically resurrected.

Not all its mysteries were prehistoric. For example, an officer returning to his Leningrad boardinghouse at the end of the war noticed a stain on his ceiling. Searching the attic for the stain's source, he found a dismembered, half-mummified body, which the militia identified as the corpse of a man. After a long, unsuccessful investigation, the militia sent a cast of the skull to the Institute of Ethnology to be reconstructed. The problem was, the anthropologists reconstructed the face of a woman, not a man. Disgusted, the militia destroyed the face and closed the case, until the boardinghouse yielded a photo of a girl. Her picture matched a picture of the face the anthropologists had made, she was identified and her murderer was convicted.

Since then the institute had reconstructed from skulls or parts of skulls more than a hundred faces for criminal identification. There was no similar method used by any other police anywhere. Some of the institute's reconstructions were merely crude sculptures in plaster; others, the creations of Andreev, were striking not only in their detail but in their animated expressions of anxiety or outright fear. The effect in court when one of Andreev's heads was revealed was always a prosecutor's moment of triumph.

'Come in, come in.'

Arkady followed the voice into the gallery of heads. The nearest cabinet displayed national types – Turkman, Uzbek, Kalmuk, etc. – assembled with the sort of vacant gazes that typify group portraits. A cabinet of monks came next, then one of Africans and so on. Beyond, in the haze of a skylight, was a table of busts of freshly memorialized cosmonauts, their paint still fresh. Not one he saw had Andreev's touch, until Arkady passed the skylight and stopped short. In the shadow at the end of the room, startled by the investigator's approach and startling him with their mute suspicion, were some semi-humans in a row. Peking Man, his lips pulled back over yellowed fangs. Rhodesian Man, trying to concentrate without a forehead. Something female with the woeful cheeks of an orangutan. A Neanderthaloid, heavy-lipped and sly. A young dwarf with vigorously curly hair, his elongated head crossed by a single brow, his hands and cut-down laboratory smock white with plaster. The dwarf slid off a stool.

'You're the investigator who called?'

'Yes,' Arkady looked for someplace to put his box.

'Don't bother,' Andreev said. 'I'm going to do the head for you. I don't do forensic work for the militia anymore, not unless the case has been unsolved for at least a year. It's a selfish rule, but you'd be amazed how often the militia is able to solve a crime on its own within a year. Someone should have told you that.'

'I knew about it.'

After a long silence, Andreev nodded and approached, bow-legged, a short arm gesturing to the busts around him. 'As you are here, let me give you a short tour before you go. Our collection of humanoids, which so caught your eye. They're fairly striking. Usually stronger than us, sometimes with a greater brain capacity, even con-temporaries of ours in some cases, but condemned for their inability to write the texts on evolution, so let us pass them by.' His rolling step brought him close to Arkady and a gilded case containing the bust of a nomadic Tartar. Arkady was surprised he'd missed it. The face was flat and square, not alive but having lived, as if its cheekbones' deep lines had been sliced by wind instead of a sculptor's knife. A mosque-shaped crown, red mustache and spade beard were ever so slightly tattered, thinned as an old man's are. 'Homo sapiens. Tamerlane, the greatest killer in history. The skull showed a left-sided paralysis. We also had his hair to work with, and some mildew on his lips where the mustache grew.'

Arkady stared at the Tartar until Andreev turned on the light inside a second gilded case, which contained an oversized man's head slumped against the rough monk's cowl. Though the forehead was high, the rest of his face, its long nose, purple lips and beard, sagged from gravity or self-loathing. The glass eyes seemed not so much dead as extinguished.

'Ivan the Terrible,' Andreev continued. 'Buried as a monk under the Kremlin. Another killer. He poisoned himself with the mercury he rubbed in to ease the pain of arthritis. He also had an occlusion of his teeth that must have made his smile a grimace. Do you find him ugly?'

'Isn't he?'

'Not unusually. He did avoid court painters in his later years, as if he wanted to bury that face with him.'

'He was only a murderer,' Arkady said. 'He wasn't stupid.'

The two men were now near the door Arkady had entered through; he was aware the gallery tour was at its end. He made no move to leave, and Andreev began studying him.

'You're Renko's son, aren't you? I've seen his picture many times. I don't see much of him in you.'

'I had a mother, too.'

'Sometimes that is a distinction.' Empathy almost showed in Andreev's face; his horse-sized teeth nearly smiled up at Arkady. 'A man who's willing to admit that should at least be listened to. Very well, let's see what

87

you brought. Maybe someone else wants to waste their time.'

Andreev led the way to a corner that held a potter's wheel under a fluorescent light. While he climbed a stool to pull the light cord, Arkady opened his box and brought the head out by its hair. Andreev took the head and put it on the wheel and softly fanned out the long brown hair.

'Young, about twenty, female, Europoid, nicely symmetrical,' Andreev said. He cut Arkady off when he started explaining about the three murders. 'Don't try to interest me in your case; three more heads hardly matter here. The mutilation is, of course, unusual.'

'The murderer thinks her face is erased. You can bring it back,' Arkady said.

Andreev pushed the wheel, and shadows swung within the orbital cavities of the head.

'Maybe she walked by here that day,' Arkady said. 'It was early in February. Maybe you saw her.'

'I don't spend my time looking at women.'

'You're a man of special powers, Professor. You can look at her now.'

'There are others here who do very nice reconstructions. I have more important work.'

'More important than the fact that two men and this girl were murdered almost in sight of your windows?'

'I only reconstruct, Investigator. I can't bring her back to life.'

Arkady put the box on the floor. 'The face will do.'

*

People whispered about the Lubyanka, the KGB prison on Dzerzhinksy Square, but most Muscovites who broke the law and got caught ended up in Lefortovo Prison on the east side of town. A guard took the investigator down in an elevator that was a pre-Revolutionary cage. Where was Zoya now? She'd called to tell him not to expect her back at the apartment. Thinking about her, he couldn't recall anything except her face at the bedroom door in Misha's dacha. The triumph on her face, as if an opponent had played a trump card too soon. Other than that, there was very little. Meanwhile another phenomenon was taking place. Iamskoy had ordered tapes from Pribluda. A head had been delivered for reconstruction. Under the guise of pretense, without his will, a real investigation was taking shape.

The subbasement. Arkady went down a hall of small iron doors that looked like furnace mouths, past a guard scribbling at a desk, by an open room stuffed with mattresses and reeking of mildew, to a closed door that he opened to see Chief Investigator of Special Cases Chuchin, the blandest figment of a man, staring, eyes aglitter, one hand clutching his belt buckle, and a woman, sitting, turning away to spit into a handkerchief.

'You—' Chuchin blocked Arkady's view of her, but Arkady was looking a second time at what he'd seen: the door swinging open, Chuchin's initial amazement, the hand closing the buckle, the red-faced girl – young but plain – turning in her chair to spit. Chuchin, the smoothest-featured of men, a mustache of sweat on his upper lip, buttoned his jacket and pushed Arkady into the hall.

'An interrogation?' Arkady asked.

'Not a political, just a whore.' Even Chuchin's voice was mild, as if he were identifying a type of dog.

Arkady had come with a request. He didn't have to request anymore. 'Give me the keys to your files.'

'Fuck off.'

'The prosecutor would be very interested in how you carry out an interrogation.' Arkady put out his hand for the key.

'You don't have the nerve.'

Arkady's hand closed on the crotch of Chuchin's pants and on the softening prick, the prick of Special Cases inside the pants, and squeezed Chuchin to his tiptoes so that the two men could see eye to eye.

'I'll kill you for this, Renko, wait and see,' Chuchin said huskily, but he gave up the key.

Arkady spread the files over Chuchin's desk.

No investigator showed another his files. Each was a specialist, and where their activities did overlap, their separate files contained the identities of personally groomed informers. Especially in Special Cases. What were Special Cases? If the KGB were to arrest all political offenders, their sheer numbers would exaggerate their importance. Better that some be arrested by the prosecutor's office for normal crimes that the average citizen could understand. For example: The historian B., a correspondent of exiled writers, was arrested for profiteering on ballet tickets. The poet F., a *samizdat* courier, was charged with stealing books from the Lenin Library.

The technician M., a Social Democrat, was arrested in the act of selling religious ikons to the informant G. This grab bag was an insult to real investigators. Arkady's attitude had always been to ignore Chuchin, as if to deny his existence. He'd hardly spoken to the man, let alone touched him.

Arkady's eye was caught by Chuchin's references to 'the informant G.,' 'the alert citizen G.,' 'the reliable source G.' Fully half the arrests involving ikons were battened by that single letter. He went to Chuchin's budget accounts. On a list of informants G. was at the top with 1,500 rubles. There was a telephone number.

From his own office Arkady called the telephone exchange. The number belonged to a Feodor Golodkin. Pasha's tape machine was by the desk. Arkady put a fresh tape on it and dialed the phone. After five rings it was picked up without an answer.

'Hello, is Feodor there?' Arkady asked.
'Who is this?'
'A friend.'
'Give me a number to call you back at.'
'Let's talk now.'
Click.

When the first cartons came from Pribluda, Arkady felt some of the exhilaration that even illusory progress brings. There were thirteen Intourist hotels in Moscow, with a total of over twenty thousand guest rooms, half equipped with listening devices, and while only 5 percent might be monitored at a time, even fewer taped and

MARTIN CRUZ SMITH

transcribed, the accumulation of material was impressive.

'You may come across some innocent who talks openly about buying ikons or meeting someone in the park, but don't expect it,' Arkady told Pasha and Fet. 'Don't bother reading transcripts of anyone accompanied by an Intourist guide. Don't bother with foreign newspapermen or priests or politicians; they're watched too closely. Concentrate on tourists or foreign businessmen who know their way around, speak Russian, have contacts here. Who have short, cryptic conversations and immediately leave their rooms. A tape of the black marketeer Golodkin is on this machine so that you can match his voice on another tape, but don't lose sight of the fact that he may not be involved.'

'Ikons?' Fet asked. 'How did we decide on them?'

'Marxist dialectic,' Arkady answered.

'Dialectic?'

'We are now in an intermediate stage of communism where there are still criminal tendencies resulting from relics of capitalism in the minds of some individuals. What more obvious relic than an ikon?' Arkady opened a pack of cigarettes and passed one to Pasha. 'Besides, gesso and gold dust were found on the victims' clothes. Gesso's a primer for wood, and about the only legal use of gold is for restoring ikons.'

'You mean this could be tied to an art theft?' Fet asked. 'Like the case at the Hermitage a couple of years ago. Remember, a gang of electricians were taking crystals from the museum chandeliers. It took years to catch them.'

'Ikon fakers, not thieves.' Pasha bummed a match. 'That's where the sawdust on their clothes came from, from woodworking.' He stopped and blinked. 'Did I just do some dialectic?'

After a day of listening to tapes, without enough energy left to confront his apartment, Arkady wandered until he found himself under the Imperial Roman main entrance to Gorky Park, where he bought himself a supper of meat pies and lemonade. On the skating rink, muscular girls in short flared skirts skated backward from a boy with an accordion. The boy pumped gasps of music. The loudspeakers were silent; the deaf woman had put away her records.

The sun set into steamy clouds. Arkady walked on to the amusement section. On a good weekend there might be a thousand kids riding the rocket ride and pedal cars, plinking wooden ducks with an air rifle or watching a magic show at the amphitheater. He'd come often enough himself as a kid with the then sergeant Belov, as a wise guy with wise-guy Misha and all the other wise guys in their group. He remembered when the Czechs opened the first foreign exhibition in the park, the Pilsen beer pavilion in '56. Suddenly, of all things, beer was popular. Everyone was pouring it into his vodka. Everyone was happy and drunk. He remembered when *The Magnificent Seven* came to Moscow, and every male between the ages of twelve and twenty started walking like Yul Brynner; Gorky Park seemed to be full of stiff-legged cowboys looking for their mounts. A time when everyone was a cowboy. Amazing! What were they now? City planners, factory managers, Party members, car owners, ikon buyers, *Krokodil* readers, television critics, opera goers, fathers and mothers.

There weren't many kids today. Two old men slapped dominoes in the dusk. Pushcart vendors huddled together in their white caps and aprons. A toddler sought the limits of an elastic band held by a grandmother.

On the Ferris wheel at the end of the amusements a couple in their eighties sat suspended halfway up while the operator, a boy with skin problems, leafed through a motorcycle magazine, damned if he was going to release the brake just for two pensioners. As the wind picked up, the cars rocked and the old woman edged closer to her husband.

'Take it up.' Arkady presented a ticket to the operator and sat in a car. 'Now.'

The wheel shrugged and revolved, and Arkady rose above tree level. Although sunlight lingered in the west, past Lenin Hills, lamps were coming on across the city and he could make out traffic lights like concentric halos; the tree-lined boulevards around the inner city, the Sado-vaya Ring reaching the park, the Outer Ring as vague as the Milky Way.

That was one of the things about Gorky Park; it was the only place in the city where you could fantasize. You had to have a special pass to join the fantasies of Mos-film, but everyone was welcome in the park. At one time Arkady had planned to be an astronomer. All he had left of that period was a wrinkle of useless information on the cortex. He'd watched Sputnik pass over Gorky Park twenty years ago. Well, no regrets. Everyone left such ghosts in the park; it was a great and pleasant grave. He and Misha, Pasha, Pribluda and Fet, Zoya and Natasha. It offended him that someone had left bodies in it.

Round again. The ancient couple a few cars ahead rode without a word, the way pre-Revolutionaries often did when they came to the capital. It was the Great Patriotic War crowd who were larded with enough self-confidence to push and shout. While their grandchildren sat outside the cathedrals of the Kremlin and picked their noses, the salute of heirs.

He shifted to get comfortable against the metal seat. Below, the park rose into hills, ran by the militia station and divided into romantic walks, off one of which '40 meters north of the footpath on a line with Donskoy Street and the river' three people had been killed. Despite the growing dark he found the clearing because a figure stood in the middle of it with a flashlight.

On the next pass by the ground Arkady jumped off. It was half a kilometer to the clearing, and he began running in long strides, alternately skidding on ice and regaining his balance. The path twisted uphill.

Zoya was right; he should have exercised. Stupid cigarettes. He reached the militia station, just as cozy as Pasha had described but empty, not even a car around, so he kept on moving as the path became steeper. Consciously he pulled his knees up and his elbows back in some sort of rhythm, out of beat with the slap of his shoes and the rasp of his windpipe. After three hundred meters of sprinting his stride was as short as a baby's. He felt as if he'd run for hours. The path leveled just as side stitches started tugging, and it would probably only be Detective Fet doing some housework, he told himself.

Where the militia van had turned off the path four days before, he slowed woodenly, following the tracks to the clearing. Ice popped underfoot. The light was gone; the searcher was gone or smart enough to block the light from the path. There was no definition to help because the clearing, stripped of snow, was totally black. No sounds. He moved from tree to tree around the clearing, stopping in a crouch, staring. He was about to move again when a beam of light shone on the shallow trench from which the bodies had been removed.

Arkady was about ten meters into the clearing when the light disappeared.

'Who's there?' he called.

Someone ran the other way.

Arkady followed. The clearing sloped down to a copse of trees, he knew. Beyond that would be a steep bank, some bowers for chess tables, another path, trees, then a jump down to the Pushkinskaya quay road and the river.

'Stop! Militia!' he shouted.

He couldn't shout more and run, too. He was gaining. The footsteps ahead were heavy, a man's. Though Arkady was once issued a gun, he never carried it. The copse neared, leaping forward like the crest of a wave. The fugitive reached the trees first, breaking through branches. There'd be lights on the lower path, Arkady thought, and many lights on the quay road. He put his arms out as he reached the trees.

He ducked when he heard an arm drawing back, but

it wasn't a punch, it was a kick at his groin. As his breath rushed out he grabbed for the foot and got a fist in the neck. He swung and missed. Another kick knocked him back. His second swing hit a stomach that was round and hard. A shoulder pinned him against a tree while fingers stabbed his kidneys. Arkady's mouth found an ear, and bit.

'Son of a bitch.' In English. The shoulder jumped back.

'Militia . . .' Arkady tried to shout, but it came out a whisper.

A kick dropped him face first into the snow. Fool, Arkady told himself. The first time an investigator hits anyone in years he loses his wife. The second time he bawls for help.

He pulled himself up, listened for the sound of branches shaking, and followed. The slope pitched toward the river. He half fell. The lower path was empty, but he saw feet dissolving in the trees beyond.

Arkady took the path in one stride and leaped, coming down on a broad back. The two men rolled through the dark until they hit a bench. Arkady tried to lock the man's wrist back, but their coats were too tangled for either to do anything until the man twisted free. Arkady tripped him and, swinging as wildly as ever, knocked him off his feet again. But as soon as they were separated, Arkady hadn't a chance. A palm slapped his face, and before he began to react the same hand as a fist shot into the ribs under his heart. He stood in feeble admiration long enough for the fist to find his heart again. Falling, he felt his heart stop.

This is a vast improvement over primitive methods, the collective's director told Arkady and his father, and pulled the cow's head into a pillory over which was a large metal cylinder that at the flick of a switch drove an oil-slicked piston square into the cow's cranium, the animal's legs flying into a comic spread. Cowhide for tankers' helmets, he remembered. Let me try it, General Renko said, and pulled another cow to the pillory. Whomp! Imagine being able to use one's hands like that.

Arkady pulled himself out of a drift and staggered, holding his chest. Trees and snow sucked him downhill to a stone wall. He eased over and collapsed onto the sidewalk of the Pushkinskaya quay.

Truck lights sailed along the sweep of the quay road. He could see no one walking. No militiamen. Streetlamps were furry balls, like the bubbles of air he gagged down. The trucks moved on and he was left alone, unsteadily crossing the road.

The river was a three-hundred-meter-wide streak of ice backed by black trees stretching toward Lenin Stadium to the west, and by unlit ministry buildings to the east. The Krimsky suspension bridge was at least a kilometer away. Close at Arkady's left was a subway bridge with no walkway. Over it rattled a train, wheels sparking.

A figure was running on the river under the bridge.

There were no stairs. Arkady slid three meters down the curving stone embankment, his ass taking the punishment of a violent landing on the ice. He picked himself up and started running.

Moscow was a low city. From the river it almost disappeared into its own somnolent ether.

The footsteps were closer. The man was powerful, not fast; even limping, Arkady still gained. There were no stairs along the north embankment either, but he saw on the embankment toward the stadium the docks for summer excursion boats.

The man stopped for breath, looked back at Arkady and moved on again. They were more than halfway across the ice, about forty meters apart. As Arkady closed in, the man stopped a second time and raised his hand with such authority that Arkady found himself halted. Ice created an illusion of luminescence. He could make out a stocky figure in an overcoat and cap. The face was hidden.

'Away,' it said in Russian.

When Arkady stepped forward, the hand lowered. He saw a barrel. The man aimed with both hands the way detectives were trained to fire a gun, and Arkady dove. He heard no shot and saw no flash, but something smacked off the ice behind him and, an instant later, rang off stones.

The figure lumbered again to the far side of the river. At the embankment Arkady caught up. Water had run down the stone wall and frozen to an uneven slickness on the ice, and there the two men struggled in the shadow of the bridge, slipping first on their feet and then on their knees. Arkady's nose bled and the other man lost his cap. A blow on the chest no harder than a tap put Arkady on all fours. His opponent stood. Arkady took two kicks in the side and, as efficient as a hammer's final measure, a shoe on the back of the head.

When he turned over, the man was gone. Sitting up, he discovered in his hand the man's cap.

Above, more sizzling wheels crossed the sky. Small fireworks for small victories.

Chapter Five

Stalin gothic was not so much an architectural style as a form of worship. Elements of Greek, French, Chinese and Italian masterpieces had been thrown into the barbarian wagon and carted to Moscow and the Master Builder Himself, who had piled them one on the other into the cement towers and blazing torches of His rule, monstrous skyscrapers of ominous windows, mysterious crenellations and dizzying towers that led to the clouds, and yet still more rising spires surmounted by ruby stars that at night glowed like His eyes. After His death, His creations were more embarrassment than menace, too big for burial with Him, so they stood, one to each part of town, great brooding semi-Oriental temples, not exorcised but used. The one in the Kievskaya District, west of the river, was the Hotel Ukraina.

'Isn't this great?' Pasha spread his arms.

Arkady looked down from the fourteenth floor of the Ukraina at the broad boulevard of Kutuzovsky Prospekt, and across Kutuzovsky's traffic at the obeisant buildings of the diplomatic and foreign correspondent complex with its center courtyard and militia kiosk.

'Like Spy Smasher.' Pasha surveyed a suite of tape machines, cartons, tables and cots. 'You really swing some weight, Arkady.'

Actually it was Iamskoy who had moved the base of

the investigation, citing the lack of space in Arkady's own office. There was no mention of who had occupied the suite before, though there was a poster of blond airline stewardesses of the Democratic German Airline taped to a wall. Even Detective Fet was impressed.

'Detective Pavlovich is taking the German tourists and Golodkin, the man you suspect of dealing in ikons. I am familiar with the Scandinavian languages. When I was considering a naval career, I thought they would be useful,' Fet confided.

'Is that so?' Arkady rubbed his neck. His whole body ached from the beating he'd taken the night before; he couldn't honestly call it a fight. It ached to fish for a cigarette, and it gave him a headache to consider being attached to a headset. His Army career had consisted of sitting in a radio shed on the fraternal socialist side of Berlin and listening to Allied transmissions. A duller job couldn't be imagined, yet his two detectives clearly shared a commonality of bliss. After all, here they were in a luxury hotel with their feet resting on a carpet instead of beating a sidewalk. 'I'll take English and French,' he said.

The phone rang. It was Lyudin reporting on the cap lost by the man who had beaten up the chief investigator.

'The cap is new, Russian manufacture, of cheap serge, and it contained two gray hairs. A protein analysis of the hairs indicates the cap's wearer to be Europoid, male, with blood type O. A pomade on the hair was lanolin-based, of foreign manufacture. Casts of the man's heel prints from the park showed the unworn factory imprint of new shoes, also Russian. We also have your heel prints.'

'Worn?'

'Badly.'

Arkady hung up and looked at his shoes. Not only were the heels worn, but the original green color of the leather showed through black polish.

'Son of a bitch!' the man had said when Arkady bit him. Americans say that. An American son of a bitch.

'These German girls,' Pasha said as he listened to a tape through his headset. 'Secretaries for the German Export Bank. Live at the Rossiya Hotel and pick up men right on the hotel dance floor. A Russian prostitute, one of our own, would be thrown out of the Rossiya on her ass.'

Arkady's own tapes had peccadilloes. He eavesdropped on the tirades of a French-speaking liberation fighter from Chad who roomed at the Peking Hotel. The would-be national leader had a sexual appetite matched only by his difficulty in procuring partners. Girls were afraid that after fornicating once with a black man, years hence they might give birth to 'a monkey'. Up with Soviet education!

The demand for so many tapes and transcripts was only to scare Pribluda. It didn't matter that sensitive material wouldn't be delivered; someone in the KGB's chain of command only had to know that the holy of holies (tapes and transcripts, those other people's secrets that only the initiated were empowered to paw) were in the hands of a rival organization. Any transgression was transgression enough. The cartons would go back, and with them, Arkady was sure, the whole investigation. He hadn't mentioned yet that the man who'd roughed him up was probably American, or that he'd taken Beauty's head to Andreev. He couldn't prove the one, and nothing had happened with the other.

He listened to the tape of one tourist while he read the transcript of another. The microphones were in the hotel-room telephones, so he heard calls and conversations alike. The French all complained about the food, and the Americans and English all complained about the waiters. Travel was so irritating.

During lunch in a cafeteria off the hotel lobby, Arkady called Zoya's school. For once, she came to the phone.

'I want to come over and talk to you,' he said.

'It's the month before May Day, you know how that is,' Zoya answered.

'I can pick you up after school.'

'No!'

'When?'

'I don't know. Later on, when I know what I'm doing. I have to go.'

Before she hung up he heard Schmidt in the background.

The afternoon was endless, though the time came when Pasha and Fet put on their hats and coats and went home. Arkady stopped work for coffee. In the dark he made out two more of His skyscrapers close by, Moscow University to the east and the Foreign Ministry right over the river. Their ruby stars glowed to each other.

Alone, listening again to tapes, he heard his first familiar voice. The tape was of an American's party given on January 12 at the Rossiya Hotel. The voice was that of a Russian guest, an angry woman:

'Chekhov, naturally. Always relevant, they say, because of his critical attitude toward the petty bourgeoisie, his deep-rooted Democratic feelings and his absolute faith in the strength of the people. The truth is, in a Chekhov film you can dress the actresses in decent hats instead of scarves. Once a year they want a film with nice hats.'

Arkady recognized the voice of Irina Asanova, the girl at Mosfilm. There was a dulcet protest against her from the actresses present.

Latecomers arrived.

'Yevgeny, now what did you bring me?'

A door closed.

'A late Happy New Year, John.'

'Gloves! How thoughtful. I shall wear these.'

'Wear them, show them off. Come by tomorrow and I'll give you a hundred thousand to sell.'

The American's name was John Osborne. His room at the Rossiya was just off Red Square, most likely a real suite with cut flowers. The Ukraina was a railway station in comparison with the Rossiya. Osborne's Russian was good and strangely suave. But Arkady wanted to hear the girl again.

More voices rushed onto the tape.

' . . . wonderful performance.'

'Yes, I gave a reception for her when the whole ballet company came to New York. Dedicated to her art.'

'With the Moiseyev?'

'Wonderful energy.'

Arkady listened to more welcomes, toasts to Russian art, questions about the Kennedys; there was nothing more from Irina Asanova. He felt his eyelids grow heavy, as if he were an unseen guest buried beneath warm coats and the drone of half-heard words, four-month-old echoes of a room and faces he'd never seen. The flapping of tape in his earphones snapped him to attention. On the chance that Irina Asanova would speak again, Arkady turned over the tape.

The same party, later. Osborne speaking.

'The Gorky Tannery already gives me ready-made gloves. Ten years ago I did try to import leather – calfskin I could undercut the Spanish and Italians with. Fortunately, I checked the goods in Leningrad. I'd been given stomach linings. Tripe. I traced the shipment back to a cattle collective in Alma Ata, which had shipped on the same day my calfskins to Leningrad and soup tripe to Vogvozdino.'

Vogvozdino? But the American wouldn't know about the prison camp there, Arkady thought.

'They contacted the authorities in Vogvozdino, who said their shipment has arrived, been made into soup and devoured with gusto. So the collective was vindicated. I must not have tripe because, certainly, Russians would not eat gloves. I lost twenty thousand dollars, and now never order soup east of Moscow.'

A nervous silence was followed by nervous laughter. Arkady smoked and found he had laid three matches before him on the table.

'I can't understand why you people ever defect to the United States. For money? You would learn that Americans,

no matter how much money they have, always find some-thing finally that they can't buy. When they do, they say, "We can't afford it, we're too poor to buy it." Never, "We're not rich enough." You don't want to be poor Americans, do you? Here you will always be rich.'

The pages from the file on Osborne were onionskin, with the KGB seal embossed in red:

John Dusen Osborne, citizen U.S.A., born 16/5/20 in Tarrytown, New York, U.S.A. Non-party member. Unmarried. Current residence, New York, N.Y. First entry to U.S.S.R. 1942 at Murmansk with Lend-Lease advisory group. Resided 1942–44 in Murmansk and Arkhangelsk on assignment from U.S. Foreign Service as transportation adviser, during which time the sub-ject performed significant services to the anti-Fascist war effort. The subject resigned from the Foreign Service in 1948 during a period of rightist hysteria and initiated a private career in the importation of Russian furs. The subject has sponsored many good-will missions and cultural exchanges and is a yearly visitor to the U.S.S.R.

The second page of the dossier mentioned offices of Osborne Fur Imports, Inc., and Osborne Fur Creations, Inc., in New York, Palm Springs and Paris, and listed Osborne's visits to Russia over the past five years. His last trip had been from January 2 to February 2. There was a penciled note crossed out, but Arkady could read: 'Personal Reference: I. V. Mendel, Ministry of Trade.'

The third page said: 'See: *Annals of Soviet-American Cooperation in the Great Patriotic War*, Pravda, 1967.'

Also: 'See: Department One.'

Arkady recalled Mendel. The man was one of those lobsters who molted and grew fatter with each season, first as supervisor of 'relocation' for kulaks, then wartime commissioner for the Murmansk Region, next director of Disinformation for the KGB, and finally, his claws as great as dredges, deputy minister of Trade. Mendel had died last year, but Osborne was sure to have more friends of the same species.

'It's your humility that makes you charming. A Russian feels inferior to anyone but an Arab or another Russian.'

Russian giggles proved Osborne's point. It was the worldly tone that seduced them. Anyway, he was a *safe* foreigner.

'When in Russia, a wise man stays away from beautiful women, intellectuals and Jews. Or to put it more simply, Jews.'

A sadistic pearl with the one necessary element, Arkady conceded: a grain of truth.

His much amused audience was wrong, however. The dossier notation, 'Department One', stood for the KGB's North American Bureau. Osborne was no agent; no tapes would have been passed on if he were. Osborne, the notation meant, was simply cooperative, a patron of Russian arts and an informant on Russian artists. No doubt more than one dancer basking in his hospitality had uttered statements in New York that found a second audience in Moscow. Arkady was relieved that there was no more sound of Irina Asanova on the tape.

Misha had invited Arkady for supper. Before going, he checked on what his detectives had been up to. Fet's Scandinavian tapes were stacked neatly by notepapers and two pencils sharpened to pinpoints. Pasha's table was a mess. Arkady glanced at the detective's transcripts of Golodkin's telephone calls. One transcript made the day before was curious. Golodkin spoke nothing but English on this call, and whoever was on the other end spoke nothing but Russian:

G: *Good morning. This is Feodor. Remember, on your last trip we were going to go to the museum together.*

X: **Да**.

G: *How do you do? I want to show you the museum today. Is today convenient for you?*

X: **Извините, очень занят. Может, в следующпй раз.**

G: *You are sure?*

The transcribed Russian of the unidentified person was perfectly colloquial. It was a matter of faith, though, that no one could really speak Russian except Russians, and apparently the black marketeer thought, contrary to the evidence, that he had to use English. Golodkin was speaking to a foreigner.

Arkady found the tape that matched the transcript and put it on the machine. This time he heard what he'd read.

'*Good morning. This is Feodor. Remember, on your last trip we were going to go to the museum together.*'

'*Yes.*'

'How do you do? I want to show you the museum today. Is today convenient for you?'

'I'm sorry, I'm very busy. Maybe next year.'

'You are sure?'

Click.

Arkady recognized the other voice at once because he'd listened to it for hours. It was Osborne. The American was back in Moscow.

The Mikoyans had a large flat – five rooms including one with two grand pianos that Misha had inherited, along with the flat, from his parents, who had performed as a team with the Radio Symphony Orchestra. The parents' collection of revolutionary cinema posters decorated the walls, together with Misha and Natasha's peasant wood carvings. Misha directed Arkady to the bathroom, one corner of which was occupied by a new clothes washer of immaculate white enamel.

'The Siberia. Top of the line. A hundred fifty-five rubles. We waited ten months for this.'

An extension cord led to an outlet, and a hose was draped over the side of the tub. Exactly what Zoya wanted.

'We could have had the ZIV or the Riga in four months, but we wanted the best.' Misha picked up a copy of *The Commercial Bulletin*, which had been lying on the toilet. 'Very highly rated.'

'And not in the least bourgeois.' Maybe Schmidt had one in his seraglio.

Misha gave Arkady a black look and handed him his

glass. They were drinking peppered vodka and were already a little unsteady. Misha pulled a lump of wet underwear from the agitator tub and stuffed the clothes into the spin dryer.

'I'll show you!'

He twisted the spin dryer's knob. With a roar, the machine began vibrating. The roar grew, as if a plane were taking off in the bathroom. Water spewed from the hose into the bathtub. Misha leaned back dreamily.

'Fantastic?' he shouted.

'Poetry,' Arkady said. 'Mayakovsky's poetry, but still poetry.'

The machine stopped. Misha checked the plug and the knob, which wouldn't turn.

'Something the matter?'

Misha encompassed Arkady and the machine with a glare. He pounded its side, and the machine began vibrating again.

'Definitely a Russian washer.' Arkady remembered an old verb which meant 'to whip one's serf' and wondered, sipping, if there would be a new one: 'to whip one's machine.'

Misha stood with arms akimbo. 'Anything new has a break-in period,' he explained.

'It's to be expected.'

'It's really rolling now.'

Shaking to be precise. Misha had crammed four underpants into the spin dryer. At that rate, Arkady estimated, moving laundry from the agitator tub to the spin dryer and on to the communal clothesline, a week's wash could be done in ... a week. Nevertheless, the machine was nearly lifting itself from the bathroom floor in its fervor. Misha took an anxious step back. The noise was deafening. The drainage hose popped off and water sprayed the wall.

'What!' Misha alertly crammed a towel against the drain hole with one hand and twisted the control knob with the other. When the knob came loose in his fingers, he fell to kicking the machine, which dodged his efforts until Arkady pulled the plug.

'Fuck your mother!' Misha kicked his stationary target. 'Fuck your mother. Ten months' – he wheeled on Arkady – 'ten months!'

He snatched up *The Commercial Bulletin* and tried to tear it in two. 'I'll show those bastards! I wonder how much they got paid off!'

'What are you going to do?'

'I'll write them!' Misha threw the journal into the bathtub. At once he was on his knees ripping out the editorial page. 'State quality label? I'll show you a quality label.' He rolled the page into a ball, threw it into the toilet bowl, pulled the flush chain and whooped triumphantly.

'Now, how do you know who to write?'

'Sshh!' Misha put a finger to his lips for silence. He took back his drink. 'Don't let Natasha hear you. She just got her machine. Act as if nothing happened.'

Natasha served a supper of forcemeat patties, pickles, sausage and white bread, hardly touching her wine but sitting in an aura of contentment.

'To your coffin, Arkasha.' Misha raised his glass. 'Which will be lined with embroidered silk, have a satin pillow, your name and titles on a gold plate, and silver handles set in the finest cedar one hundred years old from a tree I will plant in the morning.'

He drank, pleased with himself. 'Or,' he added, 'I could just order it from the Ministry of Light Industry. That should take about as long.'

'I'm sorry about the supper,' Natasha told Arkady. 'If we had someone else to shop . . . you know.'

'She thinks you're going to pump her about Zoya. We refuse to get in the middle between you two,' Misha said, and turned to Natasha. 'Have you seen Zoya? What did she say about Arkasha?'

'If we had a bigger refrigerator,' Natasha explained, 'or one with a freezer.'

'They talked about refrigerators, clearly,' Misha rolled his eyes at Arkady. 'Incidentally, you don't happen to know any murderer-repairmen who owe you a favor?'

Natasha cut her meat patty into small sections. 'I know some doctors.' She smiled.

Her knife stopped as her eyes finally picked up the control knob lying by Misha's plate.

'A little problem, love,' Misha said. 'The washer isn't quite working.'

'That's all right. We can still show it to people.'

She seemed genuinely content.

Chapter Six

Man was not born criminal but fell into error through unfortunate circumstances or the influence of negative elements. All crimes great and small could be traced to postcapitalist avarice, egoism, sloth, parasitism, drunkenness, religious prejudices or inherited depravity.

The killer Tsypin, for example, was born of a killer and a gold speculator, whose forebears included killers, thieves and monks. Tsypin was brought up an urka, a professional criminal. He wore an urka's blue tattoos – snakes, dragons, the names of assorted lovers – in such profusion that they curled out from under his shirt cuffs and collar. Once he'd shown Arkady the red cock tattooed on his penis. Tsypin's murder of an accomplice was, fortunately for him, committed during a time when only state crimes were deemed to merit the death penalty. Tsypin got ten years. In camp he added another tattoo, 'Fucked by the Party,' across his forehead. Again he was lucky. Such 'corporal' anti-Soviet propaganda had been a state crime until a week before his act, so he merely got some skin added to his head from his ass and five years added to his sentence, a term suspended on the event of the hundredth anniversary of Lenin's birth.

'I take the long view now,' he told Arkady. 'The crime rate goes up, it goes down. Judges loosen up, then they

114

break your balls. Like the moon and the tide. Anyway, now I have a good situation.'

Tsypin was a machinist. But he made his real money off truck drivers. Drivers would fill up their tanks to deliver goods to some village in the country. Just outside Moscow, however, they'd siphon some gas, sell it at a cut rate to Tsypin, change their odometers and, at day's end, return to their terminal with the always plausible story of bad roads and detours. Tsypin, in turn, sold the gas to private car owners. The authorities were aware of his activities, but as there were so few gas stations in Moscow and there was such pressure from car owners for more, profiteers such as Tsypin were covertly allowed to perform a needed social service.

'The last thing anybody wants is a crackdown, and if I knew who killed three people in Gorky Park, I'd be the first to tell you. In fact, whoever pulled something like that should have his balls cut off. We have standards too, you know.'

More urkas took the chair in Arkady's office at Novo-kuznetskaya, each repeating that no one was crazy enough to shoot anyone in Gorky Park and, from the other point of view, no one was missing. The last was Zharkov, a former Army man who traded in guns.

'What's available anyway? Red Army issue, some rusty British revolvers, maybe a Czech pistol or two. You take the east, Siberia, you might find a gang with a machine gun. Not here, nothing like you describe. Very well, who's going to fire it? Besides myself, I can't think of ten people in Moscow under the age of forty-five who could hit their grandmother at ten steps. They've been in the service, you say? This isn't America. If we've been in any real wars for the past thirty years, do let me know. They don't get a chance to shoot anyone, and besides, the training's gone to the devil. Let's be serious. You're talking about an organized execution, and you and I know only one organization equipped for that.'

In the afternoon, Arkady kept calling Zoya's school until they told him she'd left for the Union of Teachers athletic club. The club was a former mansion at the point of Novokuznetskaya just across from the Kremlin. Searching for the club's gymnasium, he became lost until he went through a door and found himself on a small balcony that at one time had been for musicians. He looked down at what had been a ballroom. Defaced cupids decorated the high ceiling. The dance floor was covered with vinyl tumbling mats, shiny and redolent of sweat. Zoya was swinging on the uneven bars. Her gold hair was pulled into a bun, and she wore sweat bands on her wrists and woollen leg warmers. When she rolled under the lower bar, her legs spread like the wings of a plane, the muscles of her back and rear scalloped under her leotard. In a sweatsuit, arms folded, Schmidt watched from the mats. She reached, thumbs to forefingers, for the upper bar, about-faced in a spin to swing down to the lower bar, grunting against wood, raised herself in a handstand with toes to the ceiling, and reversed and rolled, legs apart, back to the high bar. She was not good enough to be graceful; what she had was a manic kind of momentum, like a clock's wire pendulum wrapping and unwrapping around two poles. She swung down from the bars, and when Schmidt caught her with both hands at her waist, Zoya put her arms around him.

It was romantic, Arkady thought. Instead of a husband there should be a string quartet and moonlight. Natasha was right – they were made for each other.

Leaving the balcony, Arkady slammed the door hard so it gave the report of a gun.

He got fresh clothes from his apartment and, on his way to the Ukraina, *Annals of Soviet-American Cooperation in the Great Patriotic War* from the Historical Library. Maybe the KGB would have carted off their cartons by the time he reached the hotel, Arkady thought, and maybe Pribluda would be waiting. The major might even start with a little joke, establishing a fresh, more amiable relationship, perhaps describing their current misunderstanding as purely institutional. After all, the KGB was maintained out of fear. Without enemies, outside or within, real or imagined, the whole KGB apparatus was pointless. The roles of the militia and the prosecutor's office, on the other hand, were to demonstrate that all was well. Years hence, Arkady imagined, the three killings might be discussed in law journals as *Institutional Goal Conflicts in Gorky Park*.

There were new cartons with the old ones at the Ukraina. Pasha and Fet were gone. Pasha had left a note saying the ikon angle was a bust, but that he did have a German on something else. Arkady crumpled the note, flipped it into the wastebasket and dropped his clean clothes on the office cot.

It was raining, drops hurtling down to the frozen river, steaming off the boulevard traffic. Through the rain, across the boulevard, in the foreigners' compound, a woman in a nightgown stood at a lit window.

American? Arkady's chest ached, the center swollen pink and tender where the fugitive in the park had hit him two nights before. He mashed out one cigarette and lit another. He felt strangely light – light of Zoya, light of home, slipping out of an orbit that had been his life, falling away from gravity.

Across the boulevard the woman's window went dark. He asked himself why he wanted to sleep with a woman he'd never seen before and whose face was a blur behind a wet pane. He'd never been unfaithful, never even thought about it. Now he wanted any woman. If not that, to hit someone. Make contact, that was the main thing.

He forced himself to sit and listen to the January tapes of the businessman-provocateur Osborne. If he could fashion any link between Gorky Park and such a KGB favorite, he was sure Major Pribluda would step in. There was no reason to suspect Osborne despite the American's contacts with Irina Asanova and the ikon dealer Golodkin. It was merely as if passing through a field one day Arkady had heard a hiss beneath a rock. Here lies a snake, said the hiss. The furrier had spent January and the first two days of February shuttling between Moscow and the annual fur auction in Leningrad. In both cities he fraternized with an elite of cultural and trade officials, choreographers and directors, dancers and actors, not with the sort of shabby citizens whose bodies had been found in Gorky Park.

Osborne: *You're famous as a director of war films. You love war. Americans love war. It was an American general who said 'War is heaven.'*

In the *Annals of Soviet-American Cooperation in the Great Patriotic War*, Arkady found Osborne mentioned twice:

During the siege, most foreign nationals vacated the port. One who did not was the American Foreign Service officer J. D. Osborne, who worked shoulder to shoulder with Soviet colleagues to minimize the destruction of goods on the docks. Throughout the most intense shelling, General Mendel and Osborne could be found in the outskirts of the city laboring under fire to supervise the almost immediate repair of damaged tracks. The intent of Roosevelt's so-called lend-lease policy was fourfold: to prolong the struggle between the Fascist aggressors and the defenders of the Soviet homeland until both combatants were drained of blood; to delay opening a Second Front while he bargained for peace with the Hitler Gang; to place the fighting Soviet people in unending financial debt; and to reestablish Anglo-American hegemony throughout the world. It was individual Americans who had the vision to strive for a new global relationship.

A few pages later:

> . . . one such infiltration of Fascist raiders trapped the transportation group led by General Mendel and the American Osborne, who fought their way to safety using handguns.

Arkady remembered his father's jokes about Mendel's physical cowardice ('shitty pants, shiny boots'). Yet with Osborne, Mendel was a hero. Mendel had gone to the Ministry of Trade in 1947, and shortly after, Osborne received a license for the export of furs.

Detective Fet suddenly popped into the office. 'I thought since you were here, Investigator, I might listen to more of my tapes,' he said.

'It's late. Wet out, Sergei?'

'Yes.' Fet laid his dry overcoat on a chair and sat down at a machine. We're not even being that subtle, Arkady thought. The young man went through the motions of balancing his glasses on his knob of a nose and laying out his sharpened pencils. Probably there was a microphone in the office, and they'd got fed up with listening to a man reading and listening to his own headset and ordered poor Fet into the breach. That showed real interest. Very good.

Fet hesitated.

'What is it, Sergei?'

Familiarity made Fet uncomfortable. The detective

shifted like a small locomotive gathering steam. 'This approach, Investigator—'

'It's after hours, call me Comrade.'

'Thank you. This approach we've taken – I can't help but wonder whether it is the correct one.'

'Me, too. We start out with three dead bodies, and go off on a tangent with tapes and transcripts of people who, after all, are welcome visitors. We could be absolutely wrong, and all this could be a waste of time. Is that what you were thinking, Sergei?'

Fet seemed to have lost his breath. 'Yes, Chief Investigator.'

'Please call me Comrade. After all, how can we link cooperative foreigners to this crime when we don't know who the victims were or what they were really killed for?'

'That's what I was thinking.'

'Why not, rather than foreigners, choose a selection of ice-skate clerks, or amass the names of all the people who visited Gorky Park this winter? Would that be better, do you think?'

'No. Maybe.'

'You're of two minds, Sergei. Please tell me, because criticism is constructive. It defines our purpose and leads to unanimity of effort.'

The concept of ambiguity made Fet more uneasy, so Arkady helped. 'Not of two minds. In mind of two different approaches. Is that better, Sergei?'

'Yes.' Fet started afresh: 'And I was wondering whether you knew of some aspect in the investigation that I didn't, which has led us to such a concentration on the recordings of State Security?'

'Sergei, I have complete faith in you. I also have complete faith in the Russian murderer. He kills from passion and, if possible, in private. True, there is a housing shortage now, but as that situation improves there will be even more homicides in private. Anyway, can you imagine a Russian, a son of the Revolution, luring three persons in cold blood to an execution in Moscow's foremost cultural park? *Can* you, Sergei?'

'I don't quite understand.'

'Don't you see, Sergei, there are elements of a joke in this murder?'

Fet straightened with revulsion. 'A joke?'

'Think about it, Sergei. Put your mind to it.'

Making excuses, Fet left a few minutes later.

Arkady went back to Osborne's tapes, using earphones, determined to finish the January reels before going to sleep on the cot. In the table lamp's moon of light he set three matches on a piece of paper. Around the matches he drew an outline of the park clearing.

Osborne:

'But you can't do Camus's The Stranger *for a Soviet audience. A man takes the life of a total stranger for no reason but ennui? It's purely Western excess. Middle-class comfort leads inevitably to ennui and unmotivated murder. The police are used to it, but here in a progressive socialist society no one is tainted by ennui.'*

'What about Crime and Punishment? What about Raskolnikov?'

'My very point. For all his existentialist rambling, even

Raskolnikov just wanted to get his hands on a few rubles. You'd be as likely to find an unmotivated act here as you would be to find a tropical bird outside your window. There would be mass confusion. Camus's murderer would never be caught here.'

Around midnight he remembered Pasha's note. On the detective's table was a report clipped to the dossier of a German national called Unmann. Arkady leafed through it with red eyes.

Hans Frederick Unmann was born 1932 in Dresden, married at eighteen, divorced at nineteen, dismissed from the Young Communists for rowdyism (criminal charges for assault dropped). Joined the Army in 1952 and, during the reactionary turmoil of the following year, accused of bludgeoning rioters (charges of manslaughter dropped), then finished his service as a guard at the Marienbad stockade. Employed for four years as chauffeur to the secretary of the Central Committee for Trade Unions. Reinstated in Party in '63, remarried the same year and employed as foreman in an optics factory. Five years later, dismissed from Party for beating his wife. In short, a brute. Unmann was back in the Party and attached by Komsomol to maintain discipline among German students in Moscow. His photo showed a tall, bony man with sparse blond hair. Pasha's report added that Golodkin had supplied prostitutes for Unmann until the German ended the association in January. There was no mention of ikons.

There was a reel on Pasha's machine. Arkady jacked in Pasha's earphones and turned the machine on. He wondered why Unmann broke off with Golodkin, and why in January?

Arkady's German wasn't as good as it had been in the Army, but it served to decipher the outright physical threats that Unmann used to keep his students in line. From the sound of their voices, the German students were adequately terrified. Well, Unmann had a great job. One or two terrified kids a day, and the rest of his time to call his own. He'd smuggle cameras and binoculars from Germany, and probably bullied the students into doing the same for him. Of course, no ikons; only visitors from the West wanted Russian ikons.

Then Arkady heard a tape of a caller telling Unmann to meet him 'at the usual place'. A day later the same caller told Unmann to be outside the Bolshoi. The next day 'the usual place,' and two days later somewhere else again. No names were used, no real conversation was held, and what conversation there was, was in German. It took a long time for Arkady to convince himself that the anonymous friend was Osborne because Unmann had never appeared on the Osborne tapes. Osborne called Unmann, never the other way around, and Osborne apparently called only from pay phones. Then there would be a wrong intonation in the anonymous caller's voice, and Arkady would think his identification was insane.

He set up two machines and listened alternately to Osborne and Unmann tapes. He built an ashtray pyramid of butts. Now it was a matter of patience.

At dawn, after seven hours of listening, Arkady walked outside the hotel to revive himself. Around the empty taxi stand, hedges crackled in the wind. As he gulped air he heard another sound, a rhythmic thud from far overhead. Workmen were tapping the parapets of the Ukraina's roof for the false notes of bricks loosened by the winter.

Back in the room, he started on Unmann's February tapes. On February 2, the day of Osborne's departure from Moscow to Leningrad, the anonymous man called.

'The plane's delayed.'

'It's delayed?'

'Everything is going fine. You worry too much.'

'You never do?'

'Relax, Hans.'

'I don't like it.'

'It's a little late to like or not like anything.'

'Everyone knows about those new Tupolevs.'

'A crash? You think only Germans can build anything.'

'Even a delay. When you get to Leningrad—'

'I've been to Leningrad before. I've been there with Germans before. Everything will be fine.'

For an hour Arkady slept.

Chapter Seven

The dummy was a featureless pink plaster head in a ratty wig, but it was hinged at the ears so that the face could split open down the middle and reveal an inner structure of blue muscles and a white skull as intricate as a Fabergé egg.

'Flesh doesn't sit on a vacuum,' Andreev said. 'Your features, dear Investigator, are not determined by intelligence, character or charm.' The anthropologist set the dummy aside and took Arkady's hand. 'You feel the bones in there? Twenty-seven bones in your hand, Investigator, each articulating in a different way for a definite purpose.' Andreev's grip, strong for such a small man, tightened, and Arkady felt the veins shifting within the back of his hand. 'And flexor muscles and extensor muscles, each with different sizes and attachments. If I told you I was going to reconstruct your hand, you wouldn't doubt me. The hand seems a tool, a machine.' Andreev let go. 'The head is a machine for nervous response, eating, seeing, hearing and smelling – in that order. It is a machine with proportionately larger bones and less flesh than a hand. The face is only a thin mask of the skull. You can make the face from the skull, but you can't make the skull from the face.'

'When?' Arkady asked.

'In a month—'

GORKY PARK

'A few days. I have to have an identifiable face in a few days.'

'Renko, you're the typical investigator. You haven't heard a word I said. I barely decided to do the face at all. The procedure is very complicated, and I'm doing it in my spare time.'

'There is a suspect who will be leaving Moscow in a week.'

'He can't leave the country, so—'

'He is.'

'He's not Russian?'

'No.'

'Ah!' The dwarf's laugh erupted. 'Now I see. Don't tell me any more about this, please.'

Andreev climbed a stool and scratched his chin and looked up at the skylight. Arkady was afraid he would refuse to have anything more to do with the head.

'Well, she did come to us largely intact except for the face and I took photographs of her, so I won't have to spend any time building the neck and jawline. The muscle attachments were still on the face, and we photographed and sketched those. We know her hair color and cut. As soon as I can get a cast from a clean skull, I suppose I could begin.'

'When can you get a clean skull?'

'Investigator, such questions! Why don't you ask the cleaning committee?'

Andreev reached and pulled open a deep drawer. Inside was the box Arkady had brought the head in. Andreev knocked off the lid. Inside was a shiny mass, and it took Arkady a moment to see that the mass was moving and was composed of beetles, a mosaic of jewel-like insects feeding over and inside bright bone.

'Soon,' Andreev promised.

From the militia teletype room on Petrovka Street, Arkady sent out a new homicide bulletin, not just west of the Urals this time but all-republic, including Siberia. He continued to be disturbed by the fact that the three bodies were unidentified. Everyone had papers; everyone watched everyone else. How could three people be missing for so long? And the only connection to anyone was the ice skates of Irina Asanova, who was from Siberia.

'In a place like Komsomolsk they're ten hours ahead of Moscow,' the teletype operator said. 'It's night there already. We won't get an answer until tomorrow.'

Arkady lit a cigarette and, with his first inhale, went into a coughing fit. It was the rain and his banged-up ribs.

'You ought to see a doctor.'

'Know a doctor.' He put a fist to his mouth and left.

When Arkady arrived, Levin was in the autopsy room working over a body with maroon lips. Seeing him hesitate at the door, the pathologist wiped his hands and came out.

'Suicide. Gas, plus cutting both wrists and the neck,' Levin said. 'New joke. Secretary Brezhnev calls Premier Kosygin into his office and says, "Aleksei, my dearest comrade and oldest friend, I have just heard a disturbing rumor that you are Jewish." "But I'm not," Premier Kosygin answers with shock. Secretary Brezhnev takes a cigarette from his gold case, lights it, nods' – Levin's narrow head mimicked all this – 'and says, "Well, Aleksei, think about it." '

'Old joke.'

'New version.'

'You're fixated on Jews,' Arkady said.

'I'm fixated on Russians.' The chill of the basement sent Arkady into another coughing fit, and Levin relented. 'Come with me.'

They went up to Levin's office, where, to Arkady's amazement, the pathologist broke out a bottle of real cognac and two glasses. 'Even for a chief investigator, you look awful.'

'I need a pill.'

'Renko the Hero Worker. Here.'

The sugary cognac was soaked up by the mass alongside Arkady's heart. Nothing seemed to reach his stomach.

'How much weight have you lost recently?' Levin asked. 'How much sleep have you had?'

'You have pills.'

'For fever, chills, runny nose? For your work?'

'A pain-killer.'

'Kill it yourself. You don't know fear when you have it? Not the Hero Worker.' Levin leaned forward. 'Drop the case.'

'I'm trying to shift it.'

'Not shift it. *Drop* it.'

'Shut up.'

Coughing again, Arkady set his glass down and bent over, holding his ribs. He felt Levin's icy hand slip into his shirt and run over the tender swelling in the middle of his chest. Levin hissed. By the time Arkady's fit was done Levin had moved to the chair behind his desk and was writing on a slip of paper.

'This will inform the prosecutor's office that you have a coagulated mass resulting from contusions and hemorrhage of the chest cavity and need medical observation in case of pyrenemia and peritonitis, not to mention the possibility of a broken rib. Iamskoy will give you two weeks at a sanitorium.'

Arkady took the slip and crumpled it.

'This' – Levin wrote another slip – 'will get you an antibiotic. This' – he opened a drawer and threw Arkady a bottle of small pills – 'should help the coughing. Take one.'

It was codeine. Arkady swallowed two pills and tucked the bottle into his coat.

'How did you get that lovely bump?' Levin asked.

'Someone hit me.'

'With a truncheon?'

'Just his fist, I think.'

'That is someone for you to stay away from. Now, if you'll excuse me, I'll get back to a suicide that's quick and clean.'

After Levin left, Arkady stayed while the codeine spread like a salve through his veins. With one foot he maneuvered the wastebasket closer in case he threw up, then sat very still and thought about the corpse downstairs. Both wrists and the throat? and gas? Was that animal rage or philosophical thoroughness? On the floor or in a tub? Private tub or communal? Just when he was certain he was going to be sick the nausea subsided and his head lolled back.

A Russian kills himself; that made sense. But, honestly, what would a Russian corpse have to do with a tourist? Three corpses – that had a more wholesale, capitalist ring to it, but even so . . . When does a tourist even find time to gun down people? For what Russian treasure worth stealing? From another viewpoint, what threats could three poor workers make against a man who could simply get on a plane and fly away to America, Switzerland, the moon? So why was he pursuing such a theory, let alone conceiving it? To hand the case to the KGB? To thumb his nose at the KGB? Or, getting personal, to prove to someone that being a mere investigator actually amounted to something, perhaps even a hero, as Levin suggested? Maybe that someone would leave Schmidt and come home? Yes to all questions.

There remained one more intriguing possibility: that the investigator himself had discovered – by accident, the way a man passes a mirror and suddenly notices he is unshaven, his overcoat worn at the collar – how shabby his work was. Or worse, how pointless. Was he a chief investigator or a processor of the dead, an adjunct of the morgue, his paperwork the bureaucratic substitute for last rites? A small point that, and merely indicative of socialist reality (after all, only Lenin Lives!). More important, careerwise, everyone was right. Unless he became a Party apparatchik, he'd gone as far as he ever would. Here and no further. Was it possible – did he have the imagination – to create some elaborate case full of mysterious foreigners, black marketeers and

informers, a whole population of fictitious vapors rising
off three corpses? All of it a game of the investigator
against himself? There was a certain plausibility to that.

He fled the morgue for the rain, walking with his
head pulled into his shoulders. At Dzerzhinsky Square
crowds were running for the metro station. There was a
stand-up cafeteria next to the children's store across the
square from the Lubyanka. He had to put something in
his stomach, and he was waiting for the traffic to pass
when he heard his name called.

'Over here!'

A figure came from under a low archway to pull
Arkady out of the rain. It was Iamskoy, a blue trench
coat over his prosecutor's uniform, a gilded hat on his
shaved head.

'Comrade Justice, do you know our extremely talented
Chief Investigator Renko?' Iamskoy brought Arkady over
to an old man.

'Son of the general?' The justice had little eyes set
close to a sharp nose.

'The same.'

'Very pleased to meet you.' The justice gave Arkady a
small, knobby hand. In spite of the justice's reputation,
Arkady was impressed. There were only twelve justices
on the Supreme Court.

'My pleasure. I was on my way to the office.' Arkady
took a step back toward the street, but Iamskoy held on
to his arm.

'And you've been working, since before the sun came
up. He thinks I don't know his hours,' Iamskoy told the
justice. 'The most creative worker and the hardest

worker. Don't the two always go together? Enough! The poet lays down his pen, the killer lays down his ax, and even you, Investigator, must rest from time to time. Come with us.'

'I have a lot of work to do,' Arkady protested.

'You want to shame us? I won't have it.' Iamskoy swept the justice along as well. The archway led to a covered passageway Arkady had never noticed before. Two militiamen wearing the insignia of the Internal Security Division stood aside. 'Besides, you don't mind if I show you off a little, do you?'

The passageway led to a courtyard of gleaming Chaika limousines. More expansive with each stride, Iamskoy led the way through an iron door into a hall lit by crystal fixtures in the shape of white stars, down a carpeted stairway and into a wood-paneled room of narrow mahogany stalls. The star-shaped fixtures on this level were red, and running the length of the room was a photograph of the Kremlin at night, a red flag twisting above the green cupola of the old Senate.

Iamskoy stripped. His body was rosy, heavily muscled and, except for his crotch, nearly hairless. A mat of white hair covered the justice's concave chest. Arkady followed their lead. Iamskoy looked casually at the black swelling on Arkady's chest.

'A little rough stuff, eh?'

He took a towel from his stall and tied it like a scarf around Arkady's neck to hide the bruise. 'There, now you look like a regular metropolitan. This is a private sort of club, so just follow me. Ready, Comrade justice?'

The justice wore a towel around his waist; Iamskoy

draped his over his shoulder and pulled Arkady close, his arm around Arkady's back, whispering with a jovial confidentiality that excluded the older man.

'There are bathhouses and bathhouses. Sometimes an official needs to freshen up, correct? You can't expect him to wait in line with the general public, not with a gut like the justice's.'

They passed through a tiled corridor ventilated by hot-air blowers and into a cellar vast enough to accommodate a long bathing pool of heated sulfurous water. Around the pool, within glazed Byzantine arches, swinging screens of carved wood hid alcoves furnished with short-legged Mongol tables and settees. Bathers sat in the steamy water at the far end of the pool.

'Built during the distortions of the Cult of Personality,' Iamskoy said in Arkady's ear. 'The interrogators at the Lubyanka were working around the clock, and it was decided they should have somewhere to rest between prisoners. Water was pumped up from the underground streams of the Neglinaya, steam-heated and mixed with salts. Just as the facility was completed, however, He died and the facility was abandoned. Lately the complete silliness of not using it became apparent. It has been' – he squeezed Arkady's arm – 'rehabilitated.'

He guided Arkady into an alcove where two naked men sat perspiring at a table bearing silver bowls of caviar and salmon in crushed ice, plates of thinly sliced white bread, soft butter and lemons, mineral water and bottles of plain and flavored vodka.

'Comrades First Secretary of the Prosecutor General

and Academician, I want you to know Arkady Vasilevich Renko, investigator in charge of Homicide.'

'Son of the general.' The justice sat, ignored.

Arkady shook hands over the table. The first secretary was big and hairy as an ape and the academician suffered from a resemblance to Khrushchev, but the atmosphere was relaxed and amiable, the same as in a film Arkady had once seen of the Czar Nicholas skinny-dipping with his General Staff. Iamskoy poured out spiced Pertsovka vodka – 'pepper for the rain' – and heaped caviar on Arkady's bread. Not pressed caviar but roe as big as ball bearings, the kind Arkady hadn't seen in a store in years. He ate it in two bites.

'Investigator Nikitin, you remember, had a near-perfect record. Arkady Vasilevich has a perfect one. So I warn you,' Iamskoy said in a soft mockery of his usual voice, 'if you plan to do away with your wives, find another town.'

Tufts of steam drifted off the pool and under the screen to taint the mouth with sulfur. Not unpleasantly, though – more like an edge to the vodka. A soul didn't have to travel for a cure, Arkady thought, just bathe below Dzerzhinsky Square where heroes were overweight.

'White Dynamite from Siberia.' The first secretary refilled Arkady's glass. 'Straight alcohol.'

The academician, Arkady gathered, was a member of this inner circle not for ordinary labors such as medical research but as an ideologist.

'History shows us the necessity of facing west,' the academician said. 'Marx proves the necessity of internationalism. That's why we have to keep an eye on those bastards the Germans. The minute we take our eye off them they'll get together again, take my word for it.'

'That's who's running drugs into Russia,' the first secretary agreed strongly, 'the Germans and the Czechs.'

'Better ten murderers go free than one drug dealer,' the justice spoke up. Caviar speckled his chest.

Iamskoy winked at Arkady. After all, the prosecutor's office knew that it was Georgians who ran cannabis into Moscow and chemistry students at the university who concocted LSD. Arkady half listened as he ate dill-scented salmon, and all but closed his eyes in sleep as he relaxed on the settee. Iamskoy too seemed content to listen, arms folded; he'd yet to eat or more than sip his vodka; the talk lapped around him like water around a rock.

'Don't you agree, Investigator?'

'Excuse me?' Arkady had lost track of the conversation.

'About Vronskyism?' the first secretary asked.

'That was before Arkady Vasilevich joined our office,' Iamskoy commented.

Vronsky, Arkady remembered the name, an investigator for the Moscow Regional Office who'd not only defended Solzhenitsyn's books but denounced as well the surveillance of political activists. Naturally, Vronsky was no longer an investigator, and the mention of his name caused a queasiness in the judicial community. 'Vronskyism' was a different kind of word, though, vaguer and more chilling, a breeze from a new direction.

'What must be attacked, uprooted and destroyed,' the academician explained, 'is, generally, the tendency to place legalisms above the interests of society, and, individually, the tendency among investigators to place their interpretation of the law above the understood goals of justice.'

'Individualism is just another name for Vronskyism,' the first secretary said.

'And self-centered intellectualism,' the academician said, 'the kind that feeds itself on careerism and flatters itself with superficial success until even the basic, tacit interests of the greater structure are undermined.'

'Because,' the first secretary said, 'the solution to any particular crime – indeed, the laws themselves – are only the paper bunting on the concrete system of political order.'

'When we have a generation of lawyers and investigators who confuse fancy with reality,' the academician said, 'and when paper laws are smothering the work of the organs of justice, then it is time to pull down that bunting.'

'And if a few Vronskyites fall as well, all the better,' the first secretary said to Arkady. 'Wouldn't you agree?'

The first secretary leaned forward, knuckles on the table, and the academician turned his clown's round belly toward Arkady, who watched Iamskoy's sidelong gaze. The prosecutor must have known even as he called to Arkady on the street where the conversation in the bathhouse would lead. Iamskoy's eyes said, Concentrate . . . take care.

'Vronsky,' Arkady answered, 'wasn't he also a writer?'

'True,' the first secretary said, 'a good point.'

'A Yid, too,' the academician said.

'Then' – Arkady draped salmon on a piece of bread

– 'you could say we should keep our eyes on all investigators who are also Jews and writers.'

The first secretary's eyes grew. He looked at the academician and Iamskoy, then back at Arkady. A grin built on his mouth, followed by the pistol report of a laugh. 'Yes! For a start!'

Defused, the talk fell to food, sports and sex, and after a few minutes Iamskoy drew Arkady away for a stroll around the pool. More officials had arrived, floating like walruses in the heated water or moving as shades of white and pink behind the lattice of screens.

'You're feeling especially subtle today, confident enough to dodge the thrust. Good. I'm pleased to see that.' Iamskoy patted Arkady's back. 'At any rate, the campaign against Vronskyism begins in a month. You are forewarned.'

Arkady thought Iamskoy was steering him out of the bathhouse until the prosecutor led him into an alcove, where a young man was buttering slices of bread.

'Look, you two must know each other. Yevgeny Mendel, your father and Renko's father were famous friends. Yevgeny is with the Ministry of Trade,' Iamskoy told Arkady.

Yevgeny tried to bow from a sitting position. He had a soft middle and a wispy mustache. He was younger, and Arkady vaguely remembered a pudgy boy who always seemed to be crying.

'An expert on international trade' – Iamskoy made Yevgeny blush – 'one of the new breed.'

'My father—' Yevgeny started to say when Iamskoy abruptly excused himself, leaving them alone.

'Yes?' Arkady encouraged Yevgeny out of politeness.

'A moment?' Yevgeny pleaded. He concentrated on buttering the bread and adding dollops of caviar so that each slice resembled a sunflower with yellow petals and a black center. Arkady sat down and helped himself to a glass of champagne.

'American companies in particular,' Yevgeny glanced up from his artwork.

'Oh? That must be a new field.' Arkady wondered when Iamskoy would reappear.

'No, not at all, no. There are a number of longstanding friends – Armand Hammer, for example, was an associate of Lenin's. Chemico built ammonia plants for us in the thirties. Ford made trucks for us in the thirties, and we thought we were going to work with them again but they made a mess of it. Chase Manhattan has been a correspondent of Vneshtorgbank since 1923.'

Most of the names were unknown to Arkady, but Yevgeny's voice was growing more familiar, though he couldn't recall having seen him in years.

'Good champagne.' He put his glass down.

'Soviet Sparkling. We're going to export it.' Yevgeny looked up with a face full of childish pride.

Arkady felt the gate opening. Into the alcove stepped a man, middle-aged, tall, lean, and so dark that at first Arkady believed he might be an Arab. Straight white hair and black eyes, a long nose and an almost feminine mouth made an extraordinary combination, equine and handsome. On the hand carrying his towel he wore a gold signet ring. Arkady saw now that his skin was leathery, tanned rather than dark, tanned everywhere.

139

'Absolutely gorgeous.' The man stood over the table, and water dripped off him onto the arranged bread. 'Like perfectly wrapped presents. I won't dare eat one.'

He regarded Arkady without curiosity. Even his eyebrows seemed groomed. His Russian was excellent, as Arkady had known, but the tapes had missed the quality of animal assurance.

'Someone from your office?' the man asked Yevgeny.

'This is Arkady Renko. He's . . . well, I don't know what.'

'I'm an investigator,' Arkady said.

Yevgeny poured champagne and pushed the dish of canapés around the table, prattling as he did so. His guest sat down and smiled; Arkady had never seen such brilliant teeth before.

'What is it you investigate?'

'Homicides.'

Osborne's hair was more silver than white, and wet, it clung to his ears even after he toweled it. Arkady couldn't see whether either ear was marked. Osborne picked up a heavy gold watch and slipped it on his wrist.

'Yevgeny,' he said, 'I was expecting a call. Could you be an *ange sur la terre* and wait at the switchboard for me?'

From a chamois purse he took a cigarette and holder, joined them and lit the cigarette with a lighter of lapis lazuli and gold. The screen flapped behind the exiting Yevgeny.

'You speak French?'

'No,' Arkady lied.

'English?'

'No,' Arkady lied again.

Arkady had seen people like this only in Western magazines, and he'd always thought their gloss was a quality of the paper, not of themselves. The sheer physical smoothness was alien, intimidating.

'It's interesting that in all my other visits here this is my first encounter with an investigator.'

'You never did anything wrong, Mr ... forgive me, I don't know your name.'

'Osborne.'

'American?'

'Yes. Your last name again?'

'Renko.'

'You're young to be an investigator, aren't you?'

'No. Your friend Yevgeny talked about champagne. Is that what you import?'

'Furs,' Osborne said.

It would have been easy to say Osborne was more a collection of expensive items – ring, watch, profile, teeth – than a person; it had the correct socialist attitude and in part it was true, but it didn't take into account what Arkady hadn't expected, a sense of power under restraint. He himself was too stilted and inquisitorial. He had to change that.

'I always wanted a fur hat,' Arkady said. 'And to meet Americans. I hear they're just like us – big-hearted and open. And to visit New York and the Empire State Building and Harlem. What a life you must lead traveling around the world.'

'Not to Harlem.'

'Excuse me.' Arkady stood. 'You know many important people here that you'd like to talk to, and you're too polite to ask me to go.'

Smoking his cigarette, Osborne gave him a prolonged, non-committal stare until Arkady started for the pool.

'I insist you stay,' Osborne said quickly. 'I don't usually meet investigators. I should take advantage of this chance occasion and ask you about your work.'

'Anything I can tell you.' Arkady sat. 'Though from the accounts I read of New York anything I do will seem dull. Domestic troubles, hooligans. We have murders, but almost invariably they are committed in the heat of anger or under the influence of alcohol.' He shrugged apologetically and sipped champagne. 'Very sweet. You really should import it.'

Osborne poured more for Arkady. 'Tell me about yourself.'

'I could go on for hours,' Arkady said with zeal, and downed the champagne in a swallow. 'Wonderful parents, as well as wonderful grandparents. In school I had the most inspiring teachers and the most helpful classmates. Now the team of fellows with whom I work would each be worthy of a book to themselves.'

'Do you' – Osborne removed his cigarette holder from his smile – 'ever talk about your failures?'

'Speaking personally,' Arkady said, 'I've never had a failure.'

He loosened the towel from around his neck and dropped it on the towel Osborne had cast aside. The American looked at the discolored swelling.

'An accident,' Arkady said. 'I've tried hot-water bottles and heat lamps, but nothing is better than a sulfur bath for clearing up congestion. The doctors tell you a lot, but the old remedies are always the best. In fact, socialist criminology is the field where the greatest new advances are—'

'Getting back to that,' Osborne cut in, 'what has been your most interesting case?'

'You mean the Gorky Park bodies? May I?' Arkady tapped out one of Osborne's cigarettes and used his lighter, admiring its blue stone. The finest lapis lazuli came from Siberia; he'd never seen it before.

'Not that there's been any story in the press' – Arkady puffed – 'but I accept the fact that such a bizarre matter becomes grist for rumors. Particularly' – he wagged his finger as a teacher might at a naughty student – 'among the foreign community, yes?'

He couldn't tell whether he'd made any effect. Osborne sat back without expression.

'I hadn't heard about it,' Osborne said when the silence grew too long.

Yevgeny Mendel breezed in with the news that there were no phone calls. Arkady immediately rose and made profuse excuses for having overstayed his welcome, and thanked them for their hospitality and champagne. He picked up Osborne's towel and knotted it around his neck.

Osborne watched like a man far away and out of earshot until Arkady was at the screen. 'Who is your superior? Who is the chief investigator?'

'I am.' Arkady issued a last, encouraging smile.

After a few steps along the pool he felt exhausted. Suddenly Iamskoy was at his side.

'I hope I was right about your father and Mendel's being friends,' he said. 'And don't worry about Vronsky-ism too much. You have my unqualified support to pursue your investigations as only you can.'

Arkady dressed and retraced his steps from the bath-house to the street. The rain had become a mist. He walked up Petrovka Street to Colonel Lyudin's warm forensic lab and delivered Osborne's damp towel.

'Your boys have been trying to get hold of you all afternoon,' Lyudin said before he took the towel off for examination.

Arkady put a call in to the Ukraina. Pasha answered, and proudly told him that he and Fet were monitoring the black marketeer Golodkin's phone, and had heard a man tell Golodkin to meet him in Gorky Park. Pasha believed the caller was American or Estonian.

'American or Estonian?'

'I mean he spoke very good Russian, but slightly different.'

'Anyway, that's a violation of privacy, Pasha, Articles 12 and 134.'

'After all the tapes we've been—'

'Those were the KGB tapes!' There was a hurt silence on the other end until Arkady said, 'All right.'

'I'm no theoretician like you,' Pasha answered. 'It takes a genius to know what's against the law.'

'All right. So you stayed at that end and Fet covered the meeting. He took a camera?' Arkady asked.

'That's what took him so long, finding a camera. Because he missed them. He walked all around the park and never found them.'

'All right, at least we can use your tape and try to match—'

'A tape?'

'Pasha, you broke the law to listen in on Golodkin's phone and you weren't bothering to tape him?'

'Actually . . . no.'

Arkady hung up.

Colonel Lyudin clicked his tongue from across the lab. 'See here, Investigator. I found ten hairs on the towel. I took one and cut it and put it under this microscope to compare it with a hair from the cap you found before, which is under this other microscope. The one from the cap is gray to white and has an ovoid cross section, which is indicative of curly hair. The new one from the towel has a color more like chrome, quite attractive, and has a perfectly round cross section, which indicates straight hair. I'll go on with a protein analysis, but I can tell you right now these hairs are not from the same man. Look.'

Arkady looked. Osborne was not the man who had said 'Son of a bitch.'

'Nice goods.' Lyudin fingered the towel. 'You want it?'

The vodka and codeine were getting to Arkady and he went over to the militia commissary on Petrovka for a cup of coffee. Alone at a table, he fought the urge to guffaw. Some detectives, trying to find a camera while a mysterious character (Estonian or American!) strolls around Gorky Park unobserved. Some investigator, stealing a towel that exonerates his only suspect. He'd go home if he had a home.

'Chief Investigator Renko?' asked an officer. 'There's a call for you in the teletype room, from Siberia.'

'Already?'

The call was from a militia detective named Yakutsky in Ust-Kut, four thousand kilometers east of Moscow. In answer to the all-republic bulletin, Yakutsky reported that a Valerya Semionovna Davidova, age nineteen, resident of Ust-Kut, was wanted for the theft of state materials. Comrade Davidova was in the company of Konstantin Ilyich Borodin, age twenty-four, also wanted for the same crime.

Arkady looked around for a map; where in the world was Ust-Kut?

Borodin, Detective Yakutsky said, was a hooligan of the worst cloth. A fur trapper. A black marketeer in radio parts, which were in great demand. Suspected of working illegal gold deposits. With the Baikal-Amur-Mainline railroad construction, Borodin had a regular windfall of truck parts left in the open. When the militia had gone after him and the Davidova girl, the fugitives had simply disappeared. Yakutsky figured they either were holed up in some hut way off in the taiga or were dead.

Ust-Kut. Arkady shook his head. No one ever got to Moscow from Ust-Kut, wherever it was. He wanted to let the Siberian detective down gently. We are all one republic, he thought. 'Yakutsky' was one of the names slapped on every other Yakut native. Arkady pictured some canny Oriental face at a far-off phone. 'Just where and when were they seen last?' he asked.

'Irkutsk in October.'

'Did either the girl or the man have any training in restoring ikons?'

'If you grow up here you know how to carve.'

The connection started to fade. 'Well,' Arkady said quickly, 'send me whatever pictures and information you have.'

'I hope it's them.'

'Sure.'

'Konstantin Borodin is Kostia the Bandit . . .' The voice was faint.

'Never heard of him.'

'He's famous in Siberia . . .'

Tsypin the killer greeted Arkady in a cell at Lefortovo. He wore no shirt, but his urka's tattoos covered his body to his neck and to his wrists. He held up his beltless pants.

'They took my shoelaces, too. Whoever heard of anyone hanging himself with his shoelaces? Well, they fucked me again. Yesterday I saw you and I was all set up. Today two guys come by on the highway and try to rob me.'

'Where you were peddling gas?'

'Right. So what was I to do? I hit one with a spanner and he drops dead. The other guy drives away just as a militia wagon pulls up, and I'm standing there with the spanner in my hand and a dead guy at my feet. My God! This is the last of Tsypin.'

'Fifteen years.'

'If I'm lucky.' Tsypin sat down again on his stool. The

cell also had a cot bolted to the wall and a pitcher for washing. His door had two panels, a small one for the guard to look through and a large one for food.

'I can't do anything for you,' Arkady said.

'I know, I ran out of luck this time. Sooner or later everyone does, right?' Tsypin put on a better face. 'But look, Investigator, I've been a lot of help to you. When you really needed information I was the guy who helped you out. I never failed you because we had a mutual respect.'

'I paid you.' Arkady softened what he said by giving Tsypin a cigarette and lighting it for him.

'You know what I mean.'

'I can't help you, you know that. It's aggravated homicide.'

'I wasn't talking about me. You remember Swan?'

Not well. Arkady recalled an odd figure that had stayed in the background at a couple of meetings he'd had with Tsypin.

'Sure.'

'We've always been together, even in the camps. I've always been the moneymaker, understand. Swan's going to be hard up. I mean, I have enough on my mind, I don't want to worry about him too. You need an inform- ant. Swan has a telephone, even a car, he'd be perfect for you. What do you say? Give him a try.'

When Arkady left the prison, Swan was waiting at a street-lamp. His leather jacket emphasized his narrow shoulders, long neck and close-cropped hair. In camp a professional thief was likely to pick out an amateur con- vict, bugger him and then kick him out of bed. It made the thief, the one on top, more masculine. The 'goat', the one on the bottom, was detested as the queer. Yet Swan and Tsypin were a real couple, a rarity, and no one calls Swan a goat around Tsypin.

'Your friend suggested you might do some work for me,' Arkady said without enthusiasm.

'Then I'll do it.' Swan had the strange delicacy of a chipped and shopworn figurine, all the more striking because he wasn't handsome, let alone pretty. It was hard to guess his age, and his voice was too soft to be a clue.

'There's not much money in it – say, fifty rubles – if you come up with good information.'

'Maybe you can do something for him instead of paying me.' Swan looked at the prison gate.

'Where he's going all he can get is one package a year.'

'Fifteen packages,' Swan murmured, as if he were already wondering what to put in them.

Unless Tsypin was shot right off, Arkady thought. Well, love was no fading violet; love was a weed that flourished in the dark. Has anyone ever explained it?

Chapter Eight

Although it led the way to the twenty-first century, Moscow maintained the Victorian habit of traveling on iron wheels. Kievsky Station, which was near the foreign ghetto and Brezhnev's own apartment, pointed to the Ukraine. Belorussia Station, a short walk from the Kremlin, was where Stalin boarded the Czar's train from Potsdam and, afterward, where Krushchev and then Brezhnev boarded their special trains for Eastern Europe to inspect their satellites or to launch détente. Rizhsky Station took you to the Baltic states. Kursky Station suggested suntanned vacations on the Black Sea. From the small Savelovsky and Paveletsky stations no one worthwhile traveled – only commuters or hordes of farmers as dusty as potatoes. Most impressive by far were Leningrad, Yaroslavl and Kazan stations, the three giants of Komsomol Square, and the strangest of these was Kazan Station, whose Tartar tower capped a gateway that might take you thousands of kilometers to the deserts of Afghanistan, to the siding of a Ural prison camp, or all the way across two continents to the shore of the Pacific.

At 6 a.m. inside Kazan Station, entire Turkman families lay head to feet on benches. Babies with felt skullcaps nestled on soft bundles. Soldiers leaned slackly against the wall in a sleep so tangibly deep that the heroic mosaics of the ceiling overhead could have been their communal dream. Bronze fixtures glowed fully. At the one refreshment stand open, a girl in a rabbit-skin coat confided in Pasha Pavlovich.

'She says Golodkin used to shake her down, but not anymore,' Pasha reported when he returned to Arkady. 'She says somebody saw him at the car market.'

A young soldier took Pasha's place with the girl. She smiled through a rouge of vaseline and lipstick while the boy read the price chalked on the toe of her shoe; then, hand in hand, they walked out the station's main door as the investigator and detective trailed behind. Komsomol Square was blue before the dawn, the clicking candles of trams the only movement. Arkady watched the lovemakers slip into a taxi.

'Five rubles.' Pasha watched the taxi pull out.

The driver would swing into the nearest side street and get out to watch for militia while the girl and boy went at it in the back seat. Of the five rubles the driver would get half and the chance to sell a congratulatory bottle of vodka to the soldier afterward; the vodka was a lot more expensive than the girl. The girl would get some sips, too. Then a return to the station, a tip to the washroom attendant for a fast douche, and overheated and giddy, she'd start all over. By definition prostitutes did not exist, because prostitution has been eliminated by the Revolution. Charges could be brought against them for spreading venereal disease, performing depraved acts or leading a nonproductive life, but by law there were no whores.

'Not there, either.' Pasha returned from talking to the girls in Yaroslavl Station.

'Let's go.' Arkady threw his overcoat in the back of the car before getting behind the wheel. No frost, and the sun wasn't even up. The sky was just lightening above the neon signs of the stations. A little more traffic. It would still be black in Leningrad. Some people preferred Leningrad, its canals and literary landmarks. To Arkady, it wore a perpetual sulk. He preferred Moscow, a big open machine.

He headed south toward the river. 'You can't remember anything else about that mysterious caller who met Golodkin in the park?'

'If I'd gone instead . . .' Pasha muttered. 'Fet couldn't find the balls on a bull.'

They watched for Golodkin's car, a Toyota. Across the river, at the Rzhesky bathhouse, when they stopped for coffee and cakes, a fresh newspaper was being tacked to the public board. ' "Athletes Inspired by Impending Celebrations for May Day," ' Pasha read aloud.

' "Vow to Score More Goals?" ' Arkady suggested.

Pasha nodded, then looked over. 'You played soccer? I didn't know that.'

'Goalie.'

'Aha! See, now that explains you.'

A crowd was already gathering a block away from the bathhouse. At least half the people wore signs pinned to their coat. 'Three-Room Apartment, Bed, Bath' was a woman with a widow's stricken eyes. 'Trade Four Rooms for 2 Two Rooms' was a newly-wed determined to escape her parents. 'Bed' was a shrewd junk dealer. Arkady and

Pasha worked their way from each end of the block and met in the middle.

'Sixty rubles for two rooms with indoor plumbing,' Pasha said. 'That's not bad.'

'Any word of our boy?'

'Of course, it doesn't have heat. No, Golodkin's here some days, some days not. He makes himself a sort of go-between, you know, and takes thirty percent.'

The used-car market was near the city limit, a long trip made longer because Pasha saw a truck selling pine-apples. For four rubles he bought one the size of a generous egg.

'Cuban aphrodisiac,' he confided. 'Some friends of mine, weight lifters, went down there. Fuck your mother! Black girls, beaches and unprocessed foods. A worker's paradise!'

The car market was a lot filled with Pobedas, Zhigulis, Moskviches and Zaporozhets, some excruciatingly old but others with the aroma of the showroom. Once he had after years finally received the miniature Zaporozhets he'd paid 3,000 rubles for, a sharp owner could drive it at once to the used-car lot, sell his toy for 10,000, record a mere 5,000-ruble transaction at the government shed and pay a 7 percent commission, then turn around and spend his extra 6,650 rubles for a used but roomier Zhiguli sedan. The market was a beehive – the proviso being that each bee bring some honey of his own. Per-haps a thousand bees were on hand. A foursome of Army majors gathered around a Mercedes. Arkady ran his hand over a white Moskvich.

'Like a thigh, eh?' A Georgian in a leather coat stopped next to him.

'Nice.'

'You're in love already. Take your time, walk around it.'

'Really nice.' Arkady strolled to the back.

'You're a man who knows cars.' The Georgian placed a finger to his eye. 'Thirty-thousand kilometers. Some people would have turned the mileage back, but I'm not that way. Washed and polished every week. Did I show you the windshield wipers?' He pulled them out of a paper bag.

'Nice wipers.'

'Practically new. Well, you can tell.' He turned his back to everyone but Arkady and penciled on the bag: '15,000.'

Arkady got into the car, sinking almost to the floor through the hollowed seat. The plastic wheel was as cracked as ivory from an elephant's graveyard. He turned the ignition, and in the rear-view mirror watched a plume of black smoke rise.

'Nice.' He got out. After all, a seat could be padded and an engine repaired, but a car body was as precious as diamonds.

'I knew you'd say that. Sold?'

'Where's Golodkin?'

'Golodkin, Golodkin.' The Georgian racked his brains. Was it a person, a car? He'd never heard the name before, until the investigator revealed an ID in one hand and the ignition keys still in the other. *That* Golodkin! *That* bastard! He'd just left the lot. Arkady asked where he was headed. 'The Melodya. When you see him, tell him an honest man like me pays commissions to the state, not to punks like him. In fact, for officials of the state, dear, dear Comrade, there is a discount.'

On Kalinin Prospekt the smaller buildings were five-story rectangles of cement and glass. The larger buildings were twenty-five-story chevrons of cement and glass. Copies of Kalinin Prospekt could be found in any new city being erected, but none were quite so on the march to the future as Moscow's prototype. Eight lanes of traffic raced in each direction over a pedestrian underpass. Arkady and Pasha waited at an outdoor cafeteria across the street from the narrow building that was the Melodya record store.

'It's a little more fun in the summertime.' Pasha shivered over a sundae of coffee ice cream and strawberry syrup.

A bright-red Toyota came up the other side of Kalinin and turned onto a side street. A minute later Feodor Golodkin, wearing a sharply tailored coat, a lamb's-wool cap and cowboy boots and jeans, sauntered into the store as the investigator and detective were coming out of the underpass.

Through the Melodya's glass front they saw that Golodkin was not climbing the open stairs to the classical-music floor. Pasha stayed by the door as Arkady passed the kids flipping through the rock 'n' roll. In the rear, between divider racks, Arkady spotted a gloved hand searching the political albums. Moving closer, he glimpsed nicotine-blond hair fashionably shaggy and a puffy face scarred at the mouth. A sales clerk came out of the rear pocketing money.

' "The Speech of L. T. Brezhnev to the Twenty-fourth Party Congress." ' Arkady read the album cover aloud as he stepped by Golodkin.

'Piss off.' Golodkin elbowed Arkady, who took the elbow and bent it back so that Golodkin was forced to the toes of his boots. Three records slid out of the cover and rolled around Arkady's feet. Kiss, The Rolling Stones, The Pointer Sisters.

'One of the more interesting Congresses,' Arkady said.

Golodkin's eyes were set within red and heavy lids. For all his long hair and tailored suit, he put Arkady in mind of an eel twisting a hook first one way and then another. Taking him to the office at Novokuznetskaya was a combination of hooks. First, it officially placed Golodkin entirely in Arkady's hands. No lawyer could be summoned until an investigation was finished, and not even the prosecutor need be informed of an arrest for forty-eight hours. Also, by bringing Golodkin within earshot of Chuchin, the implication was made that the chief investigator for Special Cases had washed his hands of his prime informer, or that Chuchin himself was in some kind of danger.

'I was as surprised as you to see those records,' Golodkin protested as Arkady led him into the first-floor interrogation room. 'This is all a mistake.'

'Relax, Feodor.' Arkady made himself comfortable on

the other side of the table and put a stamped tin ashtray in front of the prisoner. 'Have a smoke.'

Golodkin opened a pack of Winstons and offered them around.

'Myself, I prefer Russian cigarettes,' Arkady said amiably.

'You'll have a laugh when you find out what a mistake this all is,' Golodkin suggested.

Pasha came into the room bearing a stack of papers.

'My file?' Golodkin demanded. 'Now you'll see that I'm on your side. I have a long history of service.'

'The phonograph records?' Arkady asked.

'Very well. Now I will be totally honest. That was part of my infiltration into a network of scheming intelligentsia.'

Arkady tapped his fingertips. Pasha pulled out a charge sheet.

'Ask anyone about me, they'll tell you,' Golodkin said.

' "Citizen Feodor Golodkin, of Serafimov Two, City and Region of Moscow," ' Pasha read, ' "you stand accused of hindering women from taking part in state and social activity, and of incitement of minors to crime." '

A nice way to describe procuring whores; the sentence was four years. Golodkin brushed his hair back, the better to glare at the detective. 'Ridiculous!'

'Wait.' Arkady lifted his hand.

' "You stand accused" ' – Pasha went on – ' "of receiving illegal commissions for the resale of private automobiles, of exploitation in the resale of living spaces, of selling for profit religious ikons." '

'All of this is perfectly explainable,' Golodkin told Arkady.

' "You stand accused of leading a parasitical life," ' Pasha read, and this time the eel twitched. The decree against parasitism was originally formulated for Gypsies, then broad-mindedly expanded to include dissidents and all sorts of profiteers, and the sentence was nothing less than banishment to a woodshed rather closer to Mongolia than Moscow.

Golodkin's grin was small and sharp. 'I deny everything.'

'Citizen Golodkin,' Arkady reminded him, 'you understand the penalties for failing to cooperate with an official inquiry. As you say, you are familiar with this office.'

'I said—' He stopped to light one of his Winstons and, through the smoke, measured the stack of papers. Only Chuchin could have given them so much documentation. Chuchin! 'I was working for . . .' He halted again despite Arkady's inviting expression. Accusing another chief investigator was suicidal. 'Whatever . . .'

'Yes?'

'Whatever I did, and I'm not admitting I did anything, was on behalf of this office.'

'Liar!' Pasha flared up. 'I should punch your lying face in.'

'Only to ingratiate myself with real profiteers and anti-Soviet elements.' Golodkin stood his ground.

'By murder?' Pasha cocked his arm.

'Murder?' Golodkin's eyes shot open.

Pasha lunged across the table, just missing Golodkin's

throat. Arkady shouldered the detective back. Pasha's face was dark with fury; there were times when Arkady really enjoyed working with him.

'I don't know anything about murder,' Golodkin blurted.

'Why bother with an interrogation?' Pasha asked Arkady. 'All he does is lie.'

'I have a right to talk,' Golodkin said to Arkady.

'He's right,' Arkady told Pasha. 'As long as he can talk and tell the truth, you can't say he isn't cooperating. Now, Citizen Golodkin' – he switched on the tape recorder – 'let's begin with an honest and detailed account of your violation of women's rights.'

Purely as an unofficial service, Golodkin began, he had provided females he'd believed of legal age to approved persons. Names, Pasha demanded. Who fucked who where, when, and for how much? Arkady listened with half an ear while he read the reports from Ust-Kut that Golodkin had thought was his file. Compared with the petty crimes Golodkin was boasting about, the information supplied by Detective Yakutsky was an adventure by Dumas.

As an orphan in Irkutsk, Konstantin Borodin, called 'Kostia the Bandit,' took apprentice courses in carpentry and engaged in restoration work at the Znamiensky Monastery. Shortly afterward, he ran away from his state school and traveled with Yakut nomads to the Arctic Circle to hunt polar foxes. The militia first took notice of Kostia when a gang of his was caught trespassing on the Aldan gold fields along the Lena River. Before he was twenty, he was wanted for the theft of Aeroflot tickets, vandalism, sale of radio parts to young people whose 'pirate' stations interfered with government transmissions, and old-fashioned highway robbery. Always he escaped into the Siberian taiga, where not even Detective Yakutsky's helicopter patrols were able to find him. The only recent photo of Kostia was a chance picture taken eighteen months before by the Siberian newspaper *Krasnoye Znamya*.

'If you want to know the truth,' Golodkin was telling Pasha, 'the girls liked screwing foreigners. Nice hotels, good food, clean sheets – it's a little like traveling themselves.'

The newspaper photo was grainy and showed about thirty unidentified men walking out of an undistinguished building. In the background, circled, surprised by the camera, a face recovered with a stare. It was heavy-boned and rakishly good-looking. There were still bandits in the world.

Most of Russia was Siberia. The Russian language admitted only two Mongol words, *taiga* and *tundra*, and those two words expressed a world of endless forest or treeless horizons. Not even copters could find Kostia? Could such a man die in Gorky Park?

'Have you heard of anyone selling gold in town?' Arkady asked Golodkin. 'Maybe Siberian gold?'

'I don't trade in gold; it's too dangerous. There's a bonus, you and I know; two percent of all the gold you can catch on a trader you boys can keep for yourselves. No, I'd be insane to. Gold wouldn't come from Siberia, anyway. It comes in with sailors, from India, Hong Kong. Moscow's not a big market for gold. When you say gold or diamonds, you mean dealing with the Jews in Odessa or Georgians or Armenians. People with no class. I hope you don't think I'd ever be involved with them.'

Golodkin's skin, hair and coat reeked of American tobacco, Western cologne and Russian sweat. 'Basically, I just do people a service. My particular expertise is in ikons. I go a hundred, two hundred kilometers out of Moscow, out into the sticks, into a little village, find out where the old men hang around and take a bottle. Look, these men are trying to stay alive on their pensions. Excuse me, but the pensions are a joke. I'm doing them a favor to give them twenty rubles for some ikon that's been gathering dust for fifty years. Maybe the old women would rather starve and keep their ikons, but the men you can deal with. Then, I come back to Moscow and sell.'

'How?' Arkady asked.

'Some taxi drivers and Intourist guides recommend me. But I can go right out on the street, I can spot the real buyers. Especially Swedes, or Americans from California. I speak English, that's my strong point. Americans will pay anything. Fifty for an ikon you wouldn't pick up from the gutter, an ikon you wouldn't know whether you were looking at the front or back. A thousand for something big and fine. That's dollars, not rubles. Dollars or tourist coupons, which can be just as good. How much does a bottle of really good vodka cost you? Thirteen rubles? With tourist coupons I can get that bottle for three rubles. I get four bottles to your one. I want a guy to fix my television, my car, do me a favor, I'm seriously going to offer him rubles? Rubles are for suckers. If I offer a repairman a few bottles, I have a friend for life. Rubles are paper, see, and vodka is cash.'

'Are you trying to bribe us?' Pasha demanded indignantly.

'No, no, my only point was that the foreigners I sell ikons to are smugglers, and I was assisting an official investigation.'

'You sell to Russian citizens, too,' Arkady commented.

'Only dissidents,' Golodkin protested.

Detective Yakutsky's report went on to say that during the 1949 campaign against Jewish 'cosmopolites,' a Minsk rabbi named Solomon Davidov, a widower, was resettled in Irkutsk. Davidov's only child, Valerya Davidova, quit her art studies after her father's death a year ago to work as a sorter at the Fur Center in Irkutsk. Two photos were included. One was of a girl on an outing, eyes sparkling, dressed in a fur hat, heavy woolen jacket and the kind of felt boots called *valenki*. Very young, very gay. The other photo was from *Krasnoye Znamya*, captioned: 'Pretty sorter V. Davidova holds up the pelt of a Barguzhinsky sable worth 1,000 R. on the international market for the admiration of visiting businessmen.' She was extraordinarily pretty, even in a dowdy uniform, and in the forefront of the admiring businessmen, his fingers brushing the sable, was Mr John Osborne.

Arkady turned back to the Kostia Borodin photo. With fresh eyes he saw that the group walking away from the circled bandit consisted of some twenty-odd Russians and Yakuts surrounding a small group of Westerners and Japanese, and this time he saw Osborne.

By now, Golodkin was urgently explaining how certain Georgians had monopolized the used-automobile market.

'Thirsty?' Arkady asked Pasha.

'From listening to lies,' Pasha said.

The windows had fogged over with perspiration. Golodkin watched one man and then the other.

'Come on, it's lunchtime anyway.' Arkady put the file and tape under his arm and led Pasha to the door.

'What about me?' Golodkin asked.

'You know better than to go, don't you?' Arkady said. 'Besides, where would you go?'

They left him. A moment later Arkady opened the door to toss in a bottle of vodka. Golodkin caught it against his chest.

'Concentrate on the murder, Feodor,' Arkady urged, and shut the door on Golodkin's bewildered expression.

Rain had washed away all the snow. Across the street at the metro station, a line of men formed at a kiosk selling beer – 'a true sign of spring,' according to Pasha – so he and Arkady bought pork sandwiches from a wagon as they queued up. They could see Golodkin watching them through a smear on the window dew.

'He'll tell himself he's too smart to take a drink, but he'll think it over, say he's doing all right and deserves a reward. Besides, if *your* throat's dry, think of his.'

'You're a subtle bastard.' Pasha licked his lips.

'About as subtle as a shove off a high place,' Arkady said.

All the same, he was excited. Imagine, the American Osborne could have encountered the Siberian bandit and his lover. The bandit could have come to Moscow on stolen plane tickets. Remarkable.

Pasha bought the beers, two full glass mugs for forty-four kopeks, golden liquid warm and yeasty. The street corner filled up, more men in overcoats using the beer kiosk as an excuse to stand around. Without any grand squares or a building high enough to hang a banner from, Novokuznetskaya had the air of a small town. The mayor and his planners had plowed Kalinin Prospekt through the old Arbat neighborhood to the west. The Kirov section to the east of the Kremlin would be the next to go, laid to rest under a new boulevard three times longer than Kalinin. But Novokuznetskaya, with its narrow streets and small shops, was the kind of place to which spring came first. Men with beer mugs greeted each other as if during the winter everyone had been invisible. At times like these, Arkady felt that a figure like Golodkin really was an aberration.

The break over, Pasha went off to the Foreign Ministry for travel histories of Osborne and the German, Unmann, and to the Ministry of Trade for exterior photos of the Fur Center in Irkutsk. Arkady returned alone to finish off Golodkin.

'It's no secret to you, I'm sure, that I myself have participated in interrogations on the other side of the table, so to speak. I think we can speak honestly, you and I. I can promise you I will be as cooperative a witness for you as I was for others. Now, these things we discussed this morning—'

'Minor matters, Feodor,' Arkady said.

Golodkin's face flushed with hope. The vodka bottle stood half empty on the floor.

'Sometimes sentences seem all out of proportion to the crime,' Arkady added, 'especially for such citizens as yourself with, let's say, special status.'

'I think we're going to work this out now that detective is gone.' Golodkin nodded.

Arkady put a fresh tape on the recorder, offered a cigarette to Golodkin, who took it, and lit one for himself. The tape started spinning.

'Feodor, I'm going to tell you some things and show you some pictures; then I want you to answer some questions. It may all sound perfectly ridiculous to you, but I want you to be patient and think carefully. Okay?'

'Go right ahead!'

'Thanks,' Arkady said; inside he felt as if he were at the top of a long dive, the way he always did when he had to go by guesswork. 'Feodor, it is established that you sell religious ikons to tourists, often Americans. This office has evidence that you tried to sell ikons to a foreign guest now in Moscow named John Osborne. You contacted him last year and again a few days ago by phone. Your "deal" fell through when Osborne decided to buy from another source. You're a businessman of a sort yourself, and sales must have fallen through for you before. So what I want you to tell me is why you got so angry this time.' Golodkin looked blank. 'The bodies in

Gorky Park, Feodor. Don't tell me you haven't even heard about them.'

'Bodies?' Golodkin couldn't have been less fazed.

'To be more precise, a man called Kostia Borodin and a young woman called Valerya Davidova, both Siberian.'

'Never heard of them,' Golodkin answered helpfully.

'Not by those names, of course. The point is that you were done out of a sale by them, that you were seen arguing with them, and that a few days later they were killed.'

'What can I say?' Golodkin shrugged. 'It's just as ridiculous as you said it would be. You said you had pictures?'

'Thanks for reminding me. Yes, of the murder victims.'

Using both hands, Arkady laid out the pictures of Borodin and of Valerya Davidova sorting fur. Golodkin's eyes were a marvel, darting from the girl to Osborne, to the circled bandit to Osborne in the crowd, to Arkady and back to the pictures.

'You begin to see how it looks, Feodor. Two people come from thousands of kilometers away and live here secretively for a month or two – hardly enough time to make enemies except for a business competitor. Then they are killed by someone sadistic, a social parasite. See, I'm describing a very rare bird – a capitalist, you might say. You, in fact, and you are the bird in my hand. The pressures brought on an investigator to close out this sort of case are enormous. Another investigator would need nothing more. You were seen arguing with the victims. You were seen killing them? That's a very fine line.'

Golodkin stared up at Arkady. Eel and eeler. Arkady sensed this would be his only chance, before the hook was coughed up.

'If you killed them, Feodor, you will receive the death sentence for homicide aggravated by profit. If you perjure yourself, you'll get ten years. If I as much as think you're lying to me, I'll send you away for all those minor matters we talked about before. The truth is, Feodor, you're not going to have any special status in camp. The other convicts have very strong views about informers, especially unprotected informers. The truth is, Feodor, you can't afford to go to camp. You'll have your throat slit before the first month is out, and you know it.'

Golodkin clamped his mouth shut, the hook deep in his guts now and not to be disgorged. He was landed and exhausted and losing color, all the vodka-courage gone.

'I'm your only hope, Feodor, your only chance. You must tell me everything about Osborne and the Siberians.'

'I wish I was drunk.' Golodkin slumped forward until his forehead rested on the table, as if his face were in the dirt.

'Tell me, Feodor.'

Golodkin wasted some time protesting his innocence, then began his tale, his head between his hands.

'There's a German, a guy named Unmann that I know. I used to get him girls. He said he had a friend who'd

167

pay a lot for ikons, and he introduced me at this party to Osborne.

'Osborne didn't really want ikons. What he wanted was a church chair or a chest with religious panels. For a big chest, good quality, he promised me two thousand dollars.

'I spend the whole fucking summer looking for a chest and finally get one. Osborne shows up in December, just like he said. I call to give him the good news, and suddenly the prick gives me the brush-off and hangs up. I go right over to the Rossiya, just in time to see Osborne and Unmann coming out, and I follow them to Sverdlov Square, where they meet up with a pair of country bumpkins, the ones in your pictures. Unmann and Osborne split, and I follow the other two and talk to them.

'There they are in the middle of Moscow reeking of turpentine. I know what's up, and I tell them so. They're fixing up their own chest to sell Osborne while I'm left in the cold with mine. I had the deal first and I had expenses. Fair is fair, I want half of what they get – a commission, like.

'The guy, this Siberian ape, puts his arm around me real friendly and suddenly there's a knife at my neck. He puts this knife right through the collar of my coat to my throat in Sverdlov Square and says he doesn't know what I'm talking about, but he better not see me again and Osborne better not either. Can you believe it? Sverdlov Square. It was the middle of January – I remember because it was the Old New Year. Everyone's drunk, and

I could bleed to death and nobody would notice. Then the Siberian laughs and they just walk off.'

'You didn't know they were dead?' Arkady asked.

'No!' Golodkin picked his head up. 'I never saw them again. You think I'm crazy?'

'You got up the nerve to call Osborne as soon as you heard he was back in town.'

'Just testing the water. I still have the chest, I can't sell it to anybody. You can't smuggle out a chest. The only customer was Osborne. I don't know what he had in mind.'

'But you met Osborne in Gorky Park yesterday,' Arkady tried.

'That wasn't Osborne. I don't know who it was, he never gave me a name. Just some American who called and said he was interested in ikons, and I thought maybe I could still unload the chest. Or break it up and sell part. All he wanted to do was take a walk through the park.'

'You're lying,' Arkady pressed.

'I swear I'm not. He was some fat old guy with stupid questions. He spoke great Russian, I'll say that, but I'm pretty much of an expert at spotting foreigners. So we walked through most of the park and stopped at a muddy field.'

'On the north side of the park off the path?'

'Yeah. Anyway, I thought maybe he wanted some privacy to ask about a girl, having a party, understand, but he starts in about some exchange student, an American named Kirwill I've never heard of. I only remember now because he kept asking. I told him, I meet a lot of people. That was it. The jerk walks off' – Golodkin snapped his fingers – 'just like that. Anyway, as soon as I saw him I knew he wasn't serious about buying ikons.'

'Why?'

'He was so fucking poor. All his clothes were Russian.'

'Did he describe what this Kirwill looked like?'

'Skinny, he said. Red hair.'

Everything was coming Arkady's way. Another American name. Osborne and a black marketeer. Two open sesames. He telephoned Major Pribluda. 'I want information on an American with the last name of Kirwill. K-i-r-w-i-l-l.'

Pribluda took his time answering. 'This sounds more like my business,' he finally said.

'I agree absolutely,' Arkady said.

A specific alien was under investigation. How could there be any doubt who should investigate him?

'No,' Pribluda said, 'I'll give you more rope. You send your Detective Fet around, I'll give him whatever I have.'

Naturally, Pribluda would release information only if it came with his own informant, Arkady knew. Good. He reached Fet at the Ukraina, then for an hour played with matches on a sheet of paper while Golodkin sipped from his bottle.

Chuchin wandered into the interrogation room and gawked at the sight of his own informer with another investigator. Arkady brusquely told the investigator for Special Cases that if he had any complaint, to take it up with the Prosecutor, and Chuchin rushed out. Golodkin was impressed. Finally, Fet arrived bearing a briefcase and the air of a reluctantly invited guest.

'Maybe the chief investigator would care to fill me in.'
He adjusted his steel-rimmed glasses.

'Later. Take a seat.'

If Pribluda wanted a report from Fet, then Arkady
would give him a good one. Golodkin liked the rebuff
of the detective, Arkady saw. He was getting his bearings,
adjusting to a new loyalty. Arkady emptied the briefcase
of photostats. There were more than he'd expected. Pribluda was generous with what he called 'rope.'

There were actually two dossiers.

The first read:

U.S.A. *Passport.* Name: James Mayo Kirwill. Birthdate:
4/8/52. Height: 5'11" [about 1.7m., Arkady calcu-
lated]. Wife: XXX. Minors: XXX. Birthplace: New
York, U.S.A. Eyes: brown. Hair: red. Issue date: 7/5/74.

The black-and-white passport photo showed a young,
underweight man with deep-set eyes, wavy hair, a long
nose and a small intense smile. The signature was tight
and precise.

Residence Visa. James Mayo Kirwill. Citizenship:
U.S.A. Born same date, same place. Profession: student of linguistics. Object of stay: studies at Moscow
State University. Dependents: none. Previous visits
to U.S.S.R.: none. Relatives in U.S.S.R.: none. Home
residence: 109 West 78 St., New York, New York,
U.S.A.

The same photo as in the passport was pasted in a box

on the right side of the visa. An almost identical signature; its fastidiousness was striking.

Bureau of Records, State University of Moscow. Enrolled Sept. 1974 for graduate studies in Slavic Languages.

Grades uniformly high. A tutorial report full of praise, but . . .

Komsomol Report. J. M. Kirwill mixes overmuch with Russian students, displays too great interest in Soviet domestic policies, mouths anti-Soviet attitudes. Rebuked by the Komsomol cell in his dormitory, Kirwill pretended to hold anti-American attitudes as well. Clandestine searches of his room uncovered material by the religious writer called Aquinas and a Cyrillic edition of the Bible.

    Committee for State Security. The subject was sounded out in his first year by fellow students for suitability for attention and was reported not worthy. In his second year a female faculty member attempted, at our directive, intimacy with the subject and was rejected. A male student was directed likewise without success. It was decided that the subject was not suitable for any positive endeavour and that only a negative list compiled by the organs of Security and Komsomol would be established. Reported for unwarranted fraternization with the subject were the Linguistic Students T. Bondarev, S. Kogan, and the Law Student I. Asanova.

Ministry of Health, Polyclinic of State University of Moscow. The Student J. Kirwill received the following treatments: general antibiotics for gastroenteritis for his first four months; injections of vitamins C and E and sun-lamp therapy for influenza; late in the subject's first year a tooth was pulled and replaced by a steel prosthetic tooth.

On a dental chart the second upper left molar was inked in. There was no note of any root-canal work.

Ministry of Interior. J. M. Kirwill exited from U.S.S.R. 12/3/76. Having displayed a temperament unsuitable for a guest of the U.S.S.R., this subject should not be permitted reentry.

So this suspiciously ascetic student, Arkady thought, had had no problems with the weak left leg Levin found on the corpse called Red, apparently had no American dental work and never came back to Russia. On the other hand, he was the same age, same general physique, had the same steel molar and red hair, and knew Irina Asanova.

Arkady showed the passport photo to Golodkin. 'Recognize this man?'

'No.'

'He may have had brown hair or red. You don't see a lot of skinny Americans with red hair in Moscow, Feodor.'

'I don't know him.'

'What about these university students? Bondarev?

Kogan?' He didn't ask about Irina Asanova. Fet was showing enough interest.

Arkady looked at the second dossier.

U.S.A. *Passport*. Name: William Patrick Kirwill. Birth date: 23/5/30. Height: 5'11". Wife: XXX Minors: XXX. Birthplace: New York, U.S.A. Hair: gray. Eyes: blue. Issue date: 23/2/77.

The photo was of a middle-aged man with curly gray hair and eyes that must have been a dark blue. The nose was short and the jaw broad. No smile. Shirt and jacket fitted over what looked like a muscular chest and shoulders. The signature was tight and large.

Tourist Visa William Patrick Kirwill. Citizenship: U.S.A. Born same date, same place. Profession: advertising. Object of stay: tourism. Traveling dependents: none. Previous visits to U.S.S.R.: none. Relatives in U.S.S.R.: none. Home residence: 220 Barrow St., New York, New York, U.S.A.

Same signature and same photo.

Entry to U.S.S.R. 18/4/77. Departure 30/4/77. Travel confirmed through Pan American Airways. Reservation confirmed at Hotel Metropole.

Arkady held up the photo of William Patrick Kirwill.
'Recognize this one?'
'That's him! That's the one I met in the park yesterday.'

'You said' – Arkady took a second look for himself – 'some fat old guy.'

'Well, big, you know.'

'His clothes again?'

'Russian, very ordinary. All new. The way he speaks Russian he could have bought the clothes himself, but,' Golodkin sneered, 'why would anyone want to?'

'How exactly did you know he wasn't Russian?'

Golodkin leaned forward, comrade to comrade. 'I've sort of made a study of it, spotting tourists on the street. Possible buyers, see. Now, your average Russian always walks with his weight sort of above his belt. Your American walks with his legs.'

'Really?' Arkady looked at the photo again. He didn't know much about American advertising; he did see a face that expressed brute strength, a man who had taken Golodkin straight to the clearing where the bodies had been found and where Arkady had lost a fight. Arkady remembered biting his assailant's ear. 'You saw his ears?'

'I don't think,' Golodkin mused, 'that there's any big difference between Russian ears and Western ears.'

Arkady called Intourist, which told him that three nights before, when Arkady was being expertly beaten, the tourist W. Kirwill had tickets for the Bolshoi. Arkady asked how to reach Kirwill's Intourist guide. Kirwill was an individual tourist, he was told, and Intourist did not supply guides for groups of less than ten people.

As Arkady hung up to face Fet's limpetlike attention, Pasha returned from his visit to the Foreign Ministry. 'We now have a witness who links two probable victims directly to a foreign suspect' – Arkady phrased his

remarks to his detectives grandiosely, the better for Fet
to pass on to Pribluda. 'It was ikons in a way, after all.
It is unusual for us to hold a foreign suspect. I will have
to discuss this with the prosecutor. Our witness may
even provide us with a second-hand link to the third
victim in the park. See, boys, it's starting to fit together.
Feodor here is the key to everything.'

'I said I was on your side,' Golodkin told Pasha.

'What suspect?' Fet couldn't hold back.

'The German,' Golodkin answered eagerly. 'Unmann.'

Arkady hustled Fet and the briefcase out the door. It
wasn't hard because at long last Pribluda's canary had a
song to sing.

'Is it true about this Unmann?' Pasha asked.

'Close enough,' Arkady said. 'Let's see what you got.'

The detective had brought all the Soviet itineraries
for Osborne and Unmann for the last sixteen months,
done in Ministry shorthand that made it seem as if
they'd been trapped in revolving doors:

J. D. Osborne, President, Osborne Furs Inc.
Entry: New York-Leningrad, 2/1/76 (Hotel Astoria);
Moscow, 10/1/76 (Hotel Rossiya); Irkutsk, 15/1/76
(guest of Irkutsk Fur Center); Moscow, 20/1/76
(Rossiya).
Exit: Moscow-New York, 28/1/76
Entry: New York-Moscow, 11/7/76 (Astoria).
Exit: Moscow-New York, 22/7/76.
Entry: Paris-Grodno-Leningrad, 2/1/77 (Astoria);
Moscow, 11/1/77(Rossiya).

Interesting, Arkady thought. Grodno was a railway town on the Polish border. Instead of flying, Osborne had gone by train all the way to Leningrad.

Exit: Moscow-Leningrad-Helsinki, 2/2/77.
Entry: New York-Moscow, 3/4/77 (Rossiya).
Scheduled Exit: Moscow-Leningrad, 30/4/77.

H. Unmann, German Democratic Republic, C.P.G.D.R.
Entry: Berlin-Moscow, 5/1/76.
Exit: Moscow-Berlin, 27/6/76.
Entry: Berlin-Moscow, 4/7/76.
Exit: Moscow-Berlin, 3/8/76.
Entry: Berlin-Leningrad, 20/12/76.
Exit: Leningrad-Berlin, 3/2/77.
Entry: Berlin-Moscow, 5/3/77.

There was no information about Unmann's interior travel in Russia, but Arkady figured that Osborne and the German could have been in immediate contact for thirteen days of January '76 in Moscow, for eleven days of July '76 in Moscow, then this winter with strenuous coincidence from January 2 through 10 in Leningrad, and from January 10 to February 1 in Moscow (when the murders took place). On February 2 Osborne flew to Helsinki while Unmann seemed to have gone to Leningrad. They had now been in Moscow together since April 3. Yet for the past twelve months, Osborne had called Unmann only by public phone.

Pasha also produced a glossy photo of the Irkutsk Fur Center. It was the same drab modern building as in the photo of Kostia Borodin. Arkady would have been surprised if it wasn't.

'Drive our friend Feodor back to his place,' Arkady told Pasha. 'There's a special chest there I'd like you to pick up and take to the Ukraina for safekeeping. Here, and take the tapes, too.'

He took the reels of Golodkin's confession off the machine. To make room for them in his pockets, Pasha had to shift his small, prized pineapple.

'You should have got one, too,' he told Arkady.

'It would be wasted.'

'I'll be available, Comrade Chief Investigator' – Golodkin put on his hat and coat – 'just for you.'

When they were gone and he was alone, Arkady felt the excitement in himself running like a motor. He'd done it. This time, with Golodkin's testimony and the threat of detention for one of the KGB's favorite Americans, he could stuff the case down Pribluda's throat.

He put on his coat, went across the street and had a vodka, already regretting he hadn't gone with Pasha so they could have shared a celebratory drink. 'Here's to us!' They weren't such bad investigators, after all. He remembered the pineapple. Pasha obviously had other plans of an earnestly erotic nature. Arkady found himself staring at the pay phone. There just happened to be a two-kopek piece in his hand. He wondered where Zoya was.

The Gorky Park investigation had been too strange. He'd escaped, and now he was returning to routine. The pay phone was ballast, a connection to the total gravity that was Zoya. What if she'd left Schmidt and gone back to the apartment? He hadn't been there in days, and had been moving around so much it would have been impossible for her to reach him. He shouldn't hide from her; at least they should talk. He cursed himself for being weak, and dialed. The apartment phone was busy; she was there.

On the metro, everyone was going home from work. Arkady was one of them and he felt almost normal, with hardly any pain in his chest. Melodramas filled his head. Zoya was repentant and he was magnanimous. She was still angry but he was tolerant. She was in the apartment by sheer chance and he talked her out of leaving. All the variations in between, and all ending in bed. Yet he wasn't excited. The melodramas were sodden, cheap and uninteresting; he was only determined to act them out.

He came off Taganskaya, through the courtyard, up the stairs two at a time and knocked on the door. The sound was hollow. He unlocked the door and entered.

Zoya had been back, that much was clear. There were no chairs or tables, rugs or curtains, books or book-shelves, records or record player, china, glasses or eating utensils. She had made a diligent sweep, a combination annexation and purge. In the first of the two rooms she'd left nothing but the refrigerator, and that was empty even of ice trays, which showed, he thought, a disappointing greed. In the second room the bed remained, so it was still a bedroom. He recalled how hard it had been to get the bed into the room. She'd left only the sheets and the blanket on the bed.

His sensation was of being oddly bruised and empty, as if a burglar had crept not into the apartment but into him, and with dirty hands ripped out ten years of marriage. Or did she see it another way, her Caesarean birth out of him? Had it been that bad all the time? She was a good thief because now he didn't want to remember.

The telephone receiver was off the hook, which was why he'd thought she was home. He put the receiver back and sat beside the phone.

What was happening to him? He was hated by someone who had once loved him. If she'd changed, he must have changed her. Him and his perfect record. Why didn't he become an inspector for the Central Committee, what was so wrong about that? Become a shit and save his marriage. Who was he to be so pure? Look at what he'd just done, his fantasy about the black market and Siberians and Americans, one phony connection after another, not to solve any crime, not for the sake of justice, just to get those bodies from Gorky Park off his hands. Bluffing, squirming and dodging to keep his white hands clean.

The phone rang. Zoya, he thought. 'Yes?'

'Is this Chief Investigator Renko?'

'Yes.'

'There's been a shooting at an apartment at Serafimov Two. A man called Golodkin is dead, and Detective Pavlovich, too.'

A trail of militiamen led from the entrance up the stairs to the second floor, through a hall of faces at cracked doors and into Golodkin's apartment, two and a half rooms of cartons of scotch, cigarettes, records and canned foods heaped on a floor thick with Oriental carpets laid one over the other. Levin was there fiddling with some instruments inside Golodkin's head. Pasha Pavlovich was on the carpets, the back of his dark overcoat wet but not too wet; he'd died immediately. By his hand and by Golodkin's lay separate guns.

A borough investigator Arkady didn't know presented himself and his notes.

'It's my guess,' he said, 'well, it's obvious that this Golodkin shot the detective in the back first, then the detective turned and, as he fell, killed Golodkin in return. The people in the other apartments didn't hear the shots, but the bullets would seem to be a match for the guns, the detective's issue PM and Golodkin's TK, though of course we'll check that with ballistics analysis.'

'The people in the other apartments, did they see anyone leave here?' Arkady asked.

'Nobody left. They killed each other.'

Arkady looked at Levin, who looked away.

'Detective Pavlovich was returning the other man here after an interrogation,' Arkady said. 'Did you search the detective? Did you find any tape-recorder reels?'

'We searched him. We didn't find any reels,' the borough investigator answered.

'Have you removed anything from the apartment?'

'Nothing.'

Arkady went through Golodkin's apartment looking for the church chest with the ikon panels, throwing armloads of parkas and skis out of the closets, cutting open cartons of French soaps while the borough investigator watched, rooted to one spot not just by anxiety that he'd have to account for the damage but out of horror for an assault on such valuables. When Arkady finally returned to the dead detective on the floor, the borough investigator ordered militiamen to start removing the goods.

The shot that killed Golodkin left his forehead concave. Pasha seemed peaceful, eyes closed, his handsome Tartar face pressed into colored threads, a sleeping rider on a flying carpet. Golodkin's chest was gone, the tapes were gone, Golodkin was dead.

As Arkady went down to the street, the militiamen on the stairs were passing from hand to hand cartons of liquor, watches, clothes, a pineapple, skis, reminding him in spite of himself of ants laboring under crumbs.

Chapter Nine

Almost all Russia is old, graded by glaciers that left a landscape of low hills, lakes and rivers that wander like the trails of worms in soft wood. North of the city, Silver Lake was still frozen, and all the summer dachas on the lake were deserted, except Iamskoy's.

Arkady parked behind a Chaika limousine, went to the back door of the house and knocked. The prosecutor appeared at a window, motioned Arkady to wait and, five minutes later, emerged as the very picture of a boyar in a coat and boots trimmed with wolf fur. His bald head glowed pink with good health, and he set out immediately along the beach.

'It's the weekend,' he said irritably. 'What are you doing here?'

'You don't have a phone here.' Arkady followed.

'You don't have the number. Stay here.'

The ice was thick and dull at the center of the lake, fine and glassy at its edge. During the summer every cottage would have its family badminton game, bright parasols and pitcher of lemonade. Iamskoy had gone to a small shed about fifty meters from the house. He returned carrying a tin horn and a pail of fishmeal pellets.

'I forgot. You must have had a house up here when you were a boy,' Iamskoy said.

'One summer, yes.'

'I'm sure, a family like yours. Blow this.' He handed the horn to Arkady.

'Why?'

'Just blow,' Iamskoy ordered.

Arkady put the cold mouthpiece to his lips and blew. A honk echoed across the ice. The second blast was louder, sounding again from the willows on the far side.

Iamskoy took the horn back. 'Too bad about your detective. What was his name?'

'Pavlovich.'

'Bad for you, too. If this profiteer Golodkin was so dangerous, you should have gone along and Pavlovich would still be alive. I've been getting calls all morning from the prosecutor general and the commissioner of Militia; they have my phone number out here. Don't worry, I'll protect you if that's what you came to ask.'

'It isn't.'

'No,' Iamskoy sighed, 'you wouldn't. Pavlovich was a friend of yours, wasn't he? You worked together before.' He looked away from Arkady to the sky, a white haze that blended into the silver birches. 'Wonderful place, Investigator. You should come up here later in the year. There are some excellent shops that have opened for the residents since you were a boy. We'll go to them together and you can pick out something you want. Bring your wife.'

'Pribluda killed him.'

'Wait.'

Iamskoy listened to a rustling from the trees right and left. Over the treetops rose strings of eiders, forming V's

184

as they gained height, the males white with black bellies and caps, the females gray. The geese circled the lake, their wings beating rapidly.

'Pribluda had Pavlovich and Golodkin followed and killed.'

'Why would Major Pribluda have any interest in this case?'

'The suspect is an American businessman. I met him.'

'How did you meet an American?' Iamskoy began emptying the fishmeal pellets onto the ground. A deep cooing and whirring of wings stirred the air.

'You led me to him.' Arkady raised his voice. 'At the bathhouse. You've been following the case very closely, as you said.'

'I led you to him? That's an enormous assumption.' Iamskoy poured the pellets in a wavy, decorative line. 'I have infinite respect for your abilities, and make no mistake, I will help you any way I can, but do not assume I "led" you to anyone. I don't even want to know his name. Sssh!' He stopped Arkady's answer and set the empty pail down.

The eiders descended on a straight course, skidding in single file over the lake ice to a halt about thirty meters from the beach. There the birds directed a short-necked, suspicious glare at Iamskoy and Arkady until the men retreated toward the shed. Satisfied, the braver geese advanced in a portly waddle.

'Handsome birds, aren't they?' Iamskoy said. 'Unusual for this area. They winter around Murmansk, you know. I had a regular colony of them up there during the war.'

MARTIN CRUZ SMITH

More geese landed even while the leaders were stepping on shore, heads swiveling in search of danger.

'Looking for foxes, always looking for foxes,' Iamskoy
said. 'You must have some very damning evidence to
make you suspect an officer of the KGB.'

'We have a tentative identification of two of the Gorky
Park bodies. We had a tape on which Golodkin had
positively identified those two people as dealing with the
American.'

'Do you have Golodkin now? Do you have the tape?'

'It was stolen from Pasha's body in Golodkin's apartment. There was a chest, too, at Golodkin's.'

'A chest. Does that exist now? Reading the borough
investigator's report of property, I saw no mention of
any chest. Well, is that all? You want to charge a major
of the KGB on the basis of a missing tape and a chest
and the testimony of a dead man? Did Golodkin ever
mention Major Pribluda?'

'No.'

'Then I fail to understand what you're talking about.
I sympathize with you. You're distraught over the death
of a comrade. You have a personal dislike of Major
Pribluda. But this is the wildest and least substantiated
charge I've ever heard.'

'The American has ties to the KGB.'

'So? So do I, so do you. We all breathe air and we all
piss water. All you're telling me is that an American
businessman is no fool. Frankly, how big a fool are you?
For your own sake I hope you haven't shared these
irrational suspicions with anyone else. They had better
not be in any report to my office—'

'I want the investigation of Pasha's murder under my personal direction, as part of the Gorky Park investigation.'

'Let me finish. The sort of American you hint at has wealth, not merely money as you understand it, and a great many influential friends here – more even' – Iamskoy put it kindly – 'than you. What could those three people in Gorky Park have that would have been worth a minute of his time, let alone make them worth killing? A thousand rubles, a hundred thousand rubles may seem a lot to you, but not to a man like that. Sex? With his influence he could cover the most bizarre embarrassment. What is left? The fact is, nothing is left. You say you tentatively identified two of the bodies from the park. Were they Russian or foreign?'

'Russian.'

'See, you're getting somewhere. Russian, not foreign, nothing that concerns Pribluda or the KGB. As for Detective Pavlovich's death, he and Golodkin killed each other, it's in the report. It seems to me that the borough investigator is doing an efficient job without your assistance. Of course his final report will go to you. But I will not let you interfere. I know you. First, you wanted to force this investigation onto Major Pribluda. Now that you think – for illogical and personal reasons – that he might be involved in the death of your colleague you'll never give up the case, will you? Once you get your teeth into a case you don't let go. Let me be candid – any other prosecutor would put you on medical leave right now. I'll compromise, I'll let you continue on the Gorky Park victims, but I will be taking a much closer interest and control of the investigation from now on. And, maybe you should rest for a day or two.'

'What if I just quit?'

'What if you do?'

'That's just what I'm doing. I resign. Get another senior investigator.'

The thought and words had come to Arkady at the same moment, as a man might realize simultaneously that he was in a trap and that there was an exit from it, a door emitting light from the other side. It was so obvious.

'I keep forgetting' – Iamskoy watched him – 'that you have this irrational streak. I've often wondered why you disdain your Party membership so openly. I've wondered why you wanted to be an investigator.'

Arkady had to smile at the simplicity of the situation, and at the peculiar power it gave him. To simply exit? What if in the middle of *Hamlet*, the prince decided the complications of the plot were too much, denied the ghost's instructions, and sauntered off stage; Arkady saw in Iamskoy's eyes just that astonishment and fury at a play cut short. He'd never had Iamskoy's total attention before, yet Arkady continued to smile until the prosecutor drew his own chalky lips into a wide grin.

'Well, let's say you do quit, what happens?' Iamskoy asked. 'I could destroy you, but that wouldn't be necessary; you'd lose your Party card and you'd destroy yourself. And your family. What kind of position do you think a chief investigator of Homicide gets after he quits? Night watchman, if you're fortunate. Not that you'd be making me look very good, either, but I can survive it.'

'So can I.'

'So, let's talk about what happens to your investigation after you leave it,' Iamskoy said. 'Another investigator will have to take over. Well, let's say I have Chuchin take over. That doesn't bother you?'

Arkady shrugged. 'Chuchin's not trained for homicide work, but that's up to you.'

'Good, that's settled, Chuchin is your successor. A venal moron takes over your investigation and you approve.'

'I don't care about my investigation, I'm quitting because—'

'Because your friend is dead. For his sake. It would be hypocrisy not to. He was a good detective, a man who would step between you and a bullet, right?'

'Yes,' Arkady said.

'Then quit, make your gesture,' Iamskoy said, 'although I must agree with you that Chuchin is hardly the investigator you are. In fact, considering his lack of experience in homicide and the pressures of success in his first case, I would guess there is only one course of action he could take, and that would be to indict Golodkin for the murders in Gorky Park. Golodkin's dead, the investigation would be wrapped up in a day or two ... you see how it all fits together. But knowing the way Chuchin's mind works, I suspect that won't be quite enough. He likes to put his stamp on things, to give the screw an extra turn. You know, I suspect he's capable of naming your dead friend Pasha as Golodkin's confederate. They died together in a shoot-out between thieves. Just to spite you; after all, if it weren't for you, Chuchin would still have his best informer. Really, the more I think about it, the more I'm sure he's going to do it. Speaking as a prosecutor, I've always found it a fascinating aspect of human nature that with the same case different investigators will come up with different solutions. All perfectly acceptable. Excuse me.'

There was no exit, after all. Arkady saw himself standing alone while Iamskoy retrieved his empty pail. Rather than take flight, the geese ran along the beach or onto the lake ice, finding a safe distance at which to coo disconsolately, eyes darting between Arkady and Iamskoy, resenting them equally. Iamskoy carried the pail back to the shed.

'Why do you care so much whether I stay on this case?' Arkady joined him.

'Histrionics aside, you're the best homicide investigator I have. It's my duty to keep you on the case.' Iamskoy was friendly again.

'If the killer in Gorky Park was this American—'

'Bring me the evidence and we will write the order for arrest together,' Iamskoy said generously.

'If it was this American, I only have nine days. He leaves May Day Eve.'

'Maybe you've made more progress than you know.'

'Nine days. I'll never get him.'

'Do whatever you see fit, Investigator. You have great talents and I continue to have faith in the outcome of this matter. More than you, I have faith in the system.' Iamskoy opened the shed door to replace the pail. 'Trust the system.'

Before the door shut, Arkady saw in the dark of the

shed two geese hanging by trussed feet, their necks wrung. The air was fetid with their ripening. Eiders were protected by law; Arkady couldn't understand why a man like Iamskoy would chance killing them. He looked back at the beach, which was crowded again with geese fighting for their fair share of the prosecutor's feed.

Arkady returned to the Ukraina and started drinking before he noticed an envelope that had been slipped under the door. He tore the envelope open and read the note inside, which said that both Pasha and Golodkin had died instantaneously from shots fired at a distance of no more than half a meter. Some shoot-out: one man killed from behind and the other in the forehead, their bodies found three meters apart. Levin hadn't signed the note, which didn't surprise Arkady.

Arkady wasn't a big vodka drinker. Most men *believed* in vodka. There was a saying: 'There are two kinds of vodka, good and very good.'

Who followed Pasha and Golodkin to Serafimov 2? Who rapped on the door of that apartment and flashed the kind of identification that would satisfy Pasha and awe Golodkin? There would have been two men, Arkady thought. One visitor wouldn't have been able to do everything fast enough, and three men would have put even the trusting Pasha on his guard. Who then shot Pasha in the back, picked up his gun and killed the ever more deeply awed Golodkin? Every answer was Pribluda. Osborne was a KGB informant. Major Pribluda wanted to protect Osborne and hide Osborne's connection to

191

the KGB, and the only way he could do both was at a distance. As soon as Pribluda accepted the case, the KGB would be acknowledging that foreigners were involved. The foreign embassy – the American embassy, nothing but spies – would become concerned and start its own inquiry. No, the investigation had to stay in the hands of the chief homicide investigator of the prosecutor's office, and it had to be unsuccessful.

There were different ways not to get drunk. Some people relied on the bite of a pickle right after a swallow; some trusted in mushrooms. Pasha had always said the trick was to get the alcohol straight to the stomach without breathing in. Arkady supposed that was what he was doing, doubled up and coughing.

In some fashion Pasha and Zoya were linked. They were twin emblems of the chief investigator, his admiring colleague and his faithful wife. If there'd been any temporary sense to her desertion, Pasha's death made it final. Marxist history was a scientifically arranged series of muffled clappers, one swinging against the next and so on, out of Arkady's reach now and beyond retrieval, but all set in motion by a fatal instability, a flaw. It wasn't the system that was at fault. The system excused, even assumed, stupidity and drunkenness, sloth and deceit. Any system that didn't wouldn't be human, and this system was more human than any other. The instability was in a man who put himself *above* the system; the flaw was in the chief investigator.

Pasha's notes were written in block print. Arkady saw, however, an effort to make them more scribbled, like his own. He knew he should get another detective to go through the rest of the German and Polish tapes and transcripts. Of course, there was Detective Fet to continue with the Scandinavian tapes, in between reports to Pribluda. There was a great deal of work left to be done, even if the investigator did nothing at all.

Who had demanded the tapes and transcripts in the first place? Who bravely threatened to arrest a foreign informant of the Committee for State Security? Who really killed Pasha?

Arkady threw a carton of tapes against a wall. He threw a second, splitting it open. A third, and then he scooped reels by the handful, releasing their long black tails in the air. 'Down with Vronskyism!' he shouted.

The only undamaged carton was the one that had been delivered that day. There were all new tapes inside. Arkady found one for Osborne's suite at the Rossiya that was only two days old.

He would do his work. He would carry on.

The first conversation on the reel was very short.

Arkady listened to a knock, the sound of a door opening and Osborne's greeting.

'Hello.'

'Where is Valerya?'

'Wait. I was about to take a walk.'

The door closed.

Arkady listened to it over and over because again he recognized the voice of the girl from Mosfilm.

Chapter Ten

The sign was a city block long, of red letters standing as tall as a man: THE SOVIET UNION IS THE HOPE OF ALL MANKIND! GLORY TO THE COMMUNIST PARTY OF THE SOVIET UNION!

Beyond the sign were the Liklachev works, where workers were 'storming' to fill the special May Day quota of cars, tractors and refrigerators by slamming in screws with hammers, setting coolant coils with hammers, hand-making whole vehicles with hammers as the welder followed one step behind with his blessing torch, though all that could be seen from the sign outside was the impressively leaden smoke of the chimneys, each puff big as a boxcar and regularly patched to the morning sky.

Arkady led Swan to a cafeteria and gave him pictures of James Kirwill, Kostia the Bandit and Valerya Davidova. The morning drunks raised their heads from their tables. Swan's black sweater made his neck and wrists seem all the more emaciated, and Arkady wondered how he would survive as an informant. Where workers drank, militiamen traveled in pairs.

'It must be difficult for you,' Swan said.

'Me?' Arkady was surprised.

'Being a man of feelings like you, I mean.'

Arkady wondered if this was some sort of homosexual

pass. 'Just ask about those faces.' He threw some ruble notes on the table and left.

Irina Asanova lived in the basement of an unfinished apartment house near the Hippodrome. As she came up the steps Arkady had the benefit of her full gaze and a look at the faint blue discoloration on her right cheek. The mark was small enough to cover with powder if she wished; uncovered, it added a lazuline edge to her dark eyes. Her patched coat flapped in the wind.

'Where is Valerya?' Arkady asked.

'Valerya . . . who?' She faltered.

'You're not the kind of citizen who reports her skates stolen to the militia,' he said. 'You're the kind who avoids the militia. You wouldn't report your skates stolen unless you were afraid they might be traced to you.'

'What am I accused of?'

'Lying. Who did you give your skates to?'

'I'll miss my bus.' She tried to pass him.

Arkady grabbed her hand, which was warm and soft. 'Who is Valerya, then?'

'Where? Who? I know nothing, and neither do you.' She pulled free.

On the way back, Arkady passed a rank of girls waiting for a bus. Compared with Irina Asanova they were as drab as cabbages.

Arkady told a story to Yevgeny Mendel at the Ministry of Foreign Trade.

'A few years ago, an American tourist was visiting the village he was born in about two hundred kilometers from Moscow when he dropped dead. It was summer and the local people didn't want to be disrespectful, so they stuck him in the refrigerator. They called here, and the people in the Foreign Ministry told them to do nothing more until they received special forms for the death of tourists. A couple of days go by, no forms. A week, no forms. These forms take time to organize. Two weeks went by, and the villagers got fed up with the tourist in the refrigerator. It was summer, after all. Milk was spoiling, and there was only so much they could fit on the American's lap. Well, you know villagers – one night they got drunk, threw the body in a truck, drove all the way to Moscow, dumped the body in your lobby, jumped back in their truck and drove off. This is a true story. The commotion here was unbelievable. There was a ring of KGB officers around the body. At three in the morning they called an American attaché from the embassy. The poor bastard thought he was going to have a private word with Gromyko, and instead here's this body. He wouldn't touch it – not without the right forms. Still no one could find the right forms. Someone suggested there were no such forms, and that set off a panic. Nobody wanted this American. Maybe they should just lose him, someone else suggested. Take him back to the village, bury him in Gorky Park, give him a job in the ministry. Finally, they called in me and the head pathologist. It turned out we had the right form, and we threw the American tourist in the trunk of the attaché's car. That was the last time I was in this building.'

Yevgeny Mendel, who had been with Osborne at the bathhouse and who appeared so often on the Osborne tapes, knew nothing about James Kirwill or the bodies in Gorky Park, Arkady was sure. No special anxiety or intelligence had stirred Mendel's soft face during the story.

'What was the correct form for an American tourist?' Mendel asked.

'In the end, they settled for a death certificate.'

Yet Yevgeny Mendel was troubled. He knew now that Arkady was an investigator, and while he wouldn't have been bothered by an investigator who had worked his way up from the general population, he knew that Arkady was from that magic circle of Moscow children of 'the High Ranks,' a creation of the same special schools and mutual acquaintances, and someone from that circle should be more than a chief investigator. Mendel, the fool of that circle, had an English suit, a silver pen beside the Party pin in his lapel, a large office high over Smolenskaya Square with three phones and a brass sable emblem of Soyuzpushnina, the agency for fur exports, on the wall. Somehow this chief investigator had *fallen*, and the social implications brought a sweat to Mendel's chin like water beads on good butter.

Arkady used this reaction. He mentioned the great friendship between their fathers, praised the valuable labor of Yevgeny Mendel's father behind the lines during the war, and insinuated that the old brute was a coward.

'He was decorated for bravery, though,' Yevgeny protested. 'I can show you the papers, I'll send them to you. He was attacked in Leningrad! He was with the American you met the other day, isn't that a coincidence! The two of them were attacked by a whole squad of Germans. My father and Osborne killed three Fascists and drove the rest away.'

'Osborne? An American furrier at the siege of Leningrad?'

'He's a furrier now. He buys Russian furs and imports them to America. He buys one here for four hundred dollars and sells it there for six hundred. That's capitalism; you have to admire it. He's a friend of the Soviet Union, that's been proven. May I speak out of school?'

'Absolutely,' Arkady said encouragingly.

Yevgeny wasn't vicious; he was nervous. He wanted the investigator to go away, but not until the investigator had a high opinion of him. 'The American fur market is in the grip of international Zionist interests,' he said softly.

'Jews, you mean,' Arkady said.

'International Jews. I regret to say that for a long time there has been an element in Soyuzpushnina close to those interests. My father hoped to break this relationship by reserving for certain non-Zionists especially competitive prices. Somehow the Zionists got wind of it, flooded the Fur Palace with their money and took the entire sable harvest.'

'Osborne was one of the non-Zionists?'

'To be sure. That was about ten years ago.'

From Mendel's window the river ice showed dark

fractures. Arkady lit a cigarette and dropped the match in a wastebasket.

'How did Osborne prove himself a friend of the Soviet Union, besides fighting heroically with your father at Leningrad?'

'I shouldn't tell you this.'

'You might as well.'

'Well' – Mendel followed Arkady with an ashtray – 'a couple of years ago there was a trade between Soyuz-pushnina and the American fur ranchers. That's what they call it – ranching. Like cowboys. It was a trade of the very best fur-bearing animals. Two American minks for two Russian sables. Beautiful minks – they're still producing at one of our collectives. The sables were more beautiful; nothing can compare with Russian sable. However, they had one minor defect.'

'Tell me.'

'They were neutered. Well, it's illegal to export fertile sables from the Soviet Union. They shouldn't have expected us to break our own law. The American ranchers were upset. In fact, they even organized a plan to infiltrate a man into Russia, steal some sables from a collective and smuggle them out. It took a true friend to inform us about his own countrymen.'

'Osborne.'

'Osborne. We showed our gratitude by telling the Zionists that from then on an equitable share of the Russian sable market was going to Osborne. For services rendered.'

*

'*The plane's delayed.*'

'*It's delayed?*'

'*Everything is going fine. You worry too much.*'

'*You never do?*'

'*Relax, Hans.*'

'*I don't like it.*'

'*It's a little late to like or not like anything.*'

'*Everyone knows about these new Tupolevs.*'

'*A crash? You think only Germans can build anything.*'

'*Even a delay. When you get to Leningrad—*'

'*I've been to Leningrad before. I've been there with Germans before. Everything will be fine.*'

Arkady looked at the date on the reel again: February 2. Osborne was speaking to Unmann on the day of Osborne's departure from Moscow to Helsinki. Arkady remembered Unmann's itinerary; the German had gone to Leningrad on the same day, apparently not on the same plane.

'*I've been to Leningrad before. I've been there with Germans before. Everything will be fine.*'

How, Arkady wondered, had Osborne killed the three Germans in Leningrad?

Listening to the new Osborne tapes, Arkady recognized the voice of Yevgeny Mendel.

'*John, you will be the ministry's guest for Swan Lake on May Day Eve, yes? You know it's very traditional, very special. It's important to be there. We will have you driven immediately to the airport.*'

'*I would be honored. Tell me all about what it will be like.*'

There was a change from winter to spring. The winter

Osborne had been maliciously entertaining; the spring Osborne was an agreeable bore, a business dullard. Arkady heard monotonous toasts endlessly repeated, an endless conversation becoming longer and duller. Yet after hours of listening, he felt a watchfulness on the tapes. Osborne was hiding among the endless words like a man standing sideways among trees.

Arkady thought of Pasha.

'A peasant goes to Paris' – Pasha had told a joke while they were riding around looking for Golodkin – 'and when he comes back all his friends get together to welcome him home. "Boris," they say, "tell us about your trip." Boris shakes his head and says, "Oh, the Louvre, the paintings, fuck your mother." "The Eiffel Tower?" somebody asks. Boris stretches his hand as high as it can go and says, "Fuck your mother." "And Notre Dame?" somebody else asks. Boris bursts into tears remembering such beauty and says, "Fuck your mother!" "Ah, Boris," everybody sighs, "what wonderful memories you have." '

Arkady wondered how Pasha would describe heaven.

Revolution Square used to be Resurrection Square. The Metropole Hotel used to be the Grand.

Arkady turned on the lights. The bedspread and curtains were of the same threadbare red muslin. A Persian carpet had a pattern indecipherable from wear. Table, bureau and stand-up closet were mottled by dents and cigarette burns.

'This is allowed?' The floor lady was anxious.

'It is allowed,' Arkady said and shut the door on her to be alone in the room of the tourist William Kirwill. He looked down at the square, at the Intourist buses lined up from the Lenin Museum to the hotel entrance and the tourists boarding in linguistically divided herds for evenings of ballet and opera. According to Intourist, Kirwill was booked for regional-cuisine-and-theater. Arkady went into the bathroom. New, neat; hygiene was the one demand of the Western traveler. Arkady took the bath towels to the bedroom, where he wrapped them around the phone and covered them with pillows.

William Kirwill's bureau revealed American underwear, stockings, sweaters and shirts, but none of the Russian clothes Golodkin had described.

There were no clothes hidden under the bed. In the closet was a locked aluminium-and-vinyl suitcase. Arkady carried it to the bed and tried to jimmy the lock open with his penknife. The latch didn't move. He put the suitcase on the floor and stamped on the lock while he worked the knife. Half the latch sprung. He hammered the knife into the other side of the lock, sprung it open, put the suitcase back on the bed and went through the contents.

There were four small books – *A Concise History of Russian Art, A Tourist's Guide to Russia, A Guide to the Tretyakov Gallery* and *Nagel's Moscow and Environs* – held together by a thick rubber band. By itself was an immense edition of Schulthess's *Soviet Union.* Two cartons of Camel cigarettes. A Minolta 35-mm. camera fitted on a hand grip; also a 10-inch-long focus lens, filters and ten unopened boxes of film. Traveler's checks to the amount of $1,800. Three rolls of toilet paper. A metal tube with a threaded cap on one end and a grooved plunger on the other that pushed up an artist's razor-bladed knife. Used socks rolled into a ball. A small case shut tight with thick rubber bands; inside the case, a gold pen-and-pencil set. A pad of graph paper. A plastic bag containing a can opener, a bottle opener, a corkscrew and a thin, flat metal bar bent at one end and doglegged at the other with a screw through the bar above the dogleg. A book of Intourist dining coupons. No Russian clothes.

Arkady went through the suits hanging in the closet; nothing but American goods. He looked behind and under all the furniture. Finally he returned to the broken suitcase. If the American was so crazy about Russian products, he could go buy some new luggage, something nice in cardboard. Arkady took the rubber band off the guidebooks and flipped through them. He picked up the Schulthess tome of color photographs, a bulky item for a light traveler. In the center, between a two-page spread of a horse festival in Alma Ata, was a loose graph paper keyed five feet to one inch. Drawn precisely were trees, footpaths, the edge of the river, a clearing and, in the middle of the clearing, three graves. Except for the difference between meters and feet, it was almost an exact rendition of the militia base-line drawing of the clearing in Gorky Park. Between the following two pages of the book he found a drawing of the whole park scaled at twenty feet to one inch. He also found a tracing of an X-ray of a right leg; a shadow marked a compound fracture of the shin, the same fracture as on the third body from the park. A dental chart and a tracing of dental X-rays showed root-canal work on the upper-right incisor, but no steel molar.

Arkady looked at the rest of the contents of the suit-case with a different eye. The metal tube that held the artist's knife was curious; what did a businessman plan to cut in Moscow? He unscrewed the cap of the tube and, with the plunger at the other end of the tube, pushed up the knife, which appeared unused. There was a faint odor from the tube. The odor was gunpowder. Looking down the hole, he could just make out the sharp point of the inside of the plunger. The tube was a gun barrel.

In Moscow, guns were hard to come by, and the most improbable weapons were concocted. One gang made shotguns out of exhaust pipes. Now that he knew what he was looking for, the investigator was in his element; he was angry that he hadn't seen it all immediately.

For apparently so devoted a photographer, this tourist took no pictures at all. Arkady removed the camera from the wooden hand grip. There was a groove along the top of the grip that the tube fit into snugly. Only an inch of the barrel protruded from the front, and the plunger at the rear. On the left side of the grip was a screw hole. For a moment Arkady was stumped. Then he broke open the plastic bag, dumped out the openers and cork-screw, and picked up the odd-shaped metal bar he'd noticed before. The main shaft was ten centimeters long, the right angle at one end about three centimeters, the dogleg at the other end about four centimeters. With his thumbnail he twisted its screw into the hole of the grip, leaving enough play for the bar to move. Now the dogleg was a trigger, and the right angle at the other end sat firmly on the barrel plunger, preventing it from sliding forward. He pulled the trigger; the right angle rose and the plunger was free. He set it again, and wrapped one of the heavy rubber bands twice from the front of the grip to the back of the plunger. Ammunition. American airports X-rayed luggage; how could bullets be hidden? Arkady opened the pen and pencil case. It was a matched set, fourteen-karat gold, impervious to X-rays. He pulled off their caps; there were two .22 bullets in the pencil cap and one in the pen cap. Using the long handle of the artist's knife, he stuffed a round into the barrel until it set tight against where the plunger's needle point would slap forward. Too loud; he'd heard hardly any report when he was fired at under the tram bridge. Somewhere was a silencer. Hidden in a box of film? Too short. He ripped open the American toilet paper. Inside the third roll, instead of a cardboard cylinder was one of black plastic, ringed by gas vents, with a threaded protrusion at one end.

In all, a clumsy one-shot firearm inaccurate beyond five meters. Closer than that, adequate. Arkady was threading the silencer onto the barrel when the door opened. He aimed the barrel at William Kirwill.

Kirwill shut the door gently with his back. He looked at the broken suitcase, the muffled phone, the gun. The quick blue eyes were the giveaway – otherwise he looked like any brute: a florid face of small, clean features, a body of beef still hard at close to fifty, heavy arms and legs. At first impression a soldier, at second impression an officer. Arkady knew this was the man with the fists from Gorky Park. Kirwill looked back, weary but alert, his raincoat open to a pink sport shirt.

'Came back early.' Kirwill spoke in English. 'It's raining again, in case you hadn't noticed.'

He removed a short-brimmed hat to shake the water off.

'No,' Arkady spoke in Russian. 'Throw the hat here.'

Kirwill shrugged. The hat landed at Arkady's feet. With one hand Arkady searched the sweatband.

'Take off your coat and drop it on the floor,' Arkady said. 'Pull your pockets all the way out.'

Kirwill did as he was told, letting his raincoat fall to the floor, then emptying his pants pockets front and back, dropping his room key, loose change and wallet onto the coat.

'Push it to me with your foot,' Arkady said. 'Don't kick it.'

'All alone, aren't you?' Kirwill said. He said it in Russian, very easily, while he nudged the raincoat over the floor. Five meters was the effective range of the gun; a meter, Arkady felt, was the effective range of Kirwill. He waved Kirwill back to a point in between, and pulled the coat the rest of the way. The cuffs of Kirwill's shirt were rolled back from heavy wrists, which showed freckles and red hair going white.

'Don't move,' Arkady ordered.

'It's my room, why should I move?'

Kirwill's passport and visa were in the raincoat. In the wallet Arkady found three plastic credit cards, a New York driver's license and car registration, a paper with the phone numbers of the American embassy and two American news services. Also eight hundred rubles in cash, a lot of money.

'Where's your business card?' Arkady asked.

'I'm traveling for pleasure. I'm having a wonderful time.'

'Face the wall. Put your hands up and spread your legs,' Arkady said.

Kirwill very slowly did so, and Arkady shoved him from the back at an angle against the wall, then felt his shirt and pants. The man was built like a bear.

Arkady backed up. 'Turn around and remove your shoes.'

Kirwill took his shoes off, watching Arkady and the gun.

'Shall I hand them to you or mail them?' Kirwill asked.

Incredible, Arkady thought. The man was actually ready to attack a Soviet investigator again in a room at the Metropole.

'Sit down.' Arkady pointed to a chair beside the closet.

He could see Kirwill gauging the chances of a rush. Investigators were issued guns and were expected to take target practice; Arkady never carried his and hadn't fired a gun since the Army. Shoot for the head or the heart? A .22 anywhere else wouldn't even slow a man like Kirwill.

Finally Kirwill sat in the chair. Arkady knelt and examined the shoes, finding nothing. Kirwill shifted, his heavyweight's shoulders leaning forward.

'Just curious,' he said when the gun barrel jerked

toward him. 'I'm a tourist, and tourists are supposed to be curious.'

Arkady threw the shoes to Kirwill.

'Put them back on, and tie the laces of the shoes together.'

When Kirwill was done, Arkady approached and kicked the chair, tilting it and the man against the wall. For the first time since Kirwill had entered the room, Arkady felt reasonably safe.

'Now what?' Kirwill asked. 'You pile the furniture on me to hold me down?'

'If need be.'

'Well, you might need to.' Kirwill assumed an air of mock ease, a recklessness Arkady had seen in other powerful men, a vanity as if their strength had no limits. The hate in the blue gaze, though, Arkady didn't understand.

'Mr Kirwill, you are guilty of violating Article 15, smuggling a weapon into the Soviet Union, and Article 218, manufacturing a dangerous weapon.'

'You manufactured it, not me.'

'You've been moving around Moscow dressed as a Russian. You talked to a man called Golodkin. Why?'

'You tell me.'

'Because James Kirwill is dead,' Arkady said to shock Kirwill.

'You ought to know, Renko,' Kirwill answered. 'You killed him.'

'Me?'

'Aren't you the guy I punched around in the park the other night? You're from the prosecutor's office, right?

Didn't you send a man to follow me and Golodkin when I went back to the park? Little guy with glasses. I followed him from the park to a KGB office. What difference what office, huh?' Kirwill's head lolled to one side.

'How do you know my name?' Arkady asked.

'I talked to the embassy. I talked to the correspondents. I read every back issue of *Pravda*. I talked to the people on the street. I watched your morgue. I watched the prosecutor's office. When I found out your name I watched your apartment. I didn't see you, but I saw your wife and her boyfriend clean the place out. I was outside your office when you let Golodkin go.'

Arkady didn't believe what he was hearing. This madman could not have watched him, followed Fet to Pribluda's office, seen Zoya. When he and Pasha queued for a beer at the corner kiosk, was Kirwill in the line behind them?

'Why did you choose this time to come to Moscow?'

'I had to come sometime. Spring's a good time, time for bodies to come up from the bottom of the river. Good time for bodies.'

'And you think I killed James Kirwill?'

'Maybe not you yourself, but you and your friends. Does it matter who pulled the trigger?'

'How do you know he was shot?'

'In the clearing in the park, the depth of the digging. For slugs, right? Anyway, you don't stab three people to death. I wish I'd known it was you in the park, Renko. I'd have killed you.'

Kirwill spoke with regret and some amusement for his missed opportunity. His Russian had no accent, yet retained a distinctly American voice. He folded his arms as if he were laying them aside. An outsized man of intelligence exerts a force of gravity, a threat of physical absorption, especially in a small room. Arkady sat down on a night table against the opposite wall. How could he have not noticed someone like Kirwill?

'You came to Moscow to ask questions among the foreign community about a murder,' Arkady said. 'You have drawings of X-rays and dental charts. You must have meant to aid the investigation.'

'If you were a real investigator.'

'There is a record of James Kirwill leaving the Soviet Union last year; there is no record of his returning. Why did you think he was here, and why did you think he was dead?'

'But you're not a real investigator. Your detectives spend as much time with the KGB as they do with you.'

There was no way of explaining Fet to an American, and Arkady didn't try. 'How are you and James Kirwill related?'

'You tell me.'

'Mr Kirwill, I operate under the directive of the Moscow town prosecutor, no one else. I am investigating the murder of three persons in Gorky Park. You came all the way from New York with information that might be of help. Give it to me.'

'No.'

'You're not in a position to say no. You've been seen dressed as a Russian. You smuggled in a firearm you've already fired at me. You're withholding information and that, too, is a crime.'

'Renko, you find any Russian clothes here? Anyway, it's a crime to dress like you? As for the gun, or whatever you're aiming at me, I never saw it before. You broke into my suitcase; I don't know what you planted in it. And what information are you talking about?'

Arkady was stopped for a moment by such massive contempt for the law.

'Your statements about James Kirwill—' he began again.

'What statements? The microphone is in the telephone, and you've taken care of that. You should have brought some friends along, Renko. As an investigator you're not too competent.'

'There are your drawings of the murder scene in Gorky Park and the X-rays and dental chart you brought, which will connect you to James Kirwill if he was one of the victims.'

'The drawings and chart are done by a Russian pencil on Russian graph paper,' Kirwill answered. 'There are no X-rays, only tracings. What you should be thinking about right now, Renko, is what the American embassy is going to say about a Russian cop who assaults innocent American tourists when he's caught' – Kirwill glanced at the open suitcase – 'apparently in the act of burglary. You didn't plan to take anything, did you?'

'Mr Kirwill, if you report anything to your embassy they will put you on the next plane home. You didn't come here to go right home, did you? You also don't want to spend fifteen years in a Soviet rehabilitation center.'

'I can handle it.'

MARTIN CRUZ SMITH

'Mr Kirwill, how is it that you speak Russian so well? Where have I heard your name before, before you and this James Kirwill? It seems to me now it's a familiar name.'

'Good-bye, Renko. Go back to your friends in the secret police now.'

'Tell me about James Kirwill.'

'Get out.'

Arkady gave up. On his way he put Kirwill's passport, wallet and credit cards on the night table.

'Don't bother,' Kirwill said. 'I'll clean up after you.'

The wallet was heavy in the palm, and stiff even without credit cards. There was handstitching along one lip of the wallet. Kirwill rocked forward. Arkady waved the gun. A spy? Arkady thought. Something as ridiculous as a secret message sewn into a wallet and a heroic roundup of traitors and foreign agents with a chief investigator bumbling around in the middle? He ripped the stitching open, keeping one eye on Kirwill. From the wallet he drew a gold metal shield embossed in blue with the figures of an Indian and a pilgrim. 'City of New York' was above the scale and 'Lieutenant' below it.

'A policeman?'

'Detective,' Kirwill corrected.

'Then you must help,' Arkady said as if it were clear, because it was to him. 'You saw Golodkin leave my office with a detective, a friend of mine, Pasha Pavlovich.' A name like that would mean nothing to an American, Arkady decided. 'Anyway, a detective I worked with many times, a very good man. An hour later, in Golodkin's apartment, both Golodkin and the detective were killed

212

by someone else. I don't care about Golodkin. All I want to do is find the man who killed the detective. Things can't be so different in America. Being a detective, you understand how it is when a friend—'

'Renko, go fuck yourself.'

Arkady wasn't aware of raising the makeshift gun. He found himself aiming the barrel at a point between Kirwill's eyes and pulling the trigger so that the doubled rubber band and plunger started to move smoothly. At the last moment he aimed away. The closet jumped and a hole two centimeters across appeared in the closet door beside Kirwill's ear. Arkady was astonished. He'd never come close to murdering anyone in his life, and when the accuracy of the weapon was considered he could as easily have killed as missed. A white mask of surprise showed where the blood had drained around Kirwill's eyes.

'Get out while you can,' Kirwill said.

Arkady dropped the gun. Unhurriedly, he collected the X-ray tracing and dental chart from the open suitcase. He kept the badge and threw the wallet aside.

'I need my shield.' Kirwill came out of his chair.

'Not in this city.' Arkady walked out the door. 'This is my city,' he murmured to himself.

No one was on night duty at the lab. Arkady matched the tracings and dental chart with Levin's records himself, aware that at the same time William Kirwill was probably disposing of his gun – a hand grip here, a barrel there – around the city. By the time he got to his office at Novokuznetskaya and wrote a report for Iamskoy, he knew that Kirwill was probably seeking asylum at the American embassy. Fine; all the more proof for the prosecutor because now it was certain that James Kirwill was the third body from Gorky Park. Arkady left the report on the desk of Iamskoy's deputy, to be found in the morning.

A bright searchlight stood in the middle of the Moskva. No, it moved. There was a sound as of stones shifting. Arkady stopped his car and watched from the embankment as an icebreaker plowed by, pushing a crest of broken ice ahead, trailing floes that rose and fell in the thrust of the wake. Water, freed, twisted in braids of black.

Arkady drove along the river until he had finished a pack of cigarettes. He was shaken by the encounter at the Metropole. He hadn't shot William Kirwill, but he'd wanted to and had come within a finger's breadth of doing so. He was shaken because he hadn't cared particularly one way or the other. Neither, he suspected, had Kirwill.

Going by Gorky Park, he noticed the lights in Andreev's studio on top of the Ethnological Institute. Although it was midnight, Arkady was welcomed by the anthropologist.

'I do this work for you after hours, so it's only fair you should keep me company. Come on, there's supper enough for two.' Andreev brought Arkady to a table where Cro-Magnon heads made way for plates. 'Beets, onions, sausage, bread. No vodka, I'm sorry. It's been my experience that dwarfs become drunk very quickly, and personally I can think of nothing more grotesque than a drunken dwarf.'

Andreev was in such good humor that Arkady hesitated to say that so far as he was concerned the investigation was as good as over.

'Ah, but you want to see her.' Andreev misinterpreted Arkady's indecision. 'That's why you came by.'

'You're finished?'

'Hardly. You can look, though.' He lifted a cloth from the potter's wheel to display his progress.

Reconstruction of the face of the girl from Gorky Park was at that midpoint which might have been a building of her features by a sculptor or a dissection of them by an anatomist. All the muscles of her neck were in place, forming a graceful pink column only wanting skin. A cat's cradle of pink muscles spread from the nasal hollow around the gum lines of naked teeth. Flat temporal muscles fanned across her cheekbones and temples. Muscles smoothed the angles of her jaw. Overall, the interlace of pink plasteline strips and daubs both softened the starkness of her skull and made it as gruesome as a death mask. She stared with two brown glass eyes.

'As you can see, I've already finished the large masseter muscles of the jaw and the muscles of the neck. The position of her neck vertebrae tells me how she held her head, a psychological clue as well. She held her head high. I saw at once by the larger muscle attachments on the right side of the vertebrae that she was right-handed.

Some things are very simple. A female's muscles are smaller than a man's. Her skull is lighter, she has larger eye sockets and less bone relief. But every muscle must be individually sculpted. Look at her mouth. See how uniform the teeth are with a medium projection, typical Homo sapiens, except for some primitive aborigines or red Indians. The main thing is, in this kind of bite the upper lip is usually dominant. In fact, the mouth is one of the easier areas of reconstruction. Wait and see, she has a lovely mouth. The nose is more difficult, a triangulation from the horizontal profile of the face and the contours of the nasal opening and eye sockets.'

The glass eyes, anchored in plasteline, bulged hysterically. 'How do you know what size eyes to insert?' Arkady asked.

'Everyone's eyes are about the same size. You're disappointed. The "windows of the soul" and all that? Where would romance be without eyes? The fact is, when we talk about the shape of a woman's eyes, we're really describing the shape of her eyelids. "She deliberately shrouded the light in her eyes but in spite of herself it gleamed in the faintly perceptible smile." '

'*Anna Karenina*.'

'A literate man! I suspected it all along. And it's eyelids, nothing but eyelids and muscle attachments.' Andreev climbed a stool and carved a piece of bread for himself. 'You like the circus, Investigator?'

'Not especially.'

'Everybody likes the circus. Why don't you?'

'Some parts I like well enough. The Cossacks and the clowns.'

'It's the bears you're sick of?'

'A little. But the last time I was there they had an act of trained baboons. There was a girl in a sequined outfit – she was too fat for it or it was too tight for her – and she'd call the baboons out one by one and they would roll around or do flips. All the time the baboons were looking over their shoulders at this big brute, a guy in a sailor outfit, who was snapping a whip at them from behind. It was crazy. This brute, unshaven, in a sort of kid's sailor costume, and he's beating the baboons every time they miss a cue. Then the fat girl comes out, does a curtsy and everyone claps.'

'You're exaggerating.'

'I'm not,' Arkady said. 'It was a performance of baboon abuse.'

'Then you weren't supposed to notice the man with the whip – that's why he was in a sailor suit.' Andreev grinned. 'Anyway, dear Renko, what's your discomfort at a circus compared to mine? I barely get to my seat before children start crawling over their parents to get at me. To them a dwarf must be part of the show. I should tell you that I do not appreciate children under the best of circumstances.'

'Then you must hate the circus.'

'I love it. Dwarfs, giants, fat men, people with blue hair and red noses, or green hair and purple noses. You don't know what a relief it can be to escape normality. I do wish I had a little vodka here now. Anyway, that's where you will benefit from me, Investigator. The previous director of this institute was a good man, round and jolly and very normal. Like all normal artists, his

217

reconstructions tended to resemble himself. Not at the start, but it crept in. Each face he did was a little rounder, even a little jollier. There was a cabinet of cavemen and murder victims here, and a happier, better-fed lot you never saw. A normal person always sees himself in others, you know. Always. I see more clearly.' Andreev winked. 'Trust the freak's eyes.'

As he slept the phone rang. The caller was Detective Yakutsky, who asked first what the time was in Moscow.

'Late,' Arkady muttered. Calls between Moscow and Siberia, it seemed to him, always began with a ritual establishment of the time difference.

'I'm on the morning shift here,' Yakutsky said. 'I have a little more information on Valerya Davidova.'

'You might want to hold on to it. I think someone else will be handling this case in a couple of days.'

'I have a lead for you.' After a silence, Yakutsky added, 'We're very interested in this case in Ust-Kut.'

'Okay,' Arkady answered, so as not to let down the boys in Ust-Kut. 'What is it?'

'The Davidova girl had a very good friend who moved from Irkutsk to Moscow. She's there at the university. Her name's Irina Asanova. If Valerya Davidova showed up in Moscow, she would have gone to the Asanova girl.'

'Thanks.'

'I'll call as soon as anything else turns up,' Detective Yakutsky promised.

'Anytime,' Arkady said and hung up.

He had to pity Irina Asanova. He remembered Pribluda breaking the frozen dress on the corpse in Gorky Park. And the Asanova girl was beautiful. Anyway, it wasn't his concern. He closed his eyes.

When the phone rang again he fumbled for it in the dark, expecting Yakutsky with more useless information. He found the receiver, lay back and grunted.

'I've picked up the Russian habit of calling late,' John Osborne said.

Arkady was awake. His eyes were open, and with the clarity only an involuntary waker has, he saw all the dark details around him: the cartons of tapes, the ominous crossing of chair legs, a shadow folded in a corner of the room, the airline poster on the wall totally legible.

'I haven't disturbed you, have I?' Osborne asked.

'No.'

'We were just getting into an interesting conversation at the bathhouse, and I was afraid we might not bump into each other again before I left Moscow. Is ten tomorrow convenient for you, Investigator? On the quay outside the Trade Council?'

'Yes.'

'Wonderful. See you there.' Osborne hung up.

Arkady could think of no reason for Osborne to show up at the quay tomorrow. He could think of no reason to be there himself.

Chapter Eleven

The first real dew of the year had turned into a damp shroud along the Shevchenko Quay. Waiting across the road from the U.S.–U.S.S.R. Trade and Economic Council, Arkady could see Russian secretaries in the staff offices and American businessmen and a Pepsi-Cola machine in the members' room. He coughed up smoke.

It was still Arkady's case. Iamskoy had called first thing in the morning to say it was interesting that an American who once studied in Moscow should have some similar physical characteristics to a body found in Gorky Park, and that the investigator should not hesitate to pursue any evidence that could establish such a link, although the investigator must not approach foreign nationals and, from this point on, would receive no more tapes or transcripts from the KGB.

Well, Arkady thought, Osborne had approached him, not the other way around. The 'friend of the Soviet Union' must not have liked learning that he was the subject of an investigator's visit to the Ministry of Foreign Trade. How to get his conversation with Osborne around to his particular trade and travels, Arkady wasn't sure; in fact, he doubted that Osborne would appear at all.

Half an hour after the agreed time a Chaika limousine coasted to a stop in front of the Trade Council. John

Osborne emerged from the building, said a few words to the limousine driver, and then strode across the road toward the investigator. He wore a suede overcoat. Set on his silver hair was a black sable hat that must have cost more than Arkady earned in a year. Gold links rather than buttons held his shirt cuffs together. On Osborne such extraordinary clothes were matter-of-fact, as subservient as skin to an enormous and totally foreign self-confidence. He had the power of not being out of place himself, but of making everything around him seem inappropriate and shabby. He and Arkady stood together for a moment, then the businessman gathered the investigator by the arm and began walking at a hurried pace along the quay in the direction of the Kremlin. The limousine followed.

Osborne began talking before Arkady could say anything. 'I hope you don't mind the rush, but I have to make a reception at the Trade Ministry, and I know you wouldn't want me to keep anyone waiting. Do you know the Minister of Foreign Trade? You seem to know everyone, and you pop up in the most unexpected places. Do you know anything about money?'

'Nothing.'

'Let me tell you about money. Fur and gold are the oldest Russian items of value. They're the oldest Russian items of foreign exchange, tribute to khans and Caesars. Of course, Russia pays tribute to no one anymore. Now, there are two fur auctions a year, in January and July, at the Fur Palace in Leningrad. About one hundred buyers attend, about ten of them from the United States. Some buyers are principals, some are brokers; the principals buy furs for themselves and the brokers buy for others. I am a broker *and* a principal because I buy for others but also have my own salons in the United States and Europe. The major furs at the auctions are mink, marten, fox, fitch, Persian lamb and sable. In general, American brokers don't bid on minks because Russian minks are prohibited in the United States – an unfortunate holdover from the Cold War. Because of my European outlets, I bid on all furs, but the only fur most American buyers are really interested in is sable. We arrive ten days before the auction to inspect the pelts. When I buy minks, for example, I look carefully at fifty mink pelts from a particular collective. Those fifty pelts will give me the worth of a "string" of a thousand pelts from that collective. Since there are eight million mink pelts harvested in the Soviet Union in a year, the "string" system is a necessity.

'Sables are a different matter. Less than one hundred thousand export-quality sables are harvested in a year. There are no "strings." Each sable has to be examined individually for color and richness. If the pelt is harvested one week early, thickness is missing; one week late and the gloss is gone. The bidding is in dollars simply as a standard of exchange. I buy about half a million dollars' worth of sable at each auction.'

Arkady didn't know what to say. This was not a conversation; it was a rambling monologue. He discovered himself being lectured to and ignored at the same time.

'As a business associate and friend of long standing, I've been honored by invitations to different Soviet facilities besides the Fur Palace. Last year, I flew to Irkutsk to tour the Fur Center there. My visit to Moscow now is of a business nature. Each spring the Trade Ministry here contacts a few buyers and negotiates a discount sale of its leftover furs. I always enjoy my visits to Moscow because of the wide variety of Russian people I've come to know. Not only my close friends in the ministries, but also artists of the dance and film people. Now, a chief investigator of Homicide. I regret not being able to stay over until May Day, but I will be leaving the night before for New York.'

Osborne opened a gold case, removed and lit a cigarette without breaking stride. Arkady realized that the monologue had not rambled. It had come directly to the point. Every item about Osborne's activities was being volunteered and dispensed with in a fashion that put Arkady in the role of the lowest government flunky. The effect was no mere appearance. Within minutes, offhand, Osborne had fully demonstrated his superiority. There wasn't a question left in the investigator's head, except those so accusatory that they couldn't be asked.

'How are they killed?' Arkady asked.

'Who?' Osborne stopped with no more interest on his face than if Arkady had remarked on the weather.

'Sables.'

'Injections. It's painless.' Osborne began walking again, a little less quickly. Mist clung on his sable hat. 'You take a professional interest in everything, Investigator?'

'But sables are so fascinating. How do you trap them?'

'They can be smoked out of their dens. Or treed by

huskies that are trained for sable hunting; then all the surrounding trees are cut down and nets are spread.'

'Sables hunt like minks?'

'Sables hunt minks. There is nothing faster on snow. Siberia is paradise for them.'

Arkady stopped and bent three matches before getting one of his Primas lit. A smile announced to Osborne that all the investigator aspired to was amusing chatter.

'Leningrad,' Arkady sighed, 'such a beautiful city. The Venice of the North, I hear it's called.'

'Some people call it that.'

'What I want to know is why Leningrad has all the great poets. I don't mean Yevtushenko or Voznesensky, I mean great poets like Akhmatova and Mandelstam. You know the poetry of Mandelstam?'

'I know he's out of favor with the Party.'

'Ah, but he's dead, and that improves his political position wonderfully,' Arkady said. 'Anyway, look at our Moskva River. Broken up like a concrete street. Then take Mandelstam's Neva River "heavy as a jellyfish." That says so much in a phrase.'

'You may not be aware' – Osborne glanced at his watch – 'that almost no one in the West reads Mandelstam. He's too Russian. He doesn't translate.'

'My very point! Too Russian. It can be a fault.'

'*That's* your point?'

'Like those bodies we found in Gorky Park you asked me about. Three people shot down with brilliant efficiency and with a Western automatic? It doesn't translate into Russian at all, does it?'

Sometimes a wind catches a parade banner and the

face painted on the banner, with no change in expression, shivers. In Osborne's eyes Arkady saw such a tremor, an excitement.

'You must have noticed some difference between a man like yourself, Mr Osborne, and a man like me. My ways of thinking are so dull, so proletarian, that it's a privilege to meet anyone so sophisticated. You can imagine my difficulty in trying to fathom why a Westerner would bother killing three Russians. This isn't war or espionage. Let me confess that I'm unequipped. Usually I find a body. The scene of the crime is a mess – blood everywhere, fingerprints, probably the murder weapon as well. A child with a strong stomach could do such work as well as I. The motives? Adultery, a drunken rage, the loan of a few rubles, maybe one woman killing another over a missing chicken. The communal kitchen is, I have to say, a hotbed of passion. Frankly, if I had the mind to be an ideologist or run a ministry or know the difference between one piece of fur and another, that's what I'd be doing, wouldn't I? So all sympathy should go to a plodding investigator who comes across a crime of executive planning, daring operation and, unless I'm very mistaken, wit.'

'Wit?' Osborne was interested.

'Yes. Remember what Lenin said. "The working class is not separated from the old bourgeois society by a Chinese Wall. And when the Revolution occurs, it will not happen that when a given individual dies, the dead man will bury himself. When the old society dies, it will be impossible to sew its corpse in a shroud and put it in a tomb. It will putrefy among us, this corpse will oppress and contaminate us." Consider, then, a bourgeois businessman who can execute two Soviet workers and leave them in the heart of Moscow, and tell me he is not a character of great wit.'

'Two, you say? I thought you found three in the park.'

'Three. You know Moscow well, Mr Osborne? You enjoy your visits?'

They were walking again, leaving dark footprints on the stones. Despite the hour, drivers had turned on headlights. Ahead, a sour yellow haze clung to a bridge.

'And you are enjoying yourself in Moscow?' Arkady repeated.

'Investigator, during my tour of Siberia I was welcomed by a village mayor who showed me the most modern structure in town. It had sixteen toilets, two urinals and a single sink. It was the communal excretory. There the village leaders gather with their pants down and shit while they make their important decisions.' Osborne paused. 'Of course, Moscow is much larger.'

'Mr Osborne' – Arkady stopped short – 'excuse me. Did I say something to annoy you?'

'You couldn't annoy me. It occurs to me that I might be taking you away from your investigation.'

'Not at all, please.' Arkady touched the suede of Osborne's arm and resumed their stroll. 'If anything, you're a help. If I could, for one minute, think not as a Russian but as a business genius, my troubles would be over.'

'What do you mean?'

'Wouldn't it take a genius to find something worth killing Russians for? That's not flattery, that's admiration.

Furs? No, he could buy them from you. Gold? How would he carry it out? He had enough trouble disposing of the bag.'

'What bag?'

Arkady slapped his hands together explosively. 'The deed is done. Both men and the girl dead. The killer shovels food, bottles, gun into a leather bag torn by the shots. He skates through the park. It's snowing, growing dark. Out of the park, he must put his ice skates in the bag and, hopefully without being noticed, get rid of it. Not in the park and not in a wastebasket because in either case the bag would be found and, at least in Moscow, reported. The river?'

'The river has been frozen all winter.'

'Absolutely true. Yet even with the bag magically gone, he must return to this side of the river.'

'The Krimsky Bridge.' Osborne gestured in the direction they were going.

'Without attracting the notice of any suspicious babushka or militiaman? People are so nosy.'

'Taxi.'

'No, very chancy for foreigners. A friend waiting on the quay road in a car; that's obvious enough even to me.'

'Then why wasn't the accomplice in on the murder?'

'Him?' Arkady laughed. 'Never! We are talking about seduction and charm. The accomplice couldn't lure flies to pudding.' Arkady turned grave. 'Seriously, the first man, the killer, thought this all out very carefully.'

'Someone saw him with the bag?'

The river edged sideways into drizzle. Osborne was concerned about a witness; that could be returned to.

'Insignificant. What I want to know,' Arkady said, 'is the reason. Why? I don't mean an object – say, an ikon. I mean, why would an intelligent man, successful and wealthier probably than anyone in the Soviet Union, why would he murder for more? If I could understand the man, I could understand the crime. Tell me, could I understand him?'

Osborne was seamless. Arkady felt himself scratching at an unmarred and slippery surface. Suede, sable, skin, eyes, they were all the same, all ... *money*. That was a word the investigator had never used in this context before. In the abstract, in thieves' fantasy, yes. But never had he come into physical contact with money. For that was what Osborne was, a man magically dripping money from his every pore. Understand a man like this?

'I would suppose not,' Osborne answered.

'Sex?' Arkady asked. 'A lonely stranger meets a beautiful girl and takes her to his hotel room. The floor ladies will look the other way for the right foreigner. The man and girl start meeting regularly. Suddenly at the end she demands money and produces a rough-looking husband. She's a regular extortionist.'

'No.'

'There's a flaw?'

'In perspective. To Westerners, Russians are an ugly race.'

'Is that a fact?'

'In general, women here have no more appeal than cows. That's why your Russian writers make such a fuss about their heroines' eyes, their veiled looks and alluring glances, because no other physical aspect invites description.' Osborne expanded. 'It's your long winters. What could be warmer than a heavy woman with hairy legs? The men are slimmer, but even uglier. Since good looks have been bred out, the only sexual triggers left are thick necks and heavy brows, like bulls.'

Arkady thought he could have been hearing a description of troglodytes.

'From your name, you have a Ukrainian background yourself, don't you?' Osborne added.

'Yes. Well, we'll put sex aside—'

'That seems wise.'

'—which leaves us a crime without a motive,' Arkady frowned.

Turning as slowly as a door, Osborne regarded him. 'Astonishing. You are full of surprises. Are you serious?'

'Oh, yes.'

'A triple killing purely for a whim?'

'Yes.'

'Incredible. I mean' – Osborne became full of life – 'literally not to be believed, not from an investigator of your training. From another kind of man, not from you.' Osborne took a deep breath. 'Let's say such an event happened, a totally random murder without witnesses, what would be your chances of finding the murderer?'

'None.'

'But that's what you think happened.'

'No. I only mean I haven't found the motive. Motives are different. The perspective, as you said. Assume a man who visits, occasionally, an island of primitives. Stone

Age people. He speaks their language, is expert at flattery, becomes friendly with the local chiefs. At the same time, he is aware of his superiority. In fact, he finds the natives ridiculously contemptible.' Arkady spoke slowly, feeling his way, remembering the vaguely worded account of the German soldiers killed by Osborne and Mendel. 'At some point, early on, he becomes involved in the murder of a native. During a tribal war, so that he's not punished but rewarded. And in time he comes to relish the memory of the act the way another man enjoys recalling the details of his first woman. There is an allure in primitive society, don't you think?'

'An allure?'

'A revelation to this man. He discovers what his impulses are, and he also discovers a place where he can carry out his impulses. A place outside civilization.'

'What if he's right?'

'From his perspective he might be. The natives are primitive, there's no doubt about that. But for all his civilized appearance, I suspect he feels the same loathing for everyone. It's only on this primitive island that he's open about it.'

'Still, if he kills randomly, you wouldn't catch him.'

'But he doesn't. First, he waits many years before indulging his violent impulse again. And he's an amateur, even if an inspired amateur, and it is a curious fact that an amateur, once he's carried out one crime successfully, almost always tries to copy himself as if he alone has the secret of a perfect crime. So there's a pattern. Also, it's carefully planned. A superior man by definition has to feel in control. Even to the record of Tchaikovsky's cannon booming through the park, yes? He raises his gun in the bag, shoots down the brute, then the second man and the girl, skins their faces and fingerprints and escapes. Planning, however, can go only so far. It's unfair, but there's always the element of chance. Some vendor who's taken her pushcart into the woods for a rest, boys hiding in the trees, lovers who will go anywhere for a bit of privacy. After all, where can lovers go in the wintertime? – ask yourself.'

'Then there was a witness?'

'What good is a witness? Their memories are indistinct after a day. After three months, frankly, I could get them to recognize anyone I wanted to. Only the killer can help me now.'

'Will he?'

'It's possible. I could hide like a frog beneath the river and he would come and seek me out.'

'Why?'

'Because murder isn't enough. Even the dullest man finds that's true when the first flush is gone. Murder is only half the act. Don't you think a superior man will personally, for real satisfaction, need to see an investigator like me reduced to impotence and futility, maybe even to admiration?'

'Would that be much of a challenge, Investigator?'

'Everything considered' – Arkady stepped on a butt – 'not much.'

They had reached the Novo-Arbatsky Bridge. From either side of it the pink stars of the Ukraina and the Foreign Ministry glowed to each other like beacons. Osborne's limousine pulled alongside.

'You're an honest man, Investigator Renko,' Osborne said in a voice mellowed to warmth as if, arduous journey over, he and Arkady had developed a tired but cozy informality. A grin was called forward as in the last-scene appearance of a character actor. 'I wish you good luck now because I have only a week left in Moscow and I don't think we will be seeing each other again. However, I don't want you to leave empty-handed.'

Osborne lifted the sable hat from his head and set it on Arkady's. 'A gift,' he said. 'When you told me in the bathhouse that you always wanted a hat, I knew I had to give it to you. I had to guess the size, but I have a good eye for heads.' He viewed Arkady from different angles. 'It's perfect.'

Arkady took the hat off. It was black as ink, with a texture of satin. 'It's lovely. But' – he handed the hat back regretfully – 'I can't accept it. There are regulations about gifts.'

'I'd be very offended if you refused.'

'Very well, give me a few days to think about it. That way we have an excuse to talk again.'

'Any excuse will do.' Osborne shook Arkady's hand firmly, then got into his limousine and rode across the bridge.

Arkady picked up his car at the Ukraina and drove on to the Oktyabrsky precinct station, where he asked about any foreigners noticed waiting in cars near the park around the time of the murders.

By the time he left, a broad orange sun had come out. It slid between the cables of the Krimsky Bridge. Bits of it glittered like coins from ministry windows.

Pools of it burned into the quay road where he and Osborne had walked shortly before.

Chief Investigator Ilya Nikitin, his thin hair combed wet straight back over his round head, squinted orientally through the smoke of the cigarette clamped between his teeth. He lived alone in the Arbat district in a narrow house where paint flaked from the walls and plaster dropped from the ceilings to be lost among the stacks of books, dusty and tagged with slips of yellowed paper, that rose two and three meters tall and five volumes thick. Arkady remembered triple-paned windows that had looked out on the river and the Lenin Hills, but the view existed only in memory. Stacks had grown in front of the windows, into the kitchen, up the stairs and into the bedrooms of the second floor.

'Kirwill, Kirwill—' Nikitin carefully pushed aside files of *Partial Amendments of the Charter of the All-Union Publishing-Polygraphic Combine* to uncover an almost empty bottle of Rumanian port. He drank while he winked and started crawling up the stairs. 'So you still come to Ilya when you need help?'

When Arkady first joined the town prosecutor's office, he inferred from Nikitin that the man was a genius and a progressive, or a genius and a hard-liner. An author of legal reforms or a Stalinist. A drinking companion of the Negro singer Robeson or a confidant of the reactionary novelist Sholokov. At the very least, a genius of gnostic hints. A figure of white or black painted by his own winks, supported by the names he dropped.

There was no doubt that Nikitin had been a brilliant chief investigator of Homicide. Though Arkady would build the case, it was always Nikitin who came into the interrogation room with two bottles and a leer, to emerge hours later with a pliant, shamefaced killer. 'Confession is all,' Nikitin explained. 'If you won't give people religion or psychology, at least let them confess to a crime. Proust said that you could seduce any woman if you were willing to sit and listen to her complain until four in the morning. At heart, any murderer is a complainer.' 'For the bribes, boychik,' Nikitin explained when Arkady asked why he transferred from Homicide to Government Liaison.

'Kirwill. Reds. Diego Rivera. The Battle of Union Square.' Twisting to look back, Nikitin asked, 'You do know where New York City is?' He slumped a step, dislodging a book, which carried two more down the stairs, then another. After a precarious moment the slide subsided.

'Tell me about Kirwill,' Arkady said.

Nikitin wagged his head like a finger. 'Correction: Kirwills. *Red Star.*' He gathered his strength to crawl through a second-floor hall narrowed by walls of books.

'Who were the Kirwills?' Arkady asked.

Nikitin dropped his empty bottle, stumbled over it with his knee and rolled onto his back, belly wedged between the stacks, helpless. 'You stole a bottle from my office, Arkasha. You're a thief. You can go to the devil.'

At Arkady's eye level was a hard crust of cheese and half a bottle of plum wine on top of a book entitled *Political Oppression in the United States, 1929–1941.*

Holding the bottle under one arm, he flipped through the book's index. 'Can I borrow this?'

'Do me a favor,' Nikitin said.

Arkady dropped the wine into Nikitin's hands.

'No.' Nikitin let the bottle slip away. 'Keep the book. Don't come back.'

Belov's office was a monument to the war. Small grainy soldiers marched across newspaper photographs. Framed headlines on newsprint as fine as tissue declared: 'Valiant Defense on the Volga,' 'Bitter Resistance Snuffed Out,' 'Heroes Praise Homeland.' Belov's mouth gaped in sleep, bread crumbs on his lower lip and the front of his shirt. A beer stood in his hand.

Arkady took the other chair and opened the book he'd taken from Nikitin.

The 1930 Union Square Rally was the largest public gathering ever organized by the CPUSA. Unemployed workers eager to hear and be heard by the vanguard of social justice thronged to the square in numbers even greater than leaders anticipated. Despite the fact that New York Police Commissioner Grover A. Whalen ordered no subways to stop in the vicinity of the square, estimates of the throng exceeded 50,000 people. The police and their agents took other measures to break, splinter or muffle the will of those in attendance. During the singing of 'The Internationale,' undercover agents of the so-called Radical Squad infiltrated the square. Provocateurs attempted with-

out success to instigate attacks against uniformed
police. No film cameras were allowed to record the
glorious rally on the instructions of Commissioner
Whalen, who sputtered later, 'I saw no reason for
perpetuating treasonable utterances, and I don't mean
to engage in censorship.' His statement typified the
contradictory roles of police in a capitalist society:
one role as keeper of the peace conflicting with its
paramount role as headbreaking watchdog of the
exploiter class.

Arkady skipped over a message of solidarity from Stalin
that was read to the excited throng.

A peaceful march to City Hall was then proposed by
speaker William Z. Foster. As soon as the crowd began
to move, however, their way was blocked by an armored police truck. Thus was the signal given by
Whalen to police troops massed in side streets. On
foot and on horseback à la Cossacks the police fell
on unarmed men, women and children. Negroes,
especially, were targets of assaults. A Negro girl was
held upright by one officer while his cohorts beat her
around the breasts and stomach. James and Edna
Kirwill, editors of *Red Star*, a journal of the Catholic
Left, were clubbed to the ground in their own blood.
Mounted police rode down equally both Party members bearing placards and citizens who were only
passersby. Party leaders were assaulted and arrested.
Kept in cells, they were allowed no lawyers or bail, in
accordance with Commissioner Whalen's declaration

that 'These enemies of society are to be driven out
of New York regardless of their constitutional rights.'

The chief investigator for Industry opened two rheumy
eyes, licked his lips and sat upright.

'I was just,' he began, grabbing at his beer as it started
to tip, 'looking at some factory directives.' He wadded
the remains of a sandwich, cast it into the wastebasket
with an effort that brought a burp, and glared at Arkady.
'How long have you been here?'

'I was just looking in a book, Uncle Seva,' Arkady
said. 'The book tells me, "Enemies of society are to be
driven out regardless of their constitutional rights." '

'That's easy,' the old man answered after a moment's
thought. 'By definition, enemies of society don't have
constitutional rights.'

Arkady snapped his fingers. 'There you are,' he said.

'That's first grade stuff.' Belov waved away flattery. 'So
what do you want? You only listen to me these days
when you want something.'

'I'm trying to find a weapon that was thrown into the
river in January.'

'*Onto* the river, you mean. It was frozen over.'

'True, but maybe not everywhere. Some factories still
discharge warm water into the river, where the ice might
never form. You know the factories better than anyone
else.'

'Pollution is an area of major concern, Arkasha. There
are firm directives concerning the environment. You were
the one who always used to complain to me about the

factories when you were a kid. You were a regular pain in the ass.'

'Clean warm water, maybe discharged under a special industrial continuance.'

'Everyone thinks they're a special case. Discharging waste water into the Moskva within city limits is strictly forbidden, thanks to people like you.'

'But industry must progress. A country is like a body. First the muscle, later the hair lotion.'

'True, and you think you're making fun of me, Arkasha, when you say something that's true. You'd rather be in a fancy city like Paris. You know why they have such big boulevards there? The better to shoot down Communists. So don't come griping to me about pollution. Agh!' When Belov rubbed his face it shifted like pudding. 'What you want is the Gorky Tannery. Under a very special continuance, they do discharge treated water. All the dye is out, understand. I have a map . . .'

Belov rooted through his desk drawers and found an industrial map, an orange-and-black affair that unfolded to tablecloth dimensions.

'Gloves, notebooks, holsters, that sort of thing. Here—' His finger descended to the quay beside Gorky Park. 'An effluent pipe. The river is iced there, but it's just a crust. Something heavy could drop through it and the crust would form again in an hour or so. So, Arkasha, what do you think the chances are that a man throws a gun in the river in the only place the ice is not a meter thick?'

'How did you know I was looking for a gun, Uncle?'

'Arkasha, I'm just old. I'm not totally senile and I'm not deaf. I hear things.'

'What things?'

'Things.' Belov looked at Arkady, then to the framed heroics on the wall. 'I don't understand things anymore. It used to be a person could believe in the future. There were cliques, errors in judgment, purges that perhaps went too far, but at heart we were all pulling together. Today . . .' Belov blinked. The old man had never unburdened himself to Arkady like this before. 'The Minister of Culture is dismissed for corruption, she made herself a millionaire, she built palaces. A minister! Didn't we try to change all that?'

Mosfilm's day of outside shooting was over.

Arkady followed Irina Asanova around the set of a log cabin and birches propped into place by wire struts. He felt electrical cables under squares of sod. Despite a sign that warned NO SMOKING, the girl smoked the cheapest cardboard-and-tobacco *papirosi* cigarette in the old lacquered holder. Her raffish Afghan jacket was open to a flimsy cotton dress and a pencil that hung from a string around her neck, and this somehow accented the grace of her neck. Her long brown hair was loose, and her eyes looked boldly at Arkady almost at his level. The mark on her cheek was faded in a red glow that had nothing to do with the setting sun. It was the glow Tolstoy described on the faces of the artillery men at Borodino, an exultant flush as the battle came closer.

'Valerya Davidova and her lover Kostia Borodin were

from the Irkutsk area,' Arkady said. 'You came from Irkutsk, you were Valerya's best friend there, you wrote her from here, and when she died here she was wearing your "lost" skates.'

'You're going to arrest me?' Irina challenged Arkady. 'I went to the Law Faculty, and I know the law as well as you. You need a militiaman present if you're going to arrest me.'

'So you told me before. The man found with Valerya and Kostia was an American named James Kirwill. You knew James Kirwill at the university. Why do you keep lying to me?'

She moved away from his questions, leading him in a circle around the make-believe cabin. For all her bravado, he felt as if he were stalking a deer.

'Don't take it personally.' She looked back. 'I generally lie to your kind.'

'Why?'

'I deal with you the way I'd deal with a leper. You're diseased. You're a member of a leper organization. I don't want to be infected.'

'You were studying law to become a leper?'

'A lawyer. A doctor, in a sense, for the defense of the healthy against the sick.'

'But we're talking about murder, not disease.' Arkady lit a cigarette of his own. 'You're very brave. You expect some Beria to come out here and eat a baby before your eyes. I must disappoint you; I'm only here to find the person who killed your friends.'

'Now you're lying to me. Your only interest is dead

bodies, not someone's friends. Your friends you'd care about, not mine.'

It was a throwaway accusation, but she'd hit home. The only reason he'd come to the studio was for Pasha.

He changed the subject. 'I've looked at your militia record. What was this anti-Soviet slander of yours that got you expelled from the university?'

'As if you don't know.'

'Pretend I don't,' Arkady said.

Irina Asanova was still for a moment, the way he'd seen her when he first came to the studio, lost in a self-confidence or self-absorption that was a world unto itself.

'I think,' she said, 'I prefer your counterparts from Security. At least there's honesty in slapping a woman. Your approach, your phony concern, shows a weakness in character.'

'That's not what you said at the university.'

'I'll tell you what I said at the university. I was in the cafeteria talking to friends, and I said I would do anything to get out of the Soviet Union. Some Komsomol creeps were listening at the next table. They turned my name in, and I was dropped from the student roster.'

'You were kidding, of course. You should have explained.'

She stepped closer so that they were almost touching. 'But I wasn't kidding, I was totally serious. Investigator, if someone right now gave me a gun and told me I could get out of the Soviet Union if I killed you, I'd shoot you where you stand.'

'Seriously?'

'I'd do it gladly.'

She pressed her cigarette into the birch beside Arkady. The white skin of the tree blackened and smoked around the ember, and bits of skin flamed and curled away. Arkady suffered the remarkable sensation of pain, as if the warm stab were being pressed against his heart. He believed her. The truth had gone from her into the tree and into him.

'Comrade Asanova, I don't know why I still have this case,' he tried again. 'I don't want it, I shouldn't have it. But three poor people were murdered, and all I ask is that you come with me now and see the bodies. Perhaps from the clothes or—'

'No.'

'Just prove to yourself that they aren't your friends. Don't you at least want to be sure?'

'I know it's not them.'

'Then where are they?'

Irina Asanova said nothing. A black burn marked the tree. She said nothing, but the causeway of truth was still open. Arkady laughed involuntarily, awed by his own stupidity. All the time he'd asked himself what Osborne could have wanted from two Russians, he'd never asked himself what they could have wanted from him.

'Where do you think they are?' he asked.

He felt her hold her breath.

'Kostia and Valerya were running from Siberia,' Arkady answered himself. 'That wouldn't be any problem for a bandit like Kostia, not with his stolen Aeroflot tickets. It's possible to buy blackmarket working papers and a residency permit here if you can afford it, and Kostia could afford it. But Moscow wasn't far enough. Kostia wanted to get all the way out. And that's impossible, except that he died with an American for whom there is no record of reentry into the Soviet Union.'

Irina Asanova stepped backward into the last rays of the sun.

'In fact,' Arkady said, 'that's the only reason you admit you knew them at all. I know they died in Gorky Park, but you think they're alive on the other side of the border. You think they got out.'

She had the radiant look of triumph.

Chapter Twelve

Divers kicked up a spinning murk, the winter's silt. Sealed floodlights were lowered into the water. A hand could be seen, then a fin as the men probed where the underwater effluent pipes of the Maxim Gorky Tannery joined the Moskva.

Above on the embankment road, militiamen with lanterns waved on the occasional early-morning truck. Arkady crossed to an unlit area where William Kirwill sat deep in the shadows in the back of Arkady's car.

'I promise nothing,' Arkady said. 'You can go back to your hotel if you want, or you can go to your embassy.'

'I'll stick around.' Kirwill's eyes glinted in the dark.

There was a splash over the embankment as another diver went in. Another floodlight rattled down on a chain, and militiamen pushed loose ice floes away from the wall with poles.

Arkady showed a thick envelope. 'These are the forensic reports on the three bodies found in Gorky Park,' he said. Arkady relied on a peculiar familiarity, the heavy-footed profanity of militiamen, the suspicious glare of militia lanterns, the professional environment of investigators anywhere. After an undisturbed day of reasoning, Kirwill should have reached the conclusion that Arkady was not from the KGB – no one from the KGB could be so genuinely ignorant.

'Let me see.' Kirwill reached.

'Who was James Kirwill?' Arkady asked.

'My brother.'

Arkady handed over the envelope through the car window; the first trade was completed. No mention of Osborne was in the envelope. If William Kirwill wanted only to help an investigation, he would have delivered the dental chart and X-ray his first day in Moscow. But he'd also brought a weapon, so he was willing to deal only as long as he didn't know whom to attack. That he didn't have his gun anymore didn't matter. He had his hands.

An officer of the River Patrol came over to tell Arkady that the divers were freezing, and that there was no bag to be found on the river bottom. Crossing the road to the wall, Arkady was pulled aside by a sergeant to speak to a young militiaman from the Oktyabrsky precinct whose beat was the quay. The boy remembered a Zhiguli sedan parked on the embankment road one January evening. Maybe February. All he could recall of the driver was a German wearing a lapel pin of a Berlin 'Leather Ball' club. 'Leather Ball' was Komsomol's term for youth football. The militiaman knew the driver was German because, being an avid collector of lapel pins, he had offered to buy the man's and got a heavily accented refusal.

'Keep looking for another half hour,' Arkady told the divers, and just ten minutes later they shouted and climbed up the rope ladder over the embankment wall hauling a muck-covered bag leaking water and eels.

The bag was leather with a rope loop. Wearing rubber

gloves, Arkady opened it under a floodlight and picked through a mix of ooze, bottles and glasses until he found, pointing up, a gun barrel. He pulled free a large, slim semiautomatic pistol.

'Comrade Investigator?'

Fet had arrived. Arkady hadn't seen him since Golodkin's questioning. The detective stood on the periphery of the flood lamps, adjusting his glasses, his eyes fixed myopically on the gun. 'Is there anything I can do?' he asked.

Arkady didn't know what role Fet had in Pasha's death. All he knew was that he wanted the detective out of the way.

'Yes,' Arkady said, 'get a list of ikons stolen within the last sixteen months.'

'Ikons stolen in Moscow?'

'And around Moscow,' Arkady said, 'and anywhere in the country this side of the Urals. And then, Detective . . .'

'Yes?' Fet edged forward.

'Then, Detective, any ikons stolen in Siberia,' Arkady said. 'You know where Siberia is.'

Arkady watched the detective mope off into the dark; he would be busy for a week, and it was remotely possible the lists might be useful.

The investigator carefully placed the gun in a handkerchief. None of the militiamen, not even the veterans, recognized its make. Arkady gave the River Patrol officer money for brandy for the divers, and carried bag and gun to his car.

He drove Kirwill to a taxi under the Krimsky Bridge.

Dawn was breaking. Outside the garage, drivers in shirt sleeves were gutting and reconstructing taxis that were on the point of collapse. Wandering among the cars, entrepreneurs sold stolen parts from over-sized coats.

Kirwill examined the pistol. 'Good gun. Argentine version of the 7.65-mm. Mannlicher. Big muzzle velocity, accurate, carried eight rounds.' Mud spurted onto his shirt as he slid a magazine from the grip. Arkady hadn't noticed when he'd roused him in his hotel room that Kirwill had dressed again as a Russian. 'Three rounds left.' He slid the slip back and handed the gun back. 'Used to be the Argentine service weapon before they went to a different pistol, a Browning. The Mannlichers were sold to gun dealers in the States, so that's how I know.'

'The pillows.' Arkady studied Kirwill's clothes. 'I didn't look in your pillows.'

'That's right.' Kirwill came close to a smile. He handed back the envelope, wiped his fingers and then pulled a card from his shirt pocket. The card had ten ink smudges. A fingerprint card. 'You missed this, too.' He shook his head and put the card away even as Arkady started to reach.

'See, I wouldn't show you that' – Kirwill spread his arms, covering the sill of the back window – 'but I've been thinking. Maybe you're just what you pretend to be, Renko. Maybe we can work something out. You say a detective of yours was shot, and you lost Golodkin, too. You're going to need all the help you can get.'

'So?'

'Your file on Jimmy—' Kirwill nodded to the folder.

'Jimmy was what you called him?'

'Yeah.' Kirwill shrugged. 'The forensic work isn't too bad, but there's no follow-up.'

'What do you mean?'

'Detective work. It's called "getting off your ass." Fifty men questioning anyone who's been in the park this winter. Asking them once, twice, three times. Stories in the newspapers, and a special police telephone line announced on television.'

'What wonderful ideas,' Arkady said. 'If I'm ever in New York, I'll use them.'

The blue eyes cooled. 'If I did identify my brother's body, what would happen?'

'It would become a case for State Security.'

'The KGB?'

'That's right.'

'What would happen to me?'

'You'd be detained to give evidence. I could withhold information about our meeting in the park, about your weapon. Your detention wouldn't be too unpleasant.'

'Could you make it fun?' Kirwill asked.

'Not great fun.' The unexpected question made Arkady laugh.

'Then' – Kirwill lit a cigarette and flipped the match through the window – 'I think I prefer this arrangement. Just you and me.'

One of the taxi drivers crossed the street to ask whether they had auto parts to buy or sell. Arkady brushed him off.

'An "arrangement"?' Arkady asked Kirwill. It was what

he'd had in mind, but hearing it from Kirwill the spoken word made him uncomfortable.

'An understanding – mutual assistance,' Kirwill said. 'Now, it seems to me that the big guy, Kostia, went down first, right? Jimmy would be second. With his bum leg, I'm surprised he was even skating. Last, the Davidova girl. What I don't get is the shots in the head, unless the murderer knew about Jimmy's root canal and knew it would be different from Russian dental work. Now, you don't suspect any dentists, do you, Renko? Or' – he produced his half-smile – 'any foreigners?'

'Anything else?' Arkady asked in a flat voice, though it had taken him days to work out the root-canal answer.

'Okay. The gesso on the clothes. Ikons, right? That's why you sent that guy off for a list. By the way, that's the guy I tailed back to the KGB. Maybe you're not a scab for them, but he is.'

'We're thinking along the same lines.'

'Good. Now, give me my shield back.'

'Not yet.'

'Renko, you're holding back on me.'

'Mr Kirwill, we are holding back on each other. We're just one step ahead of outright lying, remember. Since neither of us knows when the other is going to turn on him, we'll just have to do this step by step. Don't worry, you'll get your police shield back before you go home.'

'Detective shield,' Kirwill corrected him again, 'and don't kid yourself, I don't need it. If it makes you feel better, keep it for a day or two. In the meantime, you understand the expression "sucks"? Because that's what your legwork on this case does, not to mention that you've done zero so far on the ikon angle. I think it would be better if we worked apart and only meet to exchange information. Look, you'll only come out ahead that way. Give me some numbers where I can reach you.'

Arkady wrote out the phone numbers of his office and the room at the Ukraina. Kirwill stuffed them in his shirt pocket.

'The girl was pretty, huh? The one killed with Jimmy?'

'I think so, but why do you? Your brother was big with the ladies?'

'No. Jimmy was a professional ascetic. He didn't touch women, but he liked to be near them and he was very choosy.'

'Explain.'

'Madonnas, Renko. You know what they are.'

'I don't believe I understand.'

'Well, don't push.' Kirwill opened his door. 'I'm just starting to believe that you're for real at all.'

Arkady watched Kirwill cross the street and move among the taxi drivers, plowing in with a confident haphazardness. At an open hood, he leaned over and offered a judgment. In a second he'll be handing out cigarettes, Arkady thought. Kirwill did, and the drivers gathered around.

Arkady's intent was to use Kirwill. The American, clearly, had something else in mind.

After dropping the bag and gun off with Lyudin, Arkady went on to the Central Telephone and Telegraph Office to order the pay phones around the address of Irina

Asanova monitored. It was not unusual for someone like her not to have a phone of her own; people waited years for the privilege. What interested Arkady were other examples of penury: her secondhand clothes and boots, cardboard cigarettes. Mosfilm was full of women paid the same wages but stylishly dressed for attendance at the parties the Film-Makers Union gave for foreign guests, where the civilized appreciation of a bottle of French perfume or a wash-and-wear skirt was routine. Irina Asanova must have been invited; instead, she scrimped for kopeks. He admired her.

Colonel Lyudin was introducing Arkady to the dried and examined debris of the bag found in the river when the lab phone rang. An assistant answered it and handed it to Arkady saying, 'Comrade Renko.'

'Let me call you back later,' Arkady told Zoya.

'We have to talk now.' Her voice was strident.

Arkady gestured for Lyudin to continue. 'The leather bag is of Polish manufacture,' the forensic expert began.

'Arkady?' Zoya asked.

'A leather rope through the metal eyes around the top of the bag' – Lyudin demonstrated – 'so that it can be carried by hand or from the shoulder. Very sporty, and only for purchase to the general public in Moscow and Leningrad. Here' – he pointed with a sharpened pencil – 'a single hole at the bottom corner of the bag, the hole enlarged by more than one shot. There are traces of gunpowder around the hole, and the leather of the bag matches the leather fragments found on slug GP1.'

The bullet that killed Kostia Borodin. Arkady nodded encouragement.

'I'm filing for a petition of divorce at City Court,' Zoya said. 'The cost is one hundred rubles. I expect you to pay half. After all, I did leave you the apartment.' She paused for a reply. 'Are you there?'

'Yes,' Arkady answered sideways to the phone.

Lyudin enumerated the items on a table. 'Three key rings, a similar key on each ring. A cigarette lighter. One empty bottle of Extra vodka. One half-empty bottle of Martell cognac. Two Spartak ice skates, size extra large. A broken jar of French strawberry preserves. Not imported, I might add; it must have been bought abroad.'

'No cheese, bread, sausage?'

'Fish and eels have been in and out of that bag for months, Investigator, please. There are traces of animal fats indicating other food. Also, traces of human tissue.'

'Arkady, you have to come down right now,' Zoya said. 'It will look better and we can have a closed session with the judge. I've already talked to her.'

'I'm busy,' Arkady said into the phone, and asked Lyudin, 'Fingerprints?'

'You didn't honestly expect any, Investigator.'

'Now,' Zoya insisted, 'or you'll be sorry.'

Arkady put a hand over the phone. 'Excuse me, Colonel. Give me a minute.'

His watch held up for elaborate scrutiny, Lyudin moved away from the table with a coterie of lab assistants. Arkady turned his back to them and whispered,

'Just what grounds are you petitioning on? I beat you? I drink?'

'To begin with' – he heard her throat tighten – 'incompatibility. I have witnesses. Natasha and Dr Schmidt.'

'What about . . .' He couldn't get his thoughts together. 'What about your Party standing?'

'Ivan—'

'Ivan?'

'Dr Schmidt says I will not be adversely affected.'

'Thank heaven for that. How incompatible are we supposed to be?'

'That depends,' Zoya said. 'You'll be sorry if we have to go to public court.'

'I'm already sorry. Sorry for what else?'

'Your remarks,' she said softly.

'What remarks?'

'Your remarks, your whole attitude. Everything you say about the Party.'

Arkady stared at the receiver. Trying for a mental image of Zoya, he came up with the poster of the Pioneer with the hair as gold as corn. Then a blank wall. The ransacked apartment. Dead scenes, as if their marriage had been picked clean over the years by invisible, voracious animals. But that was thinking like Lyudin, and there was really nothing at all to grasp; the images were already becoming mixed, and he was talking to a void. Analyses of political, emotional and ironic natures all died in that void where one talked to one's soon-to-be-former wife.

'I'm sure your future will not be adversely affected,'

he said. 'I just need until May. A few more days.' He
hung up.

Lyudin clapped his hands. 'Back to work. The gun
must come out of an acid bath before ballistics can fire
a test round. However, I can tell you this much now,
Investigator. Our munitions experts are strongly of the
opinion that the gun is a Mannlicher, and of the same
caliber as the gun that fired the fatal bullets in Gorky
Park. By tomorrow I will be able to tell you the exact
model. In the meantime we will do more than is
humanly possible. Investigator Renko, are you listening?'

Going by Novokuznetskaya to check on any calls from
Kirwill, Arkady got caught in an ideological meeting.
They took place infrequently enough, and usually only
involved one man reading aloud from the front page of
Pravda while everyone else leafed through sports magazines. But this time it was a real production; the first-
floor interrogation room was filled with district investigators facing Chuchin and a doctor from the Serbsky
Institute.

'Soviet psychiatry is on the threshold of a major
breakthrough, a major statement on the entire basis of
mental illness,' the doctor was saying. 'For too long, the
organs of health and justice have worked separately in
an uncoordinated fashion. Today, I am happy to say, this
situation is nearly at an end.' He paused to place a
lozenge in his mouth and sort his papers on the table.
'It is the finding of the institute that criminals suffer
from a psychological disturbance we term pathohetero-

doxy. There is theoretical as well as clinical backing for this discovery. In an unjust society a man may violate laws for valid social or economic reasons. In a just society there are no valid reasons except mental illness. Recognizing this fact protects the violator as well as the society whose law he attacks. It affords the violator an opportunity to be quarantined until his illness can be expertly treated. Therefore you see how vital it is that investigators have their own psychological consciousness raised so that they may detect those subtle signs of the pathoheterodox before he, the deviant, has a chance to violate the law. It is our duty to spare society from injury and to save a sick man from the consequences of his acts.'

The doctor used both hands to turn to a new page. 'You would be amazed at the experiments being conducted now at the Serbsky Institute. We now have proof that the nervous system of a criminal is different from that of a normal person. When they were first brought to the clinic different subjects may have displayed wildly various behavior, sometimes mouthing irrational statements, sometimes appearing as normal as you or I. Yet all, after a few days in an isolated cell, lapsed into catatonia. I myself have placed a needle two centimeters deep into the skin of such a pathoheterodox personality and observed a total absence of pain.'

'Where did you place the needle?' Arkady asked.

A phone rang in his office, and Arkady slipped out to the stairs. Chuchin spoke into the ear of the doctor, who made a note.

*

'I had a cat once when I was a girl.' Natasha Mikoyan smoothed the mohair blanket that covered her legs. 'So soft, light as fluff, you could hardly feel her little ribs. I should have been a cat.'

She curled against the end of the sofa, the blanket tucked up to the ruffled collar of her nightgown, her small toes bare on the sofa cushions. The curtains of the apartment were drawn, no lights lit. Her hair was loose, wisps making dark commas along her neck. She sipped brandy from an enameled cup.

'You said you wanted to talk about a murder,' Arkady said. 'What murder?'

'My own,' she replied possessively.

'Who do you suspect of trying to kill you?'

'Misha, of course.' She suppressed a little giggle, as if he'd asked a stupid question.

Despite the faint light of the room, he saw changes from the week before when he'd come to dinner. Nothing much, a picture askew, ashtrays filled with the chalk ends of cigarettes, dust in the air and a smell like rotting flowers. A purse lay on the table between the sofa and his chair; lipstick and a mirror were beside it, and when she shifted and her knee touched the table the lipstick rolled back and forth.

'When did you first suspect Misha wanted to kill you?'

'Oh, for years.' She added as an afterthought, 'You can smoke. I know how you like to smoke when you're nervous.'

'We've known each other for a long time,' he agreed, and felt for a smoke. 'How do you think he's going to kill you?'

'I'll kill myself.'

'That's not murder, Natasha, that's suicide.'

'I knew you'd say that, but it's not the case here. I'm only the instrument, he's the murderer. He's a lawyer, he doesn't take any chances.'

'You mean he's trying to drive you crazy, is that it?'

'If I were crazy, I wouldn't be able to tell you what he's doing. Besides, he's already taken my life. We're just talking about me now.'

'Ah.'

She didn't appear crazy. In fact, her tone had the undertone of a daydream, and a surface of acquiescence. Now that he thought about it, he and Natasha had always been great friends, but never close.

'Well,' he asked. 'What do you want me to do for you? I'll certainly talk to Misha—'

'Talk to him? I want you to arrest him.'

'For murder? Don't kill yourself and there won't be one.' He tried to smile.

Natasha shook her head. 'No, I can't take any chances. I have to have him arrested now, while I can.'

'Be reasonable.' Arkady lost patience. 'I can't arrest anyone for a crime he hasn't committed, especially on the word of a victim who's going to take her own life.'

'Then you're not a very good investigator, are you?'

'Why did you call me? Why talk to me? Talk to your husband.'

'I like the sound of that.' She tilted her head. ' "Your husband." It has a nice judicial ring.' She curled up warmly. 'I think of you and Misha as one and the same. So does he. He always calls you his "good side." You do all the things he wishes he did; that's why he admires you so. If I can't tell his "good side" he's trying to kill me, I can't tell anyone. You know, I've often wondered why you weren't interested in me when we were at university. I used to be very attractive.'

'You still are.'

'Are you interested now? We could do it here; we wouldn't have to go to the bedroom, and I promise you it would be absolutely safe, no danger at all. No? Be honest, Arkasha, you're always honest, it's your charm. No? Don't apologize, please; I must tell you that I'm not interested either. What's happened to us' – she laughed – 'when we're not even interested anymore?'

On impulse, Arkady reached and upended her purse, spilling its contents, mainly paper packets of Pentalginum, a pain-killer containing codeine and phenobarbital, sold over the counter, the housewife's addiction.

'How many of these a day do you take?'

'The *modus operandi*, that's what catches your eye. You're so professional. Men are so professional, so quick with the stomach pump. But I'm boring you,' she said brightly, 'and you've got some dead of your own to attend to. I was only thinking of expanding your horizons. You were the only man I knew who might possibly care to. You can get back to work now.'

'What will you do?'

'Oh, I'll just sit here. Like a cat.'

Arkady stood and took a couple of steps to the door. 'I hear you're going to testify against me in a divorce court,' he said.

'Not against you. For Zoya. Frankly,' Natasha said with

gentleness, 'I never saw the two of you as a couple, never.'

'You'll be okay? I have to go.'

'I'll be perfect.' She raised the cup demurely to her lips.

At the hall elevator Arkady met Misha, who was just arriving, flushed with embarrassment.

'Thanks for calling. I couldn't get away sooner.' Misha tried to brush past.

'Wait, you better get her to a doctor,' Arkady said. 'And get those pills away from her.'

'She'll be fine.' Misha backed toward his apartment. 'She did this before, she'll be fine. Why don't you worry about your own affairs?'

Arkady spent the afternoon with paperwork, checking Hans Unmann's registry of a Zhiguli sedan and rechecking Osborne's visas. The American had traveled from Paris to Leningrad by rail, arriving January 2. Such a trip, even going "soft class" through France, Germany and Poland, must have been tedious, especially for such a high-powered businessman as Osborne. Leningrad was iced in to shipping during the winter months, though, and an airport search might have discovered the Mannlicher.

Late in the afternoon Arkady attended the cremation of Pasha Pavlovich, whose body had finally been released so that it could be placed in a pine box and rolled onto gas jets.

*

Hooligans had kicked down all the words of the red sign except for one: HOPE.

The chimneys of the Likhachev works vanished at night. On the street the stores were shut, the one that sold vodka protected by an iron gate. Drunks yelled after a militiaman. 'You fucking garbage prick-twister!' And the militiaman left the sidewalk for the street, looking for a patrol car.

Arkady walked into the cafeteria where he had met Swan before. Patrons huddled at round tables, honest hands on their bottles, sweat-stiff jackets over their chairs, raw onions and knives on their plates. The illegal entertainment of a television set was placed on the bar counter: Dynamo vs. Odessa. Arkady went right to the rest room, where Kirwill was urinating down the hole provided. He wore a leather jacket and cloth cap. Despite the bad light, Arkady could see on Kirwill's face, besides the usual dangerous tautness, a bloom of capillaries.

'Having fun?' Arkady asked.

'Standing in someone else's piss? Sure.' He zipped himself up. 'Just like the Lower Fucking Depths. You're late.'

'Sorry.' Arkady took his turn at the hole, standing two feet away and out of the puddle. He wondered how much Kirwill had already drunk.

'Mannlicher check out?'

'It looks as if it will.'

'What the hell else have you been doing today? Perfecting your aim?'

'You could do worse.' He glanced at Kirwill's shoes.

They went to a table Kirwill had claimed in a corner of the bar. A half-empty bottle of vodka stood in the center of the table.

'Renko, you a drinking man?'

Arkady considered leaving. Kirwill was unpredictable enough sober, and Arkady had always heard that Americans couldn't hold their liquor. But Swan was coming, and he didn't want to miss him.

'What do you say, Renko? Later on we'll have a pissing contest – distance, time, aim and style. I'll take a handicap. One leg. That's not enough? No hands?'

'You're actually a police officer?'

'The only one I see here. Come on, Renko, I'm buying.'

'You're quite an insulting character, aren't you?'

'When inspired. You'd rather I punched you around like I did before?' Kirwill leaned back, crossed his arms and looked around appreciatively. 'Nice place.' His eyes returned to Arkady and restlessly mimicked a childish hurt: 'I said it was a nice place.'

Arkady went to the counter and returned with a bottle and glass for himself. He laid two matches on the table between his bottle and Kirwill's, snapped one match in half, covered both so that only the match heads peeked out from his hand, and said, 'Short match pours from his bottle.'

Frowning, Kirwill pulled one out. The short match. 'Shit.'

'Good Russian, wrong expression.' Arkady watched Kirwill pour. 'Also, you should trim your hair closer at the sides. Don't put your feet up on the chair. Only Americans put their feet up.'

'Oh, I see we're going to work well together.' Kirwill emptied his glass in one gulp, head back, the same as Arkady. Again they drew matches, and again Kirwill lost. 'Fucking etiquette of the Lumpen-proletariat. Cute, Renko. Why don't you tell me what you've been doing besides letting your blood go from your brain to your butt.'

Arkady wasn't going to tell him about Osborne, and he didn't want Kirwill going after Irina Asanova, so he talked about the reconstruction of the dead girl's skull.

'Wonderful,' Kirwill said when Arkady was done. 'I'm dealing with a fucking nut. A face from a skull? Christ. Well, this is fascinating, like seeing police procedure in ancient Rome. What's next, entrails from birds, or do you throw bones? Reconstructing ikons, that's what Jimmy was up to. Your own notes mentioned a chest of ikons.'

'To be stolen or bought, not reconstructed.'

Kirwill scratched his chin and his chest; then his hand wandered into a jacket pocket and dangled a postcard before Arkady. On the blank side was a short description of a 'Religious chest, Cathedral of the Archangel, the Kremlin.' The other side showed a color photograph of a gilded chest bearing sacramental goblets of crystal and gold. Around the chest, ikon panels illustrated a battle between white and black angels.

'How old, Investigator, would you say that is?'

'Four hundred years old, five hundred,' Arkady guessed.

'Try 1920. That's when the Cathedral and everything in it was renovated, Comrade. Who said Lenin didn't have taste? Now, I'm just talking about the chest frame. The panels are original. They'd go as a set for a hundred thousand dollars and up in New York. And they do; panels get out of here all the time, but sometimes they just don't leave as ikons. Maybe a dealer exports a mediocre chest built around ikons doctored to look bad. So I spent the day following this clever idea of mine to every goddamn embassy in town, trying to find out who'd exported ikons, or a chest or a chair of ikons, in the last six months. Got nowhere. Went back to the American embassy, to the political attaché, who's the local CIA chief and a man who couldn't find his asshole with a mirror, so he could tell me in secret that smuggling a decent ikon was a good hedge against inflation. You could get a hernia trying to lift a diplomatic pouch over there. Only, no private dealers are allowed. Then I realize, of course, that you can't do any reconstruction without gold, and you can't buy or steal gold in this country, so the whole idea is out the window, and, a little thirsty, I stumbled onto this toilet you so cunningly chose to meet at.'

'Kostia Borodin could,' Arkady said.

'Buy gold here?'

'Steal gold in Siberia. But wouldn't it be too obvious, putting a new chest around old ikons?'

'They antique it. Rub off some gold to let the red bole show through. Rub in some umber. Send a detective to every art store in town to check on anyone buying Armenian bole, gesso, granulated gelatin, whiting, carpenter's hide glue, cheesecloth, extrafine sandpaper, chamois—'

'You seem to have some experience.' Arkady made a list.

'Any New York cop knows this. Also, cotton, alcohol, punches and a flat-faced burnisher.' Kirwill poured another glass for himself while Arkady scribbled. 'Surprised you didn't find sable hair on Jimmy's clothes.'

'Sable? Why?'

'That's the only kind of brush for laying gilt, a red sable brush. What the hell is this?'

Swan had arrived with a Gypsy, an old man with the face of an ancient monkey, shrunken and alert, a misshapen hat on grayed curls, a dirty bandanna tied at the neck. In every statistical survey of the Soviet Union there were no unemployed, except Gypsies. Despite every effort to raise them up or ship them out, every Sunday they could be found selling charms at the farmers' market, and every spring they would appear as if out of the ground in the city parks, brown babies at an open breast, begging for coins.

'People do not buy art supplies in art stores,' Arkady explained to Kirwill. 'They buy them at secondhand markets, on street corners, at someone's apartment.'

'He says he heard about a Siberian who had gold dust to sell.' Swan nodded to the Gypsy.

'And sable skins, I heard.' The Gypsy had a hoarse voice. 'Five hundred rubles for a single skin.'

'You can buy anything at the right street corner,' Arkady said to Kirwill but looked at the Gypsy.

'Anything,' the Gypsy agreed.

'Even people,' Arkady said.

'Like the judge who will die of a slow cancer who sent my son to camp. Did the judge think of the children my son left?'

'How many children did your son leave?' Arkady asked.

'Babies.' The Gypsy's throat choked, visibly swollen with emotion. He twisted in his chair to spit on the floor and wiped his mouth on his sleeve. 'Ten babies.'

The drunks at the nearest table moaned a song about love, arms over each other's shoulders, heads swaying. The Gypsy wiggled his hips and licked his lips suggestively. 'Their mother's very pretty,' he whispered to Arkady.

'Four babies.'

'Eight is the final—'

'Six.' Arkady put six rubles on the table. 'Ten times that if you find out where the Siberians lived.' He talked to Swan. 'There was a skinny red-headed guy with them. They all vanished around the beginning of February. Copy the list of art supplies and give one list to the Gypsy. They had to buy their stuff from someone. They probably lived on the outskirts of town, not the center. They didn't want a lot of neighbors where they holed up.'

'You're going to be a very lucky man.' The Gypsy stuffed his money into a pocket. 'Like your father. The general was very generous. Did you know we followed his troops all the way through Germany? He always left good pickings. Not like some.'

Swan and the Gypsy left just as Odessa scored on the television on the bar. The Dynamo goalie, Pilgui, stood arms akimbo as if surveying an empty field.

'Gypsies can find out things,' Arkady said.

'I have to go through the same stuff with my own informants, don't worry,' Kirwill said. 'Pick a match.'

Arkady lost and poured.

'You know' – Kirwill took his glass – 'there was a case in Tuxedo Park years back where they put together pieces of a girl's face for identification. And there's a guy in the New York medical examiner's office who does work reconstructing faces, mostly from airline crashes. He removes the bones and reshapes the skin. I guess you can work from the opposite direction. Hey, here's to your dead detective, huh?'

'Okay. To Pasha.'

They drank, drew matches and drank some more. Arkady felt the vodka insinuating its way from his stomach to his limbs. Kirwill, he was pleased to see, showed none of the feared signs of alcoholic paralysis; in fact – comfortably filling his chair, a glass cradled in one hand – he showed the signs of a practiced drinker. He put Arkady in mind of a long-distance runner just hitting stride, or a barge leisurely riding out the swell of a wave. The stench of the place would have chased away any cultured Muscovite. Better dead on the steps of the Bolshoi than alive in a workers' bar. But Kirwill seemed genuinely at ease.

'Is that true about General Renko?' he asked. 'The Butcher of the Ukraine was your father? That, as we say, is an outstanding footnote. How did I miss that?'

Arkady looked for an insult in the broad, florid face. Kirwill showed simply curiosity, even a friendly interest.

'Easy for you,' Arkady said, 'very hard for me.'

'Yeah. How come you didn't make an Army career? "Son of the Butcher of the Ukraine," you should have a star of your own by now. What are you, a fuck-up?'

'Besides incompetent, you mean?'

'Yeah' – Kirwill laughed – 'besides that.'

Arkady thought about it. This was a strain of humor he was unfamiliar with, and he wanted to choose the right answer.

'My "incompetence" is purely a matter of training; being a "fuck-up," as you put it, was my own genius. And, I repeat, very hard. The general commanded tanks in the Ukraine. Half of today's General Staff commanded tanks in the Ukraine. The political commissar for that campaign was Khrushchev. It was a charmed group: future Party secretaries and marshals. So I was sent to the right schools, had the right tutors, the right Party sponsors. If they had made the general a marshal there's no way I could have escaped. Right now I'd have my own missile base in Moldavia.'

'How about the Navy?'

'Be one of those fops with braid and a dress dagger? No, thank you. Anyway, they didn't make him a marshal. He was "Stalin's Arm"! When Stalin died, no one else could trust him. A marshal of the Army? Never.'

'They killed him?'

'Retired him. And I was allowed to degenerate into the investigator you see today. Pick a match.'

'It's a funny thing' – Kirwill picked the short match and poured – 'how people always ask how you became a cop, right? Three jobs always get that question: priests, whores and cops. The most necessary jobs in the world, but people always ask. Unless you're Irish.'

'Why?'

'If you're Irish, you're born into the Holy Name Society and you only go into one of the two branches, the police or the Church.'

'The "Holy Name"? What's that?'

'That's the simple life.'

'How simple?'

'Women are saints or cunts. Commies are Jews. Irish priests drink; the rest are fags. Blacks are sex-crazed and great fucks. The best book ever written was *The Thirteenth, Greatest of All Centuries*, by John J. Walsh, the nuns tell you. Hoover was queer. Hitler had a point. A district attorney will piss in your pocket and tell you it's raining. Those are the facts of life and the Golden Rules; the rest is horseshit. You think I'm a pretty ignorant son of a bitch, don't you?'

There was no mistaking the contempt on Kirwill's face. The amiability that had been on it a moment before – real when it was there – had vanished. Arkady had done nothing to cause the appearance of one expression or the disappearance of another. He had no more influence on Kirwill than he would have had on the sudden change in motion of a ship, or over the changing aspect of a planet. Kirwill leaned over the table, enveloping it with his arms, his eyes bright and close.

'I'm not so goddamn ignorant. I know about Russians, I was brought up by Russians. Every goddamn Russian Stalin scared out of this pisshole of a country lived in my house.'

'I heard your parents were radicals,' Arkady said carefully.

'Radicals? Fucking Reds. Irish Catholic Reds. Big Jim and Edna Kirwill, you're goddamn right you heard about them.'

Arkady glanced around the bar. Every other occupant was drunkenly intent on the television. Odessa scored again, and those who could whistled. A painful grip on Arkady's wrist tugged his head around.

'Big Jim and Edna, bleeding hearts of the Russian world. Anarchists, Mensheviks, you name it, if it was Russian and crazy, it had a home in New York City – our home. When nobody else would take them in. One permanent benefit for displaced Reds. I'll tell you this, anarchists made the best car mechanics. Very mechanically minded, anarchists – comes from rigging bombs.'

'The American left seems to have an interesting history—' Arkady started.

'Don't tell me about the American left, I'll tell you about the fucking American left. The limp-wrist Catholic Marxist movement, with all their cute magazine names like *Work, Worship, Thought* – as if any of them worked harder than lifting a sherry glass or passing a fart – or sniveling-after-Jesus names like *Orate Fratres* or *The Gregorian Review. The Gregorian Review*, I love that. A little monastic bum punching with Brother Marx. Only they were never around when the heads got busted, and the cops who did the busting trooped into church to get their clubs blessed. The priests were worse than the cops. Hell, the Pope was fascist. In America, to be a prince of the Church you had to be vicious, ignorant and Irish, that's it. Beat on Edna Kirwill's head, and she was four feet ten, and your kid's confirmed at Saint Patrick's. Why? Because for twenty years *Red Star* was the only Catholic journal with the balls to call itself Communist. Right out on the banner. That was the way Big Jim did things. He came from an old IRA family, built like a beer wagon, two hands that would cover this table' – Kirwill spread his own immense hands – 'and too fucking educated for his own good. Edna was lace Irish. Her folks had a brewery and she was going to be the family nun, that kind of family. That's why Big Jim and Edna were never excommunicated because her old man kept buying retreats for the Church, three up the Hudson and one in Ireland. Of course, we had our own retreats – Joe Hill House, Maryfarm – deep intellectual conversations around the fireplace. De Chardin was a closet capitalist, yes or no? Should we boycott *Going My Way*? Oh, we were weekend monks. Did the Gloria with tomtoms, stained glass, gilded ikons. We fucking stank of brotherhood until the war was over and the Rosenberg trial started. Then all the monks pulled their hoods over their heads and asses and ran for cover except Big Jim and Edna and the same miserable Russians we started out with – which didn't do us a hell of a lot of good with McCarthy and the FBI parked at the door. I was killing Chinese in Korea when Jimmy was born. It was a family joke. Hoover had Big Jim and Edna so trapped in the house that they'd gone back to screwing again.'

Dynamo finally scored, exciting bleary approval the length of the bar.

'Then I got this personal bereavement leave to go

home because they were dead. A double suicide – morphine, the only decent way to go. March tenth, 1953, five days after Stalin, when the Soviet Union was going to rise up from confusion and light the way to a Socialist Jerusalem. Only it wasn't going to happen; it was the same old boat-load of butchers steering the same old tub of blood, and Big Jim and Edna plain died of mortal disappointment. Still, we had an interesting funeral. Socialists didn't come because Big Jim and Edna were Communists; Catholics didn't come because suicide was a sin; Communists didn't come because Big Jim and Edna didn't clap for Uncle Joe. So it was just the FBI, Jimmy and me. About five years later someone from the Soviet embassy comes around asking if we'd like to have Big Jim and Edna moved to Russia. They wouldn't get slots in the Kremlin Wall – nothing so wonderful as that – but a nice plot in Moscow. Fairly amusing in retrospect.

'The point of all this, me talking and you sitting there like you got an egg between your cheeks – the point is that I know you and your people. Someone in this city killed my little brother. You're playing along with me now, but somewhere along the line because you want to go chasing after the guy who wasted your detective, or because your boss tells you to, or because you're the fucker behind it all, you're going to try to leave me with a hard-on and a rope around my neck. And I just want you to know that when you do I'm going to get you first. I just want you to know.'

*

Arkady drove aimlessly. He wasn't drunk. Sitting with Kirwill had been like sitting before an open furnace that burned vodka off in a vapor and left a futile energy. At every other block, red banners were being hoisted into place under floodlights. Snail-humped sanitation trucks browsed in the gutters. Moscow was sleepwalking toward May Day.

Hungry at last, he stopped for a bite at Petrovka. The militia cafeteria was empty except for a table of girls from the private alarm room. Some people paid so many rubles a month for special burglar alarms. The girls were dead asleep, heads on their forearms. Arkady dropped change into a can for hard rolls and tea, ate one roll and left the rest.

He had a sense that something was happening, but he didn't know what or where. In the halls his footsteps sounded ahead of him like another man's. Most of the officers on night duty were out on the annual push to clear the central city of drunks before May Day; conversely, on May Day it would be patriotic to be drunk. Timing was everything. Kirwill's radicals, ghosts from an obscure chronology of dead passions that Arkady doubted even Americans knew or cared about – how could they have anything to do with murder in Moscow?

In the communications room, two sergeants with loosened collars typed out radio messages that came in snatches, bits and ends, invisible litter from the outside world. Although there were no lights on the city map, Arkady stared at it.

He moved on to the detective squad room. One man, alone, was typing up court transcripts. Trials were recorded in longhand and filed in type. Bulletins on the wall exhorted 'Vigilance for a Glorious Week,' and invited 'Ski Groups to the Caucasus.' He sat at a desk and dialed Central Telephone and Telegraph. Getting an answer on the twentieth ring, he asked about phone calls from the pay phones around Irina Asanova's apartment.

A voice clotted with sleep replied, 'Investigator, I'll send a list in the morning. I'm not going to read you a hundred phone numbers now.'

'Any calls to the Rossiya Hotel from the pay phones?' Arkady asked.

'No.'

'Hold on.' The squad room had a single telephone book. Arkady scrambled through the 'R' pages to Rossiya. 'Any calls to 45–77–02?'

There was a snort of disgust on the other end, and then a long silence before the voice came back on. 'At twenty-ten, a call was placed from public phone 90–28–25 to 45–77–02.'

'Duration?'

'One minute.'

Arkady hung up, dialed the Rossiya number and asked for Osborne. Mr Osborne was out of his room, the clerk said. Osborne was meeting Irina Asanova.

In the garage, Arkady ran to his car and swung onto Petrovka Street, one-way south. There was little traffic. Assuming that she had called Osborne, Arkady thought, then it was at her initiative, even insistence. A minute was more time than needed to merely state a meeting place; she'd demanded one. Where? Not in Osborne's room, and not someplace where he would seem out of place and conspicuous. Not in a car – that could catch the eye of a militiaman, and if not in a car, then Osborne wouldn't be driving her home. Public transportation stopped at twelve-thirty. Arkady's watch said twelve-ten. The truth was, he didn't know if they were meeting, or where or when. He could only try the obvious.

He turned into Revolution Square, cut his motor and rolled to a stop in the shadow between streetlights. This was the nearest metro station to the Rossiya, also a direct line to her neighborhood. A militia emergency car raced by, blue overhead lights flashing, no siren. For once Arkady regretted the lack of a radio in his car. He felt his heart pound. He tapped the steering wheel. His excitement told him that he was right.

Revolution Square opened at its north on Sverdlov Square, at its south on Red Square. He kept watch on the shapes emerging from the glow of Red Square, a haze bright as snow crystals that filtered past the giant front of G.U.M., the Government Universal Store. But footsteps came from all directions, tugging his eyes one way and then another. Out of the steps, some strolling, some running for a train, he picked out the sound of her stride. Irina Asanova came in sight around the corner of the department store, hands in her jacket pockets, her long hair behind like a flag. She entered the metro station's glass doors directly across from Arkady's car. He saw two men, one at each side of the entrance, fall in behind her.

Inside the station, Irina had her five kopeks ready. When he entered, Arkady had to get change from a machine. By the time he was on the down escalator, she was far ahead, along with the two men she still hadn't noticed. They were in overcoats and hats, guises of drabness that could be found on every third or fourth step of an escalator that descended two hundred meters – bomb-shelter depth – beneath the city. Yet it was an hour for romance; there was a staggered swoon of couples, men one step lower than the women on whose bosoms they rested their heads. Impassive as sweatered cushions, the women stared ahead at the unreeling ceiling, to glare possessively when Irina pushed by. The two men in overcoats pushed forward behind her, as did Arkady from farther back. Where the escalator's descent ended at the low white gullet of the ceiling, Irina stepped off and vanished, and the two men in overcoats followed.

The passages of the lower station had marble floors, crystal chandeliers, rounded walls of mosaics, revolutionary panoramas of flesh-, gun- and fire-colored stones that hid the hiss and tremor of unseen trains. Arkady ran past two small Mongolian soldiers dragging a single heavy suitcase past a mosaic of Lenin addressing Bolsheviks. A musician stepped along in glassy pumps near Lenin rallying factories. Tired couples dawdled where Lenin hunched over a manifesto. Arkady couldn't see Irina Asanova, and he couldn't hear the echo of her steps over his own running. She had simply disappeared.

At the end of the passage, low arches led to a passenger platform. A train was just pulling out, strangers behind steel and glass, the old folks and veterans slipping into the seats provided for them, lovers daring to sway together, becoming a blur, a whiptail, then two red lights in the tunnel. Arkady didn't think she was on the train, but he couldn't be sure. Over the track the light-bulb numerals of a large digital clock changed from 2:56 to 0:00 and started to count up again. During rush hour, trains were never more than a minute apart, so that there was always a hushed, insistent trembling in the tunnels, and at night, even toward the end of service, no train was more than three minutes after the previous one. Platform conductors, sturdy grandmothers in blue uniforms, metal flags in their hands, made the rounds of the benches and whispered to reluctant lovers, 'Last train coming... last train.' Arkady asked about a tall, young, good-looking woman with long brown hair, and the conductor, misunderstanding, shook her head sympathetically. He darted across the passage to the opposite platform for trains in the other direction. The passengers there were a mirror of the ones he'd left, except for the Mongolian soldiers, who sat on their suitcase like a pair of prize dolls waiting to be won.

Arkady left the platforms and started back up the passage, reentering the glitter of revolutionary mosaics, sidestepping the last stragglers running for the train. He was sure he hadn't gone past her. A washwoman knelt by a bucket of ammonia scrubbing the marble floor. Lenin said he'd use gold for plumbing; marble in the subway was close enough. The washwoman's head mimicked the rotation of her hand. For the length of the passage Lenin inspired, berated, meditated in stone cartoons. Between the mosaics on one side were three doors. The chandeliers winked, signaling that the next train would be the last of the night. In the alternate light and dark, Lenins waked and faded.

Arkady opened a door marked by a red cross and found a closet of oxygen tanks, fire extinguishers, bandages and leaning stretchers, the props of emergency. A door marked PROHIBITED was locked. The second door marked PROHIBITED swung open easily and he slipped through it.

He found himself in an area the size of a locomotive cab. A red bulb was reflected by banks of meters. Another wall was a crosshatch of circuit breakers and chalk strikes. From the floor he picked what first looked like a rag. It was a scarf, black under the bulb.

An iron door was marked DANGER. Arkady pushed it open and stepped into the train tunnel. He was on a metal catwalk chest-high in the tunnel. The air was reverberant, gray from the light that seeped from the faraway platform. Irina Asanova lay on the track directly below, her eyes and mouth open, as a man in an overcoat arranged her legs. The other man, who was on the catwalk, swung a sap at Arkady.

Arkady took two hits on his arm and felt a warm numbness from the elbow down. He had learned from Kirwill in Gorky Park, though. As the other man drew back to bring a blow directly to the soft fontanel in the center of the skull, Arkady savagely brought his foot up to that larger, softer area between the legs. The man folded like a chair and dropped his weapon. Arkady gathered it up and swung in one motion, snapping the man's head back. The man sat down on the catwalk, one hand over his groin, one hand catching the dark burst of blood from his nose. Arkady looked down the tunnel to the far-off platform clock, surprised he could see it so distinctly. 2:27.

The man on the track regarded the scuffle above him with the mild dismay of a manager whose assistant has been brushed aside by an overbearing customer. His face was scarred like street snow: a professional's face. His little eyes looked over a snub-nosed TK, the KGB's pocket pistol, that was aimed at Arkady's chest. Irina wasn't moving. Whether she was alive, Arkady couldn't tell.

'No,' Arkady said, and looked again toward the passenger platform. 'They'll hear it.'

The man on the track nodded in a reasonable way and dropped the gun into his coat, then looked toward the platform clock and turned back to Arkady with a reasonable suggestion. 'Too late. Go home.'

'No.'

At the very least, Arkady had thought he could prevent the man from getting off the track and onto the catwalk, but in one step the man had his hands on the catwalk railing, and with the next he swung athletically over it to Arkady's level. Arkady flailed with the sap, his newly won weapon, hitting nothing but overcoat and railing until the man kicked him away, squeezed past his fallen colleague and advanced in terse, mechanical steps while Arkady retreated. Arkady took another kick in his stomach while he covered his tender chest in panic, then another, bringing a deep grunt. The professional face speculated, like a doctor searching for a vein. Here? There? His hands and feet were not as hard as Kirwill's, and not drawn back from reach as cleanly.

Arkady dropped the sap, smothered the next kick and pulled. The man grabbed the catwalk railing for balance, allowing Arkady to slip in a fist. A second punch, better aimed to the heart, even dropped the man. Without complaint he rose, locking with Arkady, first trying to butt and then to gouge. As Arkady twisted away, they spilled over the railing and toppled down onto the tracks.

Arkady landed on top, but felt something slap into his belt. Raising himself, he saw a knife blade sticking through the man's overcoat pocket. The man rolled free and pulled a spring-operated knife that he held thumb up, blade flat. Hatless now, exposing a sharp V hairline, he also revealed for the first time a personal interest in his work. The blade circled and stabbed, first a peck to the eyes and then a thrust to the body. The blade winked, then tapped the rails for emphasis. Arkady stumbled backward over Irina. Remarkably, as the man moved in with his knife, his eyes developed orange cores, brilliant moth eyes as if he were lit from within.

The rails trembled under Arkady's back. In a pantomime of neatness, the man folded his knife, picked up his hat and scrambled onto the catwalk. Arkady saw the distant platform numbers change from 2:49 to 2:50, and he turned into the glow of two vertical headlights. Halos spread over the tunnel walls. He felt a wind, air-propelled ahead of the train, and the rails' moan.

Irina's hands were limp and hot to the grasp. He had to lift her bodily and twist away from the train to keep from being blinded. He had never been so brightly lit. The last mote in the air stood out. Her arms fell sleepily and he staggered. A scream of locking brakes climbed to a fine peak of metallic hysteria, then abruptly dropped away as the train rushed through.

Arkady pushed Irina onto the catwalk and pressed himself into the wall.

As soon as Levin opened his apartment door, Arkady carried Irina in to a plastic-covered sofa.

'She was hit on the head or they gave her a shot of something, I haven't had time to look,' he said. 'She's very hot.'

Levin was in a robe and slippers, pajama bottoms at shanks as sharp as his nose. It was clear that he was debating whether to tell Arkady to go or not.

'I wasn't followed,' Arkady offered.

'Don't insult me.' Levin made his choice, folded his robe, and sat and took Irina's temperature. Her face was flushed and slack, her Afghan jacket reduced to the scruff and patches it really was. Arkady was embarrassed for her; he hadn't considered yet what he looked like. Levin held up her right forearm to show a bruise marked by pinpricks. 'Injections. Sulfazin, probably, from her temperature. A messy job.'

'She was probably struggling.'

'Yes.' Levin's tone underlined the stupidity of the remark. He struck a match and passed it slowly over her eyes, covering one eye and then the other.

Arkady still felt the afterthrill of near death. The subway train had stopped short of the platform, and by the time the engineers reached it and the platform conductors called the militia, Arkady had carried Irina from the station to his car. *Escaped* was the description; the word moved inside him like a flywheel out of control. Why would a chief investigator run from the militia? Any more than an unconscious girl should seem so dangerous to Levin? It was a wonderful country where everyone understood secret signs so well.

It took him some time to look clearly at Levin's flat. He'd never been here before. Instead of comfortable knickknacks, shelves and tables were crowded with lacquered men on chessboards of ivory, teak and colored glass, each board set for a game in progress. Instead of the usual embroidered babushkas nailed to the wall were photos of Lasker, Tal, Botvinnik, Spassky and Fischer, all chess masters, all Jews.

'If you have any brains, you'll take her back where you found her,' Levin said.

Arkady shook his head.

'Then you'll have to help me,' Levin said.

They took her to Levin's bed, a plain iron cot. Arkady pulled off her boots and helped Levin remove her dress and underclothes. Each article was spongy with perspiration.

Arkady thought of the many times he and Levin had stood over other bodies that were white, cold and stiff. Over Irina, Levin was strangely tentative, ill at ease and trying to disguise the fact. It was the most human Arkady had ever seen him; he was nervous around the living. Because Irina Asanova was very much alive, there was no denying that. Comatose, but hardly cold. She was a feverish pink. Slimmer than Arkady'd expected, her ribs under heavy breasts with oblong areolae, her stomach

281

concave until a rise of thick brown hair. Her graceful legs sprawled. She stared up at Arkady and through him.

While they were covering her in wet towels to bring down her temperature, Levin pointed to the faint blue mark on her right cheek. 'See this?'

'An old accident, I suppose.'

'Accident?' Levin sneered. 'Clean up. You can find the bathroom yourself, this isn't the Winter Palace.'

In the bathroom mirror, Arkady saw that he was covered with dirt, and that one eyebrow was sliced open as if with a razor. After washing, he returned to the living room, where Levin was warming tea on a hot plate. A small cabinet exhibited cans of vegetables and fish.

'They offered me an apartment with a kitchen or an apartment with a bathroom. For me a bathroom is more important.' On a long-unused note of hospitality, he added, 'You want something to eat?'

'A little sugar in the tea, that's all. How will she be?'

'Don't worry about her. She's young and strong. She'll feel sick for a day, no more. Here.' He gave Arkady a tepid cup.

'So you think it was sulfazin.'

'You can take her to a hospital if you want to be sure,' Levin said.

'No.'

Sulfazin was one of the favorite narcotics of the KGB; he'd no sooner get her to a hospital than a doctor would be calling. Levin knew that.

'Thanks.'

'Don't.' Levin cut him off. 'The less you say, the better

off I'll be. I'm sure my imagination is adequate; I just wonder if yours is.'

'What do you mean?'

'Arkady, this girl of yours is no virgin.'

'I don't know what you're talking about.'

'The mark on her cheek. They had her before, Arkady. They shot aminazin into her years ago.'

'I thought they stopped using aminazin because it was dangerous.'

'That's the point. They deliberately inject it badly into the muscle so that it's not absorbed. If it's not absorbed, it forms a malignant tumor, just as it did with her. Wake up. She's blind in one eye. Whoever cut the tumor cut the optic nerve and left that mark. That's their mark.'

'That's overstating it a little, don't you think?'

'Ask her. Talk about blind!'

'You're making too much of this. A witness was attacked and I defended her.'

'Then why aren't you in a militia station now?'

Arkady went to the bedroom. The towels on Irina were hot; he replaced them with fresh ones. Her arms and legs jerked spasmodically in sleep, a reaction to her change in temperature. He smoothed her forehead, pushing back strands of matted hair. The mark on her cheek was a faint violet cast from the rush of blood beneath the skin.

What did *they* want? he wondered. From the beginning, *they* had been there. Major Pribluda to rake up the bodies in Gorky Park. Detective Fet when Golodkin was questioned. The killers in Golodkin's apartment, the would-be killers in the metro tunnel. Rubber balls, injections, blades – all signatures of Pribluda and the host of Pribludas that was *them*. Anyway, *they* would be stationed around her place and by now *they* would have a list of her friends. *They* would get tired of watching hospitals, and the idea of Levin the pathologist wouldn't take much longer to occur to Pribluda. Levin had courage, but when she woke she had to go.

When he returned to the living room, Levin was sedating himself by scrutinizing his chessboards. 'She looks better,' Arkady reported. 'At least she's sleeping.'

'I envy her.' Levin didn't look up.

'Would you like to play?'

'What's your rating?' Levin looked up.

'I don't know.'

'If you had one, you'd know. No, thank you.' That reduced Levin to the demands of hospitality again, however, and thoughts of the woman in his bed who was being searched for. He feigned a smile. 'Actually, this is quite an interesting situation here. A game played by Bogolyubov and Pirc in '31. Black's move, only he doesn't have one.'

Only in the Army had Arkady been bored enough to play chess seriously, and then his only talent had been for defense. Both sides in this game had castled and White had control of the center, just as Levin said. On the other hand, Arkady noted an absence of game clocks in the apartment, the sign of a soul who preferred leisurely analysis to over-the-board mayhem. Also, poor Levin was fraying at the prospect of a long and nervous night.

'Do you mind?' Arkady moved for Black. 'Bishop takes pawn.'

Levin shrugged. PXB.

. . . QXP check! KXQ, N-N5 check! K-NI, NXQ! Black's knight forked White's bishop and rook.

'Do you ever take time to think before you move?' Levin muttered. 'There's a certain pleasure to be found in that.'

B-N3, NXR. Levin pondered whether to take the knight with his rook or his king. Either way the knight was doomed; then Black would have given up queen, bishop and knight in exchange for queen, rook and two pawns. The outcome would depend on White's ability to bring his bishop back into the game before Black could link his majority of pawns and double his rooks.

'You've only introduced complications,' Levin said.

While Levin thought out his move, Arkady dipped into a book-shelf, coming up with a collection of Poe. Soon enough, he saw that Levin had fallen asleep in his chair. At 4 a.m., he went down to his car, drove it around the block to find if he was being watched, and returned to Levin's apartment. He couldn't wait any longer. He dressed Irina in her damp clothes, wrapped her in a blanket and carried her down. Driving, the only people he saw were road crews 'storming' for May Day. A single man on a steamroller directed four women pouring warm tar. When he had crossed the river and was within two blocks of Taganskaya, he got out, walked alone the rest of the way to his apartment, and went through every room to be sure it was empty. Returning to the car, he drove to the apartment, switching his engine and headlights off as he turned into the courtyard. He carried

Irina upstairs, laying her on the bed, undressing her and covering her with Levin's blanket and his own overcoat.

He was about to go out to move the car again when he saw that her eyes were open. Her pupils were dilated and the whites were tinged red. She didn't have the strength to move her head.

'Idiot,' she said.

Chapter Thirteen

It was raining. The floors creaked idly. In the apartments above and below, Arkady heard the occasional footfall of housecleaning. On the hall stairs, the sideways climbing of an old woman. There had been no knocks at the door, no phone calls.

Irina Asanova lay facing him, her skin was wan as ivory now that her fever was broken. He was still in his clothes. At first he'd tried to find some other place to curl up, but there were no chairs or sofa, not even a rug, and in the end they'd shared the bed. Not that she'd known or that it mattered. He lifted his watch. 9 a.m. Slowly, so as not to wake her, he rose and walked down in stockinged feet to the side of a window and looked down into the courtyard. No face looked up. He'd have to move her, but he didn't know where. Not her place. Hotels were out of the question; it was illegal to take a hotel room in your own city. (What good reason could a citizen have for not being home?) Something would turn up.

Four hours' sleep was enough. The investigation carried him along. He felt it rising like the bulk of a wave, bearing him, bones and body, in rumpled clothes.

The girl clutched her blanket against her cheek, good for another four hours of deep sleep, he guessed. He'd be back by then. It was time to see the general.

*

287

Enthusiasts Road, where prisoners used to start their journey to Siberia on foot, went by the Hammer and Sickle tractor works to Route 89, a truck run of narrow concrete, flat mud countryside and villages set as close to the ground as potatoes east all the way to the Urals. Arkady drove forty kilometers before turning north on a macadam road toward a village called Balobanovo, past figures sowing okra and beans, and fields of uniformly brown cows, then on a dirt road through woods so dense that drifts of snow untouched by the sun blanketed the ground. Between branches he could see the river Kliazma.

At an iron gate he got out and walked the rest of the way. No cars had been through recently. In the middle of the road, last year's grass stood dead and tall. A fox dashed almost under his feet and he braced automatically for the general's dogs, but the woods were silent except for the drizzle of rain.

After ten minutes' walk, he came to a two-story house with a steep metal roof. On the other side of the circular yard, he knew, was a long stairway going down to the riverbank where there was – had been, at least – a dock with a skiff and, anchored well into the stream, a float on orange oil cans. There had also been peonies in wooden buckets along the dock, and a tub of ice manned by two aides-de-camp in white jackets and white gloves. For parties, Chinese lanterns would hang over the dock and be strung all the way up the stairs, a trail of moons rising straight to the sky. Their reflections in the water would bob like luminous sea creatures attracted to the music.

He looked up at the house. Ferrous stains reached from the gutters to the ground. A banister leaned from the steps. Weeds flourished in the yard around a rusted garden table and an empty rabbit pen. Crowding around the house and the lawn, staggering at all angles, were gaunt pines and elms gone wild in decay, adding more finishing touches to an atmosphere of total desolation. The only sign of life was a string of dead hares, flayed blue and black-red.

His knock was answered by an old woman, whose stupefaction turned into a poisonous glare and a twist in the blot of lipstick that was her mouth. She wiped her hands on a greasy apron. 'Surprise,' she said in a voice slurred by vodka.

Arkady stepped in. Sheets covered the furniture. The curtains were as gray as shrouds. An oil portrait of Stalin hung over the fireplace, which reeked of damp ashes. There were dried boughs, bottles of faded paper flowers, a gun rack with a Mosin-Nagant bolt-action rifle and two carbines.

'Where is he?' Arkady asked.

She nodded toward the library. 'Tell him I need more money,' she said loudly. 'And a woman to help out, but, first, money.'

Arkady pulled free of her fingers and went to a door built under the stairway to the second floor.

The general was in a wicker chair by a window. Like Arkady, he had a narrow, handsome face, but the skin had gone taut and translucent, the eyebrows white and untrimmed, the hair a white fluff around a high forehead knotted by veins at the temples. His frame sank within a loose peasant shirt, pants and oversized boots. His hands, pale as cream paper, rubbed a long wooden holder which had no cigarette.

Arkady sat down. There were two busts in the library, one of Stalin and the other of the general, both cast from shell casings. A framed panel of red felt displayed rows of medals, including two Orders of Lenin. The felt was dusty, the photographs on the walls were obscured by a haze of dirt, and dust collected in the folds of a divisional flag nailed to the wall.

'So it's you,' the general said. He spat on the floor, missing a ceramic bowl filled almost to the brim with brown scum. He waved his cigarette holder. 'Tell the bitch if she wants more money to go into town and make it on her back.'

'I came to ask you about Mendel. There's something I have to be certain of.'

'He's dead, that's certain enough.'

'He won his Order of Lenin for killing some German raiders near Leningrad. He was a close friend of yours.'

'He was a piece of shit. That's why he went into the Foreign Ministry. All they take is thieves and shit, all they've ever taken. Another coward, like you. No, better than you. He wasn't a total failure. It's a new world, and turds float down. Go home. Sniff after that silly cunt you married. You still married?'

Arkady took the general's holder and put a cigarette in it. He put one in his own mouth, lit both and gave back the holder. The general coughed.

'I was in Moscow for the October reunion. You could have come around and seen me then. Belov did.'

Arkady studied one of the clouded photographs. Was it of men dancing, or hanging? Another one was of a freshly turned garden or a mass grave. It had been so long that he'd forgotten.

'You there?'

'I'm here.'

For the first time the general turned his face to Arkady. There was little left in it. Muscles worked like wires directly between skin and bone. The black eyes were blind, milky with cataracts. 'You're a weakling,' he said. 'You make me sick.'

Arkady looked at his watch. The girl would be waking in a few hours, and he wanted to pick up some food before getting back to Moscow.

'Heard about the new tanks? Tried to show them off for us. Fucking limousines. That's that asshole Kosygin for you. Designed by plant directors. Plant directors! One runs a nuclear reactor; let's put in atomic shells. One makes lemonade; let's put in chemical war sprayers. Another makes air conditioners; let's air-condition the damn thing. You make toilets, we'll put in toilet seats. More useless shit than a luxury cruiser, as if we were going to be impressed! No, you build a tank with as little as possible to go wrong, and if it does go wrong you can fix it on the run. Just like Mikoyan built his planes, a good team with one brain at the top. But they kept heaping shit on us like fruit on a grave. They're all soft now. You still have that stupid moon-calf look about you?'

'Yeah.'

The old man shifted, hardly disturbing the clothes hanging on him.

'You could have been a general by now. Govorov's boy commands the whole Moscow Military District. With my name you could have risen faster. Well, I knew you didn't have the balls for an armored command, but at least you could have been one of those assholes in Intelligence.'

'What about Mendel?'

'You just don't have it. A weak sperm or something. I don't know.'

'Did Mendel shoot the Germans?'

'Ten years you don't come here, and then you ask about some coward in his grave.'

Cigarette ash dropped on the general's shirt. Arkady leaned forward and pinched an ember.

'My dogs are dead,' the general said angrily. 'They were out in the fields and came across some assholes in bulldozers. The bastards shot them! Peasant bastards! What are bulldozers doing out here? Well, the whole world . . .' He made a fist, a white knob. 'Everything going to seed. Dung beetles. Rotting. Listen, the flies!'

They sat quietly, the general's ear tilted to the rain. A bee was trapped between the second and third panes of the window, but it was stiff on its back.

'Mendel's dead. In bed, he always said he'd die in bed. He was right. Now my dogs.' He drew his lips up in a smile. 'They want to take me to a clinic, boy. There's a clinic in Riga. Very fancy, no expense spared for heroes. I thought that's why you came. I have cancer all through me, rotten with it. It's all that's holding me together, you know. And they have this clinic with radiation and heat cures and I'm invited. They won't get me there because I know I'd never come back. I've seen doctors in the field. I won't go. I didn't tell the bitch. She'd want me to go because she thinks she'll get my pension. Same as you, right? I can smell you coming like a monk with shit in your pants.'

'I don't care where you die,' Arkady said.

'That's right. The main thing is, I'll cheat you. See, I always knew why you joined the prosecutor's office. All you ever wanted to do was tear me down, come sniffing up here with all your detectives, bring the whole thing up again. Did the wife of the general die in a boating accident or was she killed? That explains your whole life right there – getting me. And I'll be dead before you do, and then you'll never know.'

'But I do know. I've known for years.'

'Don't try to fool me. You're a bad liar, you always were.'

'Still am. But I know. You didn't do it and it wasn't an accident. She killed herself. The wife of the hero committed suicide.'

'Belov—'

'Didn't tell me. I figured it out for myself.'

'Then if you knew I didn't do it, why didn't you visit me all these years?'

'If you could see why she killed herself, you should be able to see why I never came. It's not a mystery; it's just the past.'

The general sank back into his chair, his expression set for a scornful protest, and then he seemed to continue sinking beyond himself and the chair and Arkady. His face went slack. He diminished. Not gave up the ghost; the ghost retreated in him. Shirt and pants might simply have been left on the chair, unruffled as they were by movement or breath, as unruffled as his head or hands.

In the silence Arkady thought – he didn't know why – of the Asiatic folktale of life. Perhaps it was the abrupt peacefulness of the figure in the chair. The tale had it that all life was preparation for death, that death was a passage as natural as birth, and that the worst a man could do in his life was to struggle to avoid death. There was a mythical tribe where all births were without crying and all deaths were without agony. Where the hell these mythical people thought they were going after they were dead, he forgot. However, they had their advantages over the universal Russian, who went through life struggling like a man caught in a river rushing toward a falls. By the second, he could see his father growing more inert, the force in him fading to one last central stronghold. Then, just as visibly, he saw the force painfully rally. The breathing deepened, and blood, ordered like reinforcements, sent a tremor through the limbs. It was a picture of a man reconstituting himself out of sheer will, holding on within himself. At last, the waxiness of the face was gone and the milky eyes stared forward, corrupted but defiant.

'Mendel was in my class at the Frunze Military Academy, and we both had armored commands on the front line when Stalin said, "Not one step back!" Me? I understood the Germans would be spread out, ripe for infiltration. The effect of my radio reports from behind their lines was electric. Stalin listened every night in his bomb shelter. The newspaper reports said, "General Renko, somewhere behind enemy lines." The Germans asked, "Renko, who is this Renko?" Because I was only a colonel. Stalin had promoted me, and I didn't even know it. The Germans had our entire officers' list, and this new name confused them, shook their confidence. It was on everyone's lips, the first name after Stalin. And the effect when I fought my way into Moscow and was welcomed by Stalin himself, and still in battle gear followed him to Mayakovsky Station and stood by his side to hear his greatest speech, words that turned the Fascist tide even as they shelled the city overhead . . . And four days later I was given my own armored division, the Red Guard Division that marched first into Berlin. In Stalin's name . . .' His hand shot out to restrain Arkady from rising and going. 'I gave you a name like that, and you come here, a petty detective, to ask about a coward who spent his war hiding in packing cases? Some common snoop, is that all you are? Is that a life? Asking about Mendel?'

'I know all about you.'

'And I, you. Don't forget. Another milk-fed reformer . . .' The general's hand dropped. He stopped and tilted his head. 'Where was I?'

'Mendel.'

Arkady expected more rambling, but the general came to the point.

'An amusing story. They captured some German officers in Leningrad and handed them to Mendel for interrogation. Mendel's German was—' He spat cleanly into the bowl. 'So this American volunteered to do it –

295

I don't recall his name. He was good, for an American.
Sympathetic, charming. The Germans told him everything. At the end the American took the Germans for a
picnic in the woods with champagne and chocolates and
shot them. For fun. What was amusing was that they
weren't supposed to be shot, so Mendel had to make a
false report about raiders. The American paid off the
military investigators, and for that Mendel got an Order
of Lenin. He swore me to silence, but you being my
son . . .'

'Thank you.'

Arkady rose, more exhausted than he could have
imagined, and stumbled on the way to the library door.

'You'll come again?' the general asked. 'It's good to
talk.'

The cardboard box contained milk, eggs, bread, sugar,
tea, plates and cups, a frying pan, soap, shampoo, tooth-
paste and toothbrush – all bought on the return trip
outside Moscow – and he rushed to the refrigerator
before the bottom of the box broke. He was kneeling,
putting the food away, when he heard Irina behind him.

'Don't look,' she said, picked up the soap and shampoo and was gone. He heard water running into the tub.

Arkady stayed in the living room, sitting on the windowsill and feeling foolish for hesitating to enter the
bedroom when there was no real place to sit here. The
rain had stopped, yet no characters in overcoats had
emerged on the street. He was surprised because Pribluda was not subtle. Which brought Arkady's mind back

to his conversation with his father. Osborne had killed the three Germans ('I've been to Leningrad before,' Osborne had said on the tapes; 'I've been there with Germans before') in almost exactly the same manner he'd killed the three victims in Gorky Park. Arkady was interested in the military investigators paid off by Mendel and Osborne; who were they and what glorious postwar careers had they carved out?

He felt Irina at the bedroom doorway before he saw her. She was in a sheet with holes cut for her arms, a belt of his around the waist, her wet hair in a towel, her feet bare. She couldn't have been there for more than a second, but he had the sensation that her eyes had been on him for longer, the same as the first time he'd seen her, as if she were studying some oddity in her field of vision. Again she made the strangest apparel seem stylish, as if sheets were the natural thing to wear this year. Now, too, he noticed how her face was turned slightly to one side; he remembered what Levin had said about the blind eye, and glanced at the telltale mark on her cheek.

'How are you feeling?'

'Cleaner.'

Her voice was harsh from throwing up; sulfazin had that effect. Still, there was color in her face, more than most Muscovites ever boasted. She looked around the room.

'I apologize for the state of the apartment.' He followed her gaze. 'My wife did a little spring-cleaning. She took a few things out.'

'It looks like she took herself out.'

'She did.'

297

Arms folded, Irina walked to the stove with its single frying pan, cups and plates.

'Why did you save my life last night?' she asked.

'You're important to my investigation.'

'That's all?'

'What else could there be?'

She looked into an empty closet. 'I don't want to upset you,' she said, 'but it doesn't look as if your wife's coming back.'

'An objective opinion is always appreciated.'

She rested against the stove, across the room from him. 'Now what?'

'When your clothes are dry, you go,' Arkady said.

'Where?'

'That's up to you. Home—'

'They'll be waiting for me. Thanks to you, I can't even go to the studio.'

'Friends, then. Most of them will be watched, but there must be someone you can stay with,' Arkady said.

'With the chance of getting them in trouble as well? That's not what I do to friends.'

'Well, you can't stay here.'

'Why not?' She shrugged. 'No one else is. The apartment of the chief investigator seems perfect to me. It would be a crime to let it go to waste.'

'Comrade Asanova—'

'Irina. You've undressed me enough; I think you can call me by my first name.'

'Irina, this may be hard to grasp, but this is the worst place for you to be. They saw me last night, and this is one of the first places they'll come. You wouldn't be able to go out for food or clothes. You'd be trapped here.'

The longer they talked, the more the sheet attached itself to her still-damp body, the damp spots showing through.

'I won't be around that much,' Arkady looked away.

'I see two plates and two cups,' Irina said. 'It's very simple. Either you are with "them," in which case it doesn't matter where I run because you'll have me followed, or you're not with "them", in which case I can drag a friend down with me or I can drag you. I've thought it over. I want to take you.'

The phone rang. It was in a corner of the bedroom floor, black, insistent. On the tenth ring, Arkady picked up the receiver.

It was Swan saying that the Gypsy had found where Kostia Borodin did the ikons.

The place the Gypsy had found was a garage near the go-kart track on the south side of the river. A mechanic called 'the Siberian' had disappeared a few months ago. Two karts hung by hooks from the ceiling, apostrophes above a corroded Pobeda that was set on blocks. Sawdust and oil coated the floor. A worktable vise clutched a half-sawed board. Metal and car parts were piled in one corner and wood trash in another. There was a frame for stretching canvas hanging on a wall, and cans of whiting, linseed oil and turpentine. A locker with a broken door had coveralls too filthy to steal. There were no tool chests, nothing valuable and portable in sight.

Accelerating and decelerating whines came from the track outside.

'You know how to do this?' Arkady asked.

'I spent two years in Latent Prints. I'll try to keep up,' Kirwill said.

Swan and the Gypsy stood aside, the Gypsy using his pocket as an ashtray. Arkady set down a floodlight, spread his forensic case on the floor, and took out a flashlight, thin rubber gloves, black and white cards, tongs, powders (black, white and dragon's blood), camel's-hair brushes and atomizers. Kirwill put on a pair of gloves, unscrewed the garage's suspended sixty-watt light bulb and replaced it with one of a hundred fifty watts. Arkady started at the windows, playing his flashlight over dirty panes as he brushed on white powder, then moved to the drinking glasses and bottles on the shelves, applying white powder and dropping black cards into the glasses to see the prints. Kirwill started on porous surfaces with an atomizer of ninhydrin, working clockwise from the garage door.

Dusting was the sort of work that could be done well in a day or badly in a week. After all the obvious places – points of entry, handles, glasses – were covered, an investigator had to consider all the unlikely places a human finger could reach: tires, picture backs, the bottom of paint cans. Generally Arkady avoided dusting if possible. This time he welcomed it; it was normal and occupied the mind. The American detective worked with a methodical energy and a certain grace, directing muscle and concentration on minute labor. Nothing was said to spoil the immersion in work. Arkady dusted the door handles, fenders and license of the car while Kirwill sprayed the workbench, upper and under. When the Gypsy pointed out a heap of rags, Arkady and Kirwill dismissed him with a mutual glance; there were no decent prints on cloth. Arkady dusted black powder onto the margin of a photo on the wall. The actress in it had a smile that spoke of romps over sea-girt cliffs, honesty and foreign underwear. He used as little powder as possible, brushing in the direction of the ridges, from the top of a fingerprint loop to the exit.

There was the personality of the garage to consider. The area around the car and go-karts bloomed with greasy prints; a man doesn't get under an oil pan unless he's looking forward to a little oil. Woodworkers, on the other hand, were a more fastidious, almost surgical lot. There were other factors. The perfect suspect would be a nervous man with an oily complexion and lotion in his hair. But a cool, dry man could just have shaken hands with the oily one or shared the same bottle. Also, winter was an item; cold closed human pores. Wood dust could absorb latent prints like a sponge.

While Arkady returned his instruments to his kit for a magnifying glass and a fingerprint card of Kostia Borodin, Kirwill plugged in the long extension cord of the flood lamp, turned it on and began retracing his steps, shining the intense heat of the lamp where he'd sprayed before. Arkady noted that Borodin's card showed unusual double loops on each first finger and a scarred whorl on his right thumb. Gathering evidence for court he would have used a slower routine, photographing the prints and lifting them on tape, trying to gain as many points of reference between the card and the brushed prints as he could. Instead, he worked now for speed and Kirwill moved quickly as well. The light spray of ninhydrin, combined with residue amino acids of forgotten touches, dried purple under the lamp's glow. Then Kirwill retraced his route a second time, without the lamp and without a magnifying glass, comparing the ninhydrin prints with his own card of the prints of James Kirwill. They didn't exchange cards. When Arkady was done with the dusted prints, he switched to the sprayed ones, while Kirwill moved on to Arkady's work.

Three hours after they'd arrived, Arkady repacked his case. Kirwill leaned on a car fender, lighting a cigarette and being bummed for one by the Gypsy, who'd showed signs of starving for a smoke for the last hour. Arkady lit one himself.

The garage looked as if madmen had pasted moth wings, thousands of them, black, white and purple, everywhere they could reach. Arkady and Kirwill were silent, sharing the perverse sense of contentment that comes from well-done and futile labor.

'You found their prints, then,' the Gypsy assumed.

'No, they were never here,' Arkady said.

'Then why do you both look happy?' Swan asked.

'Because we did *something*,' Kirwill answered.

'This man was Siberian,' the Gypsy said. 'There was wood and paint, that's all you told me.'

'We didn't give him enough to go on,' Kirwill said.

What else was there to go on? Arkady asked himself. James Kirwill dyed his hair, but Arkady guessed that it was the girl who had been sent out to buy the dye.

'What was in that forensic report again?' Kirwill asked.

'Gesso, sawdust, what we're already looking for,' Arkady said.

'Nothing else at all?'

'Blood. They were shot, after all.'

'I remember something else on their clothes.'

'Animal-blood stains,' Arkady answered. 'Fish and chicken blood. Fish and chicken,' he repeated, and looked at Swan.

'Now, I've been to your food stores, and I haven't seen anything fresh enough to sweat out one drop of blood,' Kirwill said. 'Where do you get fresh meat around here?'

A poor grade of blood-drained and water-heavy chicken or frozen fish was commonly available. But freshly killed chicken or live fish were exorbitantly expensive and – outside of 'closed shops' for the elite or foreigners – available only from private entrepreneurs, fishermen or a local woman with a backyard coop. Arkady was disgusted with himself for not thinking of it before.

'He's good,' Swan nodded toward Kirwill.

'Find out where they got fresh meat and fish,' Arkady ordered.

Swan and the Gypsy left. The other two men remained, Kirwill weighing down a fender, Arkady sitting on the table. Arkady took out the New York detective shield and tossed it over.

'Maybe I ought to detect. I could be a fucking superman around here,' Kirwill said.

'That was a good idea, those other bloodstains,' Arkady tried to concede graciously.

'How did you get that cut over your eye? Where did you go last night after we left the bar?'

'I went back for a piss and fell down the hole.'

'I can kick the answer out of you.'

'What if you broke a toe? You'd be kept in a Soviet hospital until it was healed – six weeks at least. At no cost, of course.'

'So what? The killer's here, that will give me more time.'

'Come on.' Arkady heaved himself from the table. 'You've earned something.'

At the Central Universal Department Store music was a serious business. There was a contemplative atmosphere where a young soul could be influenced by the function of official pricing, by an approving twenty rubles for a violin and bow or a forbidding four hundred eighty rubles for a brassy saxophone. A man with a pockmarked face in a hat and overcoat picked up the saxophone, admired it, fingered the stops, and gave Arkady the vague sort of nod one passes to a colleague. Arkady recognized the face from the train tunnel. Looking around, he found another KGB plainclothesman pricing accordions. As he led Kirwill into the home-entertainment department, the two music lovers laid down their instruments and followed at a discreet distance, interested but not obtrusive.

Kirwill spun the turntable of a stereo. 'Where is this guy, Renko? He works here?'

'You didn't really think I was going to have you shake hands with him, did you?'

Arkady slipped a reel from his coat pocket and put it on a tape machine, a Rekord, the same as he had at the Ukraina. There were two headsets for the machine, for enjoyment that would not disturb a crowded apartment. Kirwill placed one set over his ears, following Arkady's lead. The pockmarked man watched from the end of a long aisle of TVs. The other was gone – phoning in a description of Kirwill, Arkady assumed.

Arkady pushed PLAY. It was the February 2 telephone call between Osborne and Unmann.

'*The plane is delayed.*'

'*It's delayed?*'

'*Everything is going fine. You worry too much.*'

'*You never do?*'

'*Relax, Hans.*'

'*I don't like it.*'

'*It's a little late to like or not like anything.*'

'*Everyone knows about those new Tupolevs.*'

'*A crash? You think only Germans can build anything.*'

'*Even a delay. When you get to Leningrad—*'

'*I've been to Leningrad before. I've been there with Germans before. Everything will be fine.*'

After the recorded click of the phone disconnect and silence, Kirwill pushed STOP, REWIND AND PLAY. He replayed the tape twice before Arkady removed it.

'A German and an American.' Kirwill removed his

headset. 'The German's named Hans. Who's the American?'

'I think he murdered your brother.'

A Padoga color set priced at six hundred and fifty rubles showed a woman speaking in front of a map of the world. The sound was off. Arkady checked the name of the factory; there was a big difference between factories.

'That's not telling me anything,' Kirwill said. 'You're just stringing me along.'

'Maybe you'll thank me later.' Arkady turned to a channel of folk dancers in pastel costumes silently skipping back and forth, slapping their hands on their knees and heels. He turned off the set, and as the screen dulled he got a clearer reflection of the two men in overcoats at the end of the aisle. The other man had returned. 'Those two' – Arkady nodded – 'I doubt they'd try anything with an American tourist, but they may not know you are one.'

'They followed us in a car from the garage.' Kirwill looked at the screen. 'I thought they were yours.'

'No.'

'Not a whole lot of people on your side, are there, Renko?'

Arkady and Kirwill split when they came out on Petrovka Street. Arkady headed for militia headquarters and Kirwill for the Metropole Hotel. Half a block along, Arkady stopped to light a cigarette. The street was filled with after-work shoppers, stoical armies in slow march past store windows. At a distance he picked out the broad figure of Kirwill moving away through the crowd as imperiously as a czar, trailing two retainers in overcoats.

Arkady went to look for the Gypsy.

The truck was painted orange on green, with stars and cabalistic signs in blue. A naked baby stumbled down the truck's rear steps to the fire, onto his mother's lap of colored petticoats, and to her brown breast. Half a dozen crones and little girls sat around the fire with an old man. The other men of the family sat on a car, all of them in dirty suits, hats and mustaches, even the youngest of them sporting a silky shadow on his lip. The sun set behind the Hippodrome.

There were Gypsy encampments in all the fields around the race-track, a spontaneous generation like flies. His Gypsy, though, was gone, disappeared as Arkady had expected. Somehow he'd known it wasn't Swan who had betrayed him.

The apartment was so quiet when he entered that he thought she was gone, but when he went into the bed-room she was sitting cross-legged on the bed. She wore her dress, which was short and tight because of his inexpert washing.

'You're looking better.'

'Of course I am,' she said.

'Hungry?'

'If you're going to eat, I'll have something.'

She was starving. She devoured a supper of cabbage soup and had a chocolate bar for dessert.

'Why did you meet Osborne last night?'

'I didn't.' She took the cigarettes from his hands without asking.

'Why do you think Osborne had those men attack you?'

'I don't know what you're talking about.'

'In the metro station. I was there.'

'Then interrogate yourself.'

'You think this is an interrogation?'

'And there are men in the apartment below recording this interrogation,' she said calmly, blowing smoke and looking through it. 'This is a house of KGB informants, and there are torture cells in the basement.'

'If you really believe that, you should have left.'

'Can I leave the country?'

'I doubt it.'

'Then what difference does it make whether I'm in this particular apartment or someplace else?'

She rested her chin on her hand and studied Arkady with her dark eyes, one blind. 'Do you really think it matters where I am or what I say . . .'

The apartment was dark; he'd forgotten to get light bulbs. When Irina rested against a wall she seemed to lean on a shadow.

She smoked as much as he did. Her hair had dried in ringlets around her face and heavy curls down her back. She was still barefoot, and her shrunken dress stretched around her breasts and hips.

As she paced, smoking, thinking up lies, his eyes turned with her. In the faint upcast light of the courtyard lamps, he saw her in parts – a cheek's curve, her lips sharp as a carving. She had generous features, long fingers, long neck, long legs. There was a flash, like light caught in water, when her gaze crossed his.

He knew she was aware of her effect on him, just as he knew his slightest advance would be surrender to her. Then she wouldn't even bother to lie.

'You know Osborne killed your friend Valerya, Kostia Borodin and the American boy Kirwill, and yet you offer him the chance to do the same to you. You practically force him to.'

'Those names are unfamiliar to me.'

'You were suspicious on your own; that's why you went to Osborne's hotel as soon as you heard he was back in Moscow. You were suspicious as soon as I came to Mosfilm.'

'Mr Osborne has an interest in Soviet film.'

'He told you they were safely out of the country. I don't know how he told you he got them out, but he did get James Kirwill *in*. Did it ever occur to you that getting out of the Soviet Union, especially for three people, is more difficult?'

'Oh, it often occurs to me.'

'And that killing them is simpler? Where did he tell you they were? Jerusalem? New York? Hollywood?'

'Does it matter? You say they're dead. In any case, you can't get them now . . .'

In the dark, lit by her cigarette, she glowed with moral superiority.

'Solzhenitsyn and Amalrik exiled. Palach driven to suicide. Fainberg's teeth kicked out in Red Square. Grigorenko and Gershuni thrown into lunatic asylums to make them mad. The ones you throw into jail separately: Sharansky, Orlov, Moroz, Bayev. The ones you throw in by the handful, like the Baltic Fleet officers. The ones you throw in by the thousands, like Crimean Tartars . . .'

She went on and on. This was her chance, Arkady knew. Here was an investigator, and she spat words as if they were bullets aimed at an army of investigators.

'You're afraid of us,' she said. 'You know you can't stop us forever. The movement keeps spreading.'

'There is no movement. Right or wrong, it doesn't matter. It simply doesn't exist.'

'You're too scared to talk about it.'

'It's like arguing about a color neither of us has ever seen.'

He was being too polite, he decided. She was building such a cold distance that she would soon be out of reach completely.

'So you were writing to Valerya before you flunked out of the university,' he began again.

'I didn't fail any courses,' she said. 'As you know, I was expelled from the university.'

'Failed, expelled, what does it matter? You got thrown out for saying you hated your own country? The country that gave you your education? That's so stupid it's the same as flunking.'

'Think what you want.'

'Then you pander to a foreigner who killed your best friend. Ah, but that's politics to you. You'd rather believe the most incredible lie from an American with bloody hands than the truth from one of your own.'

'You're not one of my own.'

'You're phony. At least Kostia Borodin was a real Russian, bandit or no bandit. Did he know what a fraud you are?'

She inhaled too strongly and the ember lit the sudden heat in her face.

'If Kostia wanted to get out of the country he had a real reason, he was on the run from the law,' Arkady went on. 'That's a reason anyone can respect. Otherwise he would have stayed. Tell me, what did Kostia think of your anti-Soviet swoons? How many times did he tell Valerya what a phony her friend Irina Asanova was? He'd say it now if he was alive.'

'You're disgusting,' she said.

'Come on, what did Kostia the Bandit say when you told him you were a political dissident?'

'That frightens you, the idea of having a dissident under your own roof.'

'Have you ever frightened anyone? Be honest! Who

cares about some so-called intellectuals who get thrown out of school for pissing on the flag? Serves them right!'

'You never heard of Solzhenitsyn?'

'I've heard about his Swiss bank account,' Arkady taunted her. She wanted to deal with a monster? She'd get a bigger one than she'd bargained for.

'Or Soviet Jews?'

'Zionists, you mean. They have their own Soviet republic; what more do they want?'

'Or Czechoslovakia?'

'You mean when Dubček brought Fascist German soldiers in as tourists and the Czechs asked us for help? Grow up. You've never heard of Vietnam or Chile or South Africa? Irina, maybe your world view is not quite large enough. You seem to think that the Soviet Union is one enormous conspiracy to keep you an unhappy adolescent.'

'You don't believe what you're saying.'

'And now I'll tell you what Kostia Borodin thought.' Arkady wouldn't stop. 'He thought you wanted the pleasure of being persecuted without having the guts to break the law.'

'That's better than being a sadist and not having the nerve to use your fists,' she said.

Her eyes were wet with anger. He was amazed. He could smell the salt in them. She was in the battle, whether she wanted to be or not. There was a little blood on the floor now, so to speak. As battles do, this one shifted to a new field, to the bedroom and the apartment's single piece of furniture.

They sat on opposite sides of the bed and crushed out their cigarettes in plates. She was ready for the next assault, her head bravely up and her arms folded tight as a locked gate.

'You want the KGB.' He sighed. 'You want torturers, murderers, apes.'

'You were going to hand me over to them, weren't you?'

'I was going to,' he admitted. 'At least, I thought I was.'

She watched his silhouette walk back and forth across the windows.

'Did I tell you just how Osborne did it?' he asked her. 'They were having a skating party, he and Valerya, Kostia and the American student Kirwill. But you know that part – you gave Valerya your skates – and you know that Osborne's business is buying Russian furs, though maybe you weren't aware that he is an informant for the KGB on the side. That bores you. Anyway, after a little skating in Gorky Park they step off into a clearing for refreshments. Osborne, a rich man, has brought everything.'

'You're making this up as you go along.'

'We have the bag he brought the food in; we pulled it out of the river. So while everyone is eating, Osborne lifts his bag toward Kostia. He has a gun in the bag. He shoots Kostia first, through the heart, then Kirwill, also through the heart. One, two, just like that. Efficient, yes?'

'You sound as if you were there.'

'The one thing I have not been able to figure out, and where you can help me, is why Valerya didn't call for help after she saw the other two killed. Granted there was a lot of music coming from the loudspeakers in the park, but she didn't even try to call. She stood still, facing Osborne, close enough to touch him while he put the gun to her heart. Why did Valerya do that, Irina? You were her best friend, you tell me.'

'You keep forgetting,' she told him, 'that I know the law. It's an article of the criminal code that all defectors are state criminals. You'd say or do anything to get them and anyone who helped them. How do I know that the attack in the Metro station wasn't staged? That you didn't plan it yourself? Or you *and* the KGB? Like the bodies you say you have – where did they come from? You say Osborne shot someone? You'd pick any innocent tourist and throw him in the Lubyanka.'

'Osborne's not in a cell at the Lubyanka; he has friends at the Lubyanka. They're protecting him. They'll kill *you* to protect him.'

'Protect an American?'

'He's been going in and out of Russia for thirty-five years. He brings millions of dollars in, he informs on Soviet actors and dancers, he feeds his friends silly little people like you and Valerya.'

She put her hands over her ears. 'Your friends, your

friends,' she said. 'It's you we're talking about. You just want to know where to send your assassins.'

'To send after Valerya? I can find her anytime I want in a refrigerator in a basement off Petrovka. I have the gun Osborne killed her with. I know who was waiting for Osborne afterward, and in what kind of car. I have photos of Osborne with Valerya and Kostia in Irkutsk. I know about the church chest they made for him.'

'An American like Osborne could buy twenty different chests from twenty different sources.' Irina didn't retreat a step. 'You yourself mentioned Golodkin. Golodkin would have given him one, and Golodkin didn't need to leave the country. Money would have been enough, and, as you say, Osborne has millions of dollars. So why would he bring Valerya and Kostia Borodin from Irkutsk? Why *them*?'

He could make out her eyes deep-set in the oval of her face, and her hand resting on the swell of her hip. He felt her exhaustion in the dark.

'During the war Osborne killed three German prisoners the same way. He took them into the woods in Leningrad, fed them chocolates and champagne, and shot them. He got a medal for it. I'm not lying; you can read about it in books.'

Irina made no response.

'If you get out of this thing, what do you want to do?' he asked. 'Become a major dissident and denounce investigators? You do it well. Reapply to the university? I'd give you a recommendation.'

'Be a lawyer, you mean?'

'Yes.'

'Do you think I'd be happy as that?'

'No.' Arkady thought of Misha.

'That director,' she murmured, 'the one who offered me the Italian boots? He asked me to marry him. You undressed me; I'm not too unattractive, no?'

'No.'

'Maybe that's what I'll do then. Marry someone, live at home and disappear.'

After hours of argument her voice was so soft it might have been coming from another room.

'What it comes down to,' Arkady said, 'is that everything I've told you is an extraordinarily elaborate lie or the very simple truth.'

He sensed her rhythmic breathing, realized she was asleep and covered her with the blanket. He moved to the window for a while, watching for any unusual late-night activity in the apartments across the courtyard or on Taganskaya Boulevard. Finally he returned to the bed and lay down on the other side.

Chapter Fourteen

Red lines were painted on the streets leading to Red Square. Army officers measured the gutters. Television towers rose.

Ten years of marriage to Zoya had amassed at 2 percent interest per year a savings account of 1,200 rubles, from which she had already withdrawn all but 100 rubles. A man can stay ahead of killers, but not his wife – former wife, Arkady corrected himself.

On the way from the bank he saw a sidewalk queue, and splurged twenty rubles on a red-white-and-green scarf decorated with Easter eggs.

Andreev was done.

Valerya Davidova, murdered in Gorky Park, was alive again. Her eyes sparkled, blood coursed through her cheeks, her lips were red and parted with anxiety, she was about to speak. She remained mute, but it took an act of rationalism to believe that plasteline was not soft flesh, that the blush of paint was not complexion, that glass couldn't see. What seemed incredible was that this apparently living head had no body; its neck balanced on a potter's wheel. Arkady didn't consider himself superstitious, but he felt his skin crawl.

'I changed the color of her eyes to a darker brown,' Andreev said, 'which brought out the color of her cheeks. It's an Italian wig, real hair.'

Arkady walked around the head. 'She's your masterpiece.'

'Yes,' Andreev proudly acknowledged.

'I could swear she was going to say something.'

'She is saying something, Investigator. She's saying, "Here I am!" Take her.'

Valerya looked up from the wheel. Not as stunning a beauty as Irina, but very pretty, with a shorter nose, a broader, simpler face. The kind of face you'd expect to see smiling from under a fox hat on a winter outing as snowflakes drifted by. A good skater, a lot of fun, full of life.

'Not yet,' he said.

He spent the day with Swan talking to butchers, farmers and any other possible source of fresh meat. It was after four when he got to Novokuznetskaya and was called to the prosecutor's office.

Iamskoy was waiting behind his desk, baby-pink fingers laced on the desk top, his shaved head glistening with thought.

'I am concerned about the apparent lack of organized progress in your investigation of the Gorky Park matter. It is not my intention to meddle with an investigator, but it is my duty to oversee one who is losing control either of himself or of his investigation. Do you think that is happening in your case? Be sincere, please.'

'I have just returned from seeing a reconstruction by Andreev of one of the victims,' Arkady answered.

'You see, this is the first I've heard about such a reconstruction. That is an example of a lack of organization.'

'I am not losing control.'

'Your refusal to say so could be a symptom. Now, there are more than seven million people in this city, among them a lunatic who has killed three victims. I don't expect you to pull the killer out of a hat. I *do* expect an investigator to conduct a right-thinking, coordinated effort. You dislike coordination, I know. You see yourself as a specialist, an individualist. An individual, however, even the most brilliant, is vulnerable to subjectivity, illness or personal problems. And you've been working very hard.'

Iamskoy pulled his hands apart and brought them back together. 'I understand you've been having some difficulty with your wife,' he said.

Arkady didn't reply; it hadn't been a question.

'My investigators are a reflection of me, all of you in your different ways. You, being the brightest, must know that,' Iamskoy said.

He changed his tone to one of decision. 'You've been working under a strain. The holiday is coming up; nothing can be accomplished now. What I want you to do, as soon as you leave this office, is to prepare a detailed summary of all aspects of the investigation so far.'

'Such a summary would take days, even if I did nothing else.'

'Then do nothing else. Take your time and be complete. Naturally, I do not want to see any references to foreign nationals or officers of State Security. Your speculations in those areas have led you nowhere. References to them would be an embarrassment not only to you but to this office. Thank you.'

Arkady ignored the dismissal. 'Prosecutor, I would like to know, is this summary to be for another investigator who will take my place?'

'What we want from you,' Iamskoy said firmly, 'is cooperation. Where there is heartfelt cooperation does it really matter who does what?'

Arkady sat in front of a typewriter with no paper in it.

On the wall, in a picture, Lenin relaxed in a garden chair, wearing a white hat and holding a cup on his lap. His eyes looked slyly up from under the brim of his hat.

The summary. There would hardly be any summary after deleting Osborne and the identification of the Kirwill boy. To a succeeding investigator it would seem that there had been no investigation at all. He could start fresh with new detectives. The only problem would be the former investigator.

Nikitin, with a bottle and two glasses, opened the door. The chief investigator for Governmental Directives wore an appropriate grimace of commiseration.

'I just heard. Bad luck. You should have come to me.' Vodka spilled into the glasses. 'You keep things in, though. I always told you that. Don't worry, we'll find something. I know some people; we'll get you something. Drink up. Not at the same level, of course, but you'll work your way up again. I'll think of something for you. I never felt you were a natural investigator.'

It was clear to Arkady that he'd missed all the important clues: those messages that would have told a more astute investigator which avenues to follow, which to turn away from. Levin, Iamskoy, even Irina had tried to warn him. It was as if by staring into the sun, one sees the benefits of following the correct channels, those avenues so brightly lit that all seeming contradictions meet and are explained.

'. . . can't remember a chief investigator being dismissed before,' Nikitin was saying. 'The whole glory of this system is that no one can lose his job. Trust you to fuck that up.'

When Nikitin winked, Arkady closed his eyes, and the chief investigator leaned forward. 'How do you think Zoya's going to take this?' he asked.

Arkady opened his eyes to see Nikitin balanced expectantly on the edge of a chair. He didn't know why Nikitin was present and hadn't really been listening to what he was saying, but it did strike him that his former mentor, this opportunist with his round face and mobile, guppy expression, would always be present. Some men die, some were dismissed. Nikitin attended them all like a grave robber.

The phone rang and Arkady answered. It was a return call from the Foreign Ministry saying that while no individuals had exported ikons or items of a religious or superstitious nature during the previous January or February, a special license had been granted for a 'religious chest' sent as a gift to the Helsinki Party Arts Council from the Leatherball Clubs of the German Young Communist League. The chest was sent by air from Moscow to Leningrad, where it was transferred to the train going from Leningrad to Finland via Vyborg. The entire trip from Moscow to Finland had transpired on February 3, and the name on the invoice was 'H. Unmann.' There was a chest, and Unmann had sent it.

Arkady placed a call to the headquarters of the Finnish Communist Party in Helsinki – no problem because international phone calls were far more reliable than local ones. From Helsinki he heard that the Arts Council had been disbanded more than a year before, and that nothing resembling a 'religious chest' had ever been expected or arrived.

'Anything I can do?' Nikitin offered.

Arkady pulled open the bottom drawer of his desk and took out the Makarov semiautomatic he'd been issued when he became an investigator and had never used, and a box of 9-mm. rounds. He slid the magazine from the grip, scooped eight rounds from the box, loaded the gun and slapped the magazine home.

'What are you doing?' Nikitin watched.

Arkady lifted the gun, pushed off the safety and filled the square-notched sight with Nikitin's face, which opened its mouth and gaped. 'I'm afraid,' Arkady said. 'I thought you'd like to be afraid with me.'

Nikitin vanished through the door. Arkady put on his

overcoat, slipped the gun into his coat pocket and walked out.

When he entered the apartment, Irina looked behind him as if he'd brought other men. 'I thought you'd arrest me now,' she said.

'Why do you think I want to arrest you?' He went to the window so he could look back at the street.

'You will sooner or later.'

'I stopped them from killing you.'

'That was easy. You still think killing and arrest are two different things. You're still a chief investigator.'

Her dress was molded to her body from wear. She walked softly in bare feet. He himself wondered whether Pribluda had taken the apartment below, and whether he and Irina stood on a tracery of microphones.

She'd swept the floor, obsessively; cleaned and empty, the apartment had a colorless and airless quality. In it she was like a fire in a vacuum.

'You may hide me today. It's only a day from your life,' she said. 'When the knock comes on the door, you'll hand me over.'

Arkady didn't ask her why she didn't leave because he was afraid she might.

Her accent was rounded, bursting with contempt.

'Investigator, Investigator, how can you investigate our deaths when you know nothing about our lives? Oh, you read magazine articles about Siberia, and the militia in Irkutsk told you about Kostia Borodin. How, you ask me, could a Jewish girl like Valerya become involved with a criminal like Kostia? How could such a clever guy like Kostia ever fall for Osborne's promises? You think I wouldn't fall for them too if they were offered to me?'

As she talked she rubbed her hands on her arms and paced the floor. 'My grandfather was the first Siberian in my family. To begin with, he was chief engineer of waterworks in Leningrad. He committed no crime, but you remember the order of the day was "All engineers are wreckers," and so he was put on a train east to serve fifteen years' hard labor in five different Siberian camps before he was freed in perpetual exile – which is to say he had to stay in Siberia. His son, my father, a teacher, was not even allowed to volunteer against the Germans because he was the son of an exile. They took away his internal passport so that he could never leave Siberia. My mother was a musician and was offered a position with the Kirov Theater, but she couldn't-accept because she was the wife of a son of an exile.'

'What about Valerya?'

'The Davidovs were from Minsk. Their block committees had a quota of "Jew sophisticates" to arrest. So off the rabbi and his family went to be Siberians.'

'And Kostia?'

'He was more Siberian than any of us. His great-grandfather was exiled by a czar for murder. From then on, the Borodins worked for the camps, capturing escapees. They lived with the Yukagir, the reindeer herders, because the herders knew first when a prisoner was trying to cross the tundra. When the Borodins caught a man they'd be friendly, as if they were going to help him escape. They'd let him talk a whole night about what he planned to do when he was free, and then they'd kill him when he was asleep, so that at least he'd tasted the illusion of freedom for an hour or so. You don't even do that.'

'It sounds cruel to me,' Arkady said.

'You're not Siberian. Osborne knows us better than you do.'

Even from the depth of her scorn, though, she watched him carefully, as if he might assume a different shape.

'The Borodins couldn't live off just catching prisoners,' Arkady said.

'They traded with the herders, worked their own illegal gold claims, guided geologists. Kostia trapped.'

'Trapped what?'

'Sables, fox.'

'He was a bandit, so how could he bring in sables to sell?'

'He came into Irkutsk and gave his pelts to someone else to sell. Each pelt was worth a hundred rubles, so he'd take ninety. No one was going to ask questions.'

'There are farms for breeding sables now; why do they still need trappers?'

'The farms are typical collectives – total disasters. Sables have to have fresh meat. The cost of distributing meat to farms in Siberia is high, and when the distribution breaks down, which it always does, the farms have to buy in the food stores. So it costs the state twice as much to breed a sable as it does to buy a wild one. But the quota is always increased because sables bring in foreign currency.'

'There must be a lot of trappers, then.'

'Do you know where you have to hit a sable with a rifle bullet at fifty meters? In the eye, or the pelt is ruined. Very few hunters could do that, and none like Kostia.'

They ate fried sausages, bread and coffee.

Arkady felt as if he were hunting, having to be very still and at the same time set out questions like bait to bring a wild animal within range.

'Where else can we run to but Moscow?' Irina asked him. 'The North Pole? China? Leaving Siberia is the only real crime a Siberian can commit. That's all your investigation is about. How did these wild Siberians get here? How did they get out of the country? Don't tell me you're going to all this trouble just because a couple of Siberians are dead. We're *born* dead.'

'Where did you hear this trash?'

'You know what the "Siberian dilemma" is?'

'No.'

'It's a choice between two ways of freezing. We were out on a lake fishing through the ice when a teacher of ours fell through. He didn't go far, just down to his neck, but we knew what was happening. If he stayed in the water he would freeze to death in thirty or forty seconds. If he got out he would freeze to death at once – he would be ice, actually. He taught gymnastics, I remember. He was an Evenki, the only native on the teaching staff, young, everyone liked him. We all stood about in a circle around the hole holding our poles and fish. It was about minus forty degrees, bright and sunny. He had a wife, a dentist; she wasn't along. He looked up at us; I'll never forget that look. He couldn't have been in the water for more than five seconds when he pulled himself out.'

'And?'

'He was dead before he stood up. But he got out, that was the important thing. He didn't just wait to die.'

The sun broke in her eyes. Night made her paler, her eyes darker.

'I'll tell you about a "Siberian dilemma",' Arkady said. 'Osborne could have bought religious chairs, chests and ikons from twenty different sources in Moscow. As you said, Golodkin already had one for him. So why would he take the risk of dealing with two desperate people running from the law? Why bother creating that fantastic lie of escape for them? What could Kostia and Valerya offer that no one else could?'

'Why ask me?' She shrugged. 'You say there was an American student named Kirwill illegally brought into Russia. Why would Osborne take *that* risk? It's crazy.'

'It was necessary. Kostia wanted walking proof that Osborne could bring persons in and out. That's what James Kirwill was. Kirwill was also perfect because he was American. Kostia and Valerya didn't think Osborne would betray another American.'

'Why would Kirwill come unless he thought he could get out?'

'Americans think they can do anything,' Arkady said. 'Osborne thinks he can do anything. Was he screwing Valerya?'

'She wasn't that—'

'She was pretty. Osborne says Russian women are ugly, but he was bound to notice Valerya. Even at the Fur Center in Irkutsk he noticed her. What did Kostia think of that? That he and Valerya were going to make a sucker out of this rich American?'

'You make it sound—'

'Is that what they had to offer Osborne? Sex? Did Kostia push her, say "Go ahead, a little screw doesn't hurt me or you, let's play the tourist for all he's worth"? Was that it? Three people killed because Osborne figured out what a sucker he was?'

'You don't know anything.'

'I know that when Kostia and James Kirwill were dying in the snow, your friend Valerya was alive and standing close enough to Osborne to touch him, and she didn't run away or shout for help. That's a real "Siberian dilemma", and it suggests only one thing: that she knew Kostia and Kirwill were going to be killed, that she was in on it with Osborne. So much for her Siberian bandit. How could he compare with a businessman from New York? So much for romance! Maybe Osborne told her he could get only one person out. She had to make a choice, and she was a sharp girl. Call for help when she was plotting with Osborne to kill them? She planned to walk over their dead bodies arm in arm with her American!'

'Stop!'

'Imagine her surprise when he shot her. Too late then to call for others to help. In hindsight it seems incredible. How obvious it is that the American was a cold-blooded killer, and how paper-thin his promises must have been. How cruel to bring this pretty, empty-headed girl all the way from Siberia so that he could kill her here. Yet you have to admit that if she wouldn't run for help when her own boyfriend and an innocent foreigner were shot to death in front of her, then she really was stupid. She really deserved to be killed just the way she was.'

Irina slapped him. He tasted blood in his mouth.

'Now you know she's dead,' he said. 'You hit me because you believe me. Yes!'

There was a knock at the door. 'Chief Investigator Renko,' a man said from the hall.

Irina shook her head. Arkady didn't recognize the voice either.

'Investigator, we know you're there, and we know about the girl,' the voice said.

Arkady motioned Irina into the bedroom, moved to the overcoat folded on the drainboard and took out his gun. He saw her eyes were fixed on it. He didn't enjoy handling the Makarov; he didn't want to shoot anyone and he didn't want to be shot in his own apartment, especially when there wasn't even a chair to sit down on. He acted calmly while in his brain his thoughts tripped over themselves. Should he shoot through the door – was that what spies did? Should he rush into the hall, gun blazing? Instead, he crept to the wall beside the door and, with his free hand, gently unlocked the door and took hold of the knob. 'Come in,' he said.

As soon as he felt a hand on the opposite knob Arkady swung the door open. A figure staggered in alone and off-balance. He caught the man with an arm around the neck and the gun at the side of the head, knocking off a woolen cap.

Arkady kicked the door shut and turned the visitor around. He was about twenty-two, big and freckled and grinning drunkenly as if he'd pulled off a colossal trick. It was Yuri Viskov, the Viskov of the Viskov appeal that Prosecutor Iamskoy had argued before the Supreme Court, the son of the Viskovs in the cafeteria.

'I'm leaving for Siberia tomorrow' – he pulled a bottle of vodka out of his windbreaker – 'and I wanted you to have a drink with me.'

Arkady managed to put his gun away while Viskov hugged him. Irina came uneasily out of the bedroom. Viskov was enormously pleased with himself. With deliberate steadiness, he carried his bottle to the glasses in the sink.

'I haven't seen you since you were let out,' Arkady said.

'I should have come around and thanked you.' Viskov brought back the glasses overfilled. 'You know how things are – you've got so many things to do when you're out of jail.'

He had brought only two glasses. While there were two more in the kitchen, Arkady sensed that the exclusion of Irina was intentional and saw how she hung back by the bedroom doorway.

'You know each other?' he asked Viskov as they raised their glasses in a toast.

'Not well,' Viskov said. 'She called someone today to ask about you, and that someone had me talk to her over the phone. Very simple. The first thing I told her was how you saved my neck. I gave you highest marks – I called you a hero of Soviet Justice, nothing less. What's more, it's true.'

'I didn't ask you to come here,' Irina said.

'I didn't come to see you. I'm a railroad worker, not a dissident.' Viskov turned his back on her, his joking mood gone, erased by a fumbling sincerity as he put his hand on Arkady's elbow. 'Get rid of her. People like her are poison. Who is she to ask about you? You were the only person to ever help me. I'll tell you, if there weren't any dissidents like her, a lot of good people would never suffer like my parents did. Just a few persons make trouble, and a lot of honest folks get arrested. It doesn't happen only to people like me, either. Everyone's out to get someone like you.' As he looked again at Irina, Arkady saw perfectly the frame of Viskov's vision: Irina, the doorway and the bed. 'The best poison is the sweetest – right, Investigator? We're all human, but when you're done, get rid of her.'

They each still had a forgotten upraised glass. Arkady touched his to the other. 'To Siberia,' he offered. Viskov continued to glare at Irina. 'Drink up,' Arkady said more strongly, and pulled free of his visitor's grip. Viskov shrugged, and they downed the vodka in a swallow.

The alcohol burned the cut in Arkady's mouth. 'Why in the world are you going there?' he asked.

'They need line engineers on the new Baikal track.' Viskov moved reluctantly at first to a new subject. 'The pay has double bonuses, triple vacation time, an apartment, refrigerator stocked with food – everything. There'll be Party creeps out there, but not as many as here. I'll start a new life, build a cabin in the woods, hunt and fish. Can you see it, a former convicted murderer with his own shotgun? That's where the future is, out there. You'll see, when I have kids they're going to grow up different. Maybe in a hundred years we'll tell Moscow to fuck off and have our own country. What do you think of that?'

'Good luck.'

There was nothing left to say. After another minute Arkady was looking down into the courtyard as Viskov trudged, shoulder against the wind, out toward the lights of Taganskaya. The night was low enough to press rain clouds against the roofs. The window glass hummed.

'I told you not to use the phone.' He watched Viskov disappear around the gate. 'You shouldn't have called him.'

Though he stilled the pane with his hand he could feel the vibration on his skin. Irina was a white reflection in the window. If it had been anyone besides Viskov, she could be dead. Arkady realized it was his arm that was shaking, not the window.

He stared at himself in the pane. Who was this man? He saw that he didn't give a damn for Viskov, whose life he'd saved only months before. He wanted only one thing: Irina Asanova. The obsession was so plain that even Viskov, drunk, saw it. Arkady had never wanted anything before; there'd never been anything worth wanting. Lust was too pale a word. It was unfair. Life was so drab and listless, such a routine of shadows. She burned so bright against this dark that she lit even him.

'He saw it,' Arkady said. 'He was right.'

'What do you mean?'

'About me. I'm not interested in your friend Valerya. I don't care whether Osborne is up to his waist in blood. There's no investigation. All I'm doing is keeping you with me.' Every word was a surprise to him; he didn't even sound like himself. 'I wouldn't doubt that everything I've done since the first time I met you was to get you here. I'm not the investigator you thought I was, and I'm not the investigator I thought I was. I can't protect you. If they didn't know you were here before, they must have been listening to my phone and so they know now. Where do you want to go?'

He turned to Irina. It took him a moment to see the dull glint of the gun in her hands. Without explanation, she put it back on the drainboard. 'What if I don't want to go?' she asked.

She came to the middle of the room and pulled off her dress. She was naked underneath. 'I want to stay,' she said.

Her body had a porcelain glow. Her arms hung by her sides, with no attempt to cover herself. She opened her lips slightly as Arkady came toward her, and her

333

eyes opened, not the lids but the very centers of the eyes themselves, when he touched her.

He entered her standing up, lifting her and setting her down on him before they kissed. At his first touch she was wet, an unfolded secret, and when they finally kissed, her fingers pulled on his head and his back. He felt drunk on her taste through the vodka and blood in his mouth. They swayed and lowered themselves to the floor, where she locked her legs around him.

'Then you love me, too,' she said.

Afterward, in bed, he watched her breast tremble with her heartbeat.

'It's a physical thing.' She spread her hand on his chest. 'I felt it the very first time I saw you at the studio. I still hate you.'

The rain beat on the windows. He ran his hand over her white flank.

'I still hate what you do; I don't take anything back,' she said. 'When you're in me, though, nothing else matters. In a way, I think you've been in me for a long time.'

There might be listeners above and below; the fear only made sensation more sensitive. The tips of her breasts remained hard.

'You're wrong about Valerya,' she said. 'Valerya had no place to run. Osborne knew that.' She smoothed his hair. 'Do you believe me?'

'The part about Valerya, not all the rest.'

'What don't you believe?'

'You know what Valerya and Kostia were doing for Osborne.'

'Yes.'

'We're still enemies,' she said.

A look of hers went through him, leaving him like the surface of water broken by a rock.

'I got you this.' He let the scarf fall on her.

'Why?'

'To replace the one you lost at the metro.'

'I need a new dress and coat and boots, not a scarf.' She laughed.

'I could only afford a scarf.'

She looked at it, trying to see its colors in the dark. 'It will have to be a wonderful scarf,' she said.

'It doesn't matter how ridiculous a lie is if the lie is your only chance of escape,' she said. 'It doesn't matter how obvious the truth is if the truth is that you'll never escape.'

Chapter Fifteen

Misha sounded panicky on the phone. Arkady dragged on his clothes. Irina was still asleep, her arm across the bed where he had lain.

'I have to meet a friend. We'll stop someplace else on the way,' Arkady said as William Kirwill got in the car.

'I have four days left here, and I wasted yesterday waiting for you to show up,' Kirwill said. 'Today you tell me who killed Jimmy or I'll kill you.'

As Arkady pulled away from the Metropole Hotel and around Sverdlov Square he was laughing. 'In Russia you have to stand in line.'

At Serafimov 2 they walked up to the second floor. The door they found had none of the locks and pasted notices that Arkady had expected. When he knocked it was opened by an old woman holding a baby with a hairless skull delicate with veins. The woman squinted at Arkady's identification.

'I thought this apartment would be sealed,' he said. 'Two people died here a week ago, the occupant and a militia detective.'

'I'm just a grandmother. I don't know anything about

that.' She looked from Arkady to Kirwill. 'Anyway, why should a good apartment be empty? People need apartments.'

There was nothing left of Boris Golodkin to be seen from the door. The black marketeer's rugs, record players and stacks of foreign clothes were gone, and in their place were a sofa still made up as a bed, a splitting carton of dishes, an ancient samovar. Pasha and Golodkin might have died in another apartment altogether.

'Did you find a chest here?' Arkady asked. 'Maybe it was in a storage area in the basement? Like a church chest?'

'Why would we want a church chest? What would we do with one?' She stepped out of the way. 'Look for yourselves. Honest people live here, we have nothing to hide.'

Frightened, the baby burrowed like a pupa into the old woman's arms. Its eyes threatened to explode. Arkady smiled, and the baby was so startled that it smiled back with gums and drool.

'You're absolutely right,' Arkady said. 'Why should a good apartment go to waste?'

Arkady met Misha at a small church off the end of Serafimov. It was Saint Something-or-Other, one of the great majority of churches long ago renamed 'museums', desanctified and euthenized by cultural restoration. A barrier of scaffolding rotted around crumbling walls. Arkady pushed the door open and stepped into the dark, catching a glimpse of puddles and bird droppings on the stone floor before the door closed. A match flared and lit a candle, illuminating Misha. Arkady could make out the four central pillars of the church, the broken bars of an ikonostasis and faint light from the ceiling dome. Rainwater dripped and ran down the pillars. The interior was once covered in ikons of Christs, angels and archangels, but the plaster had cracked and the paint had faded and all that was left were forms hovering in the candle's light. Pigeons rustled in the shuttered windows of the dome.

'You're early,' Misha said.

'Is there something wrong with Natasha? Why couldn't we talk at your apartment?'

'You're half an hour early.'

'Then we both are. Let's talk.'

Misha was strange, his mop of hair uncombed, his clothes looked slept in. Arkady was glad he'd persuaded Kirwill to stay outside in the car. 'It's Natasha?' he asked.

'It's Zoya. Her lawyer's a friend of mine and I've heard the statements she's giving to the court. You know your divorce hearing is set for tomorrow, don't you?'

'No.' Arkady was not surprised; he felt nothing about the news.

'Everyone talks about the Party the way you do, but not to have it repeated in court. You, a chief investigator. And what about me?' Misha asked. 'You were saying those things about me, a lawyer! That's in her statements, too. I'll lose my Party card. I'll be finished in court, I won't be able to go back.'

'I'm sorry.'

'Well, you never were a good Party member. I tried

every way I could to help your career, and you threw it in my face. It's your turn to help me. Zoya's lawyer is meeting us here. You're going to deny ever making anti-Party statements in my presence. In Zoya's presence, maybe, but not in mine. It's her or me. You have to help someone.'

'You or Zoya?'

'Please, for old friends' sake.'

'I would have said "best friends". Anyway, all sorts of things are said in divorce hearings and no one takes them seriously. It's too late.'

'Will you do it for me?'

'All right, give me his name and I'll call him.'

'No, he's on his way, he's meeting us here.'

'He doesn't have an office or a telephone?'

'We can't reach him now, and he's on his way.'

'We're going to talk here, in a church?'

'A museum. Well, he wanted privacy, talking to his client's husband and all. He's doing it as a favor to me.'

'I'm not going to wait half an hour.' Arkady thought of Kirwill in the car.

'He'll be early, I swear. I wouldn't ask you if I didn't have to.' Misha clutched Arkady's sleeve. 'You'll stay?'

'All right, I'll wait awhile.'

'He won't be long.'

Arkady leaned against a pillar until he found his neck getting wet from the water dripping down. He lit a cigarette from Misha's candle and walked around the pillars. The longer he was in the church, the more he could see. Perhaps old paintings were best seen in bad light, he thought. Many of the figures on the wall were winged, though he couldn't tell angels from archangels. Their wings were slim and airy. The angels themselves were birdlike; they glistened, their eyes and swords. The altar was gone. Tombs were ripped out, leaving holes like graves. Both eyes and ears became accustomed. He heard the frightened passage of a mouse. He thought he could hear not only a drop of water hit the floor but the moment when it was released from the dome. In the candle's light he could see Misha sweating, though the church was cold. He saw Misha watching the faint blue outline of the shut door.

'Remember,' Arkady said abruptly and watched Misha start, 'when we were kids – we couldn't have been more than ten – we went into a church?'

'No, I don't remember.'

'We went because you were going to prove to me that there was no God. It was a working church, it was in the middle of a service. All these old people were standing around, and priests with big beards. You went right up behind them and shouted, "There is no God." Everyone was angry, and I think a little scared. I know I was. Then you shouted, "If there is a God, let him strike me dead and let him strike Arkasha dead, too." I was very scared. But we weren't struck down dead, and I thought you were the bravest person in the world. We marched out of there, didn't we?'

'I still don't remember.' Misha shook his head, but Arkady knew he did.

'It may have been this same church.'

'No, it wasn't.'

On one wall Arkady could barely discern a seated

figure with a raised hand. Angels seemed to bubble up from it. Below it were two naked figures, perhaps a man and a woman, on what looked like a two-headed dog. Or a pig. Or a stain. Martyrs trooped over here, a man led a donkey over there, there was a secret bustling about everywhere.

'There's no lawyer coming,' Arkady said.

'He's on his—'

'There's no lawyer.'

He lit another cigarette from the first one. Misha blew out his candle, but Arkady could still see him. They both watched the door.

'I never thought it would be you,' Arkady said. 'Anyone but you.'

A minute went by. Misha said nothing.

'Misha,' Arkady sighed, 'Misha.'

He felt the drops hit, the circles spread and overlap. It must be raining harder outside, he thought. The faintest rays of light crossed the dome, fading before they reached a wall. Misha looked pleadingly at Arkady. His black curls were bedraggled and ridiculous. Tears ran from his eyes and formed a lyre on his face. 'Run,' he whispered.

'Who's coming?' Arkady asked.

'Hurry, they're taking the head.'

'How did they find out about the head?'

Arkady thought he heard a step. He killed his cigarette, backed to a wall and drew his gun. Misha stayed where he was, smiling weakly. A pigeon was bathing in a broken font. It shook the water off and rose, clapping its way between the pillars to the dome.

'You'll be all right?' Arkady asked. 'I'll call you later.' Misha nodded.

Arkady moved along the wall and pulled the door open. Another spring shower was in progress, pouring over the scaffolding, chasing people under their newspapers and umbrellas. Kirwill waited impatiently in the car.

'Arkasha, I've often thought about that church,' Misha said.

Arkady ran.

The embankment road was flooded, and he had to detour around Gorky Park. As he reached the Ethnological Institute, a black Volga was turning on its lights for the rain and pulling out. He recognized the driver. Thank you, Misha, Arkady said to himself. He went by the institute, made a complete circle at Andreyesk Prospekt and returned back along the park, a block behind the Volga.

'Now what are we doing?' Kirwill asked.

'I am following a car and you are getting out at the next light.'

'The hell I am.'

'There is a KGB officer in that black car. He is stealing a head that was reconstructed for me.'

'Then stop him and take it back.'

'I want to see who he's taking it to.'

'Then what will you do?'

'Then I will come in with a couple of militiamen and

arrest them for theft of state property and obstruction of the prosecutor's office.'

'That's the KGB, you said. You can't arrest them.'

'I don't think it's a KGB operation. The KGB announces it is taking over a case; they don't steal the evidence. The apartment we visited should have been sealed for a year; that's the way the KGB operates. The bodies in the park should have been "discovered" within a day. That's the way the KGB operates, they don't let a lesson grow cold. I think it's one major in the KGB and a few of his officers running their own private operation, protecting someone just for money. The KGB doesn't like entrepreneurs in its ranks. Anyway, the Moscow town prosecutor is the law outside the KGB, and I am still his chief investigator. You can get out here.'

They were stopped at a light at the Sadovaya Ring, three cars behind the Volga. The driver, the pockmarked man who had followed Irina into the metro station, looked down at something beside him on the front seat. He didn't check his rearview mirror. Such a man couldn't conceive of being followed himself, Arkady thought.

'I'm along for the ride.' Kirwill stretched out.

'Very well.'

The light changed. At any moment Arkady expected the Volga to turn left toward the center of the city and Pribluda's office. Instead it turned right, to the east, onto Enthusiasts Road. Some banners were already up. NO ONE WILL LAG BEHIND! said one. Arkady stayed three cars behind.

'How can you be sure he has the head?' Kirwill asked.

MARTIN CRUZ SMITH

'It's probably the only thing I'm sure of. I would like to know how he found out about it.'

The farther they went from the center of town, the less traffic and the more distance Arkady put between himself and the black car. The Hammer and Sickle Works were behind them; Izmailovo Park, too. They were leaving Moscow.

The Volga turned north onto the Outer Ring, the division between city and country. The overcast broke into thunderheads and wells of light. Suddenly on the shoulder of the highway they saw personnel carriers, heavy trucks with gunslit windows, tanks as large as trucks, caissons, trailers of angular canvas-shrouded forms. Soldiers peered into the headlights.

'For the May Day parade,' Arkady explained.

He slowed as the highway approached the Dmitrov Road. Of the cars ahead only the Volga entered the exit ramp. Arkady turned off his headlights before he hit the ramp. The motorcycle militiamen on duty there checked the Moskvich's official plate and waved him through. The Volga was about two hundred meters ahead.

Highway and city fell behind. Woods blurred the side of the road. The land became more hilly and rumpled, and the taillights of the car ahead would disappear, then reappear as the road straightened out. Crows blew past.

'What's this place called?' Kirwill asked.

'Silver Lake.'

'And this guy is just a major?'

'Yes.'

'Then I don't think that's who we're going to see.'

Water showed through a screen of ash and rowans.

Side roads, muddy tributaries, led to summer dachas. As they crossed a wooden bridge, Silver Lake was on their left. The lake had melted except for a central island of ice populated by eiders. The road moved back into trees. The taillights of the Volga were fleeting markers at the end of each curve. Yards with upended parasol tables, broken arbors, and an archery range slipped by the car.

Arkady turned his engine off and coasted onto a side road that ended in ruts beside a cabin that was nailed and shuttered up. Its lawn ran to an apple orchard unpruned and gone wild, then to a fringe of willows and on down to a beach.

'Why did we stop here?' Kirwill asked.

Arkady put a finger to his lips and gently opened his door. Kirwill did likewise, and in the near distance they heard the shutting of another car door.

'You know where they are?' Kirwill asked.

'Now I do.'

The ground was waterlogged and heavy under Arkady's feet. He could hear voices, though not words, through the trees as he crossed the lawn. He moved through the apple orchard, clutching branches, trying to pick his way through the wet leaves and detritus of winter.

The voices were stronger, agreeing on some point as he moved from tree to tree. When the voices stopped, he halted in mid-step. They began again, closer, and he dropped to his stomach and crawled to a low screen of brush. About thirty meters away, he saw the corner of a neighboring dacha, the black Volga, a Chaika limousine, the pocked man and Andrei Iamskoy, the Moscow town prosecutor. The pocked man held a cardboard box. Iamskoy wore the same wolf-trimmed coat and boots as when Arkady had visited the dacha before, as well as a lamb's wool cap on his bare skull and leather gloves that he pulled on while he talked. Arkady could snatch none of the words out of the air, for the prosecutor spoke in a low tone, but he caught the familiar power of that tone, the foresight in it and its total conviction. Iamskoy put his arm around the other man and led him to the path to the beach where Arkady had played a tin horn for the geese.

Arkady kept pace with them through the brush and willows. On his first trip to Iamskoy's dacha he had paid no attention to the woodpiles scattered among the trees on the property. The pocked man waited by one while Iamskoy went into the shed. Arkady remembered the horn, the bucket of fishmeal pellets and the ripening geese inside it. Iamskoy came out carrying an ax. The other man opened his box and pulled out the head of Valerya Davidova – or rather, Andreev's perfect nearly alive re-creation of her head. They laid her on her cheek, staring, an already executed head waiting to be executed again on a chopping stump.

Iamskoy brought the ax down and split the head in two parts. With the precision of a man who enjoys country skills, he set up the halves of the head and split them, and those smaller parts he split again. With the thoroughness of a man who likes a bracing sweat, he minced small parts into smaller, then turned the ax on its broad side and reduced the smaller parts into powder, which he brushed back into the box. The pocked man took the box down to the beach and poured the dust into the water. Iamskoy picked two marbles, Valerya's glass eyes, from the ground and put them in his pocket. He picked up the wig as the pocked man returned, filled the empty box with wood, and together they walked up the path back to the dacha.

Kirwill had followed Arkady silently. 'Let's go,' he said.

Kirwill knew. His smiled had a profound amusement.

'I watched your office, remember,' Kirwill said. 'I've seen the prosecutor before. You better run for your life.'

'Where should I run?'

By the time they got back to the orchard, smoke was rising from the chimney of the Iamskoy dacha. Through the dacha window, Arkady saw the glow of the fire. If he could stand tall enough he might be able to smell the burning hair, he thought.

'Tell me who shot Jimmy,' Kirwill said. 'You're never going to get him. You've got no evidence, no identification and now you're as good as dead. Let me get him.'

Arkady sat down against a trunk and considered the suggestion. He lit a cigarette and cupped it against the rain. 'If the person who killed your brother lived in New York and you killed him, do you think you'd get away with it?'

'I'm a cop – I can get away with anything. Look, I tried to help you.'

'No.' Arkady leaned back. 'No, you didn't.'

'What do you mean? I told you about his leg.'

'He had a bad leg and he's dead; beyond that I know nothing. Well, tell me, was he smart or foolish, brave or a coward, humorous or serious? How could you say so little about your brother?'

Standing over Arkady, Kirwill looked bigger than the trees – a trick of proportion: little trees around a big man. Rain rolled from his shoulders. 'Give up, Renko, you're not in charge anymore. The prosecutor's taking over and so am I. What's the name?'

'You didn't like your brother?'

'I wouldn't say that.'

'What would you say?'

Kirwill looked up at the rain, then down at Arkady. He took his hands from his pockets, made two huge fists and let them spread slowly, as if reassuring himself. He glanced at the house. What would he do if the dacha weren't so close? Arkady wondered.

'I hated Jimmy,' Kirwill said. 'Surprised?'

'If I hated a brother I wouldn't go halfway around the world on the chance that he was dead. But I am curious. When we dusted for fingerprints in the garage you had a card of his prints – a police card. Did you ever arrest your brother?'

Kirwill smiled. With an effort he put his hands back in his coat. 'I'll be waiting for you in the car, Renko.'

He disappeared, ducking between the trees, for all his size hardly making a sound. Arkady congratulated himself for eliminating his last, part-time ally.

Iamskoy. Now it all comes together, the man said as he climbed the gallows steps, Arkady thought. Iamskoy who refused to let anyone but Arkady Renko investigate the bodies in Gorky Park. Iamskoy who led Arkady to Osborne. Pribluda didn't have Pasha and Golodkin followed to Golodkin's apartment; there never was time to shoot them, steal the chest and carry it off. Chuchin had told Iamskoy that Golodkin was being interrogated, and Iamskoy had hours to have the chest removed and the killers waiting. And who had told Iamskoy about Valerya's head? Nobody but Arkady Renko. It was, after all, a discovery not of Iamskoy but of himself, of how stupid and groping an investigator he was, blind, deaf and stupid. An idiot, just as Irina had said.

The door of the dacha opened and Iamskoy and the pocked man emerged. The prosecutor had changed into his usual brown uniform and coat. The other man brushed soot off himself while Iamskoy locked up. They had left the fire going.

'So' – Iamskoy took a deep, invigorating breath – 'I will hear from you tonight.'

The pocked man saluted, got into the Volga and reversed onto the road. Iamskoy followed in the Chaika. Rolling over the leaves and dipping down onto the road, the limousine seemed to give a heave of satisfaction, over work well done.

As soon as the cars were gone, Arkady circled the dacha. It was a four-room cabin furnished in Finnish rustic. Front and back doors were double-locked and the windows were wired because, for the elite residents of Silver Lake, there was an alarm system tied directly to a local KGB station and regular car patrols.

He walked down to the beach. There was a glove on the chopping stump, and pink plasteline dust and a hair or two embedded in the wood. More pink dust was on the ground among the goose droppings, and more dust was being blown in the wind. He scratched the stump. There were also minute flecks of gold.

This was where Golodkin's chest had been brought. It was probably in the cabin on Arkady's first trip, he realized; that was why he was hurried off to feed the eiders. Then the chest had been chopped up on the stump. Would a large chest have been burned all at once? he wondered.

Looking through the woodpile, he couldn't find any traces of the chest. He kicked the whole pile over; at the bottom were slivers that Iamskoy had missed – fine needles of wood and gold.

'Look, Kirwill,' Arkady said to the footfall behind him. 'Golodkin's chest, or what's left of it.'

'So it is,' a different voice said.

Arkady looked up at the pocked man who had left in the Volga. He aimed the same short-barreled TK at Arkady that he had in the metro. 'I forgot my glove,' he explained.

A hand came from behind the pocked man and shook his gun loose. Another hand took him by the throat. Kirwill carried the pocked man by the arm and neck to the nearest tree, the single oak on the beach, held him against the tree by the throat and began hitting him. The pocked man tried to kick back. Kirwill's fist had the sound of a cleaver.

'We want to talk to him,' Arkady said.

Bright blood started coming out of the pocked man's mouth. His eyes swelled. Kirwill's fist accelerated.

'Let him go!' Arkady tried to pull Kirwill off.

Kirwill knocked Arkady to the ground with a backhand.

'No!' He reached for Kirwill's leg.

Kirwill kicked him in the still-unhealed bruise over the heart, and Arkady doubled up, gagging. Kirwill went on hitting the man against the tree. The blood from the man's mouth became effusive and foamy and his feet jerked clear of the ground. The nearest thing Arkady had ever seen to it was watching a hunting dog savage a bird. The pocked man's face thrashed from side to side, blood flying like spittle. His heels beat on the tree. Each blow was harder than the one before, and the impact of Kirwill's fist was into something increasingly soft and inert. Kirwill must have broken the man's ribs at the very start, Arkady thought. Kirwill went on hitting as the pocked face got grayer and grayer.

'He's dead.' Arkady got to his feet and pulled Kirwill back. 'He's dead now.'

Kirwill staggered away. The pocked man dropped to his knees and discolored face, then rolled on his side. Kirwill fell and crawled, his hands speckled red.

'We needed him,' Arkady said. 'We had to ask him questions.'

Kirwill started trying to wash his hands with pebbles. Arkady grabbed him by the back of the collar and led him like an animal down the beach to the water, then returned to the oak tree and went through the dead man's clothes. He found a cheap wallet with little money, a change purse, a push-button knife and the red identification book of a KGB officer. The name inside was Ivanov. He kept the book and the gun.

MARTIN CRUZ SMITH

Arkady dragged the dead man to the shed. When he pulled the door open, warmth and buzzing poured out. The eiders hung in rows all the way to the ceiling, feet bound, heads resting on dirty plumage. A murmur of flies crawled in and out of feathers and there was a smell of liquid decay. He threw the dead man in and slammed the door.

The wind pushed them back to Moscow.

'First he was going to be a priest,' Kirwill said. 'One of those pale boys who bleed over cut flowers, gets to Rome and hates Italians and sucks up to French Jesuits. That would have been disgusting but all right. He could have been a workers' priest, an ordinary pain in the ass. Then he raised his sights; he wanted to be a messiah. He wasn't smart and he wasn't strong, but he wanted to be a messiah.'

'How could he do that?'

'A Catholic can't. If you call yourself an Oriental yogi or a guru and drool and eat chicken heads and never change your pants, you can attract all the disciples you want. But a Catholic, no.'

'No?'

'If you're Catholic, the best you can hope for is excommunication. There are too many messiahs in America, anyway. It's a supermarket of messiahs. You don't know what the hell I'm talking about, do you?'

'No.'

At the Outer Highway they reached the Exhibition Park. Dusk curved around an obelisk.

'Russia is the Virgin Land for messiahs,' Kirwill said. 'Jimmy could have stood out here; he had a chance. He'd already fucked up at home. He had to do something big here. He wrote me from Paris saying he was coming here. He said the next time I saw him would be at Kennedy Airport. He said he was going to perform an act in the spirit of Saint Christopher. Do you know what that means?'

Arkady shook his head.

'That means he was going to smuggle someone out of Russia and hold a news conference at Kennedy. He was going to be a savior, Renko – at the least, a religious celebrity. I know how he got in here. He told me when he came back from here the first time how easy it would be to find a Polish or Czech student who looked like him. They'd exchange passports and Jimmy would return here under the other guy's name. That's how the Church runs a lot of Bibles in through Poland, he said. Jimmy spoke Polish, Czech and German besides Russian; it wouldn't have been hard. What would have been hard was not being caught here. And getting out.'

'You said he'd fucked up in the United States. How?'

'He got involved with those Jewish kids who harass Russians in New York City. At first it was just paint on the cars and protests. Then letter bombs. Then pipe bombs at Aeroflot and shooting rifles through the windows at the Soviet Mission. There's a bureau in the Police Department called the Red Squad that watches radicals; it stepped in and watched the Jews. In fact, we sold them their next bunch of blasting caps. In the meantime Jimmy went down to Georgia and bought some more rifles and ammo for them. He made two trips – one load he brought up in an altar.'

'What was wrong with the blasting caps?' Arkady asked.

'They were defective. I saved his life. He was supposed to help make the bombs. That morning I went to his apartment and told him not to go. He wouldn't listen. I threw him on the bed and broke his leg over the bed-board. So he didn't go. The Jews attached the bad caps and the bombs went off. Everyone was killed. The point is, I saved Jimmy's life.'

'Then what?'

'What do you mean, "Then what"?'

'The Jews who were left, didn't they think your brother was an informant?'

'Sure. I sent him out of town.'

'He never got a chance to explain to his friends?'

'I told him that if he came back I'd break his neck.'

There was a downpour on the Avenue of Peace. News-papers were scattered on the sidewalk.

'There was a case in New York.' Kirwill accepted a cigarette. 'There was a slasher, a mugger, who pulled a knife on people, and after he got what he asked for he'd cut them up just for fun. We knew who he was, a black guy – into jewelry mainly. I wanted him off the street, so I pulled a drop on him. You know, I had one of the victims' rings, dropped it behind this black individual and grabbed him. The stupid fucker pulled a gun and shot and missed. I didn't miss. This was in Harlem. There was a crowd, and somebody took the bastard's gun and ran. That made him a martyr, a citizen shot down on the way to church. There were marches up and down One Hundred and Twenty-fifth Street, every black minister that could shuffle his feet, plus the whole white antiwar crowd and Jimmy and his Christian Witnesses. All the Christian Witnesses had signs saying, "Sergeant Killwell: Wanted for Murder." I found out who thought up "Killwell." Jimmy never told me, but I found out.'

The river was swollen. High black water drove the last floes.

'You know what else he liked to call me?' Kirwill asked. 'He liked to call me Esau. His brother Esau.'

At the Ethnological Institute Arkady went up alone to tell Andreev what had happened to the head. From Andreev's studio he called Misha's apartment and office and got no answer. Then he called Swan, who said he had found the house used by Kostia Borodin, Valerya Davidova and James Kirwill. The woman who had led Swan to the house said she had sold them a fresh chicken and fish every day.

Arkady took Kirwill with him to see the house, which proved to be a cabin between the factories of the Lyublin-sky District and the southern arc of the Outer Ring Highway. Almost everything about the place was familiar to Arkady, as if he'd entered a creation of his own imagination. Kirwill moved through it silently, in a trance.

The two men went to a workers' cafeteria. Kirwill ordered a bottle of vodka and picked up where he'd left off about his brother, but in a different manner, almost about a different person. He told Arkady how he had taught Jimmy how to ice-skate, how to drive, how to lay gilt on a frame, how to deal with nuns, how they'd gone every summer up the Allagash River, how they'd seen Roger Maris hit his home run, how they'd buried the old Russian babushka who'd raised them both. The stories flowed; some Arkady understood and some he didn't.

'I'll tell you when I knew you were for real,' Kirwill said. 'When you shot at me in my hotel room. You aimed away, but not by much. You could have hit me. You didn't care and I didn't care. We're just the same.'

'I care now,' Arkady said.

At midnight he dropped Kirwill close to the Metropole. The big man walked away fragilely on drunken legs.

Irina had waited for him. She made love to him tenderly, as if saying, Yes, you can trust me, you can come in, you can trust your life in me.

His last conscious thought before sleep was of what Kirwill had said at the cafeteria when Arkady asked whether he and his brother Jimmy had ever trapped sables.

'No. There are pine martens in Maine and Canada, and the pelt of the pine marten is called sable, but they're pretty rare. They were trapped out by auger holes. The auger's a drill. If he's a real bastard, a trapper uses the auger to bore a hole into a tree trunk about eight inches deep. This deep. He puts some fresh meat all the way into the hole. Then he drives two horseshoe nails at an angle into the trunk so that the tips of the nails almost meet about six inches inside the hole. The auger hole does the rest. The pine marten's a good climber – slim, clever. He smells the meat, goes right up the trunk and into the trap. He can just squeeze his head past the nails pointing at the meat. He gets the meat – he always gets the meat – but by then the nails have got him. He's trying to go against the angle of the nails, and the more he struggles to get his head out, the deeper the nails dig in. Finally he bleeds to death or else rips his head off. There aren't many pine martens left. The auger holes got them.'

Chapter Sixteen

At four in the morning Arkady called Ust-Kut. 'This is Detective Yakutsky.'

'This is Chief Investigator Renko in Moscow.'

'Oh? You finally called at a good time,' Yakutsky said.

Arkady closed his eyes at the dark of the window. 'What do sables eat?' he asked.

'You called to ask me that? You can't find a copy of the encyclopedia?'

'Borodin's clothes had traces of chicken and fish blood. He was buying chicken and fish every day.'

'Sables and minks eat chicken and fish. So, if I remember, do people.'

'Not every day,' Arkady said. 'Have there been any thefts of sables in your area?'

'None, not one.'

'No unusual incidents at any of the fur collectives?'

'Nothing unusual. There was a fire in November at a collective at Barguzin, and five or six sables were killed. All the animals, however, were accounted for.'

'How badly burned were they?'

'Dead, as I said. It was an appreciable loss, actually, because Barguzins are the most valuable sables of all. There was an inquiry, but no negligence could be proved.'

'Were autopsies done on the animals to show that

they definitely were Barguzin sables and that they actually died from the fire, or exactly when they died?'

'Investigator, I assure you that only someone in Moscow could have thought of that.'

After hanging up, Arkady quietly dressed and left the apartment, walking to Taganskaya Square before using a public phone. There was still no answer at Misha's apartment. He called and woke Swan and Andreev, then walked back to his apartment and stood against the bedroom wall watching Irina.

Could he go to the prosecutor general and say that the Moscow town prosecutor was a killer? Two days before May Day? Without evidence? They'd say he was drunk or crazy, and hold him until Iamskoy arrived. Could he go to the KGB? Osborne was a KGB informant. Also, he had the blood of a dead KGB agent on his hands, thanks to Kirwill.

Dawn crept over Irina. She was a pale blue figure on a pale blue sheet, but he felt the languid warmth of her sleep. He watched as if enough concentration would imprint her image on his eyes. Her forehead was shaded by hair that became fine gold as the sun rose.

The world was a mote erratically stirred by her breath. The world was a coward plotting to kill her. He could save her life. He would lose her, yet he could save her life.

When she awoke, he'd made coffee and laid her dress at the foot of her bed.

'What's the matter?' she asked. 'I thought you liked having me here.'

'Tell me about Osborne.'

'We went through all that, Arkasha.' Irina sat up, naked. 'Even if I believed what you said about Osborne, what if I was wrong? If Valerya's safe someplace, I'd be turning in the man who helped her. If she's dead, she's dead. Nothing can change that.'

'Let's go.' Arkady threw her dress at her. 'You talk too easily about dying. I'll introduce you to the dead.'

On the way to the lab Irina continually glanced at him. He felt her searching for an explanation of this sudden about-face into an investigator again.

Arkady took her inside the forensic lab with him to collect one sealed evidence bag and one empty one from Colonel Lyudin. Lyudin regarded Irina appreciatively; some sleight of hand and her new scarf had made her Afghan jacket momentarily chic again.

Driving away, she showed her irritation with Arkady's brusqueness by staring out her side window. This was a typical lovers' spat, her manner said. A scent insinuated itself into the car. She looked at the sealed and bulky evidence bag beside her. The smell was so vague as to be barely noticed, but it had a ripeness that lingered on the tongue and in the throat. By the time they reached the river, she had opened her window to the cold.

At the Ethnological Institute Arkady led Irina up to Andreev's studio. Relieved to be out of the car, she made a display of curiosity over the cabinets containing the heads of Tamerlane and Ivan the Terrible while Arkady looked for the anthropologist. But Andreev was gone, as he'd sworn he would be.

Arkady watched Irina across the room of heads.

'Is this what you brought me to see?' She tapped the cabinet of Ivan.

'No. I'd hoped we could meet Professor Andreev. Unfortunately, he doesn't seem to be here. He's a fascinating man, you must have heard of him.'

'No.'

'They lecture on his work at the Law Faculty,' Arkady said. 'You should remember that.'

Irina shrugged and left the cabinets for the tables of anthropological exhibits, scanning faces that peered with heavy brows and glass eyes. She moved closer. Andreev's work was magical. Arkady saw Irina's delight in one apish face comically puckered, and in another one bearing a fierce scowl. At the end of the table was a potter's wheel and a high stool. Propped on a wire stand on the wheel was a Neanderthal skull half covered with strips of pink plasteline.

'I see.' She touched a bare area of the skull. 'Andreev reconstructs them—' She snatched her hand back, the words still on her lips.

'It's all right.' Arkady approached her. 'He left it for us.'

Hanging from Arkady's hand by a carrying string was a round hatbox of pink enameled pasteboard, the kind of box that had gone out of style sixty years before.

'I have heard of Andreev.' Irina wiped her fingers.

As Arkady walked toward her, the hatbox danced in a top-heavy way.

Every Law Faculty student knew of Andreev's reconstructions of the heads of murder victims. Riding along Gorky Park, the former good student Irina Asanova barely breathed the tainted air of the car. Death seeped from the sealed bag and rattled in the hatbox on the rear seat.

'Where are we going, Arkasha?' Irina asked.

'You'll see.' Arkady chose the most prosaic words, the answer to a prisoner.

He offered no explanation or compassion to distract her, no hand to hold, no sympathy. A man doesn't become chief investigator without a capacity for cruelty, he told himself.

When a whole convoy of waving soldiers passed on the left and Irina's eyes didn't deviate from straight ahead, he knew that it was for fear that the smallest slip would bring her eye round to the obscenely colored box. Over a little rough road it jostled. The box would be speaking to Irina, to her it would have a whole biography, enough and more to erupt through the rear of the car.

'Just wait,' he told her, taking a corner. The box shifted and Irina's hands jerked as if on a string.

Red May Day banners stretched across a ball-bearing plant, a tractor plant, an electric plant, a textile plant. On the banners were golden profiles, golden laurels, golden slogans. From the stacks rose steel-colored smoke. She must know now where she was being taken, he thought.

Southeast through the Lyublinsky District, no words said, an hour's worth of traveling through larger factories thinning to smaller ones, to the prefabricated gray of workers' flats, to old homes razed for development, to a country field mazed by surveyors' strings, bumping over mud heaves, past the end of the autobus line, still in the expanded city limits but beyond it to another world of low houses little more than cabins, swaying picket fences and tethered goats, wash in the arms of women dressed in sweaters and boots, a church of plaster, a one-legged man doffing his hat, brown cows crossing the road, a backyard chopping block and ax, and slowly over ruts, a house set off by itself in a yard of broken sunflower stalks, two dirty windows in front showing filthy curtains, paint curling on a carved eave – behind the house an outhouse and a metal shed.

He let her out of the car and gathered the bags and hatbox from the rear seat. At the door of the house he pulled three key rings from one of the bags, the key rings that had been found in the leather bag in the river. On each key ring one key was similar.

'Seems logical, doesn't it?' he asked Irina.

The key fit. The door stuck, and Arkady hit it with his hip, releasing an odor of mildew as it swung open. Before going inside, he put on a pair of rubber gloves and hit a light switch. Electricity was still connected to a single bulb above a round table. The house had the stench of a trap and was cold, as if it had stored winter. Irina stood in the middle of the floor shivering.

There was only one room to the house, with four triple-paned windows all shuttered and locked. Horsehair quilts in two sleeping compartments. A coal stove on an apron of ashes. Three chairs of different styles around the table. A cabinet with moldy cheese and a milk bottle long since opened by ice. On the walls, one photo of Brando and many of ikons torn from books. Under a drop cloth in a corner, paint cans, bottles of bole and varnish, rags, a cushioned pad, flat brushes, punches and brushes. Arkady pulled back the sheet from a closet to expose to the light two men's suits, one medium and one large, three cheap dresses the same small size and, on the floor, a jumble of shoes.

'Yes,' Arkady read the thought on Irina's face, 'it's like being in someone's grave. It always is.'

Three old-fashioned naval footlockers stood against the wall. Arkady unlocked them, using a different key from each ring. The first one had underwear, socks, Bibles and other religious contraband; the second, underwear, a corked vial of gold dust, condoms, an old Nagant revolver and shells; the third, a woman's underwear, glass jewelry, a foreign perfume, douche, scissors, brushes, lipstick, hairpins, a jar, an almost feature-less bisque doll, and photographs of Valerya Davidova, mostly with Kostia Borodin and one of her with a full-bearded old man.

'Her father, right?' He picked up the picture for Irina to see. She said nothing. He closed the lockers. 'Kostia must have really scared the neighbors while he was around here. Imagine them not breaking in here all this time.' The sleeping compartments caught his eye. 'Kostia must have been a difficult man, and to have to live with another man as well? This is how we live, though, so . . .

Why don't you stop me, Irina? Tell me what they were doing here for Osborne.'

'I think you already know,' she said in a whisper.

'That's speculation. There has to be a witness. Someone has to tell me.'

'I can't.'

'But you will.' Arkady put the hatbox and the evidence bags on the table. 'We will help each other, and we will solve a couple of mysteries. I want to know what Valerya and Borodin were doing here for Osborne, and you want to know where Valerya is right now. Soon it will all come clear.'

He moved one chair away, leaving two by the table. He looked around the room. It was so desperately shoddy, so little more than a carton turned on its end, packed with three lives, a thin sheet for privacy's sake, entrepreneurs blowing on their hands to stay warm.

The dim bulb yellowed Irina and hollowed her cheeks. He saw himself through her eyes, a gaunt man with wild black hair and feverishly sharp features looming over a pink box. He looked deeper into the reflection of this ridiculous man, this puppet man of Iamskoy's, as Irina had seen him so accurately from the start. Yet he could save her from Iamskoy and Osborne – and even from herself, if his nerve didn't fail.

'So' – Arkady slapped his hands – 'it is Gorky Park at dusk. It is snowing. The pretty fur sorter Valerya, Kostia the Siberian bandit and the American boy Kirwill are skating with the furrier Osborne when they leave the path and make their way fifty meters to a clearing to have something to eat and drink. Here they stand. Kostia here' – Arkady indicated the chair at one side of the table. 'The Kirwill boy here' – he indicated the other chair – 'and Valerya in the middle' – he laid his hand by the box. 'You, Irina, stand here' – he brought her closer to the table – 'you are Osborne.'

'No, please,' Irina asked.

'Simply for purposes of explanation,' Arkady said. 'I can't manage the snow or the vodka, so bear with me. Try to imagine the atmosphere, the gaiety. Three of these people believed a whole new life was about to begin – freedom for two of them, fame for the third. This was no mere skating party, it was a celebration! Was this when you – Osborne, that is – were going to give them their instructions on how to escape? Very likely. Only you know that in seconds they will be dead.'

'I—'

'You don't care about any religious chests; anyone could have gotten them for you – Golodkin, for example. If that was all these three people had done for you, a little ikon-faking and smuggling, you would have let them live. Let them talk, let them walk right straight into the office of the KGB with accusations and pictures to prove them; your friends there would have laughed them back into the street. But this other thing, not the chest but what they *really* did for you, these three people must never talk about – not in Moscow, not anywhere.'

'You mustn't do this to me,' Irina said.

'The snow is falling,' Arkady went on. 'Their faces are a little red with vodka. They trust you; you'd already brought in this American dupe Kirwill, yes? By the time the first bottle of vodka is gone, they love you. You're their savior from the West. Many smiles and toasts. Hear the music from the skating paths? Tchaikovsky! Ah, we need another bottle. Mr Osborne, you are a generous man, you've brought a leather bag full of vodka and brandy and all sorts of treats. You lift the bag high as if you are sorting around inside with your hand and bring out . . . another bottle. Go first yourself; pretend to take a real swig. Kostia is next and he more than matches you, if I know him. Valerya is a little giddy now, and it's not easy to take the bottle when she has bread in one hand and cheese in the other. Besides, she's thinking about where she'll be in a week or so, what kind of clothes she'll be wearing, how warm it will be. No more Siberia there – heaven, instead. Kirwill is already unsteady on his skates, he has that weak leg, but he's thinking too about his return home, the vindication of all his saintly efforts. No wonder the vodka goes so fast.

'Another bottle? Why not? The snow is falling harder, the music is louder. You lift your bag and sort through it, feel the bottle, feel the grip of your gun. Push the safety off. Kostia is the thirstiest, turn to him and give this famous bandit a smile.'

Arkady kicked the chair so that it slammed onto its back on the floor. Irina blinked and rocked slightly in surprise.

'Very good,' Arkady continued. 'An automatic doesn't make as much noise as a revolver, and the sound is muffled by the leather bag, the snow and the music from loudspeakers. There's probably no obvious sign of blood at first. Valerya and the Kirwill boy don't really understand why Kostia is down on the ground. You're all friends. You came to save them, not to hurt them. Turn to the American boy. Keep the bag up to his chest.'

A tear crossed the mark on her cheek.

'No expression now,' Arkady said.

He kicked the second chair to the floor. 'It's so simple. Only Valerya is left. She looks down at her dead Kostia, at the dead American, but she makes no move to run, to call out, to protest. You understand her so well. Without Kostia she's as good as dead; you'll be putting her out of her misery. A life can change that quickly. You'll be doing her a favor.' Arkady ripped open the evidence bag. An oily redolence filled the air as he pulled free a cheap, dark dress stained by dirt and blood and bearing a hole over the left breast. Irina looked to the open closet and back; he knew she recognized the dress. 'Bring the gun as close as you want; Valerya will wait, she welcomes the bullet. Bring the gun closer to her heart. Such a waste of beauty, you think' – Arkady let the dress fall across the table – 'such a waste of beauty. Dead, all three. No one is coming, the music still plays, snow will soon cover the bodies.'

Irina was shaking.

'They may be dead,' Arkady said, 'but you still have work. Gather all the imported food, the bottles, the papers from the bodies. Take the chance of firing two more times, because the American has some foreign dental work. You give Kostia a shot in the same place so that maybe the dumb militia will think they were coups de grace. Still, they can be identified. They have fingerprints. Simple. Some heavy shears, the kind used for cutting up chicken, and snip, snip at each finger joint.

But what to do about the faces? Hope they decompose? But they'll freeze; they'll be whiter than snow, but otherwise exactly the same. Smear jam on their faces so that the little animals of the park will eat them off? No, the squirrels are tucked away for the winter, and there aren't enough dogs in Moscow. But the furrier has an answer because he has a special skill. He skins them: he lifts a whole face like a little pink pelt right off each head – Kostia's, the Kirwill boy's and, last and most delicate, Valerya's. What a special moment. How many furriers have ever done that! He scoops out their eyes, and then he's done. The scraps go into the bag. Three lives erased and doubly erased. Enough! You go to your hotel, to your plane, to that separate world you came from. Everything seems perfect.'

Arkady shaped the dress on the table, folding one long sleeve over the other, draping its skirt over the table's edge. 'There is only one person you can think of who can connect you to the three bodies in Gorky Park. She won't tell, though, because she is Valerya's best friend and she wants Valerya to be in New York or Rome or California. That fantasy is the most important thing in her life. She can get through each stupid, dangerous, oppressively boring day here if she can just believe that Valerya has escaped. The idea that Valerya is drawing a free breath somewhere else is all that keeps this friend from dying of claustrophobia. You could try to kill her yourself and she still wouldn't talk. You really do know your Russians.'

Irina wavered on her feet. He was afraid she would fall.

'So the whole question is, Where is Valerya?' Arkady went on.

'How can you do this?' Irina asked.

'We are' – Arkady looked aside and spoke in a different tone of voice – 'a backward, ignorant people. It seems we always have been. We have strange talents, Irina. At the Law Faculty at the university you had lectures on forensic medicine and were introduced to the work of Professor Andreev. Perhaps you were shown some photos. It is a simple but painstaking method of reconstructing a face from a skull. Not a vague idea of what the face might have looked like or a close approximation, but the face itself. No other country has it. It's a delicate matter of rebuilding every muscle on the skull, then laying on flesh and eyes and skin. As you know, Andreev is a master, and you must also be aware of his reputation for integrity.' Arkady removed the lid from the hatbox. 'You wanted to know where Valerya is.'

'I know you, Arkasha,' Irina said. 'You won't do it.'

'Here is Valerya.'

Arkady started to lift the head out of the box. He did it slowly so that Irina could see first above the rim of the box a mass of dark curls entangled in his fingers, then the hair pulling taut between his hand and a rising forehead of fresh-complexioned skin.

'Arkasha!' She closed her eyes and covered them with her hands.

'Take a look.'

'Arkasha!' She didn't take her hands from her eyes. 'Yes, yes, this is where Valerya lived. Put it back in the box.'

'Valerya who?'

'Valerya Davidova.'

'With . . .'

'Kostia Borodin and the Kirwill boy.'

'An American named James Kirwill?'

'Yes.'

'You saw them here?'

'Kirwill was always here hiding. Valerya was here, I wouldn't come unless she was.'

'You didn't get along with Kostia?'

'No.'

'What were they doing here in the house?'

'Making a chest, you know about the chest.'

'Who for?' Arkady held his breath when she hesitated.

'Osborne,' she said.

'Osborne who?'

'John Osborne.'

'An American furrier named John Osborne?'

'Yes.'

'They *told* you they were making the chest for Osborne?'

'Yes.'

'Is that all they were doing for Osborne?'

'No.'

'Did you ever go into the shed in back of the house here?'

'Yes, once.'

'You saw what they brought Osborne from Siberia?'

'Yes.'

'Repeat your answer, please. You saw what they brought Osborne from Siberia?'

'I hate you,' she said. Arkady turned off the portable tape machine on the bottom of the hatbox and let the head fall back in. Irina dropped her hands. 'Now I really do.'

Swan entered from outside the door, where he had been waiting.

'This man will drive you back to town.' Arkady dismissed her. 'Stay with him. Don't go to my apartment; it will be unsafe. Thank you for your help in this investigation. You had better go now.'

He hoped she would understand, and that she would insist on staying. He would take her with him if she did.

She did stop at the door. 'There's a story about your father, the general,' she said. 'They called him a monster because he took German ears as trophies during the war. No one ever said he showed off a whole head. He was nothing compared to you.'

She walked out. Arkady's last view of her was in Swan's car, an ancient Zil sedan, moving up the dirt road.

Arkady went to the back of the house, past the outhouse to the metal shed, which he unlocked with one of the dead men's keys. As he entered, something brushed against his face, a light cord for a rack hanging from the center of the ceiling. When he pulled the cord, rows of powerful bulbs made the inside of the shed as bright as day. He found a timer on the wall. Turning it, he heard a faint ticking, and noticed an almost imperceptible shift in the rank of lights. The timer would swing the rack almost 180 degrees over twelve hours to simulate the rising and setting of the sun. Another cord rose to two ultraviolet lamps. There were no windows.

The remains of a round brick forge explained the shed's history. Stacks of molds and iron scrap had rusted together into metal knots. All the usable space was taken up by two cages that ran the length of the shed. Each was partitioned by wood walls into three pens, and each pen had a wooden coop. Wire covered the sides and tops of the cages. At ground level the wire was buttressed by stones and cement so that not even the slimmest and most determined animal could escape.

In the area between the two cages was a bench cross-hatched with blood and fish scales. Arkady found a prayer book beneath the bench. He imagined the dissimilar pair of James Kirwill and Kostia Borodin guarding and feeding their secret, Kirwill praying for divinity while Kostia chased snoopers.

He entered a pen and collected fine hairs from the wire and droppings from the ground.

Back in the house, he filled his extra evidence bag with items from the footlockers. As he put the bag on the table, he knocked over the hatbox and the head inside rolled out. It was a hinged plaster head without eyes, brows or mouth, without any particular features at all, merely paint and the roughest shape of a face and a wig. It was the dummy Andreev used for teaching. As Arkady lifted the head back in, the halves of its face swung open and showed the narrow inner leer of the skull.

Andreev's reconstruction of Valerya's head was now no more than flesh-colored dust and the smell of burning hair at Iamskoy's dacha. Andreev had confirmed that Iamskoy himself had called about the head and sent over the pocked man to get it. In a way, the destruction of Andreev's masterpiece had liberated Arkady; only then did he think of using a dummy. He never could have shown Irina the real head, just as he knew she couldn't look at it. Desperate, he'd had a brilliant idea. He had fooled her. Saved her and lost her.

Entering the Ukraina lobby, Arkady saw Hans Unmann leaving the elevator. Arkady sat in a lobby chair and picked up a discarded newspaper. He'd never actually seen Osborne's co-conspirator before. The German was a scarecrow, thin-mouthed and bony, with blond hair cut close under his hat. The kind of man who instinctively stares down the next person in his path, he was too much a thug to be as dangerous as Osborne or Iamskoy. When he passed, Arkady dropped the newspaper and squeezed into the elevator.

He'd expected to find the airline office vacant, so he was surprised to find Detective Fet sitting at a desk and aiming a pistol at him.

'Fet!' Arkady laughed. 'I'm sorry. I'd completely forgotten about you.'

'I thought you were him coming back,' Fet said. He was trembling so much that he had to put his gun down with both hands. His steel-rimmed glasses sat on a face bleached by fear. 'He was waiting for you. Then he got a phone call and ran out. He gave me my gun back. I would have used it.'

Transcripts and tapes were strewn around upended chairs and open drawers. How long ago was it, Arkady asked himself, that he and Pasha and Fet had childishly luxuriated in this office? It was Iamskoy who'd set them up here. Was there a microphone? Was someone listening now? No matter; he didn't plan to stay long. He sorted through the mess on the floor enough to satisfy himself that all the transcripts and tapes of Osborne and Unmann were gone, all but the one reel Arkady had kept of the February 2 Osborne-Unmann call.

'He barged in here and took over.' Fet gained in heat and color. 'He wouldn't let me leave. He thought I'd warn you.'

'You wouldn't have done that.'

Among the debris, Arkady found one of the blue books of airline schedules left behind by the office's previous inhabitants. The book was current. All international flights left Moscow from Sheremetyevo Airport, and the only plane leaving on May Day Eve was a night flight by Pan American. Osborne and Kirwill would be on the same plane.

And there was an open package from the Ministry of Trade, from Yevgeny Mendel. Inside was a photocopy of the citation won by his father, the coward, and to settle any doubts, also a tediously full report of old Mendel's heroism signed and dated June 4, 1943. No wonder Unmann had only ripped open the package, glanced at it and tossed it aside, as Arkady was going to do until he recognized on the last page, despite the smudges of time and the indistinctness of the ministry's copying machine, the bold signature of the investigating officer, Lieut (j.g.) A. O. Iamskoy. There, an Order of Lenin bought and sold in a charnel house, in the world capital of charnel houses that was Leningrad during the war! The young Northern Army junior lieutenant Andrei Iamskoy – he couldn't have been twenty – had known the young American Foreign Service Officer John Osborne more than thirty years ago, known him and protected him even then.

'You haven't heard,' Fet said tentatively.

'Heard what?'

'The prosecutor's office sent out an all-city alarm for you an hour ago.'

'What for?'

'For murder. A body was found in a museum off Serafimov. A lawyer named Mikoyan. Your fingerprints were found on cigarettes there.' Fet picked up the phone and started dialing. 'Maybe you want to speak to Major Pribluda?'

'Not yet.' Arkady took the phone away and returned it to its cradle. 'Right now you're the forgotten man. It's often the forgotten man who becomes the hero. In any case, it's the forgotten man who lives to tell the tale.'

'What do you mean?' Fet was confused.

'I want a head start.'

Savelovsky Station was ordinarily for commuters – the contented clerks and good citizens of life. This train was special, and the commuters avoided as pariahs its crowd of passengers. They were laborers, all signed to a three-year contract for work in the northern mines, some within the Arctic Circle. They would work in steam and ice, would haul ore on their backs when carts shattered from the cold, would be killed by blasting, mine collapses or hypothermia, or they would kill somebody else for a pair of boots or gloves. When they arrived at the mine, their internal passports would be taken away so that there could be no second thoughts. For three years they would disappear, and for some of them this was fine.

Arkady fit in with the workers. He shuffled along in the crowd, holding on to his evidence bag with one hand, his other on the gun in his pocket. On the train he moved with the flow into a compartment already filled with men and the stink of sweat and onions. A dozen faces studied him. They were the same tough and homely faces as on the Politburo, but roughed up and down the street a bit. They sported bruises and unusual scars, their knuckles and collars were dirty, and they carried their possessions in bundles. Basically they were criminals, men wanted for violence or theft in one town instead of the whole country. Little fish who thought they were escaping through the holes of the great socialist net, only to be funneled into socialist mines in the north. Tough fish, urkas, brothers, hard cases, men with tattoos and knives. To them a stranger was shoes, a coat, maybe a watch. Arkady claimed a space on the lower bunk.

A solid rank of militiamen pushed the last workers onto the train. The air in the compartment was unbreathable, though Arkady knew he'd get used to it. Conductors began running up and down the platform outside, eager to get this special train under way and out of their station. An all-city alarm might close the roads, airports and ordinary trains to an escaping man, but this was a whole train of escaping men. Through the compartment window, Arkady saw Chuchin, the chief investigator for Special Cases, argue with a chief conductor. Chuchin showed the chief conductor a photograph. All he had to do was look in the compartment. The chief conductor kept shaking his head. Chuchin waved militiamen onto the trains. In the next compartment someone began singing, 'Farewell, Moscow, farewell love . . .' To be pushed along the platform by militiamen was one thing; to be rousted from their compartments on their own special train was something else. Threats and curses delayed the progress of the search: 'You can't bother me, I'm already on the way to hell!' Instead of leaving their seats, they spat on the militiamen. Ordinarily, something a militiaman would reply to with a club, but contract workers were given special considerations; it was understood that saints didn't volunteer for three years in hell. Besides, the militiamen were outnumbered. They never reached Arkady's compartment; the militia were horselaughed off the cars. The chief conductor brushed Chuchin aside, and again the other conductors did their pantomime run up and down the platform. The train heaved, and Chuchin and the chief conductor slid by. The metal canopies of the platforms gave way to smokestacks and the double-beaked fences of defense factories, the terrain of northern Moscow. The train was still gathering speed when it reached the next commuter station, not slowing for the safely disdainful looks of the commuters there, rolling with a will right by a platform of militia, sounding its locomotive horn. Farewell, Moscow. Arkady took a deep breath; the air wasn't so bad after all.

The train was special too, the oldest and dirtiest the Ministry of Transport had been able to dig up. The compartment had been gutted and vandalized so many times and so long ago that there was nothing left to deface or steal. Besides, there was barely room to move. Fifteen men on four hard wooden bunks and the floor, each elbow lodged against a neighbor's. The train conductor had locked himself into his own end compartment for the duration of the trip. This was hardly the fastest way to Leningrad. The Red Arrow Express left from Leningrad Station and took half a day. This train, on the local track from Savelovsky Station, hauling its ancient cars of what the magazines called rehabilitated workers, would take twenty hours. The conductor had his own samovar, hard rolls and jam in his haven. In Arkady's compartment they broke out cigarettes and vodka. The ceiling filled with smoke. Someone told him to drink, and he drank and offered a cigarette in return.

The man with the bottle was an Ossetian, like Stalin – squat and dark, with the same sort of brows, mustache and beetle eyes.

'Sometimes they put informers on these trains, you know,' he told Arkady. 'Sometimes they still try to catch you and bring you back. What we do is catch the informer and slit his throat.'

'There are no informers on this train,' Arkady said. 'They don't want you back. You're going right where they want you to.'

The Ossetian's eyes glittered. 'Fuck your mother, you're right!'

The wheels measured the afternoon and evening. Iksa, Dmitrov, Verilki, Savelovo, Kalazin, Kasin, Sonkovo, Krasnii Cholm, Pestovo. There was no point in not drinking. They were leaving not just a day but three years behind. Better straight alcohol than vodka. These were talented eyes and hands, and how many languages? It was a multinational compartment. An Armenian embezzler – a description redundant to some. A pair of highwaymen from Turkistan. A snatchman from Mary's Grove. A gigolo from Yalta with sunglasses and a tan.

'What are you hiding in your coat?' the gigolo demanded.

Arkady had the bag of material taken from the cabin, his gun, his own ID and that of the KGB officer Kirwill had beaten to death. Nobody would have dared ask Kirwill that question; it was one that a hunter asked his prey.

'A collection of tiny pricks from the Black Sea,' Arkady answered.

He drank chifir. Chifir was tea concentrated not twice or ten times but twenty times. In the camps a starving man could work three days straight on a few cups of chifir. Arkady had to stay awake. The moment he was asleep he would be robbed. His skin became clammy with adrenaline; his heart seemed to expand. Yet he had to think calmly. Someone had killed Misha. Unmann, the scarecrow? Arkady had just missed him twice. Why a homicide alarm, though? Why would Iamskoy chance bringing in the militia? Unless the prosecutor had already cleaned up the cabin where the Gorky Park victims had lived. Unless he felt sure that his investigator would die trying to escape arrest. Or that he could be declared insane at once. Maybe he already was.

His heart was pouring out more blood than his veins could handle, so he drank some more vodka to open them. Someone had a transistor radio that reported May Day preparations in Vladivostok.

'The iron mines aren't so bad,' a veteran said. 'If you work in the gold mines, they stick a vacuum cleaner up your ass when you come out of the mine.'

There was a bulletin on May Day preparations in Baku.

'My home,' the Ossetian told Arkady. 'I murdered someone there. It was purely by accident.'

'Why tell me?'

'You have an innocent face.'

May Day preparations from around the world. The night outside was overlaid by reflections of the compartment. Arkady opened the pane a crack; he could smell fields plowed black and loamy from the winter's snows.

He missed Misha already. The curious thing was that he could hear his friend's voice as if he were still alive and commenting on the characters on the train: '*Now, this is what Communism's all about, getting people together. It's a little bit like the United Nations; you just don't get to change your clothes as often. Now, the Armenian, there's a man who's going to lose weight. Or he could just split in half like an amoeba and become two Armenians. He'd get double pay. I wouldn't put it past an Armenian. Look at the gigolo. We have discussed Hamlet, we have discussed Caesar, we are looking at a man who has the last tan of his life. Now, that's tragedy. Arkasha, won't you admit now it's all a little crazy?*

The vodka ran out. When the train stopped for water at a small town – nothing more than a station and a single lit street – the workers came off the train and broke into the town store while a pair of local militiamen stood by helplessly. When all the looters were back on, the train continued.

Kaboza, Chvojnaja, Budogosc, Posadnikovo, Kolpino. Leningrad, Leningrad, Leningrad. The morning sparks of commuter trains ran on converging wires. Dawn was mirrored by the Gulf of Finland. The train entered a city of briefcases and canals, a gray city to red eyes.

As the train pulled into Finland Station, Arkady jumped from it while it was still moving, waving the red KGB identification card taken from the man Kirwill had beaten to death. Anthems filled the loudspeakers. It was the day before May Day.

Chapter Seventeen

A hundred kilometers north of Leningrad, on a plain between the Russian town of Luzhaika and the Finnish city of Imatra, the train rails crossed the border. There was no fence. There were shunting yards and customs sheds and discreet radio bunkers on each side. Dirty snow lay on the Russian side because Russian trains on this spur burned low-grade coal, and cleaner snow on the Finnish side because the Finns used diesels.

Arkady stood with the commandant of the Soviet Border Patrol station and watched a Finnish major return to the Finnish Frontier Guard post fifty meters away.

'Like the Swiss.' The commandant spat. 'They'd sweep all the soot on our side if they had the nerve.' He made a halfhearted attempt to fasten the red tabs of his collar. The Border Patrol was an arm of the KGB but was staffed largely by veterans of the regular Army. The commandant's neck was too thick, his nose aimed sideways, and his brows were an honest mismatch. 'Every month he asks me what to do with that damned chest. How the devil should I know?'

He framed Arkady's match with his hands so that they each could light their cigarettes. A Soviet guard watched from the track, an assault rifle that looked like a plumber's tool hanging from his shoulder. Every time the guard shifted, the weapon rattled in the wind.

'You're aware that a chief investigator from Moscow has about as much authority here as a Chinaman,' the commandant told Arkady.

'You know Moscow around May Day,' Arkady said. 'By the time everybody stamps my papers I'd have another victim on my hands.'

Across the border the major led a pair of frontier guards to a customs shed. Beyond, foothills led to the Finnish lake country. Here the land was ironed flat and sprinkled with alders, ash, bilberry shrubs. Good country to patrol.

'The smugglers here bring in coffee,' the commandant said, 'butter, sometimes nothing but money. For foreign-currency shops, you know. They never smuggle anything out. I guess that's insulting. Pretty unusual, a case of yours bringing you all the way out here.'

'Nice here,' Arkady said.

'Quiet here. You can get away from it all.' The commandant pulled a steel flask from inside his jacket. 'Do you like this stuff?'

'Probably.' Arkady took the offered draw on the flask and body-heated brandy rolled to his stomach.

'Some men can't take it guarding a border – guarding an imaginary line, you know. They actually go crazy. Or they allow themselves to be corrupted. Sometimes they actually try to cross the border themselves. I should have them shot, but I just send them back to have their heads examined. You know, Investigator, if I met a man who came out here from Moscow without any clearance to sweet-talk the Border Patrol, I'd have his head examined too.'

'Frankly' – Arkady met the commandant's eyes – 'so would I.'

'Well' – the commandant's brows lifted and he slapped Arkady on the back – 'let's see what we can do with this Finn. He's a Communist, but you can fry a Finn in butter, and he's still a Finn.'

The customs shed across the border opened. The Finnish major returned carrying an envelope.

'Was our investigator right?' the commandant asked.

The major dropped the envelope with distaste into Arkady's hands. 'Turds. Small animal turds in six compartments inside the chest. How did you know?'

'The chest was out of its case?' Arkady asked.

'We opened it,' the commandant said. 'All packing is opened on the Soviet side.'

'Would the inside of the chest have been inspected?' Arkady asked.

'What would be the point in that,' the Finn answered, 'relations between Finland and the Soviet Union being what they are?'

'And what is the procedure for claiming articles from the customs shed?' Arkady asked the major.

'Very simple. Very few goods are ever in the shed; they usually stay on the train until Helsinki. No one can remove any goods without papers of identity and of possession, and also import-duty receipts. We don't have a man at the door, but we would have noticed if anyone had tried to carry out a chest. Understand, we maintain a very light force of men here by agreement with the

Soviet Union in order to avoid provocations with a friendly neighbor. Now you must excuse me; I am off duty, and I have a long drive home for the holiday.'

'For May Day,' Arkady said.

'Walpurgis Night.' The Finn enjoyed correcting him. 'Witches' sabbath.'

From Vyborg, close to the border, Arkady flew to Leningrad, and there caught the evening plane to Moscow. Most of the passengers on the flight were military on two days' leave, and were drinking already.

Arkady wrote a report of the investigation. He put it into the evidence bag along with the border commandant's statement, the envelope of droppings from the chest, fur samples from Kostia's cage, personal effects from the footlockers of the three victims, the tape of Irina's testimony in the cabin, and the February 2 tape of Osborne and Unmann. He had addressed the bag to the prosecutor general. A stewardess handed out hard candy.

Within hours Osborne and Kirwill would board their flight. More than ever, Arkady appreciated how finely Osborne timed his entrances and exits. 'Even a delay . . .' Unmann had worried the day before the chest concealing Kostia Borodin's six Siberian sables was shipped from Moscow. How long could small animals be drugged with safety? Three hours? Four? Enough for the flight to Leningrad, certainly. Then Unmann could have given them another dose on the way from the airport to the train station. The chest couldn't be flown out of the country because international air packages were X-rayed. Cars and their contents were virtually dismantled at checkpoints. The train was the answer, a local train to an undermanned border station, while Osborne drove back from Helsinki to the Finnish side of the border station before the chest even came off the train. The Soviet Border patrol did the job of opening the packing case. The Finns had done Osborne the favor of leaving the chest unguarded in a shed. Did anyone even notice him going in? Did he have a special coat made with pouches? Was there an accomplice among the Finnish guards? No matter, Osborne had never had to show papers and there was no link between him and the chest from the start of its journey to its conclusion.

Kostia Borodin, Valerya Davidova and James Kirwill had died in Gorky Park. John Osborne had six Barguzin sables somewhere outside the Soviet Union.

The plane descended from a sunset to Moscow at night.

In the airport, Arkady mailed the package. Taking the holiday into account, his report would reach its destination in four days no matter what happened to him.

The courtyard was watched. Arkady entered the basement from the alley and climbed the stairs to his apartment, where he changed in the dark into his chief investigator's uniform. The uniform was navy blue with a captain's four brass stars on the epaulets and a red star on the gold braid of his cap. As he shaved he heard the televisions in the apartments above and below. Both were tuned to the Bolshoi's traditional May Day Eve performance of *Swan Lake* in the Kremlin's Palace of Congresses. During the overture he made out an announcer's voice noting the most honored and most beloved of the evening's six thousand guests, but he couldn't pick out the names. He tucked his automatic inside his uniform jacket.

Out on Taganskaya Boulevard, it took him twenty minutes to wave down a taxi. The ride into the central city was accompanied by floodlights and banners. All year Moscow had been a dour chrysalis for red banners that sprang to life mothlike to the lights of this one night. Red wings draped every high building, and billowed over wide avenues. Letters marched: LENIN LIVED, LIVES AND WILL LIVE FOREVER! The taxi overtook them. HEROIC WORKERS . . . NOBLE AND HISTORICALLY UNPRECEDENTED . . . APPLAUDS . . . IN GLORY . . .

No public traffic was allowed in the blocks around Red Square. Arkady paid his last rubles to the taxi driver and walked to Sverdlov Square just as William Kirwill came out of the Metropole Hotel carrying a suitcase to an Intourist bus. Kirwill was dressed in a tan raincoat and a short-brimmed tweed hat, and he looked like any of the other dozen or so Americans lining up at the bus. When Arkady was still crossing the garden in the center of the square, Kirwill saw him and shook his head. Arkady stopped. Looking around, he saw militia detectives in a car behind the bus, in the hotel café, at the street corners. Kirwill set the suitcase down; it was still dented from Arkady's kicks. Another bus pulled out; the passing glare of headlights made Kirwill's presence all the more temporary. Kirwill made a point of looking in the direction of each detective in case Arkady had missed any. The Intourist driver sauntered out of the hotel, threw a cigarette on the street and allowed the tourists to board.

'Osborne,' Arkady mouthed from the center of the square.

William Kirwill took a last look at the investigator. Clearly, he'd missed the name. He wanted it desperately, but he knew that to get it he would have to kill all the plainclothesmen watching him in the square, and all the plainclothesmen that followed, and beat down the buildings of the square and all the buildings of the city, and not even his great strength was equal to that.

Swan Lake wafted from the bus radio. Kirwill was the last to board. By then Arkady was gone.

Hammers and spaceships fashioned from flowers waited in Dzerzhinsky Square for the morning's parade. Arkady jumped onto a personnel carrier of soldiers, and they rode past the empty grandstands in Red Square. Flood-lights made the Kremlin walls hover, the swallowtail battlements shiver.

Along Manezhnaya Street on the other side of the Kremlin, limousines were drawn into black, glossy, diag-onal ranks. Not just ordinary Chaika limousines but the Presidium's Zils, armor-plated and spiked with antennae. Militiamen on foot were spaced along the middle of the street, and others on motorcycles traveled back and forth from the more open space of Manezhnaya Square to the Kremlin's Kutafia Tower, where Arkady jumped from the personnel carrier. His uniform his identification, he explained to the KGB officer who approached that he had a message for the prosecutor general. He controlled his hands as he lit a cigarette, and moved away from the floodlights welling out of the sunken gardens up over the short whitewashed bridge that connected the Kutafia Tower to the Kremlin's Trinity Gate. He moved casually across the street into the high shadow of the Manezh, the czar's riding school. From there he could see the white marble roof line of the Palace of Congresses over the Kremlin wall. As a car of KGB officers went by, he heard the ballet's last movement, a valse, on the car radio. Along the Manezh, other shadows stirred – an eye here, a foot there.

Above the Trinity Gate, swarms of moths, real ones bright as crystal, climbed to the ruby star of Trinity Tower. Two soldiers emerging from the gate were backlit into their own shadows until they crossed the little bridge, where they seemed consumed like match heads by light. Another car of KGB went by trailing radio applause. The ballet was over.

To get to the airport on time, Osborne would have to pass up the official reception after the performance. Even so, there were curtain calls, bouquets for the ballerinas and the Presidium, and the inevitable struggle at the cloakroom. Chauffeurs ambled to their limousines.

Guests started to appear. Arkady watched a long line of Chinese, then Navy men in dress whites, some Westerners laughing loudly, Africans laughing even louder, musicians, women in ushers' uniforms holding flowers, a well-known satirist alone. Limousines with diplomatic flags rolled off with passengers. The rush of early goers thinned and the bridge to the sidewalk emptied. There was no apparent reason for Arkady to start for the street.

A figure walking briskly, elegant as a knife, approached the Trinity Gate. It passed through to the lights of the bridge and became Osborne pulling on gloves, eyes straight ahead to the alert faces of plainclothesmen and the open doors of limousines. He wore a sober black coat and the same sable hat he had offered to Arkady. The dark fur contrasted with his silver hair. The attention of the plainclothesmen shifted to guests following Osborne. He vanished into the Kutafia Tower, emerged on its steps and was off the sidewalk heading for a limousine that had pulled out for him before he saw Arkady coming.

Arkady felt the shock of recognition in the American, a tremor so quickly controlled that it was no more than an extra beat of the heart. They met at the limousine, facing each other over the car roof.

Osborne showed a bright, powerful smile. 'You never came for your hat, Investigator.'

'No.'

'Your investigation—'

'It's over,' Arkady said.

Osborne nodded. Arkady had time to admire the touches of gold and silk around the body, the look like wood of tanned skin, features so un-Russian. He saw Osborne's eyes travel up and down the street to see whether Arkady had come alone. Satisfied, the gaze returned to Arkady.

'I have a plane to catch, Investigator. Unmann will bring you ten thousand dollars American in a week. You can have it in another currency if you wish – Hans will handle the details. The main thing is that everyone is content. If Iamskoy does go under and you keep me clear, I would consider that another service worth even more. I congratulate you; you've not only survived but you've made the most of your opportunity.'

'Why do you say all this?' Arkady asked.

'You haven't come to arrest me. You haven't the evidence. Besides, I know the way you people operate. If this were an arrest, I'd be in the back of a KGB car and headed for the Lubyanka right now. It's just you, Investigator – you alone. Look around – I see friends of mine, but none of yours.'

So far the plainclothesmen had taken no special notice of Osborne's delay. At close distance they were characteristically beefy men vigorously hurrying ordinary guests away from the cars of the elite.

'You would try to arrest a Westerner, here of all places, tonight of all nights, without a signed order from the KGB, without even the knowledge of your prosecutor, without anyone else at all, all by yourself? You, a man wanted for murder? They'd put you in an asylum. I wouldn't even miss my plane; they'd hold it for me. So all you could have come for was money. Why not? You've already made the prosecutor a rich man.'

Arkady brought out his automatic and rested it in the

crook of his left elbow, where only Osborne could see the dull muzzle. 'No,' he said.

Osborne glanced around. Plainclothesmen were all about, but distracted by the growing stream of guests emerging through the floodlights.

'Iamskoy warned me that you were like this. You don't want money, do you?' Osborne asked.

'No.'

'You're going to try to arrest me?'

'Stop you,' Arkady said. 'Keep you off your plane, to begin with. Then, not arrest you here and not tonight. We'll take your car. We'll take a drive tonight, and tomorrow we'll show up at the KGB office in some small town. They won't know what to do, so they'll call the Lubyanka direct. People in small towns are afraid of state crimes, the theft of valuable state property, sabotage of a national industry, smuggling, the concealment of state crimes – by which I mean murder. I will be treated very skeptically and you will be treated very politely, but you know how we operate. There will have to be more phone calls made, cages thoroughly inspected, a certain chest transported. After all, once you miss tonight's plane you're already late. It's worth a chance, anyway.'

'Where did you go yesterday?' Osborne asked after a moment's thought. 'No one could find you.'

Arkady said nothing.

'I think you made a trip to the border yesterday,' Osborne said. 'I think you believe you know everything.' He checked his watch. 'I'm going to have to run for that plane. I'm not staying.'

'Then I will shoot you,' Arkady said.

'You'd be shot a second later by every man here.'

'True.'

Osborne reached for the door handle. Arkady began squeezing the Makarov's spitcurl trigger, pulling forward the releasing lever, which slid along the magazine against and then away from the leaf spring, which would slap the cleared hammer toward the 9-mm. round in the breech.

Osborne released the handle. 'Why?' he asked. 'You can't be willing to die simply to make an arrest to please Soviet justice. Everyone is bought, from the top to the bottom. The whole country's bought – bought cheap, cheapest in the world. You don't care about breaking laws, you're not that stupid anymore. So what is there to die for? Someone else? Irina Asanova?'

Osborne pointed to a coat pocket, then slowly put his hand into the pocket and drew out a red-white-and-green scarf decorated with Easter eggs, the scarf that Arkady had bought for Irina. 'Life is always more complicated and simpler than we give it credit for,' he said. 'It is – I see it in your face.'

'How did you get this?'

'A simple exchange, Investigator. Me for her. I'll tell you where she is, and you really don't have time to worry whether I'm lying or not because she won't be there long. Yes or no?'

Osborne placed the scarf on the car roof. Arkady gathered it in his left hand and raised it to his nose. It smelled of Irina.

'Understand,' Osborne said, 'we each have one basic demand for which we will destroy everything else. You will throw away your life, career and reason for that woman. I will betray my accomplices rather than miss my plane. We are both running out of time.'

The limousines were backing up. The nearer plain-clothesmen shouted and waved for Osborne to get into his car.

'Yes or no?' Osborne asked.

There was no decision to make. Arkady stuffed the scarf inside his uniform. 'You tell me where she is,' he said. 'If I believe you, you're free. If I don't, I kill you.'

'Fair enough. She's at the university, in the garden near the pool.'

'Repeat it.' Arkady leaned forward, increasing his pressure on the trigger.

'The university, in the garden near the pool.'

This time Osborne had steadied himself reflexively to take the bullet, his head tilted slightly back but his eyes locked on Arkady's. For the first time he allowed the investigator to see him. A beast looked out through Osborne's eyes, something leashed by its own hand, a creature that inhabited his coat and skin. Osborne's eyes had no fear at all.

'I'll take your car.' Arkady slipped the gun into his coat. 'You can probably buy the next one in line.'

'I love Russia.' Osborne whispered it.

'Go home, Mr Osborne.' Arkady got into the limousine.

The university glowed. Beneath a golden star within a golden wreath descended a floodlit spire and ruby stars and thirty-two floors empty of students gone for the May Day vacation. Around the wings of the university enormous gardens five hundred meters wide spread over the Lenin Hills. For May Day Eve the gardens were lit a soft dark green. In this deminight, clay paths spoked away from outsized fountains to wander through hedges, to vanish into stands of fir and spruce, or to stumble haphazardly into statues.

The front garden facing the river had a long reflecting pool foaming with water jets and tinted by colored lights. The city night was lit by mile-high beams that waved from antiaircraft installations along the embankments.

Osborne had escaped effortlessly. He had produced Arkady's heart with Irina's scarf. Yet Arkady was sure that Irina was here. It was a trap, not a lie.

The light show from the embankments lasted for half an hour. At last the colored lights of the pool died and the water jets subsided, and on the stilling surface of the pool emerged a mirror of the university spire.

He waited among the firs. Osborne's plane would be in the air now. The trees rustled, giving off a scent of resin as a breeze came up. From the far end of the pool two shadows walked toward him.

Midway to Arkady, the shadows fell and the image on the water broke. Arkady ran, drawing his gun. He made out Unmann straddling a body over the edge of the pool, then Irina as she pulled her head free of the water. Unmann pushed her under again, and she reached backward, scratching. Unmann twisted her long hair into a bun, the better to hold her still. He looked up at

Arkady's shout. The German had eyes set in hollows and protruding teeth. He let Irina go. She pulled herself out of the water and gagged against the side of the pool. Damp hair swept over her face.

'Get up,' Arkady ordered Unmann.

Unmann stayed on his knees, grinning. Arkady felt warm metal softly brush the short hairs at the base of his skull.

'Instead' – Iamskoy closed the last step behind Arkady – 'why don't you throw your gun down?'

Arkady did as he was told, and Iamskoy laid a consoling hand on his shoulder. Arkady could see the pink ends of the fingers. The gun, the same issue as Arkady's, nestled at the back of his neck. 'Don't do it,' he said to the prosecutor.

'Arkady Vasilevich, how can I avoid it? If you had done as you were directed, neither of us would be here now. This sad occasion wouldn't be. But you're out of control. You're my responsibility, and I have to clean up this affair not only for my own sake but also because of the office we both represent. Right or wrong has nothing to do with it. Which is not to denigrate your talents. There's not another investigator with your powers of intuition, your resourcefulness or your integrity. I counted on them heavily.' Unmann rose and slowly sidled forward. 'I thought I was a student of you, and you—'

While Iamskoy braced him, Unmann punched Arkady in the stomach, pulling his fist away with a curious flourish. Arkady looked down and saw a slim knife handle protruding from his stomach. He felt a sensation of ice inside himself and couldn't breathe.

'And you surprised me,' Iamskoy went on. 'Most of all, you surprise me by coming here to save a tramp. Which is interesting, because Osborne wasn't surprised at all.'

Arkady's eyes filled helplessly with Irina.

'Be honest with yourself,' Iamskoy suggested, 'and admit I'm doing you a favor. Besides your father's name, you're losing nothing – no wife, no children, no political consciousness and no future. You remember the upcoming campaign against Vronskyism? You would have been the first to go. That's the sort of thing that happens to individualists. I warned you about it for years. You see what comes of ignoring advice. Believe me, this way is better. Why don't you sit down?'

Iamskoy and Unmann stepped back for him to fall, and Arkady's knees trembled and started to give way. He pulled out the knife. It seemed to come out forever, double-edged and sharp and red. German workmanship, Arkady thought. A hot rush poured down the inside of his uniform. Without warning he swung the knife into Unmann's stomach at the same spot that Unmann had driven it into him. The force of his thrust carried them both into the pool.

They rose together from the water. Unmann tried to push away, but Arkady single-mindedly lodged the knife deeper and jerked it upward. Along the edge of the pool, Iamskoy ran back and forth for a clear shot. Unmann began boxing his ears, and Arkady clung all the tighter, lifting the other man in an embrace. Unable to break

free, Unmann tried to bite, and Arkady fell back, carrying the man down into the water with him. There the
German sat on top, squeezing Arkady's throat. He looked
up from the bottom of the pool. Unmann's face grim-
aced, fluttered, divided, ran back together and split apart
again like quicksilver, each time less coherently. It broke
into moons, and the moons broke into petals. Then a
dark cloud of red obscured Unmann, his hands went
slack and he slid out of view.

Arkady came up gasping. Unmann's body bobbed
alongside.

'Stay there!'

Arkady heard Iamskoy's shout; he couldn't move
anyway.

Iamskoy stood at the side of the pool, aiming at him.
There was the boom of a large automatic, deafening in
the open garden, though Arkady hadn't seen the gun
flash he'd expected. He noticed that Iamskoy's hat was
gone, replaced by a jagged crown that sat on Iamskoy's
shaved skull. The prosecutor wiped blood away from his
brow in a distracted fashion, but his head produced a
profusion of more blood, a fountain. Irina was behind
Iamskoy, holding a gun. She fired again, whipping Iamskoy's head around, and Arkady saw that an ear was
gone. She fired a third time, through Iamskoy's chest.
The prosecutor tried to keep his balance. On the fourth
shot he pitched into the water and sank.

Irina came into the pool to drag Arkady out. She was
lifting him over the side when Iamskoy rose to his waist
out of the water beside them. He fell backward without

seeing them, his eyes straight up to the night, and bellowed, 'Osborne!'

He sank again as if he were walking down a staircase, yet Arkady heard the shout long after he had disappeared.

Part Two

SHATURA

Chapter One

He was a conduit. Tubes flowed into him carrying blood and dextrose; tubes flowed out of him taking blood and wastes. Every few hours when he was afraid of consciousness, a nurse would inject him with morphine, and at once he would float above the bed and look down at the gray-faced sewage operation below.

He had no clear idea why he was there. It was vaguely in his mind that he'd killed someone, and it struck him as typical that it should have been a piece of butchery. He was uncertain whether he was criminal or victim; he worried some about this, but not much. Mostly he sat up in the far, high corner of the room and observed. Nurses and doctors constantly hovered and whispered at the bed, and then the doctors would walk over and whisper to two more men in street clothes and sterile masks who sat by the door, and they in their turn would open the door to whisper to more men waiting in the hall. Once a group of visitors arrived; among them he recognized the prosecutor general. The entire delegation stood at the foot of the bed and studied the face on the pillow in the somber manner of vacationers at a foreign landmark trying to decipher an inscription they could not understand. Finally they shook their heads, ordered the doctors to keep the patient alive and left. Another time a captain in the Border patrol was ushered in to identify him. He didn't care because at that moment he was busy hemorrhaging, a secret revealed by all the tubes running from his body, every plastic byway a sudden, generous red.

Later he was belted into bed, and surrounded by a translucent plastic tent. The belts didn't constrict him – he hadn't planned to use his arms – but somehow the tent kept him from floating away anymore. He sensed that the doctors were cutting back on the morphine. By day he was dully aware of colors moving around him, and by night of a burst of fear when the room door opened to the lights outside. The fear was important; he sensed this as well. Of all the hallucinations of his opiated state, only the fear was real.

Time measured by hypodermic needles did not pass; it was only an edge between limbo and pain. What existed was the waiting, not his own but that of the men by the door and the men outside it. He knew they were waiting for him.

'Irina!' he said aloud.

At once he heard the scrape of chairs and saw shapes hurrying to his tent. As its walls were drawn back, he closed his eyes and jerked his arms against its belt as hard as he could. A tube jumped free and blood spewed from the hole in his arm. Steps ran in from the door.

'I told you not to touch him,' a nurse said. She pressed the vein shut and taped the tube back into his arm.

'We didn't.'

'He didn't do this himself.' The nurse was angry. 'He's not even conscious. Look at this mess!'

His eyes closed, he imagined the sheets and floor. The

nurse was only furious, but a bloody mess in a hospital terrified and intimidated anyone else, even dull souls from the KGB. He heard them on their knees wiping the floor. They said not another word about his being awake.

Where was Irina? What had she told them?

'They're going to shoot him anyway,' one of the men wiping the floor muttered.

In his translucent tent he listened; he intended to listen to everything while he could.

In the minutes before the militia had arrived at the university garden, Arkady told Irina what her story should be. Irina had killed no one; Arkady had killed both Iamskoy and Unmann. Irina knew that Valerya, James Kirwill and Kostia were in Moscow – that was all in the tapes – but she knew nothing about any defections or smuggling. She was a dupe, a lure, a victim, not a criminal. If the story wasn't plausible or neat, it had to be said in his defense that he had put it together while Irina was holding his stomach together. Besides, the story was her only chance.

They started off the first interrogation by reading off the crimes he was accused of: the crimes were familiar, generally the same he'd accused Osborne and Iamskoy of. One wall of the tent was pulled back so that the three men could sit close to the bed. In spite of sterile masks he recognized the squat face of Major Pribluda, and behind the mask a smile.

'You're dying,' the nearest of them told Arkady. 'The least you can do is clear the name of those who are innocent. You had an excellent record until this happened, and that's the kind of record we want to remember you by. Clear the good name of Prosecutor Iamskoy, a man who befriended you and promoted you. Your father is an old man in poor health; at least let him die in peace. Wipe away this shame and meet your own death with a clear conscience. What do you say?'

'I'm not dying,' Arkady said.

'You're doing damned well, you know.' The doctor opened the drapes. He smoothed the sunshine that poured onto his white coat. The tent had been removed and Arkady now had two pillows propped under his head.

'How well?'

'Very,' the doctor said, gravely enough for Arkady to understand that the man had been waiting weeks to be asked. 'The knife penetrated your colon, stomach and diaphragm, and also took a nick out of your liver. In fact, the one thing your friend missed was what he was probably aiming for, the abdominal aorta. Still, you had no blood pressure when you came in; then we had to contend with infection, peritonitis, filling you with anti-biotics with one hand and draining you with the other. That pool you were in was filthy. The one fortunate thing was that apparently you hadn't eaten for twenty-four hours previous to being stabbed; otherwise the spread of infection would have been straight through your digestive tract, and not even we could have saved you. Amazing, isn't it, how life can turn on a bite of food, something as insignificant as that? You're a lucky man.'

'Now I know.'

The next time five of them came, again wearing sterile masks, and sat around the bed asking questions in turn so that Arkady would become confused. He chose to answer Pribluda no matter who spoke.

'The Asanova woman has told us everything,' someone said. 'You masterminded the conspiracy along with the American, Osborne, promising protection against the efforts of Prosecutor Iamskoy.'

'You have the report I sent to the prosecutor general,' Arkady answered Pribluda.

'You were seen speaking with Osborne on numerous occasions, including May Day Eve. You didn't arrest him. Instead you went directly to the university, where you lured the prosecutor into a trap and killed him with the aid of the woman.'

'You have my report.'

'What excuse do you have for your contacts with Osborne? The prosecutor always made notes after his meetings with his investigators. There is nothing in any of his notes about your so-called suspicions concerning the American. If you had mentioned it, he would immediately have conferred with the organ of security.'

'You have my report.'

'We aren't interested in your report. The report only condemns you. No investigator could have ascertained a

theft of sables in Siberia or how those sables were taken
out of the country from the flimsy evidence you had.'

'I did.'

It was the only time his answer varied. He was accused
of conspiring with Osborne for money; his divorce was
cited as proof of a mental collapse; it was known that he
had bothered Osborne for the gift of a valuable hat; the
Asanova woman had described his offensive sexual
advances; he had encouraged Osborne's scheme, hoping
for the coup of a sensational arrest in the face of a campaign against careerists such as himself; proof of his violent nature was his assault on the secretary of the District
Committee, a friend of his former wife; his link to the
foreign agent James Kirwill was made manifest by his col-
laboration with the brother agent William Kirwill; he had
clubbed to death an officer of the KGB at the prosecutor's
dacha; according to the Asanova woman, he'd had sexual
relations with the dead female gangster Valerya Davidova;
he was psychologically crippled by his father's name – to
sum up, all was known. To every attempt to anger, confuse
and terrify, Arkady told Pribluda to read his report.

Pribluda was the one man who didn't speak, the one
who was content with silent menace, a warted brooding
under wetted hair. Arkady remembered him best wrapped in a coat in the snow on that first morning in Gorky
Park. He hadn't appreciated how much space he'd taken
in Pribluda's mind until now. In their concentration,
Pribluda's eyes were startlingly candid. All was *not*
known; *nothing* was known.

*

When the guards were dismissed, a telephone was brought into the room. As the phone never rang and no one ever used it to place a call, Arkady assumed that it was a transmitter to listen to him. The first time he was allowed soft food he could hear the cart bringing it all the way from the elevator to his door. Every other room on the floor was empty.

The five men returned for interrogation twice a day for two more days, and Arkady continued to repeat his single answer until a miraculously germinating seed of understanding burst within him.

'Iamskoy was one of you,' he interrupted. 'He was KGB. You made one of your own into Moscow town prosecutor, and now he turns out the next thing to a traitor. You have to put a bullet in my head just because he made such enormous fools out of you.'

Four of the five men looked at each other sharply; only Pribluda maintained his attention on Arkady.

'As Iamskoy said' – Arkady laughed painfully – ' "We all breathe air and we all piss water." '

'Shut your mouth!'

The five men adjourned to the hall. Arkady lay in bed and thought of the prosecutor's lectures about the correct jurisdictions of the organs of justice, so much more amusing in retrospect. The five men didn't return. After a while, guards showed up for the first time in a week and placed the five chairs against a wall.

*

As soon as he was allowed to walk alone with canes he went to the window. He found he was six stories up, near a highway and practically within reach of a candy factory. It was the Bolshevik Candy Factory, he realized, off the Leningrad Road, though he couldn't recall any hospitals this far out. He tried to open the window but it was locked.

A nurse came in. 'We don't want you to hurt yourself,' she said.

He didn't want to hurt himself; he wanted to smell the chocolate from the factory. He could have cried for not smelling the chocolate.

He would feel an abundance of strength, and the next moment be ready to dissolve into tears. Part of this was the strain of the questioning. It was standard for interrogators to work as a team, massing their will against that of a single suspect, outflanking and confusing him with false charges, the wilder the better, bullying him this way and that until he was at their mercy. *That* was an honest man, a man on his knees. As a general rule it wasn't bad, so he expected them to use the technique; it was normal.

Part of the problem was his isolation. He was allowed no visitors, no conversation with the guards or nurses, no books, no radio. He found himself reading the factory markings on utensils, and standing by the window watching the traffic on the highway. His sole intelligent occupation was sorting through the many contradictory questions to determine what was happening to Irina.

She was alive. She hadn't told everything and she knew he hadn't either; otherwise the interrogation would be far more accurate and damaging. Why had he concealed her knowledge of smuggling? When had he brought her to his apartment? What happened there?

After a day without interrogation, Nikitin came. Shrewd eyes in a round face, the senior investigator for Government Liaison regarded his colleague and former pupil with sighs of disappointment.

'The last time we saw each other you pointed a gun at me,' Nikitin said. 'That was almost a month ago. You look a little calmed down now.'

'I don't know what I look like. I don't have a mirror.'

'How do you shave?'

'They bring me an electric razor with my breakfast and take it away with the tray.' Given somebody to talk to, even Nikitin, he felt positively effusive. And there had been a time years ago when Nikitin was senior investigator for Homicide that they'd been close.

'Well, I can't stay.' Nikitin produced an envelope. 'The office is in an uproar, as you can understand. They sent me over with these for you to sign.'

In the envelope were three copies of a letter of resignation from the prosecutor's office for reasons of health. Arkady signed them, almost sad that Nikitin had to rush off.

'I get the impression,' Nikitin whispered, 'that you're giving them quite a wrestle. It's not easy to interrogate an interrogator, eh?'

411

'I guess not.'

'Look, you're a clever boy, don't be modest. Maybe you should have listened to your uncle Ilya a little bit more, though. I tried to steer you right. It's all my fault; I should have been firmer. Anything I can do to help, you just ask.'

Arkady sat down. He felt immensely depressed and tired, and grateful that Nikitin was taking the time to stay. Nikitin was now sitting on the bed, although Arkady couldn't recall seeing him move.

'Ask me,' Nikitin suggested.

'Irina . . .'

'What about her?'

It was difficult for Arkady to concentrate. All the secrets he had hoarded pressed with urgency for Nikitin's sympathetic ear. His only other visitor that day had been a nurse who had given him an injection just before Nikitin's arrival.

'I'm the only one who can help you,' Nikitin said.

'They don't know . . .'

'Yes?'

Arkady felt nauseated and dizzy. Nikitin's hand, as small and plump as a baby's, rested on his.

'What you need now is a friend,' Nikitin said.

'The nurse—'

'Is no friend of yours. She gave you something to make you talk.'

'I know.'

'Don't tell them anything, boychik,' Nikitin urged.

Sodium aminate, Arkady guessed; that was what they used.

412

'Quite a lot of it, too.'

He knows what I'm thinking, Arkady told himself.

'It's a very strong narcotic. You can't be held responsible for not having your usual control,' Nikitin reassured him.

'You didn't have to bring the letters.' Arkady made a point out of speaking distinctly and loudly. 'No one needs those letters.'

'Then you didn't take a good look at them.' Nikitin produced the envelope again and opened it for Arkady. 'See?'

Blinking, Arkady reread the letters. They were confessions of all the crimes he had been accused of for the last week. 'That's not what I signed,' he said.

'They have your signature. I saw you sign them. Never mind.' Nikitin tore the letters into halves and then quarters. 'I don't believe a word of it.'

'Thank you,' Arkady said gratefully.

'I'm on your side; it's us against them. Remember, I was the best interrogator of all, you remember that.'

Arkady remembered. Nikitin leaned forward confidentially and spoke softly into Arkady's ear. 'I came to warn you. They're going to kill you.'

Arkady looked at the closed door. Its very flatness was ominous, a façade for the people on the other side.

'After you're dead, who's going to help Irina?' Nikitin asked. 'Who's going to know the truth?'

'My report—'

'Is to fool *them*, not your friends. Don't think of yourself, think of Irina. Without me she'll be all alone. Think how alone she'll be.'

They probably wouldn't even tell her he was dead, Arkady thought.

'The only way she'll know I'm afraid is if you tell me the truth,' Nikitin explained.

There was no doubt that they were going to kill him; Arkady saw no escape from that. Maybe a fall from the window, an overdose of morphine, an injection of air. Who would look after Irina then?

'We're old friends,' Nikitin said. 'I'm your friend. I want to be your friend. Believe me, I'm your friend.' He smiled like a buddha.

The rest of Arkady's vision was tinged gray by the sodium aminate. He heard the collective breathing in the halls. The floor was far below his feet. Corpses wore paper slippers; they'd given him paper slippers. His feet were so white and sickly, what did the rest of him look like? His mouth was a pesthole of fear. He brought his fists up to his forehead. Not fear – insanity. Thinking as a process was impossible; better to tell everything now while he could. But he clamped his mouth over the words. A narcotic sweat broke from his skin, and he was afraid that words were coming from his pores. He brought his knees up tight together until they cramped, so that every orifice was shut. When he thought about Irina, the words would start to force their way out like a snake, so he thought about Nikitin – not the Nikitin beside him on the bed because that was an insistent friend who had torn up a confession, but the Nikitin of before. The old Nikitin was an elusive subject, slipping and teasing the short grasp of Arkady's mind. The paranoia of the moment overwhelmed memory. The only man in the world he could trust was Nikitin, the Nikitin beside him insisted. He trembled and tried to cover his eyes and ears, working backward from Nikitin's last words to the ones just before those, and so on, in this clumsy way examining the new Nikitin for a clue to the old.

'I am your oldest and dearest and one friend,' Nikitin said.

Arkady brought his hands down. Tears covered his face, but there was a glow of relief in his head. He raised one hand as if it held a gun and pulled an imaginary trigger.

'What's the matter?' Nikitin asked.

Arkady didn't speak because the words about Irina were still waiting to spring from his mouth. He smiled, though. Nikitin shouldn't have mentioned the episode of the gun when he'd first arrived in Arkady's room; that was the connection. He aimed at Nikitin's face and pretended to fire again.

'I'm your friend,' Nikitin said with less conviction.

Arkady squeezed off a full magazine of invisible bullets, reloaded and fired some more. Something of his insanity penetrated Nikitin. After much protesting he fell silent; then, recoiling from Arkady's empty hand, he edged from the bed. Like the Nikitin of old, he moved faster the closer he got to the door.

Chapter Two

At the start of the summer Arkady was moved to an estate in the country. It was an old aristocratic affair with a brave front of white columns and French doors, porticoes to glass conservatories, its own little church used as a garage, and a clay tennis court on which the guards played volleyball all the time. Arkady was free to wander where he wished as long as he returned in time for supper.

The first week a small plane touched down on the landing strip with a pair of interrogators, Major Pribluda, a mail pouch and such items as fresh meat and fruit that were available only from Moscow.

Interrogations took place twice a day in a conservatory. No plants were left except some giant rubber trees, hunched and as out of place as formal servants. Arkady sat in a wicker chair between the interrogators. One of them was a psychiatrist and the questions were clever; as usual when questioning is friendly, there was a smarmy bonhomie in the air.

During lunch on the third day Arkady encountered Pribluda alone in a garden. His jacket hung over the back of a wrought-iron chair, the major was cleaning his gun, gross fingers dexterously handling pins, springs and rag. He looked up in surprise when Arkady took the chair across the table.

'What's the matter?' Arkady asked. 'Why do they leave you out here?'

'It's not my job to question you,' Pribluda said. His ugly, honest eyes had become a constant to Arkady, and a relief after a morning with the other officers the KGB had sent. 'Anyway, they're specialists; they know what they're doing.'

'Then why are you here?'

'I volunteered.'

'How long will you be here?'

'As long as the interrogators are.'

'You only brought a change of shirts; that's not long,' Arkady said.

Pribluda nodded and went on cleaning, developing a sweat in the sun. He hadn't even rolled up his sleeves, although he worked so carefully that there was no danger of dirtying them with oil.

'If it's not your job to question me, what is your job?' Arkady asked.

Pribluda pushed the gun's slide and barrel assembly forward and out of the guides of the receiver. From the receiver he daintily picked out the subassembly and hammer mechanism. A stripped gun always struck Arkady as a cripple undressed.

'You mean it's your job to kill me, Major. Speak up – you volunteered.'

'You speak about your life very lightly.' Pribluda slipped the rounds out one by one from the magazine like lozenges.

'That's because it's being treated lightly. If you're going

to shoot me when you run out of clean shirts, how serious can I be?'

Arkady didn't believe that Pribluda would kill him. Pribluda had gladly volunteered to, no doubt, and was primed to do so hour by hour, but Arkady didn't believe that it would happen. So the next morning when the interrogators and Pribluda rushed by car to the landing strip, Arkady followed the kilometer's distance on foot. He arrived in time to see Pribluda outside the plane arguing furiously with the interrogators inside. The plane left without him, and he got back into the car. When the driver asked him if he wanted a ride back, Arkady answered that it was a nice day and he'd walk.

Except for the gentlest undulations the surrounding countryside was flat. In the morning sun his shadow stretched thirty meters along the road, the shadow of a rare tree over a hundred meters. There were few woods to speak of, mostly the occasional rubble and shag of berry bushes. Grass gone wild contained all manner of flowers and young grasshoppers bright as jade. Lying down in the grass, Arkady knew that he was seen by field glasses from the observation walk on top of the main house. He never thought of trying to escape.

Arkady and Pribluda ate at the only table set in a dining room of ghostly dustcloths. In his dirty clothes the major grew testy, loosening his shoulder holster and pulling his shirt away from his armpits. Arkady watched with interest. A man about to be shot always regards the shooter with great interest, and with the fatal shot indefinitely delayed, Arkady had an opportunity to study his would-be executioner closely.

'How do you plan to kill me? From behind, the front? The head or the heart?'

'The mouth,' Pribluda said.

'Outside the house? Inside? A bathroom is easy to clean.'

The major truculently refilled his glass with lemonade. No vodka was allowed at the house, and Arkady was the only one who didn't miss it. After long days of volleyball the guards played table tennis late into the night to go to sleep.

'Citizen Renko, you are no longer a senior investigator, you no longer have any rank or standing of any nature, you are nothing. I can simply tell you to shut up.'

'Ah, but it goes the other way, Major. Now that I am nothing, I don't have to listen to you.'

Almost what Irina had said to him, he thought. How easily perception changes. 'Tell me, Major,' he asked, 'has anyone ever tried to kill you?'

'Only you.' Pribluda pushed his chair away and left his food uneaten.

Out of frustration, Pribluda began working in the garden. Stripped to an undershirt, his pants rolled up above the handkerchiefs tied around his knees, he savaged weeds.

'It's too late to plant anything but radishes, but we do what we can.'

'What's your quota?' Arkady asked from the porch. He squinted up at the sky in search of the plane returning from Moscow.

'This is enjoyment, not work,' the major muttered. 'I'm not going to let you ruin it. Smell that.' He lifted some peat-rich soil to his snout. 'There's no earth anywhere in the world that smells the same.'

The sky was empty, and Arkady turned his gaze down to the major and the handful of dirt. The gesture reminded him too much of Pribluda digging through the bodies in Gorky Park. Arkady thought again of the major's victims at the Kliazma River. Yet here they were in a country garden, Arkady with scars from his ribs to his groin and Pribluda on his knees.

'They found Iamskoy's money. That's what's holding everything up,' Pribluda offered. 'They took his dacha apart board by board, and dug up the whole place. They finally found it under some shed, I hear, where he kept dead ducks and geese. There was a fortune, though I don't understand why he bothered. What was he going to spend it on?'

'Who knows.'

'I said you were innocent. I said right from the start that you were innocent. Detective Fet was a pissant informant, so I'm proud to say I acted on my own instincts. Everyone said no senior investigator would carry out the sort of investigation you claimed to have done contrary to the orders of a prosecutor. I said you would because only I knew how you tried to ruin me. Everyone else said that if Iamskoy was as corrupt as you claimed, then you must be too, and that it was just a case of thieves falling out. I said you'd ruin a man for no good reason at all. I know you. You're the worst kind of hypocrite.'

'How's that?'

'If I follow orders, then you call me a killer. What did I care about those prisoners from Vladimir Prison? There was nothing personal – I didn't even know them. All they were to me were enemies of the state, and I had the job of getting rid of them. Not everything in the world can be done with perfect legality – that's why we are given intelligence. You must have figured out I had orders. But on a whim, out of some hypocritical superiority, you want to bring a case against me – in other words, to kill me for doing my duty. So you're worse than a killer; you're a snob. Go ahead, laugh, but admit there's a difference between duty and sheer egotism.'

'You have a point,' Arkady conceded.

'Aha! Then you knew I was following orders—'

'Whispers,' Arkady said, 'you were following whispers.'

'Whispers, then – so what? What happens to me if I hadn't done it?'

'You leave the KGB, your family doesn't talk to you, you're an embarrassment to your friends, you can't go to special stores anymore, you're moved to a smaller apartment, your children lose their tutors and fail the university examinations, you drop off the rolls for cars, you're never trusted in any new job you're given – and, besides, if you hadn't killed them, someone else would. I had a lousy marriage, no kids, and I didn't especially care if I had a car.'

'My point exactly!'

Arkady went back to watching a jet-vapor trail climb the sky. Nothing that concerned him, unless they planned to bomb him. He listened to Pribluda spading and the soft patter of seeds. As long as he was alive, Irina was alive.

'If I'm innocent, maybe you won't have to shoot me.'

'No one is completely innocent.' The major dug.

The plane ferried in more interrogators, food and changes of clothing for Pribluda. Sometimes the interrogators were different, sometimes the same; some used drugs, some hypnosis, each stayed a night and left. Now that he had fresh clothes, Pribluda dressed every day – when the interrogators were out of sight – in a standard gardening outfit of rolled-up pants, undershirt, handkerchiefs wrapped around his knees and brow, and scuffed shoes. He kept his gun close by, hanging from a stake. Dogged rows of radishes, lettuce and carrots appeared.

'It's going to be a dry summer, I can feel it,' he told Arkady. 'Have to plant a little deeper.'

He would curse and trudge behind when Arkady went on one of his long strolls around the grounds.

'No one's going to run away,' Arkady said. 'You have my promise.'

'There are bogs. They can be dangerous.' The major stayed ten meters behind. 'You don't even know where to step.'

'I'm not a horse. If I break a leg, you won't shoot me.'

For the first time, Arkady heard Pribluda laugh. The major was right, though. Sometimes Arkady would start one of his walks still so doped on sodium pentothal that he could have walked into a tree without knowing it. He walked the way a man walks when he feels it is the only way to find himself. Away from the house and the precautionary towels on the couch for times when an injection made him throw up. Interrogation is largely a process of rebirth done in the clumsiest fashion possible, a system in which the midwife attempts to deliver the same baby a dozen times in a dozen different ways. Arkady walked until the day's poison was diluted with oxygen; then he would sit under a shade tree. To begin with, Pribluda insisted on sitting in the sun; it took him a week to accept the shade.

'I hear this is the last day for you' – Pribluda smirked – 'the last interrogator, the last night. I'll come for you when you're asleep.'

Arkady closed his eyes and listened to the insects. Each week it was a little hotter and the insects were a little louder.

'You want to be buried here?' Pribluda asked. 'Come on, I'm losing patience, let's go.'

'Go cultivate your garden.' He kept his eyes shut and hoped the major would leave.

'You really must hate me,' Pribluda said after a while.

'I don't have time for it.'

'Don't have time for it? You have nothing but time.'

'When I'm awake and not so drugged that I can think, I don't have time to worry about you, that's all.'

'Worry about me; I'm going to kill you.'

'Don't be upset, you won't.'

'I'm not upset.' Pribluda's voice rose. With better control, he added, 'I've been looking forward to it all year. You're crazy, Renko.' He was disgusted. 'You forget who's in charge here.'

Arkady said nothing. Over the field were the triumphant screams of small birds mobbing a crow; they looked like a bar of music moving through the air. He had determined by the short-range Antonov airliners flying overhead, their steady frequency, and their direction toward the balmy south that he was within an hour of Domodovo Airport, itself just outside Moscow. The psychiatrists sent to question him were all from the KGB's Serbsky Clinic in Moscow, so he assumed that Irina was there.

'Well, what do you think about, then?' Pribluda asked in exasperation.

'I think that I never knew *how* to think. I feel as if I'm making it up as I go along. I don't know. At least, for the first time, it's not making *me* up.' He opened his eyes and grinned.

'You're crazy,' Pribluda said seriously.

Arkady got to his feet and stretched. 'Want to get back to your seeds, Major?'

'Fuck your mother, you know I do.'

'Say you're human.'

'What?'

'We'll be back,' Arkady said. 'All you have to do is say you're human.'

'I don't have to do anything. What kind of game is this? You're so crazy, Renko, it makes me sick.'

'It shouldn't be so hard to say you're human.'

Pribluda walked in a tight circle as if screwing himself into the ground. 'You know I am.'

'Say it.'

'I'll kill you for this – for this alone,' Pribluda promised. 'To get it over with' – his voice fell to a monotone – 'I'm human.'

'Very good. Now we can go.' Arkady started toward the house.

The new interrogator was the doctor with fluttery hands who had once addressed the meeting at the prosecutor's office.

'Let me give you my analysis,' he told Arkady at the end of their session. 'For every truth told us by you and the Asanova woman there is a lie. Neither of you was directly a member of the Iamskoy-Osborne clique, but you were each indirectly involved, and you were and still are involved with each other. With your wide experience as an interrogator and her long experience as a suspect, you hope to confuse and outlast us. You have unreal expectations. All criminals have unreal expectations. You and the Asanova woman are both suffering from the pathoheterodoxy syndrome. You overestimate your personal powers. You feel isolated from society. You swing from excitement to sadness. You mistrust the people who most want to help you. You resent authority even when you represent it. You think you are the exception to every rule. You underestimate the collective intelligence. What is right is wrong, and what is wrong is right.

The Asanova woman is an obvious, classic case, easily
understood by anyone and thus easily dealt with. Yours
is a far more devious and dangerous case. You were
born with a famous name and great advantages. Despite
strong indications of political egoism, you rose to a
position of significance in the system of justice. After
heroically combating a powerful superior, you entered
into a criminal conspiracy with this woman to hide
important facts from this inquiry. What was her actual
relationship with Osborne? What transactions took place
between you and the American intelligence agent
William Kirwill? Why did you let Osborne go? I've heard
your answers. I believe the healthy part of you wants to
give me the real answers, and with sufficient therapy you
would. But it would be pointless. We *have* the real
answers. Further interrogations in this vein, I am convinced, will only feed your unhealthy delusions. We have
to think of the greater good. So I am recommending
that an example be made of you, and that you pay the
extreme penalty as quickly as can be arranged. You and I
have one more session scheduled for tomorrow morning
before I leave for Moscow. I have no more questions for
you. However, if you have any new information, it will
be your final opportunity. Otherwise, goodbye.'

Pribluda carefully emptied the pail. Water, sparkling
like an icicle, ran through a ditch and into a cutoff for
a row of lettuce until Arkady pushed soil from the ditch
into its wall, rerouting the water to the next cutoff. He
moved on his knees from row to row, reshaping a whole
series of tiny dams until the whole garden was afloat. 'A
veritable Nile,' he said.

'Agh, the ground's too dry. A dozen big buckets for a garden this size?' Pribluda shook his head. 'That's a drought.'

'The private agricultural sector of the Committee for State Security will never go dry, I'm sure.'

'You laugh. I came from a farm. Drought is a serious thing, and I can feel a drought coming. I confess I joined the Army to get away from the farm' – Pribluda lifted a shoulder, a graceful gesture for a man of his shape – 'but at heart I'm still from the country. You don't even have to think; you can feel a drought coming.'

'How?'

'Your throat tickles for three days. That's because the dust is not lying down. There are other ways.'

'Like?'

'The earth. The ground is like a drum. It's true – you can hear it. As a drumhead gets hotter and drier, what happens? It gets louder. The same with the ground. Listen.' Pribluda slapped his foot down. 'Sort of hollow. The water table is falling.' He stomped among the pails, delighting in a newfound ability to entertain, stomping harder the more Arkady laughed. 'This is peasant science. Hear the earth? You can hear how dry its throat is. You thought you cosmopolitans knew everything.' Pribluda did an ungainly dance, kicking the pails over until he tripped himself up and sat down with a clown's grin.

'Major' – Arkady helped him up – 'you're the one who should see the psychiatrist, not me.'

Pribluda's grin vanished. 'It's time for your last session,' he said. 'You're not going?'

'No.'

'Then I have to.' The major looked away. He pulled on his shirt, rolled down his pants, wiped the dust off his shoes and put on his jacket, trying to make himself presentable. Then at the same time they saw that his gun and holster still hung from a stake in the middle of the flooded garden.

'I'll get it for you,' Arkady said.

'I'll get it.'

'Don't be silly. You have shoes on, I'm barefoot.'

With the major shouting at him, Arkady stepped through the mud and picked the holster off the stake. The major was silent as he made his way back to dry land. When Arkady handed the gun over, Pribluda swung the barrel against the side of Arkady's head. 'Don't touch my gun.' He was furious. 'Don't you know what's going on here, don't you know anything?'

Arkady and Pribluda no longer worked in the garden together, and the vegetables withered, as water was restricted. Under vacant skies the fields yellowed in midgrowth. The house stood with all its doors and windows open in hopes of a breeze.

Zoya came. She was thinner, her eyes pinched, though she displayed a smile.

'The judge said we should give it another go,' Zoya explained. 'She said nothing was final if I changed my mind.'

'You've changed your mind?'

She sat by the window and fanned herself with her

handkerchief. Even her girlish braid of golden hair seemed thinner, older – like a wig, he thought.

'We just had troubles,' she said.

'Ah.'

'Maybe it was my fault.'

Arkady smiled. Zoya said maybe it was her fault the way a bureaucrat would discuss a change in department policy.

'You're looking better than I expected,' she said.

'Well, there's nothing to do here but get healthy. I haven't had any interrogations now for weeks. I wonder what's going to happen next.'

'It's very hot in Moscow. You're lucky to be here.'

Zoya went on to say that while they'd never be able to go back and live in Moscow, she had been assured that a suitable job could be found for him in a pleasant town away from the pressures of the capital. Perhaps as a teacher. They could teach together. Also, maybe it was time to start a family. In fact, it might even be possible for her to return here for a longer conjugal visit.

'No,' Arkady said. 'The truth is we aren't married and we don't care for each other. I certainly don't love you. I don't even feel responsible for what you are.'

Zoya stopped fanning herself and stared dully past Arkady at the other wall of the room, hands on her lap. Strangely, losing weight and roundness made her gymnast's muscles bulkier, her calves into biceps.

'Is it another woman?' She all too obviously remembered to ask.

'Zoyushka, you were right to leave me, and now you should stay as far away as you can. I don't wish you ill.'

'You don't wish me ill?' She seemed to rouse herself, and repeated what she'd said more fiercely and more sarcastically. 'You don't wish me ill? Look at what you've done to me. Schmidt has left me. He's asked for my transfer to another school, and who can blame him? They have my Party card; I don't know what they're going to do with it. You've ruined my life, as you plotted to from the day I met you. Do you think it was my idea to come here?'

'No. In your own way you've always been fairly truthful, so I was surprised to see you.'

Zoya pressed her fists against her eyes and worked her mouth so tightly that the red of her lips could not be seen; after a moment she took her hands away, trying to smile again, her blue eyes wet and bright when she spoke. 'We just had marital troubles. I was not understanding enough. We'll start fresh.'

'No, please.'

Zoya grabbed his hand. He had forgotten how callused her fingers were from exercises. 'It's been a long time since we slept together,' she whispered. 'I could stay tonight.'

'Don't.' Arkady pried her fingers off.

'Bastard.' She scratched his hand.

They flew Zoya out before supper. The experience of seeing the woman who had once been his wife turn herself inside out before him was profoundly depressing.

That night he woke with an overwhelming desire for Irina. His room was black around a window of stars. He stood at the window, naked. A touch, even the light friction of the sheet, would have brought a rush of pleasure and relief, and he would have felt no shame. But easing the desire would have erased her image. Stronger than an image, it was an apparition of Irina asleep on a blue bed. It had been in his dream, then in his room; it passed through the window and hovered outside. He could feel the warmth of her through the glass. She was the shock of life.

Not of ordinary life. Ordinary life was an endless queue of backs, of the next man's breath. In ordinary life people went to offices and did terrible things, and went home and, still in the jumble of a communal apartment, drank, swore, made love, waged war for a bit of dignity and somehow survived. Irina rose above this mob. She flaunted extraordinary beauty in a ragged jacket, she wore a mark on her cheek as honesty, she didn't care for petty survival. In many ways she was not a person at all. Arkady understood other people well; as an investigator it was his talent. He didn't understand Irina, and he suspected he might never penetrate vast areas of her unknowability. She had appeared as another planet and taken him in tow. He had followed, but he didn't know her, and it was he who had switched allegiance.

In the past months he had made himself almost dead, a defense of impassivity against the probes of the interrogators. It was a necessary suicide, his bow to killers. But it was a death all the same. Now this image of her had appeared, and for one night, at least, he was alive, too.

*

The peat fires began the following month. For days the whole northern horizon shifted under a purple haze. The provisions plane was turned back before landing one afternoon, and the next morning the southern horizon was also covered in smoke. A fire truck showed up with an engineer and firemen in rubber helmets and capes that made them look like medieval soldiers. The engineer ordered the house abandoned. There was to be no evacuation to Moscow; the roads were either cut off or blocked, and every able person was being enlisted in the battle against the fire.

It was truly a battle. Just thirty kilometers from the house was a command post of hundreds of firemen, Army engineers and 'volunteers' being organized as infantry around mobile water tanks, excavating machines and tractors. The group from the house – Arkady, Pribluda, a score of guards, housekeepers and cooks – were made into a reserve line of shovel wielders, with Arkady in the middle. But as soon as they crossed the first firebreak and went into action, the line started to fall apart. There was the underbrush to deal with, which spread out the line and frustrated it. There were sudden changes of wind and smoke that blinded and gagged the men and left them walking in different directions entirely. There were ancient ditches into which a man or a whole tractor suddenly dropped. The rest of the line would march into a new wall of smoke, exit behind two tractors and not know which to follow. Men in charred clothes appeared from nowhere running for safety, or bravely shoveling a new firebreak directly in the face of the flames. Of the people Arkady had started with, he recognized only Pribluda.

The fire was unpredictable. One bush would catch slowly like a biscuit of fuses; another would erupt whole into a torch. The problem was the peat. By now Arkady had a fair idea that he was close to the town of Shatura. Shatura was famous for building the first electric power station after the Revolution, and the fuel for the station was peat. The ground itself caught on fire; below the surface, it burned through seams of peat, so that even beaten out, each blaze was parent to a fair ring of new flames. An excavating machine collapsed through burned-out and hollowed turf, releasing methane gas that exploded among the fire fighters like a bomb. The intense heat was staggering. Every man coughed up cinders and blood. Helicopters crossed overhead releasing tons of water that fell as a suffocating rain of steam and smoke. Men with tearing eyes held on to each other's belts in a blind chain.

The plan was to contain the fire, but the peat fields were too immense, and firebreaks were useless against an enemy that attacked underground. As each successive line of defense retreated, the men at the earlier lines were more entrapped. Arkady no longer knew which way to retreat. Shouts of confusion sounded through the smoke in every direction. A ridge of torn earth ended in a burning tractor; shovels lay where they had been thrown. Pribluda, face smeared black, sat with fat legs outstretched, gagging and exhausted. The major held his gun limply, and his voice was so weak that Arkady could hardly understand him.

'Get out of here. Save your skin,' Pribluda said bitterly. 'This is your big opportunity. You can pick the papers off some poor dead guy if you don't burn yourself. This is the chance you've been waiting for. We'll catch you anyway; I'd shoot you if I didn't know that.'

'What are you going to do?' Arkady asked.

'I'm not so dumb as to wait and fry, I'll tell you that. I'm no coward.'

Pribluda looked more like a hamstrung pig than anything else. High walls of smoke closed in as the wind turned. Arkady had always felt that Pribluda was not going to kill him; he had no idea whether he would die in the fire. At least that would be a natural death, not nine grams of lead in the back of his head from his fellow man.

'Run!' Pribluda coughed.

Arkady pulled the major up and lifted him onto a shoulder. He could no longer see the tractor or trees or sun. He started to his left, the last clear path he recalled.

Weaving under the weight of Pribluda, tripping on debris, soon he couldn't tell if he was moving left, right or in a circle, but he knew that they would die if he stopped. It was the claustrophobia of not breathing, of keeping his mouth shut as if there were a hand over it, that he hadn't expected. The vacuum in his lungs sucked on his windpipe. Through the slits of his eyes he made out only a red furze of fire. When he could go no further and was so deep in smoke that he had to shut his eyes entirely, he ordered himself another twenty steps, and when the smoke was worse, another twenty steps beyond that, and then another ten, and another five. He stumbled into a ditch of brackish water. The ditch was as tall as a man; the water was shallow, and between it and the lip of the ditch lay a channel of thin, acrid air. Pribluda's lips were violet. Arkady turned him on his back in the water and rocked back and forth, pumping air into him. Pribluda revived, but the heat became worse.

Arkady walked him through the ditch. Embers fell on them, settling in their hair and burning curlicues in their shirts. The ditch rose and ended, and at first in the haze Arkady thought he had worked his way back to the field he had started from that morning. Then he saw that the excavation machines, water tanks and fire engines were black and gutted, some upended from explosions when their fuel ignited, and that what seemed shapeless hillocks on a charred field were the bodies of men who had died the day before. Some of them apparently had taken refuge from the smoke in a peat cutter's shaft; now they were skeletons. Peat was anaerobic compost, organic decay so old that all its oxygen had been used up. Few microbes survived in peat – perhaps twenty or thirty a cubic meter. Exposed to air and water, the microbes instantly reproduced to many millions, a voracious pool of starved life that bored through flesh like lye. The walls of the shaft were gouged by efforts to escape this sanctuary. A rubber cape lay across the white slick of an arm and one hand. From two of the bodies on the ground above, Arkady took intact water containers, made masks out of his shirt, wet them, tied them on Pribluda and himself, and started out again as the smoke approached.

They moved to keep the smoke at their backs. At one point Arkady stumbled near a shaft, and Pribluda, ahead of him, turned and caught his hand before he dropped into it. They continued across more burning plains, more scenes of calamity and heroism strewn randomly with a generous hand, deaths in a war that would never be reported in any newspaper except for a paragraph that admitted to some windblown cinders in the Moscow area.

Finally they came to a palisade of burned trees. 'There's no place left to go, the smoke is everywhere.' Pribluda watched the encircling darkness. 'Why did you lead us here? See, the trees are burning again.'

'That's not smoke, it's night. Those are stars,' Arkady said. 'We're safe.'

The house was untouched by the fire. In a few days rains came, violent storms that drowned the fire, and afterward the guards played volleyball again and the plane brought fresh supplies, even ice cream. The plane also brought the prosecutor general, who never removed his raincoat and talked with his head down, his hands clasped behind his back.

'You want the entire system of justice to bend to you. You're only one man, one investigator, and not even an important one. Yet reason and persuasion have no effect on you at all. We know the full scope of the complicity of the woman Asanova with the foreign agent Osborne and the traitors Borodin and Davidova. We know that you are withholding information about the Asanova woman, and about your relationship with her. An investigator who does that deliberately spits in the face of his country. At the end of patience, you will learn, is a great anger.'

The next week the doctor from the Serbsky Clinic returned. He made no effort to analyze Arkady but went off with Pribluda to what had been the vegetable garden. Arkady watched from an upstairs window. The doctor spoke to Pribluda, argued and finally insisted. He opened a briefcase to show Pribluda a needle the size used for horses, placed the briefcase in his hands and returned at once to the airstrip. The major walked off out of sight.

In the afternoon Pribluda rapped on the door of Arkady's room and invited him to go mushroom hunting. In spite of the heat he was wearing his jacket, and he had two large bandannas for the mushrooms.

Less than a half hour's walk was a copse that had escaped the fire and where rain had magically brought from dry ground new grass, flowers and, almost overnight, mushrooms. Many of the trees were great oaks over a hundred years old and arching high over a mossy floor. A mushroom hunt always focused the eyes on the twist of a leaf, the discolored bark of a tree, freshets of wildflowers, the industry of beetles. Mushrooms themselves took on the aspect of animals; camouflaged, still as rabbits, they waited for the hunter to pass. They popped into view and then seemed to vanish. They were best seen at the corner of the eye, a homely brown one here, among the leaves a stationary herd of orange mushrooms, another with the ruffed gill of a small dinosaur, yet another trying to hide a scarlet head. They were called not so much by name as whether they were best picked, salted, dried over a stove, fried, eaten plain, with bread, with sour cream, washed down with vodka – but what kind of vodka, clear, anise-flavored, caraway, cherry pit? A man hunting mushrooms had a whole year ahead to think of.

As Pribluda happily rooted, Arkady studied his low forehead, the fringe of brown hair turning gray, his Russian thumb of a nose, warty jowls, butcher-block body, the badly cut jacket over his holster. The woods were deep in shadow before Arkady realized that they had missed dinner.

'That's all right,' Pribluda said, 'we'll have a feast of mushrooms tomorrow. Here, see what I found.' He held his bandanna open to display the varied collection inside, told Arkady in detail how each would be prepared, and at what holiday they would be served. 'Let me see yours.'

Arkady opened his bandanna and let his day's pickings – all slender greenish-white mushrooms, sickly bright in the shadow – spill to the ground.

Pribluda jumped back. 'They're all poison! Are you crazy?'

'The doctor told you to kill me,' Arkady said. 'You didn't do it on the way here, so will you do it on the way back? Are you waiting for the dark? Will it be a shot in the head or a needle in the arm? Why not mushrooms?'

'Stop it.'

'There won't be any feast tomorrow, Major. I'll be dead.'

'He didn't have orders, he just suggested it.'

'Is he a KGB officer?'

'Just a major, same as me.'

'He gave you a briefcase.'

'I buried it. That's not the way I kill a man.'

'It doesn't matter what way; a suggestion like that is an order.'

'I've demanded a written order.'

'You!'

'Yes, me,' Pribluda said defiantly. 'You don't believe me?'

'So a written order will come tomorrow and then you'll kill me. What difference does it make?'

'I have a sense that there was some conflict over the decision. The doctor is too rash. I want definite written instructions. I'm not a killer. I'm as human as you are.' Pribluda kicked the pale mushrooms away from his feet. 'I am.'

On the way back, Pribluda was more forlorn than Arkady. Arkady breathed deeply, as if he could drink the night down. He thought of the old enemy trudging alongside. Pribluda would shoot him when the written order came, but he had taken a chance by not doing it at the first word. It was a very small thing to a condemned man, but it was something to Pribluda, the sort of mark that stayed on one's record.

'Venus.' Arkady pointed out a brilliant star on the horizon. 'You're from the country, Major, you must know the stars.'

'This is no time for stargazing.'

'Pleiades over there.' Arkady pointed. 'There's Cepheus, Pisces above him, Aquarius over there. What a fantastic night. Except for the fire, this is the first night I've been out of the house since I got here. The tail of Taurus way over there.'

'You should have been an astronomer.'

'Obviously.'

They walked for a while in silence, except for the sound of their tread, crackling when they crossed burned fields, rustling through grass. The house appeared, bright in its own yellow haze. Arkady made out men running from the house with flashlights and rifles. He stepped away from the brightness the better to see the night.

'We're all going out of orbit, Major. We're all together. Someone pulls me, I pull you, who will you pull?'

'There's something I have to know,' Pribluda said. 'If we'd known each other a year ago, would you still have gone after me?'

'For the two men you killed on the Kliazma River?'

'Yes.' Pribluda's eyes fixed earnestly on Arkady.

Arkady heard shouts, though the voices were too far off to be understood. His own long silence became embarrassing to him, and it was unbearable to Pribluda. 'Maybe,' Pribluda answered his own question, 'if we'd been friends then, I wouldn't have done it.'

Arkady turned to the footsteps approaching and the flashlights' glare sweeping over his face. 'Anything's possible,' he said.

From the remembered habit, one of the guards knocked Arkady to the ground with a rifle butt.

'You have new visitors,' another told Pribluda. 'There's been a change.'

Chapter Three

In October Arkady was flown to Leningrad and taken to what looked like an enormous museum but was in fact the Fur Palace. He was led to an amphitheater of tiers of desks surrounded by a white colonnade. On the stage five uniformed KGB officers – a general and four colonels – sat at a dais. The Palace smelled of dead meat.

The general had an ironic tone. 'Now, they tell me this is a love story.' He sighed. 'I would have preferred a simple tale of national interest.

'Every year, Arkady Vasilevich, men come from all the nations of the world to sit at these desks and spend seventy million dollars for Soviet furs. The Soviet Union is the world's leading exporter of furs. We always have been. The reason is not our minks, which are inferior to the Americans', or lynx, which are too few, or karakul, which, after all, is sheepskin; the reason is Soviet sable. Gram for gram, sable is worth more than gold. How do you think the Soviet government reacts to losing its monopoly on sable?'

'Osborne has only six sables,' Arkady said.

'I'm amazed, I've been amazed for months by how little you know. How can so many men – the Moscow town prosecutor, the German Unmann, officers of State Security and the Militia – be dead, thanks to you, and you know so little?' The general thoughtfully pulled on an eyelash. 'Six sables? With the aid of Assistant Deputy Minister of Trade Mendel we have determined that with the collusion of his dead father, the Deputy Minister of Trade, the American Osborne spirited away seven other sables about five years ago. They were ordinary sables from production collectives around Moscow. The Mendels thought that Osborne could not breed high-quality animals. The young Mendel never would have dared help the American acquire Barguzins. That's what he said, and I believed him.'

'Where is Yevgeny Mendel now?'

'He killed himself. He was a weak man. The point, however, is that Osborne had seven ordinary-quality sables five years ago. We estimate conservatively an average increase of fifty percent a year, giving him now about fifty sables. His conspiracy with the Siberian Kostia Borodin has gained him six more. Barguzin male sables. Using the same estimate, Osborne will have over two hundred high-quality sables in five years, over two thousand in ten. At that point I think we can forget about the historic Soviet monopoly on sable. Citizen Renko, why do you think you are still alive?'

'Is Irina Asanova alive?' Arkady asked.

'Yes.'

Comprehension spread through Arkady. He wasn't going back to the house in the country, and he wasn't going to be killed. 'Then you can use us,' he said.

'Yes. Now we need you.'

'Where is she?'

'Do you like to travel?' the general asked gently, as if he were causing pain. 'Have you ever wanted to see America?'

Part Three

NEW YORK

Chapter One

The first sight of America was of the running lights of a tanker, the night-fishing lights of trawlers.

Wesley was tall, young and balding, smooth-featured as if rolled like a pebble, with a faint and meaningless expression of affability. He wore a three-piece suit of blue material. Scents of lime and mint came from Wesley's mouth, cheeks and armpits. For the entire flight he had crossed his legs and smoked a pipe and answered Arkady's questions with grunts. There was something awkward and milk-fed about Wesley, like a calf.

The two men had a section of the plane to themselves. Most of the other passengers were 'meritorious artists,' musicians on tour who argued about the watches and perfumes they'd already bought at the Orly stopover. Arkady had not been allowed off the plane there.

'You understand the word "responsibility"?' Wesley asked in English.

The passengers crowded to one side of the plane as they approached farmland, faint lines between the fields of dark.

'That means you're going to help me?' Arkady asked.

'It means that this is an FBI operation. It means,' Wesley said earnestly, as if he were selling Arkady something, 'that we are responsible for you.'

'Who are you responsible to?'

A childish excitement filled the plane as it flew over the first American community. It seemed to be a community of cars. Cars filled the streets and nestled close to houses that seemed too outsized for people.

'I'm glad you asked that question.' Wesley tapped his pipe into the ashtray in his armrest. 'Extradition is a complicated matter, especially between the United States and the Soviet Union. We don't need any more complications than we already have. You understand "complication"?'

A steeper descent created the illusion of gathering speed. A great expressway would appear – an infinite track of colored signals – and then vanish into a maze of highways. It seemed impossible there could be so many paved roads. Where could they all go to? How many cars could there be? It looked as if the whole population below was driving or moving or evacuating.

'In the Soviet Union a complication is anything you don't want,' Arkady said.

'Exactly!'

Seams of light merged into shopping centers, main streets, boatyards. THANKSGIVING SALE, said a billboard. The plane slipped even lower over a residential area. Lit playing fields of brilliant grass appeared. The blue of backyards was empty swimming pools. The first distinct American stood in the glow of a house door, looking up.

'Let me tell you a complication we're not going to have,' Wesley said. 'You're not going to defect. If this were a KGB operation, then you could defect. You could come to us and we'd be happy to give you asylum. Anyone else on this plane, for example, can defect.'

'What if they don't want to defect and I do?'

'Well, they can and you can't,' Wesley said.

Arkady felt the shudder of the wheel bays opening. He searched for a trace of humor in Wesley's smile. 'You're making a joke,' he suggested.

'I certainly hope not,' Wesley said. 'It's the law. Before any defector is allowed to stay in the United States, his or her case is determined by the bureau. We've already made a determination in your case, and we've determined that you can't stay.'

Arkady thought he might be having a problem with the language. 'But I haven't tried to defect yet.'

'Then the bureau will be happy to be responsible for you,' Wesley said. 'Until you try to defect.'

Arkady studied the agent. This was a kind of man he'd never encountered before. The face was human enough – the brows, lids and lips moved when appropriate – but Arkady suspected that inside the skull on the cortex of the brain lay a uniform pattern of spirals.

'You can defect, but you'd have to defect to us,' Wesley said. 'Anyone you run to will hand you over to us. Of course, we'll send you right back to the Soviet Union. So when you're in our hands there's really very little point in defecting to us, is there?'

The airliner passed over drab row houses bathed in a fearful public light. The streets rolled away and the plane was on a long run over a bay, and then an island of lights reared into the sky. A thousand towers of light as profligate as stars rose from the water, and a wonderful sound of relief and appreciation went through the passengers at this effect.

'Then you won't help me,' Arkady said.

'Absolutely, any way I can,' Wesley said.

Landing lights skidded by the windows. The airliner touched down and reversed thrust.

By the time the plane taxied to the Pan Am terminal the aisle was full of musicians, musical instruments, bundles of gifts and string bags of food. Now the Russians were preparing their faces of boredom-with-American-technology, and though everyone had to pass by Arkady and Wesley, no one looked at them; no one wanted to be contaminated when they were so close, only a few steps from a remarkable walk-through tube that attached the plane directly to the terminal. Instead they all watched each other.

When all the other passengers were gone, service attendants bounded into the plane through a door in the rear and Wesley led Arkady down the service ladder to the tarmac under the Ilyushin's rear engines. The engines whined and the red light on the tail blinked. Was the plane going right back to Moscow? Arkady wondered. Wesley tapped his shoulder and pointed to a car maneuvering over the runway towards them.

They didn't pass through American customs. The car took them directly to an access gate, and then onto a high-speed expressway.

'We have an understanding with your people.' Wesley settled comfortably into the shadow of the rear seat with Arkady.

'My people?'

'The KGB.'

'I'm not with the KGB.'

'The KGB says you're not with them, too. That's what we'd expect them to say.'

There were abandoned cars by the side of the road. Not recently abandoned cars; they looked like the wrecks of ancient wars. 'Free Puerto Rico' was written on the side of one. The cars moving on the road were of a hundred makes and colors. The drivers were of all colors too. Ahead was the same startling skyline he had seen from the plane.

'What is the understanding you have with the KGB?' Arkady asked.

'The understanding is that this will be a bureau operation as long as you can't defect to the bureau,' Wesley said. 'And since you can only defect to us, you can't defect.'

'I understand. And you think I'm with the KGB because they say I'm not.'

'What else would they say?'

'But if you believed I was not with the KGB, that would change everything?'

'Absolutely! Then what the KGB says would be true.'

'What do they say?'

'They say you were convicted of murder.'

'There wasn't any trial.'

'They didn't say there was. Did you kill someone?' Wesley asked.

'Yes.'

'There you are. It's against the immigration laws of the United States to admit a criminal. The laws are very strict unless you're an illegal alien. But we could hardly allow in someone who comes right up to the bureau and announces he's a murderer.'

Wesley's head bobbed affably in the shadow while he waited for more questions, but Arkady was silent. The car dipped into a tunnel for Manhattan. Police watched through the smeared glass booths in the tunnel's greenish light. Then the car emerged on the other side into streets that were narrower than Arkady had expected, and so far below the bright haze of the skyline that they had a disorienting underwater quality. The streetlights had a lighter tungsten pallor.

'I just wanted you to know exactly where you stood,' Wesley said at last. 'You're not here legally. You're not here *illegally* either, because then you'd have a leg to stand on. You're simply not here at all, and there's no way you can prove otherwise. I know it's insane, but that's the law for you. Also, it's what your people wanted. If you have any complaints, you should take them up with the KGB.'

'Will I see the KGB?'

'Not if I can help it.'

The car stopped at the corner of Twenty-ninth and Madison in front of the glass doors of a hotel. Imitation gas torches flanked a marquee that said THE BARCELONA. Wesley handed Arkady a key attached to a plastic plaque bearing the hotel's name, but held on to it for a moment when Arkady took it. 'Her room number is on the key.' Wesley let go. 'You're a lucky man.'

Arkady felt a strange dizziness as he got out of the car. Wesley didn't follow. Arkady pushed open the glass doors. The hotel lobby had a maroon carpet, pink marble columns and brass chandeliers with electric candles. A man with dark pouches under his eyes rose from a chair to wave a newspaper at Wesley outside, then glanced at Arkady and sat back down. Arkady rode up alone in a self-service elevator with the message 'Fuck You' carved into the door.

Room 518 was at the end of the fifth-floor hall. The door to 513 opened a crack as Arkady went by, and as he turned, furious, the door shut. He went on to 518, unlocked it and entered.

She was sitting on the bed in the dark. He couldn't tell what kind of dress she had on, Russian or American. Her feet were bare.

'I made them bring you,' Irina said. 'I cooperated at the start, because they told me that they were going to kill you. Finally I decided you were as good as dead as long as you were over there. I wouldn't even leave the room until they brought you . . .'

She lifted her face to him, showing the tears in her eyes. This is finally all we have to offer each other, Arkady thought. He touched her lips and she said his name against his hand. Then he saw the telephone on a side table. Iamskoy was listening to them, he thought irrationally – Wesley, he corrected himself. He tore the telephone cord from the wall.

'You never told them,' she whispered as he returned. 'You never told them who really killed Iamskoy.'

Her face was changed, thinner, making her eyes larger. Was she even more beautiful?

'How did they ever think you were one of them?' she asked.

Here, floors were softer, beds harder. She toppled to one side, carrying him in her. 'And here you are.' She kissed him.

'Here we are.' Arkady felt a manic force building inside him.

'Almost free,' she whispered.

'Alive.' He laughed.

Chapter Two

Wesley and three other FBI agents brought a paper-bag breakfast of coffee and doughnuts to the hotel room. Arkady had a cup. Irina was changing in the bathroom.

'I understand the NYPD liaison is a Lieutenant Kirwill,' Ray said. A small, natty man of Mexican background, Ray was the only agent who didn't put his feet on the coffee table. 'A problem?'

'No problem,' Wesley said. 'A little personal involvement.'

'Mental case from what I hear,' George said. George was the man with angry circles under the eyes that Arkady had seen in the lobby the night before. Sometimes the others called him 'the Greek.' He picked his teeth with a matchbook.

The English that Wesley spoke seemed to be some new form of Latin, mechanically double-faced, limpid to the point of transparency and open to infinite interpretation.

'You have to understand the history of socialist radicalism in New York City, as well as the fascinating tradition of Irish-Americans on the police force. Or you don't have to understand anything,' Wesley said, 'because all that's important is that Kirwill wants to save the Red Squad.'

'What is the Red Squad?' Arkady asked.

There was an uncomfortable moment until Wesley graciously said, 'The New York Police Department has a Red Squad. They change the name every ten years or so – Radical Bureau, Public Relations, Public Security. Right now they call it the Security Investigation, but it's always the Red Squad. Lieutenant Kirwill has the Russian desk on the Red Squad. And you are the Red.'

'What are you?' Arkady asked the agents. 'What did you bring us to America for? How long are we going to be here?'

Al broke the silence by changing the subject. The oldest agent, he had skin as freckled as a lily's and an avuncular manner. 'There was some stink about his brother, and Kirwill got bounced off the squad. Now his brother's dead in Moscow and Kirwill's back on the squad.'

'Kirwill will try to make his comeback at our expense,' Wesley said. 'We have excellent relations with the Police Department, but they'll stab us in the back if we give them the chance – the same as we'd do to them.'

'Ten years ago, the Red Squad was the elite of the detectives.' Al brushed doughnut sugar from his stomach. 'They were investigating everyone. Remember the Jews shooting at the Soviet Mission? The Red Squad stopped them. The Hispanics who wanted to blow up the Statue of Liberty? The squad infiltrated them.'

'They were very successful,' Wesley agreed. 'The squad was there when Malcolm X was assassinated. Malcolm's bodyguard was a squad agent.'

'What happened to the Red Squad?' Ray asked.

'Watergate,' Wesley said.

'Shit, them too,' George muttered.

There was a silent moment of sympathy before Al explained. 'During the Watergate hearings, it turned out that Nixon's special assistant for security, a guy responsible for hiring other guys for dirty work, was a John Caulfield. Caulfield was from the Red Squad; he used to bodyguard Nixon when he lived in New York before he became President. When Caulfield was in the White House, he brought in another old friend from the Red Squad, a guy named Tony Ulasewicz.'

'The fat guy who spied on Muskie?' George asked.

'For CREEP,' Wesley said.

'He was a funny guy?' George asked. 'Kept a coin changer on his belt for public phones? Sure!'

'Well, Watergate was the end of the Red Squad's glory days,' Al said. 'The political climate changed after that.'

'Political climate'll fuck you every time,' George said.

'Are we prisoners? Are you afraid of us?' Arkady asked.

'What does the Red Squad do now?' Ray filled the pause.

'They chase illegal aliens.' Wesley looked at Arkady. 'Haitians, Jamaicans, whatever they can get.'

'Haitians and Jamaicans? Pretty pathetic,' George said.

'When you consider what the squad used to be.' Wesley sighed. 'When you consider they used to have millions of names on file, had their own special headquarters on Park Avenue, went into secret training with the CIA.'

'The CIA?' George asked. 'Now, that's illegal.'

*

Nicky and Rurik, the two men from the Soviet Mission, insisted on seeing Arkady. They were unlike any KGB agents he had ever seen before. They had good suits, better than those of the FBI men who greeted them, had excellent manners, spoke well, had American informality. They were more American than the Americans. Only a thickness through the waist, a childhood of potatoes, gave them away.

'I'll speak in English' – Nicky lit a cigarette for Arkady – 'so everything will be in the open. Because this is détente in action. Our two nations have joined, through the appropriate agencies, to bring to justice a heinous murderer. This madman will be brought to justice and you can help.'

'Why did you bring her here?' Arkady asked in Russian. Irina was still out of earshot.

'In English, please,' Rurik said. He was taller than Nicky and his red hair was cut full, American style. The FBI agents called him 'Rick.' 'She was brought at the request of our friends here in the bureau. They have many questions. You have to understand, Americans are not used to tales of corrupt Communists and Siberian bandits. Extradition is a delicate matter.'

'Especially the extradition of a wealthy and well-connected man.' Nicky looked at Wesley. 'Isn't that right, Wes?'

'I think he has almost as many friends here as he had over there.' Wesley provoked a laugh from all the agents, Soviet and American.

'Let's assume you're happy,' Rurik told Arkady. 'Our counterparts here are treating you well? You have a lovely room off a fashionable avenue. I can just see the top of the Empire State Building from your window. Excellent. So let's assume you will make the girl happy. Calmer, easier to deal with? It should be pleasant work.'

'You're very lucky to get this second chance,' Nicky said. 'This will make all the difference in your reception when you go home. In a couple of days you can have your apartment back, a job – maybe even something from the Central Committee. You're a very lucky man.'

'What do I do for all this?' Arkady asked.

'What I said,' Rurik answered. 'Make her happy.'

'And stop asking questions,' Wesley added.

'Yes,' Rurik agreed, 'stop asking questions.'

'Let us remind you,' Nicky said, 'that you are no longer a chief investigator. You are a Soviet criminal who is alive only because of our favor, and that we are your only friends.'

'Where's Kirwill?' Arkady asked.

The conversation stopped as Irina emerged from the bathroom wearing a black gaberdine skirt and a silk blouse open to an amber necklace. Her brown hair was up on one side in a gold clasp and she wore a gold bracelet. Arkady suffered two shocks: first, that Irina should be in such rich clothes; second, that they should look so *right* on her. Then he noticed that the mark on her right cheek, that faint blue vein of pain, was gone, lightly covered by makeup. She was perfect.

'Okay, let's go.' Wesley rose, and all the men gathered their overcoats and hats from where they'd thrown them on the bed. Al took from the closet a full-length black fur coat and helped Irina into it. It was a sable coat, Arkady realized.

'Don't worry,' Irina mouthed to Arkady as she was being led out.

'We're sending someone to fix that.' George pointed to the phone. 'Keep your hands off it. That's hotel property.'

'Private property' – Nicky slipped his arm through Wesley's as they left – 'is what I love about a free country.'

Alone, Arkady inspected the room, which was like a dream in which everything was a little askew. His feet sank into the carpet. The bed had a padded headboard. The coffee table was a wood-grained plastic that yielded under the fingers.

Ray returned and repaired the telephone. When Ray was gone Arkady discovered that the phone would only take incoming calls. He found another microphone in the ceiling fixture of the bathroom. The television was on a stand that was bolted to the floor so he couldn't steal it. The door to the hall was locked from the outside.

The door burst open as the FBI agent called George backed through, propelled by a hand.

'This man is under federal protection,' George protested.

'I'm police liaison, I have to check you got the right Russian.' Kirwill filled the doorway.

'Hello,' Arkady said from the other side of the room.

'This is a bureau operation, Lieutenant,' George warned.

'This is New York, asshole.' He brushed George aside. Kirwill was dressed exactly the same as the first time Arkady saw him at the Metropole Hotel, except that now his raincoat was black instead of tan. The same short-brimmed hat was tilted back from the broad, creased forehead and gray hair. The tie was loose at his neck. Closer, Arkady saw stains on the raincoat. Kirwill's face had a red flush of alcohol and excitement. He clapped his big hands together with satisfaction, beaming at the same time his blue eyes darted around the room. Compared with the FBI men, he was disheveled and out of control. He rewarded Arkady with a malicious grin. 'Son of a bitch, it's you.'

'Yes.'

Kirwill wore a comic expression of amusement and woe. 'Admit it, Renko, you fucked up. All you had to do was tell me it was Osborne. I'd have taken care of him in Moscow. An accident – no one would have known. He'd be dead, I'd be happy and you'd still be chief investigator.'

'I admit it.'

George spoke on the room phone without dialing.

'They think you're a very dangerous man.' Kirwill jerked his thumb in George's direction. 'You shot your own boss. You stabbed Unmann. They think you killed the guy out at the lake, too. They think you're just about a homicidal maniac. Watch out, they're triggerhappy.'

'But I'm being guarded by the FBI.'

'That's who I'm talking about. It's sort of like getting together with the Rotary, only they kill you.'

'Rotary?'

'Forget it.' Kirwill kept moving, walking around the room. 'Christ, look where they put you. This is a whore's nest. Look at the cigarette burns in the carpet by the bed. Feel the flowers on this wallpaper. I think they're giving you a message, Renko.'

'You said you were liaison?' Arkady switched to Russian. 'You have what you asked for, you're in control.'

'I'm liaison so they can keep an eye on me.' Kirwill stuck to English. 'See, you never gave me Osborne's name, but you gave my name to everyone else. You fucked me.' He enunciated precisely. 'You fuck me. She fucks you. Who do you think fucks her?'

'What do you mean?'

'I'm a little disappointed in you,' Kirwill went on. 'I didn't think you'd go along with this, even to get here.'

'Go along with what? This extradition—'

'Extradition? Is that what they told you?' Kirwill guffawed, a great gape of amazement.

Three FBI agents Arkady hadn't seen before rushed in, and together with George they had the courage to shoulder Kirwill into the hall. The detective was too busy wiping tears of laughter from his eyes to resist.

Arkady tried the door again. It was still locked, and this time two voices from the hall told him to leave the knob alone.

He paced around the room. From the southwest

corner one step to the bathroom, one step from the
bathroom to the bed and night table, one step from
the table to the northwest corner, two steps to a pair
of single-paned windows looking out on Twenty-ninth
Street, three steps across the windows to the side table
with the phone, half a step to the northeast corner, one
step to the hall door, one step from the door to the sofa,
two steps from the other end of the sofa to the southwest
corner, half a step to the closet door, half a step from
the door to the bureau and another step from the bureau
back to the southwest corner. In the room were two
wooden chairs and the plastic wood-grained coffee table,
the television set, a wastepaper basket and a cracked ice
bucket. The bathroom had a toilet, a sink and a shower-
bath that suggested that a very small person could stretch
out in great comfort. All the fixtures were pink. The
carpet was olive green. Pastel blue wallpaper sprouted
flowers of pink fuzz. The bureau and chairs were painted
cream and smudged by cigarette burns. The bedspread
was mauve.

Arkady didn't know what he'd expected from Kirwill.
He thought they'd reached something approaching
human understanding in Moscow, yet here they seemed
to be enemies all over again. Even so, Kirwill was real in
a way that Wesley was not. Arkady had the sense that at
any moment the hotel room would sag and collapse like
the props on a stage. He was furious with Kirwill and
wanted Kirwill to come back.

He paced the room more nervously than before. The
closet had only two dresses, not even an extra pair of

shoes. A blouse was redolent with Irina's scent. He crushed it against his face.

The day had a yellow light, brittle with filaments and cracks.

Looking right, the farthest he could see was across Madison Avenue to a sign that said THE HAPPY HOUR. Directly across from the hotel was a store that sold oil-paper umbrellas from China. Above the store were thirteen floors of offices. Looking left, he made out the worn-out grass and sepia stones of a churchyard. Dried leaves drifted like soot through the streets.

Secretaries typed and men in shirt sleeves and ties talked on phones in the office windows across the street. The offices had ivy plants and paintings. A steel pushcart served coffee in the halls. A pair of black men painted the office directly across from Arkady. What looked like a portable radio the size of a suitcase stood in their window.

A nimbus of condensation outlined his fingers on the glass.

I am here.

'Do you like game shows?' Al turned on the television when he brought a sandwich for Arkady.

'I don't particularly like games.'

'This one is great, though,' Al said.

Arkady didn't understand the show at first. There was no game; all the contestants did was guess how much money the prizes – toasters, stoves, vacations, houses – were worth. Everything – knowledge, physical ability, luck – was eliminated except avarice. The simplicity of the concept was stunning.

'You're a real Party member, aren't you?' Al said.

The shadows outside moved only when his eyes were looking elsewhere. Then they would shift from one side of a window ledge to the other, or leap en masse to another building. Who knew which way they would go next?

At dusk Irina returned, throwing packages onto the bed and laughing. Arkady's anxieties vanished. She made the room come to life; it even seemed attractive again. The most banal words rose from the dead.

'I missed you, Arkasha.'

She'd brought cartons of spaghetti with meat, clam and white sauces. The sun set while they ate their exotic fare with plastic forks. It occurred to him that for the first time in his life he was living in a building that did not smell, however faintly, of cabbage.

She opened the packages and proudly displayed the wardrobe she had bought for him. Like her clothes in the closet, these were of colors and cuts and a quality of manufacture new to Arkady. There were pants, shirts, socks, ties, a sports jacket, pajamas, an overcoat and a hat. They examined the stitching, the linings, the French labels. Irina tied her hair up in a bun and modeled everything for him with a grave face.

MARTIN CRUZ SMITH

'Is that supposed to be me?' Arkady asked.

'No, no. An American Arkady,' she decided, parading with an insouciant swagger, the hat pulled low over one eye.

While she modeled the pajamas, Arkady turned off the room light. 'I love you,' he said.

'We will be happy.'

Arkady unbuttoned the pajama top, opened it and kissed her breasts, neck and mouth. The hat fell off and rolled under the table. Irina dropped the pajama bottoms herself. Arkady entered her standing up as he had the very first time in his own apartment, the same but slower and deeper, sweeter.

Night washed all the garish colors from the walls.

In bed, he taught himself again about Irina's body. The women he had seen walking on the street below had a narrow look. Irina was taller, more sensual, more animal. Her ribs were not as painfully drawn as in Moscow; her nails were longer and painted. Yet from the softness of her lips to the hollow of her neck, to the dark hardness of the tip of her breasts, from the sweep of her stomach to the rising mound of damp curls, she felt the same. Her teeth bit the same; the same beads of perspiration sat at her temples.

'In my cell I would imagine your hands' – she took his hand – 'there, and there. Feeling them, not seeing them. It made me feel alive. I fell in love with you because you made me feel alive, and you weren't even there. At first they said you told them everything. You

466

were an investigator, so you had to. The more I thought
about you, though, the more I knew you wouldn't tell
them anything. They asked me if you were insane. I said
you were the sanest man I'd ever met. They asked if you
were a criminal. I said you were the most honest man
I'd ever known. They ended up hating you more than
they did me. And I loved you more.'

'I am a criminal.' Arkady lay on her. 'I was a criminal
there and I'm a prisoner here.'

'Gently.' She helped him.

She'd brought back a miniature transistor radio that
filled the room with an insistent, percussive music. Boxes
and clothes were spread across the floor. On the table,
plastic forks stood in cardboard containers.

'Please, don't ask how long I've been here or exactly
what's happening,' Irina said. 'Everything is being done
at different levels, at new levels we never knew about.
Don't ask questions. We're here. All I ever wanted was
to be here. And I have you here with me. I love you,
Arkasha. You mustn't ask questions.'

'They're sending us back. In a couple of days, they
said.'

She clutched him, kissed him and whispered fiercely
in his ear, 'It will all be over in a day or two, but they'll
never send us back. Never!'

*

467

Her fingertips traced his face. 'You could have a cowboy's tan, with sideburns and a bandanna and a cowboy hat. We'll travel. Everyone has a car, you'll see.'

'I should have a horse if I'm a cowboy.'

'You can have a horse here. I've seen cowboys in New York.'

'I want to go out West. I want to ride the range and be a bandit like Kostia Borodin. I want to learn from the Indians.'

'Or we could go to California, to Hollywood. We could have a bungalow by the sea, a lawn, an orange tree. I'd be happy if I never saw snow again in my life. I could live in a bathing suit.'

'Or nothing at all.' He caressed her leg, then laid his head against it and her fingers stroked his chest. They had to talk in fantasy because of the microphone. He couldn't ask her why she was so sure she wasn't going back. She begged him not to ask about anything else. Anyway, when it came to America all they could conceive of was fantasy. He felt her fingertips trace the scar the length of his stomach. 'I'll keep my horse by the orange tree in back of the bungalow,' he said.

'Actually,' Irina said while she was lighting her cigarette from his, 'it wasn't Osborne who tried to have me killed in Moscow.'

'What?'

'It was all Prosecutor Iamskoy and Unmann the German. They were in it together; Osborne knew nothing about it.'

'Osborne tried to kill you twice. You were there, I was there, remember?' Abruptly Arkady was furious. 'Who told you Osborne had nothing to do with it?'

'Wesley.'

'Wesley is a liar.' He repeated in English. 'Wesley is a liar!'

'Ssh, it's late.' Irina put her finger to his lips. She changed the subject; she was patient, and in spite of his outburst she was pleased with herself.

But Arkady was disturbed. 'Why did you cover up the mark on your cheek?' he demanded.

'I just decided to. They have makeup in America.'

'They have makeup in the Soviet Union, and you didn't cover up the mark there.'

'It didn't make so much difference there.' She shrugged.

'Why does it make a difference here?'

'Isn't it obvious?' Irina was angry in her turn. 'It's a Soviet mark. I wouldn't cover a Soviet mark with Soviet makeup, but I will with American makeup. I'll get rid of everything Soviet. If I could have a doctor cut into my brain right now and take out everything Soviet, every memory I had, I'd do it.'

'Then why did you want me here?'

'I love you and you love me.'

She trembled so much that she couldn't speak. He wrapped the sheet and blanket around her and held her. He shouldn't have gotten angry at her, he told himself. Whatever she was doing was for the two of them. She had saved his life and brought him with her to the United States at what cost to herself he had no idea, and he had no right to argue. He was, as everyone reminded him, no longer a chief investigator but a criminal. The two of them were criminals, and all that was keeping them alive was each other. He found her cigarette where it had rolled onto the carpet and burned a new hole, and held it to her lips so she could smoke. They could both enjoy good Virginia tobacco now. How wonderful was a lover's accuracy that he could mention that hidden mark and so easily wound her.

'Just don't tell me that Osborne didn't try to have you killed,' he said.

'Things are just so different here,' she said. She began shaking again. 'I can't answer any questions. Please, don't ask me any questions.'

They sat up in bed and watched the color television set. On the screen, a professorial type was reading a book at a lawn table next to a swimming pool. Out of the bushes jumped a young man with a water pistol.

'My God, you frightened me!' The reader almost fell over in his chair and his book dropped into the pool. He pointed to it and said, 'I'm nervous enough as it is, and you pull a stupid trick like that. Lucky that was just a paperback.'

'This is Chekhov?' Arkady laughed. 'This is the same scene you were shooting at Mosfilm when we met.'

'No.'

The man with the water pistol was followed by girls in bathing suits, a man dragging a parachute, a dance band.

470

'No, this isn't Chekhov,' Arkady agreed.

'It's good.'

He thought she was joking, but Irina was totally absorbed by the screen. He could tell she wasn't following the story that was developing; there was no need to, the screen provided its own appreciative howls of laughter. She was, he saw, captured by the electric blue of the pool, the plush green of an avocado tree, the purple of bougainvillea around a driveway, the high-speed mosaic of a freeway. She had found, in a way he never could, what was important on the screen. Its glow reached out and filled the room. When a woman sobbed, Irina saw her dress, her rings, her hair, plush cushions on wicker furniture, a red-cedar terrace and the sunset over the Pacific.

She turned and saw Arkady's dismay. 'I know you think it's not real, Arkasha. You're wrong – here it is real.'

'It's not.'

'It is, and I want it.'

Arkady relented. 'Then you should have it.' He laid his head on her lap and closed his eyes as the television murmured and laughed.

He realized Irina was wearing a new scent. There were few perfumes in Russia, and they were solid, workaday smells. Zoya's favorite was Moscow Nights. That was a real tractor among perfumes. Moscow Nights had been called Svetlana for Stalin's favorite daughter until she eloped with a swarthy Indian. Moscow Nights was a rehabilitated smell.

'Can you forgive me for wanting it, Arkasha?'

He heard the anxiety in her voice. 'I want it for you, too.'

Irina turned the set off and Arkady let the window shade snap up like an explosion. The office building across the street was a grid-iron of dark and empty windows.

He laughed for Irina's sake and turned on the transistor radio she had bought. A samba. Her courage returned, and they danced on the gray carpet, followed by their shadows on the gray walls. He picked her up and spun her around. Blind eye and good eye, both widened with pleasure at the same time. So in one eye sight was gone and the soul remained, even though the mark was gone.

With her above, her hair covered both their faces, a coverlet that swayed as he rose.

With her below, she was a boat bearing them both away.

'We're castoffs and castaways,' Arkady said. 'No country will let us land.'

'We're our own country,' Irina said.

'With our own jungles.' Arkady pointed to the flowered wallpaper. 'Native music' – he pointed to the radio and to the hidden microphones – 'and spies.'

Chapter Three

A brown spider fell into the sunlight and became white.

Irina had left early with Wesley and Nicky.

Its white cable hung from thin air.

'How can you Russians smoke before you even had breakfast?' Wesley had asked.

It swung to a web high in the corner. Arkady hadn't even noticed the web before – not until it glittered in the sideways slant of this particular morning sun. Spiders would be sun worshippers, of course.

'I love you,' Irina had said in Russian.

The spider hurried up and down its threads, front limbs fretting at this and that. Nobody gives them credit; they are such perfectionists.

Which made Arkady say 'I love you' in Russian in return.

How much difference was there between a Russian spider and an American spider?

'Let's go, big day,' Nicky had said when he opened the door.

Did they spin their webs in the same direction? Did they brush their teeth the same way?

Which made Arkady afraid.

Did they communicate?

*

The sidewalks were crowded with well-dressed crowds. The sun stood at their backs and counted the seconds until they got to work.

How long had Irina been in New York? Arkady asked himself. Why did she have so few clothes in the closet?

It would be snowing in Moscow. If they had a sun like this they'd be on the embankment, stripped to the waist, basking like seals.

The painters were at work again across the way. The clerks on the next floor would pick up a phone, say no more than a word or two and set it down. In Moscow an office telephone was an instrument for gossip considerately provided by the state; it was hardly ever used for work, but it was always busy.

He turned on the television to cover the sound while he worked on the lock with a hairpin. It was a well-made lock.

Why would painters work with the windows shut?

In the church garden old men in dirty clothes shared a bottle in slow motion.

The television showed mostly detergents, deodorants and aspirin. There were short interviews and dramatic sketches in between.

When Al brought in a ham-and-cheese sandwich and coffee, Arkady asked him what American writer he liked – Jack London or Mark Twain? Al shrugged. John Steinbeck or John Reed? Nathaniel Hawthorne or Ray Bradbury? Well, that's all the ones I know, Arkady said and Al left.

The offices emptied for lunch. Wherever the sun

reached the sidewalk, someone stopped and ate out of a paper bag. Paper wrappers floated five or ten stories up between buildings. Arkady threw the window up and leaned out. The air was cold and smelled of cigars, exhaust and frying meat.

He saw the same woman in a white-and-black imitation fur coat go in and out of the hotel with three different men.

Cars were huge and dented and had a plastic gloss. There was an intense level of noise, of things being hauled and raised and hammered, as if, just out of sight, the city was being torn down and the cars were being instantly and carelessly manufactured.

The colors of the cars were ridiculous, as if a child had been allowed to color them.

How to categorize the men in the church garden? Social parasites? A 'troika' of drinkers? What did they drink here?

London wrote about the exploitation of Alaska, Twain about slavery, Steinbeck about economic dislocation, Hawthorne about religious hysteria, Bradbury about interplanetary colonialism, and Reed about Soviet Russia. Well, that's all I know, Arkady thought.

People carried so many paper bags. Not only did these people have money, they had things to buy.

He took a shower and dressed in his new clothes. They fit perfectly, felt incredibly fine and made his own shoes immediately ugly. Nicky and Rurik, he remembered, had Rolex watches.

The clothes bureau had a Bible. Far more surprising

was the telephone book. Arkady tore out the addresses of Jewish and Ukrainian organizations, folded them and put them inside his socks.

Black police in brown uniforms directed traffic. White police in black uniforms wore guns.

Irina had hidden the criminals Kostia Borodin and Valerya Davidova. She was implicated in the state crimes of smuggling and sabotage of industry. She knew the Moscow town prosecutor had been a KGB officer. What was waiting for her in the Soviet Union?

Cabs were yellow. Birds were gray.

Rurik came by with a gift of miniature vodka bottles – 'airline bottles' he called them.

'We have a new theory. Before I say it, though' – he raised his hands – 'I want you to know I'm not insensitive. I'm Ukrainian like you. I'm a romantic, too. Let me confess something else. This red hair of mine, it's Jewish. My grandmother was a convert; she had a whole head of it. So I can identify with all kinds of people. But there is a feeling in some quarters that this sable affair is part of the overall Zionist conspiracy.'

'Osborne's not Jewish. What are you talking about?'

'But Valerya Davidova was the daughter of a rabbi,' Rurik said. 'James Kirwill was associated with Zionist terrorists here who shot at innocent clerks in the Soviet Mission. The retail fur and garment industries in the United States are basically Zionist monopolies, and they are the ones who will ultimately profit from the introduction of sables here. See how it fits?'

'I'm not Jewish, Irina's not Jewish.'

'Think about it,' Rurik said.

Al collected all the miniature bottles.

'I'm not KGB,' Arkady said.

Al was embarrassed about being put on the spot. 'Maybe you are, maybe you aren't.'

'I'm not.'

'Does it make any difference?'

Dusk came, the offices emptied and Irina didn't return. There was an evening service at the church. The prostitutes were busy bringing men into the hotel. Arkady thought of the women and their business as the final tide of the street's life reached up to him.

In an hour, shadows became impenetrable spaces between streetlamps. Figures on the street appeared as night animals. Heads turned to a siren's operatic call.

Why had Kirwill laughed?

Arkady was used to different agents. It didn't strike him as strange that the new one wore a dark suit, tie and visored cap, and he was relieved to finally be allowed out of the hotel room. No one stopped them. They went down in the elevator, walked through the lobby and west on Twenty-ninth Street and across Fifth Avenue to a dark limousine. Not until Arkady was ushered into the rear of the car by himself did he realize the other man was a chauffeur. The interior of the limousine was a dove-gray plush, the driver and passenger separated by a glass panel.

The Avenue of the Americas was a dark street deserted except for the illuminated store windows, the mannequins' life of luxury, as unearthly as the whole city was on this first trip outside the hotel. At Seventh Avenue they turned south and went a few blocks before the limousine turned into a side street and into a truck bay. The chauffeur let Arkady out of the car, led him to an open elevator and punched a button with his thumb. The elevator rose to the fourth floor, where they stepped into a brightly lit hall swept by miniature television cameras from opposite corners. The door at the end of the hall clicked open.

'You go alone,' the chauffeur said.

Arkady entered a long, dim workroom. Sorting tables ran the length of the room, and racks of what first appeared to be clothes or rags became, as his eyes adjusted, a mass of furs. There may have been a hundred racks, most of them hung with thin, dark pelts – sable or mink – as well as stacks of larger, flattened hides – lynx or wolf from what he could see. There was an acrid smell of tannic acid and over each white table a low fluorescent lamp. Halfway down the room one lamp went on and John Osborne laid a pelt on the table.

'Did you know that the North Koreans sell fur?' he asked Arkady. 'Cat pelts and dog pelts. Amazing what people will buy.'

Arkady walked down the aisle toward the table.

'Now, this pelt by itself is worth about one thousand

dollars,' Osborne said. 'Barguzhinsky sable, but you probably guessed that; you must have become a bit of an expert on sables. Come closer, you can just see the hint of frost on the hairs.' He brushed the fur back from the stiff skin, and then picked up a small automatic and aimed it at Arkady. 'That's close enough. This will be a beautiful coat, full-length, maybe sixty pelts in all.' He brushed the pelt again with the gun. 'I think someone will pay a hundred and fifty thousand for the coat. How different is it really from buying cat skins and dog skins, though?'

'You'd know better than I would.' Arkady had stopped one table away from Osborne.

'Then take my word for it' – Osborne's face was hidden in the shadow of the lamp – 'because this building and the surrounding two blocks are the largest fur market in the world. So I'll tell you, there's no more comparison between this' – he stroked the glossy pelt – 'and a cat skin than there is between Irina and an ordinary woman, or between you and an ordinary Russian.' He tilted the lamp and Arkady had to raise his hand to keep from being blinded. 'You're looking good, Investigator – very good in a decent suit of clothes. I'm sincerely glad to see you alive.'

'You are sincerely surprised to see me alive.'

'That, too, I admit.' Osborne let the lamp drop. 'You once said you could hide from me, that you could hide beneath the Moskva River and I would come and seek you out. I didn't believe you, but you were right.'

Osborne left the gun on the table while he lit a cigarette. Arkady had forgotten the almost Arab darkness, the lean elegance and silver hair. And, of course, the touches of gold in the cigarette case and lighter, the ring, watchband and cuff links, the amber flames in the eyes, the dazzling smile.

'You're a murderer,' Arkady said. 'Why would the Americans let you meet me?'

'Because the Russians let me meet you.'

'Why would we let you?'

'Open your eyes,' Osborne said. 'What do you see?'

'Furs.'

'Not just furs. Blue mink, white mink, standard mink, blue fox, silver fox, red fox, ermine, lynx, karakul. And Barguzin sables. Over two million dollars' worth of furs in this room, and there are fifty more like it along Seventh Avenue. This is not a matter of murder; it's a matter of sables and always has been. I didn't want to murder the Kirwill boy and Kostia and Valerya. After the help they'd been to me, I would have been perfectly happy if they had gone on living quietly anywhere in the world. But what would you have done? The Kirwill boy insisted on publicity; he had an obsession for telling his story to the world upon his triumphant return to New York. Maybe he wouldn't have told about the sables in his first press conference, but he surely would have by his tenth. Here I was fighting the world's oldest monopoly, I had put in years of effort and risk; should I make myself vulnerable to the self-aggrandizement of a religious fanatic? What sane man would have? I confess I did not mind doing away with Kostia, either. No, he would have extorted money from me the day after he got here. Valerya, though, I regret.'

'You hesitated?'

'Yes.' Osborne was pleased. 'I did hesitate before I shot her, you're correct. I find that confession gives me an appetite. We'll have something to eat.'

They rode down in the elevator and found the limousine waiting in the bay. The car took them north on the Avenue of the Americas. Much more than Moscow would have been at this hour, New York was awake; Arkady could feel it in the snake rush of traffic. Above Forty-eighth Street the avenue was flanked by stark office towers of glass, not unlike Kalinin Prospekt.

At Fifty-sixth Street, the car stopped and Osborne led Arkady into a restaurant, where they were ushered to a banquette of red velvet by a maître d' who greeted Osborne by name. There were fresh-cut lilies on each table and enormous sprays of flowers in alcoves, French Impressionist oils on the wall, crystal chandeliers above, pink tablecloths and an obsequious captain. The other diners were older men in pinstriped suits and younger women with lacquered faces. Arkady still half expected Wesley or the police to burst into the restaurant and arrest Osborne. Osborne asked whether Arkady wanted something to drink; Arkady declined, and Osborne ordered a Corton-Charlemagne '76. Was Arkady hungry? Arkady lied and said no, and Osborne ordered a grilled gravlax with dill sauce and pommes frites for himself. Just the silverware on the table was dazzling. I should be putting the knife through his heart, Arkady thought.

'The Russian émigrés pour through New York, you know,' Osborne said. 'They write down that they're going to Israel, but at Rome they make a right turn and come here. I help quite a few, as many as is practical; after all, some of them know quite a lot about furs. Some of them, though, I can't do anything for. I mean the ones who were waiters in Russia. Do you know anyone who could hire a Russian waiter?'

The wine had a golden color. 'You're sure you don't want any? Anyway, there are more than enough émigrés. Very sad, most of them. Candidate members of the Soviet Academy of Science who are sweeping school halls or fighting each other over scraps of translation work. They live in Queens and New Jersey and have little houses and big cars they can't afford. Of course, one can't criticize; they're doing the best they can. They can't all be Solzhenitsyns. I'd like to think I did something to promote Russian culture in this country. I sponsored a great deal of cultural exchange, you know. Where would American ballet be without Russian dancers?'

'What about the dancers you informed on to the KGB?' Arkady asked.

'If I hadn't, the dancers' friends would have. That's the fascinating thing about the Soviet Union: everyone informs right from the nursery. Everyone has dirty hands. They call it "vigilance". I love that. Anyway, that was the price. If I wanted to promote goodwill and understanding by bringing Soviet artists to the United States, the Ministry of Culture wanted me to inform on who I brought. I did have to inform on some would-be defectors, but generally I just tried to weed out as many bad dancers as possible. I have high standards. I probably had a beneficial effect on Soviet dance.'

'You don't have dirty hands, you have bloody hands.'

'Please, we're at the table.'

'Then tell me how it is that the American FBI lets you, a murderer, a man who informs for the KGB, walk around this city and come here to eat.'

'Oh, I have enormous respect for your intelligence, Investigator. Think about it just for a second. I know you will understand.'

Surrounding conversations wafted among tablecloths and cut flowers and the discreet rattle of a pastry cart. Osborne waited confidently for Arkady's understanding. The understanding came, faintly to begin with, then with a more definite shape, and Arkady was struck by its utter logic and palpable symmetry, as a deer's eye would be if a lion half in shadow stepped fully into the sun. Whatever hope he had left died when he spoke.

'You're an informer for the FBI,' Arkady said as the thought fully formed. 'You informed for the KGB *and* for the FBI.'

'I knew that you of all men would understand.' Osborne smiled warmly. 'Wouldn't I have been a fool to inform for the KGB without informing for the bureau? Don't be disappointed; that hardly makes America as bad as Russia. It just happens to be the way the bureau operates. Ordinarily the bureau relies on criminals, but I hardly get involved in that sort of operation. I simply passed on gossip. I knew the gossip would be appreciated by the bureau because the same gossip was so much appreciated in Moscow. The bureau was even more desperate for it. Hoover was so afraid of mistakes that he had as good as gone out of the business of watching the Russians for the last ten years he was alive. The KGB had a man in the bureau's Central Files, and Hoover didn't even dare clean the section out because he was afraid the news would get around. I made it a point to work only with the bureau's New York office. Like any other national firm, the best men are in New York, and they're so touchingly middle-class, so happy to mix with me. And why not? I wasn't any "hit man" from the Mafia, I didn't ask for money. In fact, they always knew they could come to me for a helping hand when they had personal financial trouble. I gave them extraordinarily good prices on coats for their wives.'

Arkady recalled Iamskoy's lynx coat and the sable hat Osborne had offered him.

'I'm as patriotic as the next man,' Osborne said, and nodded at the people at the table behind Arkady. 'Or rather, as the next man happens to be chairman of the board of a grain company that has just established a dummy distillery in Osaka that will funnel his grain to the Soviet Union's Pacific ports, I'm even *more* patriotic than the next man.'

A plate of grilled gravlax was set in front of Osborne, at its side a dish of pommes frites almost as thin as Russian string potatoes. Arkady was starving.

'You're sure you wouldn't like to share this with me?' Osborne asked. 'It's absolutely delicious. At least some wine? No? It's a curious thing' – he went on talking while he ate – 'it used to be that whenever Russian émigrés arrived in America they would start a restaurant. They served wonderful food – beef Stroganov, chicken Kiev, paskha, blini and caviar, sturgeon in jelly. That was fifty years ago, though. The new émigrés can't cook at all; they don't even know what good food is. Communism has erased Russian cuisine. Now, there's one of the great crimes.'

Osborne had coffee and a tart from the pastry wagon. The desserts wore marbleized sugar and soft toques of whipped cream.

'You won't have a bite? Your former prosecutor, Andrei Iamskoy, would have devoured the entire cart.'

'He was a greedy man,' Arkady said.

'Exactly. It was all Iamskoy's doing, you know. I'd been paying him for years for one thing and another – introductions, small indiscretions, ever since the war. He knew I wouldn't be returning to the Soviet Union and decided to strike for a final grand sum; that's why he led you to me in the bathhouse. Every time I thought I'd shaken you loose, he whipped you on a little more. Not that you needed much encouragement. He said you were an obsessive investigator and he was right. A brilliant man, Iamskoy, but greedy, as you said.'

They left the restaurant and walked up the avenue, Osborne's limousine keeping pace beside him in the street, just as another limousine had once followed them on the Moskva River embankment. After a few blocks they reached a pair of equestrian statues rearing over the entrance to a park. Central Park, Arkady said to himself. They entered, the limousine still behind them, a few snowflakes drifting before its headlights. Were they going to kill him in the park? Arkady wondered. No, it would have been easier to do that in Osborne's workroom. A brightly painted horsedrawn carriage trotted by an old-fashioned light standard. Arkady smoked to damp his hunger.

'Filthy Russian habit.' Osborne lit a cigarette of his own. 'It will be the death of us. Do you know why he hated you?'

'Who?'

'Iamskoy.'

'The prosecutor? Why would he hate me?'

'There was some business about an appeal to the Supreme Court where he got his picture into *Pravda*.'

'The Viskov appeal,' Arkady said.

'That's the one. It ruined him. The KGB didn't set up one of their own generals as Moscow town prosecutor in order for him to start publicizing the rights of convicts. After all, the KGB is like any other bureaucracy, and a powerful man, especially a rising star, has powerful enemies. You gave them just the weapon they needed. Iamskoy was slandering Soviet justice, they said, or promoting a personality cult for himself, or mentally ill. There was going to be a big campaign about it. That appeal ruined him, and you forced him into it.'

In Central Park a former chief investigator learns why the dead Moscow town prosecutor hated him, Arkady thought. Yet what Osborne said sounded right. He remembered the bathhouse conversation with Iamskoy and the secretary to the prosecutor general and the academician and the justice. The hints about the coming campaign against Vronskyism had been aimed at Iamskoy, not at Arkady!

He heard rock music, and through the branches his eyes found the colored lights of a skating rink some distance away. He could make out motion on the ice.

'You should see the park in the snow,' Osborne said.

'It's snowing now.'

'I love the snow,' Osborne confided.

The flakes were scattered around each lamp and in the headlight beams. A brass silhouette saluted Arkady from a pedestal.

'I'll tell you why I love the snow,' Osborne said. 'I've never told anyone this. I love it because it hides the dead.'

'You mean in Gorky Park.'

'Oh, no. I mean Leningrad. I was an idealistic young man when I first went to the Soviet Union. Yes, like the Kirwill boy, maybe worse. No one worked harder to make Lend-Lease succeed. I was the American on the scene, I had to keep up with the Russians, had to do more, on four hours' sleep a night, half starving for months at a time, shaving and getting into clean clothes only when I had to go to Moscow to the Kremlin so that I could beg some secretary to Stalin, some drunkard with grease on his chin, to allow me to add some food and medicine to the trucks we were trying to get into Leningrad. Of course, the siege of Leningrad was one of the great battles, one of the turning points in human history, the army of one mass murderer throwing back the army of a fellow mass murderer. My role, the American role, was to keep the carnage rolling as long as possible. We did it, too. Six hundred thousand Leningraders died, but the city didn't fall. It was a war that went from house to house; we'd lose a street in the morning and gain it back at night. Or gain it back a year later and find all the dead from the year before. You learned to appreciate a deep snow. When the shooting stopped they

487

talked to each other with loudspeakers. The Russian loudspeaker would tell the German soldiers to shoot their officers; the German loudspeaker told the Russians to shoot their children. "Better to shoot them than make them starve to death. Give up, bring your rifle and we'll give you a chicken," the Germans said. Or, "Andrei So-and-so, your two daughters have been found eaten by your Soviet neighbors." This insulted me because I was responsible for getting food into the city. When some Wehrmacht officers were captured, Mendel and I brought some chocolates and champagne and took them for a picnic. We thought we'd release them later and they'd go back over the German lines with stories about how well fed we were inside the city. The Germans laughed at us. They had a thousand stories about the bodies they found as they fought their way into the city. They laughed at me in particular. They were curious about the American who fed the Russians. Did I seriously think, they asked, that it was the few rations we dropped from planes or got through on sleds that were keeping a million people alive? They roared with laughter. Couldn't I think of anything more available? Didn't I already have the answer? they said. I found I did, and then I killed the German officers. But I had the answer.'

They came out of the park onto Fifth Avenue, a dividing line between the public and the rich. Chandeliers glittered in windows; doormen stood under canopies. The limousine coasted to a side street to wait while Osborne led Arkady into the nearest building. A uniformed elevator operator took them to the fifteenth floor, where there was only one door. Osborne unlocked it and motioned Arkady in.

Enough light entered from the windows for Arkady to see that he was standing in the foyer of a large apartment. Osborne flicked a light switch and nothing happened. 'The electricians were here today,' he said. 'I suppose they're not finished.'

Arkady entered a room with a long dining table and only two chairs, and on through a pantry with open, empty cabinets, and into a study with a television still in its packing case and light fixtures ripped from the wall. He counted eight rooms, all nearly stripped except for a rug or chair as a token of more to come. There was also a familiar scent.

He was drawn to the living room, where casement windows framed the park below, far more beautiful from a height. He saw the deep black of lakes and ponds, and the white oval of the skating rink. Around the park was a palisade of apartments and hotels, overhead a vault of clouds.

'What do you think of it?' Osborne asked.

'A little empty.'

'Well, in New York the view's the most important thing.' Osborne took another cigarette from his case. 'I sold my Paris salons. I had to put the money somewhere, and a second apartment here is as good as anything else. To be honest, Europe simply isn't safe for me. That's been the most difficult part of the trade – the guarantees of physical safety.'

'What trade?'

'For the sables. Fortunately, I've stolen something worth giving back.'

'Where are the sables?'

'American fur ranching is done largely around the Great Lakes. But maybe I lied to them; maybe I have the sables in Canada. Canada is the second largest country on earth; it would take them a while to search it. Or maybe I have them in Maryland or Pennsylvania; there's some ranching down there. The problem is that in spring all my new kits will be thrown, all of them sired by my Barguzhinskys, and there'll be that many more sables to account for. That's why the Russians have to trade now.'

'Why tell me?'

Osborne joined him at the window. 'I can save you,' he said. 'I can save you and Irina.'

'You tried to kill her.'

'That was Iamskoy and Unmann.'

'You tried to have her killed twice,' Arkady said. 'I was there.'

'You were a hero, Investigator. No one wants to take that away from you. I sent you to the university to save Irina, after all.'

'You sent me to be killed.'

'And we saved her, you and I.'

'You killed three of her friends in Gorky Park.'

'You killed three of my friends,' Osborne said.

Arkady felt cold, as if the windows had opened. Osborne was not sane, or not a man. If money could grow bones and flesh it would be Osborne. It would wear the same cashmere suit; it would part its silver hair the same way; it would have the same lean mask with its expression of superior amusement. They were high above the street. The apartment was empty. He could kill Osborne, he had no doubt of that. He didn't have to listen to another word.

As if Osborne had heard Arkady's thoughts, he pulled out his gun again. 'We have to forgive each other. Corruption is part of us, it's the very heart of us. It was born in Iamskoy, Russian Revolution or no Revolution. It was born in you as well as me. But you haven't seen the entire apartment . . .'

Arkady in front, they walked down the hall to a room he hadn't entered before, and whose windows also overlooked the park. There were a bureau and a mirror, a chair and night table and a large, unmade bed. The scent he had recognized when he first entered the apartment was strongest here.

'Open the second drawer of the bureau,' Osborne said.

Arkady did so. Laid neatly inside were new men's underwear and socks. 'So someone's moving in,' he said.

Osborne pointed to the sliding doors of a closet. 'Open the door on the right.'

Arkady slid the door open. Hanging from a rack were a dozen new jackets and slacks. Despite the faint light, he saw duplicates of the jacket and trousers he was wearing. 'There was no point in not getting extras,' Osborne said.

Arkady slid the other door open. It was full of dresses, gowns, bathrobes and two fur coats, and its floor was covered by a woman's shoes and boots.

'You're moving in,' Osborne said, 'you and Irina. You

will be my employee and I will pay you well – better than well. The apartment is in my name, but the first year's mortgage and maintenance is already paid. Any New Yorker would gladly trade places with you. You'll have a new life.'

This conversation wasn't possible, Arkady thought; it had taken some supernaturally wrong turn.

'Do you want Irina to live?' Osborne asked. 'That's the trade; the sables in exchange for Irina and you. Irina because I want her, and you because she won't come without you.'

'I'm not going to share Irina with you.'

'You're already sharing Irina with me,' Osborne said. 'You shared her with me in Moscow, and you've been sharing her with me ever since you arrived here. I was in her bed that morning in Moscow when you talked to her outside her apartment. She slept with you last night, and she slept with me this afternoon.'

'Here?' Arkady stared at the rumpled sheets luminous in their disarray.

'You don't believe me,' Osborne said. 'Come now, you're too good an investigator to be so surprised. How would I ever have met James Kirwill without Irina? Or Valerya or Kostia? And didn't it seem strange to you that Iamskoy and I didn't find the two of you when you were hiding her in your apartment? We didn't have to look; she called me from your apartment. How did you think I found her when you took your trip to the Finnish border? She came right to me. You didn't ask yourself these questions? Because you already had your answers. I've confessed – now it's your turn. But you don't like that. At the end of an investigation you only want to find a monster and the neatly assorted dead. God forbid that you should discover yourself. You'll learn to live with yourself, I promise. The Russians will just throw you and Irina on their Jewish quota; they do that with a lot of problems they want to get rid of.'

Osborne laid the gun on the night table. 'I didn't want you, but Irina wouldn't stay without you. It was maddening. All she ever wanted was to be here, and then she threatened to go back. Now, I'm glad you're here; it makes everything complete.' He opened the night table and brought out a bottle of Stolichnaya and two glasses. 'I find the situation seductive. What two men can know each other as well as a killer and his investigator? It's your very duty to define the crime; you give definition to the criminal. I take shape in your imagination before we even meet, and as I run from you, you obsess me in return. We have always been partners in crime.'

He poured vodka to the brim, so that the liquid swelled softly at the top, and gave one glass to Arkady.

'And what killer and investigator can be closer than two men who share the same woman? We are partners in passion as well.' Osborne lifted his glass. 'To Irina.'

'Why did you kill the people in Gorky Park?'

'You know why; you solved it.' Osborne's glass was still raised.

'I know *how* you did, but why?'

'For the sables, as you know.'

'Why did you want your own sables?'

'To make money. You know all this.'

'You already have so much money.'

'To have more.'

'Just more?' Arkady asked. He poured his glass onto the bedroom carpet, drawing a spiral with the vodka. 'Then you're not a man of great passion, Mr Osborne; you're only a homicidal businessman. You're a fool, Mr Osborne. Irina sells herself to you and gives herself to me. A businessman should only expect the skin, yes? You should know about taking the skin. We'll live here at your expense and laugh in your face. And who knows when we'll disappear? Then you'll have no sables, no Irina, nothing.'

'Then you accept my offer of help,' Osborne said. 'Today is Wednesday. On Friday the Soviets and I will trade – you and Irina for the sables. You will allow me to save you?'

'Yes,' Arkady said. What choice was there? Only Osborne could save Irina. Once they were safe they could run away. If Osborne tried to stop them, Arkady would kill him.

'Then I drink to you,' Osborne said. 'It took me a year in Leningrad to discover what humans will do to survive. You are here only two days and you're already a different man. In two more days you'll be an American.' He drank his glass in one swallow. 'I look forward to the coming years,' he said. 'It will be good to have a friend.'

Alone in the elevator, Arkady sagged under the weight of the truth. Irina was a whore. She had slept with

Osborne and God knew who else to earn her passage from Russia. Spread her legs as if they were wings. Lied to Arkady – lied with accusations and kisses – called him an idiot and then made him one. Worse, he had known. Known from the beginning, known from moment to moment, known more as he loved her more. Now they were both whores. Him in his new clothes, no longer chief investigator, no longer criminal – then what? The three bodies in Gorky Park. 'What about them?' Osborne had asked. And what about Pasha? He was staggered at all the frauds he had committed. The first fraud of the investigation so that he could force Pribluda to take over. The second one so that he could have Irina, the final one so that Osborne could have her.

The elevator door opened and he walked through the lobby. I'm Osborne's partner, he answered himself. As soon as he reached the sidewalk, the limousine rolled in front of him. Blindly he got in and the car moved south, toward the hotel.

Yet he still loved her. He would turn his back on the bodies in Gorky Park. She had whored her way to America, and he would whore to help her stay. The Barcelona Hotel had been well chosen for such a pair. He let his head loll against the seat. Snowflakes trembled on the moving shadows of the window. No questions, she had begged, so he'd asked no questions and made his mind a blank. How many closets of clothes did she own? How long had she been in New York?

His mind moved back. He'd never broken, he'd never talked. But the KGB and the FBI and everyone else knew about Irina and Osborne. Who was there to tell them besides Irina? And further back. How many years had she slept with Osborne? No, there wouldn't have been other men. Osborne was too proud for that.

On Broadway they passed the ape grins of movie marquees. Pornography theaters displayed cardboard blow-ups of smudged bodies. 'Live acts!' said a sign. A doorway embraced a black woman in a blond wig, a white woman in a red wig and a young man in a cowboy hat. In Times Square there was a nervous pair of police on every corner. Billboards exploded with color and smoke. Snow flew like ash over the crowds. A jogger dodged between prostitutes.

Yet Irina loved him. She would return to Russia or stay in America, depending on what he did. He remembered her at Mosfilm, her Afghan jacket and split boot. So she'd slept with Osborne in Moscow, but she wouldn't take any gifts. Not even money and she was hungry half the time. The only present she'd accept was America. What had Arkady given her, a scarf with Easter eggs? Only Osborne could give her America, only Osborne would give him the truth. Osborne had the power of gifts.

America, Russia, Russia, America. America was the best of all illusions. It defied expectations. Even here in its lights, close enough to crush dollars in your hands, it remained an illusion. He wouldn't have come if he'd known about Irina and Osborne, he told himself. But he'd always known about Irina and Osborne, he answered himself. Who was he to talk about illusions?

She'd go back if Arkady said so; even Osborne agreed. What were Irina and Osborne like in bed?

Irina, Osborne, Osborne, Irina. He could see them in bed, the two of them a serpentine. The three of them.

He came out of his reverie when the limousine pulled to the curb. He noticed they were far south of Twenty-ninth Street. Both rear doors swung open; on each side a young black man leaned into the car aiming a revolver at Arkady's head with one hand and holding a detective's shield with the other. The glass panel between the back seat and the limousine driver slid down to show Kirwill behind the wheel.

'What happened to the chauffeur?' Arkady asked.

'Some bad man hit him on the head and stole his car.' Kirwill grinned. 'Welcome to New York.'

Kirwill consumed hot beef sandwiches and shots of whiskey with beer chasers. The two black detectives, Billy and Rodney, drank rum-and-Cokes in the opposite booth. Arkady sat across from Kirwill, his glass empty. He wasn't in the bar, he wasn't free, his eyes still saw the sheets sprawled on the apartment bed. He sat with Kirwill the way a man might sit indifferently in front of a fire.

'Osborne could say "I killed them",' Kirwill explained. 'He could say, "I shot them in Gorky Park at three p.m. on February first. I did it and I'm glad." He wouldn't be extradited. With any decent American lawyer the case would drag on for five years. It takes twenty years to get a Nazi war criminal out of here. Say, five years for the first trial, another five years for an appeal. In the end he could still go to the federal appeals and buy a mistrial. Win or lose, that's fifteen years. Sables fuck; they don't

fuck like minks but they fuck, and in fifteen years the
Russian sable monopoly will be ancient history. That's
fifty million dollars in foreign exchange. So forget extradition. The other two choices are killing Osborne and
stealing the sables back, or else dealing. The bureau is
protecting Osborne, and the Russians don't know where
the sables are, so they'll deal. Look, give the man credit.
Osborne pissed on the KGB, he pissed on them and then
he shook it. The man's a fucking American hero. What
are you, some fucking Russian subversive? But I'm going
to help you, Renko.'

Kirwill and his two black detectives looked like exotic
thieves, certainly nothing like Moscow militia. The stolen
limousine was only a few blocks away.

'You should have helped me in Moscow,' Arkady said.
'I could have stopped Osborne then. You can't help me
now.'

'I can save you.'

'Save me?' The humor roused Arkady. Yesterday he
might even have believed Kirwill. 'You can't save me
without the sables. Do you have the sables?'

'No.'

'You're going to save me, but you can't save me. This
is not very hopeful.'

'Leave the girl – let the KGB take it out on her.'

Arkady rubbed his eyes. Him in America and Irina
in Russia? What an absurd conclusion that would be.

'No.'

'That's what I figured.'

'Well, thank you for your kind thought.' Arkady

started to rise. 'Maybe you should take me back to the hotel now.'

'Wait a second.' Kirwill pulled him down. 'Have one drink for old times' sake.' He filled the shot glass in front of Arkady, searched in his pockets and came up with some cellophane bags of peanuts that he shoved across the table. Billy and Rodney watched Arkady with great curiosity, as if he might drink with his nose. They were tall and jet-black, and wore bright shirts and necklaces. 'If the bureau can lend you to an admitted murderer, it can lend you to the New York Police Department for another five minutes,' Kirwill said.

Arkady shrugged and drank the whiskey in one swallow. 'Why is the glass so small?' he asked.

'It's a form of torture designed by priests,' Kirwill said. He looked at the other detectives. 'Hey, at least let's have a bowl for the nuts. Can one of you get off his ass?' As Billy went to the bar, Kirwill turned back to Arkady and said, 'Wonderful spade.'

'Spade?' Arkady asked.

'Spade, nigger, blood, dude, coconut. Hey, now, Rodney,' Kirwill said when the other black detective laughed and shook his head, 'if he ever becomes an American the man will have to get his terms straight.'

'Why don't you like the FBI?' Arkady asked.

The manic power that was Kirwill made a slight revolution. The grin twisted. 'Well, for a lot of reasons. Professionally, because the FBI doesn't conduct investigations, they pay informers. Doesn't matter what kind of case – spies, civil rights, Mafia – all they know is informers. Most Americans are touchy about informing, so the bureau specializes. Their informers are mental cases and hit men. Where the bureau touches the real world, suddenly you get all these freaks who know how to kill people with piano wire. Say a freak got caught, and now he's willing to fry his friends. He tells the bureau what it wants to hear and makes up what he doesn't know. See, that's the basic difference. A cop goes out on the street and digs up information for himself. He's willing to get dirty because his ambition in life is to be a detective. But a bureau agent is really a lawyer or an accountant; he wants to work in an office and dress nice, maybe go into politics. That son of a bitch will buy a freak a day.'

'Not everyone who informs is a freak,' Arkady muttered. He saw Misha standing in the church, took another drink and pushed the image aside.

'When their freaks are finished testifying, they move them and give them new names. If the freak kills someone else, the bureau moves him again. There are psychopaths who've been moved four, five times – totally immune. I can't arrest them; they've got better pardons than Nixon. That's what happens when you don't do the job yourself, when you use freaks.'

The detective returned from the bar with a wood-grained plastic bowl. Kirwill opened the peanuts into it. 'While you're up, Billy,' he said, 'why don't you call the pens and find out if they've released our friend Rats yet.'

'Shee-it!' Billy said, but went to the phone booth.

'What's "shee-it"?' Arkady asked.

'Two scoops of shit,' Rodney said.

500

'Osborne says he is an informer for the FBI,' Arkady said.

'Yeah, I know.' Kirwill looked up as if his eyes were on the moon. 'You can just imagine the day when John Osborne walked into the bureau. They probably stepped on their cocks they stood so fast. Someone like him – been to the Kremlin, been to the White House, high society – won't take a penny, could buy and sell any man in the bureau. Hobnobs with all sorts of pinkos here and Reds there. He's your dream freak come true.'

'Why didn't he go to the CIA?'

'Because he's smart. The CIA has thousands of sources of Russian information, a hundred men going in and out of Russia. The FBI was forced to shut its Moscow office. All it had was Osborne.'

'All he could give them was gossip.'

'That's all they wanted. They just wanted to get on some congressman's lap and put their hot lips to his ear and whisper that they'd heard from their own special source that Brezhnev had syph. Same as they whispered about the Kennedy boys and King. That's what congress-men are willing to pay for, that's what federal budgets are all about. Only, now the bureau has to pay; Osborne is calling in his notes. He wants the bureau to protect him, and he's not going to change his name and hide. He's got the bureau by its delicate pearl-sized balls and he's just started to squeeze.'

Arkady had finished the nuts while Kirwill talked. He poured himself another drink. 'But he stole the sables and has to give them back.'

'Really? Would the Soviet Union give them back if the KGB stole them? He's a hero.'

'He's a murderer.'

'Says you.'

'I'm not KGB.'

'Says me. In this particular world we're the odd men out.'

'They didn't let him go.' Billy returned from the phone. 'Now they want to hold him for drunk-and-disorderly. They'll charge him in an hour.'

Billy's voice reminded Arkady of a saxophone. 'Your two men' – he studied Billy and Rodney – 'aren't they painting an office across the street from my hotel?'

'See,' Kirwill told them, 'I said he was good.'

When they left the bar, Billy and Rodney drove off in a red convertible. Kirwill and Arkady walked through a series of streets connected at odd angles through a part of the city Kirwill called the Village. There was just enough snow to make streetlamps stand out and the night air taste better. On Barrow Street they stopped in front of a three-story brick house with marble steps and vines wedged between nearly identical houses. Arkady knew without being told that it was Kirwill's house.

'In the summer that wisteria gets out of hand, a regular purple hell,' Kirwill said. 'Big Jim and Edna had a Russian who lived here with us whose English wasn't too good. When his friends visited he told them to look for a house "covered with hysteria". Close enough.'

The house looked slightly suspended in the dark.

'We had a lot of Russians. The babushka who took care of me used to do the five little piggies on my toes.

She'd say, "This little Rockefeller went to market, this little Mellon stayed home, this little Stanford had roast beef . . ."

'The bureau used to have two guys sitting in a car here all day and all night. They tapped the phone, they put bugs in our walls from the other houses, they questioned anyone who came to the door. The anarchists made bombs on the roof. There was a kind of suspense about the whole place you don't find in a lot of homes. Jimmy took over the top floor later. Very Nearer My God to Thee. He put an altar up there – crucifixes, ikons. Christ was Jimmy's bomb. Big Jim and Edna exploded, Jimmy exploded, and me, I'm down to one Russian.'

'And you still live here?'

'In a fucking haunted house. This whole country's a fucking haunted house. Come on, there's someone we have to get.'

Kirwill's car was blue, old, fastidiously clean. He drove south on Varick, waving casually to a police squad car they passed. It struck Arkady that by now Wesley must know he was missing and there had to be some panic at the Barcelona Hotel. Was there a bulletin out to police cars? Would they suspect Kirwill?

'Even if Osborne is an important informer, I don't understand why the FBI would allow him to see me,' Arkady said. 'No matter what, he is still a criminal and they are an organ of justice.'

'Other towns go by the book. There's no book in New York. If a diplomat hits your car, shoots your dog, rapes your wife, he goes home quietly. There's a small Israeli army, a small Palestinian army, Castro's Cubans, the bureau's Cubans – all we can do is play chambermaid and clean up the mess.'

Driving through a strange city at night, his imagination filled in what wasn't seen. In the shadows Arkady placed the chimneys of the Likhachev works, the walls of the Manezh, the side streets of Novokuznetskaya.

'The bureau is playing this one differently, though,' Kirwill said. 'They have safe apartments in the Waldorf, why put you in the Barcelona? That's good because the security stinks, and I can get Billy and Rodney right on top of you. It's fishy, though, because it suggests that Wesley doesn't want any record even in the bureau that you were ever here. What did Osborne say to you? He mention any kind of deal?'

'We just talked,' Arkady said. The lie came without hesitation, as if from another set of nerves and another, glibber mouth.

'He talked about himself and the girl, if I know him. He's the kind that takes a lot of pleasure in applying the screws. Leave him to me.'

Lower Manhattan's public buildings were a nighttime collection of Roman, colonial and modern architecture, with one floodlit exception, a single mammoth building that consumed an entire block and seemed familiar to Arkady. It was a building in Stalinist Gothic without Stalin's Oriental frills, a sleeker necrolith without a ruby star which rose out of sight of its lights. Kirwill parked in front.

'What is it?' Arkady asked. 'What can be open now?'

'It's the Tombs,' Kirwill said. 'Night Court's open now.'

They pushed through brass doors into a lobby full of beggars with purple bruises, jackets with exploded pockets and lapels, the sideways suspicion of kicked dogs. There were beggars in Moscow, but they were seen only in railway stations or when they were flushed out by a militia campaign. The entire lobby was theirs. The information counter was filled waist-high with trash. One long side of the lobby was papered with trial times; the other side had a line of aluminium phones. Huge ceiling fixtures hung far out of reach. A pair of older men in shabby overcoats and carrying briefcases eyed Arkady.

'Lawyers,' Kirwill explained. 'They think you might be a client.'

'They should know their clients better.'

'They don't know their clients until they come through these doors.'

'They should meet their clients in their offices.'

'This is their office.'

Kirwill steered him through the crowd and a double set of brass doors into what Arkady recognized at once was a courtroom. It was close to midnight; how could any court be in session?

A single judge in a robe sat at a high desk before a wooden panel engraved with the words 'In God We Trust' and an American flag covered in plastic. A stenographer and a clerk were at lower desks, and one man sat at a table sorting through stacks of blue-covered charge sheets. Attorneys wandered from the table of papers to the judge or to the side bench where the offenders waited. These were of both sexes, all ages and mostly black; all the attorneys were young, white, male.

A velvet rope separated the proceedings from a front row of men in leather jackets and jeans. They wore police shields on their belts and expressions of infinite boredom, some with eyes rolled back, others with eyes closed. Families of the defendants sat in the back rows among beggars who had come to drowse. Here was the city's sleep; it started and spread from this court, a fatigue overcoming any outrage, outlasting even the fixed pose of cynicism. Judge, offender, friend, every face was slack. A young coffee-colored woman with a baby in a snowsuit sat peacefully by Arkady. The baby's eyes reflected the bright squares of the ceiling lights. The window blinds were drawn. Occasionally a guard would stir to evict a snorer; otherwise the court was virtually silent because when an offender and the arresting officer were called to stand at the table, the attorneys talked to the judge in voices too soft to carry. Then the judge would set a price. Sometimes the price was $1,000, sometimes $10,000. The judge listened, never looking up, his head turning from one attorney to the other. They're *bargaining*, Arkady realized. A case could take five minutes or only one before a price was set. In Moscow, he saw cases of drunkenness settled as quickly, but these were accusations of robbery and assault. As the next offender was called, the previous one smirked through the velvet rope, placing a comb in his hair just so, leaving before the man who had arrested him.

'What is "bail"?' Arkady asked.

'It's what you pay to get out of jail,' Kirwill said. 'You can look at it as a bond, or a loan, or a tax.'

'That's justice?'

'No, but it's the law. They didn't bring Rats out yet – that's good.'

Some of the detectives walked to the back of the courtroom to say hello respectfully to Kirwill. They were big, unshaven men, muscle and fat tucked into plaid shirts and belts with detective shields – nothing like the slim agents of the FBI. One pointed to the next defendant slouching before the judge and said, 'Fucker mugged a lady in Battery Park, so the Robbery Squad caught it. Then they thought she was raped, so they gave it to the girls on the Rape Squad; then they thought she was going to die so they passed her over to us on Homicide. But she didn't die and she wasn't raped, so they gave her back to Robbery – only, their shift is over and the paperwork's all over the fucking place and if it doesn't get here in one minute he walks.' 'A psycho,' the second detective said. 'Already did murder as a juvenile for torching his mother. We have to protect everyone who reminds him of his mom?' 'What's the point?' the first detective asked. 'What's the sharp and nasty, smooth and greasy, barbed and two-pronged fucking point?' Arkady shrugged, he didn't know. Kirwill shrugged. Accepting the homage of the other detectives, he was their intelligence, their broad shoulders, their alcohol-washed blue eyes. 'No point,' he said, 'that's the point.'

Kirwill led Arkady out of the court and back through the lobbies. 'Where are we going now?' Arkady asked.

'Going to get Rats out of the pens. You've got something better to do?'

Kirwill buzzed at a steel door. Two eyes peered through a slot and the door opened to the Manhattan Pens. The pens were the court detention cells. Seen from an angle, the green bars were solid walls with protruding hands. Head on, they opened into cells of yellow tile where a dozen or more men waited their turn in court as docilely as machinery, the only movement their eyes as Arkady and Kirwill passed. Kirwill stopped at a cell occupied by a white man bizarrely dressed in woolen gloves cut off at the fingers, muddy boots, an overcoat of many pockets and a woolen cap pulled over matted hair. His face had the raw flush and dirt of liquor and exposure, and he was trying to control the trembling in his left leg. Outside the cell were a mustached detective and a pinch-faced young man in a suit and tie.

'Ready to go home, Rats?' Kirwill asked the man in the cell.

'You aren't taking Mr Ratke anywhere, Lieutenant,' the man with the tie said.

'This is an assistant district attorney, he's going to grow up and be a high-paid defense lawyer,' Kirwill explained to Arkady. 'And this is a very sheepish detective.'

In fact, the detective did look as if he wanted to crawl behind his mustache and hide.

'Mr Ratke is being arraigned in a few minutes,' the attorney said.

'On a drunk-and-disorderly?' Kirwill laughed. 'He's drunk, what do you expect?'

'We would like some information from Mr Ratke.'
The attorney had the nervous courage of a small dog. 'I
would like to draw the lieutenant's attention to the fact
that recently there was a major theft at the Hudson Bay
Company, the perpetrators of which are still unknown.
We have reason to believe Mr Ratke was attempting to
sell goods from that robbery.'

'Where's the evidence?' Kirwill asked. 'You can't hold
him.'

'I dint steal it!' Rats shouted.

'Anyway, he's being held for drunk-and-disorderly,'
the attorney said. 'Lieutenant Kirwill, I've heard about
you and I don't mind going head to head with you.'

'You pulled him in on a D-and-D?' Kirwill read the
name on the detective's badge. 'Casey, is it? Didn't I
know your father? There was a detective.'

'Rats was already in, and they needed someone to
stand up with him—' Casey wouldn't meet Kirwill's eyes.

'I could understand a uniformed man doing it, but
you?' Kirwill asked. 'Money problem? You need over-
time? What is it, alimony?'

'Detective Casey is doing me a favor,' the attorney
said.

'For your father's sake, I'll send you the money,' Kirwill said. 'Anything to keep a good Irish boy from kissing
ass. I'd hate for this kind of story to get around.'

'Lieutenant Kirwill, there's no point belaboring the
issue,' the attorney said. 'The detective has agreed to be
the arresting officer for the arraignment. I don't know
what your interest in the matter is, but we are definitely

holding Mr Ratke. As a matter of fact, we should be going into court—'

'Fuck this.' Casey waved his hand and walked off.

'Where are you going?' the attorney demanded.

'I'm gone.' The detective didn't look back.

'Wait!' The attorney ran after him and tried to get between Casey and the door, but the detective wouldn't stop to argue.

'You don't have to work with these fucking Hibernian ball-busters,' he said and slammed the door as he left.

The attorney returned.

'You still lose, Lieutenant. Even if we can't arraign him, Mr Ratke is in no condition to go home by himself, and no one has come forward to claim him.'

'I'm claiming him.'

'Why? Lieutenant, what are you doing all this for? You interrupt the caseload, you intimidate a fellow detective, you antagonize the district attorney's office – all for a drunk. If an officer can do this, what's the point in having a court?'

'No point, that's the point.'

Kirwill and Arkady got Rats all the way to the main lobby before he started screaming with d.t.'s. The beggars in the lobby were startled, wakened somnambulists. Kirwill put a hand over Rats's mouth and Arkady carried him. Rats was the first American he'd met who really stank.

They got him into the car, and at Mulberry Street Kirwill went into a delicatessen and came out with a pint each of whiskey and port and more bags of nuts. 'It's against the law to buy booze from a deli,' Kirwill said. 'That's why it tastes so good.' Rats drained the port and promptly went to sleep on the back seat.

'Why?' Arkady asked. 'Why did we go to all that trouble to get a drunk? Wesley and the FBI must be looking for me – maybe the KGB as well. You'll be in a great deal of trouble. So why?'

'Why not?'

The nuts salted the tongue and the whiskey spread through Arkady's limbs. He saw that Kirwill was enormously pleased with himself. For the first time he began to see some humor in the situation. 'You mean there actually is no point?' he asked.

'Not at this place at this time. Let me show you around.'

'What if they find us before you take me back?'

'Renko, you have nothing to lose, and God knows, I don't. We'll take Rats home.'

Arkady looked at the filth-encrusted figure asleep on the back seat. He'd dined with Osborne, had a taste of American justice and didn't want to face Irina yet. 'Why not?'

'That's my boy.'

Snow and gilt Chinese characters swayed above Canal Street.

'What I couldn't figure out right from the start,' Kirwill said, 'was how you became a cop.'

'You mean an investigator.'

'A cop.'

'Whatever.' Arkady was aware that some odd compliment, perhaps even an apology, had been paid. 'I saw a case once when I was a boy – one of those cases that could have been murder or suicide.' He paused in surprise at himself, because he hadn't meant to say that. An investigator is trained by rote to answer this particular question by referring to fatherly investigators he has known, to stopping shirkers and wreckers, and to protecting the Revolution. Tonight there were demons in his head. 'It was right after the war and there were large reputations at stake,' Arkady went on. 'I'd never heard so many people blurting out the truth. Because the victim herself was such an inescapable truth, there was no way they could set her back on her feet, and because the investigators had special permission to deal with the truth.'

They passed mysterious storefronts with names like Joyeria, Knights of Columbus, Head Shop.

'I'm not making myself clear,' Arkady said.

'Try.'

'Let's say a meritorious artist one night asks his wife to get out of the car to push some glass off the road and then runs her down. A girl, a Young Communist, soon to be married, tucks her old grandparents into bed, seals the windows and turns on the gas before going out for the evening. A hard-working peasant, an honored agronomist, kills a flirt from Moscow. These are worse than crimes; these are things-that-aren't-supposed-to-happen. They're the *truth*. They're the truth about a new kind of Russian: a man who can afford a mistress and a car; a young girl who has to bring her husband home to live in one room with two old people; a peasant and nothing but a peasant who knows he'll never leave a village a thousand miles from the rest of the world. We don't put this in our reports, but we're supposed to know it. That's why we have to have special permission to deal with the truth. We play with the statistics, of course.'

'You mean fewer murders?' Kirwill asked.

'Of course.'

Kirwill passed the bottle and wiped his mouth with the back of his hand. 'What's the point?' he asked. 'We love it. The number one cause of death for young men in America is murder. That body's hardly hit the ground before it's a star on television, everybody has a chance to be a star. We've got wars and better than wars – psychos, rapists, queers, cops, chainsaw massacres. Step outside and get shot, stay inside and watch television. We're talking art form. Bigger than Detroit, better than sex, native art and industry rolled into one, what the Renaissance was to Italy, chopsticks to the Chinks, Hamlet without the slow parts – we're talking car chases here, Arkady, me boy. The guys getting killed for real are lost in the shuffle, life's losing stuntmen. How can you care when you can see a better murder in slow motion, plus special effects, with a beer in one hand and a tit in the other? Better than real cops. All the real cops are in Hollywood; the rest of us are fakers.'

The Holland Tunnel took them under the Hudson. Arkady knew that he should be anxious because by now Wesley really must be thinking he was defecting; yet he felt strangely elated, as if he found himself speaking a language he had never been taught.

'Our Soviet murders are secret,' he said. 'We're backward in terms of publicity. Even our accidents are secret, officially and unofficially. Our killers generally only boast when they're caught. Our witnesses lie. Sometimes I think our witnesses are more afraid of the investigator than the killers are.' From the New Jersey side of the river he looked back at Manhattan. At the end of a million lights, two white towers reached into the night. He wouldn't have been surprised to see two moons above them. 'For a time, I thought I wanted to be an astronomer, but then I decided astronomy was a bore. The stars only interest us because they're so far away. Do you know what would really interest us? A murder on another planet.'

Signs pointed to the New Jersey Turnpike, J. F. Kennedy Boulevard, Bayonne.

Arkady's throat was dry and he took a long drink. 'There are not many road signs in Russia, you know.' He laughed. 'If you don't know where a road goes, you shouldn't be on it.'

'Here we live on road signs. We consume maps. We never know where we are.'

The whiskey was gone. Arkady laid the empty bottle gently on the car floor. 'You had a babushka!' he said abruptly, as if Kirwill had just mentioned it.

'Her name was Nina,' Kirwill said. 'Never became American, not to her dying day. There was only one thing American she liked.'

'What was that?'

'John Garfield.'

'I don't know him.'

'Nothing like you, much more proletarian.'

'This is a compliment?'

'He was a great lover. To his dying day.'

'What was your brother like?'

Kirwill drove for a while before answering. Arkady liked the way the white dashes of the road seemed to leap into the headlights.

'Sweet. A virgin. It was tough having the parents he had, even tougher having them dead. The priests feasted on him, put the Holy Grail in his hand and a passport to heaven up his ass. I used to bust up his altar every time I came home. Stuffed Mark Twain and Voltaire down his throat. It was like throwing rocks at Saint Sebastian. But chasing him to Russia, how do you forgive yourself that?'

Bayonne was a terrain of oil tanks and fractioning columns silvered and brightly illuminated, a lunar encampment.

'We used to go fishing up on the Allagash in Maine, Jimmy and me. It's all timber-company country up there, just one road in and out. Great fishing – pike, bass, trout. Ever fish from a canoe? We even went up there in winter. I took Big Jim's old Packard and put on some oversized tires. We floated over the snow in that car. Ever hear of ice-fishing? You punch a hole in the ice and put some lines down?'

'It's been done in Siberia.'

'Just drink enough to stay warm. Snowed in? No problem. The cabin had canned goods, fireplace, wood-burning stove, and all the goddamned wood you could chop. There was deer, moose, one game warden every thousand square miles. No one else but loggers and

French Canadians, and you speak better English than they do.'

A bridge took them over a river called the Kill Van Kull. Below, a tanker slipped toward the sea, its passage betrayed by a single unblinking red eye.

'Staten Island,' Kirwill announced. 'We're back in New York.'

'It's not Manhattan?'

'No, it's definitely not Manhattan. So near and yet so far.'

They drove by row houses. A plaster saint blessed a lawn.

'Could Jimmy have gotten those people out, Arkady? Tell me the truth.'

Arkady remembered the bodies under the snow in the park, all in a row, not even a step of escape, and the log cabin, the sheets over the sleeping compartments where Jimmy Kirwill read the Bible while Kostia rode Valerya. 'Sure,' he lied. 'He was brave enough. Why not?'

'You're all right,' Kirwill said after a while.

A bridge carried them back to New Jersey over a narrow strip of water the road signs called the Arthur Kill. Along it were docks, tracks and the flares of more refineries. Arkady had lost his sense of direction, but as the moon was to his left he guessed they were headed south. Was there a bulletin out for him in New York? Were they searching for Kirwill, too? What was Irina thinking?

'How far are we going?'

'We're almost there,' Kirwill said.

'Your friend Rats lives here? I don't see any houses.'

'It's all marshland,' Kirwill said. 'Used to be herons here, ospreys, barred owls. A lot of clamming, years back. And frogs. At night the peepers would drive you just about deaf.'

'You used to come here?'

'Used to bring a boat in. I came with one of our anarchists. He was in love with outboard motors. He was also in love with weeds. Naturally, we spent most of our time marooned. To me it was a typical Russian outing.'

Now they were on an industrial access road that ran by the factories. In the headlights the swamp showed all the viscous hues of a palette, greens, yellows, reds.

'You're worried, I can tell,' Kirwill said. 'Don't be. I'll take care of Osborne.'

Then what will happen to Irina and me? was Arkady's first thought. See how grotesque it is to be saved by Osborne; you hope he lives.

'Turn here.' Rats popped up, awake in the back seat.

Kirwill swung onto a strip of blacktop that ran down to the Kill.

'There's more involved than you and Osborne,' Arkady said.

'You mean the bureau? They can protect Osborne anywhere else, not in New York.'

'No, I don't mean the bureau.'

'The KGB? They want his head, too.'

'Stop!' Rats said.

They got out of the car. In one direction, marshland extended to the faint and moving lights of a turnpike; in the other it slipped down to boatyards. They followed Rats on a path that sank spongily under their shoes.

517

'I'll show you.' Rats looked back. 'I'm no thief.'

In the boatyards, harbor craft stood on timber stilts. Guard dogs barked under a lamp, joined by dogs from another yard where timbers rose in creosote-soaked pyramids. On the Kill a garbage scow was on a night run. Across on Staten Island were a few lights, a window, a blue storage tank couched in trees and, along the water, what appeared to be houses, boats, trucks and cranes piled one on top of another.

Arkady reached the relative security of planks set in mud before Kirwill. Snowflakes glittered on sedges and rushes. Rats bounded energetically ahead to a tarpaper shack with a stovepipe. As Arkady approached it he stepped on small bones that oozed like teeth out of the mud. Rats opened the shack door, lit a kerosene lamp and invited him in.

Arkady hesitated. For the first time since he'd been in America he was not surrounded by lights. There was only the glow of the highway, another distant haze blocked by Staten Island, and overhead the familiar half-dome of darkness and the dizzy glitter of snow. The emptiness poured into him.

'Why did we come here?' he asked Kirwill. 'What do you want from me?'

'I want to save you,' Kirwill said. 'Listen, the Barcelona's full of prostitutes; the bureau can't keep track of who goes in and out. By tomorrow night I'll have Billy and Rodney in the room above you. They'll wait until it's good and dark and then drop a ladder outside your window. You and the girl wear something that won't show and hit your ceiling when you're ready. They'll take you down the service elevator and out the basement. Simple operation – up and out, the Red Squad's done it before.'

'The Red what?'

'The Red Squad. They told you about us.'

'How do you know they told me about the Red Squad?' Arkady waited for the answer, then gave it. 'You have a microphone in our room. That's what your detectives Billy and Rodney are doing across the street; the radio in their window is the receiver.'

'Everyone has a transmitter in your room.'

'But they don't know me as a friend. As a friend, tell me, does everyone gloat over every word? Is it possible to listen antiseptically? Excuse me for being so stupid, I must ask you now what you were doing at the apartment Osborne took me to. Why was the electricity off there? Tell me if I'm wrong, but you were running more microphones through that apartment – one in every room right with the wiring? Ah, Lieutenant, you've been busy. You didn't miss the bedroom, did you?'

'They're setting you up, Arkady. The bureau and the KGB together. There's no record of you being in this country – I checked. Not in this country, not in the Barcelona, nowhere. Whatever I'm doing is for your protection.'

'Liar! You broke your own brother's leg for his protection. You know all about Osborne and Irina and me.'

'But I can save you. I can get you both out, and Wesley won't even know you're gone until the morning. There'll be a car waiting for you a few blocks from the hotel with money, new identification, maps. You can be in Maine in nine hours. I still have that cabin. I stocked it for you, and I replaced the Packard with a jeep. There are skis and rifles. If things get tight, you can head for Canada – it's not far away.'

'This is an insane joke of yours, because you can't help us.'

'I can. See, this way Jimmy still wins. He stills gets two Russians out. Otherwise, his whole life and death was a waste. This way there's some point to Jimmy's having lived.'

'There's no point. He's dead.'

'What are we arguing for? Then let me do it for you. We're friends.'

'No, we're not. Take me back to the hotel.'

'Wait.' Kirwill held on to Arkady's arm.

'I'm going.' Arkady pulled loose and started for the car.

'You'll do what I tell you.' Kirwill grabbed him again.

Arkady hit him. The corner of Kirwill's mouth split and bled, as if with surprise as much as the force of the blow. Kirwill still held Arkady's other arm.

'Let go, now,' Arkady warned.

'No, you've got to—'

Arkady hit him again and the blood smeared over Kirwill's lip. Arkady expected a display of the lieutenant's professional expertise: the powerful hands that crushed ribs and struck at the heart, the kick that disabled a knee, the legendary fury. But he had learned something since Gorky Park, and he thought it might be a little more even this time. A fight to the death had a growing attraction, and that's where Kirwill – *Killwell*, as his own brother called him – could help; that's what he was best at.

'Fight back,' Arkady demanded. 'This is how we started, remember.'

'No,' Kirwill said, but he hung on.

'Fight.' He knocked Kirwill to his knees.

'Please,' Kirwill asked.

This was a new and grotesque figure, Kirwill in the mud, begging.

'Let go!' Arkady shouted. His arms dropped. 'Just let me go. There's not going to be any escape to any fairy-tale cabin. You know that. You know we could hide for ten years, and the KGB would find us and kill us if they don't get the sables. They'll never let us go without the sables. They'll give us to Osborne to get the sables. So don't tell me your stories – you can't save anyone.'

'Just look,' Kirwill said.

Arkady looked at the shack. Rats still waited at the door, too frightened to run.

'Look inside,' Kirwill said.

Arkady felt sweat pouring over his chest. His face was freezing. With each step the ground sucked at his feet.

Rats held the lamp up. Arkady stooped through the low door and pushed aside a dangling roll of flypaper. The walls and roof of the shack were boards and plastic sheets, insulated with newspaper and rags. Loose planks were the floor. A rug and blankets lay on one side. In the middle, a potbellied stove displayed a pan of congealed beans. In the windowless structure the smell of decaying meat was overpowering.

'I dint steal it.' Rats backed away, terrified of Arkady. 'Unnerstan' English? I trap. Thass what I am, thass what I do.'

Cans of grease and tallow lined an orange-box shelf. There was a shelf of medicine: digitalis, nitroglycerin, ampules of amyl nitrite, Contact, Scope.

'Muskrats is good food, nashural foood. It's just the name what puts people off. The fur's firs'-rate. People is so dumb; most of the coats they wear is muskrat. I take ten, twenny hides a week to town. I'm set up, I don't need to steal nothin' an' I dint.'

Rats stumbled against the stove, and the pan of beans fell over a cardboard box of metal utensils. Ajax and Handiwipes. He back-shuffled around cases of Bisquick, Gravy Train, Roach Mottel, a postcard of John Glenn tacked to tarpaper. Jars of Vaseline, A&P Instant Coffee, a tannic acid solution made from Red Rose Tea. Wading boots and a net.

'It was mine, in my trap. Never saw nothin' like it. Wasn't no mink, it was differ'nt. Thass why I took it to town, to fine out what it was.'

Backward past plastic bags of Kraft marshmallows, Wonder Bread and Alba Milk Powder. Stained clothes on a line. A fatigue jacket on a hook, a Citibank calendar and more encrusted curlicues of flypaper. Then a clothesline of muskrat hides, glossy pelts hanging from flat, naked tails, the heads and short, webbed feet still attached.

'The man at the market said it ain't even American.

So maybe iss yours afterall. All I'm sayin' is I caught it, I dint steal it. I'll show you where, right across the water. I'm a happy man, I don't need trouble.'

Rats took the fatigue jacket from the hook.

'If iss yours, iss yours.'

On the hook was a pelt much longer and narrower than the muskrats, the fur a lustrous blue-black with a characteristic touch of 'frost' at the tips, its tail bushy and rounded, the hide stiff and meticulously tanned, but one paw had been almost gnawed through in desperation when the animal had tried to escape the trap. A sable.

'I'll take you right there,' Rats told Kirwill, who stood inside the door. 'We'll go soon as there's light. Dawn, juss you an' me go.' He giggled, and his eyes darted from Arkady to Kirwill, ready to take them into his confidence. 'I gotta secret. Where I got that fur? There's plenny more.'

Wesley pulled the emergency stop, and the elevator car hovered between the fourth and fifth floors of the Barcelona. In the car were Arkady, Wesley, George and Ray. It was 3 a.m.

'We did have a bulletin out for an hour,' Wesley said. 'Lieutenant Kirwill is totally insane, attacking a civilian driver and taking his car. Who knew what danger you were in? Then I realized there was nothing to worry about; you'd never try anything as long as we have Miss Asanova. As long as we have her, we have you. So we waited, and here you are. Where have you been?' He released the emergency stop. 'I promise you, it doesn't matter.'

George and Ray pushed Arkady along the fifth-floor hall until he shook them off and turned on them, and then they looked back at Wesley, who waited at the elevator. 'Gently,' Wesley said.

Arkady went the rest of the way down the hall alone. Al was waiting inside the room. Arkady threw him out and put a chair against the door.

Irina sat in bed watching, exhausted and afraid. He had never seen her more afraid. He noted the way the sheets lapped against the green silk nightgown she wore, the way her long hair fell over her shoulders. Her arms were erotically bare, her eyes large. The faint blue mark on her cheek was unmasked, the touch of guilelessness. She didn't dare speak; she hardly dared breathe. An idiot shouldn't be so frightening, Arkady thought. He sat on the bed beside her and tried to keep his hands from shaking.

'You slept with Osborne in Moscow. You sleep with him here. He showed me the bed. I want you to tell me about it. You did intend to tell me about it sometime, didn't you?'

'Arkasha,' she said so softly that he could hardly hear what she had said.

'One man is not enough for you?' Arkady asked. 'Or Osborne does something for you that I don't? Something special, a particular position? Backward, forward? Please inform me. Or he possesses a sexual magnetism you can't resist? Are you attracted to a man whose hands are covered with blood? See, my hands are bloody now. Not the blood of *your* friends, I'm afraid – only the blood of *my* friend.'

He held his bloody hands up for her to see. 'No' – he read her reaction – 'not satisfactory, not stimulating enough. But Osborne tried to kill you; maybe that's the difference. That's it! Why would a woman sleep with a killer unless she wanted to be hurt?' He slipped his fingers into her hair, twisted it and raised her head. 'Is that better?'

'You're hurting me,' Irina whispered.

'You don't seem to like it.' He let go of her hair. 'Then that's not it. Maybe it's money that excites you; I understand it excites many people. Osborne showed me around our new apartment. What rich people we're going to be in such an apartment, so full of gifts and clothes. But you've earned them, Irina. You paid with the lives of your own friends. No wonder you're showered with gifts.' He fingered the neck of her night-gown. 'Is this a gift?' He ripped the neck open, tore the gown down the middle and pulled it open from her breasts. Above her left breast he saw her pulse beat in terror, the same pulse he felt when they made love. He ran his hand lightly over her stomach: his pillow, Osborne's pillow.

'You're a whore, Irina.'

'I told you I'd do anything to get here.'

'Now I'm here and now I'm a whore too,' Arkady said.

The touch of her made him both furious and weak. He forced himself to stand and look away; as he did so, as if the very movement had upset a brimming cup, he found tears pouring from his eyes and over his face. I will kill her or cry, he said to himself. Hot salt poured into his mouth.

'I told you I would do anything to get here,' Irina said behind him. 'You wouldn't believe me, but I told you. I didn't know about Valerya and the others. I was afraid, but I didn't know. When could I have told you about Osborne? After I began to love you, after we were in your apartment? Forgive me, Arkasha, for not telling you I was a whore after I began to love you.'

'You slept with him there.'

'Once. So he would get me out. You had just appeared for the first time, and I was afraid you were going to arrest me.'

Arkady raised his hand. It dropped of its own dead weight.

'You slept with him here.'

'Once. So he would take you with me.'

'Why? You were going to be free, have your apartment, your clothes — why ask for me?'

'They were going to kill you in Russia.'

'Maybe. They hadn't killed me yet.'

'Because I love you.'

'You should have left me there! I was better off there.'

'I wasn't,' Irina said.

He'd never even known he possessed such tears. He remembered Unmann's knife standing from his stomach — the only other time anything had flowed from him so strongly. The pain was not so different.

'I wasn't better off with you there.' As Irina sat up the torn gown fell from her.

Were they listening? Arkady wondered – all those miniaturized ears within the bed, the sofa, the medicine cabinet. The window shade hung like a vulgar eyelid. He snapped it up and turned the lights off.

'If you go back there, I'll go with you,' Irina said from the dark.

His tears were springs of rage as hot as blood. Blind, he saw in his mind the Viskovs in their cafeteria near Pavelettsky Station, the old man bearing a plate of caviar paste and smiling with steel teeth, his mute wife beaming. He saw them by the millions with their steel teeth. 'They'd kill you for certain,' he said.

'Whatever you do, I'll do.'

He sank on his knees by the bed. 'You didn't have to sell yourself for me.'

'What else did I have to sell?' Irina asked. 'It's not as though I'd sold myself for a pair of boots. I sold myself to escape, to become alive. I'm not ashamed, Arkasha. I would be ashamed of myself if I hadn't. I'll never say I'm sorry that I did it.'

'With Osborne, though—'

'I'll tell you about it. I didn't feel dirty afterward, the way young girls are supposed to feel. I felt burned, as if one layer of skin had been taken off.'

She pulled his head between her breasts. His arm went around her. His clothes were heavy and soaked through, and he sloughed them off, like memory.

At least this bed was theirs, he thought. Perhaps nothing else on earth was, but by rights this bed was, with its torn gown and torso of an overcoat, with its canopy of dark. Somehow they loved each other more.

They were exhausted, dead, and now were alive again in this whore's bed, in this alien night.

Arkady felt Irina's deep sleep against his side.

In the morning Rats would take Kirwill to the sables.

'They're on the Arthur Kill,' Kirwill had said on the way back, 'and I'll tell you, it makes a lot more sense stashing them here than a thousand miles away. First, everyone automatically assumes he has them up in mink country. Second, he keeps them right here under his own control; he doesn't have to depend on someone answering a long-distance call. Third, maybe there's a hundred thousand square miles around the Great Lakes, but there are a lot of mink ranchers up there, too. It's one giant mink cooperative, did you know that? Sables need fresh meat. Big cooperatives find out about that kind of food being shipped into any part of their woods. But New York's the fresh-meat capital of the universe; you can't keep track of what goes where. And the west side of Staten Island is all woods and swamps, a couple of refineries, a few local people who mind their own business and no cops. The only thing that can possibly go wrong is a hole in a cage, a sable escapes, someone catches it and tries to sell it, a furrier in Manhattan calls the cops, and I, of all people, happen to hear about it. The only thing that can go wrong. The fates are good to you, Arkady. It's going your way now.'

In the afternoon Billy and Rodney would check into the hotel room above. Once it was dark all Arkady and Irina had to do was climb up a ladder that would be dropped outside their window. Just pick a time when the street was clear and rap on the ceiling. No one would see them from the empty office buildings. Then they'd take the service elevator from the sixth floor to the basement, and go out the rear entrance to a waiting car. There'd be keys, money and carefully marked maps in the glove compartment. Once they were on their way Kirwill would contact the KGB and offer Nicky and Rurik the same trade Osborne had: the sables for Irina and Arkady. What could Rurik and Nicky do? The prisoners were already gone. As soon as the FBI discovered the escape, the old trade would be off, and Osborne would make the sables disappear again to who knew where. It always came down to the sables. The KGB would quickly trade with Kirwill and race to Staten Island.

He smoked, blocking the match's flare from Irina's face.

Irina didn't know. How could he describe plans for escape when they were surrounded by microphones? Besides, she lived in expectation of Osborne's trade, an expectation that was daylight seen from a black pit. There was no reason to frighten her until the new plan went into motion; then he could just motion her to follow him. Before she knew it, they'd be in the car.

Everything depended on a drunk. Perhaps Rats had found the sable pelt and concocted the entire story. Or he'd have another attack of delirium tremens and be unable to lead Kirwill to the sables. Osborne must be aware that a sable was gone; had he moved the others already?

Then he and Irina might not get away. Perhaps the FBI watched the windows of their room all the time. Arkady had never driven an American car; who knew how it worked? They could get lost. Maps, at least in the Soviet Union, were deliberately inaccurate. Perhaps he and Irina were so plainly Russian that everyone would recognize them as fugitives. Besides, he was an ignorant man in a foreign country.

At least, he no longer had to believe Osborne. As Irina said, you believe what you have to. She had no pretense; all she wanted from Osborne was America. An investigator demanded more of a killer, an ascent to a dark view, a landscape of sheets, contact with the soul of evil. What Arkady demanded, Osborne could provide.

At the ceiling, smoke spread like thought into a cumulus.

Russian/investigator/killer/American. No one knew Osborne as well as he did – not even Irina or Kirwill. Arkady knew that Osborne had spent a fortune bringing his sables secretly from the Soviet Union. He'd never give them back. He'd be an American hero if he kept them. Osborne's only crime was Gorky Park, and the only person who could connect him to it was Irina. He'd tried to kill her in Moscow. Nothing was changed, except that now he had to kill Arkady as well. Osborne would send Nicky and Rurik in the wrong direction, and would kill Arkady and Irina the moment they were out of FBI custody. It was the one thing Arkady was sure of. But Osborne would be one day late.

In her sleep, Irina's face pressed against his chest. As

if she's blowing life into me, Arkady thought. He ground out his cigarette.

Falling asleep, he imagined what it would be like in Kirwill's cabin. Was there tundra in Maine? They'd have to get coats and tea – as much tea as they could buy. And cigarettes. What did Kirwill mean, 'like Siberia with beer cans'? No matter; Arkady found himself smiling at the prospect. He didn't enjoy hunting much, but he loved to fish and he'd never been in a canoe. What else would they do? He'd ask Irina to tell her life from the beginning, leaving nothing out. When she got tired, he'd tell about himself. Their life would be two stories. How long they'd have to stay he had no idea. Osborne would want to find them, but he'd be busy hiding himself from Kirwill – they could wait. They'd get some books. American authors. If he got a generator they could have lights, a radio, a record player. Seeds for a garden: beets, potatoes, radishes. He could listen to music while he planted – Prokofiev, New Orleans blues. In hot weather they could go swimming, and in August there'd be mushrooms.

He dreamed he was on the bank of the Kliazma River at dusk. In the distance Chinese lanterns led down a long stairway to a dock and wooden tubs colored with peonies. A raft on orange oil cans invited swimmers.

Everyone had left the dock and come up the bank – guests, musicians, the aides-de-camp. His father and some of his friends were in a skiff, which swung around and around in the middle of the river. His father took a knife and dove into the water.

Although the water was opaquely black, Arkady could see his mother clearly because she was in her best white dress. She seemed suspended in her own dive, her stockinged feet just below the surface of the water, her body perpendicular, one arm reaching down to the river bottom. When they brought her in, he saw that her wrist was hacked by his father's efforts, but that he had finally given up and left the rope that was tied to her wrist. It was the first time Arkady had seen a dead person. His mother was young – his father too, though already a famous general.

Painfully, as always in these dreams, he analyzed the crime. At first he believed his father had killed her. She'd danced and laughed, gayer than he'd seen her in weeks, giddy when she walked off by herself. But she was strong and the best swimmer of the whole group, practically a mermaid. There were no signs anyone had forced her down in the water; the boat had not been used, there were no bruises. Slowly he came to realize that the wooden tub full of rocks and the rising meter's length of rope, its end tied in an expectant slipknot, had been placed on the river bottom by no one but her. Each day of the summer she had added another stone to the tub, weighting it ever more securely. When the time came – in the middle of the evening's entertainment – she had walked off with bright eyes, slipped into the river downstream, swum to her rope and dived.

As a child he knew nothing about the purge of the engineers, of the Army, of the poets, of the Party, or of the suicide of Stalin's own wife, but even a child felt the time's antic fear, when lanterns became goblins. The kindest uncles became traitors. Women cried for no reason. This photograph was cropped, that one burned. It was difficult to accept that she had followed all those who disappeared because she herself hadn't disappeared; she was there in the water for all to see. That was why his father had tried so desperately to remove the evidence of the mocking rope and turned her death into an accident or – as Stalin did with his own wife – even murder. In the dark water she seemed still to be the exclamation mark of her accusation, escaping as she swam down, at least in dreams.

Chapter Four

When Arkady woke, snow was blowing horizontally by the windows and it appeared as if the room was spinning. Wesley and George and Ray stood over the bed. They were all in heavy coats. The chair that had been propped against the door was on the floor. Ray carried a suitcase and George held a gun. Irina woke and pulled the sheet over herself.

'What do you want?' Arkady asked.

'Get dressed,' Wesley said. 'We're going.'

'Where?'

'Today's the day,' Wesley said.

'Osborne's trade is supposed to be tomorrow,' Arkady protested.

'It's been moved up. It's right now,' Wesley added.

'But it's not supposed to be until tomorrow,' Arkady said again.

'It's been changed.'

'Arkasha, what does it matter?' Irina sat up, clutching the sheet. 'We can be free today.'

'You're free right now. Just do as I say,' Wesley said.

'You're taking us to Osborne?' Arkady asked.

'Isn't that what you want?'

'Get out of bed,' George said.

'Leave us alone and we'll dress,' Arkady said.

'No,' Wesley said, 'we have to make sure you aren't concealing anything.'

'She's not getting out of bed with you here,' Arkady said.

'I'll shoot you if she doesn't.' George aimed the gun at Arkady.

'It's all right.' Irina held Arkady's hand when he began to move.

'It's a precautionary measure,' Wesley said.

'I have your new clothes here.' Ray opened the suitcase at the foot of the bed. There was a complete outfit of clothes for each of them.

'How big are the balls on a KGB agent?' George asked Arkady.

Irina got out of bed naked, keeping her eyes on Arkady. She moved in front of the window and slowly made a complete turn, her arms away from her body.

'I am not KGB,' Arkady said.

'I think you'll find the sizes correct,' Ray told Irina.

'Comrade Renko?' Wesley motioned for Arkady to get out of bed.

Arkady stood, his eyes on Irina. Whatever fat he'd had he'd lost to the doctors; country life with Pribluda had added muscle. George aimed a short-barreled revolver at the midpoint of the scar that began at Arkady's ribs and disappeared into his pubic hair.

'Are you going to shoot me now and be done with it?' Arkady asked.

'This just relieves us all of worrying about anything secreted in your own clothes or shoes,' Wesley said. 'It makes things easier for everyone.'

Irina dressed, taking no more notice of the Americans than if she and Arkady were alone.

'I have the jitters myself,' Wesley told Arkady.

There were undergarments, brassiere, blouse, slacks, sweater, socks, shoes and parka for Irina: underpants, shirt, pants, sweater, socks, shoes and parka for Arkady.

'Our first snow in America,' Irina said.

Everything fit, as Ray had said. When Arkady reached for his watch, Wesley gave him a new one.

'The time is exactly six-forty-five.' Wesley strapped it to Arkady's wrist. 'It's time to go.'

'I'd like to brush my hair,' Irina said.

'Be my guest.' Ray gave her his comb.

'Where are we going?' Arkady asked.

'You'll be there soon and you'll see,' Wesley said.

Had Kirwill found the sables yet? Arkady wondered. How could he find anything in this snow? 'I want to leave a message for Lieutenant Kirwill,' he said.

'Fine. Give it to me,' Wesley offered.

'I mean, call him and talk to him.'

'Gee, I really feel that would gum things up, especially considering last night,' Wesley said. 'You don't want to gum things up.'

'What does it matter, Arkasha?' Irina asked. 'We're free.'

'The lady is absolutely correct,' George said and put his gun away to prove it.

Ray helped Arkady into the parka.

'There aren't any gloves.' He felt in the pockets. 'You forgot gloves.'

The agents were momentarily nonplussed.

'You can buy gloves afterwards,' Wesley said.

'After what?' Arkady asked.

'It really is time to go,' Wesley said.

Last night's small, hard flakes were now fleecy and moist. In Moscow there would have been battalions of old women sweeping the snow. Arkady and Irina were put in the back of a two-door sedan with George. Wesley was in front with Ray, who drove.

The storm produced a steamy confusion: snowplows on garbage trucks before a parade of headlights, police waving orange batons, streetlamps whittled to half-silhouettes. Traffic slowed to a painstaking crunch of tires; pedestrians were hunchbacked. Inside the car the windows fogged; there was the closeness of heavy coats. Arkady would have to climb over Wesley to reach a door; George and his gun were on the other side of Irina.

'Cigarettes?' Wesley opened a pack and offered them to Arkady. There was a light, girlish blush of excitement on his face.

'I thought you didn't smoke,' Arkady said.

'Never. They're for you,' Wesley said.

'No, thank you.'

'They're wasted if you don't take them.' Wesley seemed distressed.

George angrily took the cigarettes.

They drove on the West Side underneath an elevated highway that partially sheltered them from the snow. Ships loomed up suddenly between docks.

'Where did you go with Kirwill last night?' Wesley asked.

'Is that why we're doing this today instead of tomorrow?' Arkady asked in return.

'Kirwill's such a dangerous man I'm surprised you're still alive,' Wesley said, and repeated to Irina, 'I'm surprised he's still alive.'

Irina held Arkady's hand. Occasionally snow plunged through great holes in the highway overhead, and she leaned against him as if they were on a sleigh ride.

Inside Arkady's new parka, his new shirt felt stiff, like the slippers they put on the dead. Cigarettes were what executioners offered, he thought; gloves were what they forgot.

Should he tell Irina? he wondered. He remembered her telling about Kostia's father, the bastard who had tracked escapees in Siberia, how this manhunter would pass himself off as an ordinary trapper and befriend an escapee, share a warm meal and a bottle of vodka, and while the runaway dozed with his head full of dreams, would humanely slit his throat. Irina, Arkady recalled, had approved. Better to die with the illusion of freedom, she felt, than with nothing at all. What could be crueler than taking away even that?

And what if he was wrong? What if Osborne really was going to trade his sables for Irina and Arkady? For a moment he could even delude himself!

Osborne would do the shooting, Arkady decided. That would be clean and honest, and the agents were clean and honest types. Arkady and Irina would be trespassers? Enemy agents? Extortionists? It didn't matter. Osborne was expert at this sort of work. In comparison Wesley was a paper shuffler.

The elevated highway faded behind them and the sky opened up, pouring down its milky snow, and Irina tightened her grip on Arkady's hand in excitement. She was so beautiful that he felt foolishly proud.

Maybe something would happen; maybe the car ride would take forever. Then he thought of Kirwill's transmitter in the hotel room. Maybe Billy and Rodney had heard everything and were in the car behind. It occurred to him that Kirwill and Rats had planned to cross the Kill in a small boat. They couldn't have done so in this weather. If Kirwill had given up, maybe he was with Billy and Rodney.

'Why are you smiling?' Irina asked.

'I discover that I have an incurable disease,' Arkady said.

'That sounds interesting,' Wesley said. 'What is it?'

'Hope.'

'I thought so,' Wesley said.

The car stopped, and Ray bought a ticket at a booth in front of a green building that said DEPARTMENT OF MARINE AND AVIATION. Arkady could see straight through the bottom of the building to the black water of the harbor. They had reached the end of Manhattan. To one side was an older ferryhouse, its graceful cast-iron columns outlined by snow. A car pulled up behind them, its driver a woman who put a newspaper in front of her face; with her other hand she held a coffee cup and a cigarette.

'What will you do if they stop the ferries?' Arkady asked.

'If there's a hurricane, they have trouble in the slips.

Snow never stops the ferry,' Wesley said. 'We're right on schedule.'

Sooner and faster than Arkady expected, a ferry coupled with the building. Gates opened, and apparatchiks and workers emerged holding umbrellas and briefcases up against the storm, trying to pick their way through the snow as they dodged the cars driving off the boat. Then the waiting cars boarded. Wesley's was first in the middle of three rows, rolling right through the ship to the opposite bow. Pedestrians boarded on overhead ramps. The ferry still pressed against the ferryhouse; the swell from the inbound engines rose along the wooden pilings of the slip. The boat filled quickly. Most of the drivers took the stairs up to the saloon level. At the sound of two bells, a crewman in a pea jacket lifted a cylinder from the deck and let it drop back to unlock the inbound rudder. The inbound engines died and the outbound engines cut in. The ferry eased out of the slip and into the water.

Arkady guessed the visibility at a kilometer. The ferry moved into a veil of quiet that muffled the noise of its own engines. They were surrounded by a snow that seemed to fold into the water. The ferry would have radar, there was no danger of collision. A large wave, perhaps a wake, grew from the water; the ferry only sighed, passing through it. Where was Kirwill? Arkady remembered him running across the frozen Moskva River.

Ray rolled down a window and breathed deeply. 'Oysters,' he said.

'What?' George asked.

'Smell reminds me of oysters,' Ray said.

'You hungry or horny?' George asked, and glanced at Irina. 'I know what I am.'

The interior of the ferry was painted a bright mussel-orange. There was a black anchor, a hawser, rock salt and pipes between the rows of cars, cases of life preservers overhead and lifeboats over the stairs. VEHICLE OPERATORS NOTICE STOP ENGINE SET BRAKES PUT OUT LIGHTS DON'T BLOW HORN DON'T SMOKE U.S. COAST GUARD REGULATIONS was in red letters. All that would have kept the car from rolling directly off the front of the boat was a slack cable. There was a fold-up gate a child could have pulled apart.

'Do you mind if we get out?' Arkady asked Wesley.

'Why would you want to get out in the cold?'

'For the view.'

Wesley's forehead, smooth as a pebble, lolled to one side. 'It is a wonderful view. I especially love views on days like today when you can hardly see anything at all. It gives the view some point,' he said. 'But I'm a fatalist. Some people were not meant to have sunny days. Also I'm a pessimist. Did you know that the deck of this ferry is one of the favorite suicide spots in all New York? True. Or you might accidentally slip under that gate. See how wet the deck is? And get sucked under into the propeller or freeze in the water. Well, it's going to be safety first while I'm in charge.'

'Then I will smoke,' Arkady said.

It was a Russian snow, thick as cotton. One moment the storm was a single entity, a ring around the boat; the next, it broke into separate squalls spinning like tops on the black water. The cable at the bow had a skin of frozen spray.

Valerya, Kostia the Bandit and James Kirwill didn't know what was waiting for them in Gorky Park. At least they skated to their deaths in innocence. If he told Irina, what could the two of them do? Overpower three armed agents? Make a commotion? Who would notice two passengers out of five in a car in a snowstorm in the middle of New York harbor? Would Irina believe him if he told her? Would Valerya, Kostia and James Kirwill have believed him as they skated by?

The storm parted toward the east. Gliding past them was a verdigris colossus on a stone pedestal, a torch uplifted, a crown of rays on her head, astonishingly familiar even to Arkady. Then the storm closed and she was gone.

'Did you see it?' Irina asked.

'For an instant,' Arkady said.

'Don't go away.' Wesley got out of the car and vanished up the stairs.

The surface of the bay had the deep motion of heavy breathing. Railroad cars crossed on a barge pushed by a tugboat; gulls rose from floating garbage.

Arkady noticed Ray concentrating anxiously on a side-view mirror. He was looking at someone. Someone had followed, after all. Arkady kissed Irina's cheek and glanced down the line of cars behind. At the far end of the ferry were two figures. A gust obscured them, and when Arkady looked again they were gone. One had been Wesley, though, and the other the red-haired KGB agent called Rurik.

The snow rushed down, the black water flowed by, and a red buoy danced in between, tolling its bell. A small town on the hills of an island emerged from the storms as Wesley returned.

'This is it,' he told Irina as he got into the car.

'Where are we?' she asked.

'The name of this town is St George,' Wesley said.

'It's Staten Island,' Arkady said.

'Well, yes, it is,' Wesley said. 'And it's part of New York City, no matter what people say.'

Arkady saw that for Irina the shabby docks and snow-covered roofs could have been a tropical island of palm trees and orchids. Or whipped cream set on the sea. She was near the destination of a wonderful journey.

Water surged ahead of them into the slip and crew-men hooked the ramps to the bow. When the cable dropped, the gates swung up and the cars rolled off.

St George was practically a Russian village. The streets were deeply rutted in snow and the traffic was almost stationary. The cars were old and rusted, the people drably dressed in hoods and boots. The houses were small, with real chimneys and real smoke. There was a statue with snowy epaulets. But the shops had fresh meat and poultry and seafood.

A plowed boulevard led away from the town to newer suburbs – prefabricated houses separated from each other by chain link fences. A church looked like a rising spaceship; a bank looked like a gas station.

They reached the highway that Arkady had been on the night before. There was very little traffic. Three cars behind them, Arkady made out Nicky and Rurik. He couldn't see Kirwill's detectives.

Slightly asynchronously the windshield wipers batted at the flakes. Was the snow falling or was the car rising? Arkady felt the cool skin of the car and every revolution of its wheels, the residue of whiskey in his stomach, the sweat under his arms, the sweat on George's palms, the dark blood rushing through each man in the car, and their breath moving the turgid smoke.

Ray turned off before the bridge over the Arthur Kill. A single car followed. They plowed their own way on a narrow road that ran along the Kill, by gas domes and power lines and through a marsh of silvered rushes.

Arkady felt his life simplifying, its halves closing. Extraneous elements like Billy and Rodney no longer existed. The signs along the way were in a strange language, but the road was inevitable.

Arkady understood. Osborne would kill him and Irina while the KGB was misled a thousand miles away from the sables. Yet here were Nicky and Rurik being led right to them. Better than understanding, Arkady saw. All mutual informers were mutually expendable. Worse was a man who did too many favors for both sides and demanded too much in return. What choice did Wesley have? Osborne refused to go into hiding; the bureau would have to protect not only him but a whole growing industry of sables. Seeing at last, Arkady noted the symmetry. As certainly as two eyes and two hands, there was a balance of two energetic armies with mirror hearts. Osborne would kill him and Irina, and then Wesley-George-Ray-Nicky-Rurik would kill Osborne.

They passed a corral, where a black horse stood in the snow and watched them go by.

Irina's fingers threaded through his. Although she'd tied the knot tight around her wrist, his mother's hand was open, as if she were reaching for more water.

Trucks rusted, dropping their own orange flakes in the snow outside a barn.

Even the maddest killer – Osborne – was only an individual, unpredictable, finally vulnerable. Policy, like snow, reduced the world to essentials. There, in a field, was a piece of farm machinery, a row of curved blades turned into a scribble.

Now the unctuous bowing of weighted trees.

The second car fell far behind. Arkady felt it, however, like a bead of sweat on his back.

Was there any comfort, he wondered, in seeing the outlines of life?

His sweat was as cold as snow.

Ray turned through a gate into a salvage yard. It appeared as though a sea of snow had lapped up from the Kill, bearing anything of iron with it. Entire ships, gutted hulls, locomotives rode on a white tide. Buses were piled on trucks, New York Central RR cars stood on end, anchors rested on mobile homes. Painted everywhere were signs: NO TRESPASSING THIS MEANS U AND BEWARE OF DOGS. There was an office shingled with license plates, but no one came out to stop them. Arkady noticed they were following tire tracks that looked three or four hours old; Ray drove as if he would be lost without them. The car swung uncertainly between atolls of boxcars, counterweights, cranes, around mountains where snow overlaid the erratic details of turbines and screws, past the loose slopes of chains and scrap. The tracks led away from the yard and through sycamore and linden trees, then into a field of mechanical cranes and vines. Throughout the trees, as if they had dropped there from the sky, were more abandoned cars and buses.

Because it stood before a background of snow, the chain-link fence seemed to spring at them. It was topped by triple strands of barbed wire, and all the tall trees within twenty meters inside it were cut to stumps. Arkady had no doubt that the fence had a concrete base. And there were insulators on the poles, so it was electrified. His eye was caught by a small brown bird that hopped from fence to insulator fence. The power was off. On a phone box was a sign, ATTACK DOG KENNELS, PHONE FOR DELIVERIES, BEWARE OF DOGS. The fence gate was wide open, inviting them in.

The road seemed to deliberately meander through the trees. At one curve the tracks they were following divided into two separate tracks. One earlier car had continued on the road; another had veered off, making its own path through brush.

Kirwill was waiting at the next curve. He faced them, one arm high, before a large tree, an elm. Ray stopped the car a meter in front of him. Kirwill didn't move, his eyes boring into the car and through it. Snow had settled deep on his shoulders and hat and in the cuff of his upraised hand. Stretched out dead in the snow at his feet were two large gray dogs. Arkady noticed that what protruded in a bundle from Kirwill's open coat were his entrails, pulled out and covered with snow. Snow obscured the two pink holes over his breast. His face was totally white. Now Arkady saw the ropes around his waist and wrist that tied him to the tree. When they got out of the car, they saw the blood scattered everywhere. The dogs were similar to Siberian huskies but leaner, longer-legged, more wolflike. One dog's head was crushed. Kirwill's eyes were paler than ever, the irises collapsed. He had an expression of weariness, as if he had been condemned to carry a tree on his back all his life.

'Jesus!' Ray said. 'This wasn't planned.'

'Don't touch him,' George warned.

Arkady forced Kirwill's eyes shut, buttoned his overcoat together and kissed his cold cheek.

'Get away from him, please,' Wesley said.

Arkady stepped back. Irina looked almost as white as Kirwill, the mark on her cheek sharp and dark. Did she finally understand? Arkady asked himself. Did she see Kostia in Kirwill? Did she know who Valerya would be? Did she finally realize how short a distance they had come from Gorky Park?

Osborne came out of the trees behind them carrying a rifle, a third gray dog at his side. The dog had black-outlined eyes and ruff and a muzzle of dried blood.

'He killed my dogs,' he explained to Arkady, pointing the rifle with one hand at Kirwill. 'That's why I gutted him, because he killed my dogs.'

He spoke to Arkady as if no one else were present. He was wearing hunting clothes, laced boots, a green jaeger hat and pigskin gloves. The rifle was a bolt-action sporting model with a sight and a handsome burled stock. A heavy knife was sheathed on his belt. Arkady noticed that no more snow was falling; not a flake drifted down, not even from the overheavy branches. There was a ceramic clarity to the scene.

'Well, here are your friends,' Wesley said.

Osborne, however, studied the dead man. 'You were going to keep Kirwill away from me,' he told Wesley. 'You were going to protect me. If it weren't for the dogs, he would have had me.'

'But he didn't,' Wesley said, 'and now he's out of the way.'

'No thanks to you,' Osborne said.

'The main thing,' Wesley said, 'is that we brought your friends. They're all yours.'

'They brought the KGB too,' Arkady said.

Wesley, George and Ray, who had already started to back away from Arkady and Irina, stopped.

'Good try,' Wesley said to Arkady. He looked at Osborne. 'You were right and I was wrong. The Russian is clever, but he's desperate and he's lying.'

'Why do you say that, Arkasha?' Irina asked. 'You'll ruin everything.'

No, Arkady thought, she still doesn't understand.

'Why do you say that?' Osborne asked Arkady.

'Wesley met with one of them on the ferry. He got out of the car to talk to him,' Arkady said.

'There was a blizzard on the ferry,' Wesley said in a reasonable tone. 'He could hardly see out the car, let alone any secret meetings.'

'Did you recognize anyone?' Osborne asked Arkady.

'It was hard to see,' Arkady admitted.

'Why do you even ask him?' Wesley said.

'But I know a red-haired, anti-Semitic KGB officer when I see one,' Arkady said, 'even in a snowstorm.'

'I'm sorry,' Wesley told Arkady, 'but no one will believe you.'

Arkady paid no attention to Wesley; neither did Osborne. They could have been alone. What two men better deserved to be alone than a killer and his investigator? Men who approach each other from the opposite sides of the dead – also from the opposite sides of a bed. That was a double intimacy that not even Irina could share. Who else could feel the profound weight of the snow still in the sky and almost hear Tchaikovsky in the air? Arkady let Osborne enter through his eyes. Test my words, Arkady thought; sniff them, chew them. I feel you inside me moving like a wolf's pads on snow. Try the hate now; it's lodged behind the heart. Inevitability is always in the stomach. That was all that Kirwill lacked. I have it. Now do you know?

Wesley stared at the two men and, at the last moment, motioned to Ray.

Without taking any apparent aim, Osborne fired his rifle. Wesley's head snapped, half its smooth forehead missing; he landed on his knees and then his chest. While Ray tried to free a revolver from a shoulder holster inside his jacket and coat, Osborne ejected a shell, fed a new round into the rifle breech and fired again. Ray sat down, looking at his bloody hand. He lifted it away slowly and looked at the hole that went through the middle of his chest, then sagged to one side. Osborne's dog attacked George. The dog was in midair when

George shot it, and was dead before it fell. Osborne was bleeding from his shoulder. Arkady became aware that another shot had been fired from farther away. George rolled behind a tree. Arkady pulled Irina down into the snow, and Osborne vanished into the trees.

They remained face down in the snow until they heard George and then other footsteps run by. There was shouting back and forth in English, some of it with a Russian accent. He recognized Rurik's voice and Nicky's. Arkady crawled to Ray and shook the revolver out of his coat. Car keys fell out, too.

'We can take the car,' Irina said. 'We can get away.'

He put the keys in her hand and kept the gun. 'You get away,' he said.

He ran into the woods in the direction the other men had gone. He found the revolver safety on the left by the cylinder and pushed it off. The tracks in the snow were easy to follow: George's, Osborne's and two more joining from opposite directions. He heard them just ahead, yelling and swatting at branches. There was the crack of a rifle shot followed by rapid fire of handguns.

The fight moved away. When Arkady crept forward again, he found Nicky belly up in the snow, dead, his legs twisted as if he had spun when he fell. A little further on he found a U in Osborne's tracks where he'd doubled back for the ambush.

The shooting stopped and there was quiet. Arkady moved from tree to tree. His breathing sounded terribly loud. Occasionally wind would brush snow from a branch and it would plop onto the ground and make him jump. He heard other sounds, which at first he thought were birds – sharp voices in agitation that came and went with the wind. The woods ended in a second, inner chain link fence with canvas baffles. Halfway through the fence, tangled in canvas and insulators, was Kirwill's car. The driver had been trapped inside. The rear windows crystallized around a hole, and in the front seat Rats sat upright. He was dead; the blood that had poured from his torn woolen cap had dried in stripes.

Arkady came to another gate. It was open, and through it went tire tracks almost filled in by snow and the fresh tracks of running men. Inside were Osborne's sables.

The layout of the compound was rectangular, about a hundred meters by sixty, and simply laid out. At the nearer end were a round corrugated steel unit for wastes and a lean-to for dogs; three chains hung from a ring. The tire tracks led to the far end, where Osborne's limousine was parked outside a one-story cement bunker. The bunker seemed long enough to house refrigerators, an area for preparing food and an area for quarantine. The foot tracks ran to the sable sheds. The generals in the Fur Palace had underestimated; Arkady counted ten raised, open sheds, each of them twenty meters long, with a wooden roof that sheltered two rows of cages and a central aisle. There were four cages to a row, which meant about eighty sables altogether: eighty sables in New York City. He couldn't see the animals clearly; they were excited and moving about too much. Nor could he see Osborne, George or Rurik, though there were few places to hide – only plastic cans at the end of each shed and concrete drainage troughs under each row of cages.

The American revolver was odd and short-barreled, obviously not meant for marksmanship, and he was a terrible shot anyway; he'd never be able to hit anyone from the bunker or the lean-to. He ran for the nearest shed.

First he heard the shot and then he felt the bullet. It should be the other way round, he thought. He stumbled but regained his feet. It's tough to put a pistol slug through the chest of a crouching man, he thought; now, a rifle slug would have done the job. When he dove under the shed, pain stretched on a line over his ribs.

Above him the sables shrieked in outrage. They climbed zinc-coated mesh walls, paced, leaped, were never still. They looked like cats, then weasels, furred ears turning in alarm, tails bristling with anger, moving so quickly that they were only black configurations within the cages. It was the life in them that was startling. They were wild, not tame, furiously alive, hissing and trying to reach him through the silver mesh. On his back, Arkady looked down the row of sheds and saw two different pairs of human legs. An upside-down face with dark, morose eyes joined one pair of legs; then a revolver joined the fact. It was George. He fired, and a spray of animal feces exploded over Arkady from the drainage trough. Arkady aimed back. Still too far. He rolled over the trough toward the next shed, closer to George, and was aiming again when there was a rifle shot. Arkady could see George's legs walking backward, his head still hanging down, his revolver dangling from a finger. With his other hand George seemed to be trying to reach his back. His legs worked more and more stiffly, and his head hung lower as he backed into a plastic can at the end of the shed. The can tipped over, spilling a pink soup of fish heads and horsemeat over the snow. George lay down in it.

'Arkady Vasilevich,' Rurik said.

Rurik stepped out of Arkady's shed and stood over him, a Makarov automatic hanging in his hand. Now we will hunt down Osborne together, Arkady thought, but Rurik was a better judge of enemies and trained not to hesitate. With the ironic sympathy of a final arbiter – we're all human, especially we Ukrainians – the KGB officer raised his gun and aimed at Arkady with both hands. Before he could fire, his scalp rolled back from his skull, gray flecks stuck to his red hair, and Rurik dropped, knees and face forward, into the snow. This time the sound of the rifle shot came afterward.

From his back, Arkady looked along the sheds and saw Osborne's legs at least six sheds away. It was the scope. Osborne could look through a whole line of sheds and pinpoint his targets. He could do so a lot more easily to a target under the sheds, Arkady supposed. He rolled under one more shed, closer to Osborne, and got to his feet.

Arkady approached around two more sheds, passing George in the puddle of sable food. At the next shed, as Osborne appeared and raised his rifle, Arkady ducked into the wooden aisle between the cages. Some of the sables hid in the coops inside their cages; others followed Arkady, darting from one end to the other, jumping against the mesh. Each cage, he noticed, had its own chart, food slot and padlock. As long as he and the sables kept moving he had a chance. If he could get close he had five or six shots in the revolver against a bolt-action rifle. He beat his hand against the cages as he ran, stirring up the sables. He could feel the rifle scope, frustrated, attempting to sight on him without hitting the animals.

Arkady covered the distance between sheds in two steps and jumped into the next aisle, shouting at the sables as he hit the cages. Their tails trailed behind them as they leaped from wall to ceiling to floor, spitting, some urinating in fury. His hand bled; one had bitten him through the mesh. Then he was down on the aisle floor, shot, a bullet through his thigh. Not bad, clean through; he was up again. He noticed he had passed an empty cage, where Osborne had taken the chance and fired, though the slug must have been deflected or he would be dead. There were new planks in the roof of the shed, and the mesh was freshly repainted, a crowbar and toolbox in the aisle. It must have been the cage from which the sable escaped. He saw Osborne running to catch him as he came out of the end of the shed. Arkady would dive under the cages into the waste trough instead and fire first. But he stumbled, losing control of his leg as shock spread through it.

Then he heard Irina shouting. She stood inside the compound gate calling his name. She couldn't see him. Osborne called for her to stay where she was.

'Investigator,' Osborne yelled, 'come on out! You can keep your gun and I'll let you both go. Come out or I'll shoot her.'

'Run!' Arkady shouted to Irina.

'I'll let you both go, Irina,' Osborne said. 'You can get in the car and go. The investigator's wounded and needs medical attention.'

'I won't go without you!' Irina called to Arkady.

'You can go together, Arkady,' Osborne said. 'You have my promise. But come out now, right now, or I'll shoot her. Right now.'

Arkady was back at the empty cage. He picked up the crowbar and inserted its narrow end through the shackle of the padlock in the neighboring cage. The sable inside stilled and watched. Arkady let his weight drop on the bar and the shackle snapped. As the cage door swung open, the sable jumped off Arkady's chest onto the aisle and out the shed. He had never seen anything move so quickly over snow. The sable darted over the snow on soft, furred paws, its tail whipping the snow behind. Arkady inserted the bar into the next padlock and pushed down again.

'No!' Osborne cried.

Arkady caught the sable as it came out of the cage and held it against him as it clawed to escape. Osborne stood at the end of the aisle, rifle raised. Arkady threw the sable at him. Osborne stepped aside, raised the rifle again and fired. Arkady dropped to the aisle floor as his leg gave way and fired. The first two shots took Osborne through the stomach. Osborne worked another round into the breech. Arkady's next two shots hit Osborne in the heart. The fifth shot caught Osborne in the throat as he went down. The sixth shot missed altogether.

Arkady dragged himself out of the shed. Osborne was on his back, looking not as chewed up as man should be with so many bullets in him. He still held his rifle. Oddly, Arkady saw him as not quite dead, not even dressed in the hunting outfit but in a finer suit with more touches of elegance. Arkady sat beside him. Osborne's eyes were closed, as if he'd had time to compose himself. Arkady felt the heat leaving the body and the chilling process already under way. Wearily he stripped Osborne's belt from his body and tied it around his own leg. Slowly he became aware of Irina standing over them. She stared. Was there, after all, an expression on Osborne's face as if he'd won?

'He told me once that he loved the snow,' Arkady said. 'Maybe he does.'

'Where do we go now?'

'You go.'

'I came back for you,' Irina said. 'We can get away, we can stay in America.'

'I don't want to stay.' Arkady looked up. 'I never wanted to stay. I only came because I knew Osborne would kill you if I didn't.'

'Then we'll both go home.'

'You *are* home. You're American now, Irina, you're what you always wanted to be.' He smiled. 'You're not Russian anymore. We always were different, and now I know what the difference was.'

'You'll change, too.'

'I'm Russian.' He tapped his chest. 'The longer I'm here, the more Russian I am.'

'No.' She shook her head angrily.

'Look at me.' Arkady pulled himself to his feet. One leg was numb. 'Don't cry. See what I am: Arkady Renko, former Party member and chief investigator. If you love me, tell me truthfully how American I could ever be. Tell me!' he shouted. 'Tell me,' he said more softly, 'admit it, don't you see a Russian?'

'We came all this way. I won't let you go back alone, Arkasha—'

'You don't understand.' He took Irina's face in his hands. 'I'm not as brave as you are, not brave enough to stay. Please, let me go back. You will be what you already are, and I will be what I am. I will always love you.' He kissed her fiercely. 'Go on, run.'

'The sables . . .'

'Leave them to me. Go ahead.' He pushed her. 'It shouldn't be so hard on the way back. Don't go to the bureau; go to the police or the State Department, anything but the FBI.'

'I love you.' She tried to hold on to his hand.

'Do I have to throw stones?' he asked.

Irina released him. 'I'm going, then,' she said.

'Good luck.'

'Good luck, Arkasha.'

She stopped crying, brushed her hair from her eyes, looked around and took a deep breath. 'For snow like this I should have felt boots, you know,' she said.

'I know.'

'I'm a good driver. The light seems to be getting better.'

'Yes.'

She took a dozen steps. 'Will I ever hear from you?' She looked back, her eyes haggard and wet.

'No doubt. Messages get through, right? Times change.'

At the gate she stopped again. 'How can I leave you?'

'*I* am leaving *you*.'

Irina went through the gate. Arkady found the cigarette case on Osborne and smoked and listened to the branches drumming in the wind until he heard a car start up in the distance. The sables heard it, too; they had sharp ears.

So, Arkady thought, there had been three trades. First Osborne's, then Kirwill's and now his. He would return to the Soviet Union so that the KGB would let Irina stay in America. He looked down at Osborne. Excuse me, he thought, but what do I have to trade besides myself? The sables, of course. They would have to be disposed of, too.

He pulled the rifle out of Osborne's hands and hobbled back to the shed. How many bullets did he have? he wondered. The day was turning bright and pure. The sables had quieted; their eyes pressed against the mesh.

'I apologize,' Arkady said aloud. 'I don't know what the Americans will do with you. It's been proven we can't trust anyone.'

They clung to the mesh watching him, their coats black as coal, their eyes still with attention.

'They have elected me executioner,' Arkady said. 'And they'll get the truth from me, brothers; they aren't men who'll accept lies or fairy tales or fancy stories. I'm sorry.'

He could hear their hearts beating, running away with them, the same as his.

'So . . .'

Arkady dropped the rifle and picked up the crowbar. Ineptly, on one leg, he broke a padlock. The sable jumped free, and a second later was at the fence. He got better at it, just a thrust and a pull at each cage. Cigarettes were good aspirin. He thrilled as each cage door opened and the wild sables made their leap and broke for the snow – black on white, black on white, black on white, and then gone.

HAVANA BAY

Martin Cruz Smith, former journalist and magazine editor, is now a full-time writer. He is the author of nine previous novels, including *Gorky Park*, *Polar Star* and *Red Square* – the Arkady Renko trilogy which has sold millions of copies worldwide. *Havana Bay*, his long-awaited new Arkady Renko novel, is now available in Pan Books. What follows overleaf is the first chapter . . .

Chapter One

A police boat directed a light toward tar-covered pilings and water, turning a black scene white. Havana was invisible across the bay, except for a single line of lamps along the seawall. Stars rode high, anchor lights rode low, otherwise the harbor was a still pool in the night.

Soda cans, crab pots, fishing floats, mattresses, Styrofoam bearded with algae shifted as an investigation team of the Policía Nacional de la Revolución took flash shots. Arkady waited in a cashmere overcoat with a Captain Arcos, a barrel-chested little man who looked ironed into military fatigues, and his Sergeant Luna, large, black and angular. Detective Osorio was a small brown woman in PNR blue; she gave Arkady a studied glare.

A Cuban named Rufo was the interpreter from the Russian embassy. 'It's very simple,' he translated the captain's words. 'You see the body, identify the body and then go home.'

'Sounds simple.' Arkady tried to be agreeable, although Arcos walked off as if any contact with Russians was contamination.

Osorio combined the sharp features of an ingenue with the grave expression of a hangman. She spoke and Rufo explained, 'The detective says this is the Cuban method, not the Russian method or the German method. The Cuban method. You will see.'

Arkady had seen little so far. He had just arrived at the airport in the dark when he was whisked away by Rufo. They were headed by taxi to the city when Rufo received a call on a cellular phone that diverted them to the bay. Already Arkady had a sense that he was unwelcome and unpopular.

Rufo wore a loose Hawaiian shirt and a faint resemblance to the older, softer Muhammad Ali. 'The detective says she hopes you don't mind learning the Cuban method.'

'I'm looking forward to it.' Arkady was nothing if not a good guest. 'Could you ask her when the body was discovered?'

'Two hours ago by the boat.'

'The embassy sent me a message yesterday that Pribluda was in trouble. Why did they say that before you found a body?'

'She says ask the embassy. She was certainly not expecting an investigator.'

Professional honor seemed to be at stake and Arkady felt badly outclassed on that score. Like Columbus on deck, Captain Arcos scanned the dark impatiently, Luna his hulking shadow. Osorio had sawhorses erected and stretched a tape that read NO PASEO. When a motorcycle policeman in a white helmet and spurs on his boots arrived, she chased him with a shout that could have scored steel. Somehow men in T-shirts appeared along the tape as soon as it was unrolled – what was it about violent death that was better than dreams? Arkady wondered. Most of the onlookers were black; Havana was far more African than Arkady had expected, although the logos on their shirts were American.

Someone along the tape carried a radio that sang, '*La fiesta no es para los feos. Qué feo es, señor. Super feo, amigo mío. No puedes pasar aquí, amigo. La fiesta no es para los feos.*'

'What does that mean?' Arkady asked Rufo.

'The song? It says, "This party is not for ugly people. Sorry, my friend, you can't come." '

Yet here I am, Arkady thought.

A vapor trail far overhead showed silver, and ships at anchor started to appear where only lights had hung moments before. Across the bay the seawall and mansions of Havana rose from the water, docks spread and, along the inner bay, loading cranes got to their feet.

'The captain is sensitive,' Rufo said, 'but whoever was right or wrong about the message, you're here, the body's here.'

'So it couldn't have worked out better?'

'In a manner of speaking.'

Osorio ordered the boat to back off so that its wash wouldn't stir the body. A combination of the boat's light and the freshening sky made her face glow.

Rufo said, 'Cubans don't like Russians. It's not you, it's just not a good place for a Russian.'

'Where is a good place?'

Rufo shrugged.

This side of the harbor, now that Arkady could see it, was like a village. A hillside of banana palms overhung abandoned houses that fronted what was more a cement curb than a seawall that stretched from a coal dock to a

ferry landing. A wooden walkway balanced on a black
piling captured whatever floated in. The day was going
to be warm. He could tell by the smell.

'*Vaya a cambiar su cara, amigo. Feo, feo, feo como
horror, señor.*'

In Moscow, in January, the sun would have crept like
a dim lamp behind rice paper. Here it was a rushing
torch that turned air and bay into mirrors, first of nickel
and then to vibrant, undulating pink. Many things were
suddenly apparent. A picturesque ferry that moved
toward the landing. Little fishing boats moored almost
within reach. Arkady noticed that more than palms grew
in the village behind him; the sun found coconuts, hibis-
cus, red and yellow trees. Water around the pilings began
to show the peacock sheen of petroleum.

Detective Osorio's order for the video camera to roll
was a signal for onlookers to press against the tape. The
ferry landing filled with commuters, every face turned
toward the pilings where, in the quickening light floated
a body as black and bloated as the inner tube it rested
in. Shirt and shorts were split by the body's expansion.
Hands and feet trailed in the water; a swim fin dangled
casually on one foot. The head was eyeless and inflated
like a black balloon.

'A *neumático*,' Rufo told Arkady. 'A *neumático* is a
fisherman who fishes from an inner tube. Actually from
a fishing net spread over the tube. Like a hammock. It's
very ingenious, very Cuban.'

'The inner tube is his boat?'

'Better than a boat. A boat needs gasoline.'

Arkady pondered that proposition.

'Much better.'

A diver in a wet suit slid off the police boat while an officer in waders dropped over the seawall. They clambered as much as waded across crab pots and mattress springs, mindful of hidden nails and septic water, and cornered the inner tube so that it wouldn't float away. A net was thrown down from the seawall to stretch under the inner tube and lift it and the body up together. So far, Arkady wouldn't have done anything differently. Sometimes events were just a matter of luck.

The diver stepped into a hole and went under. Gasping, he came up out of the water, grabbed onto first the inner tube and then a foot hanging from it. The foot came off. The inner tube pressed against the spear of a mattress spring, popped and started to deflate. As the foot turned to jelly, Detective Osorio shouted for the officer to toss it to shore: a classic confrontation between authority and vulgar death, Arkady thought. All along the tape, onlookers clapped and laughed.

Rufo said, 'See, usually, our level of competence is fairly high, but Russians have this effect. The captain will never forgive you.'

The camera went on taping the debacle while another detective jumped into the water. Arkady hoped the lens captured the way the rising sun poured into the windows of the ferry. The inner tube was sinking. An arm disengaged. Shouts flew back and forth between Osorio and the police boat. The more desperately the men in the water tried to save the situation the worse it became. Captain Arcos contributed orders to lift the body. As the diver steadied the head, the pressure of his hands liquefied its face and made it slide like a grape skin off the skull, which itself separated cleanly from the neck; it was like trying to lift a man who was perversely disrobing part by part, unembarrassed by the stench of advanced decomposition. A pelican sailed overhead, red as a flamingo.

'I think identification is going to be a little more complicated than the captain imagined,' Arkady said.

The diver caught the jaw as it dropped off from the skull and juggled each, while the detectives pushed the other black, swollen limbs pell-mell into the shriveling inner tube.

'*Feo, tan feo. No puedes pasar aquí, amigo. Porque la fiesta no es para los feos.*'

The rhythm was ... what was the word? Arkady wondered. Unrelenting.

Across the bay a golden dome seemed to burst into flame, and the houses of the Malecón started to express their unlikely colors of lemon, rose, royal purple, aquamarine.

It really was a lovely city, he thought.

Light from the high windows of the autopsy theater of the Instituto de Medicina Legal fell on three stainless-steel tables. On the right-hand table lay the *neumático*'s torso and loose parts arranged like an ancient statue dredged in pieces from the sea. Along the walls were enamel cabinets, scales, X-ray panel, sink, specimen shelves, freezer, refrigerator, pails. Above, at the observation level, Rufo and Arkady had a semicircle of seats to themselves. Arkady hadn't noticed before how scarred Rufo's brows were.

'Captain Luna would rather you watched from here. The examiner is Dr Blas.'

Rufo waited expectantly until Arkady realized he was supposed to react.

'*The* Dr Blas?'

'The very one.'

Blas had a dapper Spanish beard and wore rubber gloves, goggles, green scrubs. Only when he appeared satisfied that he had a reasonably complete body did he measure it and search it meticulously for marks and tattoos, a painstaking task when skin tended to slide wherever touched. An autopsy could take two hours, as much as four. At the left-hand table Detective Osorio and a pair of technicians sorted through the deflated inner tube and fishnet; the body had been left tangled in them for fear of disturbing it any more. Captain Arcos stood to one side, Luna a step behind. It occurred to Arkady that Luna's head was as round and blunt as a black fist with red-rimmed eyes. Already Osorio had found a wet roll of American dollar bills and a ring of keys kept in a leaky plastic bag. Fingerprints wouldn't have survived the bag, and she immediately dispatched the keys with an officer. There was something appealingly energetic and fastidious about Osorio. She hung wet shirt, shorts and underwear on hangers on a rack.

While Blas worked he commented to a microphone clipped to the lapel of his coat.

'Maybe two weeks in the water,' Rufo translated. He

added, 'It's been hot and raining, very humid. Even for here.'

'You've seen autopsies before?' Arkady asked.

'No, but I've always been curious. And, of course, I'd heard of Dr Blas.'

Performing an autopsy on a body in an advanced stage of putrefaction was a delicate as dissecting a soft-boiled egg. Sex was obvious but not age, not race, not size when the chest and stomach cavities were distended, not weight when the body sagged with water inside, not fingerprints when hands that had trailed in the water for a week ended in digits nibbled to the bone. Then there was the gaseous pressure of chemical change. When Blas punctured the abdomen a flatulent spray shot loudly up, and when he made the Y incision across the chest and then to groin, a wave of black water and liquefied matter overflowed the table. Using a pail, a technician deftly caught the viscera as they floated out. An expanding pong of rot – as if a shovel had been plunged into swamp gas – took possession of the room, invading everyone's nose and mouth. Arkady was glad he had left his precious coat in the car. After the first trauma of the stench – five minutes, no more – the olfactory nerves were traumatized and numb, but he was already digging deep into his cigarettes.

Rufo said, 'That smells disgusting.'

'Russian tobacco.' Arkady filled his lungs with smoke. 'Want one?'

'No, thanks. I boxed in Russia when I was on the national team. I hated Moscow. The food, the bread and, most of all, the cigarettes.'

'You don't like Russians, either?'

'I love Russians. Some of my best friends are Russian.' Rufo leaned for a better view as Blas spread the chest for the camera. 'The doctor is very good. At the rate they're going you'll have time to make your plane. You won't even have to spend the night.'

'Won't the embassy make a fuss about this?'

'The Russians here? No.'

Blas slapped the pulpy mass of the heart in a separate tray.

'You don't think they're too indelicate, I hope,' Rufo said.

'Oh, no.' To be fair, as Arkady remembered, Pribluda used to root through bodies with the enthusiasm of a boar after nuts. 'Imagine the poor bastard's surprise,' Pribluda would have said. 'Floating around, looking up at the stars, and then bang, he's dead.'

Arkady lit one cigarette from another and drew the smoke in sharply enough to make his eyes tear. It occurred to him that he was at a point now where he knew more people dead than alive, the wrong side of a certain line.

'I picked up a lot of languages touring with the team,' Rufo said. 'After boxing, I used to guide groups of singers, musicians, dancers, intellectuals for the embassy. I miss those days.'

Detective Osorio methodically laid out supplies that the dead man had taken to sea: thermos, wicker box, and plastic bags of candles, rolls of tape, twine, hooks and extra line.

Usually, an examiner cut at the hairline and peeled

the forehead over the face to reach the skull. Since in this case both the forehead and the face had already slipped off and bade adieu in the bay, Blas proceeded directly with a rotary saw to uncover the brain, which proved rotten with worms that reminded Arkady of the macaroni served by Aeroflot. As the nausea rose he had Rufo lead him to a tiny, chain-flush lavatory, where he threw up, so perhaps he wasn't so inured after all, he thought. Maybe he had just reached his limit. Rufo was gone, and walking back to the autopsy theater on his own, Arkady went by a room perfumed by carboys of formaldehyde and decorated with anatomical charts. On a table two feet with yellow toenails stuck out from a sheet. Between the legs lay an oversized syringe connected by a tube to a tub of embalming fluid on the floor, a technique used in the smallest, most primitive Russian villages when electric pumps failed. The needle of the syringe was particularly long and narrow to fit into an artery, which was thinner than a vein. Between the feet were rubber gloves and another syringe in an unopened plastic bag. Arkady slipped the bag into his jacket pocket.

When Arkady returned to his seat, Rufo was waiting with a recuperative Cuban cigarette. By that time, the brain had been weighed and set aside while Dr Blas fit head and jaw together.

Although Rufo's lighter was the plastic disposable sort, he said it had been refilled twenty times. 'The Cuban record is over a hundred.'

Arkady bit the cigarette, inhaled. 'What kind is this?'

' "Popular." Black tobacco. You like it?'

'It's perfect.' Arkady let out a plume of smoke as blue as the exhaust of a car in distress.

Rufo's hand kneaded Arkady's shoulder. 'Relax. You're down to bones, my friend.'

The officer who had taken the keys from Osorio returned. At the other table, after Blas had measured the skull vertically and across the brow, he spread a handkerchief and diligently scrubbed the teeth with a toothbrush. Arkady handed Rufo a dental chart he had brought from Moscow (an investigator's precaution), and the driver trotted the envelope down to Blas, who systematically matched the skull's brightened grin to the chart's numbered circles. When he was done he conferred with Captain Arcos, who grunted with satisfaction and summoned Arkady down to the theater floor.

Rufo interpreted. 'The Russian citizen Sergei Sergeevich Pribluda arrived in Havana eleven months ago as an attaché to the Russian embassy. We knew, of course, that he was a colonel in the KGB. Excuse me, the new Federal Security Service, the SVR.'

'Same thing,' Arkady said.

The captain – and in his wake, Rufo – went on. 'A week ago the embassy informed us that Pribluda was missing. We did not expect them to invite a senior investigator from the Moscow prosecutor's office. Perhaps a family member, nothing more.'

Arkady had talked to Pribluda's son, who had refused to come to Havana. He managed a pizzeria, a major responsibility.

Rufo went on. 'Fortunately, the captain says, the identification performed today before your eyes is simple and conclusive. The captain says that a key found in the effects was taken to the apartment of the missing man where it unlocked the door. From an examination of the body recovered from the bay, Dr Blas estimates that it is a Caucasoid male approximately fifty to sixty years of age, one hundred sixty-five centimeters in height, ninety kilos in weight, in every regard the same as the missing man. Moreover, the dental chart of the Russian citizen Pribluda you yourself brought shows one lower molar filled. That molar in the recovered jaw is a steel tooth which, in the opinion of Dr Blas, according to the captain, is typical Russian dental work. Do you agree?'

'From what I saw, yes.'

'Dr Blas says he finds no wounds or broken bones, no signs of violence or foul play. Your friend died of natural causes, perhaps a stroke or aneurysm or heart attack, it would be almost impossible to determine which for a body in this condition. The doctor hopes he did not suffer long.'

'That's kind of him.' Although the doctor appeared more smug than sympathetic.

'The captain, for his part, asks if you accept the observations of this autopsy?'

'I'd like to think about it.'

'Well, you accept the conclusion that the body recovered is that of the Russian citizen Pribluda?'

Arkady turned to the examining table. What had been a bloated cadaver was now split and gutted. Of course, there had been no face or eyes to identify anyway, and finger bones never did yield prints, but someone had lived in that ruined body.

'I think an inner tube in the bay is a strange place to find a Russian citizen.'

'The captain says they all think that.'

'Then there will be an investigation?'

Rufo said, 'It depends.'

'On what?'

'On many factors.'

'Such as?'

'The captain says your friend was a spy. What he was doing when he died was not innocent. The captain can predict your embassy will ask us to do nothing. We are the ones who could make an international incident of this, but frankly it is not worth the effort. We will investigate in our own time, in our own way, although in this Special Period the Cuban people cannot afford to waste resources on people who have revealed themselves to be our enemy. Now do you understand what I mean?' Rufo paused while Arcos took a second to compose himself. 'The captain says an investigation depends on many factors. The position of our friends at the Russian embassy must be taken into account before premature steps are taken. The only issue we have here is an identification of a foreign national who has died on Cuban territory. Do you accept it is the Russian citizen Sergei Pribluda?'

'It could be,' Arkady said.

Dr Blas sighed, Luna took a deep breath and Detective Osorio weighed the keys in her palm. Arkady couldn't help feeling like a difficult actor. 'It probably is, but I can't say conclusively that this body is Pribluda. There's no face, no prints and I doubt very much that you will be able to type the blood. All you have is a dental chart and one steel tooth. He could be another Russian. Or one of thousands of Cubans who went to Russia. Or a Cuban who had a tooth pulled by a Cuban dentist who trained in Russia. Probably you're right, but that's not enough. You opened Pribluda's door with a key. Did you look inside?'

Dr Blas asked in precisely snipped Russian, 'Did you bring any other identification from Moscow?'

'Just this. Pribluda sent it a month ago.' Arkady dug out of his passport case a snapshot of three men standing on a beach and squinting at the camera. One man was so black he could have been carved from jet. He held up a glistening rainbow of a fish for the admiration of two whites, a shorter man with a compensating tower of steel-wool hair and, partially obscured by the others, Pribluda. Behind them was water, a tip of beach, palms.

Blas studied the photograph and read the scribble on the back. 'Havana Yacht Club.'

'There is such a yacht club?' Arkady asked.

'There *was* such a club before the Revolution,' Blas said. 'I think your friend was making a joke.'

Rufo said, 'Cubans love grandiose titles. A "drinking society" can be friends in a bar.'

'The others don't look Russian to me. You can make copies of the picture and circulate them.'

The picture went around to Arcos, who put it back into Arkady's hands as if it were toxic. Rufo said, 'The captain says your friend was a spy, that spies come to bad ends, as they deserve. This is typically Russian, pretending to help and then stabbing Cuba in the back.

The Russian embassy sends out its spy and, when he's missing, asks us to find him. When we find him, you refuse to identify him. Instead of cooperating, you demand an investigation, as if you were still the master and Cuba was the puppet. Since that is no longer the case, you can take your picture back to Moscow. The whole world knows of the Russian betrayal of the Cuban people and, well, he says some more in that vein.'

Arkady gathered as much. The captain looked ready to spit.

Rufo gave Arkady a push. 'I think it's time to go.'

Detective Osorio, who had been quietly following the conversation, suddenly revealed fluent Russian. 'Was there a letter with the picture?'

'Only a postcard saying hello,' Arkady said. 'I threw it away.'

'*Idiota*,' Osorio said, which nobody bothered to translate.

'It's lucky you're going home, you don't have many friends here,' Rufo said. 'The embassy said to put you in an apartment until the plane.'

They drove by three-story stone town houses transformed by the revolution into a far more colorful backdrop of ruin and decay, marble colonnades refaced with whatever color was available – green, ultramarine, chartreuse. Not just ordinary green, either, but a vibrant spectrum: sea, lime, palm and verdigris. Houses were as blue as powdered turquoise, pools of water, peeling sky, the upper levels enlivened by balconies of ornate ironwork embellished by canary cages, florid roosters, hanging bicycles. Even dowdy Russian cars wore a wide

variety of paint, and if their clothes were drab most of
the people had the slow grace and color of big cats. They
paused at tables offering guava paste, pastries, tubers
and fruits. One girl shaving ices was streaked red and
green with syrup, another girl sold sweetmeats from a
cheesecloth tent. A locksmith rode a bicycle that powered
a key grinder; he wore goggles for the sparks and shav-
ings flying around him as he pedaled in place. The music
of a radio hanging in the crook of a pushcart's umbrella
floated in the air.

'Is this the way to the airport?' Arkady asked.

'The flight is tomorrow. Usually there's only one Aeroflot flight a week during the winter, so they don't want
you to miss it.' Rufo rolled the window down. 'Phew, I
smell worse than fish.'

'Autopsies stay with you.' Arkady had left his overcoat
outside the operating theater and separated the coat now
from the paper bag holding Pribluda's effects. 'If Dr
Blas and Detective Osorio speak Russian, why were you
along?'

'There was a time when it was forbidden to speak
English. Now Russian is taboo. Anyway, the embassy
wanted someone along when you were with the police,
but someone not Russian. You know, I never knew
anyone so unpopular so fast as you.'

'That's a sort of distinction.'

'But now you're here you should enjoy yourself.
Would you like to see the city, go to a café, to the Havana
Libre? It used to be the Hilton. They have a rooftop
restaurant with a fantastic view. And they serve lobster.

Only state restaurants are allowed to serve lobster, which are assets of the state.'

'No, thanks.' The idea of cracking open a lobster after an autopsy didn't sit quite right.

'Or a *paladar*, a private restaurant. They're small, they're only allowed twelve chairs but the food is much superior. No?'

Perhaps Rufo didn't get a chance to dine out often, but Arkady didn't think he could even watch someone eat.

'No. The captain and sergeant were in green uniforms, the detective in gray and blue. Why was that?'

'She's police and they're from the Ministry of the Interior. We just call it Minint. Police are under Minint.'

Arkady nodded; in Russia the militia was under the same ministry. 'But Arcos and Luna don't usually go out on homicides?'

'I don't think so.'

'Why was the captain going on about the Russian embassy?'

'He has a point. In the old days Russians acted like lords. Even now, for Cuban police to ask questions at the embassy takes a diplomatic note. Sometimes the embassy cooperates and sometimes it doesn't.'

Most of the traffic was Russian Ladas and Moskviches spraying exhaust and then, waddling as ponderously as dinosaurs, American cars from before the Revolution. Rufo and Arkady got out at a two-story house decorated like a blue Egyptian tomb with scarabs, ankhs and lotuses carved in stucco. A car on blocks sat in residence on the porch.

''57 Chevrolet.' Rufo looked inside at the car's gutted interior, straightened and ran his hand over the flecked paint. From the back. 'Tail fins.' To the front bumper. 'And tits.'

From the car key in the bag of effects Arkady knew that Pribluda had a Lada. No breasts on a Russian car.

As they went in and climbed the stairs the door to the ground-floor apartment cracked open enough for a woman in a house-dress to follow their progress.

'A concierge?' Arkady asked.

'A snoop. Don't worry, at night she watches television and doesn't hear a thing.'

'I'm going back tonight.'

'That's right.' Rufo unlocked the upstairs door. 'This is a protocol apartment the embassy uses for visiting dignitaries. Well, lesser dignitaries. I don't think we've had anyone here for a year.'

'Is someone from the embassy coming to talk about Pribluda?'

'The only one who wants to talk about Pribluda is you. You like cigars?'

'I've never smoked a cigar.'

'We'll talk about it later. I'll be back at midnight to take you to the plane. If you think the flight to Havana was long, wait till you go back to Moscow.'

The apartment was furnished with a set of cream-and-gold dining chairs, a sideboard with a coffee service, a nubby sofa, red phone, a bookshelf with titles like *La Amistad Russo-Cubana* and *Fidel y Arte* supported by erotic bookends in mahogany. In a disconnected refrigerator a loaf of Bimbo Bread was spotted with mold. The air conditioner was dead and showed the carbon smudges of an electrical fire. Arkady thought he probably showed some carbon smudges of his own.

He stripped from his clothes and showered in a stall of tiles that poured water from every valve and washed the odor of the autopsy off his skin and from his hair. He dried himself on the scrap of towel provided and stretched out on the bed under his overcoat in the dark of the bedroom and listened to the voices and music that filtered from outside through the closed shutters of the window. He dreamed of floating among the playing fish of Havana Bay. He dreamed of flying back to Moscow and not landing, just circling in the night.

Russian planes did that, sometimes, if they were so old that their instruments failed. Although there could be other factors. If a pilot made a second landing approach he could be charged for the extra fuel expended, so he made only one, good or not. Or they were overloaded or underfueled.

He was both.

Circling sounded good.

NIGHT WING

When was I born?
Where did I come from?
Where am I going?
What am I?

– the Hopi questions

For Knox and Kitty

Chapter One

The red man tobacco sign – an Indian profile with a corroded eye – stared west. Two pick-up trucks rusted in a bower of yellow creosote bushes. Out of a headlight socket flicked the quick ribbon of a lizard tongue.

It was noon in the Painted Desert. A hundred degrees.

The tobacco sign and car hoods welded together in upright rows were the walls of Abner Tasupi's shed. A square of sheet steel was the roof. Sometimes, Abner fixed cars and, sometimes, he sold Enco gasoline straight from a drum. Usually, the drums were empty and he spent the day listening to his transistor radio. They had Navajo disc jockeys on a Gallup station. While he hated Navajos, there were no Hopi disc jockeys. There were lots of Hopis up on the Black Mesa, but not a one that dared come visit him.

Well, one.

Youngman Duran sat in the shed between the erupting springs of a car seat. A half-empty jug of Gallo port nestled between his legs.

'I'm sorry,' Abner apologized to his only friend, 'but they got to die.'

'Anyone I know?'

Stripped down to underpants and a leather kilt, Abner squatted in the centre of the dirt floor grinding cornmeal. He was past ninety and his brown body was hard like an insect's. His grey hair, cut short above the eyes, hung down to frame a flat face with broad cheekbones and wide, peeling lips.

'Come on, Abner, you can tell me. Hell, I'm not a deputy for nothing.'

Youngman was a third of Abner's age. His hair was shorter, pitch-black and tucked under a dirty Stetson. Sweat ringed the crown of his hat and sweat stains from his armpits and back merged to turn most of his khaki shirt into a dark sponge. He shifted his seat, trying to get comfortable without sticking himself with a seat spring. Youngman hated port wine but real alcohol was hard to find on the reservation. Besides, he liked Abner.

Abner gathered ground cornmeal in his hands and started pouring it inside of the door and, moving backwards, around the corners of the room.

Youngman pulled out a pack of damp cigarettes.

'Everyone you know.'

'Well, that's a start, Abner, that's a start.'

The shed always struck Youngman as a flood mark where the junk of different civilizations was left high and dry. A box of sparkplugs and points. Tire irons and jacks. Soup and bean cans on a drum converted into a stove. T-shirts stuffed into holes in the wall, where ears of blue corn hung from braided husks. On an orange crate shelf stood a line of kachina dolls, each a foot tall, one crowned with wooden rays of the sun, another wearing eagle fluffs, the crudely carved kind, fifty to a hundred years old or more.

'You know, you get $1000 for one of those dolls in Phoenix. Might as well do it before someone comes and steals 'em.'

'No one comes around here, Flea.' Abner finished pouring corn. 'I don't worry about that.'

'Well, they figure you're going to hex 'em, Abner.'

On a steamer trunk were mason jars of peyote and datura, ground jimson weed. Youngman resisted the temptation to dig in. He'd been strung out before; he'd spent seven years trying to stay strung out. But that was the Army. Now he only smoked a little grass and drank wine. The highs weren't so high, but he didn't come so close to touching bottom. Abner was different. Abner was a priest. And Abner was right, people stayed away from him.

'Just what the hell do you mean, everyone's going to die? You're lucky you're talking to me. Anyone else would take you serious, Abner. You know that.'

The lid was off the datura jar. The steamer trunk was bandaged with travel stickers reading 'Tijuana', 'Truth or Consequences', 'Tombstone'. There could as well have been one that said 'Mars'. Abner had picked up the trunk in a pawn shop; he'd never been farther than Tuba City.

'It's a hot day and the Gallo brothers worked real hard, Abner. Have some.'

Abner shook his head. Old man's been in the datura, Youngman thought. A fat dose of ground seeds was poison. A small dose of dried roots lifted the brain like a car on a jack. There were a lot of ways to die on a reservation. Drink. Datura or locoweed. Sit in the middle

3

of the highway at night. Just let the time go by while the seconds accumulated like sand in an open grave.

Abner opened the trunk.

'Damn it. You promised me you'd never make medicine around me, Abner.'

'You don't believe in it,' Abner smiled back.

'I don't but I don't like it, either. I just want to sit down with you and get a buzz on. Like usual.'

'I know what you want to do,' the old man kept smiling. 'Too late for that now.'

'Look, we'll go take a ride. We can shoot some rabbit maybe.'

Abner lifted a blanket from the bottom of the orange crate. Under it was a rabbit in a cage, nose pressed against the slats. Youngman didn't know Abner to indulge in luxuries like fresh meat. Mostly the old man lived on pan bread, chilis, corn, and maybe a dried peach.

Inside the trunk were what Abner'd always called his 'secret goods'. Paho sticks. Feathers. Jars of dried corn, yellow, red, and blue. Abner poured small mounds of the corn on top of the trunk in front of the kachinas.

'It's just I don't want them coming after you,' Youngman said, 'because they're going to send me to deal with you. Those people are nuts. They believe your routine.'

From another part of the trunk, Abner rummaged through a Baggie of feathers until he came up with the black-and-white tail feathers of a shrike. He stood a feather in each mound of corn. The effect was of an altar. Abner stepped back to appreciate his handiwork.

4

'I want to leave the centre for the Pahana tablet. Nice, huh?'

'What's the Pahana tablet?'

'You don't know?'

'No.'

'You don't know much, then.' Abner rubbed his hands.

'I know you're tripping on that dream dust of yours. How much datura did you eat? Tell me.'

'Not much,' Abner shrugged his thin shoulders without turning around to answer. 'You'll need a lot more, Flea.'

Youngman was disappointed. 'Making medicine' was the perfect example of a fool's errand. No amount of 'medicine' had yet made a poor, ignorant Indian rich, hip, and white. At least, not in Arizona. As for kachina dolls, everyone knew they were kids' toys, nothing else.

The row of kachinas stared woodenly back with expressions of painted mischief.

'Yeah. I need a handful of uppers, some speed, a snort of coke, smokin' acid, and a can of Coors just to start feeling the Spirit.'

'Even so,' Abner maintained, 'you're a good boy.'

Youngman scratched between his eyebrows. There were times when he felt that he and Abner were conversing through an incompetent translator, although they were both using Hopi with the same white corruptions. Mentally, he kicked himself. He shouldn't have stopped by Abner's decrepit shack, he should have gone straight on to the Momoa ranch like he was supposed to.

Abner brought out a soda bottle stoppered with

5

aluminium foil. He removed the foil and poured into his palm a kind of sand Youngman had never seen before. It was very fine and black and shiny as eyes. When his hand was full, Abner squatted and, letting a thin stream of the black sand slip between his fingers and thumb, drew a swastika in a corner of the floor. The lines were ruler straight and the angles could have been done with a T-square. Empty, his hand was smudged with oil.

Damn it, Youngman thought. The last thing he wanted to do was arrest the old man.

'You been around the Peabody mine, Abner? That's not sand.'

'You're really a good boy. Not too dumb, either.' Abner refilled his hand and started another swastika. 'No, it ain't from Peabody.'

A month before, Abner had been caught dumping cartons of rattlesnakes into the Black Mesa stripmine. The guards would have shot him if Youngman hadn't arrived in time to make the arrest himself. And then let Abner go.

'Tell me not to worry about you, uncle.'

'Don't worry.' Abner concentrated on his drawing. 'It'll work. I didn't get this from any white mine, I got it from the dead people.'

The black sand had a viscous quality, almost liquid. Youngman sipped wine. Abner drew two more swastikas, forming a perfect square of them, the corners perfectly aligned to the four directions, Youngman had no doubt.

'What are you up to, Abner?'

Abner went to his steamer trunk and filled his arms with bottles of black powder, which he carried to the centre of the square of swastikas. He squatted and opened one of the bottles, filled his hand, and started drawing again. A funny thing about priests, old and feeble as they got, once they hunkered over their so-called medicine they might as well be locked into place by magnets; it took two men to budge them. All a matter of balance, of course. The new pattern Abner drew was a curl of black sand that grew into a spiral.

'Don't you get angry at me, Flea.' Abner refilled his hand. 'But I think about this a lot and I just decided something had to be done about this world. First of all, there are the goddamn Navajos. Those bastards gotta go. Then, I think, all the Federal Courts and the Indian Bureau. Them, too.' Powder hissed from Abner's hand, widening the spiral. 'They're killing us, Flea. They are, always have been. Now it's them and the companies. Peabody Coal. El Paso Gas. I'm going to fix them, Flea. It's all up to me and I'm going to take care of them, Flea.'

Abner stopped to open another bottle.

Youngman had to smile at the continued sound of his own Hopi name. He never heard it except from Abner.

'You're going to stop El Paso Gas?'

'I'm not sorry about that, just about the people.'

'Sure.'

That would shake El Paso's corporate structure, Youngman thought, knowing that a spaced-out ninety-

year-old Hopi medicine man out in the middle of the
desert was going to take them on. I'll drink to that, he
added to himself.

'I seen the shovels digging up the Black Mesa,' Abner
spat out the door. 'I hear about them taking the water.'

'Water's going to Los Angeles. Hey, Abner, why don't
you lay off your medicine and share some of this juice.'
Youngman offered the wine. Abner shook his head.

'Then Los Angeles has to go, too. Them and Tucson,
Phoenix, Albuquerque. All them cities.'

'A lot of people. You tell anyone else about this?'

Abner twisted on his knees, his arms outstretched like
the points of a compass, and the black spiral swung
around itself once, then a second time, curved delicately
to the right, and veered into a larger circle in the opposite
direction.

From where he sat, Youngman could see the stripped
trucks outside. Oxidized carapaces like the remains of
prehistoric animals. Hell of a lot of fossils in this country,
he thought. Including Indians. He twisted the cap back
on the wine.

'How're you going to do it, Abner? Get a rifle and
start popping cars on the highway? Dynamite? How're
you going to stop everybody?'

'Not stop them, end them.' Abner looked up. He had
small, powerful eyes, black centres with mottled whites.
'I'm going to end the world.'

The two whirls of black sand were complete. The
smaller curled around itself three times, the larger one
four. Together, they were a pair of serpentines five feet

across. Although Abner had had to stop and begin again many times between handfuls of sand, there was no sign of a break or a falter. Not the slightest flaw in the concentric lines. In the dark of the shed, Abner's art was as pure and glistening as a double-coiled snake.

Nervous, Youngman looked out the door, past the trucks and his jeep. The sky was as blue as water, as deep as turquoise set in a silver conch. Air moved like a dancer with a dragging foot over the sandy ground, rattling dry seed pods. On the northern horizon stood the wall of the Black Mesa. To the south, Phoenix was two hundred miles distant; east, Albuquerque was 150. They could have been on different planets. That's what he'd been after, Youngman reminded himself, a different planet. He dug the last cigarette out of his pack.

Abner went to his trunk for bottles of a bright red sand.

'How're you going to end the world?'

'Different.' Abner gestured for Youngman to give him a puff on the cigarette. 'First world was ended by fire. People were led wrong by a woman and a snake. The Creator sent down flames and opened up the volcanoes. Everything was on fire and burned up, except for a few good Hopis.'

Abner started drawing a ring of the red sand within the swastikas and around the double serpentine.

'Second world was good until people got too prosperous, too fat. They only cared about getting rich. The Creator saw what was happening and he stopped the world from turning. The earth went out of its orbit and everything froze, everything was covered with ice. Everyone died except the few good Hopis.'

Youngman blew out a sigh of smoke. The story was the litany of his youth, heard over and over again.

'Third world was perfect.' Abner measured out the arc of red sand. 'Cities were full of jewels and feather rugs. People forgot the simple way. Women became whores. Men started fighting, flying from city to city to make war. The Creator got fed up. He put a few good Hopis in hollow reeds and covered the world with rain and water.'

From the altar, the dolls listened with rigid attention. A cloud-faced star god. A horned corn god. A round-headed clown. A dancer holding a plumed serpent. Dumb witnesses on a steamer trunk.

The red ring was done. Abner got a bottle of white sand and another of orange.

'At last, the land rose and the Creator let the Hopis come ashore in the desert.' He opened the bottle of orange sand first. 'He said, "This is your Fourth World now. Its name is Tuwaqachi, World Complete. Its colour is sikyangpu, yellow-white. Its direction is north, towards the Black Mesa. Its caretaker is Masaw, the god of death. From now on, you will have to follow the simple way." '

The figure Abner drew between the serpentine and the ring was the outline of a running dog.

'Coyote Clan,' he told Youngman. 'You.'

'Swell,' Youngman said, uncomfortably.

Abner unstoppered the bottle of white sand and stepped carefully to the other side of the serpentine.

'So, we have worlds before and worlds after. For us, after the Fourth World there will be a Fifth.'

'Maybe,' Youngman suggested, 'maybe, you're rushing things a little.'

'The prophecies, you mean? Well, this world is supposed to end with atomic bombs, that's what some of the other priests say. I've been waiting for it but I don't think it's going to happen very soon. You can't depend on that. So, I'm going to end it now.'

'When?'

'Today.'

On the edge of the red ring, Abner finished the white outline of a bird. Then he excused himself and went out of the shed behind a bush to urinate. Youngman waited, wishing for nothing more than another cigarette. Abner returned, sniffing.

'It's a good day, huh? How's the machine running?'

'The jeep? It's okay. Look, I have to go see the Momoas now but then I'm going on into the hills. You want to come with me?'

Abner shook his head and chuckled. His eyes were slightly glazed.

'You didn't go out there to take a leak,' Youngman said. 'You ate some more of that junk.'

'Want some?'

'No.'

'You will.' Abner went on chuckling.

The old man had acted strange before. Never as bad as this. Even if he grabbed Abner and took him into the mesa, though, who would dare help? Who wouldn't run?

'The other priests know about your plans?'

'I asked them over. Some of them, they're busy making up tourist junk. Some of them, they wanta watch game shows on TV. I'll do it without them.'

Abner unstoppered another bottle of black sand. He swayed delicately as he stepped around his painting, but he was steady enough when he bent over to draw a final figure within the ring of red. Painstakingly, he let the oily sand shape itself into a man without a head. A ragged cape hung from his shoulders; from the cape extended fingers. Abner opened a leather pouch and took out small bones, which he placed as a necklace. Where eyes and a mouth would have been, he put round corn cob sections. Under the eyes, trails of broken mirror glass, so that the headless figure seemed to be staring and crying at the same time.

'Almost done.' Abner stood up, satisfied.

He wiped his hands on a rag and rummaged in his trunk until he came up with a buck knife and a leather belt. Putting a foot on one end of the belt, he snapped it taut along his leg as a strap and slapped the knife blade back and forth across it.

'If you're going to end the world, one more day won't make a difference,' Youngman said. 'Wait until tomorrow.'

'Radio said maybe rain tomorrow night.'

'So?' Youngman almost laughed.

'New clouds coming, Flea,' Abner said seriously. 'Dreamed them up. My clouds don't like rain.'

Abner felt the edge of his knife. Then he crossed to

the rabbit cage, lifted the animal out and strung it by its rear legs with a leather thong from the top of the shed door. The rabbit jerked from side to side and rolled its eyes.

'What do your clouds like?' Youngman asked.

Abner grabbed the rabbit by the base of the ears and twisted its head back, stretching the neck. He laid the knife across the white fur of the neck, and then his arm dropped.

The old man stared hesitantly, standing awkwardly in the frame of light, one hand still gripping the squirming rabbit. Reflection made the blade luminous. Youngman felt the stare like a blind hand running over his face, as if recognition had suddenly been lost.

'What do they like?' he repeated.

The rabbit clawed the air. The knife blinked, turning in Abner's hand.

The old man was crazy, Youngman thought. Senile. Finally over the edge after a lifetime of datura, grass, peyote, and bad booze. Tripped on stories, prophecies, lies, and frustration. Not that Youngman especially loved Abner, he told himself, any more than a man could love a gnarled ironwood tree or a stone chimney. When the tree fell or the chimney split, though, there had to be a sense of loss. As if a touchstone had been taken away. But a medicine man plotting war in a junkyard shed against the offices of the Indian Bureau, against the power shovels and million-dollar bank-rolls of the mining companies? That was not only pathetic, it was downright comic. Abner still thought the Hopis were the

Chosen People. They weren't chosen, they were marked for erasure.

Abner's eyes said he wanted to answer and that he couldn't.

'You won't believe me, Flea,' he finally said.

'Then why did you start raving about all this?'

'Because you're my friend. You're part of it and you have to help. Don't worry,' Abner became more reassuring, 'we'll kill them all.'

'Just tell me what to do.'

'Later, when I'm dead.'

The wind that penetrated the shed grew an edge. Youngman thought about re-opening the wine.

'If you can wait that long, Abner, I guess I can.'

As Youngman stood, the glossy coils of the serpentine seemed to shift. An illusion in the shadow. For Abner, though, from the altitude of datura, Youngman guessed the spirals were moving and gaining speed. He was still nagged by the suspicion that Abner might take a gun and start sniping at cars on the highway.

'But if you're ending the world different this time,' Youngman added, 'I'd be curious how.'

'Different.'

'No floods, fire, ice, bombs. Guns, then? How?'

'This time, Masaw will end it,' Abner said. 'I'll see him tonight.'

'Tonight, you're going to see him? The god of death, huh?'

Abner's concentration slipped to his painting and the unfinished figure with crying eyes and round mouth and no head inside a ring of red sand. The black body and cape shone, soft as fur.

'If I do things right,' he said.

Youngman lifted his hat and ran a hand through his hair. He felt helpless, at a total loss.

'Okay,' he gave up. Leaving the shed, he stopped in the doorway next to Abner and the hanging rabbit, half in shadow, half in light. 'If anyone can do it, you can.'

On the way to his jeep, he heard the rabbit's whimper cut short.

He had been born into the Coyote Clan, the only son of an unemployed construction worker and a perpetually angry woman. Joe Duran, bear-sized, arms like posts, never brooded over lack of work. Once for a year he hauled bricks at White Sands for the Air Force, an experience he felt bestowed on him enough of labour's honours. What Joe Duran did best was drink and hunt. He could go up the Dinnebito Wash with five rounds and stagger home with four kills. 'Saved the last round for myself,' he'd tell Youngman. The third thing he did best was clown. Whenever clowns were needed for a ceremonial, Joe Duran was always the first tapped. Disguised in white powder, he would stumble drunkenly through a line of priests, or run after women spectators waving a wooden penis, or walk suicidally backwards along the edge of the mesa. Which struck everyone as terribly funny, although it was no different from the way Joe Duran acted any other day, and in time, of course, he drove his angry wife crazy. Youngman remembered watching his father wearing clothes backwards and standing on his immense hands on the highest point of the mesa, laughing while Youngman's mother pitched knives and rocks. Finally, as a last grasp for sanity, she took up with a Navajo in Window Rock. Joe Duran followed them, killed them with his deer rifle, kicked the dead Navajo out of bed, lay down beside his wife and blew his own brains out. It was a common melodrama of reservation life.

Youngman was trucked off to mission school. Life there was comfortable enough. He had food, friends, a bed. In class, he stayed as mute as he could, watching. The teachers listed him as 'slow, possibly retarded'. Until the age of fourteen, when the school received some donated sets of oil paint. Then, he was very much noticed.

He had a glib facility, a hunter's eye for colour. He didn't speak much more than he had before, but he would sit in front of an easel every waking minute, painting landscapes, nothing but landscapes. They were shown and, to his surprise, they were bought. Youngman experimented with watercolours, tempera, and acrylic, obsessed not so much with art as with the revelation that he could make money. In one step he strode past every other Indian he knew, and past his father in particular. Within two years, he developed a technique with acrylic and varnish that gave his desert landscapes a hard, jewel-like finish that was totally cynical and artificial. Youngman, alone, knew what he was doing. Not painting the desert. Killing it. On his canvas, birds were as bright and dead as souvenir pins, and falling rain had the quality of rocks. It was a style only whites could appreciate, but they were paying. At the galleries in Santa Fe and Phoenix, they paid a lot.

Flattered by whites, he responded in kind. He cut his hair and dressed in sports jackets. Found himself becoming a good-looking man though not pretty, his features were too angular for that. Only occasionally was he betrayed by a dark hostility in his eyes, his mother's gift.

The University of New Mexico offered Youngman a full art scholarship. This was the second step up, Youngman told himself. He could be anything.

The summer before his first year at the university, Youngman returned to the reservation. The Snake Dance was being held at Shongopovi. For fun, Youngman joined the runners whose race across the desert signalled the start of the ceremony. For the first time in seven years, he wore a leather kilt and moccasins. He had always had stamina. Midway through the race, his moccasins were soaked through with blood. The pain encouraged him. He overtook the local boys at the base of the canyon and sprinted up the narrow trail to win. The Snake Clan was about to award Youngman the prize when they were stopped by a priest of the Fire Clan.

'This boy is not Hopi. Give the prize to a Hopi. Otherwise, all my clan will leave.' The priest was Abner.

'I am Hopi and I won,' Youngman protested.

'You are empty. I see inside you and nothing is there. This prize is only for real people.'

Humiliated, Youngman returned to Albuquerque, to college. But college was not what he'd expected. In most subjects he was stupefyingly ignorant, even for an Indian. Of history, literature, science, or social studies, he knew next to nothing. Worse, he came fast to the dead end of his talent. As long as he painted the desert, however fraudulently, the images came easily. Faced with anything else, even an elementary life class, he revealed himself as a complete incompetent. It was as if he knew a single song with a single variation and otherwise was dumb. But there were a number of ways to take out his frustration. The university had other Indians, mostly Navajos who regarded a Hopi as inferior. Youngman picked fights with Navajo gangs, with white football players, with just about anybody. After a single year of failing grades, he was drafted. After one year in the Army, he was court-martialled and put in the stockade at Leavenworth, where he served the next six years of his life.

At the age of twenty-seven, Youngman was released and went to Los Angeles. He joined the Mexicans working as Indian extras in films, mixed colours for paint stores, and delivered cars for Hertz. One morning, delivering a rented Continental to Burbank, he was driving through the canyons that segment L.A. into an archipelago of concrete islands. Pulling off the freeway, he left the car to walk into the canyon, which had the colour and texture of crumpled brown paper. Sitting still, he watched the shadows slide like cats over the hills.

Day cats that leisurely stretched and curled on the warm earth. And still he sat. Towards sunset, thousands of fire-control sprinklers fanned the parched walls of the canyon with water bought and diverted from the rivers of Arizona. Round as marbles, the water rolled through the air and shattered in the last rays of the sun. One drop after another, million after million, exploding unheard against the moans of the freeway. Water that fell as rain in the Rockies, that flowed as the Colorado River through the Grand Canyon, heading for the desert but rerouted to a sprinkler system. He laughed until he nearly cried.

Youngman delivered the car ten hours late, was fired and, the following morning, returned to the reservation, not much better off than when he'd left.

His first year back he spent relearning how to live. He taught himself again his own first language, which dry holes would yield water to a digging stick, how to mend clothes with a bone needle and to tell the difference between the tracks of a running deer and an unwary one.

At the end of the year, a pick-up truck of old men pulled into his camp.

'You're still here,' they told him. 'We expected you to be gone long ago.'

'I'm still here.'

'Are you going to stay?'

'Yes.'

'Then we will have to do something about you. You're a troubled person. Never at rest. We can't tell you to leave because we know our obligations. So we are going

19

to put you to work. From now on you're a deputy. You go up to Hotevilla tomorrow and sign up. Maybe, someday, we can get some good out of you.'

The old chiefs got back into their pick-up and left.

That was two years ago. Being deputy consisted largely of disarming drunks and making sure no tourists brought cameras into the pueblos when dances were held. Youngman had all the time he wanted to escape into the wilderness. He stayed out of trouble because he had the obligation to uphold the law. The old chiefs weren't so dumb.

Youngman downshifted and climbed the jeep through a copse of junipers on to a dirt road. The Momoa ranch was in the hills above Dinnebito Wash. As the road wound its way up, the temperature dropped. Scrub gave way to more junipers, oaks, and piñon trees. In the hills was water, and water was wealth.

'You finally come,' Joseph Momoa welcomed the deputy. 'Where the hell you been?'

Joe Momoa and his family had five thousand acres of timber and grassland that included two springs and pasturage for five hundred cattle and seven hundred sheep. His house was panelled in redwood and sat under a television aerial as large as a radar dish. The barn had been converted into a six-car garage and game room. Joe himself had been converted into a prosperous Mormon, along with his wife and his sons Joe Jr. and Ben. The Momoa men were alike in their aggressive bulk, flannel shirts, and flashy Acme boots. Joe drove an air-conditioned pick-up. His sons hot-dogged it on candy-coloured motorcycles. Among Hopis, they were Rockefellers.

'What have you got to show me?' Youngman asked.

'You'll see.'

Joe led the way on a loping path under piñon branches. Bastard doesn't even walk like an Indian any more, Youngman thought with a sense of irony. For more years than he cared to dwell on, he hadn't walked like an Indian himself.

'Piñon nuts oughtta bring in $10,000 this year,' Joe said automatically.

'How much in pines?'

Joe shot a scowl over his shoulder. Pines grew above the Momoa spread and every year hundreds of the trees were trucked out secretly and illegally.

'That's your problem,' Joe Jr. said one step behind Youngman.

They descended to a meadow of corrals and pens. Youngman could see sheep milling in their area. Cattle were lined up at their trough. The dogs on guard cowered at the sight of the Momoas.

'Now, you take a look at that.' Joe pointed to the middle corral.

At first, Youngman thought the corral was empty, but as he came through the gate he saw three quarterhorses lying on their sides. Their eyes were open and rolling. One struggled to its knees and Youngman could see that what first appeared to be a dark blanket over its back was caked blood and flies.

'Get a horse blanket,' he ordered Ben Momoa.

'Pa?' Ben took a step back.

'Do what he says.' Joe took a blanket from the top rail of the corral and threw it to his son.

The kneeling horse lolled its head in the manner of an animal drugged by locoweed. Flies heavy with blood bounced into the air as Ben waved the blanket at them. Youngman brushed the flies away from his face.

'What the hell happened?' he asked.

'You tell us,' Joe said.

The withers and haunches of the horse looked as if they had been shredded by a straight razor wielded by a madman. Youngman patted the horse's head, ran his hand down the mane and stopped short. From neck to tail the horse's back was pink flesh, dry blood and hanging strips of skin. The cuts weren't deep.

'Keep waving that,' Youngman told Ben.

'I'm gettin' sick.'

Not deep, more like gouges from a V-shaped leather punch. And there were more than Youngman could count. Some blood had dried in streaks down the horse's legs and belly, but the horse had lost a lot more blood than that. The animal was groggy, but not in apparent pain. Youngman checked the tail. It was brown with dried blood; it should have been totally matted.

'Well?' Joe demanded.

Youngman looked at the horse's hooves. They were smooth, not the way they'd be if the horse had struck out at anything. Youngman walked over to the other horses. They were in worse shape. The flies on them formed moving, buzzing hunchbacks. He examined their hooves too. They were as smooth as marble, but the horses were dying from loss of blood. Three horses, half their skin flayed off, that didn't fight back.

'I don't know,' Youngman said.

He took a deep breath, stepping away from the mutilated horses. They didn't even try to swat at the flies. Youngman scanned the ground.

'Ever let your dogs in here?'

'With horses? Never.'

Youngman could see nothing but hoof marks in the dirt. No deep ones, nothing suggesting excitement, nothing suggesting that anything but horses had been in the corral.

'Found the horses like this this morning?'

'Right.'

Youngman looked up at the clear blue sky. Eagles? Ridiculous. As his eyes dropped, he noticed something he should have seen before. Where blood stained the ground were wider, blacker stains. He picked up some of it between his fingers. It was sticky and smelled of ammonia.

'Jesus.' He wiped his fingers on clean earth. 'Well, I can't figure it. Any of it.'

'Coyotes,' Joe said firmly.

'Coyotes? Your sheep, maybe. Or a calf. Not horses, no way. You'd've heard your dogs. The whole corral'd be torn up. There'd be tracks. No coyote bites like that.'

'Then a cat.'

'No.'

'Then what?'

'I told you I don't know.'

'There's nothing left, damn it. I lost three horses, I'm goin' to have to shoot 'em. This is six hundred dollars in quarterhorse ripped up here an' I want some action. I want you to start up a hunt an' I don't mean some half-assed trackin'. A real hunt. The Navajos have a helicopter. You get it an' we'll go over these hills an' shoot every coyote an' cat we see.'

'You're not going to get the animal that attacked your horses that way.'

'I say I will, an' even if I don't we'll clean up these hills the way they should of been a long time ago.'

'Look, I know how you feel about losing some horses.'

'The hell you do. You don't have a horse to your name. Now you get on the stick an' fix up a helicopter for my boys an' me. We got the rifles. Lots of 'em.'

Youngman could see it. A helicopter over Dinnebito Wash, with the Momoa boys blasting away like machine gunners at anything that moved. Wouldn't they have a good time.

The kneeling horse slumped on to its side. Flies settled on it in thick spirals.

'No Navajos, no helicopter,' Youngman said.

'Tribal council meets in two weeks.' Joe's face reddened. 'I'll tell 'em about your drinkin'. I can smell it on you.'

'Get a vet's report on the horses.' Youngman walked away. 'If he says a cat did this, or a coyote, we'll talk about it again.'

'Junior!' Joe yelled.

Joe Jr. stepped in Youngman's way. He had forty pounds on Youngman, but after a moment's glare Joe Jr. swallowed it and moved aside.

'What we need here is a real deputy,' Joe Momoa shouted after Youngman, 'not a bum. Real deputies like the Navajos have. An' I know you, Duran. You're not even a real Hopi.'

At the house, Youngman got into his jeep. Instead of taking the road down the way he'd come, he drove higher into the hills. Without much effort he put the Momoa family out of his mind, but the sight of the horses lingered. There were mountain lions in the hills. The heights were their refuge. The cats were running away from man, not towards him.

Piñon trees and junipers fell away and in their place stood forests of Chihuahua pines, then Ponderosa pine as straight as the teeth of a comb and thickets of alder. The air developed a cold edge.

Momoa was right in a way. Properly speaking, Youngman wasn't Hopi, he was Tewa Pueblo. The Tewas were the tribe that had driven the Spanish out of New Mexico. Two hundred years ago, when the peaceful Hopis were being overrun by Navajos and Apaches, the Hopis asked the Tewas to come and fight the Hopis' war. The Tewas came, and fought, and stayed. The name of the Tewa hero was Popay. Flea. The same as Youngman's.

By the time Youngman reached the shoulders of the hills, dusk was filling in the wash. The desert was a faint purple. Sun still hit the tops of the hills and would for another hour. Youngman replaced his boots with moccasins Abner had made for him. He gathered his rifle and bedroll and hiked for twenty minutes until he came to a stream which he followed to a spring, where he lay down on a moss-covered rock and dipped his face in the water.

As he lifted his head, he saw a rabbit watching him from under a pine branch. Youngman's hand slipped into his rifle sheath. He could have the rabbit for supper and take the legs to Abner in the morning. The rabbit brushed a forepaw across its whiskers. With his elbow on the rifle stock, Youngman levered a bullet into the breech. He slid the rifle out. The rabbit hopped forward, a perfect target against a green background. Water rolled down Youngman's face, off his chin, hitting the water. Abner already had a rabbit, it occurred to Youngman, and he wasn't so hungry himself.

'Scat!'

After a supper of Monterey Jack and tortilla, Youngman draped his roll over his back to keep warm. The stars overhead were sharp and hard. Once, he swung a flashlight beam around the stream to catch the eyeshines of the nocturnal animals congregating there. Spider eyes were silver, toad eyes were red. Moving, they made tiny trails of lightning.

Youngman hadn't been forced to stay in the Army; Hopis could choose conscientious objector status. But he stayed and screening tests showed he had a highly developed sense of spatial relationships, so he was upped to sergeant, trained to read aerial photographs through three-dimensional viewers, and shipped to Andersen Air

Force Base in Guam. Every day, and every night, three-plane squadrons of eight-engine B-52's flew off Guam to North Vietnam, each plane carrying twenty tons of bombs. Their targets were picked from photographs taken by reconnaissance U-2's shuttling back and forth from Thailand and Guam. Day photos could be transformed into maps with code numbers and co-ordinates. Night photos were infra-red puzzles and no one was better than Youngman at deciphering the mottled reds, greens, and blues that signified the heat of human activity, the cool of forest canopies, and the chill of water at night. The enemy could burn refuse, or hose down power stations. Youngman was never fooled, and the long-distance rain that he sent out was always accurate. It was a fascination to him, a game. A year into his tour he received his first service decoration and a rest-and-recreation leave in Bangkok, where he was offered Vietnamese finger necklaces and scalps at reasonable prices. And a purse of private parts sewn together.

That night in Bangkok, while Youngman slept between two whores, he heard his father laughing. So that was the joke, Youngman thought. That was the joke all along. Joe waving a wooden penis. Dancing backward, one leg over the mesa edge. The finger necklace. Standing on his hands. The bombers easing their weight from the runway. The wrinkled purse. The beautiful maps of fire. The deer rifle in the mouth. People liked to kill each other. That was funny.

'No.' Youngman sat up between the whores.

He returned to Guam and, a month later, was court-martialled for deliberately misreading recon photos and sending night raids of B-52's to bomb the China Sea. Youngman's answer was that he'd decided to take the war seriously, and he didn't feel like making war any more. He could have gotten twenty years, but bombers habitually dropped their loads into the sea either because a raid had been aborted or, just as often, because a pilot was near the end of his six-month tour. Also, Youngman's unusual assignment from the Army to Guam muddied the jurisdiction of the court. He got two years.

At the start, it wasn't so bad. There were Indians at Leavenworth Stockade; he educated himself through the library and he had a soft job in the photographer's studio until, with a month left in Youngman's sentence, a guard emptied a water pistol full of urine on him. It was only a routine joke by a bored prison guard, but Youngman tore the slicer off a photo cropper and cut the guard's arm to the bone. When Youngman came out of the prison stockade a month later, he received two more years to serve, the first quarter in solitary, a close, unlit cell painted black. Towards the end of his second sentence, when Youngman was on a roadgrading crew, one of the other Indians bolted, idiotically since there was nothing to run to except miles of flat, freshly turned Kansas prairie. As the guard in charge of the crew raised his shotgun to fire, Youngman knocked him down and said he would bring the escaping man back. Youngman was gaining on his friend when he was cut down from the back by two loads of 30–30 pellets. He spent two months in the hospital, and received two more years.

From then on, the guards left him alone and he made no more friends.

His first winter back on the reservation, he happened by Abner's garage. The Fire Clan priest had long been run off the mesa as a witch, but he recognized Youngman.

'Your car broke down someplace?' Abner stepped out of the garage wrapped in a blanket.

'Haven't got a car.' Youngman set his backpack down. There was a rain barrel by the oil drums. He cracked the ice on the top to scoop up a drink.

'Long walk to the mesa.'

'Not going to the mesa,' Youngman answered.

'Well, there's no place to stay out here,' Abner said belligerently.

'There's every place to stay out here.'

The old man put his back to the chilled sun to see his visitor better.

'You with the Bureau or the companies now, which?'

'With no one.'

'Then what are you doing?'

'Walking.' Youngman turned to swing his pack to his shoulder. 'Just walking. Okay?'

'Wait.' Abner stopped Youngman from leaving. 'Sit a second.'

Youngman shrugged and squatted, keeping the pack balanced on his shoulder. Abner squatted facing him. After a couple of minutes, Youngman let his eyes slide from Abner's and studied the terrain, which at first seemed as flat as a drumhead and only with patience yielded the shadow of leafless bushes and the faults of arroyos. When he finally looked back at Abner the old man was grinning.

'I said a while ago you were empty inside,' Abner told him. 'I see now that you are real, a full person.'

'So?'

'So, I got some wine inside.'

From then on, Abner said, they were friends.

In the hills above Dinnebito Wash Youngman lay down and let night sounds fill his head. He fell asleep watching a star called Hotomkam travel west.

While the sun had been setting, a baby was born. Blind and hairless, it fell into a cradle formed by the membrane between its mother's legs. Instinctively, it chirped through milk teeth while its mother spread her baby's wings and sniffed scent glands that would distinguish it from all other infants in the dark. Only then did she allow it to climb to a waiting nipple. As it fed, she watched with bright eyes and over-sized ears as the rest of the colony stirred from their torpor. Life was spreading. In the next niche, a male wrapped his wings around a female, his stomach to her back and his teeth dug into the nape of her neck, copulating. The female's own weight locked the tendons of her toes into a grip on the cave roof that even death could not release. Near by, two males fought, screaming and drumming their wings against the roof. They circled each other, hair stiff around their jowls, until they rushed together, using their wings as clubs. One fight set off others, circles of tension that grew as daylight faded. The large members of the colony, the females, looked on with mild interest. The mating couple disengaged, the male to join other males, the female to preen. A week-old baby unfolded stubby wings and chattered. The great colony's mating, fighting, and births coincided until the shaft of light that fell through the cave roof narrowed to a thin stream and a different, greater need took hold. Others of their order might seek the twilight; these would wait for the dark. In the manner of upside-down spiders, wings mantled, padded claws reaching for rock, all the hundreds of adults moved sideways or backwards towards the ebbing light at the sinkhole. Squat faces fringed with whiskers concentrated on the mark of a dissolving day. As that mark faded, a ten-year-old female unfurled her wings and flew upward. One after another, the rest followed, in seconds more than a thousand streaming up through the sinkhole, climbing and trumpeting cries that directed them to their proper position in the flight. Biologically, they were miracles of evolution. Fourteen-inch wings, their membranes five times more sheer than surgical gloves, propelled them as fast as swallows. Downy fur, grey on the back and brown in front, cut wind resistance. Colour-blind eyes magnified the light of emerging stars so that the canyon glowed for them and, ahead, the desert was brushed with silver. They drifted above the canyon ridge like a cloud but as they reached the desert they flew ever lower, until they were a tide flowing a bare three feet above the desert floor. In front and around them spread a net of silent cries and echoes that returned to large, tender ears marked by a separate tragus. Each bat flew so close to its companions that their tide seemed a solid mass, and yet the tide flowed unchecked through cactus and brush. The terrain was new to the bats but not altogether different from their Mexican home. Hungry, their flattened spade-shaped noses soaked up the animal smells on the night wind. A stream of moths approached the bats, scattered and escaped. The bats swung into the wind, where smells were rich and travelled far. A night hawk following the moths changed its course, abruptly wheeling upward and away. Unlike birds, the bats couldn't soar. They only flew and they flew only for the Food, their wings beating air fourteen times a second in a steady, purposeful rhythm until the warm smell they sought tinged the air. Minute particles of sweat and plasma transferred from the air to the folds of their nostrils. The tide swung again and the all-but-silent screams increased in urgency. A thousand mouths opened, revealing the distinctive chin and long canines and, unlike teeth of any other bat or animal in Creation, incisors which were as curved and sharp as blades. Biologists called the bats Desmondontidae, a name suggesting those teeth and despair. Vampires.

Chapter Two

The morning sun warmed Abner's shed, a dirty-white Public Health Service van, and five tourists who anxiously watched Youngman's jeep drive up. Youngman put most tourists in two categories. Soul-toters, who tended to be young, scruffy, and desperate to 'get into' Indian religion. And camera-toters, who were older, cleaner, and only desperate to get back to air conditioning. The three women and two men beside the van were definitely of the second category, although a little bit better dressed than most, in expensive casual outfits. One of the men had been sick down the front of his pastel shirt. Youngman got out of his jeep. He didn't see Abner.

When he asked if he could be of any help, one of the women put her hand over her mouth.

'Abner's giving you trouble?' Youngman tried a smile on her. 'Don't pay him any mind, he's that way with everyone.'

'No, he's . . .' The man with the spoiled shirt pointed towards the shed. 'God help him.'

By now, Youngman wasn't listening. He ran around the van, past the creosote bushes with their rusting trucks, and into the shed.

The doorway and the ground around it where the rabbit had been killed were splattered with blood. A trail of blood went around the sand painting and through the ring of red sand to the drawing of the caped man, where the blood painted in a head around the mouth and crying eyes. At the figure's right hand, the red border was broken, swept aside and marked by a prayer stick decorated by shrike feathers. Another prayer stick pinned a cigarette pack Youngman had thrown away the day before into the figure of the coyote. And in the centre of the painting, sprawled over the double serpentine, lay Abner, dead, still in his kilt, wearing a mask of raw rabbitskin. His own skin, from his feet to the crown of his head, was sliced away so completely that bone showed at his fingers and knees.

Youngman wasn't the only person staring with disgust and awe. Just inside the door was another tourist in a windbreaker, a short man with a confident bearing and a smooth, marbled face. On the other side of the painting was the Health Service nurse, a blonde girl in faded jeans.

'When did you get here?' Youngman asked her.

'Ten minutes ago.'

The tourist knelt by Abner. He cleared his throat and took a Bible from inside his windbreaker, but before he could speak Youngman hauled him up by his collar.

'No missionary work here.'

'Red or white,' the man held up his Bible, 'a person deserves a final blessing.'

'He was a priest of the Fire Clan,' Youngman said.

'Maybe he was Christian as well.'

'Not even dead,' Youngman turned to the girl. 'Did they touch anything?'

'No,' she answered angrily. 'And they're not missionaries.'

'We're with a foundation.' The tourist adjusted his jacket. 'We only try to help—'

'Same thing,' Youngman cut him off. 'Why are you here?'

'Miss Dillon volunteered to show us around the reservation and take us to your famous Snake Dance. We arrived a few days early so we thought we'd get some camping in as well. I'm John Franklin.' Franklin had an amplified baritone, the kind that carried well in a boardroom. In Abner's shed it was too loud.

'Did you examine the body?' Youngman asked the girl.

'There was nothing I could do for Abner, so I looked for tracks. In case we have a rabid coyote running loose. I didn't know when you were going to be around. That's why we stopped here, so I could ask about you.'

'Did you find any tracks?'

'None.' Anne Dillon had a tanned, oval face with deep-set eyes. She was almost as good a hunter as Youngman and he knew it well.

'I took a look at the body,' Franklin interjected. 'The blood looks quite fresh to me. This attack of wild dogs or whatever must have occurred right before we arrived.'

With his boot, Youngman nudged Abner's leg.

'He's stiff. About ten hours dead.'

Youngman led the way back to the van, where the

other missionaries huddled as if the morning weren't already warming up to its regular oven quality.

'Everything is all right,' Franklin reassured them. 'I believe this is the Deputy Duran that Miss Dillon mentioned.'

'What kind of cameras do you have?' Youngman asked.

Franklin had a Nikon and the rest had similar 35mm cameras, except for Mrs Franklin, a frightened lady with blue-rinsed hair, who held up an SX-70.

'That's what I want. A flash attachment, too, if you have it.'

Youngman took the Polaroid alone into the shed. He took two pictures of Abner and four pictures of the shed, left them to develop behind the altar on the trunk and returned to the van.

'Thanks.' He handed back the camera and $8. 'That's for the film and bulbs.'

'You don't have to—'

'I think you better go now.' He made a cigarette while they got into the van, Anne behind the steering wheel. He watched them drive away until they were out of sight, then he killed the cigarette and went to the shed.

'Damn it, Abner.'

Youngman stood for ten minutes, only his eyes moving. He blocked the sound of the wind and stripes of light that came through the walls and, most of all, any memory of the white campers, because Abner had done his best to turn his junkyard garage into a sacred kiva and it was in terms of a kiva that Youngman had to think and see.

In front of the altar was a wooden plaque of bread, raw meat, tobacco, and cornmeal; some of the cornmeal was scattered over the floor. A fire had been built next to the altar. In the ashes, Youngman found pine needle strings and juniper bark. He dropped the charred bark when he saw the rabbit in a corner of the shed. The rabbit was flayed but not dressed, and the throat was slit for the blood to drain out alive, paint for Abner's god.

The truth was, the deputy understood the rabbit and the painting little better than Franklin had. Youngman had been away from the reservation too long and part of him, no matter how long he stayed now, would always be white. He'd lost the thread. He didn't believe in anything, let alone the gods of a medicine man who pumped gas. All he knew was that Abner said he was going to end the world.

He squatted by Abner and lifted the mask. Abner's mouth gaped full with clotted datura. If death was gruesome, Abner didn't know; or he had known and been prepared. Anyway, he couldn't have felt a thing.

'Uncle,' Youngman asked, 'what are you up to? What the hell are you doing?'

Abner gazed up at his friend, all eyes and teeth. The skin that wasn't sliced was punctured by small claw marks. Despite rigor mortis, some of the wounds were still damp.

The smell. Youngman recoiled. The same smell as in

Joe Momoa's corral. Around Abner's body, the serpentine was stained with ammoniac pitch.

Abner's eyes were dry. Relaxed pupils had folded into slits. Goat eyes.

'I don't get it, Abner. I don't know what or why? You don't want to help me?'

Abner's teeth, like most reservation Indians', were thin posts corrupted by decay. The jaw held a stiff grin.

'Okay, uncle.' Youngman closed the eyes.

He wrapped the body in a sheet and carried it to the back of the jeep. He returned to the shed for the photographs. Proper police procedure preserved the site of any suspicious death. For whom and for what, he asked himself? He was about as much police as there was, unless Arizona troopers were called in. For a dead Indian, they'd come in one week, maybe two. It wasn't a murder. There were animals in the desert. Things happened.

The sand painting was beautiful, complete and beautiful and totally mysterious. From where Youngman had moved Abner, in the middle of the rank stain, was the sprawled negative silhouette of a body.

'Son of a bitch.' Youngman kicked the sand painting. Red grains, blue grains, yellow and white sprayed the walls. When the ground looked like a desecrated work of art, he began kicking the black outline of the silhouette, Ammoniac pitch stuck to his boots. He picked up loose sand and poured it over the outline. The outline faded, but showed through the sand. He looked up. A desert skin was watching him from an orange crate shelf on the wall. Fly wings protruded from the lizard's jaws. It jumped as Youngman ripped the shelf from the wall. He broke the shelf over his knee, dropped the halves on to the stained floor, and lit a match. And snuffed it between his fingers. Wasn't going to do any good to burn the place down.

'Dead. Just plain dead.'

As Youngman came out of the shed, he heard the coughing of thunder north from the mesa. A ladder of dark clouds climbed into the sky. Within the clouds, lightning exploded like bombs. A wind scurried ahead of the storm.

The deputy put his jeep in gear and pulled out towards the clouds. A ball of sagebrush bounced by in the opposite direction.

The faces you could see in clouds, Youngman thought. Sad faces with grey and blue cheeks. Puffed up. Eyes closed and ready to cry. Just water, no atomic rain. No end of the world.

'You blew it,' he said to the man in the sheet. 'You didn't end the world, only yourself. A man your age ought to know the difference.'

The thunderheads kept climbing. The hot air of the desert was a wall that the clouds had to scale, until there were two walls, one warm and invisible and the other a cool, boiling blue. The invisible wall retreated, the dark one advanced, casting twenty miles before it an opalescent shadow.

Beneath the feet of the clouds was a washboard road, a clapboard store, an outdoor freezer, and a mud-and-log hogan. Gilboa was the name of the place. It wasn't a town any more. The U.S. Postal Service no longer delivered mail; the half dozen inhabitants of Gilboa had to go to Shongopovi on the mesa for letters. Maps ignored it, as did the utilities and telephone companies. For that matter, the washboard road vanished at either end about ten miles out, erased by wind and sand.

Fat globules of water rode on the wind. The real storm hadn't begun yet. Youngman stopped in front of the hogan, picked up Abner in his arms, and went inside. After he laid the dead man out on the floor, he reached up and gave a hanging light bulb a twist.

The deputy's office consisted of a roll-top desk and chair. Two-way radio. A metal locker for his gun shells, two bottles of Jim Beam, plastic bag of marijuana, and underwear. Dirt, a lot of dirt because he was away from his office for weeks at a time. Two maps – one of the reservation, another an Arizona State Highway map – were pinned to the wall. They rustled from the breeze Youngman let in to air the hogan out.

He slid up the desk's ribbed top and took a report form out of one of the pigeon-holes. The forms were bought surplus and the rubber-stamped heading 'Phoenix Police Department' was crossed out in pencil. He found a leaky ballpoint in another pigeon-hole.

NAME – Abner Tasupi. OCCUPATION – garage owner. D.o.B. – unknown. RACE-SEX – Indian-male. CRIME – death. Under MODUS OPERANDI, Youngman entered 'attack of undetermined animal, possibly rabid.' Then he went out to his jeep.

Dust devils wove back and forth over Gilboa's road. A hundred yards away and across the road, lightning illuminated Selwyn's Trading Post. The store was a tombstone of past aspirations. From the clapboard wall a peeling sign promised 'Tourist Rooms-Gas-Candy-Dry Goods-Indian Curios'. The tin Coke sign had a broken thermometer. The twin screen doors were patched with electrical tape.

The front of the store carried flour, pinto beans, cheese, blankets and cloth, axe and hoe heads, buck knives and ammo. An eyeless elk was mounted over the counter. Under the counter were pawned jewellery and whisky in pints. Selwyn was in the rear room with John Franklin and the other whites. An old Hopi woman and four half-breed girls were on the floor, pots and ropes of clay at their feet. Anne was away in her van, searching for firewood before the rain hit.

Selwyn had once been a Quaker missionary. He wore his white hair long, touching the velour shirt which draped open over his gut. A turquoise necklace nestled in the hair of his chest.

'You don't have to tell me these people need help. Next you're going to tell me the desert is dry. I know! Excuse me,' Selwyn burped against the back of his hand. 'Look, I've dedicated my life to these Indians. Speaking absolutely frankly, I personally have poured love and blood over them.'

'That's very admirable.' Mrs Franklin launched a smile into Selwyn's alcoholic haze.

'What do I get in return? A spit in the eye. Look, you

41

folks can hallelujah lizards and get more gratitude. Now I told the Bureau people when they came through a dozen years ago or so, throw your money away on going to the moon. I was willing to testify as an expert. Pardon.' He frowned at a piece of tobacco he picked from his tongue because he couldn't remember when he'd smoked last. 'There wouldn't be a Gilboa if it wasn't for me. Did you know that? It's my generator provides the power here, not just for me but for that freezer they throw their goddamn deer in and for that bum they have for a deputy. You see it? They hate me 'cause I help them. I sell them food on credit. They hate me more for that. And this is the best example of all. These stupid women are making pots. Pots! I mean, every trading post in Navajo country has women in the back making blankets. Now blankets sell, damn it, for $2000, $3000 a rug. My luck, all these savages know how to make is pots. For Christ's sake,' he rubbed his eyes, 'hasn't anyone got a fag?'

When there was no answer, he opened his eyes and followed his visitors' gaze to the deputy leaning in the doorway.

'Good.' The trading post owner left the missionaries for Youngman. 'You always have a fag.'

Youngman had heard all Selwyn's complaints many times. The 'stupid women' making pots were Selwyn's wife and daughters.

'Sure.' He tapped out a cigarette for Selwyn. Youngman could see Franklin's group bracing for a fight. Incredible. Like his store, Selwyn was a wreck in the desert, barely anchored enough in the sand not to roll into an arroyo or whatever else could serve as a gutter. Who would tolerate any white so collapsed except Indians? 'There you go.' Youngman held a match to the shaking cigarette.

'Thanks,' Selwyn muttered. 'These bible-thumpers they send out now can give haemorrhoids to your ears.'

'That so?'

'Telling me about Indians, for Christ's sake. Stick around. They'll get their asses out of here and we'll have a taste.'

Selwyn's wife giggled and Franklin cleared his throat because Selwyn's voice had strayed to normal speaking level.

'We'd intended to buy some supplies for our campout,' Franklin said. 'With our change in schedule, we didn't have a chance to in Flagstaff.'

'I gotta go,' Youngman told Selwyn. 'But I need some cornmeal, rope, a white sack.'

'Who died?'

'Abner.'

'Shit, you don't say.'

'That was that Indian gentleman we saw this morning?' Franklin asked and was ignored.

'You're not going to give him a regular funeral, are you?' Selwyn asked Youngman.

'Why not?' Franklin was outraged.

'Because he was a goddamn witch, that's why!' Selwyn wheeled on Franklin.

'You don't believe in that, surely.'

'Believe? Brother Franklin, you don't know where the hell you are, do you? Hey, honey,' Selwyn shouted to his wife, 'any witches out here?'

The woman dropped her giggling. She folded her hands on her lap and studied her pots.

'Witches?' Selwyn laughed. 'Well, the saints and apostles stop at the reservation line. What do you think this place is fit for? Indians, drunks, bums. Jesus, I was full of "thees and thous" and the Spirit when I came out here forty years ago. Bet I was just as big an asshole as you, Brother. That's hard to believe, too. Full of the Word, I was. Then one day, I found some of my congregation axing up an old woman. That was something. "Why are thee killing this woman?" I ask. Almost got myself axed trying to stop them. Well, the reason they did her in was because the night before she'd turned herself into a wolf and killed a man.'

'You didn't believe them.'

'Of course not. I'm not one of these ignorant savages. On the other hand, well, I stay away from haunted pueblos, you know, and when the Indians axe up a witch, which they do every year or so, I keep my mouth shut.' Selwyn paused. 'You people keep giving me these pathetic looks. Don't look at me, look around you. You give yourself some eye-strain trying to see to the end of that sand and you go get yourself lost in these canyons. While you're there, you ask yourself what kind of gods live in a place like that.'

'We aren't totally unenlightened persons,' one of the other campers spoke up mildly. 'Every society believes in a different Creator. Whatever names they give Him, the Creator is always much the same throughout the world.'

'Yeah? You mean the Skeleton Man.'

'Who?'

'Skeleton Man. Masaw. You call him what you want. Pluto. Satan. I know a man,' Selwyn's eyes glistened like yellowed china, 'thinks this is hell on earth right here. Maybe you'll come to think so, too.'

'Deputy, if this man we found this morning was a so-called witch,' Franklin said, 'is there any possibility that he was killed?'

'Not Abner,' Selwyn answered for Youngman. 'He was too big a witch. Sure, they'd chase him off the mesa. But they'd no sooner touch him than cut off their own hands. He'd come right out of the grave for them. Come like a wolf, or a—'

'The man you found,' Youngman interrupted, 'was an old hermit. That's all. Nobody killed him, and if I hear any rumours that someone did I'll know where those rumours started. Right, Selwyn?' He gripped the store-owner above the elbow. 'Excuse us, please.'

Youngman pulled Selwyn into the front room.

'You get yourself something to drink, old man.'

'I talk too much when I'm sober.'

'You're not sober, you're just not drunk enough. You know better than to start babbling about witches. "Come out of his grave . . ." Jesus.' He found a pint under the counter, unscrewed the top and poured whisky into Selwyn's mouth. A gust of wind made the screen doors

45

slap open. Liquor rolled down the side of Selwyn's chin as he started.

'Just the wind,' Youngman said.

'He could.'

'Then you say yourself a prayer tonight.'

'He could do a lot of things.'

'Not any more.'

Lightning jigsawed over Gilboa. As a bolt hit the outdoor freezer, the inside of the store turned silver, then black from the backflow of electricity. The generator started again. The lights inside the store cast a waxy glow. Youngman hurried to pick up the goods he'd come for.

'Put it on my bill.'

'What else?' Selwyn was feeling better. 'Maybe I can still get one of those sob sisters in there to buy a pot.'

Like sails, the clouds split. In half an hour, they'd drop three inches of water, a quarter of the year's total rainfall, enough to turn arroyos into rapids and break open the armoured seeds of smoke trees, ironwood and blue paloverde. Gilboa's road turned into rutted mud and waves spewed from the jeep's tyres as Youngman drove the hundred yards to his hogan.

A Land-Rover was parked in front of the office. He had to run through the mud before putting his shoulder to the door.

Abner was still lying in the corner but the sheet was pulled back and kneeling over the exposed body was another white man.

'You missionaries don't give up easy.' Youngman shut the door.

The white looked up. He was Youngman's age, deeply tanned, with close-cut red hair, wide blue eyes, wide smile, dressed in rough khakis and big, so big that the body at his feet looked like a doll. His hands were covered by rubber gloves and, instead of a Bible, they held a scalpel and a glassine envelope.

'Won't be a minute.' The voice was modestly official.

'You won't be a second. Stand up.'

Reluctantly, the visitor did as he was told, stooping to prevent his head from touching the ceiling. He rolled the glove off his right hand and held it out to Youngman.

'I apologize for what this must look like. My name's Hayden Paine.' He held his hand out for ten seconds before dropping it. 'Well. Just give me a chance to clean up and I'll explain everything.'

'If I were you, I'd start talking now.'

Paine smiled, totally at ease despite his bloody gloves, the closeness of the hogan, and the drumming of the rain.

'I'm stopping at all the law enforcement and health offices on the reservation. This will satisfy you, I believe.' He handed Youngman a folded paper. While Youngman read it, Paine crouched by an aluminium case. He removed his second glove and dropped both into a plastic bag, washed his hands with alcohol and cotton, and tapped the glassine packet.

'To Whom It May Concern,' Youngman read the letter, 'Mr Hayden Paine is conducting a medical survey that may be of great benefit to our nation. He has full authority to travel the reservation, and to call on the assistance of all officers of the reservation in conjunction with his survey.' The letterhead had an embossed seal of a sun, mountains, and crossed sheaves of corn. It was signed by 'Walker Chee, Chairman of the Navajo Tribal Council'.

'I have more identification if you want it.' Paine locked his case.

'I don't want it. You're on the wrong reservation.'

'This is Hopi territory, I know, but—'

'You haven't explained anything yet. You were desecrating a body when I came in and you still haven't told me why.'

'The medical survey, as explained in—'

'There's no explanation in the letter. What kind of survey?'

Paine showed no more than a slight social embarrassment. He took the letter back.

'It's very technical, sheriff.'

'Deputy.'

'Deputy. I'm doing a serologic study of antibodies. By identifying antibodies in the blood samples of the local population, I'll be able to identify diseases endemic to this area. Some diseases can't be found any other way. It's a complicated process and if I tried to explain it further, I doubt you'd understand. No layman would,' Paine added quickly. 'All I can say is that this kind of study is necessary to raise the level of health here. I've been having the most trouble getting samples from the older people on the reservation and when I saw the body here I took the opportunity. I meant no discourtesy to the dead man or to you, believe me. If anything, I need your help.'

Paine's voice had risen to a shout as the drumming of the rain increased in volume, punctuated by kicks of thunder. Paine waited impatiently for the din to fade. Youngman liked the rain; anyone who lived in a desert would. More than that, the downpour forced Paine to be quiet. It forced him to drink his own rain of words. To Indians, words were a white weapon. Indians always found it interesting to watch a white try to be silent. Youngman folded his arms and waited. Silence could be informative.

Paine maintained a broad smile. He was about thirty. His tan was a veneer marred only by a smudge of lost sleep around the eyes. A minute passed under the hard rain.

Paine sighed. He had a big chest and heavy arms, light copper hairs down to the wrists, which were marked by curved scars. A bolt hit outside, probably on the Land-Rover, Youngman thought. Paine only glanced aside at the crash. Confident and self-controlled. The storm continued to work to its climax. It wasn't so much rain that opened desert seeds as violence. Paine's smile had relaxed to amusement.

The blue eyes were clear as pools, untroubled and unruffled. Totally neutral. There was no pigment in blue eyes, Youngman remembered. It was all refraction. Dead eyes, Abner called them. Used to call them. Paine held the mutual gaze patiently, still amused. Water ran under the floor boards of the hogan. Five more minutes passed while lightning concentrated on the meagre elevation of Selwyn's store.

Selwyn's generator faltered. The bulb in the hogan dimmed to the power of a cigarette, and at that level slowly pulsed with each feeble beat of the gas-powered generator. Youngman watched Paine's eyes slide towards the body. Paine's hands curled into fists and uncurled. The eyes slid back. Youngman saw the blue eyes shadow and the pupils narrow to points. He picked up his rifle. The bulb faded to a single orange filament.

Youngman reached into Paine's shirt pocket and took out the glassine envelope. Paine's hand clamped around the deputy's wrist.

'I need it!' Paine shouted.

The muzzle of Youngman's rifle burrowed under Paine's jaw. Paine rocked slightly back, his head against the wall. His fingers let go of Youngman, who screwed the barrel into the jaw.

'You lied,' Youngman said in a flat voice. He was sure the other man understood. 'I don't know what about, but you lied.'

He took two steps back and lowered his aim to the doctor's belt buckle. Paine gestured with his hand and stopped himself at the glint of the hammer's rise.

'You're making a mistake! Deputy, I need that sample! You don't know what you're doing! Please!'

Youngman's foot shoved the aluminium case over the floor.

'Go play with the Navajos. They'll believe anything.'

Paine's expression said he couldn't hear Youngman over the thunder, so Youngman opened the hogan door. The storm spilled in. The road outside was a shallow river.

'Don't blame me, then,' Paine warned. At least, Youngman thought that was what he said because with the door open not even a shout was intelligible. Paine gathered his case and went into the rain, having to stop to unlock the Land-Rover. Youngman watched from the hogan doorway and noticed the Health Service van pull in behind his jeep. Why, Youngman asked himself, would anyone lock his car in a place like Gilboa? He waited until the Land-Rover moved away, lights on and wipers thrashing the windshield. At a distance of fifty feet, only its rear lights could be seen through the rain.

Anne Dillon threw open the door of the van. Youngman climbed in, as wet as if he'd stood under a shower, and dropped his hat and rifle on to the firewood on the back seat.

The van was better insulated than Youngman's office. A person could talk.

'I see you're still busy promoting tourism.' She turned to Youngman. 'I'm sorry about Abner.'

'So am I.'

'But what I came for was an apology.'

'I apologize.'

'That's not good enough. I finally get these foundation people to come all the way out here from the mid-west and the very first thing you do is insult them and embarrass me. Since when are you the guardian of all

51

that's sacred around this place? You made a fool of me. Then you apologize and I'm supposed to forgive you.'

'Well, you'll try. You'll try like hell.'

Anne's eyes were blue, but rayed with spots of brown. Sometimes, very analytical eyes.

'You know, Youngman, that's an incredibly cruel thing to say. I don't have to love you. I can try like hell to stop doing that.'

'What does it matter?' he asked.

'What does that mean?'

'I mean, you've got one more week before you leave the reservation for good and go back to your trust fund and backgammon or whatever rich folks do in Phoenix. I thought we were going to have the week together but it looks like you're busy with your birdwatchers, or missionaries, whoever they are. What is it they do anyway? Give money to the needy? Or only to the romantically needy? Where does their money come from?'

'Some religious groups, mostly corporations.'

'Better yet. A romantic tax deduction. That's tops. Speaking as one of the needy, you understand. So do that, have your kicks. Better yet, share your kicks with them. White Goddess of the Hopi, patron of eye salve.'

'If we'd had the whole week together, is this what you were going to tell me?'

'What else?'

He watched the rain smashing into the windshield because she was staring at him. It took him a while to notice her eyes welling.

'No,' Youngman said. 'I wouldn't have said any of that. I'm a jerk, and I'm goddamn jealous.'

She pulled him against herself. Her fingers dug into his back and he felt a tear hot on his neck.

'Jealous I accept,' Anne whispered. 'The rest you can stuff.'

'I'll have a whole week to stuff it.'

'I wish they hadn't come, now. They're waiting for me.'

As they kissed, his hand slipped into her shirt and brushed a breast softly so that its tip hardened against his palm.

'It won't be a whole week with them, just four days,' she said.

Anne shifted, stretching out on the seat.

'Maybe I should go with you,' Youngman covered her.

'Um, that kind of romantic needy they're not ready for. That's just my hang-up. Can they see from the trading post?'

'They can't see a thing.'

Anne had come to the reservation two years before, using volunteer paramedical service as her escape from Phoenix and a family fortune that was based on buying desert cheap and selling it dear as test range acreage to the Air Force. Life for the Dillons was the south-western dream: Arabian horse shows, golf in Scottsdale, a box at the Sombrero Playhouse, and monogrammed tennis balls from Neiman-Marcus. In Anne's eyes, the dream was a kind of sleeping sickness that infected everyone she knew. This whole class of sleepwalkers lived out their lives seemingly unconscious of Chicano barrios, black slums, and Indian poverty. By the time she was in college she'd diagnosed one peculiar syndrome of this 'sleep', the idea prevalent in this privileged class that somehow they were the true natives and that everyone else, particularly the poor of different colours, was an interloper. Hence, Chicanos were more likely to be called Mexicans. Blacks were Nigras. A dead Indian was an interesting item of Western lore, but a live Indian was a social ill. And it was easy to live out this dream because accepting the rights of these less fortunate groups – especially the land and water rights of these Indians – led inevitably to uncomfortable sensations of guilt. Phoenix did not believe in guilt, it was not part of the lifestyle.

Guilt. Anne worked out of Hotevilla Pueblo on the mesa. Driving a hundred miles at a time throughout the mesa and into the desert to provide antibiotics and basic surgery to outlying pueblos, she had a great deal of time to consider social guilt as a motivation. Early on, she decided it stank. Indians stank, the pueblos stank, and the chronic running sores she dealt with day after day had a tendency to stink. After six months she thought she was ready to quit and trade in her jeans for tennis whites. From nothing less than perversity, she stayed for another six months and curious things happened. Either Indians stopped stinking, or she stopped smelling them. Increasingly she found herself surprised to be treated as a white by white tourists visiting the reservation. And she met Youngman.

Their paths had crossed a number of times before,

enough to form an unspoken dislike between them. On this occasion she'd gone to the hill country around Moencopi, an area claimed by both the Hopis and Navajos, to treat a boy bitten by a rabid coyote. Navajo police and Youngman arrived to destroy the animal, which had taken refuge in a storehouse. While the Navajos waited outside the storehouse with their rifles, the Hopi deputy went in with a blanket and a pistol. At the cost of one bite through the blanket, he shot the coyote. For the next four days, Anne treated the boy and the deputy with a series of painful injections in the abdomen. On the very first day she told Youngman he deserved the pain for going into the storehouse instead of waiting. He answered that the family's chickens and rabbit pens were at the top of the storehouse and if the coyote had broken into them half the family's yearly food supply would have been wiped out. She was on hand with medicine, so what did he have to lose? Except pain.

Within a month, she was meeting Youngman regularly at different places on the mesa and in the desert. They reversed the usual order of a relationship, starting with the physical release of sex, and then talking and releasing loneliness. Love, each felt, came in spite of them. Now, with her leaving the Health Service and the reservation, love was nothing less than a burden, the embarrassing souvenir.

She clung to him, holding him inside her. But the storm was fading into squalls. Cold, liquid shadows ran over her arms.

'I've got to go. You can wait another four days, can't you?'

'Selwyn's girls haven't seduced me yet.'

'Not for lack of trying. They'd kill me if they had a chance.'

'Well, watch out for falling pots.'

'I really have to go,' Anne kissed him and pushed him up.

They sat up and pulled their clothes back together. The rain was easing, almost over.

'Who was that you kicked into the street?'

'Nobody. He had some phony story about a study of antibodies in the blood to find diseases.'

Anne buttoned the rest of her shirt in silence.

'How do you know it was phony?' She brushed her hair back.

'I just did.'

'Youngman, that's exactly the study the Health Service was supposed to do years ago. And you kicked him out? Don't you know how many Hopis I have to treat for pernicious anaemia or blood parasites?'

She felt her anger rising, she couldn't help it.

'It was a phony story.'

'How many go blind every year from venereal disease, or deaf from aural atresia? Why didn't you let me talk to him? He didn't have any accreditation?'

'A letter from Window Rock,' Youngman admitted. He didn't mention what Paine was doing to Abner, he didn't want any defence.

'Oh, that was it. He only had a letter from the Navajos

and that wasn't good enough for you. Thank you very much. Maybe I would have had a different opinion.'

With every word, she felt him withdrawing and shutting her out. What's the use, she thought. Together, they were the perfect example of centrifugal force. Why was she exhausting herself against it? Youngman fumbled in the glove compartment for cigarettes.

'Smoke your own,' Anne said.

'Yours are stale.'

'So?'

'Might as well smoke them now.'

Besides his stubbornness, his habits of poverty also irritated her. In fact, smoking up stale cigarettes was one of his prison traits.

'You don't trust Navajos, you don't trust whites. Are you paranoid? You hate outside help so much, why do you tolerate me?' she asked.

'I love you.'

'It's that simple?'

'What could be simpler?'

'Well, I'm leaving this place for good in seven days, Youngman. Are you coming with me?'

'To Phoenix?'

'It doesn't have to be Phoenix. It can be anywhere. Mexico, if you want.'

'And what would I do there?'

'You happen to be one of the very few Hopis who could make it off the reservation. You know photography, painting. I have enough money for the two of us until you get started.'

'You could stay here, you know.'

'I have stayed. I've been the audience for all your battles against the imaginary slights of anyone who tries to help you. Like the way you treated Franklin.'

'He's going to help me?' Youngman laughed.

'His foundation represents, among other sources, a number of drug companies. What the Hopi people need is a donation of medical supplies and money for a clinic of their own. I was hoping that the last thing I did before I left was guarantee that donation, but so far I've spent most of the morning apologizing for you.'

'Don't!' Youngman's face darkened. 'Don't ever apologize for me to those people.'

Anne looked out the side window, towards a rainbow that was already fast evaporating. She was more depressed than angry. 'Those people' were the pahans, Anglos, whites. By some fluke, Youngman didn't include her with her own type. The day would come of course, when he would . . . and she was begging him to follow her off the reservation? How crazy was she?

'Maybe it is just sex,' she whispered to herself.

'Maybe.' Youngman's hearing was too good.

She was damned if she was going to cry in front of him again, so she found her key and started the engine.

'We'll desert camp for a couple of days and go on to Joe Momoa's to fish. We'll come down to the Snake Dance with the Momoas. I'll see you there.'

'Don't go.'

'Why not?' Anne rested her hands on the steering wheel.

Youngman didn't know. He'd said it quickly, not as a conclusion of any thought but from a sudden rush of images through his mind. Joe Momoa's horses, a sand painting, Abner's eyes, a stain of black pitch. The smell of that pitch.

'Look,' Anne touched Youngman's hand, 'when I get back we'll go off for a couple of days alone.'

'It's not that.'

'Then what?'

Mostly the smell. Once inhaled, it seemed to work into the blood.

'Something Abner said yesterday.'

'Oh.' She could see them. Two Indians drunk under the sun. 'That's it?'

'Why don't you just go to the mesa now and wait for the dance? If they want to see a lot of Indians, that's the place to go.'

'They want to go camping.' Anne shook her head and put the van into gear. When she said nothing else, Youngman climbed out and shut the door.

He looked through the window. His black hair hung damp across his forehead. From the driver's seat of the van, he seemed hardly bigger than a boy.

Anne could think of nothing else to say except that he was wrong. He was too bitter, too silent, too lean, too dark. Too Indian.

Youngman watched her drive to Selwyn's and then went back into the hogan.

The dead were supposed to be buried before sun-

down. Youngman didn't believe in that sort of stuff but
Abner did and Abner, after all, was the dead man.

Youngman pulled up a floor board where there was
still a pool of water underneath and washed Abner's
hands and face. With the white paint from Selwyn's, he
decorated Abner's arms and legs with dotted lines and
over Abner's left eye drew a half moon, the insignia of
a priest. He combed Abner's hair and strung feather
fluffs to the hair, wrists, and ankles. He filled the dead
man's palms with cornmeal. Luckily, rigor mortis was
past because he had to bind the fingers tight around the
cornmeal. He rubbed the rest of the cornmeal over
Abner's face, which was difficult where the flesh was
shredded. With his knife he cut holes into the white
cotton sack so that it made a 'cloud mask' for Abner's
head. Nothing went to waste in the desert, not even the
dead; they are obligated to return as rain. After he wrapped Abner in the sheet, he bent and tied the legs into a
kneeling position. Abner made a small corpse. Youngman carried him under one arm and a planting stick
with the other out to the jeep.

Youngman drove about fifteen miles out of Gilboa
until he reached a rise crowned yellow by paloverde
trees. There he dug down through two inches of wet soil
and three and a half feet of dry sand, laid Abner in the
grave in an upright position facing east, and sat down
for a smoke.

'Well, uncle, you should have some family here to say
a few words. I guess you're stuck with me. Frankly, I'd
rather ask you some questions than give a speech. I sure

as hell don't know if you were a good man or not. To tell you the truth, I don't even know how important that is.

'You fool them. Don't come back as a cloud. You come back as a cactus, huh.'

Within the eyeholes of the cloud mask Abner's lids were shut. A pink spot appeared on the mask around the cheek. As that spot blossomed, other spots grew. Abner was still bleeding.

'Hey, old man, you're dead,' Youngman said.

Not only the mask was turning red, the sheet was as well. Points of rosy red that spread. Youngman didn't have the nerve to lift the mask so he lowered himself into the grave and pulled open the sheet. All the wounds that covered Abner's chest and arms were wet and running. Maybe the ride in the jeep opened the cuts, Youngman told himself. But dead cuts don't bleed. He reached inside the sheet to Abner's wrist, which was wet and cold and had no pulse. Then he saw Abner's hand. It had snapped the string that had closed it and lay open on clots of blood-soaked cornmeal.

As the sun set, an evening wind followed, swaying the branches of the paloverde trees like yellow froth. Youngman filled in the grave and covered it with stones to discourage scavengers. On top of the stones he stood a planting stick, the symbolic ladder from the grave to the spirit world. Wind rattled the stick against the rocks.

'Relax, Abner. Let go of that stick.' The stick stilled. 'Try being dead for a while. You might prefer it.'

Youngman drove the same way back to Gilboa. He

stopped once to look behind. By then, the last flush of sunlight was hitting the rise, turning the paloverde trees a brilliant red.

According to the Koran, Jesus created the first bat. During the fast of Ramadan, when no believer may eat from sunrise to sunset, Christ was in the hills outside Jerusalem and couldn't see the western horizon. Taking clay in his hands he made a winged creature into which he blew life. This creature – a bat – flew into a cave from which it emerged each nightfall to flutter around Jesus and tell him of the setting sun.

The ancient Egyptians regarded bats, because of their nipples, as examples of maternal care. The Chinese character for bat was also used for 'happiness', and some South Pacific peoples prized bats as sexual totems.

But in the New World, the bat was god. His Mayan name was Zotzilaha. Whole cities and peoples bore his name and throughout Mexico temples carried his image: a striding man with the wings, face, teeth, and tongue of a bat, holdings a severed human head in one hand and a heart in the other. Zotzilaha, the Bat God who controlled fire, was transformed into the Aztec's supreme Sun God, Huitzilopochtli, who demanded sacrificial mounds of human hearts cut out by priests attired in bat-skin capes. In 1519, the year prophesied for the return of a lost White Brother, Cortez arrived in Mexico. Armed with a prophecy, and aided by rebellious tribes, he took Moctezuma prisoner. The Spanish chronicled attacks of 'bloodsucking' bats, but by then the Aztec Empire had fallen.

Gods die, peoples change, and nature persists. For centuries after Cortez, the vampire bats held sway in the Mexican jungle and in the last twenty years, for no reason discernible to man, had been reported moving steadily north. It was a migration of the night, recorded only by random and unscientific accounts of slaughtered goats, cattle, even people in the Sonora mountains.

Now in a new environment of desert and mesas, the vampires hunted as they always did, with patience and intelligence. They passed over two flocks of unsheared sheep and a dead rabbit, poisoned and set out for coyotes. Arroyos were dark ribbons in the moonlight. Tiger salamanders stirred in the damp beds of the arroyos, feeding off insects and being fed on by night snakes. The bats slipped untouched by the spines of fifty-foot saguaros. The petals of night-blooming cereus spread milky white.

A different sound mixed with the high-pitched chatter of the bats. It travelled on the breeze from miles away, a nasally plaintive country-and-western song. As one, the thousand bats veered, their own chatter increasing in intensity, the membranes of their powerful wings stroking faster. This certain kind of sound, they knew, meant Man. Man and his animals, conveniently gathered. A lake of life.

Two miles ahead, Isa Loloma, fourteen years old, his arms and back aching from a day of shearing sheep and binding their greasy wool, sat in the cab of a Dodge pick-up sipping from a warm can of orange soda and listening to his transistor radio. The truck had no engine. Its wheel hubs sat on blocks. Its whole purpose was simply to scare away coyotes and that purpose it served very well. Isa's nights were long and lonely.

The night played tricks. Sometimes the Navajo station out of Gallup would fade and in its place would come stations from Houston or Kansas City. Voices would talk to him about steak palaces and local astronauts. Then he only had to lay his hands on the truck's steering wheel and close his eyes to imagine that he was driving his own Eldorado down the freeway of some Anglo city, that he was wearing a custom shirt with mother of pearl snaps and sitting on an alligator skin wallet stuffed with twenty dollar bills.

Tonight, the Gallup transmission droned steadily on. Every Piggly Wiggly Supermarket in Bernalillo County, the voice from the ether said, was pleased to honour food stamps. There was going to be a social dance at the Tuba City Chapter. Sports results were brought courtesy of Massey-Ferguson tractors.

Isa made the soda last. When his eyelids started to grow heavy, he climbed out of the truck and rubbed his legs and ran in place to start his blood moving. Still yawning, he drew his father's old Browning Auto-5 shot-gun from the blanket on the cab seat. The sheep were quiet. He'd take one turn around the flock and come back for a nap.

Something fluttered by him. A night hawk, he thought. The only problem with sheep was during the spring, when coyotes came in for the lambs, or during shearing if the clipping was done badly and cut up the sheep, then the smell of blood would make coyotes bold. But Isa was a good clipper. He left the sheep shorn down to their pink skin without a nick.

He walked for about fifty yards before he became very awake. He could hardly see the sheep, although he heard a constant rustling. The sheep were there, he knew they wouldn't leave the grass. There was that rustling, a busy, papery rustling that came from every direction. He fought a first, childish impulse to run. And then, just a few feet in front of him, he saw the pale blur of a sleeping sheep's head. Baby, he scolded himself.

Strangely, he could make out the legs but not the body of the sheep. He could see the head of another sheep, but not its body either. A wing grazed the boy's long hair, fanning his cheek. Something touched his foot. There was a rusted flashlight with weak batteries in his pocket. He aimed the flashlight at the nearer sheep. A pale, yellow beam picked out the steadily breathing nostrils of the sheep. The light slid back over the curly head.

At first, the sheep's flanks seemed to be covered by a grey blanket. Then two of the bats raised their eyes to the beam and he saw the blanket was a dozen bats lying on a sheet of blood. The next sheep had its own blanket of bats and, as Isa swung the flashlight around, he saw that all the sheep were covered in the same manner, sleeping under the feeding. The bats were larger than any he'd ever seen before and the ones he'd disturbed only glared at him with open mouths. He shone the light downwards and kicked off a bat that was climbing up his pants.

With all his strength, Isa swung his father's shotgun at the sheep.

The bats, as a community, were first aroused by the explosion of the shotgun. Two bats were dead. Those closest scattered, only to land a short distance away. The community as a whole drew in, ringing the source of the noise. There were no leaders, except in that the communal instincts would first be carried out by the most aggressive individuals, the females, among a very aggressive species of animal. The instincts were to protect the Food and to repel an aggressor, which they could clearly see was a single man. In a sense, then, more Food. The ring drew tighter.

The Food was a marvellous thing. There were few animals in the world, and no other at the bats' level of intelligence, whose very organ and sense were so designed and attuned solely for the taking of sustenance, and perhaps this was true because no other animal was so uniquely surrounded by it. From every other warm-blooded animal they could feel the pulsing of the Food, or taste it in the air so rich with sweat and exhalations. As a result, to the bats there were no natural enemies, not even man. There could be no enemies, when all was the Food.

A bat darted by the boy, easily dodging the stroke of a shotgun stock. Another bat flashed by him, slicing his nose. The boy turned in a circle, flailing the air. The agitation, his laboured breathing and the pounding of his heart, excited the bats. A whirlpool of them swirled around him, just out of reach of the shotgun. From straight above, one dived and tore open his ear. He fell and at once his back was covered with bats, which clung to his shirt as they ripped through to the skin. Another bat landed on his hand and the boy dropped the shotgun, rose, and began to run.

They followed the running boy until he reached the truck, dived through its door and rolled the window up. For a while, the bats clustered on the hood and windshield. Then, one by one, they returned to the sheep. To the feast.

Chapter Three

'When I die and go to hell,' Selwyn squinted at the sun, 'that place is going to look awful familiar.'

He clutched the flask in his breast pocket as Youngman steered around a hole in the road. Selwyn's wife Esther and one of his half-breed daughters rode in the back of the deputy's jeep. The teenage girl was dolled up for social attention in a black dress trimmed in red. Looming ahead was that centre of the Hopi universe called the Black Mesa. From the giant mesa four fingers stretched southward into the desert. They were called, from west to east, Third Mesa (with the pueblos of Hotevilla and Oraibi), Second Mesa (with the Shongopovi and Shipaulovi pueblos), First Mesa (Hano and Walpi), and Antelope Mesa (with the ruins of Awatovi). Seen from the road below, the mesas appeared a single, flat-topped wall of stone reaching to the horizon in either direction. Only two fragile clouds intruded on the sky.

'Did Anne tell you where she was going to camp?' Youngman asked.

'Didn't ask. She wouldn't give me the time of day or the year anyway, Romeo. She's after your balls, you know that. Rich white girl, that's the worst. I mean, she is not for you. Now, take my girl Mae here. You could do worse.' He weighed Youngman's lack of interest. 'Typical.

They want blankets, I have pots. They want white girls . . .'

'Hey, Selwyn, you never told me. Why did you give up the missionary business?'

'Never did. It gave up on me. I got another germ, see?'

'No.'

Selwyn took advantage of a relatively smooth stretch of the unpaved road to suck his flask.

'It's my theory that religion is like a disease. A great religion's like an epidemic. Take Christianity, Mohammedanism, Buddhism. Just like epidemics. Start in one place, always spread along the trade routes, flourish for a few hundred years and die out. Or get overrun by a new epidemic. I was sent here like a germ, to infect you people. Instead,' he shrugged, 'you infected me.'

'With what?'

'A very dry mouth,' Selwyn tipped his flask again.

As they neared it, Third Mesa jutted out towards the road, an escarpment of rock sheared cleanly at its top except for decaying, box-like structures of adobe. Old Oraibi was still inhabited, barely, as if by the survivors of some disaster.

Esther nudged Youngman's back.

'I have to do Mae's legs. Pull over at Spanish Place.'

Youngman pulled off the road beside a mesquite tree and a weathered tin sign that read, 'Warning. No outside visitors allowed in Oraibi. Because of your failure to obey the laws of our tribe as well as the laws of your own, this village is hereby closed.'

69

Selwyn went behind the sign to urinate. Mae's white cotton leg wrappings had come undone, revealing a pair of fifty-nine cent athletic socks. While Esther wound the traditional wrapping again, Youngman stretched his legs up on the windshield and smoked.

There was nothing much to distinguish this strip of the highway from any other, although some Hopis said it was here that they greeted a Conquistador named Pedro de Tovar and his troops in 1540.

He was supposed to be the Pahana, the White Brother whom the Hopis had left a thousand years before, when they first began their long diaspora out of Mexico. Oraibi was established in 1100; the other pueblos followed as other clans arrived at the Black Mesa. Together, they waited for the bearded White Brother whose arrival would signify the completion of the world. Pahana didn't arrive the year he was expected; in the person of Cortez, he was busy bringing down the Aztec Empire. Keeping watch, the Hopis cut a notch in a stick for each year their Brother was late.

There were twenty notches when de Tovar appeared on the horizon. Hastily, the Hopis prepared for this epic culmination. Fire Clan and Bear Clan priests ran down to the desert and drew a line of welcoming blue cornmeal before the horses and armoured men. De Tovar looked on in confusion, and so it fell to the Catholic priest to make a decision. 'Why are we here?' he yelled. 'Santiago!' the troopers answered, lanced the Hopis in their way, and rushed up the mesa, quickly subduing the pueblos.

For the greater glory of God, the Hopis were made

Christians and slaves. They were sent down mines in search of gold, silver, mercury, and oil-saturated shale that burned like coal. Indians found conducting pagan rites were whipped and torched with burning turpentine. For one hundred and forty years, the Hopis endured their error about de Tovar, until the Tewa called Popay sent to them a knotted cord indicating the night of rebellion throughout the pueblos of the south-west. At the Black Mesa, the moment of revolt was signalled by the call of a screech owl. The Castillo soldiers were slaughtered at the church doors, the priests were knifed at the altar, their steel pikes were buried and the church razed to its last stone. In all, over five hundred Spanish died during their retreat to Mexico, and although the Hopis were subsequently overrun by Spanish and Mexicans and Americans the tribe became infamous for its reluctance to convert again.

They settled down to wait for the real, the true Pahana.

Selwyn emerged from behind the sign zipping his fly.

'The Bible says that Jesus went into the wilderness and there he fasted for forty days.' He shook his pants. 'Sort of interesting exactly how long the Son of God could take living like a Hopi, huh?'

'You're a cynical bastard, Selwyn.'

'Not compared to you. I just talk that way. Booze keeps me innocent.'

'Except for your kidney.'

Two cars came flashing up the road to the mesa. The first was a new Buick Le Sabre, shiny in spite of its patina of dust. As the car went by, Youngman caught sight of its driver, a square-faced Indian in a business suit talking on a car phone as he steered. A sticker on the bumper read '*Dine Bizeel*'. 'Navajo Power'.

'Walker Chee!' Mae looked in awe after the car of the Chairman of the Navajo Tribal Council.

'Headpounder.' Youngman used the Hopi epithet for Navajos, earned by the Navajos' old habit of crushing the skulls of their prisoners.

The second car was a Cadillac. Behind the wheel was a man unknown to Youngman, a white in shirtsleeves and a tie. He glanced at the Indians on the side of the road, sun-glasses making one decisive swipe.

Inside the Land-Rover, after a night of signal tracking, Paine was asleep. Sweating and dreaming in the morning heat.

He was back in Mexico.

He and his father were immunologists under contract to the Instituto Nacional de Investigaciones Pecuarias, working out of the agency's Vampire Bat Research Station in Mexico City. The research station's aim was to control *derrienque*, rabies transferred by vampire bites. The Paines' particular mission was to find why only vampires were largely immune to the lethal virus they carried.

Paine's closed eyelids glistened. He was back in the Sierra Madre del Sur, near the Guatemalan border. In the cave. He and his father and Ochay were following the beams of their helmet lamps, feeling their way along a ridge two hundred feet above the cavern floor. The cavern wormed its way half a mile into the mountain. Its general shape was ovoid, the walls below the ridge smoothly curved to the floor, the walls above arched another hundred feet up to giant stalactites and the bat roosts. Paine was team leader and point man. He was attached to a nylon rope strung through saw-toothed pitons he hammered into the limestone wall. Joe Paine and Ochay were close behind, unattached, moving hand over hand along the rope, both men bearing a red canister of poison on their backs. No vinyl coveralls this trip because of the climbing, only goggles and gas masks to endure ammonia rising from the bat dung. Without a mask, a man could survive a maximum ammonia concentration of one hundred parts per million for an hour; near the mouth of the cave they'd registered the concentration at four thousand.

'Deeper, we're not there yet,' Hayden Paine said.

Dr Joseph Paine was getting too old for this kind of work. Grey hair sprouted like owl feathers from under his sailor's cap and the oppressive weight of the canister bowed his knees. As a point of pride, though, he refused to restrict himself to lab work in the capital. Besides, he could control his son.

Ochay probably wouldn't have come without the old man along. All the Mexicans from the station knew the son was a crazy glory seeker who chose the largest roosts in the most inaccessible mountains. Of the ten original members of the team, only Ochay and Hayden Paine had escaped bites or falls or ammonia exposure. The whole expedition would have been scrapped if the old man hadn't arrived.

In the lead, Paine dug in the crampons of his boots. The ridge of slick limestone was twenty inches across; a glistening stalactite, half-born from the wall, completely blocked the way.

Behind Paine, his father pulled his mask away to talk.

'That's it for today. We can tie the canisters here and come back tomorrow.'

Paine ignored the advice. With his left hand he swung his axe hard around the protrusion into the wall on the other side. He tugged the axe handle. It seemed solid enough. Clutching it, he swayed around the stalactite and stretched himself to where the ridge continued. As he hammered a fresh piton, the echoes of his blows resounded along the recess of the cavern. A few bats squealed in complaint.

Two million bats occupied the cave. White ghost bats. Carnivorous spear-nosed bats. Nectar-sucking bats. Minute insectivorous bats of a dozen varieties. Meat-eating *Vampyrum spectrums* with three-foot wingspreads. Fishing bats. And the colony all the others roosted far away from, the true Vampires, *Desmodus*.

'Pass the tanks,' Paine ordered.

Joe Paine and Ochay hooked the canisters to the rope. From the far side, Paine watched the tanks jiggle around the stalactite and with anxious tenderness he pulled the poison on to the ridge.

'Come on.'

'I can't make it,' Ochay answered.

'The vampires are farther on.'

'I can't—'

A shriek cut them off. There was a scuffle on the cave roof where the *Vampyrum spectrums* hung. Ochay's hand lantern followed the fall of a pink *spectrum* infant to the floor.

The floor was a world of its own, a steaming brown soup of digested nectar, meat, insects, and blood. Twenty per cent protein, it supported pools of bacteria. Over a million mites, scavenger beetles, toads and mountain crabs to a square yard. Giant cockroaches and venomous snakes. For them all, guano was a steady rain of food, or food for their food. The fall of an unlucky bat was a bonanza for them, and seconds of agony for the bat.

'Let's go.' Paine yanked the rope.

Joe Paine slid around the stalactite first and then Ochay. The latter was shaking.

'You're taking too many chances.' Joe Paine clung to the wall. 'Ochay—'

'If I can do it, so can he.'

'But we're running out of air. I suggest—'

'But you're not the leader of this team. I am.'

Paine pushed on. As they went deeper into the cave, the ridge narrowed to twelve inches, to ten, to six. Paine had to drive in a piton every second step, while his father and Ochay struggled behind with the canisters.

'He's scared,' his father whispered to Paine. 'You should understand that. He's scared of you. I think I'm scared of you now, too.'

'I can do it without you.'

'Could you?'

In overhead grottoes, shapes twisted, ears attuned to human voices. Even through his mask, Paine could smell the change in the ammonia, getting fouler, more penetrating.

'This is the last cave you go into. I'm going to see to that,' Joe Paine said.

'We're almost there.'

It was the end of the rope, not the diminishing air, that finally halted Paine.

'Madre de Dios,' Ochay was sobbing.

Paine had brought a selection of wet and dry poisons in the expedition's trucks. For a cavern as large as this, he'd selected Cyanogas. The bottom half of each tank was compressed air, the top half a compartment of poisonous dust. He strapped the two canisters together so that they'd lie flat and lowered them by a separate rope from the last piton until their tops hung level with the ridge. After he adjusted the tank nozzles to achieve a ninety-degree range, he set the timer on each nozzle at thirty minutes. When the timers ticked down, the tanks would release a hundred-foot spray of Cyanogas which, in contact with the cavern's moisture, would change into hydrocyanic acid, lethal to every life form it touched, including the men who brought it. The strapping and adjustments Paine made with a mechanical deliberateness.

'Por favor . . .' Ochay pleaded.

'We're heading back,' Joe Paine told his son. 'Maybe

when you and I get to Mexico City, we'll keep on going to the States.'

Paine wasn't listening. He remained alone to make certain both timers were ticking down. When he was sure, he shone his hand lantern up to where the roof seemed to be covered by jagged brown stones. Then one of the stones spread its wings and shifted to bare its teeth at the light. Paine turned the lamp away before any more vampires were disturbed.

He released himself from the rope and knotted it to the last piton. His father and Ochay were about thirty feet away. They were making better time going than coming, already nearing the pearly stalactite they'd claimed they couldn't clear. He checked the gauge of his air tank. Twenty minutes. Just enough time.

From the sudden lack of tension on the strung rope, before he'd seen it happen, Paine knew someone was gone. With his lantern, he picked out legs flailing in mid-air, blackness, and the solid impact of a body hitting at the end of a long dive. Then the beam found Ochay, who'd cried all during his climb and never uttered a word when he slipped. He was sinking into the ooze.

'Spider!' Joe Paine shouted. 'Spider on the rope.'

The rope jerked again in Paine's hands and went slack.

'Hayden! Hurry up!'

Joe Paine hung three feet below the ridge on a thin shelf. Paine moved arm over arm along the rope.

'I'm slipping.'

Paine could see his father's fingers spread flat over the slick rime of the limestone, giving ground. A tarantula, ten inches across at the legs, darted along the ridge towards Paine. He stomped it under his boot.

'Give me your hand.' He reached down.

'Can't reach.'

Paine wrapped the piton rope twice around his left wrist and leaned as far as he could. His father heaved himself up, stretched a hand that was too short and too wet for Paine to get a grip on. The two men looked at each other for a moment and then Joe Paine started sliding. He slid down the incline of the cave, dropping ten or fifteen feet at a time and then sliding again until, very small in the beam of Paine's lantern, he hit the bottom.

'Hayden! Throw me something!'

Paine wrenched the rope, almost losing his own balance as pitons sprang out of the soft limestone. He tied the slack rope round his axe and threw the axe down. It swayed at its limit fifteen feet over his father's head.

'They're all over me! Jesus, they're eating me alive!'

Ochay's axe was still on the ridge. Paine slammed it deep to the limestone and hung himself by it. His own axe now angled five feet over his father. He pulled his mask off.

'Get to the wall! Climb!'

'I can't see! Hayden, they're . . . Oh, God! . . . No!'

'Climb!'

'Oh, God!'

Silence, until the last call.

'Hayden!'

He woke, shaking as if in convulsions, a cramped

hand locked around the leg of a truck seat. On his hands and knees, still trembling, he crawled to the Rover's food locker and poured a quart of water over his head. He dug his fists to his eyes, erasing his father and Ochay and the others. It took him a minute to open and spin out the valiums.

Had to sleep. Had to sleep. But, please, God, no more dreams. If he could just last until night.

'Don't forget to pick me up on the way back,' Selwyn said as he and Esther and Mae got out of the jeep at the base of the mesa, where Esther's sister's family of eight lived in an aluminium trailer, which was a runway of small children between the beer cooler and the television. Wearing gift shop headdresses, the children converged on Selwyn and began pommelling him with rubber tomahawks.

'And never inter-marry,' Selwyn groaned.

Youngman drove alone back into the desert where the Snake Clan was rounding up snakes.

Cecil Somiviki and his younger brother Powell were sitting on the open tailgate of Cecil's station wagon. Between them was a canvas sack that constantly shifted from the movements of the snakes inside – diamondback and prairie rattlers, bullsnakes, whipsnakes, garter snakes, but mostly small Hopi rattlers. The brothers were both stripped down to bathing suits and leather breech clouts; Cecil had a Stetson on and Powell wore sun-glasses. From time to time, the older brother doused the sack with water to keep the snakes cool.

'What's new?' Cecil greeted Youngman. He was tribal sheriff and, on the side, sold propane gas to the pueblos from his station wagon.

'Abner Tasupi died.'

'Son of a bitch! How'd that happen?'

'Some kind of animal attack. He was all chewed up.'

'Son of a bitch!'

Powell said nothing. He was nineteen and he frowned studiously over the tribal newspaper *Qua' Toqti*, *The Eagle's Cry*, as if conversation was a distraction below his dignity.

'Man, he was a crazy mean fucker. Oh, he was wild. Well, that's the best thing I heard today.'

'He was just an old man, Cecil.'

'He was a killer. Everybody knows that. A witch.'

'You don't believe that shit.'

'I don't believe it, but it's true. Why do you think we kicked him out? Oh, he was always up in Maski Canyon where the ghost pueblos are. Come back after he made up some corpse poison. I bet he killed fifteen, twenty men, more. There was a man he hated, he'd turn hisself into a black dog and pull the poor bastard right over the edge of the mesa. Even the headpounders were afraid of him. By the way, that Walker Chee was around and he wants your ass.'

'It's not the first time.'

'This time he says you roughed up some pahan. I don't want to know about it, but stop it. And what about

Joe Momoa? Why are you always rubbing folks the wrong way? You always pick the wrong folks, too. Learn to get along, for my sake.'

A Snake priest came up to the station wagon. He had his arms outstretched and three or four rattlers in each hand, the diamondbacks pale and heavy, a sidewinder rough-scaled and horned, all of them twisting ineffectually. Cecil opened the sack while Powell picked up an eagle feather. As a Hopi rattler raised its mouth out of the sack, a wave of the feather made the snake duck. The priest dumped the snakes in, bummed a cigarette, and trotted back out into the desert.

'Did Momoa have a vet up at his place?' Youngman asked.

'I heard from Joe yesterday. All he said was he was going to shoot some night varmints in the Wash. Maybe he meant you.' Cecil smoked; ashes drifted over his belly. 'You were away, you don't know nothing about Abner. Hear about the time Arizona Public Gas sent some men down to Jeddito Wash? Abner gets wind of it. Does hisself up like Masaw. Sure. Crazy son of a bitch digs up a grave and dresses in a dead man's clothes, covers hisself in rabbit blood and goes over to Jeddito to make medicine.'

'Did it work?'

'What do you think? Those pahans see some nut in rags and blood shrieking his head off, you think they're gonna stick around? Shit, man.'

Powell cleared his throat.

'Listen to this in the paper. "Although the pahans

have drained the Gila River dry, although the pahans
have stolen four times their legal share of water from
the Colorado River, although they have raped Lake
Powell and the Little Colorado River, although they have
stolen wholesale the San Juan River, the water table level
under Phoenix is still falling so fast the city may be a
ghost town in twenty years." '

'Asshole,' Cecil yawned. 'Before there's a dry swimming pool in Phoenix, they'll be up here to drain you
for spit.'

'That's just the kind of remark I could expect from
you.' Powell was the star pupil of his mission school. He
talked like a typewriter. 'We don't have any leadership,
just old men and the non-political types like you two.
That's why we have to join Chee; at least he's a leader
who knows how to read a contract. That's why the
Navajos have power plants and coal leases. Chee could
get this reservation on the move again.'

'Yeah, he'll move us right into a toilet an' slap the lid
on if he gets the chance.' Cecil rooted behind the snake
sack for a couple of beers. He handed a can to Youngman. 'You get anyone dumb enough to bury Abner?'

'Me.'

'Oh, oh. Well, you get that shed of his then. But what
about his medicine? He was into all kinds of powers no
one else could handle.'

'I don't believe in that stuff.'

'No one does. But you better take care of it, or give
it back to the Fire Clan. They're all up in Shongopovi
today.'

Youngman took the road up to the mesa, passing the turn-around area for Cal Gas trucks that couldn't navigate the road any farther, going by orchards that produced small, wizened peaches, past corn stalks that would grow no higher than a man's chest, on up to the new plywood-and-cement houses in Shipaulovi pueblo where Cecil lived and around the edge of the mesa for two more miles. Entering Shongopovi pueblo always brought about an immense depression in Youngman. More than almost any other pueblo, Shongopovi was the home of the old 'Traditional' people. Retreating from Navajos, retreating from whites, making a last stand on the very rim of the mesa.

A garbage dump. A hundred forlorn houses of stone and earth set on rubble. Flanked by slopes of concrete outhouses. Not a blade of grass and not a real street, only flies dozing in alleys, a wrinkled face at a broken window, and shadows chipping at adobe. Inhabited ruins around a dusty plaza suspended over the desert. No one ever took the long fall, of course. At Shongopovi, everyone shuffled into oblivion.

The sun was blinding. Youngman parked on the plaza in front of the house belonging to Harold Masito, a priest of the Bear Strap Clan, and went through a screen door into the cool, dark interior. Harold was on a sofa bed mending prayer sticks. The walls were decorated with colour snapshots of his grandchildren and a needle-point portrait of John Kennedy.

At one time, Harold had been one of the strongest men on the reservation. The muscles were gone now, leaving his big frame bent and his face shrunken around a heavy nose and jaw. He was one of the men who'd made Youngman a deputy.

'Abner is dead.' Youngman sat down respectfully on a folding chair.

'Huh,' Harold nodded. Carefully, he bound a fluff around the base of the stick.

'Two nights ago. You were a friend of his, so I thought you ought to know.'

'That so?'

Harold went on to a different prayer stick, arthritic fingers straining to be steady.

'That's so. I had to bury him alone. He asked you and the other priests to go out to his place before he died.'

'I'm not Fire Clan.'

'But you used to be his friend. The least you could have done was made a visit. Two years, you didn't visit him once and now he's dead.'

'You're angry.'

'Hell, yes. What am I, some bum. Some bum buried Abner. That doesn't make any sense to me, uncle. Abner was somebody, he deserved a lot better than that. A lot better than everybody turning their backs on him and leaving him to die alone in the desert. Even when I was a kid, Abner was a great man.'

'Abner was a great man,' Harold said after a space of five minutes. 'But then he became crazy, dangerous. Before that, he was a very great man as you say. Maybe the greatest man in the world. Hungry?'

Harold went out the back screen door to where his wife was tending a horno, a stone oven. He returned with flat, steaming pan bread.

'Got no butter. You want margarine?'

'No thanks, uncle.'

The old man sat on the sofa in thought. The bread cooled in his hands. Finally, Youngman lost patience.

'You treated him like dirt, worse than a pahan. You and the Fire Clan and all the elders. Now the poor guy is dead and you still act the same way. Well, why?'

'Abner was old, old,' Harold sighed. 'Older than me. Hard to think he's dead, but he's among friends. I was his friend, as you say. It bothers me what we did, but it was necessary. And if he's dead, like you say, then he's got friends.'

'Uncle, that's not what I asked. Just give me an answer. How could you treat Abner like that?'

'You're more Tewa than Hopi. You're a warrior—'

'Knock it off, uncle.' Youngman inched forward on his chair. 'I was no warrior. I was a goddamn convict in Leavenworth. Abner deserved better company than that for a funeral and I want to know why that's all he got. I want a reason.'

Harold picked up a prayer stick, then put it down and looked at Youngman.

'See, he talked to Masaw all the time and Masaw crawling up the mesa wall, that scared people. And Abner he'd go off to the pueblos of the dead people and come back smelling of the dead, and that was unpleasant for the rest of us.'

'You mean, Abner was a witch. That's it? The whole thing? You all, all the priests, you believed that.'

'You know how it is,' Harold said. 'Everything will be all right as long as we tend to things. As long as we do the ceremonies right, there'll be rain and Masaw will protect us from our enemies. Okay. But Abner he went too far.'

'Too far?'

'He had Masaw walking around here every night. I seen him.'

'Masaw?'

'Right. From far off, 'cause if he touches you, then you're dead. You see what I'm talking about? Even Death gets hungry. It has a stomach to fill.'

'I'll tell you what I saw. I saw the body of an old man. Not a witch. An old man who was a friend of mine and who had been a friend of yours and everyone else on the mesa. And if he acted crazy lately, maybe it was because all the priests up here, all his old friends made him that way.'

'You did a good thing to keep him company this last year.' Harold Masito averted his eyes from Youngman. 'It makes me feel good to know we were right about you. Was there anything else?'

Youngman sighed.

'Well, uncle, there was. His possessions. What should I do about those, or who should I give them to?'

'I see. I'm afraid you're late. The Fire Clan priests they already went down into a kiva and they won't be up for a couple days. Anyway, they took the clan tablet from Abner a year ago.'

'What tablet?'

'The Fire Clan tablet. Abner can't stir up too much trouble without that.'

Youngman wasn't interested in stories about a tablet and there was nothing left to do in Harold's house. He thanked Harold for talking. At the door he stopped.

'One more thing, uncle. Did you hear anything about Abner wanting to stop the world?'

'No,' Harold answered curtly. He picked up a prayer stick and a fluff. The fluff escaped from his gnarled fingers and floated upwards, slowly spinning. 'You sure he's dead?'

Youngman went back out on the plaza. The sun was directly overhead, trying to melt the mesa. Youngman blinked through sun-glasses at a silver water tower and his eyes fell to boys playing with a handmade top on a roof, and to the plaza. Rough ladders marked three holes spaced across the dusty plaza. The ladders led down to *kivas*, underground chambers. From the bow standard and horsehair on the two nearer ladders, he could tell they were occupied by Antelope and Snake priests who had already been in hiding for six days for the Snake Dance.

From a house two doors away, two men emerged. One was Walker Chee and the other was the white who'd been driving the Cadillac. Chee filled the doorway. Navajos were different from Hopis: they were bigger, fleshier, and their heads seemed squared at the corners. Chee

MARTIN CRUZ SMITH

embellished these attributes with hair razor-cut to the collar of a dark, three-piece suit, a silk tie, and thick fingers studded with turquoise rings. The white took off sun-glasses. His features were broad and pink, drawn with the eraser end of a pencil. Neither man noticed Youngman in the shadows.

The white frowned.

'You said the deal was set.'

'Just a few more days, Piggot.'

'A few more days and a few more days, that's all I've heard. I have crews standing by. What fucking game are you playing? And you were going to bring maps of the canyon. What happened to the maps?'

'The maps aren't important,' Chee said.

'You know how expensive that kind of map is?'

'We don't want maps here. Not here. Back off and leave it to me.'

'You're stalling, Mr Chee. I'm trying to figure out why.'

A village elder joined the two men and Youngman took the opportunity to try to slip away unseen. He got to the middle of the plaza.

'Deputy, I want to talk to you,' Chee called.

Youngman came to a stop.

'Excuse me.' Chee left Piggot and the elder and approached Youngman alone. The tribal chairman moved with proprietary ease, ushering Youngman out of earshot of anyone else. Youngman was aware of being smaller and, in comparison, grubby. There were perhaps a thousand flies buzzing around the plaza. Not one of them would dare land on Chee. Chee dispensed a smile.

'You're Deputy Duran, right?' he asked softly.

'Yes.'

'And you pushed around a Mr Paine yesterday, is that correct?' Chee lowered his voice.

'I pointed out to him that he was on the wrong reservation.'

Eyes began appearing in the windows around the plaza. The white man was searching the soles of his shoes.

'Are you going to tell me I'm on the wrong reservation?' Chee asked.

'Are you confused?'

'No, I'm not. That's how you and me differ. See, I got loads of my own Indians just like you. Dumb and poor. You get satisfaction out of that, fine. I heard about you before, Duran. You are the best living example of ignorance in Arizona, did you know that? You can't help yourself and you can't anyone else. I bust my balls to bring some money to the mesa. I go to Washington, New York, Houston and show 'em an Indian doesn't necessarily have to be drunk or dumb and as soon as I get someone out here to help us some jerk like you shows up and screws me. Now you think I do it so I can get my face on a magazine cover. Great, that's your opinion. But there are three power plants and twelve proposed power plants on my reservation that say an Indian can do more than pose for nickels. And I've started the medical programmes that'll mean we don't have to be the most disease-ridden people in this country. And the irrigation programmes I've fought through the courts are just as much for Hopis as Navajos. So, do me a courtesy, Deputy, until you get as smart as the average toad, you hide yourself away the next time you see anyone who has anything to do with me. That a deal? And don't you eavesdrop on me ever again.'

While Youngman stood and burned for an answer, Chee gestured to the white and the two men walked away from the plaza. The deputy heard the word 'troublemaker' dropped, discarded the way a man would throw away an inferior item. Seconds later, the Buick and Caddy nosed into view and conspicuously squeezed through alleys to the mesa road.

Youngman could hear the soft roll of fat tyres in the dirt. Why did he hate Chee? Because Chee was right?

'You're laughing,' Stone Man said. 'Is there anything funny?'

Stone Man was the village elder Chee had been talking to. He wore a rag around his head. His flesh was ropy. Youngman had the sense, and the fear, that he was looking at his future self.

'Not a thing, uncle. I guess all the Fire Clan priests are already in the kiva.'

'Yes. I think Abner Tasupi was the last to go down.'

'Abner? That's not possible.'

Youngman walked across the plaza to a kiva almost on the edge of the mesa. The clan feathers on the ladder were stirred by a wind that blew straight out of the San Francisco Mountains, visible on the other side of the desert at a distance of seventy-five miles. A kiva was a link to that Underworld from which the first Hopis crawled; in other words, it was a dark, tobacco-rank chamber in which destitute people secluded themselves to prepare the ceremonies that would keep their miserable world together. Juniper bushes tied to the ladder below the entrance hole blocked Youngman's view. Stone Man followed him.

'Abner's dead.'

'Oh.' Stone Man concentrated. 'Well, you know, I only seen him from the back. You know, I seen eight fellows go down and I just thought the last one was Abner.' He watched Youngman nervously toe the stones around the opening. 'You say he's dead, I must be wrong.'

Paine had stayed in Mexico after his father's death. None of the Mexicans from the research station would work with him again but since the programme was lavishly funded by American Agency for International Development money he was allowed to operate alone for a year. When he'd arrive in his Land-Rover full of lab equipment and poisons the hill Indians would desert their village, a sight that always struck Paine as obscenely ridiculous because he came to kill death, not spread it. They'd watch, hidden, as Paine, his face strapped into a gas mask, carried into a cave canisters of barium carbonate, or arsenic trioxide, or thallium sulfate. When he left, the Indians would celebrate in the comic belief they'd driven off a demon.

Even when the Mexicans did cut off his funds, it didn't matter. Heart researchers wanted to study the vampire's circulatory system, sonar researchers wanted to test the vampire's ears, and psychologists were fascinated by the vampire's intelligence. No bat mastered a Skinner box faster than a vampire.

All the time, Paine was heading north following the survivors of the vampire colony from the cave where Joe Paine had died. One vampire roost, however large, was generally only part of a larger vampire colony. By implanting miniature radio transmitters on captive bats, he traced the survivors to new caves. When he poisoned those caves, the survivors would move to others.

Their hours and movements became his. The distinctive marks of their feeding were the compass points of his life. A cave of their poisoned dead was his defeat, because his tracking equipment always recorded more survivors and yet more caves and Mexico itself seemed a lightless hall of caves, which at night it very much was.

In this fashion, he tracked his bats up the Sierra Madre Occidental, along the oceanside Sierra de San Francisco and north to the foothills of Sonora. The hunt took two years and he did not know whether any of the original survivors still existed, but vampires were long-lived, intelligent, and adaptable. Finally, he had pursued his prey to the end of that hall of caves to the last cave before the American border. That evening, he tracked the silent chorus of a major colony of vampires crossing the border.

No true colony of vampires had ever been reported

in the United States, which was a classic puzzle to zoologists. From Northern Mexico to Argentina, through the Andean highlands to the swamps of Guyana, vampires flourished. At the U.S. border they'd always halted. No one knew why.

But Paine's bats didn't come back.

He recognized his great opportunity. Since there were no other vampire bat colonies in Arizona for his to merge with, at last he could destroy them all. Paine didn't anticipate his next problem, however. No one would believe him. County medical officers, when asked about vampire bat attacks, laughed in his face. He stopped asking about bats and used more general queries about night-time attacks and unfamiliar wounds, still without success. The vampires had disappeared.

Paine started again with the Indian reservations, working north through the Gila River, Maricopa, Apache, Colorado, and Hualapai, finishing with the largest of all, the Navajo.

He had found Walker Chee on the Black Mesa. The Navajo Tribal Chairman was leading a group of white men around the lip of what had been part of the mesa and was now the Peabody Coal Company stripmine. The mine was an enormous inverted pyramid dug by layers, a pyramid all the more dizzying because it was such a sudden and overwhelming vacuum within which eight-storey electrically powered shovels were dwarfed to the size of toys. Paine hung back by two limousines parked away from the lip as Chee strutted back and forth, pointing out elements of the operation to the visitors.

'Over there, you can just see it,' Chee pointed to a chimney on the far side of the mine, 'is the pulverizing plant. The Peabody people use fossil water to make a slurry of the coal and the slurry is gravity-fed by pipeline 275 miles around the Grand Canyon to the generating plants in Nevada.'

One of the whites kicked a stone into the mine. He turned to Chee; he had the sort of pink head on which sun-glasses became the most dominant feature.

'About the Peabody folks. You're givin' them some trouble, aren't you?'

'No trouble, Mr Piggot. Renegotiating. We get fifteen to twenty-five cents royalty per ton. The state of Montana gets a minimum of forty cents. We just want to bring our royalties into line. You take oil—'

'That's why we're here,' the man called Piggot said.

'We've been getting a fifteen per cent royalty. Arabs demand a minimum of fifty per cent . . .'

Paine watched the power shovels browsing a quarter mile deep in the pit. Steel cables dragged jaws over blasted ore. The jaws swung up, overflowing, wheezed, rotated to dump trucks, and regurgitated tons of low-grade coal. They looked like brontosaurs lethargically feeding in a dry lagoon.

'You wanted to see me.' Chee stepped aside from his group to Paine.

'Yes. I understand that all medical queries have to go through you.'

'Right.' The Navajo scratched his vest. It was hot by the strip mine. His eyes stayed hooked on Piggot.

'I've been doing a kind of biological survey—'

'Some other time,' Chee suggested impatiently. 'I have an office, you know. Make an appointment.'

'Well, I have a photo to show you.' Paine blocked Chee's view with a manila envelope.

'Excuse me.'

'Just take a look.'

'Some other—'

Paine slid the photograph from the envelope. The picture was a colour blow-up of a vampire bite, a clean crater two millimetres deep into richly vascularized human dermal tissue.

'Where the hell did you get that?' Chee reacted with anger.

'I—'

Chee grabbed Paine by the arm and forcibly led him another fifty feet from the lip of the mine. He started whispering furiously.

'What are you up to? Who gave that picture to you? I'm trying to do business here and all I need is some white son of a bitch like you busting up a million-dollar deal with some story about plague. You know what those men over there are going to do if they hear the word "plague"? You ever seen a limousine vanish?'

'I didn't say anything about plague,' Paine said.

The long moment that followed turned exquisite for Paine. In fact, his picture was of a Mexican Indian who'd been bitten months before but he calculated swiftly and accurately.

'You have a photo like this, too,' he told Chee. 'You

have somebody with wounds like this and he has plague. Do you know what made those wounds?'

Chee didn't answer.

'Then you're very fortunate,' Paine said, 'because I know, and you're going to hire me.'

That encounter with Chee at the stripmine was only the first. After, were more meetings at Window Rock and on the mesa, transfers of an unpublicized autopsy report from Chee and lists of equipment demanded by Paine.

Now, in the dozing heat of midday, Paine was searching for fleas.

The desert's arroyos were still slightly dark, as if bruised by yesterday's rain. Yucca stems vibrated through waves of warm air.

The Painted Desert appealed to Paine. He appreciated the false sterility that masked such desperate adaptations of life as limbless lizards and giant saguaros. More than that, he savoured the loneliness, the sense that he could go days, months if he wanted, without seeing another human soul. Other people, no matter how different, were mirrors of one's self. Paine wanted no reflections.

He drove over a sand dune to hard ground, where he stopped and climbed to the roof of the Land-Rover. He'd seen one vulture earlier. This time through his field glasses he spotted two about half a mile up and two miles away, spiralling down a thermal. A third vulture joined them. Paine slipped down into the cab, throwing the glasses aside to get the truck into gear.

A matter of minutes could make his work a hundred

times more difficult. Paine pushed the Rover up to thirty, running over mesquite and crashing through sand drifts. Already, without glasses, he saw more vultures descending the thermal. A deep arroyo about six feet wide stretched in front of Paine. He swerved right, found a rise, and shoved his foot to the floor. At forty, the Rover cleared the arroyo, bounced stiffly, and continued over a drift.

Paine hit his horn. A mile off on a surprisingly green knoll was a truck in the middle of sixty or seventy vultures. Sheep carcasses covered the hill. Horn blaring, Paine drove into the scavengers, scattering them off his fenders. Red eyes staring out of black faces, the vultures hopped away, trying to gather air in their four-foot wingspread. Paine braked and jumped out of the Rover, cocking his .45 as he hit the ground. He fired, taking the head off one bird. The rest scattered in a black wave, lumbering up. Paine fired again, straight up, just to keep them moving.

Death, he'd long ago learned, was not a moment of calm. Without the squabbling of vultures, the hill still resounded with the vibrant activity of flies. When he left the vultures would return, and mice and smaller birds, a whole chorus of scavengers great and small. He only hoped he was in time.

From the back of the Land-Rover he took his aluminium case, which he spread open beside a lamb that had been reduced to head, feet, and a thousand flies fighting for room to lay their eggs. He tied on a surgical mask and slipped on rubber gloves. Around his waist he strapped a belt of his own design. In addition to a holster for his automatic, the belt carried in leather-and-felt cups an odd number of jars, syringes, scalpels, operating scissors, glassine envelopes, and a jeweller's eyeglass.

The truck stationed on the hill didn't even have wheels, it was on blocks. The windows and windshield were smeared with blood from the inside. Paine grasped the handle of the door and stepped aside as he opened it.

No one fell out. There was no body in the cab, although the seat and floor were covered with dried blood. Paine was disappointed, but at least the profusion of bloodstains was a good sign.

He walked among the sheep. As many as a hundred carcasses littered the hill, most of them ripped open by the activity of coyotes and vultures. The ground was torn up. He lifted a carcass with his boot and uncovered soil discoloured by a dark pitch smelling of ammonia. That was better. He moved on in this pastoral setting until he found a ewe less disturbed than the rest. Although she was disembowelled, her intestines strung out on the grass, a fluttering of her nostrils showed she was still clinically alive. Paine squatted next to her. Some vultures landed to pick at farther away sheep. He paid them no attention.

The forward area of the ewe's chest was striped by shallow gouges seeping blood. Paine held a jar upside down almost flush over the wounds. Between the open lid and the wounds he stroked a paper card. A minuscule activity began developing in the jar. He moved the jar and card over all the wounds and then screwed the top on the jar. He fixed the jeweller's loupe in his right eye and held the jar up to the sky. Eight, nine fleas hopped against the glass.

There were over two hundred different species of fleas in North America alone. Magnified, the parasites of the Order Siphonaptera shared a basic equipment: wingless bodies, powerful legs, bristles in rows, and the sucking mouths that bestowed their Latin name. There were four species in the jar. Mice that had nibbled on the wounds had left rodent fleas. *Xenopsylla cheopis*, eyeless fleas with double rows of bristles. The coyote that had ripped open the ewe had deposited two species: common dog fleas, rounded, with a moustache-like mouth comb; and blunt-headed, eyed carnivore fleas. There were two specimens of the last species. They had eyeless, helmet-shaped heads. A mouth comb like mimic teeth. Bat fleas.

For a moment, Paine was stunned by the magnitude of his luck. Overhead, the vultures watched him squat by other sheep and collect more specimens, and when he stowed them in his truck and drove away the birds all descended again through the rising air of the thermal to finish that work nature designed them for.

Controlling his excitement, Paine drove slowly.

Life was unfair. Usually, only the poor and geniuses realized this but Hayden Paine was admitted to the fact with his father's death. It was Joe Paine who was the really first-rate immunologist, Joe Paine who back in 'forty-four led the Rockefeller Institute team that identified a mysterious paralytic disease killing hundreds of thousands of cattle annually as vampire-transmitted rabies. All the other authorities claimed the bat was an impossible vector. Under a microscope, the so-called *derriengue* virus didn't look exactly like rabies. Besides, rabies invariably killed its host, yet the majority of vampires thrived on the virus that infected them. It took Joe Paine to prove that the rabies virus had mutated under the influence of its bizarre host and that the vampire alone of all species on earth was not vulnerable to rabies.

Joe Paine's abilities hardly ended there. Chee was terrified of plague? In 1967, the Paines, father and son, were in Saigon to study a disease raging among the refugees of the beleaguered city. Joe Paine overcame American and Vietnamese obstructions to identify the disease as bubonic plague carried by rat-infested rice. A small item among the horrors of war: there were 5547 cases of plague in Vietnam in 1967.

But always for Hayden Paine it came back to the caves. He suffered from claustrophobia. One step into the dark and his heart doubled its beat. The condition had come on gradually, accreting with experience. In the first year of vampire work with his father, the claustrophobia paraded as nervous energy. The second year, without understanding why – he'd been on spelunking expeditions with his father even as a boy – Paine had trouble breathing. By the end of the second year, adrenalin flowing like nitro through a bloodstream dark with lack of oxygen, he began passing out. The third year was the worst.

In an age of sophisticated torture there is no more effective tool than claustrophobia. It combines elements of suffocation, desertion, blindness, and isolation from reality. All these elements operate in a cave, except that they are reality. When Paine entered a bat cave, his heart was already racing, each beat a muffled alarm. As the light of the entrance evaporated, his lungs became twin vacuums and his limbs numbed. With every step he felt the cave closing behind him. The glow of his helmet lamp was a ghostly moon without reference to him, like a glowworm in a coffin. Past the threshold of panic, he forced himself deeper into the cave, seemingly more steady as his sanity folded in. Within goggles, his eyes bulged. Even as he tried to concentrate on the techniques of ropework or spreading a mist net of superfine thread, he tasted his hot and salty terror. Then someone would set off a flash and the cave would erupt into a whirlwind of panicked wings. When the sound of the wings and the lower-pitched cries of the bats made a dizzying roar, only then, occasionally, would Paine let go his scream of terror.

He wasn't stupid enough to think he was a coward. Unfortunately, he was intelligent enough to know the reason he returned to the caves was to mimic his father, and that in imitating a better man, he was a farce.

No matter how many caves he went into and how competent he seemed, the secret panic blossomed. Until he took risks just to keep his eyes from straying to the enveloping dark. No one knew except his father, which was why Joe Paine had to go along when others hung back.

So, unfairly, in that Mexican cave, it was the better

man who'd died. Not without a parting gift, though. Like dross from a fire, Paine's panic fell away and was gone.

The desert sand had the quality of compacted ash. A desert, to Paine, was a land that was burned and constantly burning. For Paine, a relief compared to night.

After thirty miles of driving, he stopped in the shade of a canyon of stark, yellow walls and set up his laboratory. Like his belt, it was a construction of his own design. Aluminium poles screwed horizontally on to the top rear of the Rover and telescoped backwards fifteen feet to supporting poles rooted in the dirt. Over this structure he hung a fine wire mesh tent that zipped tight around the open doors of the Rover and at an entrance flap at the other end. He staked the mesh taut to the ground through eyeholes spaced every six inches; the whole effect was of a cocoon growing out of the truck. Inside this cocoon he set up tables and equipment. From the Rover's refrigerator, bowls of blood culture gelatines. Test tubes. Rubber-stopped jars of killing solution. Microscopes and slides. A square black box two feet high with a front hooded by black crêpe. Alongside the box, he placed the jar of specimens from the sheep.

He pulled the black hood aside and uncoiled an extension cord from inside the box to a dry cell battery he'd placed under the table. A frosted white light panel – the type used for X-rays – glowed underneath an acetate map of the Navajo–Hopi reservation. Paine removed the map. With a clean scalpel he cut into the flesh of his little finger and milked three drops of blood on to the glowing panel. Over the blood-specked panel he set a clear plastic cover that had one circular, threaded opening. He picked up the specimen jar, shook it gently, counted the fleas at the bottom of the glass, and carefully unscrewed the lid, sliding a paper card between lid and jar. He turned jar and card over and slid the card away as he screwed the jar into the plastic cover. Then he set a microscope over the panel and pulled the crêpe hood over the back of his head.

Magnified by 20X, the fleas lurched uncomfortably within the confines of the panel and cover. The heat of the glowing panel, though, spread the rich vapour of an abattoir. Antennae twitched and the hair of their palps stiffened. The sighted dog and carnivore fleas were first to move towards the balloon-like drops of blood, but the blind *X. cheopis* and bat flea joined the rush. There was enough for all. Sheaths pulled back from sucking stylets, which plunged into the walls of the blood.

At 50X, the bodies of the fleas were transparent. Paine watched a stream of red flow through stylet, esophagus, and pour into the stomach. The walls of the pharynx and gullet expanded and contracted, pumping the blood in. He studied dog flea, carnivore flea, and *X. cheopis* before focusing on one of the two feeding bat fleas. A red stream flowed through the stylet, swirled and flowed back out again into the blood drop. The bat flea was sick, vomiting up its food, dying slowly from starvation. At 75X Paine could see why. A gelatinous mass was blocking the esophagus, distending it so that the valve action was malfunctioning, sucking as much blood out of the flea's stomach as it brought in. The second bat flea suffered from the same blockage.

Paine unscrewed the jar from the cover and slipped in a gloved hand. He tweezered one bat flea and crushed it in the bowl of blood culture gelatine. The second bat flea he picked up carefully in the tweezers and held over a slide as he squeezed the stomach. A red strip shot over the slide. Paine dropped the flea in a killing solution. He screwed the jar back on the cover.

Paine moved to another table that was almost dwarfed by a fluorescence microscope. The microscope had ordinary compound optics built into a sway-backed system of mercury-discharge lamp, radiation shields, and ultra-violet filters that flooded the slide stage with blue-violet light. It was an ungainly, hot, and power-draining apparatus, but Chee had insisted on no more communication between Paine and the Navajo labs at Ship Rock except by radio. And the fluorescence microscope was a bacteriologic laboratory in itself.

Paine prepared a slide smear of the contents of the bat flea's stomach, dried it, and dyed it with fluorescent stain. He set the slide on the stage, pulled the hood over his head, turned on the lamp, and focused.

The stain was still taking effect. Paine waited, only fearing that the pounding of his heart would disturb the delicate focus. In spite of the canyon shade, the heat of the lamp rolled sweat down his neck and chest.

On the slide, invisible organisms were becoming visible against a dark background. They were short bacilli, slightly resembling safety pins.

Plague bacilli. The bats carried plague.
Chee had hired the right man.

On the way back to Gilboa, having left his wife at her
brother's trailer, Selwyn was roaring drunk.

'So, big Walker Chee took you to the cleaner's, huh?
Did a war dance on you and hit you over the head with
his Phi Beta Kappa key. You always have your leg half
down a scorpion hole before you watch where you step?
You're not just dealing with another savage, boy. You're
fighting Peabody Coal and Kennecott Copper. My friend,
you are a turtle on the superhighway of progress. Know
what happens to turtles on highways?'

Youngman handed back Selwyn's bottle. He was feeling a little run over already.

'You're right, aren't you, Selwyn?'

'Right, I'm right. Watch the road. Bad enough you're
drinking my booze, don't get me killed. You know, Tonto,
I can't believe Abner's dead. I think I'll drink to Abner.'

'I thought you hated Abner.'

'Me? Never! A wonderful guy. Weird but still a great
individual.'

'Not Quaker, either.'

'Let's drink to the Quakers. Now, goddamn it, you
stay on the road.'

Youngman steered the jeep off the road and between
a close-set pair of barrel cactuses. He kept on an angle
away from the road while Selwyn clutched the windshield.

'Where we going?' Selwyn shouted.

'You want to drink to Abner, we'll go drink to Abner.'

The jeep shook as Youngman raced over the stones of a dry wash. Ahead, the land developed those stubby rises of piñon and mesquite trees that south-westerners like to call hills. The jeep's speed created a false breeze.

'My bladder!' Selwyn warned.

Youngman wasn't listening. He needed a blast of air in the face and the physical tension of handling a fast-moving vehicle on sliding, exploding rocks without losing control.

'Hang on.'

'Holy . . .!' Selwyn exhaled as the jeep flew up a side of the wash and landed on two wheels, then four.

Youngman, more relaxed, slowed down as he wended his way through the mesquite trees. Where water was next to non-existent, mesquite was the familiar scruffy bush, but where there was any decent water table mesquite became a true tree with olive-green leaves. Half a mile on, his eye caught the brilliant yellow of paloverde branches through a screen of mesquite, like the plumage of yellow birds.

'We going where I think we're going?' Selwyn muttered.

The jeep's trail of dust curled through the hills. Inch-long cholla spikes clicked under tyres. To Selwyn, drunk or sober, the desert was a labyrinth. He had never understood why the Hopi weren't a tribe of people continually lost and meandering about in the wilderness. Somehow, to him, Youngman picked out one rise of paloverde trees from all the rest.

'Bring your bottle.' Youngman stopped the jeep.

'I always hated that son of a bitch, you know that.'

'Come on.'

They leaned against each other and stumbled up through the trees. Youngman remembered that he should have brought something, a bowl of cornmeal or a candy bar, for Abner's spirit to eat. Selwyn tripped.

'You can make it,' Youngman said.

'Look, if I could walk I'd be going in the other direction.'

Youngman put Selwyn's arm over his shoulders and half-carried him up the slope. They ducked the low branches and waded through poppies, while Selwyn's curses grew in intensity. A real wind came up. The trees bowed.

At the top of the rise, Selwyn slipped from Youngman and fell to his knees. All around the grave were dirt and rocks, and the grave itself was empty.

'He's not dead,' Selwyn said. 'I knew it. The bastard rose.'

Youngman walked around the hole. Not even the winding sheet was left.

'He's dead. Somebody dug him out.'

'I don't see any shovel marks or any footprints. He came out. I told you he was a witch.'

'A grave-robber doesn't have to leave his name. It was those bastards up on the mesa, Abner's old friends. Or that pahan who tried to get at Abner before. Paine.'

'No, he rose. He's not dead, Sweet Jesus, he's not. Feel that wind. Christ, he's walking around. He's out there.'

'Michael, row the boat ashore, allelujah, Michael row the boat ashore, allelujah! The river Jordan is deep and wide, allelujah, Milk and honey on the other side, allelujah!'

The song mixed with the sounds of tin plates and utensils being distributed, and the sizzle of hamburger patties in the camp-fire. John Franklin directed his choir with a cigarette. The campers sat on bed-rolls; their silhouettes, cast by the fire, wavered over the side of the van.

'Excellent,' Franklin applauded. 'Wasn't that excellent, Miss Dillon?'

Anne mustered a faint smile.

'My voice isn't what it used to be. La!' One of the ladies tried a high note.

'I'm hungry. That desert air sure does it to you.'

'George, you'd be hungry under water.'

Anne passed out potato chips and rolls. Since they'd started out from Gilboa, her pious charges had yet to help with the cooking or cleaning up. As long as they doled out some money to the reservation, she reminded herself.

'You can do your own toasting.'

'I sure like my burgers rare.'

'Is that coffee ready yet? Gee, it gets nippy here at night, doesn't it?'

'Rough it, Henry,' Franklin said, a moment before

Anne answered with a phrase that sounded vaguely the same.

'Hey, will you listen to that!'

Everyone fell silent. Anne had set up camp in late afternoon in an area that had seemed comfortably closed in by bouquets of ocotillos. The night dissolved the ocotillos, while the fire brought closer a grim ring of saguaro cactus. A call trailed over the desert.

'An owl,' Anne said. 'They roost in holes in the cactus.'

Mrs Franklin continued to stare into the dark. She hadn't recovered from the sight of that old Indian they found dead the day before. She'd seen dead folks before; Lord knew, she'd made enough calls to hospitals. But that was dying like a person. That Indian had died like some animal, well, like a pigeon in a gutter, she thought. Such things shouldn't happen. And the desert bothered her. The starkness disoriented her. She was accustomed to the soft clouds and stately green trees of her Minnesota lake country. In contrast, the desert was a graveyard, and the saguaros like tombstones.

'It is beautiful,' she lied. 'Do we have any more wood for the fire?'

'Leave it alone, Claire,' one of the other wives answered. 'It's romantic.'

'Don't be a dude, Claire.'

'I'm still cold,' she said.

Anne walked away from the camp in search of wood. She didn't expect to find any, not even a greasewood tree, but after a day of driving in a crowded van, she was happy to be alone for a couple of minutes in the dark. A moon hung out of reach above the upraised arms of a dead saguaro. Anne was about a hundred feet from the camp when she heard a step behind her.

'It's me,' Franklin said. 'I thought you might need some help.'

'There's no wood out here.'

'I know.' Franklin oozed complicity, and then shifted to concern. 'Have you been giving any more thought to my offer, Miss Dillon?'

'No. I don't see myself as a secretary.'

'Oh, it could be much more interesting than that. Actually, you'd be more of a personal aide. You'd love the travel. There's going to be a World Council of Churches convention in London this winter. You'd meet a lot of good Christians.'

'That would be a change.'

'While Franklin decoded Anne's insult, his wife called from the van.

'Never mind, John, don't bother.' She watched her husband and the girl walk back. 'A blanket will do.'

At the fire, Anne served up hamburgers and dished out beans from a pot resting in the centre of the coals. Franklin said the blessing.

'Miss Dillon,' said the hungry man called Henry, 'I can't help thinking about that deputy we ran into. Are all the Hopis as unfriendly as that? It seems to me after all the work you've done for his people that he was less than grateful. What's the point of donating work or money if these people are going to bite the hand that feeds them?'

Between bites there was a general echo of agreement around the camp fire.

'I don't think foundations can depend on gratitude,' Anne said.

'We all certainly know that,' John Franklin remarked. 'What we really want from you is an assessment of their character. Now, take that deputy as an example. How do you explain him?'

'I don't know what you mean, "explain him".'

'He's the only Hopi that we've met so far, unless you count the women making pots. He seems to be a friend of yours, you've talked about him enough.'

'You'll meet other Indians.' Anne tried to dodge the question. 'The Momoa family, people at the Snake Dance.'

She didn't like the turn the conversation was taking. Franklin wanted to punish her because she had refused his offer, and the others were joining in. Or maybe Youngman's paranoia was contagious. But the boredom that had been settling in on the group was definitely gone.

'Is he a good friend?' Claire Franklin asked.

'Yes. You have to get to know him, though.'

'Well, apparently you do, dear. How ever did you manage it?'

'My answers may not be your answers.' That was a poor evasion, Anne realized. 'See, I've lived here for a while.'

'Alone?' one of the other women asked with the thrill of possible titillation in her eyes.

'We haven't lived here.' Franklin gave the interrogation a more dignified tone. 'We haven't had the privilege. Now, you mentioned us helping these people. In fact, I tend to doubt we would have the benefit of your company unless you thought you could put forward a case for some sort of aid. But for us to help these people, you have to help us. Tell us about your deputy.'

'All I can tell you,' Anne said after a moment's thought, 'is that he's a desert person. A desert creature. It takes a very different kind of animal or plant to survive out here. Something very tough and self-sufficient. Well, take the bushes here as a kind of example. They grow wide apart from each other, and one of the reasons is that each bush spreads a poison around itself that will kill off another seedling. It has to be that way, because if the bushes grew closer to each other there wouldn't be enough water for either.'

'He sounds more like a scorpion, the way you describe him,' Franklin said.

Anne looked at their silly, food-stuffed faces. Any appetite she'd had for their company was gone.

She dropped her empty plate to the ground. 'I'm going to catch the weather report.'

As soon as she was in the van she closed the windows to shut out the sound of their voices. Her fingers reached for the radio, and then left it silent.

'You think there's something going on between our Miss Dillon and that deputy?' Henry's wife wondered aloud.

Anne stared through the windshield. Was Youngman

like that, as impossible to approach as she'd said? Was killing love a form of self-preservation?

'I hope it doesn't rain tomorrow,' Claire Franklin sighed. 'A day in a van is not my idea of a vacation.'

'It might rain tonight. Hear the breeze?'

'Pass the ketchup, please.'

'I hear it, but I don't feel it.'

'Can you imagine, Miss Dillon and that deputy?'

'Why didn't you and Miss Dillon bring back any wood, dear?'

'It sounds like wings, actually.'

'There's nothing like a hamburger cooked out of doors.'

'You know, she was pestering me about that donation.'

'We have enough people who need help closer to home.'

'I still don't see the ketchup.'

'Look at the moon.'

'I don't see it.'

'That's what I mean. It was there a second ago.'

'Never mind, I found the ketchup.'

'Just keep your hands off her, John, that's all I'm going to say,' Claire Franklin whispered.

'Listen to that.'

'Oh!' Mrs Franklin jumped to her feet and swung at the air. 'A bat!'

'I didn't see anything.'

'For heaven's sake, dear.' Franklin was disgusted. 'It isn't going to nest in your hair.'

'That's an old wives' tale.' Henry pitched the ketchup

bottle aside. 'I don't know, maybe that means they only bother old wives.'

'There's another!' Claire ducked.

'All right, all right.' Franklin stood up holding a blanket. 'Show me.'

A muffled sound streaked over the camp fire. Claire Franklin swayed, her hands up to her head. She took her hands away. A gouge ran from her left eyebrow to her right temple and from the wound, over her eyes, ran a sheet of blood.

'John!' she screamed. 'Help!'

Franklin swung the blanket, and stumbled as something like a fist hit him between the shoulder-blades. He felt teeth slice into his back.

'John.' Henry, like the others, didn't understand what was happening. 'John, boy, what's the matter?'

Then the sound, first like a scattering of dry leaves, then like a tide rushing over steps, poured over the camp. It spread and blanketed the camp. Ten, twenty bats on a body. Hundreds swirling overhead.

'Maude!' Henry pitched on the ground, two bats on his neck, and watched one rip open his hand. Beyond was his wife, on one knee, screaming in a coat of bats. A bat fixed on her cheek. Another bat landed on the ground. It drew up its wings and scuttled towards Henry like a spider.

The ground was covered with running bats. Claire Franklin rose from the ground, a statue in red. Another figure, seemingly two-headed, ran through the fire. Franklin and another man spun like maddened dancers.

'Here!' Anne shouted from the van door.

Henry staggered against the door, closing it. He leaned against the van even harder as others tried to push him down or pull him away, climbing over him and each other.

'Get back! Let me open it!' Anne shouted from inside.

They didn't hear her. She heard them. Shrieking. Anne had never seen such huge bats before and, since the campers had stopped fighting the bats to fight each other, the bats swarmed over them at gross leisure. The efforts of the campers became grotesque, as if they were swimming in slow motion. Swimmers no longer identifiable one from the other. Just screams and gaping eyes and a hand that smeared blood over the window.

Anne kicked the door open. Two figures rushed in, and the second slammed the door shut and locked it.

'The others . . .'

'Shut up.' Franklin pushed her away.

The others beat on the windows, but futilely. A combination of horror, confusion, and loss of blood started to take its effect. One, a woman in a coat of bats, clutched her left arm and toppled backwards. In a second, her face was covered. Smothered.

'We have to let them in.' Anne struggled against Franklin.

'And let the bats in, are you crazy?'

'You can't let them die.'

'You got us into this. Help me hold her, Henry.'

A wet forearm reached across Anne's throat. At first, she thought they were strangling her, but they were

115

only pulling her into the back seat, away from the door handle.

Claire crawled under the van to scrape the bats off her back. A steady stream of them slid under the vehicle after her. Another figure knelt, hands in prayer, arms and body under clusters of bats. Finally, the screaming subsided, overlapped by the scuttling of claws on the roof of the van, and by the cries of the bats, too high-pitched for human detection but a subtle, incessant pressure on the consciousness.

Franklin started the motor and turned on the headlights.

A figure walked towards the van swinging a burning stick. His shirt and hair were on fire. A cloud of bats hovered over him.

The van started, lurched over Claire, and stalled. The burning man beat his stick against a window while the generator whined and caught. The van ripped through an ocotillo bush.

'You can't leave them,' Anne said.

'Shut her up,' Franklin ordered.

Anne fought off Henry. Everything she touched was raw flesh.

The van rammed a saguaro, smashing the right headlight as blood continued to pour into Franklin's eyes. But he managed to find room to gain speed. A bat or two fluttered ahead. He pushed the accelerator to the floor mat, dodging the tall saguaros and running over smaller cactus and bushes.

By chance, he found the dirt road Anne had taken to

the camp site. The road was uneven but straight and the van rocked at sixty, outdistancing the last of the bats.

Thank God, he thought over and over again. Thank God.

For half an hour, Franklin raced after the beam of his single headlight. Henry had lapsed into shock, while Anne numbly let her head loll with the weaving of the van. In the middle of a nightmare, she wanted no feeling. Franklin glanced at her through the rearview mirror.

'I'll do the call on the radio,' he said.

'There's no radio. It's back at the camp, everything's back there.'

'The least you can do is give me a cloth. I'm still bleeding.'

'Then let me drive, I know the road.'

'Have you turn around? No way. And when we get out of here, you leave the talking to me. Just remember, you're the one who got us into this. Did you ever see bats like that before?'

'No one ever saw bats like that before,' she said in a flat voice.

'Except here,' he laughed bitterly. 'How's Henry doing?'

'Not much pulse, but more than the ones you left.'

'Look, you can thank me that you're alive. We barely got out of there. I did what had to be done. When we reach help, I'll do the explaining.'

'Go to hell.'

How could bats act like that? Franklin asked himself. Rabies. The girl didn't have any medical supplies with her and, besides, she wasn't bitten. She had nothing to worry about. He was the one who needed help.

A white rag of cloud hung in the moonlight. Franklin kept wiping blood from his eyes. The road was disappearing now under stretches of windblown sand. A mesquite tree slapped at the windows.

'You don't know the way,' Anne said. 'You have to let me drive.'

'I'm the one who may die,' he blurted out, and hearing the words in his mouth became aware of the chill creeping through his body. He didn't think of the night air or of lower blood pressure, only of the rank clamminess and a smell something like ammonia. The tyres skidded on sand.

'Watch where you're going,' Anne warned. She leaned forward. Franklin was breathing noisily through his mouth and his eyes were glassy under red lids. 'You're going into shock. You have to pull over. Do it slowly.'

Clinging to the wheel as if to life, he concentrated on overtaking the single beam of light, which was narrowing and turning red.

'Slow down.' Anne spoke deliberately in his ear. 'You have to let me take the wheel.'

As Franklin had lost the power of speech, he concentrated all the more on the ruby shaft of light. It glittered with night insects, with wings and eyes, with warm promises. Incredibly, he was overtaking the light. The red road expanded and welcomed him.

'I'm going to take the wheel now.' Anne reached over his shoulders. As her forearm touched his collarbone his shirt stirred, and a bat raised its head from the damp burrow it had made in Franklin's chest to give Anne a scarlet grin.

The road curved. The van went straight, shearing off two giant saguaros at the base and ploughing through tamarisk trees before it hit a dune and rolled on its back.

Chapter Four

Isa Loloma felt cold. He was in the months of the Hawk Moon and snow was covering him. The snow fell on his eyes and on his brain and between his ribs on to his heart.

Isa Loloma, dry and hot, fought in his fever against the straps that held him spreadeagled on a hay wagon in the sun outside Youngman's hogan. His wrists and ankles were raw. On his shoulders, the back of one hand and, worst, on his neck were bulging, reddish buboes. Lymph nodes become swollen moons of disease, around which the rest of Isa's life would gravitate.

His parents were in the hogan.

'I went up in the morning like always to get him.' Richard Loloma twisted the brim of his hat. 'Sheep was all dead. I figured a cat got at them. The boy was okay except for some scratches and acting crazy. We put him to bed but he went and got a fever and those bumps, so we come in to see Abner.'

'It'll ruin us probably without the sheep. I don't know, maybe we can get some new sheep,' Irene Loloma said, 'but he's the only boy we got.'

The father turned his hat in his hands, two inches at a time, while Irene respectfully clasped her hands against her apron, as if she and her husband were in a marble hall of justice instead of standing on dirty floor boards.

'Abner's dead,' Youngman said. 'Miss Dillon's off in the desert. Did you give him aspirin?'

'He can't keep it down.'

'He's real hot,' the man added. 'He gets shaking and you can't hold him down.'

Youngman didn't want to look at the boy. He didn't know anything about medicine. There was a clinic in Tuba City and the Lolomas could reach it by afternoon. All the same, he pulled himself from the chair. If it made them feel better, he told himself.

'You'll check him out?' the woman asked.

'Yeah, yeah.'

He was hung over from Selwyn's bad whisky and the white sun hammered on his forehead. Youngman stood by the hay cart squinting when he saw the boy's sweat and the glossy, pink swelling on the boy's neck, and then the lines of Youngman's face went flat. The boy started shaking and straining, twisting like a bow until only his shoulders and heels touched the cart. His mother reached to comfort him.

'No!' Youngman said. 'Get back.'

'Why? I was—'

'Don't touch him, don't get within five feet of him. Go to the trading post and get some blankets. On the way back go to the freezer. There's a cut up elk of mine in there. Wrap the meat in the blankets and bring it back to me.'

'Sure,' Richard Loloma said uncertainly.

'Wait, one more thing. You get any flea bites lately, either of you?'

'No.'

Youngman returned to the hogan and radioed Cecil Somiviki. Cecil's wife answered and said the sheriff was away at Shongopovi washing snakes for the dance.

Youngman sat in front of the radio. It was a Saturday. If he kept radioing Arizona Public Health for forty-eight hours he might get them to answer, just maybe get a doctor. The nearest town was Flagstaff. It was swimming pool and drowning season there; they weren't going to send one of their ambulances way into the reservation.

Then, there were the Navajo clinics at Tuba City and Ship Rock.

He turned to a band he'd never used before, the one to the Navajo capital.

'Calling Window Rock. This is Hopi Deputy Duran calling Navajo Police. Come in, please.'

'This is Window Rock. Did you say Hopi? Over.'

'I'm at Gilboa.'

'We know where you operate from, Duran.'

'I have a possible case of bubonic plague here.'

An hour later, a white 'Navajo Air' Beechcraft eight-seater, trimmed in blue with a yellow Navajo sun on the tail, taxied directly in front of the hogan. Two Navajo police in glossy black-and-white plastic helmets stood by while gloved and masked doctors removed the cold meat Youngman had laid beside the boy to keep him cool. Isa was slid on to a chrome table and zippered into a transparent oxygen tent attached to an air cooler and germ scrubber on the bottom of the table. His parents watched with fascination, as if their son were being transformed into someone alien. They kept glancing at Youngman for reassurance, but Walker Chee was in charge.

'It's not necessarily plague,' Chee told Youngman. 'We run a watch on all the possible carriers of the plague flea. Rats, prairie dogs, rabbits, ground squirrels. We've got it pretty much under control. Kid probably has cat scratch fever.'

'Sure. I'm just a little surprised you came with the doctors, what with all the power plants you have to run a watch on,' Youngman said.

'Anything I can do to help.' Chee was in a turquoise jumpsuit with monogrammed pockets. He lit a small cigar. 'You were right on the ball giving us that call. I was wrong about you. A lot of guys would've let these folks go on to a medicine man and then, God forbid we have a case of the plague here, we could have had a problem of more infection. You are definitely going to get a good report out of this.'

'That's wonderful,' Youngman said in a monotone. He watched the doctors briskly roll the boy to the plane. Very smooth.

In spite of his dislike for Chee, Youngman had to admit he was impressed. At thirty-eight, Chee governed an area larger than many states. If his flashy smile and suits made the cover of *Business Week*, maybe it was because he deserved it. He had brought in those power plants, and medical clinics, and power shovels to rip coal out of the mesa, and uranium surveys of the desert, and a semiconductor assembly plant in Ship Rock, and an Indian community college, and teams of white investors from Phoenix and Dallas. Youngman was very impressed that a man like Walker Chee, who was not a doctor, would personally supervise the care of a Hopi boy. Also, sceptical.

'Don't have any cases on your land?' Youngman asked.

'Of plague? None in the whole Navajo nation.'

'Any last year?'

'Why do you ask?'

'Because I remember three years ago you had twenty cases of bubonic plague.'

The doctors returned to fumigate the hay cart with sulphur dioxide.

'Let me level with you, Deputy. The life of any individual on my nation's land or your nation's is valuable to me. You can't put a price on people. But, with all the other stuff on our agenda – unemployment, education, and general health care – I just wish a couple of cases of plague were the biggest problem we had.'

Finished with the cart, the doctors trotted up to Chee. One was a young Navajo, the other was older and white. The two Navajo police pushed the Loloma couple forward. Youngman recognized the bigger policeman, a muscleman called Begay.

'What's going on?' Youngman asked.

'Don't worry,' Chee slapped his back, 'there's enough room in the plane for all of us.'

'Why?'

'Quarantine, of course. Just a couple of days at the clinic until we get lab reports. The doctors can tell you, this is standard procedure set down by the government. It's purely for your protection.' Chee gave the faintest nod to his police, who slipped by the Lolomas to either side of Youngman.

'Go ahead, ask the doctors.'

Youngman was wearing his .38. He rested his hand on the grip as casually as he could.

'It's definitely plague, then?' he asked the white doctor.

'Hold on.' Chee raised his hand. 'I told you, they can't make a diagnosis now. Look, Deputy, you asked for my help here. Since I'm giving it to you, you do what I say. You hop like a bunny over to that plane.'

As the sleek plane dominated Gilboa, Chee dominated other Indians. Usually, sheer force of personality was enough, there were other ways. He took a step back, and the doctors followed suit.

'What bit him?' Youngman asked.

'Huh?'

'You say you keep a watch on flea carriers. I saw those wounds. You tell me what animal bit him.'

Chee was momentarily sidetracked.

'Folks say a cat or coyotes got the sheep. Probably the same thing got him. We'll know when the kid talks.'

'If he talks, and that could be too late for someone else. You talk, doctor, tell me what kind of wounds those were.'

'Well,' the pahan doctor seized the opportunity to cover anxiety with professionalism, 'a good question.

125

They can't be teeth marks because they're more like the gouges you see from claws. There aren't the puncture marks you expect from canine teeth. On the other hand, they can't be claw marks because they're far too sharp. There isn't the bruising you expect to see, and the pattern is of a single crater instead of four or five lacerations as is the usual pattern for claws. In fact, the only way I could describe them is a gouge one might receive from two grooved razors held close together.'

'Cat, coyote, rat, prairie dog? Mouse? What?'

'I can't say. I never saw wounds like that before,' the doctor said.

'What does all this prove?' Chee lost patience.

'I've seen wounds like that before,' Youngman said. 'And I've seen the stains that go with them.'

Begay moved closer.

'You're going to check out where the boy was attacked, aren't you?' Youngman talked fast. 'You'll never find the place without the Lolomas or me. Let's see if we can find something else. Since you want to be a help.'

Paine got to the camp site too late.

' "Wee, sleekit, cow'rin, tim'rous, beastie," ' he slid up the door of a 12in by 20in lucite cage next to what was left of Claire Franklin, which was dried blood, a skull crushed on a tyre track, and an abdominal cavity gutted and as empty as a drum. Almost empty. ' "Thou need na' start awa sae hasty, wi' bickering brattle. I wad be laith to rin an' chase thee, wi' murd'ring prattle." '

Paine kicked the dead woman's back, and a kangaroo mouse jumped from the stomach into the cage. The cage door slapped shut.

The rest of the three corpses were as badly mutilated by scavengers. The effect scavengers created, it always seemed to Paine, was an after-the-party air. Bits of skin and clothes were strewn here and there in the dirt like torn streamers. Bodies, a coffee pot, hamburger buns and marshmallows scattered in weary repose. Only flies and ants still at work, and a horned toad waiting for the ants. A scene for Bosch, he thought.

He opened a Coke from the campers' food chest and sat down.

'The reason I've asked you here, the topic for today is, What do you think of Death? You're all worn out, I know, but it's more than likely you have some constructive insights. Group therapy may be new to you. It's not to me, so I will lead this session. A topic we might begin with is whether from your vantage point you see death as a mere continuum of life, whether you see yourselves as now existing in part at least as a vulture or a prairie dog, a communion of flesh in the Catholic view. I realize people hate to talk about it. They avoid the subject, it's a conversation killer. If it helps I can tell you this. All the really deep, all the really great thinking on the subject of death is done during a plague. Granted, millions die during a war, but all the thinking is wasted on patriotism and strategies. Take a plague. Strategies are useless and patriotism is ridiculous. Pure death, nothing but death is finally met.

'For example, you probably recall what bad poetry Robert Frost wrote about a woodpile rotting in the woods. No real sense of life or death. Just mildew. Compare it to Nashe's *In Time of Pestilence*. "Brightness falls from the air; queens have died young and fair; dust hath closed Helen's eye. I am sick, I must die. Lord have mercy on us." '

Paine chugged soda down a dry throat.

'Death is an intimate thing. That's so easy to forget. Just like sex, a very intimate thing. Nowadays, people like to be deceased, not in "death's embrace".

'The fascinating thing about plague, you see, is that it's death personified. I mean, death as a person. A lover. There was a case reported in *A Journal of the Plague Year* of a dying man who ran through the streets of London kissing pretty girls, deliberately infecting them. Killing them. People said he was mad. It's my opinion, however, that at the time he was running through the streets he had given up his soul and he was Death with two legs and two lips.

'I think you're beginning to understand. Plague is a kiss. Without that kiss, that flea bite, plague dies. Now that's the amazing part. Death can die, too. Yes, love makes us all vulnerable. Even Him.'

Paine finished the Coke and dropped the aquamarine bottle on the ground. He picked up the caged mouse on his way to the Land-Rover and looked at distant spires of rock.

' "Twinkle, twinkle little bat, how I wonder what

you're at. Up above the world you fly, like a tea tray in the sky." '

The Bell UH-I 'Iroquois' copter rattled fifty feet above its shadow as metal pipes rained down on the dead sheep. The centre of each pipe was baited with meat, the open ends were lined with insecticide.

'Don't see those ammonia stains you're talking about.' Walker Chee surveyed the carcasses through binoculars.

'We're not close enough. Go down,' Youngman yelled over the engine noise.

'Not on your life!'

The copter peeled off into a wide circle. Inside, the patrolmen rolled canisters to the bays, and as the copter passed over the sheep and Isa Loloma's truck again Begay dumped more poison, bags that exploded on contact with the ground in a dust of cornmeal spiced by a lethal anticoagulant called warfarin.

'I have a meeting with Piggot at my office in one hour. Let's step on it,' Chee told the pilot.

'I can show you the same bites and stains on the horses in Joe Momoa's corral,' Youngman said to the doctors.

'No,' Chee answered.

'Whatever attacked the boy and the sheep attacked the horses.'

'Says you.'

'Then what attacked them?' Youngman pointed back at the receding hill. 'A cat goes after a flock, it picks out one sheep. Coyotes'll scatter sheep over kingdom come. That's eighty sheep back there, slaughtered.'

'Duran,' Chee shook his head, 'you see one sick kid and you scream "Plague". You see some dead sheep and horses and you say it's a mystery. We've been dealing with plague control for years. We've done it with the Indian Bureau and experts from the Centre for Disease Control in Atlanta. Plague is spread by rodent fleas. Any rodent within miles of that hill is as good as dead now. We know how to handle this problem, if you'll just let us get on with it.'

'Those sheep weren't killed by prairie dogs.'

'But plague is spread by rodent fleas. Get it through your head, Deputy. I haven't got time to check out every vulture lunch you find.'

'Because you got to get back to your whites.'

'Right. Because it was the white oil company that gave us this helicopter so we could dust those sheep for you. Because it's the white utilities give us satellite pictures to help our irrigation programme. Yeah, you figured it out. Because in spite of you people, I'm going to bring some money into red hands. If you don't like it, you can always step outside.'

Chee lit a cigar for his grin.

'You're scared, Duran. You're scared of anyone successful, especially another Indian. I could show you some computer technology we're setting up at the clinic that would knock your eyes out, but I've changed my mind. I'm not going to have you pestering the doctors. Besides, this desert is quarantine enough for you. Just wash yourself down with some green soap and burn your clothes before you go near anyone. I can't help you.'

Chee settled back, listening to the jet's whine and the rotors' strokes, a rider secure in his element. Youngman watched the ground.

Anne sawed through the distributor cable and carried it with her to sit in the shade of the overturned van. Henry was sprawled unconscious on the sand. Franklin watched through slitted eyes. Both of his legs were broken from the accident. The two smaller fingers of Anne's left hand were broken and tied together. She peeled insulation off the cable with Franklin's penknife.

He spat cactus pulp on to the ground.

'It's no use.'

'It's all we have. We left everything with the bats.'

When she'd peeled all the insulation off, she separated the copper strands, coiling and putting aside all but one. Beside her was the one item of use she'd found in the van, a fishing pole they'd planned to use on Joe Momoa's trout stream. One end of the single copper wire Anne formed into a quarter-inch loop, through which she passed the free end of the wire. With every movement of her broken fingers, pain throbbed to her elbow. Worse, her fingers were slippery. On her fourth try she attached the wire loop to the end of the fishing pole and drew the free end through the pole's top eye.

Franklin looked on without interest. The trauma of his injuries was secondary to the fact that he refused to eat or drink. The mathematics of survival in the desert were simple. Without shelter or water, a healthy man would last one day. Since Franklin was only losing ten pounds of body fluid a day in the shade, he had about two more days to go. Henry, with a fever, little pulse, a coma, Anne gave hours.

'Pray for me,' Franklin asked.

'No.'

She put a pebble in her mouth to control her own thirst. It took her ten minutes just to hook the wire and tie on the fishing leader. An experimental tug on the leader snapped the noose at the end of the pole shut.

'Yea, tho' I walk through the Valley of the Shadow of Death—'

'You're wasting energy.'

'Should I save it?' he said. 'This is easy for you. It's always easy for heroes. I have it a little more difficult, my dear. I am a bad man,' he laughed weakly, 'and I believe in God. It's a contradiction that I've been able to maintain during life, but as I near death my situation becomes sharply uncomfortable.'

'And you're wasting lung moisture with every word.'

'The very least of my problems. You know that bat that was on my chest—'

'You were in shock long before you showed it. You wouldn't have felt a knife in your chest.'

'The Bible tells us bats shall roost on false idols. It's an omen.'

Anne's broken fingers had puffed up. She wrapped them up again with her middle finger for support.

'You're going to leave us, aren't you? When the sun goes down. Trading post can't be more than forty miles away and you know the way. You can make it in a couple of nights.'

'Maybe they'll send someone out for us,' she said.

'No. I remember you told us we wouldn't see a soul until we reached the hills. We're not expected back for three more days. What do you think, two more days before anyone gets worried? Before your deputy comes looking for you? A week, then. I'm sure you've figured this out already. You'll go tonight while you still have the strength.'

Earlier, she'd climbed the dune the van had hit. From there she could see, north, the distant edge of the mesa. South, the blue haze of the San Francisco Peaks. In between, nothing, not a hogan nor a shepherd, nothing but wasteland and the thick shimmer of superheated air which, where the ground was flat and barren, presented the illusion of water.

She sat and reformed the noose at the end of the pole.

'You are a beautiful woman. You shouldn't die out here.'

'I won't.'

'Maybe an Indian can live out here—'

'That's right. You learn to live. You learn to live differently.'

Anne removed her sweat-damp shirt and tied it into a hat. Her bare breasts, nipples dark against pale, freckled skin, shifted with each movement. She put on Franklin's wind-breaker, picked up the fishing pole, and left the van.

Fifty yards away, by the shallow gully of a dry arroyo pitted with burrows, she stopped and waited ten minutes, until her presence became part of the arroyo along with a beetle climbing over minuscule boulders and a nose that repeatedly sniffed the air before emerging as a mouse on the run. Upsidedown, a spider travelled seemingly on air from one side of the gully to the other. A Chihuahua whiptail lizard as long as Anne's finger dug for scorpions.

She felt the sun's hands on her back, a ball of sweat running down between her shoulder blades. The colours of the desert, when one spent enough time looking at it, were the colours of a woman. At a distance, the texture of skin stretched over the soft curves of hips, white in the sun, pale dun in semi-shade, in deep shade the blue of the underside of breasts. If she were naked, Anne thought, she could become indiscernible against the skin of the desert.

The lizard's tongue flashed like a ribbon. There were no male Chihuahua whiptails, only females that reproduced by cloning as if males were as needless a luxury as leaves on a cactus. Working industriously, sensing a scorpion below, the lizard didn't see a five-foot-long whipsnake gliding over the arroyo bed.

The whipsnake slid with his head held high and moving slowly from side to side the better to gauge the distance of his strike. He was smooth-scaled, striped on the side and creamy as marble on the belly. Concentrating on his prey, he nosed the copper noose.

The lizard darted down the arroyo as Anne pulled the leader. The whipsnake swayed in the noose until Anne set it down and crushed its slim head under a rock.

Half the snake meat she'd cook, half would be eaten raw for the moisture.

She refused to die.

Sixty million years ago, as the long Day of the Dinosaurs faded, an explosion of versatility was taking place among a newer class of life called mammals. Some mammals grew great, striving to fill the niche being vacated by the dinosaurs. Others developed speed afoot or fins to swim. A few tree shrews, small insectivores gifted with nimble fingers and voracious appetites, developed loose folds of skin along their ribs that enabled them to glide between branches.

Gliding was made easier as their three outer fingers grew longer and webbed. Teeth changed, the incisors crowded out by larger canines. The collarbone extended, ribs flattened out, and the sternum became ridged to support powerful chest muscles, while the heart and lungs swelled. The upper arm shrank more. Thumb and forefinger shrank. Webbed outer fingers grew still longer, the third finger as long as the animal's head and body. Gliding became flying, and there were bats. By the Age of Man, there were an estimated two thousand forms of bats.

Paine listened for them in the dark.

He sat bathed in the yellow glow of the Rover's interior light idly flipping a copy of *Playboy* he'd picked up in the office of Chee's doctor in Window Rock. The sheen of the pages transformed the nudes. Breasts were as glossy as fingernails. The centrefold blonde was as slick as soap.

On top of the Rover, a unidirectional microphone rhythmically swung back and forth 360 degrees. In the centre of the mike were six aluminium tubes, each designed to vibrate sympathetically like a tuning fork to a single frequency, however soft, at a distance of a thousand yards. The calls of many different bats might make one tube hum; only the echolocating call of the vampire could make all the tubes respond. Inside the truck, the pistol grip of the microphone shaft twisted next to Paine's ear. One wire trailed from the grip to a battery and a second wire led to a distortion-free signal amplifier that, in turn, was jacked into an oscilloscope on the seat beside Paine. Across the green face of the scope was a white line as straight as a ruler.

Chee's doctor had given Paine an injection. He was full of sewage now; a sludge of 3000 million formalin-killed plague bacilli coated with aluminium hydroxide floated through his veins. What he wanted was new ears for new voices.

The night was so full of voices. Owls, frogs, hawks, lizards, mice, insects, coyotes, the entire desert was a reservoir of mews, barks, howls, and screams. Cries heard and unheard. Which was why he had to use the oscilloscope, because human hearing ended at the meagre frequency of 20,000 cycles per second.

From the magazine page a pouty face stuck out its tongue.

Animals adapted in different ways to survive. In humans adaptation was outwardly evidenced by the size of the skull and sexual apparatus. The distended penis, enlarged breasts, full lips, and buttocks. Among bats? The wings. And the ears so magnified and as convoluted as crowns. The ear tragus as separate as a dagger. A cochlea wound round and round like a seashell and interlaced by muscles that allowed the ear to hear the echo clearer than the call, a call that could go to 200,000 cycles per second, ten times the range of man.

Touch was what most mammals relied on in the night, when colours changed to shades of grey. Rodents packed themselves into the security of close burrows. Humans groped, hoping for the feel of soft skin, surrounded by fantasies and limitations, blind in the dark.

Paine put the magazine aside, and smiled.

Jezebels, Ochay would have said. Every day until his death, the Mexican was either kneeling in prayer or pressing religious tracts on the other members of the team.

After his death, Ochay had his revenge. High in the sierras, Paine's truck almost pitched into a ravine and he lost his personal library of Milton, Shakespeare and Lewis Carroll. All that was left was Ochay's New Testament, a well-thumbed copy with the most horrific

judgements and prophecies thoughtfully underlined. It
was Paine's only reading matter for the next six months.

All of Revelations was underlined. St John the Divine
howling in the wilderness, stuffing the luggage of future
madmen. 'They have as king over them the angel of the
bottomless pit . . . The rest of mankind who were not
killed by these plagues did not repent of the works of
their hands . . .' Better the chains of Marley's ghost than
Ochay's book, Paine had thought more than once,
though there were parts he did find interesting. 'Then I
saw an angel standing in the sun and with a loud voice
he called to all the birds that fly in midheaven, "Come,
gather for the great supper of God, to eat the flesh of
kings, the flesh of captains, the flesh of mighty men, the
flesh of horses and their riders, and the flesh of all men,
both free and slave, both small and great." '

The oscilloscope shivered and cast a 'print' of white
dots. Only one microphone tube was responding; a
wrong 'print'. The Arizona sky was full of small insectivorous bats – guano bats, cave bats, red bats, pygmy
canyon bats, fringed bats, and death's head bats, which
bore white 'eyes and mouth' on their black belly fur –
all wheeling in their nightly chase after grasshoppers
and moths, blasting the air with high-intensity cries
somewhere around 140,000 cps. The sensitive tubes or
Paine's microphone would tremble sympathetically at
73,000 cps, because the larger vampire bats were 'whispering' bats, sending out low-intensity cries not through
their mouths but through their nostrils. Like breath. The

microphone continued its steady sweep. The oscilloscope line returned to level.

Over the last few nights, the bats seemed to be coming from the west. The most likely origin was the San Francisco Peaks. He as good as crossed off the bat roosts of Mansion Mesa to the south-east.

Sympathy was a concept Ochay and St John never could grasp, Paine thought. For them, the reach to God or the skid to hell, anything but the reality of the world. But sympathy was one of the most interesting of all biological phenomena.

Metal humming to bat song. Flesh with the crispness of magazine paper. Those were simple examples of mechanical sympathy. Sympathy between life forms was more subtle.

The truth was that death was no rending of the skies asunder, no clash of angels, no chariots of fire. Death was a filaria worm that was brought by a fly bite, grew on the pigment in human skin, and crawled out through the eye. Or a cancer virus that seemed to leap off the slide and begin metastasizing in mid-air. Or leprosy bacilli that turned limbs into withered ornaments. The joke was that among immunologists there was no immunity, and among parasitologists there was no prevention. Did the body recoil or throw up defences against the seductive attraction of the invader? Rarely. As a statistical fact, among researchers the flesh yielded with tender anticipation. With sympathy. Cancer researchers had the highest cancer rate. Filaria researchers went blind. The specialist in leprosy became a lazar. The very point to saying a disease or parasite was endemic to a region was that there they were everywhere, and that there was no escape. Especially when you were not trying to escape, but rather relentlessly pursuing. Where intimacy was a professional necessity. People were always amazed at immunologists who studied the progression of a disgusting disease through their own bodies. Yet, if you were going to catch it, what the hell else could you do about it? The cancer blossomed, the worms fattened, and the man pared himself for specimens. An occupational hazard. You became, quite literally as the invasion spread, exactly what you studied. 'Which is why,' Joe Paine used to point out in Mexico City, 'we're so damn clever.'

The oscilloscope line trembled, just barely.

Paine watched the microphone's rotating shaft and the needle turning in the compass. The oscilloscope line was flat, shuddered, and was flat again. A tremor, not even enough for a print. Paine tapped the compass nervously.

'We're so clever,' Joe Paine used to say, 'because our subject is rabies. We picked one with a cure.' Which was about the only mistake Paine could remember his father making. Because the subject was bats.

His head jerked. The oscilloscope line was flat, flat, flat . . . a tremor . . . flat, flat, flat . . . a print. A faint one of low intensity slashing down an octave with three harmonic streaks. From the west, according to the compass.

Inside the stationary sleeve of the microphone shaft,

microswitches rode over cams. Four indents set the revolutions of the shaft. He twisted the sleeve one click to an arc of 180 degrees running west from north to south.

On the oscilloscope, the prints were slightly stronger and twice as frequent. Those would be the lead females, casting soft, regular, searching whispers ahead of the main group. About eight hundred yards off, he estimated, and travelling around twenty miles per hour. On a clipboard map, he noted the direction and time of contact.

Despite the cool night air, he perspired. Most bat prints were graceful shadows shaped like bells or diamonds. The voice of vampires was ragged, almost human. More bats came within range of the microphone. North-west, he decided, and twisted the sleeve another click, cutting the arc to ninety degrees. The oscilloscope line was shivering almost constantly. They were coming right at him.

Paine got out of the Rover and snapped an ultra-red filter on a searchlight mounted in his door. The oscilloscope started beeping, triggered by the intensity of the signals. He got into the Rover and rolled up the windows. He twisted the sleeve another click to forty-five degrees, and the oscilloscope turned into a solid band of strong and nearing slashes.

Paine pulled the battery plug from the microphone shaft and directed the microphone manually by the grip. The oscilloscope image exploded into snow, overloaded by input. He switched off the scope and the interior light, picked up sensitized, electronic binoculars and switched on his searchlight. He swung the beam up.

They came over, ten at a time, then twenty, then more than he could count, about twenty-five feet above the Rover, hundreds of them, one of the biggest vampire colonies he'd ever seen. Not fluttering like insectivorous bats, but rowing easily with long wings, covering the sky, colouring it with red wings the shape of knives.

The rider steered his heavy motorcycle down the mountain road. The road was bad, half the time on the edge of a drop, and if he hadn't known it as well as he did he would have been reduced to a crawl in the dark. He maintained speed, as much from fear as anything else.

The lip of the road, weakened by rain, crumbled under his tyres. He straightened out and downshifted. He was happy to have to concentrate on the road and when he reached a point where it was almost totally washed out he skilfully gunned the bike up the inside bank until he reached good road again.

He was lucky, he told himself, luckier than his brother. Someone had had to stay out by the corral at night to shoot whatever was attacking the livestock. His brother wanted to go and try out his new 30–30, which he took with a pump shotgun, two remote control lamps, and a bed roll. His brother never fired a shot. At midnight, he staggered in the kitchen door, bleeding from his head to his boots and screaming, 'Bats!'

Which was crazy.

And he was luckier than his folks. The old lady took sick first. The old man had to tend both and then the old man took sick. None of which had to be serious if the storm hadn't come along and knocked out the phone line. Jesus, how many times had he told them all they should have a radio at the ranch just in case? Maybe a million. If he didn't get a doctor in time it was going to be their fault. A little planning went a long way. For one thing, the whole damn road had to be repaired, graded some places, if they intended to get trucks up for the piñon harvest. He'd probably have to run everything for a while.

He slowed to pick his way through some branches that had fallen across the road. A black line like a coach whip was tangled in the branches. He stopped and twisted the bike's handlebars, swinging the beam until he found a telephone pole on the outside edge of the road. The line was the telephone wire.

He walked his bike to the pole and opened his engraved leather saddlebags. He really was lucky, but luck didn't mean a damn thing unless you were prepared. Inside the bags were the line repairman's lamp helmet, gloves, belt, and phone he'd taken when he quit Southwest Bell. It wasn't stealing; everybody took things. Nobody was going to quarrel if he saved a few lives. He strapped on the belt and helmet, tried the light, which was faint but good enough. Eagerly, he climbed the pole stakes up to the disconnected wire.

On top of the pole, he had his first misgivings. He never had been so good at line work and the helmet lamp seemed much fainter thirty feet in the air than it had on the ground. If he just took his time, though, he could still save hours off trying to reach help on his bike. There weren't any other homes with phones around Dinnebito Wash and there wasn't a public phone until you were almost in Tuba City. He hitched his belt around the pole a notch tighter. The night was so damn dark; although he often liked dark nights for hunting coons, sometimes even deer. He'd stay in a blind until he heard noise and then hit the flood lamp. The animals would freeze, their eyes orange and panicked, and he'd put a bullet right through their lights.

The gloves were stiff from disuse. He was afraid he was going to drop the line phone if he made a mistake. The phone itself was simple enough: it had a dial on the grip and two wires attached to roach clips. His boots couldn't get a firm hold on the stakes and that slowed him. Also, the roach clips were so rusted shut from disuse he had to scrape them clean with his buck knife. He was about to sink the clips in the wire when he found he wasn't alone. Hanging upside down from the wire about ten feet away, a bat was watching him.

The clips slipped from his gloves but he recovered quickly. It was the biggest bat he'd ever seen, dull brown, with a squat nose and fringed head. Just a single bat, though, and after swallowing on a dry throat he laughed at himself. He hooked his knife on his belt to free both hands and clipped the phone on to the wire. The helmet beam slid up the wire. Five more bats hung on the wire. There hadn't been any bats on the line when he first climbed the pole, he was sure. He wasn't afraid, but he did wish he'd brought up a varmint pistol. There was one in his saddlebags. He looked down at the bike. His beam barely reached the ground, but he could swear that it was alive. At first, he thought, with toads milling and hopping after the road, and then he looked straight down and saw that the whole bottom half of the pole was covered by them and they were climbing up, sideways and backwards, and he knew what they were and, however irrationally, what they were after. His heart knew and began beating on his ribs. The line swayed, tugging the phone in his hand. The line, in a matter of seconds, was solid with bats. He saw one with a baby clutched to its chest. The baby twisted its head to look at him.

'No!'

Something hit him in the centre of the back and slapped him against the pole. He dropped the line phone to swing. Teeth bit through his pants. He punched downwards and his arm came up sliced from the elbow to the wrist. He stared at it, amazed. In a hanging march, the bats on the wire walked towards him. He tried to unhook his belt, but his gloves were too clumsy. He shook his left glove off and at once a bat covered the back of his hand. There were more on his back and others securing themselves to his legs. The bites were sharp but not terribly painful. More cold than anything else. He shook the bat off his hand and now his fingers were red and slippery. He'd always had luck on his side and if he could just get to his bike . . .

He kicked, and his other boot slipped from its stake. He hung from his belt and watched the bats crawling, head downwards, from the top of the pole. His legs kicked and churned like a man running in place for a short time, and for a long time after that they slowly rose and fell like a marathon runner staggering towards the end of his race under an unfair burden.

Chapter Five

A line of men chanted 'ho-o-hah!' against the backdrop of the desert. They were painted all in black except for white across their foreheads and mouths and spots on their arms and backs. Eagle feathers decorated their long hair, and fox skins hung from their blue kilts. With every sideways step, the turquoise strings around their necks and the tortoise-shell rattles tied to their knees clapped in time.

'There's my jerkwater brother.' Cecil Somiviki pointed out a dancer to Youngman. 'The one in the wig. So scared he's ready to shit silver dollars.'

About five hundred Hopis sat on roofs and ladders, eating piki bread and drinking Cokes, the young men dressed up like dark cowboys, girls in ceremonial trim. A delegation of Navajos, each glittering like a presentation case of silver jewellery, stayed together, but the white tourists, exhausted by their climb from the parking lot a thousand feet down in the squash fields and their foreheads burned pink over dusty sun-glasses, spread around the edge of the dirt plaza. Youngman looked for Anne. Walker Chee was there, a velvet sash tied around his razor-cut hair.

'Headpounder's still after your ass,' Cecil muttered. 'Well, I can't fire you today anyway. Oh oh, lady!' He reached across Youngman and grabbed an Instamatic a white woman had wrapped in her scarf. 'No photos, ma'am, you read the signs.'

She had swallow wing sun-glasses and zinc cream on her nose.

'Signs?'

Her smile turned into an oval as Cecil opened the back of the camera and ground the film cartridge under his boot. He dropped the camera into a sack and gave her a numbered piece of paper.

'Collect it after the dance.'

'This is a religious ceremony,' Youngman told her.

'Outdoors?' she squawked. 'Come on.'

'Remember,' Cecil said, 'no tickee, no camera.' He and Youngman moved on along the perimeter of the crowd, keeping their eyes out for more cameras, or tape recorders, or sketch pads. 'Damn Bear Strap Clan's supposed to be catching these yoyos down in the parking lot.'

The ladder from the Snake Clan kiva flew pennants of feathers and horsehair. Youngman was surprised to see feathers still flying from the Fire Clan kiva as well.

'Yeah,' Cecil answered his question, 'those old boys been down there for days. Hey, we got ourselves another amateur anthropologist.'

A white teenager clutched a torn airline bag that, under Youngman's hands, revealed a Panasonic recorder and a Glad Bag of grass.

'Far out.' Cecil took the recorder. 'What's the matter

with you today, Youngman? Usually you're the one who finds all the goodies.'

In the centre of the plaza was a standing bower of green cottonwood branches and a hole covered over by a board. The dancers stamped on the board, warning the spirits below that messengers were on their way requesting rain, singing, 'Ho-o-ah, ho-o-ah, ho-o-aha, ho-o-ha!' One of the dancers held up the 'messengers', handfuls of snakes.

Youngman and Cecil worked their way to the front of the crowd, while those dancers called 'gatherers' fanned out around the edge of the plaza. Their job was simply to gather any loose snakes before they got into the crowd. Antelope priests kept time with pebble rattles. Youngman felt adrenalin hitting him like Scotch. Cecil even was suddenly excited; except for his job, he would have been dancing. The crowd took a step back.

'Sonovabitch, sonovabitch,' Cecil kept repeating to himself.

The first dancer bit his snake about ten inches behind the head and supported the rest of the snake's body with his left hand. By the dancer's right shoulder was another dancer with an eagle feather 'snake whip'. The tail of a six-foot diamondback dragged over the ground. They had to dance a snake four times around the cottonwood bower in the centre of the plaza, and then pick up another snake and start again. That's how they got rain.

'They pull the fangs, you know,' Youngman heard a white father telling his son.

Crouched, dancing on the balls of his feet, Powell
Somiviki went by.

'Shit, he's got the snake on the wrong side,' Cecil said.

Powell's eyes rolled nearly out of sight. His knees
wobbled. From the left side of his mouth and out of
reach of the eagle feather, a blood-coloured rattler
pushed its snout along Powell's cheek. The snake's gaping
mouth displayed two yellowish fangs. Youngman
watched the snake wrap its tail around Powell's arm,
trying to coil for a strike. Powell danced away while the
snake sought its angle.

'Sonovabitch,' Cecil said.

'Dad, I saw—'

'They milk them,' the father answered.

A black rattler darted away from the dancers and
across the plaza, followed casually by a gatherer.
Although the gatherer caught up, he didn't stop the
snake, a fact that wasn't appreciated by the crowd until
the big rattler was escaping between their legs. Shouting,
they jumped against the houses or ran towards the road.
The gatherer scooped up the snake by the tail and carried
it back.

Powell was on his knees on the other side of the plaza.
He'd only fainted. The sidewinder still hadn't coiled suf-
ficiently around Powell's arm to strike and the dancer
with Powell helped by unwrapping the rattler's tail and
reversing the head in Powell's mouth.

'See what a college education does for you,' Cecil
sweated. 'You don't know right from left. Stupid—'

The dance went on. Walker Chee excused himself to

visit one of the outhouses along the side of the mesa. When he came out, Youngman was waiting.

'How's the Loloma boy?'

'I gave a report to the elders.' Chee tried to slip by.

'How is he?' Youngman blocked the way.

'He's in good hands. By the way, you people are missing a great thing here. You could auction off the Snake Dance to the television networks, you'd pull in a million dollars a year. For doing nothing, just what you always do. This could be the biggest attraction in the country.'

Youngman was amazed. Talking to Chee was like trying to catch a lizard by the tail. Even if you pinned him down, he got away.

By the time Youngman returned to the plaza, one of the dancers was bitten. A bullsnake had him by the neck until the shadow of an eagle feather passed over the snake's eyes and it let go, hitting the ground with a thump. Powell danced over the bullsnake, a new rattler in his mouth, the rattler's muzzle resting on Powell's shoulder and its tail swaying almost in time to Powell's steps. Man and snake, two parts of nature, intimately joined and not by chance; the legends spoke of the snake wife. What the whites, what even Navajos would never understand, Abner always said, was that the Snake Dance was a dance of life, not of death.

'That boy, he did okay,' Cecil winked at Youngman.

When the last snake was brought back to the cottonwood bower, the head of the Snake Clan made a circle of cornmeal with lines leading east, west, south, north, to the sun and to the underworld. While he prayed, the dancers threw their snakes into the circle where they writhed in a heap. Finally, all the dancers scrambled for snakes, each grabbing as many as he could carry, and ran from the plaza, down the narrow path that hugged the mesa wall, to the desert, where they would run for miles more before releasing the reptiles.

Youngman, Cecil, and a second deputy called Frank gave back confiscated cameras and directed tourist traffic out of the parking lot in the squash field and when the lot was almost empty they had some cold beers on the tailgate of Cecil's station wagon.

Anne hadn't shown. Obviously, Youngman thought, she had better things to do.

'Not the worst Snake Dance I ever seen. Not the best,' Cecil directed the spray of his beer away, 'but not the worst.'

'Your brother looked good,' Frank burped.

'A little shaky at the start,' Cecil frowned. 'Like I told him, though, you can't fight it. You got the belief in you, you'll be okay.'

'Who was it got bit?' Youngman tried to get into the spirit.

'What's his name . . . Butterfly. No, Butterfly's brother. Oh, I'm gonna rag him tomorrow,' Cecil laughed. 'Wasn't it swell to see Powell with those snakes?'

Cecil scratched his crotch with satisfaction. Frank was the deputy from Walpi pueblo; he had enough white blood to give him whiskers and a long nose, and behind his back friends called him Horseface.

'See when they let those snakes get in the crowd?' he nudged Youngman. 'That fat blonde. Thought she was gonna stay in the air for a month at least.'

'A laugh riot,' Youngman said.

'They wanna come and see the dance, they take their chances,' Cecil said. 'No one asked 'em. This ain't Gallup. They wanta get drunk, see some phony dances and Roy Rogers, they can go to Gallup.'

'You know Roy Rogers got Trigger stuffed in his house?' Frank turned serious.

'No!' Cecil was disgusted. 'What for?'

The few vehicles left in the lot were Hopi panel trucks and Walker Chee's Le Sabre.

'Wonder what Chee's hanging around for?' Youngman accepted a smoke from Frank.

'Business,' Cecil said in a small voice.

'Business?'

'That's what I hear. Bastard's got no respect at all.' Cecil spat on the ground.

'What kind of business?'

'Oh, some shit about letting the headpounders do all the policing of the joint lands. Doing us a favour, as usual. Hell, it wasn't joint land until the Navajos got to their friends in the Bureau and stole the land from us. By the time the head-pounders and the Bureau get finished we're gonna have just enough land to piss in from a squat.'

'Speakin' of Chee, I ran into a funny guy a couple weeks back,' Frank said. 'Big pahan with reddish hair, said he was a doctor. Drove a funny truck.'

'I met him,' Youngman said. 'What made him funny?'

'Nothing, first time I saw him. Second time, I ran into him down at Five House Butte. He asked me about bats. He ask you about bats?'

Cecil and Frank stayed to open some more cans while Youngman walked back to the pueblo. The noise of family get-togethers came out of screen doors, along with aroma of fried rabbit. Through one window he could see Chee and some other Navajos with the old men of the pueblo. Youngman sat alone where the plaza ended in thin air. He let his feet hang off the edge.

The sun burned level with his eyes. He looked down between his boots, where a juniper tree struggling on an outcrop obscured the long drop. With field-glasses, he might have been able to see the dancers returning from the desert. Dark spots moving at a lope through shadows that could lie across half a mile of sand. The air was a haze, purple to the east, golden to the west. Beyond the desert, on the other side of the mountains, the towns would just be lighting up. Winslow, Flagstaff, Tucson, Phoenix. Boulevards, palm trees, motel neon, swimming pools, all lit, all powered by water that was bought, stolen, divided, over-estimated and disappearing. Ho-ah-ha, everybody wants rain.

Bats, though. Why would the pahan who was after a slice of old Abner want bats? If he did want them, why wasn't he at the Carlsbad Caverns where there were millions? What was so secretive about looking for bats?

Everyone had seemed to be all right at Momoa's ranch, he thought. And wondered why he'd bother thinking of Momoa until he remembered that was where Anne was heading. Abner and the Loloma boy were both attacked east of Gilboa. She was going west. And she had a radio.

The only problem she had was him. He remembered the first time he and Anne camped together, up on Dinnebito Wash. Camping was a formal word for it. Just catching enough trout to eat. Making love on a blanket.

On the second night, she'd started talking about her family, and on the third night she asked about his.

'No family and no stories,' he said.

'I saw those sketches you did. That terrible bloody face in all of them. It looked full of symbolism to me.'

'Symbolism, hell,' he answered. 'That's Masaw.'

To entertain her, he told her stories about Maski Canyon. The story about how Masaw escaped bloody and burned from a flaming pit that could never be put out. The story about the city of the dead. When she asked him to take her there, he put her off.

'What you mean is, this place doesn't really exist, does it?' she laughed.

'Something like that.' He took the easy way out.

'Like "somewhere over the rainbow?"'

'Let me put it this way. If you're there, you're lost.'

One thing bothered her.

'How can you do the drawings if you've never seen Masaw?'

'Abner tells me what to draw.'

'He sees Masaw?'

'Abner has connections.'

'Abner's going to poison himself with datura some day.'

'That, too.'

Wrong, as it turned out, Youngman thought.

Abner and Anne, the only two people he cared about. One dead and the other leaving. But only leaving the reservation, not him necessarily. Not unless he insisted on staying, and what for? To end up as shrivelled as Stone Man or a pariah like Abner? Chee almost had him out of his job already. Cecil refused to investigate what had happened to Abner's body.

Why not go with Anne? Or, phrased the way most whites would like to put it, why live like an Indian? Why live dirty on scrub land, sweating all day and freezing at night. With some vocational training he could work nine to five in an air-conditioned office and own two suits and an economy car and have two weeks vacation. Or, if he had sufficient cunning, become a professional Indian like Chee. Not that Anne would ever put the question that way. For her, it was merely a matter of love. Of 'commitment', as she put it. But Youngman was already committed. Being born a reservation Indian was the same as committing a crime and being sentenced to life in isolation. Quarantined with the perverse sickness that made life among whites the same as suffocation. The evidence-symptoms of this crime-disease: self-pity, suspiciousness, stupidity, and pride. Was there an Indian of the twentieth century, Youngman asked, who wasn't schizophrenic? And who didn't use it as an excuse? Did anyone do it as well as him?

Youngman heard steps crossing the plaza and Harold Masito sat beside him, smoking a handrolled cigarette of mesa tobacco, stuff that was three times stronger than store-bought. The Bear Strap priest wore his shirt formally buttoned at the neck. In the sideways angle of the sun, his face was as rough as sandstone.

'No clouds yet.' He stared at the mountains.

'Not yet.'

'You trying to think 'em up? Can't think 'em up. We do our part and the rains come. Couple days, maybe more. Not instant. Maybe we get a breeze tonight. Get a real rain, not like yesterday.'

'I was thinking of Abner, really,' Youngman said. 'Abner and bats.'

They sat in silence for a minute, watching a mesquite ball roll over the ground far below. It bounced over some soda cans that had been pitched from the mesa. The cans could be used. Cut up and put over corn shoots in the spring.

'I been thinking about Abner, too,' Harold said. 'We shouldn't never chased him off the mesa.'

'You thought he was a witch, remember.'

'He was. But he had the power. Only kind of power we got is Masaw, this land. Abner could talk to Masaw and we chased Abner out, and now we keep losing the land. Me, I thought I was a pretty brave fellow. I shouldn't of been scared of Abner. You weren't.'

'I didn't think he was a witch.'

'And now?'

'No. Someone else seems to, though. They robbed his

grave. You wouldn't know anything about that, would you?'

'You mean, he's not in it.'

'Yeah. That's not mysterious to me. The only thing I can't figure is what killed him. I never saw wounds like that before. Weren't any tracks.'

Harold passed the cigarette.

'Tracks are only there when you see 'em. Abner did things right. I seen him last night, in dreams. That's why I come out here to you now.'

'Oh?' Youngman was bitterly amused. 'Now that you'll talk to him, what did Abner have to say?'

'He said for me to help you 'cause you don't know how to read.'

'Uncle, I can't do much but I can read, thank you.'

'Words.'

'Yeah.'

'You find any words when you found Abner?'

'No.'

Harold grunted as if he'd made a point.

'So what was I going to read?' Youngman asked with exasperation. 'Some scribbles of sand on the floor? Look, it's a little late for you to come around on Abner's behalf. I didn't chase him off the mesa, you did. With witch stories—'

'He stole the tablet.'

'What?' Youngman was stopped short.

'He stole the Fire Clan tablet so the Pahana couldn't come back. The real White Brother has a corner of the tablet and when he comes we're supposed to put the tablet back together and everything will be okay. We always had that tablet even before we got to this world so we'd know the Pahana when he got here.'

'Before this world?'

'From the Mayan world. Abner could read Mayan.'

'Oh.' Youngman kept a straight face. 'He never mentioned it to me.' How about Greek and Latin, he thought to himself.

'We had to leave the Mayans 'cause life was too easy there.'

'Sounds like a good reason.'

'Here with Masaw we have to tend to the ceremonies to get any rain and corn at all. That's how we stay close to the right way. I know it's hard but we were chosen—'

'Not chosen,' Youngman lost his patience. 'Fucked. We are the God-fucked of the earth. Look at us! Walking around in rags, eating corn other people wouldn't throw to pigs, sleeping in hovels, and what do we do but spend all our time congratulating ourselves on being the most God-fucked and hopeless people on earth. Because that's what we are and nobody did it to us, we did it to ourselves. And we're so fucking dumb we're proud of it.'

As soon as the words were out of his mouth, Youngman was ashamed. Harold regarded him with shock.

'I'm sorry, uncle. That was unfair and stupid. Okay? You were telling me about the tablet Abner stole.'

'There is such a tablet.'

'I'm sure there is,' Youngman tried to mollify Harold.

'We took it to Washington to President Taft, I remember, to see if he was the Pahana.'

Let me guess, Youngman thought.

'Was he?' he asked.

'No.' Harold stayed downcast.

Youngman found himself disconcerted by the memory of the altar Abner had set up in his shed. Abner had left a place on the altar for the tablet.

'Anyway, it doesn't matter,' Harold's face brightened, 'now that Abner gave it back to Masaw. The Pahana missed his chance. You aren't going to leave the reservation, are you?' Harold added.

'Why should I?' Youngman was surprised.

'Talk is you're going to get fired. Chee's in there saying he's going to give us a lot of help but he wants you fired.'

'The elders wouldn't do that and neither would Cecil.'

'Not up to Cecil. And Chee, he's a good talker. And maybe it's 'cause you took up with that white girl. You think there was no bad feelings about that?'

'Just between her and me.'

'Well, that's the way it is,' Harold shrugged and slapped his palms down on his knees. 'Gotta get back. My boy he brought up some ice cream in an ice bucket. You finish this.' He gave Youngman the last of his cigarette.

Fired, Youngman thought. He hadn't thought much of his job until now. Except that it wasn't worth a damn and if he couldn't hold a job like that what could he do?

'Abner told me another thing in that dream,' Harold said.

'Yeah?'

'He said for you to show me those pictures you took of him.'

Youngman sat and exhaled a stream of pungent smoke that fluttered against the air. The prospect of being fired remained in his mind but it did occur to him that he hadn't told anyone about the pictures he took of Abner dead in the shack. No one else knew about them except Anne and the campers. Maybe they'd talked to Selwyn.

'Okay,' he said slowly, 'I'll bring them. I don't have them on—'

He touched his shirt pocket and felt something flat, and brought out the Polaroid snapshots of Abner spread-eagled on the ground. Youngman thought he'd filed them away with the death report; he'd been sure he hadn't put them in his pocket.

'I guess I was wrong. What do you want them for?'

'To read for you.' Harold took the pictures.

He'd forgotten to file the snapshots, that was all, Youngman told himself.

The old Bear Strap Clan priest studied the photos slowly, one by one.

'Coyote is you. Shrike is Masaw's bird, brings him messages. Fire is . . .,' Harold frowned, 'fire is broken. Spirals and swastikas are backwards. They're backwards. He did it.'

Harold's face fell like a wall crumbling. His eyes were first surprised and then furious.

'We shouldn't of chased him, we should of killed him.'

'Read the rest for me,' Youngman asked.

Harold ripped the photos in half and threw them into

the wind that rose up the mesa wall. Youngman tried to snatch some out of the air, but the shredded pictures skipped away, over the drop to the desert.

'Not going to read any more.' Harold stood. 'Not going to help you. So long.'

Youngman stared at the bits of paper fluttering higher into the sky. Now, he'd never know what Abner did.

'Maybe the Fire Clan priests can help,' he turned to say, but Harold was already slipping into his house.

The last light of the day was fading. The square stone-and-mud houses of the pueblo were turning to smaller squares of light, the off-white of gas lamps. Voices and the sounds of meals echoed through the alleys. Cottonwood leaves drifted over the plaza.

Youngman stirred himself, stretched, and headed for the road to the parking lot. Cecil had invited him for dinner. Near the end of the plaza, though, Youngman found himself standing by the third kiva, where the totem of the Fire Clan hung from the top rung of the ladder that led down to the underground chamber. It was very unusual, practically sacrilegious, for the priests to stay in the kiva during a Snake Dance. It was definitely worse for anyone to disturb them, though.

He stood by the ladder, listening for a word, the shake of a rattle, a murmur of movement below. He blocked from his mind the sounds of the houses, the shuffle of wind. The kiva was totally silent. Juniper branches tied to the ladder below the entrance hole blocked any view of the chamber, but Youngman caught the odour of spoiled food.

He shook the ladder tentatively. There was no response. Stone Man had said eight priests were in the kiva; one of them should have noticed the ladder. Although they could have left last night or the night before without anyone noticing. The kiva could be empty. He watched a black beetle with wings marked scarlet climb from the entrance up the ladder. A carrion beetle.

A laugh reverberated in an alley. The plaza was still empty except for Youngman. A second beetle came after the first.

Youngman started down the ladder. As his boots pushed through the juniper branches he was sure he'd be greeted by angry challenges. There were no challenges, not a sound but the creaking of the ladder rungs. He shook another insect from his hand. The kiva was cold. Not cool. Cold that made his shirt cling to his back. And dark. The pale shaft of light that came through the entrance hole faded before it touched the floor. When Youngman reached bottom, the light died on his face. He could see nothing but the grey dome of the kiva ceiling curving into black space. The air was thick, hard to breathe, and slightly sweet.

He lit a match.

He was surrounded by a circle of men sitting against the walls of the kiva. All the men were stripped to the waist. Some held prayer sticks. One who stared at Youngman had his lap covered by cornmeal and coloured sand. There wasn't a mark on them, except that their skin had turned black as if singed and foam had dried to a crust on their mouths and chests, and they were dead.

The Navajo helicopter sat in the floodlights set up around the plaza. A rack of germ-killing ultra-violet lights was aimed at the kiva, from which climbed, clumsy as a moon-walker, a figure in airtight vinyl coveralls. The cloth of the suit was impregnated with diethyltolua-mide rat repellent. The face plate showed eyes and an oxygen mask. A similar figure followed and, together, the two men carried a sagging cocoon of the same shiny material to the helicopter. It was the fourth sealed bag they'd carried to the helicopter from the kiva. They went back for more.

'Ten o'clock.' Walker Chee looked at his watch. He, Youngman and Cecil, and the village elders watched from Stone Man's roof, a hundred feet away. The entire village, many of them wrapped in blankets against the night chill, were on the roofs and silently watching the floodlit scene. 'Lucky this didn't happen this afternoon.'

'Yeah,' Youngman agreed. 'All we'd need is a few hundred whites racing out of here saying there's an epidemic.'

'Wait a second, you don't know what you're talking about.'

'I want to know what you're both talking about,' Cecil interrupted. 'Epidemic of what?'

'He doesn't know what he's talking about,' Chee

answered. 'They could've died of anything. He said they looked burned.'

'I said they *looked* burned. They weren't burned,' Youngman corrected him.

'Anyway, another copter is on its way. All I meant before was that it's lucky we don't have to inoculate that crowd you had this afternoon. That's,' Chee glared at Youngman, 'how wild rumours get started.'

'And just what the hell are you going to inoculate them against?' Youngman demanded.

'We'll use general antibiotics like streptomycin.' Chee turned to the elder. 'I'm just trying to help you people. Sheriff, are you going to get your deputy off my back?'

A sixth silvery cocoon was being carried from the kiva. The same pueblo elders who had been buying the most important sales pitch of Walker Chee's life just hours before studied the Navajo chairman now with open suspicion.

'A lot of people here don't take to needles of no kind,' Cecil said. 'Matter of fact, seeing's how this fucks up the Rain Dance, not a good idea for you to be giving orders here.'

'This is a lot more serious than any Rain Dance!' Chee lost his temper.

'Tell us,' Youngman suggested. 'Start with how you're going to want this whole village quarantined.'

'Look,' Chee told Cecil, 'you want a jailbird for a deputy, that's your business. I don't have to deal—'

'You gonna want this place quarantined?' Cecil asked.

'As a precautionary measure – ' Chee found faces

watching him from all the near roofs. 'It's a normal measure.'

The seventh cocoon was laid out in the helicopter. One of the two figures in overalls waved to Chee. The second figure returned to the kiva with a flame thrower. A stream of fire spewed into the underground chamber.

Stone Man recoiled. 'I saw eight priests go down there.'

Chee took a hand radio from his belt and spoke into it.

'Doctor, you got all the bodies out of there, didn't you?'

The radio answered in the affirmative, although Youngman hadn't seen either of the men in airtight coveralls use a radio of their own. Which meant they had collar mikes and earphones.

'Good,' Chee said. 'There weren't any more bodies, just seven,' he told Stone Man.

'Did they see a small stone tablet?' Stone Man asked.

Chee shrugged, but passed on the question.

'Every item was accounted for. There was nothing like you describe,' the radio answered.

'Give me the radio,' Youngman said.

'You're out of the picture.' Chee shook his head. 'Your people fired you tonight.'

'Give him what he asks for.' Stone Man stared at the desecrated kiva. Tears stood in his eyes. 'Do it.'

Youngman put his hand out.

'Duran,' Chee lowered his voice, 'you saw those bodies. There weren't any wounds on them. No swelling, buboes, nothing. Don't try to make something out of nothing. Don't start a panic.'

'Thank you.' Youngman took the radio. 'Doctor, which one are you? Raise your hand.'

The figure without the flame thrower raised his right hand.

'Doctor, what killed the men in the kiva?'

The voice that answered was nasal and clipped, a white voice. The doctor who had come to Gilboa for Isa Loloma, Youngman guessed.

'There are no clear indicators. The evidence of froth does lead us to believe there were pulmonary complications.'

'A disease, then.'

'Or toxic agents. Maybe a disease.'

'A highly contagious disease.'

'Not necessarily. The situation of the chamber is highly abnormal. Close quarters, shared food, lack of hygiene, etc. A disease that isn't normally contagious at all could become so.'

'Did you see any fleas or flea bites?'

'Not so far.'

'Swollen places?'

'No swellings at all. I can assure you there was no indication of bubonic plague, if that's what you're getting at. These precautions we're taking are normal prophylactic methods in dealing with a possibly contagious and undetermined disease. Again, I must mention toxic agents. What they ate or breathed. The public hygiene of the pueblo itself leaves a great deal to be desired.'

'Okay, doctor, let's cut the shit for a start. We had a nurse up here who spent two years teaching me about your goddamn indicators. The indicators of those priests were, one, froth, which means their lungs were infected. Two, cyanosis, black skin, which means their lungs were so congested there was no oxygen in their blood. Three, seven men died in two days. In other words, they were killed by pneumonic plague, which is a hell of a lot more infectious than bubonic plague.'

'What's the difference?' Cecil asked.

'You don't need any fleas. Just one man with plague and a cold in his lungs so he can kill his friends with a cough. It's about a hundred per cent fatal. Right, doctor?' Youngman added to the radio.

The figure in coveralls took a long time answering.

'As long as the men were dead, had stopped breathing out any bacilli, and they weren't handled improperly, the chances of further infection are practically nil.'

'Then it was pneumonic plague.'

'That's premature speculation. We'll do autopsies, the same as we did on the boy—'

Chee's signal to the doctor was too late.

'So,' Youngman glared at the Navajo, 'you son of a bitch.'

'The main thing is to avoid a panic,' Chee said.

' . . . pathogenic signs on the boy's body would indicate the possibility of bubonic plague,' the radio went on. 'There were flea bites we suspect were vectors, points of entry for the bacilli. I must stress, he was an isolated case.'

'Until tonight.'

'Perhaps,' the voice conceded, 'until tonight.'

'Even eight cases don't make an epidemic,' Chee said.

Youngman looked at the two figures in bright coveralls, the flame thrower, the bank of floodlights and rack of ultra-violet lights, the helicopter stuffed with man-size sacks. An invasion of twentieth century apparatus such as Shongopovi had never seen before.

'But if it is,' Youngman said, 'if it is an epidemic, Chee, you're ready, aren't you? That's what interests me. You're so goddamn ready.'

'So? You're lucky I'm here.'

'Maybe.' Youngman gave the radio back. 'Cecil, Joe Momoa usually makes it to the Rain Dance, doesn't he?'

'Never misses it. And Joe Jr and Ben, they come in on their bikes.'

'See them today?'

'Nope.'

'Neither did I.'

'If you had any phones here – ' Chee said.

'You do,' Youngman said, 'in your car.'

Youngman, Chee, the white doctor, and the Navajo patrolman called Begay flew out to Dinnebito Wash in the second helicopter. Headlights probed the dark at 150 mph because the last radio report was there was still no answer on the Momoa phone.

'So I'm a son of a bitch, am I?' Chee asked Youngman. 'If that's true why am I helping you?'

'Because you're in a corner, because you're hiding something. Because you're scared.'

In the twin beams, the desert slid by as two pale tracks spotted with brush, undulating as the copter flew over a dune. Youngman tapped the pilot on the shoulder.

'Stone chimneys coming up, better climb a little.'

'I don't see anything.'

'Climb anyway.'

The copter rose fifty feet. A slight tilt to the aircraft swung the beam and picked up a red column of sandstone reaching to the skids. The copter hopped another fifty feet.

Youngman had no good memories of riding in helicopters; he had no good memories of the Army. Like the Army, copters were too complicated and illogical, loud and wasteful. Sitting beside Youngman, the doctor he'd spoken to over the radio on the plaza was distributing vinyl coveralls from a box stencilled, 'Centre for Disease Control – Sterile Until Opened or Damaged'.

'I don't mind lying to you,' Chee said, 'and I don't mind being a son of a bitch. That's what it takes. You hear me?'

'For what?' Youngman stretched his legs as best he could.

'To be like them. Like the whites. You're not so dumb you haven't figured it out yet. You don't like it but don't try to lie to me. You know.'

'I don't know what the hell you're talking about.'

'Yeah? I'm saying we're on the same side. It's you and

170

me, Duran, you and me on the same side against the whites.'

'You're prejudiced?'

'You're not? Is anyone not? Whites aren't? I'm in Houston, Phoenix, Dallas every other week and I got loads of wonderful white bankers who stand up when I come in an office. And I know that each and every one of them would rather deal with a sharp stick up the ass than me. They take me to lunch – not at their private clubs, hear – and feed me steak and lobster and when I'm gone they spit it out. They hate me to begin with and they hate me more because I make them pay. I make them pay millions. Nothing's changed, Duran. They still want to steal it all. They want to starve us out, but they can't do that now, Duran, and you can thank the Arabs for that. They're running out of coal and gas and oil, and they're running out of time. Not enough time to starve us and so they have to buy. You know what else I found out? They're no smarter than us. But they have money and they have Washington and they keep one thing in mind: it's them against us. If we don't stick together, Duran, we're dead.'

While Chee talked, the doctor pantomimed how to get into the coveralls. Feet first. Ankles snapped tight. Air tank slung over the back. Air hose attached and hung down over the collarbone. Collar mike and ear phone wired to breast pocket radio. The suit zippered from the thigh to the collar. Tape over zipper. Youngman had expected some precautions to be taken on the night flight. Nothing like this, though.

'They know they can't fool me. So,' Chee said, 'all they can do now is go around my back. Get some opposition against me in the tribal council. Just as good, get around me to the Hopis. They're counting on you to stab me in the back.'

Two helicopters, that interested Youngman. One copter as a gift, that was possible. Two? Hueys were a quarter of a million dollars new. Used, they still weren't cheap. No one gave away two Hueys, not even to Walker Chee.

'We're on the same team, Duran. That crap about different tribes is out. You don't like me and I don't like you. Tough, we're going to have to live with it. There's something else you have to live with. I'm the only Indian in four states, maybe the only one in the country, who can save us. Not Rain Dances, not witch doctors, not bleeding heart liberals. Me! Because I know bank statements and interest rates and bribing the right bureaucrat and because I'm a son of a bitch. The best one we have.'

'That's why you didn't take me into quarantine at Ship Rock? You didn't want me talking about an epidemic and "stabbing you in the back?" '

'Now you're being dumb again.' Chee pulled his suit on. 'You can see I'm doing everything I can to stop an . . . any more cases.'

'And getting me fired, that was the good report you were going to put in for me?'

'That can change, Deputy. If you get on the team, there shouldn't be any problem.'

The ground had swelled into foothills and the copter lights cut through piñon groves and sloping meadows.

'Time for the masks,' the doctor said.

'Wait until Joe Momoa gets a look at us,' Chee joked. 'We'll scare him to death.'

The rows of a piñon plantation rolled under the bay door. Then a rocky field, a stream with stones pale as eyes. Another piñon grove. A road, more piñons, an empty corral, and the Momoa house, all its lights blazing. The copter passed over the house twice before settling in a landscaped yard.

A bat hovered over a cactus. In the moonlight, the flowers of the cactus were white and fleshy and almost fluorescent, and gave off an odour of musk. The bat thrust its nose through a soft bush of anthers to lick up nectar on its long tongue.

'They're back!'

'No,' Anne fed more brush to the fire. 'He's a cactus bat. He pollinates them.'

'Like a butterfly,' Franklin laughed and coughed. 'A desert butterfly.'

On all fours, she blew an ember into a flame. Startled, the bat wheeled away from the cactus and into the dark.

'How's Henry?' Franklin pushed himself up on his elbows. 'Where is he?'

Anne had kept the fire going all day, sending a futile smoke signal into the sky. Now she wanted light. The flaring brush lit up a pile of stones about twenty yards from the van.

'There. I buried him this afternoon while you were asleep. You've been asleep all day.'

She'd noosed a gila monster earlier. She cut off the fatty tail, stuck a stake through it, and laid it in the fire. Her broken fingers were swollen and purple. Chopped cactus filled the sack she'd made from her shirt. Franklin rubbed the bristle on his chin; any other time, being alone with a young woman would have roused him like a goat. Any other time.

'God, those stars are bright.' He let his head sink back.

'They're always bright. Here they're clear.'

'Blinding, those stars.'

Anne picked up the last of the raw snake meat.

'You have to eat.'

'No.'

'Suck on it, at least.'

He waved her away.

'You're going to survive this, aren't you, Miss Dillon? You can actually live out here.'

'Someone spent a lot of time showing me how to.'

'And you think someone's going to rescue you. That Indian deputy, right?'

She was about to tell him to shut up when she decided there was no point in lying.

'Yes, I think he will. Maybe he'll rescue both of us.'

'No, this is fine with me. Funny, I was fast enough to shut the door on Claire, and now I really don't care.'

'You have to try.'

'Tell me,' he twisted his face towards her, 'do you forgive me for leaving my own wife to die? Do you?' He waited a moment. 'No, and I don't think anyone else would. If I die here I'm lucky.'

Anne turned over the lizard tail. The beady skin peeled off in the fire, revealing a waxy fat, lightly veined.

Franklin pushed himself up on one elbow.

'I saw God, you know, while I was sleeping. Well, it was a lot like this. I was out in the desert, lost, alone, and I saw a camp fire. As I went towards it I could make out a man squatting, his face to the fire. He was a big man and he had a blanket or something over his shoulders. I called out and, without looking back at me, he waved me to come closer to the fire. He was cooking supper and I was hungry, so I ran to the fire. In fact, I was reaching for the food when I really saw him. He was twice as big as a man but what was most remarkable about him was his face. It was huge and covered with blood. His nose was broken, I could see that, but that couldn't account for all that blood. Yet, he was friendly. He said I could stay. He seemed to know who I was. I asked who he was, and he said he was God. That's all.'

'That's Masaw, the Hopi god. You just read about him before you came camping, that's why you had the dream.'

'I never did get to those books,' Franklin shook his head slowly. 'Thanks, I feel better now.'

Franklin was dying from dehydration. Anne couldn't understand why he wouldn't drink. The bat bites were superficial, the broken legs accounted only for pain, and she'd seen no signs of internal injuries or haemorrhaging. Still, he couldn't keep even cactus juice down and he didn't seem to be in agony. He was simply, deliberately, drifting away.

For that matter, she didn't understand why Henry had died.

She did realize her own survival had a time limit. Her pants were hanging loosely around her hips. She no longer had the strength to walk back to Gilboa even if she spaced the journey over three nights. So she'd hold out. Youngman would come. In fact, she was positive, Youngman was searching for her already.

'Someone's going to find us,' she said.

Franklin didn't answer. He was stretched out on his back, almost relaxed, staring at the sky. Anne knelt beside him and wrung her shirt so that cactus juice dripped.

'Suck this. Just get your mouth wet.'

His eyes were open but light years away.

'You don't have to swall—'

As her elbow touched his chest, she jumped away. She'd thought the shirt was only puffed from the position of his body; it wasn't. She put her fingers on the centre of his shirt and felt soft, spongy flesh. Anne undid the buttons and pulled the shirt open. Franklin's sternum was swollen into a round, pink bubo. She pulled the shirt all the way open. There were even larger buboes under his armpits.

'So bright,' he muttered.

The front door was open. The head of an eight-point buck decorated the hall. In the living room, a chandelier with crystal pendants lit more heads, a rifle rack, oils of sporting scenes, religious samplers, Navajo rugs, and a glass case of silver jewellery.

There was no point in calling out to the Momoas through the air masks; the men could communicate by radio only among themselves. In the airtight suit, Youngman felt clammy and warm. The men looked like visitors from another planet; Youngman felt like one. He picked up the phone.

'It's dead.'

'There's our answer,' Chee said. 'Have any bad storms up here lately?'

'Couple days ago.'

'There's a pole down. End of mystery.'

'Probably.' Putting the phone down, Youngman's foot nudged an open bottle of Pepsi from under the sofa. There was still some soda in the bottle and some had dried on the carpet. 'Let's go on.'

The downstairs bathroom was empty and neat. In Joe Momoa's den, on his desk, was a pile of first-of-the-month bill payments ready to be mailed. Youngman looked in an aquarium tank. The big fish looked healthy. Two small fish, half-eaten, floated on the surface. The aerator bubbled. He tapped fish food into the water.

No one was in the kitchen. The doctor opened the copper-tinted refrigerator.

'Food's fresh. Not even the milk is separated.'

The copper-tinted cabinets were polished, butcher block tables wiped free of the smallest crumb.

'Bear meat.' Begay looked in the freezer. 'That's the way to live.'

'Look at this.' Youngman pulled a blood-stained rag out of a trash can.

'So?' Chee said. 'That could be from anything. Maybe the bear.'

By then, Youngman was already through the louvered doors of the laundry alcove. He opened the top of the dryer and started flinging clothes on to the kitchen floor.

'What the hell are you up to?' Chee asked.

'We'll see.'

Youngman spread the clothes over the tiled floor. Two shirts and a dress were discoloured brown.

'That could be anything, could be rust marks,' Chee said. 'Right, doctor?'

'Possible.' The doctor put the stained clothes in a sack.

'Damn right,' Chee said. 'If Joe comes in and sees this mess, he's going to have your hide, Duran. Of course, he'll have to stand in line.'

They turned to a sound at the kitchen's outside door. Youngman heard a sigh of relief over his radio, he couldn't tell who from. Begay opened the door. A collie entered, its tail low and wagging, shuffled to a empty food bowl, and returned to the men.

'Momoa's?'

'His wife's,' Youngman said. 'Joe wouldn't let a work dog in the house any more than he'd let a horse.'

The collie sniffed the clothes on the floor. As if it were reminded of something, the dog started whining and backing into the hall. Three or four times, the dog went back and forth between the kitchen and the hall.

'Oh, shit,' Begay said. 'What a bitch. Oh, Christ.'

For the first time, Youngman felt a bond with the Navajo patrolman. A feeling, a certainty, that the house wasn't empty.

The dog led them to the second floor and along a carpeted hall to a master bedroom, where Mrs Momoa lay peacefully dead on a king-size bed. Her dress was puffed into strange shapes from the buboes around her neck and under her arms. A jar of aspirin and a thermometer were on the night table.

In another bedroom decorated with quarterhorse trophies they found Joe Jr. Because he was naked, they saw immediately the buboes around his groin. His forearms and the back of his neck were bandaged. The doctor turned him over and removed the bandages. There was no skin on the flesh underneath.

'Like the Hopi boy—'

'Shut up,' the doctor told Begay. 'Bring the lamp closer.'

'Those are like the wounds on the boy,' Youngman said.

'I know,' the doctor snapped. 'I did the autopsy. Let me . . . Very unusual. Unique. These are actually a great many crater-like wounds. Damn! They cleaned them, otherwise we'd get a little of the saliva to go by. Deputy, you're such a hotshot, maybe you can tell me what kind of animal makes a bite like this.'

'Bats.'

The doctor gaped up through his visor.

'What the hell are you talking about?' Chee pushed Youngman away from the bed.

'Whatever bit Joe Jr, the horses here, and Isa Loloma attacked them in the dark and didn't leave any tracks on the ground. The only animal I know that flies and has teeth is bats.'

'You ever seen a bat bite like that, ever?' Chee demanded.

'No,' Youngman admitted.

'Then you don't know what you're talking about. Do you?'

'I don't know, but I'm sure.'

'You're sure about an impossibility,' the doctor interrupted. 'The immediate concern here is how long ago you saw these people, Deputy.'

'Four days.'

'This is the most virulent form of plague I've ever seen, if you're correct. If he is correct, Mr Chee, you've got problems.'

After searching through the rest of the house, they carried the two bodies in sacks to the helicopter and went on to the renovated barn. The upper section had been re-done as a panelled rec room with ping pong and billiard tables. In a place of honour was a framed photo of Joe with Senator Goldwater. Joe himself was in the bathroom beside a toilet full of vomit. His limbs were limp, but his torso was still stiff from rigor mortis. Chee commented optimistically on the lack of buboes, and the doctor pointed out black spots on Momoa's face. Capillary haemorrhage, another sign of plague.

'The young man, the one with the wounds, died first. I'd guess that he transmitted fleas to the others,' the doctor said as they dragged Joe into the rec room to stuff him in a bag. 'As long as they didn't have any visitors, we may get by.'

'Of course, we'll get by,' Chee agreed.

'Like hell,' Youngman said.

He stood in front of the maps on the rec room walls. Most of the maps were Joe's Mormon items: Biblical Israel, the diaspora of the Jews, and the travels of Brigham Young. On another wall was a large topological map of the reservation. The Painted Desert was in the middle, the Black Mesa at the top, Dinnebito Wash to the north-west, Antelope Mesa to the east.

'You've got three stiffs here,' he marked Dinnebito Wash with the pool chalk, 'seven here,' he marked Shongopovi on the Black Mesa, 'one here,' he marked the desert east of Gilboa where the boy had been attacked. 'And one more here you don't even know about,' he added a mark for Abner south-east of Gilboa, 'because he died from loss of blood before he got a chance to develop any disease.'

Youngman connected the marks, drawing a rough equilateral triangle about thirty-five miles to a side.

'In other words, in an area around five hundred square miles something you can't even identify has killed or fatally infected twelve people and you two are still doing charades. Have you contacted Phoenix yet? Washington? Anyone?'

'No,' the doctor admitted unhappily.

'There's no cause for alarm,' Chee said.

'Then take your space suit off. Go ahead.'

'Don't be childish. What I meant was, there's no reason to start a scare. We have a few deaths here, not anything else.'

'You have an epidemic. Just the start of one, but that's what you've got. Not "a problem", doctor. Not just a few deaths, because there'll be more rolling in. Damn it, look at that map. You tell me there hasn't been any plague activity among animals and the truth is you don't know what animals are spreading plague. Spreading it already over half my reservation. Yours'll be next. Quarantine the whole Hopi Nation, is that your answer? Quarantine the Navajo Nation? Arizona and New Mexico, too?'

'You're a panic starter, that's what you are.'

'Yes. That's exactly what I'm going to do, unless we make a deal.'

'Ah. You want us to fly you out to Albuquerque, put a little money your way?'

'No. You assume only the family here was infected, and I think you're right. But someone was supposed to be here. Whites, in fact, a group of campers who were going to bunk here and fish Joe's stream. They didn't make it, or one of those campers, a nurse, would have tended the family.'

'She couldn't have helped them,' the doctor said.

'Well, she would have given them more than aspirin.

Anyway, she isn't here and she hasn't checked in any place else, and that puts her,' he pointed to the middle of the triangle, 'there. There are seven people in that van. I want both your copters in the desert tomorrow looking for them. From then on I shut up, that's the deal.'

'You're crazy. We had two cases of plague of our own up towards Moenkopi yesterday—'

'Oh, you did? You didn't tell me. So that makes it fourteen cases and, what, about six hundred square miles. And you were keeping that a secret?'

'Those copters have to be on hand for emergencies. Not running errands for you.'

'But that's the deal. Otherwise, I'll call every health department official in the state tomorrow. By the way, why do you want to keep this such a secret?'

'Begay,' Chee stepped back, and the patrolman stepped towards Youngman.

'Begay,' Youngman said, 'come any closer and I'll rip that cute cloth helmet right off your head. Want to take a chance on plague just for Chairman Chee?' While Begay hesitated, Youngman drew a revolver from the deep pocket of his coveralls. 'Joe always kept a loaded Colt 44 behind the dryer in his laundry room. He believed in safety.'

'Okay,' Chee shrugged, 'it looks like we have a Mexican standoff.'

'No, it looks like you give me two copters.'

'A compromise. One copter, up until an emergency.'

'Both, until we find them. Look, Chee, I know when

I've hit a nerve and right now your nerves are singing. What are you trying to hide? You can tell me, we're on the same team, right?'

'Okay,' Chee put a glove up, 'just to shut you up. And I mean about everything. About tonight or anything else, you know nothing and you say nothing.'

'Two copters at dawn at Gilboa. Only pilots and doctors.'

'Excuse me,' the doctor interrupted, 'we have ten minutes of air left in our tanks, and you did say there were four members of this family. We've only found three.'

'We'll check the garage downstairs,' Youngman said. 'After you.'

The garage was empty, but lit. The end wall was padded for handgun practice; a fresh paper target hung from a clothesline. Tyre chains, fan belts, and wrenches arranged by size filled up the side walls. Joe's lovingly polished pick-up sat in the middle of the floor, along with a BMW cycle.

'Ben's Harley is gone,' Youngman noticed.

'Then he left before the others got sick.'

'No, someone had to go for help with the phone wires down.'

'You were the only one to say there might be sick folks up here.'

'He didn't make it.' Youngman was still thinking. He stayed slightly apart from the others, with his hand on the gun. 'Ben used to work for the telephone company. He stopped to fix the wires.'

He didn't bother adding that the phone was dead. Their air tanks were running out. After one circuit around the house, they returned to the copter on the lawn and dumped Joe's body inside with his wife and son.

'We forgot to turn the lights out.' Begay looked back at the house. 'Weird. We should of turned the lights out.'

Begay was right. The lights in the garage, the rec room, kitchen, every bedroom and hallway had been left on by the Momoas. The house blazed against the dark hills.

The collie had followed the bodies to the copter and sat forlornly by the skids.

'Everything's under control here, doc, wouldn't you say?' Chee remarked.

The question was an order. Youngman, his gun on his lap, was fascinated by Chee's desperation.

'Fourteen deaths in two days is not "under control",' the doctor said softly.

'With co-operation, though, we can handle it.'

Through his visor, Youngman watched the doctor's eyes move from Chee to him and to the dog.

'You better put that dog in a sack,' he said.

'The sack's airtight,' Begay protested. 'He'll suffocate.'

'That's the idea. Dogs have fleas.'

By flying over the hill road on the way back, they found Ben Momoa. His Harley Davidson 750 was leaning against a telephone pole. Ben hung by a repairman's belt from the top of the pole. In the helicopter's lights, his clothes shredded and black with blood, he might have been the sacrifice of a gruesome rite.

Chee himself went down in a sling to hoist Ben up.

'Maybe I can do the same thing for you sometime, Duran,' he shouted up.

The moths heard them coming, heard the net of whispers cast before their coming. Some of the insects dropped to the ground and others began desperate evasive manoeuvres. But the bats passed by them, ignoring the moths, listening for the echo of a different prey altogether.

The inner ear of the bats contained, in fact, two separate organs of sense: one for mid-air orientation, another for hearing. The one for hearing, the spiralled cochlea, was proportionately about a thousand times longer than a human's and rich in 'trigger' hairs. The hairs stirred to the slightest echo, which was simultaneously interpreted as an insect or an obstacle or another bat, opposite from a human system which heard a voice clearer than its shadow. And when the echoes were reflected from something large and warm and alive, from the Food, the cries and the echoes increased to machine gun rapidity.

Mixed with the echoes was the bleat of a goat.

There were four goats tethered to a tamarisk tree, three of them asleep. The fourth shifted its hooves nervously, ears pricked to the rustle of the wind. As the rustle settled down, so did the goat and nibbled at the tree's bark. Some grass even grew around the tree; wherever a tamarisk stood there was bound to be water. Then the goat backed up as something hopped towards it. Curious, the goat thrust its nose forward and the thing hopped into the air and flew.

By now, more than a hundred bats were on the ground. Membranes folded, resting their weight on their hind legs and the wrists of their wings, they hopped or ran rapidly around the tree. There was a feeding order and there were preferences. Better young and tender Food than old, better pregnant and blood-gorged Food than male, best the oestrous Food with an overflowing scent that turned hunger into a frenzy. The big bats, the females, surged forward. The Food thrust its nose out again, slit eyes bulging, and the nearest bat stared back in return first at the eyes and then at a dark patch on the Food's shoulder before leaping, stroking the air twice and landing on the patch. Two incisors scooped away hair and skin, and the bat's long red tongue darted to meet the blood filling the crater and tinging the air with warm sweetness. The outer edges of the tongue curled down around two grooves on the underside of the tongue, forming the sucking channels. A second bat landed, lighter than a touch, on the other shoulder. The Food ran back and forth on the end of its rope. The other Food remained sleeping as blankets gathered over them. More incisors bit. Ground and air seemed to close in on the goats and envelop them. The first bat was already releasing a black, pitchy urine, and the rest of the bats swarmed to tap the Food. Filling themselves, they paid no notice to the tamarisk tree and the hanging bulbs that bathed them in ultra-violet light, or to the Land-Rover sitting thirty yards away, where Paine opened a window vent just enough to insert the barrel of an air gun. Running the length of the barrel was an ultra-violet-sensitive sniper scope. The cross-hairs rested first on one bat and then on another, leisurely choosing the right specimens for dissection. From their activity, the bats didn't seem to be affected by plague, but only the scalpel and microscope would tell.

It would take hours for all the bats to feed. He could pick his shots.

Chapter Six

Youngman kept seeing the bright lights of the Momoa house through his sleep. He woke in the dark remembering the red-haired man who wanted part of Abner. Who asked Frank about bats.

Paine was from Chee. Chee knew all along.

By sunrise, Youngman had covered his jeep with brush on a hill about a mile out of Gilboa. He lay on his stomach under a mesquite tree and watched through field-glasses.

The helicopters came straight out of the sun, making Youngman's eyes water. They landed in tandem on the street in front of the hogan and two figures emerged from each copter, wearing white and carrying medical bags. They came out of the shed ten seconds later holding handguns. Four uniformed Navajo patrolmen joined them from the copters; Youngman recognized Begay. They ran to the trading post, where they stayed five minutes. Then they returned to the copters, climbed on, and took off. The copters circled low around Gilboa, trying to pick up tyre tracks and not finding any because Youngman had covered them. After a while, they quit and headed north towards the mesa in case he'd gone that way.

Youngman drove back to his hogan. He wasn't feeling

clever. He should have extracted Chee's promise in public, or set the meeting place at a pueblo, or told Cecil what was up. Instead, he'd stupidly isolated himself in the middle of the desert.

The first thing he did was try to radio Cecil, only the Navajos had pocketed half the tubes from the radio, so he threw his rifle and bed roll into the jeep and drove on to the trading post. Selwyn was in his bathrobe at the counter. He lifted his hand proudly and showed off a dead fly.

'Where's your radio transmitter, Selwyn?'

'Broken. I showed it to those Navajos and they tried to fix it, but they couldn't. It's broken for good, I guess. You just missed them. They're looking for you.'

'Give me some rifle shells and some .44's, too.' Youngman still had Joe's Colt. 'And Spam, a six pack, and salt tablets.'

Selwyn swept the fly away and started filling the counter.

'Regular radio's working. I heard about that fire at Momoa's place.'

'What fire?'

'Whole family burned up,' Selwyn dusted off the beer cans. 'Last night. You didn't hear about that? Well, you wouldn't care, you hated that bastard as much as me.'

Youngman wiped a display case and squinted through the glass.

'You still got those transistor radios. I'll take one and some batteries. Put it on my account.'

'Sure, what else? You know, Youngman, I hope some-one invents cash soon.'

Youngman took the goods and went out to the porch.

'Been up since five,' Selwyn followed him, bathrobe flopping around bare feet. 'One of the first signs of growing old, insomnia. You in trouble, Youngman?'

The deputy was searching the sky in case one of the copters doubled back. The shadows of dawn were already drying up.

'You in trouble, huh?'

'Yeah, but no more than anyone else. Take care of yourself, old boy.' Youngman stuffed his purchases except for the transistor radio into his bed roll and slid behind the wheel. 'I always meant to tell you, nothing wrong with your daughters. Keep their windows shut tonight.'

'What?'

But the Indian's jeep was gathering speed, headed on the road west.

Anne listened to the van radio through the shattered windshield.

She'd buried Franklin in the hour before dawn and spent a day's worth of strength. She'd spent the next day's strength simply washing herself with gasoline siphoned from the fuel tank. By now, they had to be searching for her, though. By now, Youngman was coming.

The radio accompanied her reverie.

. . . As you all know, yesterday's Rain Dance at Shongopovi was marred by the tragic death of seven elders at the pueblo. At first it was feared that the deceased were victims of swine flu, which is particularly dangerous to persons of advanced age. Autopsies showed, however, that the seven died of food poisoning from spoiled foods left in their ceremonial chamber. Other tragic news comes from Dinnebito Wash, where the popular family of Joe Momoa died in a fire at their ranch home. The fire started in the basement, according to official spokesmen of the Tuba City Fire Department, and then spread rapidly through the ventilating system. Four persons died. And now here's a message from Hubbell's Trading Post, where you'll always find . . .

Heat waves began percolating from the sand. Anne's knees were cut up from scrambling after lizards. Tentatively, she felt her armpits and groin for swelling. Nothing yet. It was funny, she thought. She'd always been aware of the endemic plague in the desert and not once had she seen a real case. Then a week before she leaves the desert, a man dies of plague before her eyes and she doesn't even recognize the signs. The lassitude. Fever. Buboes. The word 'bubo' was funny. Like bauble. An adornment.

Motionless, she again experienced the sense that she was vanishing into the desert. Part of her found this disorienting but comforting. This 'oneness' was the Hopi Way, and she was amused that she'd only felt it on the point of death, and she considered that this might be the secret of the Hopis' super-religiosity, because they were always on the point of extinction.

Another part of her continued to calculate survival. Usually, there was rain within two or three days after a Snake Dance. It was the time of year, of course. With enough water to drink and cloud cover, she might be able to walk the desert. On the other hand, it might be wiser to collect as much rain water as she could and stay by the van since that was what Youngman would be looking for. He'd be coming from Dinnebito Wash if he'd gone there to meet her at Momoa's. Only, Momoa was dead.

The sand rippled. A small mirage lapped at the two new graves. By noon, she knew, the whole desert would look like an ocean, like the ocean it once was a million years ago. Momoa was dead, she repeated to herself. Burned. So if she and Franklin and the others had reached the ranch and bunked over, they would have died in a fire anyway.

The radio went on, draining the last of the van's battery.

... That was Johnny Cash's latest. Johnny's going to be at the All Indian Powwow in Flagstaff, by the way, and you're not going to want to miss that. A time to get together with old friends and make new ones. Hey, who says you can't get a good recapped tyre for half the price you'd pay for a new one ...

A skink twisted its head to study Anne. She didn't have the energy to reach for her fishing pole. If Momoa was dead, how would Youngman know she didn't get out of the desert? She tried to concentrate, but half her mind was wandering on its own. Answers slipped away from her grasp.

... A health advisory note I want to pass along. Officials say they haven't determined the source of the food poisoning incident on the mesa. There may be more cases. This is serious. Signs to look out for, they say, are stomach pains, dizziness, fever, or any suspicious marks or swellings, or throwing up or diarrhoea. If you have or you know anyone who has these symptoms, contact the medical clinics in Ship Rock or Window Rock or here in Tuba City at once. Say, wouldn't you like to get in on the CB radio run ...

No mention of a missing camping party. No mention of rain. It occurred to her it was important for her to be rescued, not only for her own sake but to warn about the plague. About the bats. Bats didn't carry rodent fleas so the bats and the plague were unrelated, but ... The effort of thought was tiring her out. It was so much easier to watch the growing mirage, to lose herself in it, to let her mind float. Hallucination was a sign of dehydration; a lack of water changed the whole chemical balance of the body, but it was so seductive. She enjoyed thinking she might see Youngman coming, wading towards her through a dusty surf.

Her mind went on in a crueler direction. There was a story Youngman once told her about a young man who went to the Maski Canyon, arriving at night at a fine, big pueblo built underneath the ground. Smoke rose from chimneys, children ran up and down ladders and beacon fires burned on the roofs. The young man was not only welcomed in this strange pueblo beneath the earth, he was washed and fed and taken to a great dance hall where festivities were just beginning. He'd never seen such laughing and dancing, and beautiful girls who ran around singing and joking, pointing to each other and shouting, 'Hapa! Hapa! Is! Is!' 'Dead! Dead! This! This!' The fun went on for most of the night, and when he was tired he was led to bed by the two most beautiful girls. They removed his clothes and theirs. He kissed their lips and breasts and spread their legs, making love to each girl in turn until they all fell asleep, the girls lying on top of him. He woke, shielding his eyes because the daylight was much brighter than he expected, and he saw that the reason was there was no ceiling. The room which was so fine at night was now filled with sand. Parts of the wall were collapsed and the windows were broken, and bits of the rafters that were left were falling down in the wind on to the floor. He sat up, and bones fell from his chest. The entire room was full of skeletons, two of them embracing him in their arms. In fear and disgust, he broke their clutch and ran . . .

Youngman wasn't coming, she told herself. No one was, not in time. Not until she was something to be shovelled instead of loved. Her head rocked back and forth and she heard the clicking of lizard claws running over the bus. She didn't hear the fading voice of the radio.

> ... Another health advisory to pass along. A jack rabbit turned in to health authorities has proven to have an animal form of plague. Hopi Deputy Young-man Duran turned in the rabbit and he is now being sought by authorities so they can administer necessary injections of vaccine. This is an infectious disease and people are advised not to approach the deputy, only to inform authorities of his whereabouts ...

Instead of staying on flat ground, Youngman deflated his tyres and crossed as many dunes as he could on the chance he might be able to spot the van. Or smoke signals or the glint of a mirror. Or vultures. From time to time, he turned on the transistor radio to monitor what Chee was doing, and also because he knew if the campers came out of the desert Chee would broadcast their arrival. The jeep whined, sliding sideways down through mesquite, chewing the brush in its wheels.

Youngman felt no bitterness towards Chee for lies and betrayal; it was as pointless as the desert being bitter at the sun. Survival was not a matter of morals. A snake didn't debate the ethics of eating a ground squirrel; it was eat or die. The Navajos, 135,000 of them, were surviving. The Hopis, 6000 of them, were not. They could blame the Navajos, blame the pahans, blame witches. It was the desert, their own home, that was killing them. It was a changing desert, drier since the Navajos and whites stole the rivers, seized water the same way a snake bit.

Staying alive supplied its own morality. By that standard, Chee was a hero and Youngman was, perhaps, a coward. That's what they called him in the Army. Heap big coward.

The jeep would only do fifty. Youngman kept his foot down, relying on his steering. Running away, it could be termed, he thought. Avoiding the responsibility of falling into lockstep once again. That's why he'd come back to the desert in the first place, to escape a world he didn't fit into. Probably, he admitted to himself, that was why he'd fought quarantine. Not from courage but because the threat of confinement, any kind of confinement after the years in the stockade, was enough to make him shake like a boy. He wasn't even brave enough to face quarantine knowing that he had the answer. The answer to the bites, the running blood, the lack of tracks, the lights at Momoa's, the night Abner died. He had it, and his only solace for not turning back was that no one would believe him because it was impossible. An impossible nightmare.

At midday, the sun seemed to pulse yellow and huge. Not only shadows, objects themselves shrank. It was a time when even lizards crouched under rocks. Prairie dogs and sand boas dug deep away from the heat.

Youngman was crossing a dry, alkali hole when he

heard the jeep's engine block crack, and he shifted to neutral and rolled an extra hundred yards. The hood was too hot to touch so he kicked it open. The block was close to red hot, and crawling under the jeep on his back he found a hole in the radiator that a rock had punched and drained the radiator dry.

He rolled away and closed his eyes. Gilboa was thirty miles to the east, the mesa forty miles north. There was a federal highway forty miles west. He'd done it. He'd finally reached nowhere, with no way out but to follow his own tracks.

The only question was, was it worth it?

Hayden Paine stood on the roof of his Land-Rover.

Field-glasses accentuated heat waves. Saguaro cactus seemed to undulate and dance, mesquite and yucca became floating islands, a canyon twenty miles off turned into a stately sailing ship standing above its own reflection. Occasionally, he thought he caught true movement out of the corner of his eye. He'd turn the glasses and the movement would fade, a chimera. Besides, his interest was the canyons. He hadn't come to them as much as he'd been drawn. Each sunset, he'd tracked the path of the bats on his oscilloscope. Each sunrise, he'd driven another ten miles on a predicted path and tracked the bats again on the flight homeward. Studying the black and brick-red escarpments of the canyons, his excitement grew.

He climbed down to the table and isolation box he'd

set up on the ground. His trap of the night before was successful. Four goats, bought from a Navajo near Tuba City, were dead, drained until their blood pressure failed. Paine, in return, had killed four bats.

The isolation box was a simple one without air filters, good only for pathology. Two latex gloves with accordion wrists reached through a lucite panel to syringes and dissecting tools. Pins spread the dead bat's wings. Fleas hopped against the walls, because a dead host was no host at all. A colourful sun umbrella shaded Paine while he worked.

For an hour, he painstakingly examined the bat, shaving the fur in search of swellings and extracting blood specimens for analysis. Human plague normally began when the usual rodent population host died from animal plague. The fleas sought new hosts. But the bats weren't dying off; if anything, they seemed to be flourishing. Despite the imprisoned fleas and other bat parasites hopping around it, the bat in the glove box showed no signs of illness. Was it possible for an animal to play the role of a plague bacillus host and itself remain healthy? Was it conceivable that the vampires, drawing blood from different human populations, had picked up plague antibodies in a natural system of inoculation? One answer was that the same bats that had spread fatal *derriengue* in Venezuela were themselves vigorous and thriving.

The desert canyons drew his attention again. He'd always hunted vampires before in the semi-tropics among lush vegetation. Paine assembled his maps and carried them on to the Land-Rover, where the heat of the truck burned through the soles of his boots. The temperature was 120°F in the shade. Bats could survive a cave temperature of close to 100°F, but there had to be enough moisture to keep the membranes of their wings from drying out. The Geological Survey's topological map showed only a labyrinth of rugged, apparently barren canyons that, according to one map supplied by Chee, were called Cañon de Maski. He swung around slowly, taking in the Painted Desert through his field-glasses.

Heat waves had settled into a steady simmer as if the sand was on the point of bursting into flame. Straight cacti were twisted into corkscrews. To the north-east, the Black Mesa was a thin black line drawn in a blue sky over the horizon. Directly to the east, something was running. It was the same moving object Paine had seen before he examined the bat. He played with the focus. Sometimes the object would dissolve altogether into thin air, then it would coalesce for a second and be almost distinct. It was definitely coming closer and it was doing so on two legs. Paine understood the mechanics of the desert. A man could run in desert heat without water for one hour before prostration dropped him. In the high altitude of Arizona, maybe forty minutes. So the man wasn't there, Paine was seeing a mirage. Even as he decided so, the figure broke into floating spots and disappeared. Paine stared through the glasses for another five minutes. The man was gone.

The heat on the Rover was unbearable. Paine retreated to swallow two salt tablets with a pint of water and to study his other maps, which were in a plastic binder inscribed *Earth Resources Observation Systems – Landsat II, III*. The maps themselves were splotches of colour on acetate, undecipherable unless laid over a second map of man-made boundaries. They were among the most expensive maps ever charted. The power companies had paid more for them than Chee was paying Paine and the truth was that, by the maps, an investment of millions could rest on Paine. Another truth was that he would have done the work for nothing.

Paine had put the maps away when he found himself unconsciously raising his field-glasses to the east. The running man was a mile off. He was covering ground in long, easy strides, a pack of some kind strapped to his back, a wide brimmed hat shading his face. From time to time, heat waves or terrain would rise to his chest but he kept coming, his arms swinging loosely. Once, he dissolved into blue, only to reappear closer than before. Paine could see him without glasses. A dark, lean man. The pack, a bed roll wrapped around a rifle. He kept coming, shifting against the distorted background, legs rhythmically pumping. Following the Land-Rover's tracks, Paine realized. Skirting a dune, past a withered barrel cactus. Paine recognized the face.

The Indian only slowed down the last twenty yards, looking at Paine silently enough to remind Paine that they were enemies, before he slumped in the shade of the Rover.

Paine had waited too long. If he'd seen a vehicle approaching over the desert, he would have driven off; a man on foot he simply hadn't believed. And this was the last man Paine wanted to see. The Indian closed his eyes and luxuriantly breathed the relatively cool air of the shade through his mouth. The soles of his boots were punctured by thorns and stained with blood.

Paine was nervous. The damn Indian had used the silent treatment before. At last, the Indian sat up to remove his boots.

'What do you want?' Paine was brusque. 'What are you following me for?'

'You have a cold beer?' Youngman asked.

He washed his feet with one beer and drank two other cans. Including the six-pack he'd drunk up on the run, he was still minus five pounds.

'Paine, you look like you're seeing a ghost.'

'You should be one. I saw you out there two hours ago.'

'And you didn't come after me?'

'I thought you were a mirage.'

'You hoped I was one. Well, don't get uptight. I'm happy enough to see you.'

Youngman's laugh was at himself. It reinforced Paine's suspicion that he was constantly underestimating the deputy. Obviously, Chee had too, because Duran was scheduled to be locked up this morning. The idea of a man escaping on foot across the Painted Desert did amuse Paine.

'How long could you have run?'

'Maybe five more steps. How far is it to that table?'

'I was just doing a wildlife study—'

Youngman got to his feet and walked to the shaded

table. Paine followed him anxiously. Chee said Duran knew nothing, but Chee also said Duran was an ignorant drunkard, a typical reservation Indian.

The bat was still spread out in the glove box. Its wings had dried into dark parchment around which were laid the organs of a gutted stomach cavity. The stomach itself looked like a worm.

'Mind?' Youngman asked.

Paine shrugged.

Youngman inserted his hands into the gloves and picked up the scalpels in the box. He peeled back the bat's lips, exposing two broad incisors that filled half the upper jaw. The rest of the jaws were taken up by heavy, dagger-shaped canine teeth; the bottom incisors and back molars were practically non-existent. Youngman skewered the stomach on a scalpel and ran it across the dead bat's teeth, which sliced the stomach in two.

'It was the teeth.' Youngman smiled. 'It was the teeth I couldn't figure out.'

The Indian knew. How, Paine couldn't start to guess. He didn't understand his own reactions because he thought he would have killed anyone who interfered and instead he felt as much relief as anger. He balanced between the two emotions.

'Why did you follow me, Duran?'

'I'll tell you while I drive.'

Anne was poised on the end of the three-metre board, from which she could see all the swimming pools in

Phoenix so that the entire city seemed to be set in turquoise, and she remembered a story by John Cheever called *The Swimmer* in which a man set out to swim a Connecticut county by following a line of swimming pools.

'Jump!' her father called from the outdoor bar. 'Come on, honey!'

Tables were set out beside the pool for guests and a mariachi band played in the garden. Anne noticed that her mother had switched from roses to a rock garden of cactus and succulents. Water lilies floated on the pool, the same as they'd done for her graduation party. This was her graduation party, she remembered.

'You have to jump, dear,' her mother called.

Of course, her parents wanted her to take that job at the Heard Museum downtown. There were wonderful kachina dolls at the Heard. Anne considered using her medical training on one of the reservations, though. Indians were fascinating.

She dived, flying on widespread arms until she plunged into a brilliant blue pool, tasting the pure water, watching the lily pads float overhead like spots before the eyes. Leisurely, she came to the surface and pulled herself out of the pool. The top of her bathing suit had come off, but no one seemed to notice, which struck her as odd. She pushed her wet hair away from her eyes and saw Youngman at a table with a big, red-haired guy. They had a tall drink waiting for her so she joined them.

'I love you,' Youngman said. 'I'm taking you out of here, any place you want to go.'

This was flattering but the party had only begun. The other man put a wet towel around her.

'Haven't you got a dry one?' she asked.

'You need a wet one.'

Ridiculous, she was soaked. Still, she didn't want to make a scene, and Youngman seemed so pleased. He smiled so seldom and now he was gushing like a boy.

'Drink a little bit more, just sip it. You're going to be all right and as soon as you can go, we're heading out. Just you and me, okay? Right now, we have to get your temperature down.'

'How did you get here?' Anne asked. It wasn't like her father to invite Indians to social occasions.

'The smoke from the fire. You led us here. You did a great job.'

Chatter mixed with the tinkling of glasses while the mariachis strolled between the tables. Anne was afraid someone would request 'Guadalajara'. The song always made her dizzy.

'Turn off the radio,' Youngman said, and the other man went into the rock garden, where one of the guests had inappropriately parked a van. Her mother would be furious. 'His name is Paine.'

'I don't see any signs of infection. Besides the broken fingers and heat prostration, she's okay. If we can just get her fever down. Lucky she didn't get more sunburn or she couldn't have made it,' Paine said.

'She's lost about twelve pounds in body fluid too. I've seen her looking better,' Youngman tried to joke.

'Thank you.' She covered her breasts.

'No.' Youngman took the towel away and replaced it with a fresh, wet one.

'The others.' Anne looked, embarrassed, at the guests.

'Dead. You buried them. We found the camp. You're the only one left. Thank God, we found you when we did.'

'I didn't think you were coming.' Anne knew how sensitive Youngman could be about mixing with whites.

'I should have come sooner.'

Anne was concerned because Youngman seemed so worried. His face was dusty and haggard, and the whites of his eyes were red.

'Are you all right?' she asked.

'So far, I haven't caught it. That's another reason we have to get out of here.'

Paine tried to ask her a question but there was a commotion as all the other guests left, taking their chairs and tables away. She was confused, trying to find her father. No one was even saying goodbye. She didn't want to be left alone.

'Can you hear me, Anne?' Youngman asked her. 'Can you answer us?'

She nodded. Anything to keep him from going.

'Was it bats?'

One of the departing women turned and started screaming. It was the reverend's wife, screaming so loudly that Anne put her hands over her ears but the scream filled her brain, overflowed it, and came out of her own mouth.

The late afternoon was strangely cool and quiet. A breeze filtered through the mesh walls of Paine's field tent. He called it a 'cocoon'. Growing out of the back of the Land-Rover the way it did, Anne thought the resemblance was more to a queen bee. She lay on a bed roll, sipping weak tea, her head propped on a specimen case. Paine was scrambling powdered eggs on a Coleman stove. Youngman stayed beside her.

'Tomorrow you'll be in good enough shape to get out of here.' He took her hand. 'And that's just what we're going to do. Far away. Paine's driving us to the highway tomorrow.'

'You changed your mind.'

'Yeah, and all it took was you almost getting killed. If you still want me to go with you.'

Against her drawn face, Anne's eyes were larger than ever. Almost lost in one of Paine's shirts, she looked more like a child than ever. Youngman thought a hug would break her.

'You're sure?' she asked.

'My reservation days are over and I'm going to join the living. I finally figured it out. You're my ticket from here because I love you enough to be where you are, wherever that is. Look what happens when I let you out of my sight.'

'I knew you'd come for me, Youngman, really I did.' She took his hand.

'Just relax. Tomorrow, we'll make a fresh start out of here, to begin with.'

Paine joined them with two plates of curdled looking eggs. He hadn't wanted any company. On the other hand, the presence of the deputy and the girl made Paine aware of the loneliness he'd lived in so long. He was drawn to them the way a permanently cold person might idly be drawn to a fire, realizing he could see the glow without feeling the warmth.

'How did you guess?' He handed Youngman a plate.

'The answer wasn't hard. It was just impossible. The attacks were made by a night animal that didn't leave tracks, an animal that could fly to the top of a telephone pole and had teeth. But that kind of animal doesn't kill people, not with teeth like that. Never saw any animal with teeth like that. But I thought about a family of people dying and huddling inside a house with all the lights on and I remembered about a Mr Paine asking a deputy down at Five House Butte if he'd seen any bats. From then on I knew I was right even if I couldn't prove it. You proved it for me.'

'We have a lot to thank you for,' Anne told Paine.

'Like hell,' Youngman interrupted. 'He's just involved in one of Walker Chee's rip-offs. You think he's doing this for the poor Indians? To clean up a reservation? No, but to tidy things up for a new stripmine or keep the tourists rolling in, now that's worth Mr Paine's hire.

That's all he is. A hired man. You tell me if I'm wrong, Paine.'

Before Paine answered, his radio came alive with call numbers. When he tried to ignore the signal the radio called him by name even more insistently. He glanced at the Indian before moving to the table where the radio sat. Although the signal was ragged with static, Youngman already recognized Walker Chee's voice.

'Get back here to Window Rock,' Chee said.

'You called me at the wrong time.'

'That's an order. We'll set up some defence systems. I've explained everything to my friend Mr Piggot and he'll get us all the equipment we need.'

Paine turned with the mike so that he could watch the deputy and the girl. The girl listened intensely, the deputy smiled in a different direction.

'Like what?' Paine asked.

'Anything. Piggot has connections.'

'Like what?' Paine repeated.

'We'll set up a defence perimeter . . .'

'Around the desert?'

'At special points. We'll get nets . . .'

'How high? How wide?'

'And arc lamps, floodlights . . .'

'Lights are where people are, they don't mind lights.'

'Let me finish,' Chee said. 'The big thing is we'll have small planes with DDT. As soon as radar picks up the bats . . .'

'It won't. Vampires fly under radar.'

'God damn it, we wouldn't be in this fix if you'd finished the fucking bats like you said you would.'

'I will.'

'You say that every day and every night is worse.'

'I've been tracking them. I'm getting close.'

There was a pause before Chee came on again.

'Where are you right now?'

'I can't say exactly.'

'But you're close to the bats, you said. Where do you think they are?'

'I can't be positive about that, either. But, I'd guess,' Paine watched Youngman's eyes slide towards him, 'Mansion Mesa.'

'Mansion Mesa. Okay, Paine, I'm ordering you to start for Window Rock now.'

'No.'

'You haven't been paid yet, Paine.'

'I haven't killed the bats yet. Signing off.'

'Paine—'

Paine flicked the receiver off and wrapped the mike cord around his hand.

'We're nowhere near Mansion Mesa,' Youngman said. 'That's forty miles south-east of here.'

'That's right.'

Paine ripped the mike cord from the radio.

'But now you can't tell them where the bats really are,' Anne said.

'Now no one can tell them.' Paine threw the mike as far as he could.

'That's all right.' Youngman poured himself some coffee. 'He can't tell them where to find me.'

'Youngman was right about you,' Anne told Paine. 'You're here for the companies. Well, I'd like to know just what company I should be grateful to for saving my life.'

'What does it matter?' Youngman shrugged. 'I don't care. I'm finished here. As soon as we get to the highway that'll be the end for us.' He lifted his mug. 'Cheers.'

Anne removed her hand from Youngman's. Momentarily, she felt as distant from him as she did from Paine. She was not distant, she thought. They were. Paine, large, a tan that was ghostly pale in contrast to Youngman's skin, hulking but somehow absent. Youngman, dark and lean, and encased in so much cynicism that he seemed almost untouchable. Together they'd rescued her and now she felt almost superfluous to either of them.

Youngman pulled his rifle close to his knee while Paine slipped a CO_2 cartridge into an air gun.

'You kill bats, that's what you do for a living?' Anne asked.

'Uh huh.'

'There's a good living in that? Bat killing?' Youngman asked.

'From Mexico south, pretty good.'

'And you kill them with that?' Youngman looked at the air gun.

'No. With that.' Paine pointed the gun at a red canister marked DANGER in English, French, and Spanish that leaned against the rear door of the Rover. 'Cyanogas.

211

That's if you have to go into the cave. You never go into the cave if you can help it. If you can help it, you get them through an old food source.'

'Like?'

'Cattle, usually. Bats will return to a herd they've already fed off. They sort of "own" different herds in a territorial way. You smear "Vampirol" on an old wound.'

'I like it.' Youngman lit a cigarette. 'Vampirol. Sounds like something for unwanted body hair.'

'It's honey and strychnine. It works, but it's a slow way of killing them.'

'Do you hate bats?' Anne asked.

Paine laid the gun down and went into the Rover. He returned with a bottle of Napoleon brandy and three paper cups.

'We're out of their usual flight path.' He filled the cups and gave one to Anne. 'Let's—'

'This is a party?' Youngman was amazed. 'What the hell makes you think I want to drink with you?'

'Sorry, Chee told me you were a wino.'

'What else?'

'A shiftless, ignorant reservation bum.' Paine held the cup out.

'You know what a piñon is? A white nut.'

'So?'

Paine kept the cup steady. Anne expected Youngman to push Paine's hand away, but instead he took the cup.

'Honey and strychnine, huh?'

'That's the easy way of doing it.'

Paine threw back his brandy in a swallow.

'Crazy, fucking pahan.' Youngman muttered and downed half of his cup.

'What's that?' Paine refilled his cup.

'I was just saying we get all kinds of white nuts around here. Usually, they want to bag a mountain lion or a wolf. First time I ever met one who was after bats.'

'You don't think much of them.'

'Never thought about them.'

'Think about them. Think about an animal that aerodynamically is more manoeuvrable than a fly. That possesses a system of echolocation more sophisticated than the navigational technology of a military bomber. That sees in the dark as well as a cat. That, unique in nature, has made the leap of efficiently converting the blood of other vertebrates into its own blood.'

'A hell of a salesman, isn't he?' Youngman made an aside to Anne.

'I'm not talking about just a drop of blood,' Paine said. 'When a wild vampire bat feeds, it can drink one and a half times its own weight in blood. Because of the anticoagulant in the vampire's saliva, its victim loses as much blood again in excess of what the bat drinks. Over a year, a single vampire can drain twenty-eight quarts of blood, the entire blood volume of a good cow, or of about six humans.'

'Is that so? How can any animal drink 150 per cent of its own weight and get off the ground?'

'They piss. They piss while they're drinking. The blood meal is absorbed by the cardiac region of the stomach and the blood fluid goes right on through.'

'There were these tarry stains around Abner and the horses that were attacked.'

'Piss.'

'Yeah, that's efficient,' Youngman laughed. 'I'll give the little fangers some credit. A little smelly.'

Paine smiled agreeably.

'You ought to go into a cave of vampires some time. One year in Mexico, I gassed a hundred caves. I killed over 55,000 vampires. Interesting killings.'

Anne studied the dark red of her brandy. It was Youngman who finally filled the silence.

'So what is it? You have a high boredom level or you're totally insane? A white man of your talents could make a million selling insurance. Why vampires?'

'The study of vampire bats—'

'You didn't say "study", you said "killing". Anne asked you before. You hate bats?'

Paine refilled Youngman's cup.

'It's a job. I'm a professional, a man for hire, you said so yourself.'

'What if Chee doesn't pay you? Doesn't that worry you?'

'He'll pay me. Pay me double when I'm through.'

Paine threw down another cup of brandy.

'Idiot Chee, trying to keep this secret,' Youngman remarked.

'No, no, he was just acting normally.'

'That's normal?'

'Seventy years ago there was an outbreak of plague in San Francisco. State officials refused to believe it. A federal investigator arrived and was beaten up by a mob. California only accepted help after Washington threatened to quarantine the whole state. That's normal.'

'But it's not normal for vampire bats to be here. Why are they?'

'Most bats around here migrate over the border by the seasons. Vampires were just south,' Paine answered evasively, 'and I suppose they finally joined in. Arizona, Texas, New Mexico have caves with millions of bats in each. It's a regular paradise for them.'

'For you, too, then. Funny how the bats and you showed up at the same time. And then the bats start spreading plague? That's one hell of a lot of coincidence. I mean, you're not exactly good luck, are you?'

'There's something I don't understand,' Anne said. 'I thought it was a fact that only rodent fleas could transmit plague.'

'It's a commonly known fact,' Paine said. 'Like only dogs carry rabies.'

'What's rabies got to do with plague?'

'Bats. Every year, hundreds of thousands of cattle die from a paralysis like hydrophobia, rabies. In 1950, the disease spread to Trinidad and it spread to people. They killed all the dogs on the island, but people still got it. In fact, it wasn't until vampire bats started attacking them in the daytime that people realized what the real source was, a little late for the eighty-nine victims already dead.'

'How did bats pick up rabies?' she asked.

'A wild animal they fed off. The interesting part was that the rabies changed in the bats to a slightly different variant of the disease. And that the majority of the rabid vampires were immune to the disease themselves.'

'I thought any animal with rabies died.'

'Then you see my point. Any other animal would. At any rate, you said that only rodent fleas carry plague. The truth is that dozens of different fleas are capable of carrying plague and those fleas can be found on man, monkeys, cats, dogs, camels, sheep, even birds. And bats. How could the vampires avoid becoming plague hosts here? Every warm-blooded animal is their food and plague is endemic to the animals of this area. When you consider the method of feeding, the oral contact, the profusion of blood and the attraction of blood for fleas—'

'Save it,' Youngman said. 'Save it for Chee and his friend Piggot, or the Army, or whoever has enough money to be worth scaring. You're wasting it on us.'

'But someone should be told,' Anne said. 'What about the Centre for Disease Control?'

'Yeah,' Youngman laughed, 'they did a bang-up job on Swine flu.'

'Chee is handling that kind of information flow,' Paine answered Anne. 'Anyway, even if they did get a team here from the CDC in Atlanta, they don't know how to handle vampires, and they'd end up trying to reach me in Mexico. I'm here already and I know where the bats are.'

'Well, I don't understand you! You talk about an epidemic of plague but we heard you send Chee the wrong way. Are you that crazy?'

Paine was dismayed. The convivial, nearly party air he thought they'd all been enjoying was fading all too suddenly under the force of the girl's outburst. He lifted his paper cup. There was nothing in it. When he set it down he did so clumsily because he was trying to avoid her angry stare and the cup fell over and rolled towards her.

'That's all right.' Youngman picked up the cup and poured some more brandy in it for Paine. 'I understand you. You're the bat killer. You want to do it yourself.'

Two helicopters moved one behind the other towards the sun. In each ship were four men dressed in airtight vinyl suits, and four bombs and DDT. Paine was right about one thing, Chee realized. As soon as the oil companies heard the words 'vampire bat' they'd panicked.

'This is the way we stop a fire in an oil field,' Piggot said. 'We blow it up.'

'I don't know. Maybe we should have waited so we could bring Paine.'

'Look, we had troubles with fruit bat swarms at our Indonesian wells. We just blasted their roosts. You don't wait for any so-called expert to do it for you. Or any goddamn ecology study. This is where the vampires are so this is where we're going to start, and we're going to keep on until we blow up every goddamn bat cave around here if we have to. That is, if you want any oil revenues. I take it you do.'

'You're talking about millions of bats. The Hopis aren't

going to stand for that kind of slaughter, not on their land.'

'You want to pull out, Chee, just say the word and we'll turn around.'

Chee couldn't pull out, as both men knew. Tribal funds were sunk in low-cost housing, Nevada mortgage speculation, land reclamation, and banking. The operating budget for the next year had a projected deficit of two million dollars, a deficit that would bring Indian Bureau investigations of misuse of federal money. In his own mind, Chee'd done nothing wrong. He hadn't started world-wide inflation, or caused the Nevada mortgages to be forced. But he knew investigations would scare off private investors he'd courted all around the country. On the other hand, the consortium of oil companies Piggot represented was willing to hand over two million dollars for a twenty-year lease on the Maski Canyon and a 10 per cent royalty on any oil produced. To begin with, Chee thought his only problem was that the canyon was in joint Navajo-Hopi territory. Then the bats came, and the plague.

A furious red sun was poised over the horizon. Begay was in the lead copter with the white doctor who'd been at the Momoa ranch, and after Youngman's 'impossible' suggestion had made telephone queries from San Diego to Mexico City until he'd found a zoologist who recognized the wounds, and then gone straight to Piggot. Chee fired him. It didn't matter. As the doctor expected, Piggot paid well enough for the information.

'All I'm saying,' Chee rephrased his protest, 'is maybe

we should wait and co-ordinate with Paine. In case some bats get away.'

'Chee, you know how many geologists know more about oil than me? Maybe a thousand and they're all piss-poor and a lot of them work for me and the reason is that I have nerve. That's all the oil business is. Nerve and faith. That's why I'm taking a chance on you. You thought some bats were going to scare me off a strike? See how you wasted time on your expert? You should have come to me at the start.'

'But he knows these bats.'

'And I know dynamite.'

'It's almost sunset. The bats are going to be coming out.'

'Good. We blow up the ones coming out and seal the rest in for the DDT to finish off.'

'There are a lot of bats.'

'That's why we're going to this one first. Look, Chee, you want to be an important man, a hero, and you want to be rich. You go along with us and that's what you'll be, and you know it.'

Chee shut his mouth. Piggot was using almost the same argument Chee had used on Duran, only Chee's argument was a fraud and Piggot's was the bottom line. It was always the same bottom line on a white man's contract. The helicopters were Piggot's, not given to Chee, only loaned for geological surveying.

'Two miles at ten degrees south. We have visual contact,' the lead copter reported.

'Let's coast.' Piggot took the mike.

Both copters swayed slightly sideways to get a better look at Mansion Mesa, a relatively small mesa with an irregular top and crumbling talus walls that did suggest a decrepit and over-sized mansion set down in the middle of the desert. In the full furnace gaze of the setting sun, the mesa glowed orange-hot. A layer of volcanic rock made the mesa top uninhabitable for humans, but the centre of the mesa was hollow, a vast cavern occupied by blind salamanders, beetles, cockroaches, coral snakes, pseudo-scorpions, and hundreds of colonies of different bats.

'You're sure anything lives in that?' Piggot asked Chee. 'Yes.'

'We better swing by first,' Piggot ordered over the radio.

The two copters made a circuit around the walls of the mile-wide mesa, watching their silhouettes swim over the walls. The sound of turboprop engines boomed off the rocks.

'Bats!' the first copter called.

On the south wall, about twenty feet from the mesa lip, perhaps a dozen bats straggled into the daylight and dived to the shadow line rising from the desert floor.

'We're going around again,' Piggot ordered.

'That's the main entrance,' Chee disagreed. 'You don't know how fast the sun drops. We have to do it now.'

The copters made a second circuit, closer this time, their rotors almost grazing the mesa walls. As they came around to the south, without spotting another entrance, Chee saw that the sun had dropped to its waist. A shadow line of misty blue was directly under the cave entrance and a thin but solid string of bats fluttered out.

'Okay, this is going to be harder than we hoped,' Piggot spoke into the mike. 'We can't just drop the bombs. We're going to have to fly by and sling them in. The dynamite has a ten-second delayed contact fuse, so you don't have to worry as long as you don't go into a stop hover. We'll stand off and, in case you miss, we'll go in with our load. Let's do it right the first time, though. And don't forget your helmets. There's a chance some of them bats are infected and we don't to take any chances.'

Piggot was already taking chances, Chee thought.

'Tell them to go.'

'Hold on, chief. I said we were going to do it right. Look, the bats aren't even coming out now.'

The shadow line was halfway up the cavern mouth and rising even as Chee watched. The lead copter backed off a hundred yards while the one carrying Chee and Piggot drifted fifty yards alongside. There was a pause as the men in each aircraft fastened the helmets of their coveralls. They wouldn't be in them long enough to require air tanks. Chee started sweating immediately as more bats emerged. The shadow line touched the top of the cavern entrance. Most of the desert was now a blue pool.

Ready, the radio announced.

'A hundred dollar bonus for every man who bowls a strike,' Piggot told them.

Chee watched Begay get strapped to each side of the

221

Huey's open bay. A satchel charge was handed to Begay. The two copters seesawed in the air. More bats were coming out of the cavern, speckling the air.

'What are they waiting for?'

'Relax,' Piggot told Chee.

Begay gave a thumbs up. The lead copter dipped its nose and advanced towards the mesa.

'Keep it at five knots until he throws it and then scram. Good hunting!' Piggot called.

The copter aimed towards the cavern at a twenty degree angle. Begay and the charge were obscured from the second copter's view. A small cloud of about a hundred bats slipped from the cave. Steadily, resolutely, the copter swung towards the mesa wall.

The next seconds were confused in Chee's mind and always would be. The cavern erupted not with hundreds of bats or thousands but with tens of thousands of guano bats, cave bats, red bats, canyon bats, fringed bats, in all close to 500,000 bats as Mansion Mesa spilled out its colonies, the way the mesa always released its bats at sunset, until the helicopter, the mesa, and half the sky were erased by a moving, screaming cloud and Chee's copter almost spun to the ground as it listened to a radio shouting, 'Bats! The bats . . .' The sound of their wings overpowered even the howling of the copter's jet engine. Chee never heard the crash of the lead copter into the mesa wall, only that pounding like heavy rain until the charge went off at the base of the mesa, scattering what was left of Begay and the copter over the sands.

Chapter Seven

The day began hot and windless. There was no movement or shade, or even dimension to be seen. Only the
searing white light that evaporated life.

At six a.m., a general plague alert had come over the
Rover's AM radio, followed an hour later by evacuation
orders for everyone between the Black Mesa to the north
and Castle Butte to the south, and Dinnebito Wash to
the west and Route 87 to the east. By eight a.m., the
orders from Window Rock were reversed and occupants
of the previously mentioned area were instructed to stay
where they were, to avoid public gatherings, fumigate
their homes and themselves, not to approach any wild
animals or any sick domestic animals, to report any
unusual wounds or boils or fever. Also, to burn their
dead and to stay in, doors and windows shut, at night.
In effect, a quarantine of approximately 2500 square
miles. And at night, a siege.

'Just the start.' Paine spread a map. Circles and dates
marked every incident concerning the vampires or
plague. 'Winslow and Flagstaff are only thirty miles outside the area. Wait and see what happens when the
plague reaches there.'

'What are these other marks?' Anne asked.

'The X's are sound trackings of the vampires. The

triangles are major bat colonies. Mansion Mesa south, Stephen Butte east, San Francisco Mountain caves west. There are millions of bats in the mountain caves. If the vampires move in there and the fleas spread?'

'What then?'

'You can drop Arizona, Utah, and New Mexico off the map of the United States for a start.'

'We're dropping them now, we're getting out.' Youngman returned from pouring the last jerry can of gasoline into the Land-Rover. 'Once we get past Route 89, there's a dirt road I know that'll get us up to the Grand Canyon paths. No one will know we came out of the quarantine.'

'I only promised to take you to the highway,' Paine said.

'You heard the radio. We'd be picked up in a minute on the highway now and stuffed into a ward full of people with plague. That's no escape. We're going to the Grand Canyon, all of us.'

'I'm not leaving the desert,' Paine said.

'That's up to you. We are, and so's the truck.'

'I need the Rover.'

'Not like we do.'

While the two men argued, Anne walked off by herself and sat beside a withered saguaro. The pulp of the cactus was eaten away, leaving the ribs as open as a cage. Farther on, the iterated S's of a sidewinder's track decorated the sand. Beyond was flatness extending to the horizon, which was clear and extraordinarily fine even through the vibration of heat waves. A line so long and unbroken and without any margin, the same line she had concentrated on when she was dying. Dying, she had decided this was the place to die. And the way to die, because she'd lied to Youngman, she'd given up hope of any rescue and being free of that hope, and knowing she'd survived as well and as long as she could alone and without help, she'd reached an unexpected clarity of thought. A clarity of life. Franklin had reached it before his death. It was a sudden gift of the desert, not so much a conscious understanding as an extension of the senses so that she could feel the dry breeze cool within her, see the distant mesas sitting like brown women, be a very part of the desert. It was an absolution from her executioner, this awareness. Perhaps it never was the Indians or the petty ego-satisfaction of volunteerism that had brought her into the desert and to this point. Perhaps it was a lifelong drift towards reality. Because Phoenix was a dream, a false oasis. Youngman wasn't false, only his aspirations of leaving the desert were. Her visions had been real, seeing him run over the sand because he was a desert animal and he'd never leave it without killing more than half of himself. If she wanted him, she would have to take him whole. Why had he and she been spared the bats and the plague? Why had the desert done that for them? She scooped up sand and let it run like water over her broken fingers.

Youngman lifted his rifle, levered a bullet into the breech, and aimed at Paine's head.

'Give me the keys.'

'You'll have to kill me.'

'To save us, I'd do it. Throw the keys.'

'There are more lives at stake. Your people, the Navajos, everyone in the desert. And that's just the start.'

'It's not the end of the world,' Youngman said. He would have fired at that point, but he was suddenly looking at a memory of Abner. Then Anne interrupted.

'Besides you,' she asked Paine, 'who else can stop the bats?'

'No one. There are experts in vampire control in Mexico City, but it would take them a week to organize a team. By then the bats will move to a new cave and the plague will be out of control. It may be out of control now.'

'How?'

'A bullet,' Paine looked at Youngman's gun, 'only kills the person it hits. Every victim, man or animal, bitten by the bats becomes a vector, a spreader of the plague. Ask your friend how fast the plague has spread in a couple of days. From a few square miles to a few hundred square miles. Geometrically. The more area it covers, the more the rate of spread accelerates. You can probably imagine what will happen if one human vector reaches a major city or an airport. Or even a motel near the Grand Canyon.'

'Is it possible Youngman or I do have the plague?'

Paine took longer to answer.

'It's possible.'

'And you know where the bats are.'

'Almost exactly. I've been tracking their flight paths for five nights. I know the area of their cave. Of course, they could move to a different cave any time, unless I stop them now.'

'Don't listen to him,' Youngman said. 'You don't have plague now. We can get to California. We'll never have to hear about the reservation again. Remember what you told me? We could go any place in the world together.'

Anne shook her head.

'I'm staying.'

'You're going. You don't know what you're talking about.'

'I know what I'm talking about. For two years I've gone around this reservation doing nothing but handing out band aids and eye salves. That's next to doing nothing, Youngman, and that was two years of my life. Maybe I did something good for the people, I hope I did. Now you want me to be responsible for letting those people die? To throw away those years? To run away the first time I can really matter? If you want to run, go ahead. But I'm not going with you.'

'I can make you go.' Youngman swung the rifle towards her.

'No. That you can't do.'

'Paine is crazy.'

'He can stop the bats.'

'Get in the truck.'

Anne said nothing but held his eyes on hers, not fighting his stare because she didn't have the strength for that. Instead, yielding, letting his eyes go as deep as they dared, until the rifle dropped.

Youngman made a final attempt.

'I'll trade you. I'll stay here and wait while he drives you out past the quarantine. Then I'll help him when he comes back. He may have maps. He doesn't know the desert.'

'Then that settles it,' Anne said. 'We're all needed. We'll do it together as a team. If,' she asked Paine, 'that's all right with you?'

'A team?' Paine took the rifle from Youngman. 'A team is perfect.'

Maski Canyon was a maze of many canyons, some of eroded Kaibob sandstone with walls gouged and pitted by sandbearing wind, others of sheer black Hermit shale, others of lava with slick obsidian seams. At one time, the canyon had grass as well and a people, ancestors of the Hopi, who raised corn and grazed goats in this impenetrable natural fasthold. Then, slowly, the wells died and the thin soil dried and blew away and the ancestors disappeared. Anyone lost in this forgotten home was accounted dead by the Hopi, who retreated across the desert to the Black Mesa; by the Navajo, who could find more grass among sand dunes; and by the pahans of Washington, who willingly ceded an outcrop of hell.

Until Landsat. The Landsat satellite was launched by the National Aeronautics and Space Administration on 2 January 1975. Since then, fourteen times a day, the satellite circled the earth measuring the radiation intensity of the ground in 1.1-acre units. Within its multispectral scanner an oscillating mirror reflected light to detectors which converted the light into electrical voltages. The voltages were in turn converted into number values ranging from 0 to 63. Landsat beamed its data to a Goldstone, California station where the data was recorded on tape and shipped to the Goddard Space Flight Centre, where the number values were reconverted back into back and white film, which was then printed through filters into colour photographs. The photographs were stored at the Department of the Interior's Earth Resources Observation Systems Data Centre in Sioux Falls, South Dakota. Although the photographs were costly, they were much in demand by developing countries eager to find signs of mineral deposits, by meteorologists mapping weather patterns, by civil engineers responsible for highway planning, and especially by petroleum companies. A group of such companies based in Houston noticed that one photograph of generally oil-dry Arizona displayed an almost insignificant and inexplicable leap in radiation intensity. Night photographs of the area, a stretch of the Painted Desert held jointly by the Navajo and Hopi tribes, showed an even sharper 'dot' of radiation. Contact was made with the more progressive Navajos and helicopters were loaned for purposes of closer aerial study with infra-red film. The cause of the radiation leap, they found, was not radiation at all but fire, a fire in a stark series of canyons that looked from the air like interlocked teeth, canyons with no trees or anything else to burn. Except oil. From deep underneath the surface, from an unsuspected oil pool, there was a seep. At some time, lightning had struck the seep and set it on fire, a fire that could have been burning for hundreds of years without anyone knowing. The burning seep was unusable, but where there was one there were likely to be others and there was sure to be oil.

From a distance of a mile, in the desert's midday, Maski Canyon looked like the remains of an enormous creature that had fallen, burning, to earth. Instead of the flat top of a mesa, angular crags jutted at the sky. Through a shroud of dark lava broke seams of rust-red Supai sandstone and streaks of dull mica. There was no vegetation and, except for a flock of carrion crows, no life.

'Stop,' Youngman said.

The Land-Rover rolled to a halt.

No reflection and no shadow, Paine thought as he stepped out of the truck. As if the canyon absorbed all light or cancelled it out.

Youngman climbed down, staring at the cliffs ahead. In a way, he was very amused. But Paine was heading in this direction when Youngman ran him down the day before. Youngman should have guessed.

'You know these canyons?' Paine asked him.

'He does.' Anne joined them. 'All the Hopis do.'

'Give me your glasses,' Youngman told Paine.

Paine gave Youngman the binoculars and the deputy focused on the face of the mesa, sweeping slowly from left to right.

'It has religious significance,' Anne said. 'I didn't know the place actually existed at all.'

'Superstitions,' Youngman cut her off. 'Ignorant witch stories. Nothing to concern you. You say the bats are up there?'

Paine pointed to a ragged gap in the cliffs.

'They fly through there. If we can get the truck up that far, we can go the rest of the way on foot.'

Youngman studied the walls of the gap and let the field-glasses fall slowly to the base of the mesa, to a stripe of brick-red sandstone where he found what he had been searching for, a black double spiral about ten feet across and twenty feet above the ground.

'There must be a thousand caves up there, Paine. How are we going to find the right one?'

'They'll lead us to it once we get the truck up – ' Paine became aware of Anne's concentration on Youngman. 'Is there something about the canyon I should know?'

'You worry about the bats.' Youngman handed back the glasses. 'I'll handle the rest. What about the truck?'

'Okay.' Paine opened a map on the Rover's hood. 'According to this aerial survey Chee gave me—'

'You got it from Chee? Interesting,' Youngman remarked.

'There is a path wide enough for a truck in this sector.'

Youngman glanced at the map and back at the canyon.

'Not a path. That's a stream of volcanic dust. You'll sink up to your windshield.'

'Well, the only other map I have is a satellite photo.'

'Then bring it out. Let's see it,' Youngman said when Paine hesitated.

Paine did as Youngman said, laying out the yard-wide acetate satellite photo on the ground. Hues of computer-emphasized colour seemed to melt into the sand.

'These are hard to interpret,' Paine began.

Youngman turned the photo around.

'Sun here,' he held a finger up. 'Sandstone canyons are the pink blotches. Shale is orange, lava collected the most heat so it's red. These darker spots are exposed obsidian.' Youngman went on for a minute translating the shades of colour into ridges, canyons, cooler dry wells, and turquoise fields. 'This dot is the burning oil. I spent a year looking at this kind of photo, except they were taken by reconnaissance planes. We always looked for burning oil.' He ran his finger along the eastern edge of the canyons. 'There are two ways up to the ridge. Maybe both blocked, maybe one. You and Anne take the truck half a mile west along the base of the .canyon, you'll find a break. Go slow. The only danger is volcano dust on your way but you don't want to get trapped. I'll go east. There's a faster way there, but it's usually blocked by rocks.'

'She was right,' Paine said. 'We do make a good team.'

Youngman said nothing but waited for Paine and Anne to get into the Rover.

'I wish you'd come with us,' Anne said.

'Later.'

He waited until the Rover grew small along the western base of the canyon and then he began running east, towards the double spiral on the sandstone.

Paine downshifted and turned the Rover up the path Youngman had told him about. Except for a rubble of loose micabright slate, he couldn't see any obstacles ahead and he was encouraged.

'The Indian was right. Youngman, I mean,' he looked at Anne to see whether he'd offended her. Her mind was elsewhere. He said louder, 'Youngman's quite an interesting guy.'

'I suppose he is.' She watched the path. The Rover was steadily climbing, shooting slate from all four wheels. The walls ahead were pale, ossified sandstone.

'But he doesn't have to be,' she added. ' "Interesting" is really a very small word. A bored word. Vampire bats are "interesting", plague is "interesting", Indians are "interesting". All of them are, from a distance, as a thrill. Life is "interesting".'

'Death is, too,' Paine said firmly.

Anne glanced at him; there were times when she glimpsed more than the gulf in communication between them.

For an hour, the Rover picked its way into the canyon and then the path turned slowly, inexorably back down to the desert.

Under the double spiral drawn on the canyon wall, growing as the only vegetation on a small hillock, was the datura. Almost as tall as a man, the plants bore pale violet, trumpet-shaped flowers. Youngman sank to his knees before them.

Right where Abner always said they were, he thought. Because no Hopi could enter Maski Canyon without datura in his mouth. It was the 'way', as much as any road.

All his life, he had turned his back on the 'way' and everywhere he turned the 'way' was in front of him. His manipulation of Paine and Anne, sending them on a useless road so that he could be alone, was minor in comparison to what Abner had done to him. Because here he was; after everywhere, he was here. But, he told himself, he still didn't believe.

A black-and-white shrike feather vibrated among the coarse leaves of the datura.

Still, a person had obligations. Youngman tore up one of the plants and hacked off a yellow-white root. He cut off a button-sized segment from the root and stuffed the rest in his pocket. He put the button in his mouth, and gagged. The taste was alkaloid and bitter, and at first he thought he was going to throw up, but after he rolled it under his tongue the nausea ebbed. Youngman got to his feet, turned right, and ran along the base of the canyon to where sheets of pocked lava came down to the desert in overlapping folds which hid a road of graded earth and mica. Without breaking stride, he turned into the canyon.

The datura, he noticed with relief, had no effect. He breathed the thin air comfortably and watched the sky narrow by steps into blue wedges between canyon walls.

The road was tortuous, a series of seeming cul de sacs, and cruelly steep. There was shadow but no shade. The walls radiated an enervating heat that seared the windpipe and lungs. Youngman breathed through his nose at the start of the climb, but after a half an hour the oxygen demands on his legs were too much and he opened his lips. In minutes, his tongue thickened into a wooden lump, while the datura button swelled. His eyes fell from the sky to the vari-coloured walls, and from the walls to the ruts that marked the road.

It was the Castillo priests who built it three centuries ago, their ox carts burdened by double loads of flammable stone that had bitten into the road. Their knotted whips that came down on the Hopis struggling to control the overloaded carts, because oxen were valuable and souls were cheap. For fifty years, until the priests were killed and whips burned, their bells melted, their mission razed, and their road abandoned.

Sunspots danced before Youngman's eyes. As he dropped to rest he saw waiting for him, sitting high on a sandstone outcrop that jutted over the road, the silhouette of a small man wearing nothing but a ragged cape.

'Hello, Flea,' Abner said.

'Hello,' Youngman pulled himself to his feet and walked under the outcrop. Looking up at Abner he was looking directly into the sun, but he could make out dimly the features of his old friend and the dried blood on Abner's chest. Abner had been smoking mesa tobacco and listening to a transistor radio. He put out the cigarette and turned off the radio.

'Surprised to see me?' he asked.

'Not really.' Youngman spat the datura from his mouth. 'Since I was stupid enough to eat that, I expected to see something.'

'You can't see anything here without datura,' Abner reprimanded him mildly. 'You shouldn't fight it.'

'I'm fighting you, uncle.'

Abner cocked his head and smiled.

'It was a real powerful painting, wasn't it, Flea? Swastikas backwards, spirals backwards, everything in reverse to start all over again. Letting Masaw out of the fire. You were in it, too, remember, Flea?'

'Why me?'

'You're Coyote Clan.'

'That's not why.'

'Then,' Abner granted, 'because you're the only one I can trust. You hate the pahans.'

'I hate too many people, but I don't kill them.'

'The same thing, Flea, if you know how to put your mind to it. You will. You have to.'

'No.'

'Why,' Abner asked slyly, 'do you think you're here?'

Youngman stared up without an answer. Sunlight clung like dust to Abner's blanket. This wasn't happening, Youngman reminded himself.

'Sorry about the priests in the kiva,' Abner changed

tone. 'They wouldn't let me have the Fire Clan tablet, Flea.'

'You were dead before they were.'

'It was their fault, they should have helped me out. It's important when you end the world, and you have to have the tablet. Harold understood.'

'Harold's here?'

'No.'

'Any bats here?'

As the silhouette on the rock shifted, sunlight ran like liquid down the blanket. A change in the wind brought the stench of ammonia. Abner ignored Youngman's last question.

'It makes my heart glad to see you again, Flea. You know why I'm ending the world.'

'You told me before. The strip mining on the mesa. The Indian Bureau. Navajos.'

'Masaw says they're coming here.'

'Masaw said that to you?'

'You know, if the headpounders want to sell their part of the Black Mesa to rip up and carry off, that's okay. You can't expect much religion from a Navajo anyway. But, you know, we're the only real people in the world and Masaw is the only real god. This canyon is his home. The first thing you ever learned is how he came out of the fires here to watch over us. Isn't that the first fact you learned in your life?'

'It's what I heard.' That was true.

'Then you agree, the day a company can buy Maski

Canyon, it's time to wipe everything out and start all over again.'

'You mean, wipe everybody out.'

'Not everybody. We'll go underground again, the way we always do between worlds. And when everybody else is dead, we'll have plenty of room when we come back up, Masaw promised.'

Youngman thought about it.

'Let me tell you. An hour back, when I saw where I was, I would have killed Walker Chee. If he had been there with me, I would have done it, because one thing I never thought I'd be doing is helping him take Maski Canyon. He's going to get it. You're right about all that, uncle. They'll take it if it kills us, and it probably will. They'll kill Masaw for sure. They'll blow him up with blasting powder and bury him under oil rigs. I felt that. But now. Now, I just feel sad. You know, my life has just been one circle. Starting here, going out, so far out I never saw the curve, and then ending here. A circle. What's funny is that I even thought I could get away again, and I can't. So, I'm here with you, uncle. And what are you, uncle, but a hallucination, a raving hallucination trying to scare away the rest of the world.'

'Masaw said you'd be like this at the start, Flea.'

'Stop it. Masaw isn't killing people. Bats are. The plague is. Hopi people are dying. What kind of a god kills his own people?'

'It's not unusual.'

Youngman thought he could make out a smile again on Abner's face.

'The reason you're here,' Abner went on, 'is that Masaw wants you to help kill the pahan.'

'You're not here at all, uncle. I'm just imagining you.'

'You don't need to kill the pahan yourself,' Abner said, soothingly. 'Only keep him out of the cave until the sun goes down. Then Masaw can come out.'

'What if I want Masaw to tell me all this himself?'

'You have the datura. Let your mind open and you will see.'

Youngman backed away from the rock.

'No. I see you, but you're not there. I'm talking to myself, you're not there.'

'You're a good boy, Flea.' Abner started to make a cigarette. 'We know you'll do what you should.'

'You're not there!' Youngman shouted. He picked up a rock and threw it at the outcrop with all his might.

A large crow flew into the sky, screamed over Youngman's head, and dived away, out of sight.

The outcrop was bare.

Long after the desert below was ocean dark, the promontories of Maski Canyon stood in the sun. Looking away from the desert into the canyon, Anne saw a labyrinth not so much of other ridges and canyons as of shapes. Of canyons that flying sand had scooped out of sandstone, leaving them as clean and round as shells, of rivers of volcanic ash, of lava chimneys that twisted up by the hundreds.

Medical bulletins were coming more frequently now over the Rover's AM radio.

We have good news for folks in the plague area. Public Health authorities have informed us that the plague situation covering the south-west corner of the Navajo and Hopi reservations is now under control. A state and federal effort to bring in vaccine by helicopter is being mobilized at this very hour. Health facilities at Ship Rock and Window Rock are being expanded to treat the sick. If you are outside the plague area and you think you may be infected, do not, repeat, do not go to Tuba City. Stay where you are. The growing co-ordinated effort is being personally led by Navajo Tribal Chairman Walker Chee, who emphasizes that co-operation between the two Indian nations is essential. Rebroadcasts of this bulletin in Navajo and Hopi will follow. If you are in the plague area, it's probable you can carry on life as normal with certain precautions. Do not approach any wildlife that appears sick. If any livestock appears sick, kill all your livestock and pets by rifle at a distance not less than thirty feet. Under any circumstances, continue to wash twice a day with green soap, use insect repellents, and fumigate your house. Do not go out after dark for any reason. Avoid caves. Keep your windows and doors bolted at night. Most important, do not try to leave the plague area. State troopers stationed along Route 89, on the approaches to Flagstaff and Winslow, along the Black Mesa and east along Oraibi Wash have orders to turn back evacuees. Anyone not obeying their orders will be shot . . .

As the tide of shadow rose, Youngman and Paine finished the erection of the wire mesh tent from the back or the Rover. When he'd pounded the last stake into the ground, Youngman ran his fingers along the fine metal wires of the tent.

'They can bite through this.'

'Yes.' Paine set a heavy battery next to Youngman. Together, they attached two wires to the mesh wall. Youngman noticed that where the walls joined the back of the Rover was an insulating collar of thick rubber. When the attachments were complete, Paine set the battery at 115 volts and threw a switch, setting off a deep tocking. 'Now they can't.'

Youngman's quickest touch of the mesh sent an electrical jolt up to his elbow.

'I know what I'm doing.' Paine turned the battery off.

. . . a change in previous announcements. For precautionary reasons, the northern limit of the plague alert area now includes these pueblos on the southern rim of the Black Mesa: Hotevilla, Bacopi, New Oraibi, Oraibi, Toreva, Shongopovi, and Walpi. Also, the towns of Moenkopi and Tuba City are now considered in quarantine. Again, these are precautionary measures and not reasons for alarm –

Youngman turned the radio off. As darkness swung over the ridge, Paine slid into the driver's seat. The unidirectional microphone was already set up on the roof and the oscilloscope glowed green next to Paine. Youngman and Anne crowded into the rear of the truck. Paine checked his watch.

The first stars began to appear, growing in intensity every second. Hotomkam in Orion's Belt. Choochokam, the Pleiades.

'I've got their flight pattern down pretty pat.'

Paine turned the microphone grip back and forth in an arc of 15 degrees. He wiped the palm of his other hand and fine tuned the amplifier, and tuned it a second time.

Anne had grown used to the sounds of the desert at night. There were none on the ridge or from the canyon. Not an insect or a bird.

The oscilloscope's white line was straight. A string of ice.

'If they moved to a new cave – ' Anne began to say.

The line shivered. A faint pattern emerged. Three harmonic lines slashing from one octave to another.

'Under three minutes after sunset,' Paine looked at his watch. 'We're very close to the cave. To,' he checked the compass reading on the microphone shaft, 'west-north-west, and bearing straight at us. They're packed tight, very tight.'

Youngman heard nothing, but the oscilloscope line shook violently. He looked at Paine, whose face was triumphant.

'Listen.' Paine snapped off the scope.

There was a wind, Anne thought with surprise. No, rain, she corrected herself, but no rain was falling. A milling of wings, she realized, but sharper. Wings without feathers.

Youngman thought they sounded like steps in the sky.

'Look,' Anne said.

From west to east the stars were vanishing, eclipsed by a whispering tide that swept over the ridge at a height of thirty feet. It moved over the Rover, blotting out starlight. They were faster than Youngman had expected, more than he had thought possible and he cringed reflexively, bowed by their shadow and the close and heavy strokes of wings. A minute passed and the bats were still coming overhead. Paine closed his eyes: for a moment the old panic was back burning like a red bulb but he mastered himself and the panic faded. Anne concentrated on the blind eye of the scope. Youngman watched the line of the bats funnelling down into the desert, a sinuous line dipping and curling into the night wind.

'When will they return?' he asked long after the bats had disappeared and Anne was making a supper of powdered egg tortilla on a hot plate.

'I don't know.' Paine laid his air gun, three darts, and a pocket-sized radio receiver on a table. 'It all depends how quickly they find food out there. A couple of hours at the least but they're bound to find some abandoned livestock. I've set the beeper on the microphone so we'll know when they get close.'

'They may find something besides livestock. Everyone in the quarantine area is abandoned.'

'True, but that isn't what you asked. Anyway, we'll be ready for them when they return.'

'We will?'

'This,' Paine held up one of the darts, 'contains a miniature radio transmitter. It weighs about a gram and only throws a signal for two hundred yards, but I think that'll be sufficient to find a cave as close as theirs. The trick will be to plant them on the backs of the bats so they can't bite them off.' Paine slid the receiver's button to ON, checked three frequencies of tones from the darts, and slid the button back to OFF, speaking softly to himself, ' "Where the bee sucks, there suck I. There I couch when owls do cry. On the bat's back I do fly." '

Supper. Paine ate his spongy tortilla voraciously and with great good humour. Anne busied herself in a charade of domesticity. The bright light of the Coleman lamp dissolved the fine mesh of the tent, so that the three seemed to be having a picnic in the open air.

'Now that we're all in this together,' Youngman pushed his food aside, 'I think it's time you told us just what we're up against, Paine.'

'You know. Infected bats.'

'I know from what I've seen so far that I don't think we're going to come out of this.'

'Youngman—'

'Wait a second, Anne.' He considered telling her and Paine about his hallucination of Abner, but there was no point. He wasn't going to eat any more datura. 'If we're going to die up here with Paine, I want to know why. I want his reasons. I want to understand. I want to understand everything.'

'It's very complicated,' Paine said.

'You said the same thing the first time we met. You were lying then.'

'All right,' Paine conceded. He shifted uncomfortably, searching for words.

'It's like a war,' Anne suggested. 'That's obvious enough.'

'No,' Paine shook his head, 'not in a biological sense. It's simply a meeting. A meeting of life forms.'

'A competition,' Anne said.

'No. An interdependence. Vampires and plague and man.' He looked at their faces. 'You did want the truth, didn't you?'

'Go on,' Youngman said.

'It could be argued that the two dominant life forms on earth are bacilli and mammals.' Paine chose his words slowly. 'The three most successful forms of these groups are the plague bacillus, man, and bats. Functioning together. The plague, to begin with. The plague bacillus has always been here. As a minor disease.'

'It wasn't as dangerous?'

'To the caveman who caught it, yes, but how many other men could he infect? Or a farmer? Or a hunter? Do you see what I mean? There was plague, but there were no epidemics, not one in the history of the world until the coming of higher civilization. Until men got together in cities, until men traded, until men congested.

Then starts the reign of the plague above all other diseases. Because of man, nothing else.'

'The plague does okay,' Youngman said. 'What do we get out of it?'

'Unions. Before the Black Plague hit Western Europe, the majority of the population was in servitude. When the plague passed and half the population was dead there was a labour shortage. Men who had been slaves could sell their labour. Individual rights began. Democracy began with the plague.'

'Then public hygiene is the end of democracy, according to you,' Anne said.

'Sewage disposal and rat control didn't stop the plague. The first pandemic of the plague killed a hundred million people in the sixth century. Seven hundred years later, the Black Plague killed a quarter of the world's population. In between? Believe me, there was no great improvement in open sewers. The plague has its own pulse, its own cycle. It rests in places like this and waits.'

'Bats,' Youngman nervously felt for a cigarette, 'what about them?'

'What about them? Don't be angry, but what do you know about bats? Little, fluttery creatures, flying mice, freaks of nature? Not vampires now, just bats in general.'

'Something like that,' Anne acknowledged.

'Because you don't know how wonderfully successful a life form they are. One out of every five mammals on the face of the earth is a bat. Bats are more widespread over the earth than any other mammal, except man. We rule the day, not the night.'

'Aren't they related to rodents?' Anne exchanged a glance with Youngman.

'Someone else. The two glorious specimens descended from tree hopping insectivores are man and bats. We climbed down and they flew out, although we share the same hand in different forms. For twenty years, Leonardo da Vinci tried to design wings for a man to fly like a bird. His perfected design was the bat wing. We share more. More than twenty kinds of virus. The human bed bug first came from bats when we shared the same caves. And the closest of all bats to man is the vampire.'

'Well,' Youngman sighed, 'I know you're a super exterminator of bats but your humour is a little strained.'

'Not humour. Irony. It's true. You see this is an amazing concept, the vampire bat. Incredibly advanced. Of all bats, it's the only one that mates the year round, like humans. Of all bats, it has the longest gestation period. Eight months. Of all bats, its children take the longest to develop and teach. It's the only bat that can jump or run. The only bat that cannot live in harmony with any other animal, including other bats. Need I add, also the only bat unafraid of man. The first western scientist ever to see the vampire feed was Charles Darwin. He didn't know what to make of it.'

'So,' Youngman finally remembered to light his cigarette, 'know your enemy.'

'Know your cousins. And since a vampire can live close to twenty years, a fairly long-lived cousin. So, don't call me a super exterminator. You exterminate fleas. You kill bats.'

'All of which shoots your theory of interdependence to hell, right?'

'No. The vampire lives off large mammals that sleep in herds. It lives off cattle and horses. There weren't any cattle and horses in the New World until the Spanish brought them. What do you think the vampires lived on before then? Name me the one large American mammal that slept together in herds, or villages.'

A light-headed sensation came over Anne.

'You mean, people?'

'Yes, that's exactly what I mean. People. Which is why all the old vampire roosts were found next to villages. Of course, we can only speculate on the details of this relationship. Whether one vampire colony would establish territoriality over a particular village and defend its feeding ground against other colonies.'

'What did the people get out of it?' Youngman asked.

'Gods.'

He knows about Masaw, Youngman thought.

'What kind of gods?' Anne picked up.

'The Mayan gods, for example,' Paine said, to Youngman's relief. 'You can still see the statues in the Yucatan. Statues with the heads of vampires. The curved incisors and the long tongue are very well represented. No one knows quite why the Mayans deserted their cities. Maybe it was the collapse of their slash-and-burn agriculture. Maybe it was simply enervation, a loss of blood. Wherever there were more vampires, there were more bat gods. More public sacrifices, more ritual bloodletting, until Aztecs paste their hair with blood and cut their ears into a vampire's fringe and wear a cape of bat skins. Maybe cattle herds are a secondary form of sacrifice for us.'

'Then, what you're telling us,' Anne said, 'is that we can't change anything? There should be plague and there should be vampires?'

' "Should" isn't the issue. The only thing that will ever eliminate plague or vampires is the elimination of man. We'll go together.'

'Then what we're doing here is pointless,' she said. 'In the long run, in your biological scheme, we mean nothing. Then why are you here?'

'Because,' Paine couldn't think of a better explanation, 'it's what I do.'

There was a long silence before Anne commented.

'Good Lord.'

For a long time, no one said anything.

Slowly, the star Hotomkam wheeled upside down over the canyon. Choochokam slid over the horizon. Youngman smoked, wishing he had some mesa tobacco. Exhausted, Anne slept in the middle of the narrow tent. Paine methodically unloaded and reloaded his dart gun.

'Maybe we should be listening to the news,' Youngman suggested.

'Why?' Paine asked. 'They're broadcasting nothing that you couldn't predict.'

'I predict they'll start bombing caves,' Youngman lowered his voice.

'They will,' Paine agreed, 'for a cave or two. Until they find out they're only scattering bats. We want the vampires together just two more nights—'

'Speaking of that, Anne's not going into the cave with us tomorrow. Just you and me. She can't carry anything in her condition and she'd only be in the way.'

'Okay.'

'No, I want more than that. Your promise Anne stays with the truck, or you go alone.'

'Very well, you have my promise she won't go into any cave.' Paine put the dart gun down. A moth had been circling over the tent above the light. Suddenly, the insect began to fly erratically, zigzagging and dropping. Paine turned his head to the amplifier's beeper even before it sounded.

'Wake her up!' he told Youngman and dived into the rear of the truck.

'Anne,' Youngman shook her shoulder. 'They're here.'

'Three hundred yards off,' Paine returned. In one hand he held a thin, five-foot wooden pole. In the other, a two-ounce vial of defibrilated blood.

'You're sure they're going to stop,' Youngman took the pole. The last two feet of the pole were wrapped in calf hide.

Rubbing her face, Anne was already beside the battery.

'They didn't see us in the truck before. This time we're out.' Paine poured the blood over the calf hide. 'Be careful you don't tear the mesh.'

'I know what to do.'

'When I say "Juice",' Paine snapped his fingers at Anne.

Youngman realized that he had yet to see the bats close up. Paine had, Anne had. The deputy inserted the pole through the mesh so that the blood-soaked calf skin was outside the tent. The mesh was incredibly frail. He felt his heart pumping blood and adrenalin, and had a sense of the frailty of his own skin. He couldn't remember ever being afraid of an animal before.

The amplifier beeper became louder and more insistent, turning into one sustained whine.

Paine stood in the middle of the tent, calmly waiting.

Anne stared upwards.

First, they heard the whisper of the false wind, then a leathery rustle. A shape flashed overhead, through the light before Youngman could make it out. Two more shapes. Ten. Eye reflections like candles. A hundred, more than Youngman could see. Anne stared, transfixed. The walls of the tent swayed. Youngman couldn't hear the beeper's cry any more for the wing beats.

'They're going past!' she shouted.

'No.' Paine pointed with the gun to a dark shape scuttling along the ground.

The river of bats poured overhead and curved, turning into a whirlpool of dipping wings. The whirlpool flattened into a tremendous wheel spinning over the tent. Youngman found himself crouching. Paine seemed to stand taller, turning on one heel. Anne looked into a face two feet outside the net. Bristles marked each cheek. Its dark eyes were slanted on either side of a squat nose with double-folded nostrils. Its ears were long and ribbed. Youngman saw that the top of the Rover was covered by bats. One, its wings wrapped into two long 'legs', jumped on to the mesh directly over Paine. More bats appeared all around the edge of the tent. Two leaped from the ground and agilely climbed the tent walls. More jumped from the Rover and others landed from the air on the tent. Youngman's arm jerked. On the bloody end of the pole was a bat. Its incisors sliced off a half-dollar-sized patch of hide. A long red tube-like tongue curled and delicately lapped the pole. He heard the soft explosion of the air gun beside his ear and saw the fin of a dart protrude from the back fur of the bat. Forty or fifty bats crawled on top of the tent, and more climbed up the walls using thumb claws as hooks. A quarter of them had face fur matted with dried blood. The pole Youngman held bowed with the weight of three more bats. Paine pushed the dart gun's muzzle into the mesh and fired again. The top of the tent sagged. More bats climbed up from the ground, bringing a smell of retching ammonia. Youngman heard the lowest register of their excited screams, a distinct clicking in his ears. Inches from his shoulder, they started sawing through the mesh with their teeth. Paine took his time aiming his last dart, knocking a bat out off the wall to pull the trigger on one with a strip of hide hanging from its mouth. As he lowered the gun a bat landed between his shoulder-blades. Without thinking, Youngman ripped the bat off Paine and crushed it under his boot.

'Juice!' Paine shouted.

The tear was at the far end of the tent. Another bat was coming through when Youngman reached the rifle in his bed roll and blew it apart. Blood, bone and gristle splattered the inside of the tent. He shot two more coming through before Paine slid the wooden pole through each side of the tent and twisted it shut.

'Turn on the battery!' Youngman shouted at Anne, who knelt beside the battery, her hand limp on the starter knob.

The bats were cutting through the roof and the walls. Youngman emptied his rifle on them and picked up the handgun he'd brought from Momoa's. A rip three feet long appeared down one wall. Youngman walked into the bats flooding through, using up his bullets until he reached the mesh and gathered it shut in his hands. As he watched, his hands became covered with bats.

Then a thrill of electricity washed through his body, leaving his brain a darkness surrounded by convulsions.

Chapter Eight

A blue sky surrounded Anne's face.

'How are you feeling?' she asked.

'Grand,' Youngman muttered.

'Pretty good for a man whose heart stopped.'

'Is it going, now?'

He raised himself from her lap and winced. His hands, he noticed, were bandaged to the wrists. The mesh tent had been taken down and the red canister of poison was gone. Paine, also, was gone.

'Where is he?' Youngman asked.

'Paine left to look for the cave. You saved our lives last night, Youngman.'

'I don't remember a damn thing.'

'It was my fault,' she said. 'I was scared, I couldn't turn on the battery.'

He pulled himself away from her arms and stood. The ground swayed slightly under his feet. Youngman squinted at the sun; it was close to noon.

'But he should have waited. He can't carry all the stuff alone. And he didn't take the Rover?'

'He waited until he was sure you were going to come around. Youngman, he left the truck for us to leave. He never wanted us along. In fact, he took your rifle and he said he'd shoot you if you tried to follow him. I think he would. He's crazy.'

Youngman slumped to one knee as much from surprise as weakness.

'You didn't know that?' he asked Anne.

He turned his stare from Anne to the road, where Paine's footprints led up the canyon.

'When did he go?'

'An hour ago, maybe more.'

'He should have left at dawn.' Youngman shook his head. 'He don't know where he's going. Not enough time.'

'Youngman, let's go home. He's a professional, he can do the job by himself. He's the only one who can.'

'One of us is.' Youngman still looked in the direction Paine had gone, where the road screwed through the dull-red walls of the canyon.

'We'll wait and see,' he said.

Paine set the grinding weight of his pack down on the road, leaving the Cyanogas, rolled mesh, battery, wires and tools in the pack and taking only his receiver, rope, axe, and rifle. He was a mile from where he'd left the Rover and he assumed Anne and Youngman were now well out of the canyon. No more repeats of his father and Ochay. He was alone and free and his mind was clean.

The abandoned road continued to work its way through the canyon and under overhanging lava formations that had obscured it from aerial photographs. Steep walls of rust-coloured sandstone crowded in on either side of the road. Occasionally, the sandstone would part to reveal a raw seam of shale that glittered like sequins. Or a strip of chalk-white limestone. And sometimes Paine would step back from the shadow of a man's torso and look up to see only a still figure of lava poised on a rim. Of this geological richness, all that interested Paine were signs of limestone which would be most likely to lead to a cave adaptable to bats.

The radio signals weren't coming. He was sure that the darts were good hits and the bats were close but the walls of the road muffled any kind of transmission. Unless he left the road and got up higher he might miss the cave completely.

He moved slowly until he came to a ragged shank of basalt that ran forty feet up the fifty-foot wall. Paine scaled the basalt and from it chipped handholds that carried him to the top of the wall. All his skills were with him. He pulled himself up to a view of the entire eastern half of the canyon.

Maski Canyon defied the usual arid cycle of land erosion. Instead of uniform canyons and buttes, the varied rocks of different hardness created a bewildering, serrated puzzle. It must have begun as a volcanic eruption, he thought, been covered by sedimentary rock and then torn apart by winds that left gaping mouths of stained sandstone, dykes of basalt uplifted like teeth and, where sandstone had been stripped away from rivulets of lava, those upright almost human figures of black rock. The eastern half of the mesa covered about five square miles, he estimated, and the western half, a higher plateau of the same sort of formations, seemed nearly as large. The burning oil seep was in the western plateau.

Like Milton, he thought. 'A dungeon horrible, on all sides round as one great furnace flamed, yet from those flames no light, but rather darkness visible.'

Paine smiled to himself. He felt great, the way he always did when he knew he was right. On top of the world.

He moved from one cliff to another, jumping deep fissures, hauling himself by rope where a glassy wall of obsidian offered no holds. Wherever he found limestone he followed it until it either vanished or hollowed into a cave. There were caves, hundreds of them just as the Indian said, but none big enough or damp enough to support a colony of bats, and no signals reached his receiver. Paine was undiscouraged. There were bats and he was close to them.

From time to time he glimpsed shapes slipping through the basalt dykes. Crows. Beside a high nest, he found a dung beetle regally surveying a mound of bird droppings as high as a man's waist; Paine had seen storms moving across the desert, but when rain last fell here he couldn't even guess. There was no apparent plant life and, except for the solitary beetle, not even insects.

He crossed a natural bridge of gutted sandstone and discovered thirty feet below, sunk in shadow, the same road he had been on before. Paine was surprised it came so far. He checked his watch. Five o'clock; two hours to sunset. It was much later than he'd thought. He was confident, though. He still had time.

On the other side of the bridge, the composition of the rock changed to basically volcanic. Paine had to thread his way through fields of lava chimneys and arms that snagged his clothes. At one point, at his feet, he discovered a crude double-spiral scratched through the dark lava to an underlying level of white limestone. How the Indians had known there would be a different kind of rock beneath the lava he didn't know; that was a problem for anthropologists. For him, the limestone was a good sign.

As he emerged from the lava field, he got his first signal. The signal grew stronger as Paine continued moving. He tried the other two frequencies of the receiver; the second could barely be heard, but the third was the clearest of all. Paine followed it through a series of basalt dykes. He jumped from one side of a crevice to a stone chimney and landed running excitedly on the other side of a crevice. Before him loomed a huge white dome of limestone.

All three frequencies were coming in loudly; he turned the receiver off. The limestone dome was fifty feet across and in the middle of it was a sinkhole twenty feet across where erosion had broken through. The edge of the sinkhole was green with lichen and moss. On his stomach, moving with great caution, Paine crawled up the dome to the hole and looked down.

He'd found them. The shaft of light that slanted down through the sinkhole into the cave dropped into a tarry pool two hundred feet below. The pool was shallow, a new one, but the unmistakable odour of ammonia rose into the air. Paine switched his receiver on for confirmation, just for a second. The short, raucous tone brought a stirring of claws six inches beneath his chest on the thin underside of the dome. All three tones from the same cave. He had them all.

As his eyes became accustomed to looking down into the dark of the cave, Paine saw that it was circular, about three hundred feet wide, with the general shape of a natural amphitheatre. From the level floor, all the walls arched smoothly to the dome. If there were a thousand bats in the colony now, the cave would accommodate three times as many. Somewhere on the floor was a spring or access to a water table. Paine sniffed. Because the ammonia was not overpowering, he smelled another faint but familiar odour. Oil. Another seep. Chee would be overjoyed.

The irises of Paine's eyes continued to dilate. The vertical lines on the cave floor near the pool were not irregular. They were straight. They were crude ladders, maybe ten, with most of their rungs broken. More shapes emerged. In the deepest shadow of the cave was a slightly darker shadow. A square. More squares spread around and above it, reaching halfway up and a third of the way around the wall of the cave. Windows. Windows and doors for five storeys of adobe houses, an enormous underground gallery. The reason Paine hadn't seen it sooner was not only the dark. The houses themselves had disintegrated almost into rubble. Roofs were crushed, walls had fallen in, dust lay like a heavy shroud. Paine reasoned that to escape enemies a people might hide for a short time in such a place. This was not the construction of a short time, though. This had been a small city.

Intrigued and puzzled, Paine edged around the entire lip of the sinkhole, spreading his arms and legs to minimize his weight. He'd thought he would have to lower the Cyanogas canister through the sinkhole from a piton driven into the dome, an operation that risked breaking through the flimsy limestone shell or, at least, scattering the bats. If any point of the ruins, however, came within a hundred feet of the cave ceiling, he could place the canister there. The ruins told him there was another way into the cave because there had to be human access.

But no point on the ruins was high enough for the gas spray to be totally effective. Which satisfied Paine well enough; it was usually a bad idea to change methods, and one misstep among ruins as old as these seemed could mean disaster.

The sinkhole it would be, then. Right on top of the bats.

He left the way he'd come, through the lava field to the sandstone bridge, where he descended by rope to the road. By now, he was asking himself questions.

The road comes all this way? To what?

He didn't want to stop, but his habit of thoroughness was too strong. A trap was no good if there were two exits, and somehow people had gone in and out of the cave.

As Paine reversed himself and ran up the road in the direction of the cave, his receiver came gradually alive again. Not as loud as the signals above the cave, but distinct.

Youngman knew about the canyon and the road. Paine's face flushed. The bastard must have known about the cave all the time.

The road ended directly in front of what seemed to be an entrance to a mine. A cart wheel of solid wood that had been slowly decaying for hundreds of years lay beside an opening eight feet high and wide enough for two carts to enter abreast. The signals came from inside. He checked his watch. It was getting late, but he had to be certain.

As Paine stepped in, he touched the walls. They were cool and damp and left his fingertips black. One sniff explained all. Oil-saturated shale, that was what the mine was for. Soft shale so pregnant with oil it could be hacked into bricks that would burn brighter than coal.

The mine burrowed ahead and with each step the signals grew stronger. This had to be the other way into the cave. One hundred and fifty feet in, though, the mine came to a dead end. Yet the signals were stronger than before and Paine could smell ammonia. He pushed tentatively against the end wall, and it disintegrated in his fingers. His arm went through the rotting threads of a hanging blanket that had been the only separation between the shale mine and the limestone cave. Carefully, he pulled his arm out and peered through the hole he'd made. Before him, lit by the sinkhole, stretched the gigantic hall of the cave, the shallow pool of digested blood, the ghostly ruins of the pueblo and, overhead, both deadly and vulnerable, a ceiling of bats. They didn't use the mine.

Paine broke into a run when he reached the road. It was six o'clock, not enough daylight left for him to poison the bats before they flocked. In fact, there was just enough time to retrieve the backpack and escape from the bats' usual flight pattern towards the desert.

The road wasn't straight for more than a hundred feet at a time. To Paine, it seemed to wind malevolently, as if it were trying to slow him down, but at least he saw his pack sitting where he'd left it. A crow flew away from the pack as Paine approached.

From habit, Paine checked the pressure of the Cyano-gas canister as soon as he reached his backpack. The tank was good. The battery had its charge and the wire mesh was rolled as neatly as before. The crow had been searching for food, that was all. Paine slipped the pack on to his shoulders and started his return to the dome.

In spite of the uphill grade and the weight of the canister Paine maintained a rapid walk. The road was a murky blue under the sunlit tops of the walls, though rarely the low sun did penetrate a gap and throw Paine's hunchbacked shadow high up a wall. Once, a second shadow joined his and Paine looked up to see a crow running along the cliffs.

Paine cast his rope over the sandstone bridge and hoisted himself up from the road. From there, he worked his way through the lava field and circled to the west side of the sinkhole, where he huddled beneath a stone shelf and watched the last rays of the sun burning out on the dome.

Now that he knew exactly what he was going to do, Paine felt a rising confidence. He opened his pack and laid out his helmet and wire clipper. He wouldn't need gas mask or gloves. An easterly wind rose, driving his smell away from the cave. Everything was going well.

As the sun set, the eastern horizon turned a fleshy pink shading into purple. No bats emerged from the sinkhole. Other bats might greet the dusk, but vampires waited for true night. Then Paine heard them, the sound of their stirring, of wings and the rain of nitrous urine lightening them for flight. The distant mesa tops lived briefly as golden clouds, stars swam into sight and, in seconds, the world tipped into the dark.

Paine held his breath. For a final minute, the air above the canyon was still, and then the first bats rose from the sinkhole, spiralling up like leaves from a fire. The rest came like a black pillar mounting five hundred feet into the sky.

His bats.

Paine held on to the rock as if he were going to be sucked into the swirling column. Part of him was. Along with his father, Ochay, the years in Mexico. You are what you kill, Joe Paine had said. Too true. The bats and Paine had joined, become the head and tail of a single creature leading and pursuing itself. One beast conceived in death and nurtured by obesession. Mantled in evil. He'd lied to Anne. There was, past biological frameworks, a sense to everything. There was mutual grace in nature. The carnivore eliminated the weak, herbivores and birds transmitted seed, insects cleansed the soil, flowers lent beauty. Each in turn lent something in return for its life, all but one. There was that single instant, a freak, which gave nothing in return for its all-consuming thirst. The vampire, alone. Claustrophobia was not what Paine had suffered, it was a shudder in the presence of evil. He'd come to understand that but what he hadn't foreseen was that evil had its own gravity. Not until it had drawn him in and used him to push the bats where they had never been before, and multiplied a thousandfold its own energy and horror. Apocalypse needed no pale horse or fiery dragon, not with the bats as its engine and the plague as its seed. All thanks to Paine. All due to him.

But the end of the chase had come, and after the end he would be free.

Flattening into a cloud turning again and again into itself, spreading into a crescent until the centre moved forward and then forming one swift and undulating line, the bats flew east into the desert.

Paine gave the bats ten minutes before he unrolled the wire mesh and cut it in equal sections with the clipper. He wanted a snug fit over the sinkhole, no slack. One section of mesh he neatly re-rolled and carried to the far edge of the sinkhole, where he hammered a side of mesh into the dome with pitons. On all fours, he moved to the lip of the sinkhole nearer the rock shelf and tapped in more free pitons. He didn't need to drive the L-shaped pitons deep, just enough to keep the mesh tautly in place when it was spread. Underneath, he heard the anxious shifting of baby bats clinging to the ceiling. He knew of but couldn't hear the high-pitched distress call of the babies, calls that were too weak and too far behind the hunting wave of bats. Paine attached two electrical wires to the rolled mesh and led them back to the battery under the rock shelf. He set the battery voltage at 300, turned it on long enough to listen to one tock, and switched it off. That part of the trap was set.

The rock shelf itself was granite, harder than limestone. With a piton, Paine searched out a vertical fissure and then hammered the piton into the fissure. He tied his two fifty-foot ropes together, making a single hundred-foot length. One end, he tied to the piton. The other end, he knotted in a bowline through the canister handle. He twisted the timer on the canister valve. Every complete revolution set back the Cyanogas spray sixty minutes; he gave the timer twelve full turns, its limit.

Then, he turned the canister on its side and, lying on his stomach, started to roll it up the dome to the sinkhole. The granite shelf was fifty feet from the sinkhole; the tank would hang fifty feet below the sinkhole into the cave, well out of the bats' way when they returned, and when Paine would spread the net and throw the battery switch and wait. Until seven forty-five a.m., to be precise, when the first lethal vapour of the canister would rise. Nothing could be simpler.

Stars came out in clusters of light. Paine rolled the canister slowly up the dome. At the lip of the sinkhole, he gave the tank a final push that tilted it into the cave.

He grabbed the rope and let it play through his hand gradually, lowering the tank. Cautiously, he moved away from the sinkhole, halfway down the dome, before he played any more rope through his hand.

The rope stopped. The heavy tank was only about ten feet down into the cave, Paine estimated, but the rope must have snagged on something at the lip of the sinkhole. He tugged the rope. It wouldn't move.

Paine crawled back up the cave dome. Underneath his hands and knees, he felt the anxious scuttling of the infant bats, unsettled by the ominous appearance of the tank. 'Patience,' he whispered to them.

At the sinkhole, he found the problem. The rope had cut into and stuck in the soft limestone of the lip. He didn't like resting all his weight on his knees, but he pulled the rope free and raised the tank to set the rope at a different place.

There was another problem he saw as the tank rose. Somehow, the rope from the handle had twisted around the valve and jammed the timer. Paine lifted the canister gently out of the cave and set it on the edge of the sinkhole.

A single yank loosened the rope and Paine freed the valve. He lowered the tank into the cave again, watching with satisfaction as it descended into the dark, playing the rope tenderly until the canister had vanished, gently swinging in the shadows.

Paine leaned back and took a deep breath.

He heard the dome crack around him. He was already twisting as the sinkhole widened and the limestone under him dropped away. His hands clutched at rocks that crumbled with each grasp into a pale sand that streamed over him.

Paine fell. Feet first, to begin with. Then he spread his arms and legs like a man soaring and dark blew into his face. In front of him, he saw the canister rope measuring his dive.

He stopped short swinging fifty feet below the sinkhole. His wrist was tangled in the rope at the canister handle. The canister rocked coldly against his cheek, which was crushed over an eye. He tried to raise himself, but the arm caught in the rope was pulled out of his shoulder socket. His other arm couldn't reach around the canister.

He dangled.

The babies scuttled around the ceiling. In time, though, they settled down and waited.

Along with Paine.

Chapter Nine

'He didn't make it,' Youngman said. 'He'd be back by now if he made it.'

The two stars of Natupkom, Castor and Pollux, swung high overhead. Rising from the earth was Talawsohu, the Morning Star. Twice during the night, he and Anne had followed the flight of the bats. Their departure by sight. Their return, five hours later, by Paine's oscilloscope. That was five hours ago.

'I told him to wait.'

'Paine knows what he's doing. Here, eat something, you look terrible.' She offered him a slice of bread smeared with margarine. 'I'm sorry that's all that's left. And some beers.'

He shook his head. Even in the green glow of the scope, his skin was tinged with the ash of fatigue.

'He would have shot us if we went after him.'

'He won't shoot any more, he's past that.'

'He's all right. The best thing we can do is get to the highway so Chee will know to send a helicopter here and pick Paine up.'

Youngman turned the radio on again. The stations in Tuba City no longer played music. Long periods of dead air were punctuated by bulletins. Tuba City was nearing its second day of quarantine . . . Fifteen dead at Shongopovi, twelve at Walpi . . . Utah and New Mexico state lines were closed . . . the evacuation of Flagstaff was orderly . . . the situation was in hand . . .

'I'm going out to watch.' Youngman kissed Anne's hand. Let me know if you see anything on the screen.'

He got out and stood in the back of the Rover, looking up the road. Paine wasn't coming back. Instead of leaving for the cave when he should have, Paine had overstayed on the ridge. Even asleep, Youngman had done as Abner had asked. As Abner had predicted, how long ago? A week? Only that long? And a week from now, who or what would be left? What would have happened to anyone if a week ago a deputy had been able to read a dead man's sand painting?

As Youngman felt for a cigarette, his bandaged hand fell on his pocket. He drew out the datura root.

On his own, Youngman knew he didn't have the strength to go to the cave. He could barely walk and his hands were almost useless.

If only Paine had been right. If Paine had been the one man who could stop the bats.

Youngman bit into the root. The largest bite he could manage, although he didn't know how much he could handle. If he poisoned himself, Anne would drive him out of the canyon. If it was narcotic, they could go after Paine. What was there to lose? He let the bitterness pour down his throat.

After Talawsohu came Ponochona, the Dog Star, and night was complete, darkest before dawn. All night ceremonies ended with the appearance of Ponochona, and then the priests would wait for the sun to tell them whether the ceremonies had been carried out correctly. One error would cause the rising sun to bring in its right hand a rainbow of reversed colours. Youngman waited, his arms and legs rigid his mouth open, his heart slowing with every beat. His head lolled against the truck and his eyes followed the course of the stars, bright bats wheeling in a middle distance. The lights were all colours and in between were mixed auras, like coloured grains of sand. He measured out minutes to the rare beats of his heart. A morning breeze blew on the left side of his face and traced its way with infinite slowness to the right. Showers of turquoise obscured the stars and then the desert burst into flames that leaped from end to end of the eastern horizon. The canyon began sailing into the flames.

The flames covered Youngman and warmed him like a light blanket of gold. His body burned up and released him, letting him float upward. For a long time, he enjoyed nothingness, and for a long time he felt consciousness returning. Below him he found the world spinning slowly between two kachinas, one with a face of clouds and the other tarnished brown by the sun. They bowed to Youngman and gave the world a push.

The world was different. An ocean lapped against a canopy of trees. Between the trees he could see familiar rows of corn and elsewhere were square obelisks and temples like statues alive with stone faces of tigers and snakes and bats writhing, their mouths gaping. The corn was fat and the wells were full of clear water but the people were leaving, walking along the axis of the earth for hundreds of years until they stopped at an inland sea surrounded by volcanoes. On the sea islands grew pyramids and on the pyramids were steps mounted by blood-encrusted priests and guarded by soldiers dressed as animals. Yet some of the people left again, again walking the world's axis north until they reached the edge of a desert. Under his eyes new cities grew. Mesa Verde, Aztec, Wupatki, Keet Seel. Each built and at the height of its prosperity abandoned until the people were gathered for their last great migration into the desert itself. Into four groups they divided themselves and in four directions they left, making a cross over the land until more hundreds of years passed and they wheeled right, forming a swastika. As this swastika wheeled, they broke into smaller groups, all returning but all moving in circles until the land was a giant's pattern of moving swastikas and serpentines. A pueblo would live for an instant. Another group would find it and a spiral map of their predecessors' path and then turn in the opposite direction, one eddy twisting from another, yet always directed to the finally permanent gathering at the centre of the world. And there at the rim of the Black Mesa they finally did appear, at Orabi and Hotevilla and Shongopovi, without water, without fertile land, without friends, at the mercy of their gods.

Youngman saw himself, on his back, hands and feet outstretched, and covering the desert spinning slowly within a nimbus of yellow light.

He had finally arrived. He was ready.

'Feeling better?' Anne joined him.

'More myself.'

He took a deep, comfortable breath. The breeze of the dawn swayed a ringlet of soft hair at her temple and the slanting rays of the sun made her blue-brown eyes luminous.

'You know, you're very beautiful.' He got up.

'Yes, that's more like yourself. Come on, we'd better get ready if we're going to go.'

She climbed on the hood and handed down the unidirectional microphone to Youngman, who stowed the mike, amplifier, and oscilloscope in the rear of the truck. The equipment was almost weightless to Youngman. He looked at his hands and peeled off the bandages.

'What are you doing?' Anne saw the open cuts.

'Anne, I know how to stop them. I'm going to the cave.'

'You don't know where it is.'

'I have an idea.'

'Paine is—'

'Paine is dead. It's day, Anne. He's not back because he is dead. Isn't he?'

'If he is,' she faltered, 'it's all the more reason for us to go. I'm sorry I got you into this.'

'You didn't. Believe me, you didn't.'

Two hours before, he'd been almost in shock. The Youngman she saw now was casually using mutilated hands to remove his shirt.

'That was a very fast recovery, Youngman. Just about unbelievable. What is your idea?'

'Abner opened the ring. I'm going to shut it again.'

' "Shut the ring?" That doesn't make any sense to me, Youngman. You're talking like a medicine man. Make sense.'

'You mean, something called Cyanogas made sense.' Youngman ripped the back from his shirt to tie it Hopi-fashion around his head.

'Yes.'

'Paine made sense?'

'Yes.'

'And Paine is dead.'

Anne caught her words behind her teeth. The raw light of the rising sun threw blue shadows of the Rover and Youngman and her from the edge of the ridge to across the road. Youngman was talking suddenly on different levels.

'I don't understand,' she said.

'Don't understand. All I want is your trust.'

'But how can I trust you when I don't understand what you are doing?'

'That's why it's called trust. Your trust in something unscientific and unwhite. Don't you think it's about time we found out whether you do?'

'This is a good time,' she agreed. 'It's very unfair. We could hardly stay together if I say "No" right now. It's unfair because I love you.'

'Sometimes love isn't enough.'

Anne walked away so as not to see him. He decided to give her five minutes to make up her mind. She returned after only one.

'Let me put it this way,' she said. 'At the moment, for asking me a question like that, I don't love you, I hate you. I'll go with you, though. I wouldn't let you go without me.'

Which was not the same thing as complete trust, Youngman knew. But, a start.

The road had been built for high-wheeled Mexican ox carts, not a Land-Rover. Although Youngman released some air from the tyres and gained a couple of inches in roof clearance, hours were lost hacking with a shovel against crowding sandstone walls and low natural bridges. He didn't care how slow their progress was, how much backing up and road clearing they had to do; if Anne was going with him Youngman was determined to bring the shelter of the truck as well.

It was midday, halfway to exhaustion, when they came to the end of the road.

'What is it?' Anne pulled the hand brake.

'A mine.'

'I never heard of a mine up here.'

'Well, it hasn't been used for a while.' He intercepted the question in her eyes. 'About two hundred years.'

As they got out of the Rover, Anne began to call for Paine and Youngman stopped her.

'We'll find him.'

An ancient wooden wheel rested by the mouth of the mine entrance. There was no sign of Paine and the ground was too hard to pick up tracks. Anne looked anxiously around the cliffs that crowded against the narrow road. Along the edges of the cliffs, dark lava outcrops looked down.

'A mine and a road only Hopis know about? What's the secret?' she asked. 'What makes you think the bats are here?'

'I could be wrong. Want to stay here?'

'Together.' She fell in behind him.

As they stepped into the cave, black wings bolted over their heads. Youngman put his hand over Anne's scream and they watched four crows climbing into the sky.

'You okay?'

'A little edgy.'

Youngman took the flashlight away from her.

'Stay here.'

He went in alone.

It was as cool as a tomb. Not uncomfortable, though. Just as Abner had described it so many times. The walls of dank, velvet-black shale that the Castillo priests had whipped their Hopi slaves in to work. The ruts of overloaded carts. As Youngman went deeper he heard his footsteps resounding and muffled by the sweating walls. The entrance, and Anne, faded into a blur. Youngman swept the mine floor with his beam, looking for Paine. Nothing.

As he came to the end of the mine, a breeze tinged with ammonia drew by him. When he turned off his flashlight, a fainter light glowed on the end wall. The wall was a rotting blanket and the light was a hole.

Youngman took one look before he ripped the blanket apart and stepped through.

He could see he was in a tremendous limestone cave lit by an exposed sinkhole in its ceiling. Youngman had to crane his neck to see all of the ceiling and everywhere he looked were bats so thick they seemed to hang in layers, and as one bat shifted all the bats around shifted so that their daytime languor was marked by constant ripples. Over the floor was a brackish pool of urine and faeces. And there was the pueblo. And, beside the pool, a man clutching a red canister.

Youngman emerged from the mine ten minutes later dragging a rope. At the end of the rope, still locked together, were Paine and the canister. Paine's red-headed scalp hung sightly askew, like a cap, over his raw forehead. Stripes of pitch marked his shredded clothes. In the daylight, he seemed out of place, bizarre as a nightmare. Grotesque and reeking of ammonia. Youngman cut the wrist free and laid the dead man beside the cart wheel. Only then did he dare look at Anne.

'They're here.' She was staring at the mine.

'Oh, yeah. The bats are here.'

He watched her start to fall apart and pull herself back together. The dead-white pallor of her face turned into tears of anger.

'How did it happen?'

'There's a sinkhole over the cave. He fell in, tried to catch the rope and got his arm caught.' Youngman held up the frayed end of the rope. 'Maybe the rope broke before the bats came back, maybe he didn't feel a thing.'

Youngman doubted it. A good rope didn't saw itself apart, not unless there was something at the other end struggling and twisting for a long time.

'The tank, he didn't use it.' Anne wiped her eyes. 'It's the Cyanogas. We can use it for him. See, Youngman, we'll do what he was going to do.'

'No.'

'What do you mean?' Anne righted the canister. 'He told us all about it. He said it was foolproof.'

'Anne.'

'We'll do it his way. Just set the timer. It's easy.'

'Anne,' he knelt beside the canister with her and slapped the timer on the valve. It spun around. 'The fall broke it. It won't work.'

'Then how, damn it! What's your great idea? What did you bring to use?'

'Nothing, Anne. It's all here.'

While her eyes followed him furiously, Youngman went to the Rover for a blanket, which he laid over Paine. The smell of ammonia didn't only come from Paine any more, the mine was breathing it.

'You saw the bats.' Anne controlled herself.

'They're in a big cave at the end of the mine.' Youngman nodded at Paine's body. 'He had a lot more gear in his pack than the canister when he started out, you said. I think I know what he was up to at the sinkhole.'

'Can we reach the bats, that's all I want to know?'

'We can kill them. Isn't that enough?'

Youngman climbed on to the roof of the truck, from

which he saw a lava torso jutting from a cliff twenty feet above. He lassoed the torso.

'I'll be back,' he called.

He pulled himself up the wall to the cliff, where he stopped to rest out of Anne's sight. The narcotic datura was wearing off and his hands burned from the short climb. He bit off more of the root. Just enough to dull the pain, he hoped. When he'd licked his fingers with his dry tongue, he started scrambling up the dome of the cave.

Before he was halfway up the dome, he felt better, stronger. At the sinkhole's edge, he found metal mesh rolled over pitons and ready to be spread. Electrical wires and a severed rope led to a rock ledge, where he discovered Paine's battery and backpack of equipment. Youngman spread the mesh tight on the pitons, covering the hole, and started the battery going to electrify the mesh. From the backpack, he selected only the pick axe.

As he straightened up, the datura rushed to his head and he saw the sky become choked with clouds. All the clouds were red, spewing blood.

Youngman had been expecting something like that. He turned his back to the clouds and, his eyes down, worked his way to the road.

Anne was gone when he lowered himself on to the truck. She came out of the mine before he had a chance to call for her.

'There you are,' Youngman was relieved. 'I blocked their way out of the sinkhole. Paine had everything set up.'

'I saw you. I went in the cave.'

'Okay, good. Then you saw the bats.'

'I saw the houses, too. Youngman, those tales you told me about an underground city, they weren't just tales, were they?'

'Ruins of a pueblo, that's all. The desert is full of them.'

'Not in a cave. And the story about that flaming pit. If we went on another hundred yards would we find that, too?'

'What would it matter? So we found some ruins. We came here to find the bats and we did. You're not going to be scared of some old Indian witch stories.'

'It matters,' Anne said, 'because you knew what was in there and you didn't tell me. Do you believe in those stories? Do you?'

Youngman took a long time answering because he wanted to lie, it would have been such a comfort to lie, for her, for him. But Anne would hear the lie and despise him for it, as she should. So in the end, he didn't answer her at all.

'We're wasting time,' he said instead. 'Get all the blankets you can find in the truck.'

They hung a new blanket from the crossbeam that divided the mine from the cave, not only to block the light of the flashlight but to muffle the sound of their work. While Anne held the flashlight, Youngman swung the pick axe into the mine wall.

'See this,' he picked up the first chunk of shale dislodged. 'Saturated with oil. It'll burn like charcoal if we get it hot enough.'

'We're going to smoke them to death?'

'No. There's an oil seep somewhere in the cave, I smelled it. If we hit the seep, we'll get more than smoke.'

'That's going to take an awful lot of shale.'

'That's right.' Youngman dropped the rock on a blanket. He dug the pick axe into the wall again. Again. And again. The shale was soft and absorbed the blows rather than split. But a small pile of glossy chunks accumulated on the blanket. The pile grew. Holding the flashlight so that its beam was a target for the axe, Anne felt her resentment breaking down under the blows. Youngman took his shirt off. He didn't swing the axe as much as attack the wall with it. She watched the muscles of his arms and back jump with each stroke.

'You almost died two nights ago, Youngman. How can you do this now?'

'Well, hard labour's a funny thing,' he said between swings. 'You never forget how.'

The datura was working for him now. He was in control.

Anne took over with the axe while Youngman dragged the first blanket load of shale from the mine into the cave. By the angle of the light from the sinkhole, he could tell it was about two o'clock. He dragged the blanket across the cave floor to the pueblo ruins. His first step on a ladder rung splintered the entire ladder, but he was able to scale a mound of debris on to the remains of a plaza above the first-storey houses. A vapour of dust swirled around his feet. In the curve of the wall, four more storeys of ruins loomed over him. Youngman let the rocks spill from the blanket. A ring was what he needed, a solid ring of fire within the cave.

'Flea,' one of the doors whispered to him.

Youngman stumbled down from the rubble. The bats ignored him.

He went on with the digging, deliberately concentrating on the task at hand. The ring would have a circumference of 150 feet and he'd need fourteen piles of shale about ten feet apart, each pile about a foot high. His body became covered with black dust striped by rivulets of sweat. The same dust Abner had used. When he looked down on his chest he saw himself painted in spirals.

After carrying three more piles to the ruins in the cave, he was on the point of collapse. While Anne went to the truck for the last bottle of beer, he choked down more datura.

A cold sweat of shock poured from him. Within his head, he felt the datura coalescing bright and hot, like a second brain.

'Let me do some of the work,' Anne offered when she returned. 'You're going to kill yourself at this rate.'

'We're doing fine,' he said calmly.

'Youngman, let's run. Get out of here while we can.'

Pain and feeling drained from his hands, and he took the beer.

'Just don't go in the cave,' he said. 'Even if I call you, don't go in.'

He was done with the ruins. The next load of shale he dragged to the foot of the rubble, the sort of detritus of adobe and stones marked by an occasional pot shard that some people called history. The light from the sink-hole had swung high on to the plaza of the ruins, illuminating a standing tablet with the figure of a headless man. One corner of the stone tablet was broken off; it was the Fire Clan tablet stolen from the kiva of dead priests. Youngman was unsurprised until he started to gauge the time from the angle of the beam from the sinkhole, when he realized the tablet and the plaza were at the western end of the cave. The sun had moved to the east, backwards.

'Check the time on the truck clock,' he told Anne when he returned to the mine. 'Don't go by the sun, just the clock.'

'It's six o'clock,' she reported a minute later. 'But it's very light.'

Ninety minutes to sunset.

'Take the blanket off Paine,' he said.

He filled two blankets for a double load before he went into the cave again, where he started to widen the circle of piles around the pool on the cave floor. So far, he still hadn't seen any clear signs of the oil seep and he no longer smelt it. Overhead, the roof showed no more than a slow rousing of the bats, but he dumped the first pile as quietly as he could.

The second load of shale hissed out of the blanket as red sand. He felt the datura surge through his head.

'Flea. Flea, what are you doing? You have the datura.

282

We can talk. You're one of us. What are you doing now, Flea?'

The voice wasn't Abner's.

Youngman returned to the mine. Numbed, his body was starting to fail him and each blanket took longer to fill. The wounds on his hands were long since split open, making the axe hard to grip.

'Stop. There's only an hour left,' Anne told him. 'There must be enough shale in there.'

'Has to be a ring.'

'Why?'

He missed the wall and the force of his swing threw him against the shale. He fell on the blanket, blind until Anne wiped blood and sweat from his eyes.

'There's a towel in the Rover. I'll be back in a second.'

Alone in the mine, Youngman ate more datura and rubbed some into his hands. When Anne returned, he was hard at work again. The new cut on his brow had stopped bleeding.

'At least, let's bring the Rover in here and use it to cart the shale,' she said. 'The truck will fit.'

'It won't go under the beam into the cave, not unless we let all the air out of the tyres.'

'Then, let's do it.'

'No.' Youngman continued slashing at the glow of her flashlight on the black wall. 'You're going to get out of here in a hurry. You don't want to steer down that road on wheel rims.'

'You mean, *we're* going to get out of here.'

Dragging the next two blanket loads, Youngman

found the mine corridor becoming longer and narrower. His legs moved stiffly until he reached the cave, which was suffused by a cool, water-blue light.

Instead of shale piles, one great double serpentine covered the entire floor of the cave. The coils shifted with the lazy power of a huge snake, a snake without a head.

'I watched out for you, Flea. For her, too. For your sake. For the new world I'm making for you. That's why I'm doing all of this. For you.'

I understand, Youngman thought.

One spiral of the serpentine uncurled and reached out for Youngman to draw him in.

'Let me show you the new world, Flea. Let me show you.'

I'm sorry, Youngman thought. It's too late.

As the spiral coiled around him, he picked up the sharpest rock in the blanket and twisted its point into his bloody palm. He ground it into his hand, probing until the jagged point found the last neurons of pain, and then he clutched the rock tight in the open wound. The spiral receded and the whole length of the serpentine faded. He looked up through the blue mist to the ceiling of the cave, where a thousand hanging faces looked down.

Youngman emptied the blankets and hurried back to the mine. A wind followed and Anne's flashlight went out, plunging them into darkness.

'It didn't even dim,' she said. 'What do we do now?'

'Bring the truck up to the mine entrance and turn on the headlights. Run them on the battery.'

In the glare of the headlights, Youngman carved out two more piles of shale. The axe became too heavy to lift and in full view of Anne, he lifted the last of the datura root to his mouth. She shouted at him from the Rover, but her voice echoed confusingly through the mine.

'Getting dark,' he finally understood.

The two piles of shale he dragged into the cave were the last, the ring was complete. The voice was silent, but the ceiling had changed. There was a steady simmering among the bats, waves of arousal and short flights from one part of the roof to the other. He could hear the 'clicks' of their lower pitched chatter.

Youngman went out of the mine to the Rover. The road was dark under the cliffs barely trimmed in orange.

'The sun's going,' Anne said.

'Where's the siphon?'

'You didn't ask me to find it.'

'I know, but where is it?'

Youngman's face was black with dust, except for the red of his eyes. He was unrecognizable. Anne found a kit panel in the back of the Rover and in the panel a siphon tube with a bulb. Unasked by Youngman, she also took out two empty jerry-cans. She was halfway through filling up the second can when the siphon tube went dry.

'Nothing more in the tank. It's empty. How do we get out of here?'

'Roll. There's enough in the fuel line to get us started.'

'Okay,' she agreed. 'Be careful. I love you.'

'Yes. Keep the lights on so I can see my way out.'

'I'll be here.'

Youngman picked up a can in each hand and was about to go when he remembered something.

'Have you got a match?'

She put a book of matches in his pants.

'Good luck.'

He went into the mine. At the midway point, the mine curved and he left the illumination of the headlights behind him. The mine had been straight before. The jerry-cans grew heavier. Youngman could lift his feet no more than an inch. He reached the cave and, between the pool and the ruins, started pouring from the heavier can a line of gasoline connecting the ring of shale piles.

The sinkhole was a halo of light around which the cave ceiling vibrated. By the hundreds, bats spread their wings in anticipation of sunset and a steady rain of urine sprinkled the floor. Youngman concentrated on drawing his steady line of gasoline.

'Flea, look.'

Smoke drifted from the chimneys of the pueblo. The ladders stood strong and upright and poles with clan feathers marked the handsome houses. Up five storeys, windows were lit in welcome and on the inside walls Youngman saw the shadows of people. The smell of bread and the sounds of life spread through the cave.

'Stop, Flea. And look.'

The halo around the sinkhole diminished to a crescent. Around it, bats gathered so thickly they hung from each other and beneath the sinkhole massed a stationary cloud of wings. The musical laugh of a woman came from the pueblo.

He retraced his route across the peublo. He could hear children, the sound of men gambling, the gossip of girls, the boiling of stew in an oven. Each pile of shale was a bough of cottonwood and the broken Fire Clan tablet was whole and surrounded by prayer sticks. Gasoline hit the ground as blue cornmeal. From one house came a song he hadn't heard in years. 'Somewhere, somewhere, far away, Sibopay. What was I at Sibopay? When was I born? Where did I come from? Where am I going? What am I? I asked myself at Sibopay.' Out of the corner of his eye he saw people at the windows, faces that vanished when he looked up and reappeared as he looked away. After a day without food, the aroma of fresh piki bread was overpowering.

'Join them, Flea. They wait for you. Your people, Flea. Waiting for you.'

A white-bellied shrike flitted over Youngman's head and flew towards a row of stars. When it reached the stars, the bird's wings turned to leather and the stars became the last drops of sun on the rim of the sinkhole.

Youngman stumbled down from the pueblo. He only had to finish dousing the shale piles leading back to the mine.

'Flea, stay with us.'

Gasoline spilled over his pants. The more he poured,

the heavier the can grew, until he was dragging it along the ground.

Wing tips grazed walls, roof, and cave floor. By the hundreds, more bats dropped and spread their webbed hands. The cave was filled with thousands of them, a wheeling, living shadow going round and round, colour-blind eyes fixed on a final candlelight of sun on the sinkhole, waiting for their moment of emergence. Wings, eyes, mouths flashed past Youngman, rose like a wave to the sinkhole and fell away from the light.

Youngman poured out the second can of gasoline in a straight line in front of the mine exit. He'd light the ring of shale piles first and ignite the exit as he left. A bat flew over his shoulder. He didn't hear the bat's whisper or its change in tone. Two more bats flew by his face, their eyes turned on him. Another went by. He felt a slight nick. Blood flowed from his ear. A whisper spread through the cave up to where the hanging, pink newborn cried. Youngman shook his head at another bite along his neck. It was too dark now to see the bats coming at him anyway.

He pulled out the book of matches. As he started to light one, a wing knocked the book out of his hand. He went down on his hands and knees and felt the ground. Wings and teeth landed on his back. Something scuttled towards him along the floor. His fingers closed on the matches. Deliberately, he peeled another match from the book and struck it. A bat darted away from the flame and Youngman threw the match. He rolled away, crushing the bats on his back.

From the first burning shale pile, two blue flames raced to the other piles, meeting on the ruins. From each pile rose a flame thirty feet high. A new line of fire appeared and shot into the pool in the centre of the cave, which ignited into flat, glassy flame. A line of red swept into the ruins. Others blossomed into life from the ring and zigzagged over the floor and up the walls. Behind him, blocking the mine, was a sheet of fire.

The bats that weren't burning rose to the sinkhole and the electrified mesh. As a cloud, they boiled over the flames. Youngman turned in amazement. The entire cave was on fire, a palace of lights. More oil seams erupted in flame from the walls and the shale fires grew, spewing dense, black smoke.

For Youngman, bats and smoke became one, a one that took the shape of a giant crouched beneath the roof, a face of flames in agony over a ragged, black cloak. Blind, milky eyes stared in disbelief.

'FLEA! . . . WHY? . . . IT WAS FOR YOU . . . FOR YOU!'

'I know!' Youngman cried. Tears started from his eyes.

'EVERYTHING . . . FOR YOU!'

A truck pulled in front of Youngman and its doors swung open. Anne was at the wheel, shouting.

'Youngman! Youngman, here!'

Through the fire, he saw the pueblo melting. Adobe walls split into red dust. Windows raged. Inside, figures of flame danced wildly, running from room to room without escape.

'Youngman!' Anne screamed.

He fell into the truck and at once she swung the Rover around, clumsily on slashed tyres.

She aimed directly for the fire blocking the mine and broke through. Within the mine, the Rover careened off the walls. The last gas in the truck's fuel line ran out as they crashed on to the road, and from there they rolled, down, down, almost to the desert when the dome of the cave rose on a fireball into the sky.

Chapter Ten

The explosion ran like a pulse through a subterranean network of seeps and around the cave smaller caves erupted in series. Along a tracery of shale seams on the surface, blue flames spread like couriers, running parallel, converging and spreading again. Where vertical seams met, flames spewed through the canyon walls in search of more shale, which cracked and exposed rich veins of oil. Fire licked its way up the higher western plateau of the canyon, touching off fireballs that dwarfed the first, that rose into the night to rain fire on to the canyon. So the fire continued to spread, by the blackened teeth of basalt mines and across lava fields of twisting forms. The first fire engines and mobile lab from Tuba City tried to fight their way to the bat cave, only to retreat when the fire began to cut off the road behind them. They pulled back a full mile from the base of the canyon as Parks Department helicopters cruised overhead to release trails of phosphate-enriched water.

In the minutes before dawn, the fire subsided even as it widened. From one end to the other, Maski Canyon was lit by blue flames.

Youngman and Anne watched from the fire engines and emergency vehicles that huddled on the desert floor.

Standing on the hood of his car, Piggot watched the flames' progress through field-glasses.

'That first explosion lit up the mesa. Sounded like a bomb.' Walker Chee stepped on a cigarette butt. 'Whole canyon must be laced with oil and shale.'

Like camp fires, Youngman thought. The canyon was alive with blue camp fires. His face was blistered. His neck and ear were bandaged and a blanket covered his back.

Another oil seep erupted, orange turning to blue. Turbines wheezing in desperation, a helicopter peeled away from the rising flame.

'Useless. Absolutely useless.' Piggot jumped down from his car and threw his glasses on to the rear seat. 'That'll burn for years, maybe for ever. Kiss it goodbye, Chee.'

'Where're you going?'

'Venezuela, Indonesia, Alaska.' Piggot got into the front seat. 'Somewhere, someone wants to do business. All I gotta do is find him.'

'We have a contract!' Chee shouted after the moving car. He watched the rear lights of the Cadillac vanish before he turned back to the canyon, where he could watch two million dollars going up in smoke.

One of the Disease Control mobile labs took the space vacated by Piggot. A young investigator in vinyl coveralls, his fresh cheeks dusted with soot, eyed Youngman and Anne curiously before reporting to Chee.

'There's no way of telling when we can check out that cave. The main thing is, are all the bats dead?'

'Ask him.' Chee shrugged and walked away in disgust.

The investigator was eager but tentative about approaching Youngman. The Indian he saw was dark, as red-eyed as an animal, and naked to the waist.

'They're dead,' Youngman said.

'I hope that's correct. If they are, then the major vector of the disease is eliminated and the rest will be basically a quarantine operation.' The investigator studied Youngman more carefully. 'If you understand what I mean.'

The investigator's uncertainty reminded Youngman of Paine.

'I try,' Youngman said.

'And I hear that a man was left in the cave?'

'In the mine.'

'A friend?'

'Yes.' Youngman looked at Anne. 'The Hopi people owe him a great debt.'

The investigator made notes. He asked Anne about the fire, the cave, and the bats; she answered that they'd set the fire with gasoline, the cave was ordinary in all respects and that there was no chance of any of the bats escaping. While she talked, she slipped her arm through Youngman's. When he closed his notebook, the investigator was very pleased.

'Thank you. There's an ambulance on the way for the two of you. You'll be in a hospital for a couple of days of observation but I bet you can use the rest. You've had an amazing escape.'

'Do you think so?' Youngman asked flatly.

'Well . . . yes,' the investigator blurted. 'Unbelievable.'

'Good.'

The investigator went in some confusion back to his truck, and drove off to the rank of fire engines sitting out the dawn.

Youngman spread his blanket over Anne so that they could lean together. Around the canyon the sky paled.

'You're going to make Paine a hero, aren't you?' Anne said.

'He was.'

Or Abner was, and Harold, even Chee. Give them their due, everyone was right, Youngman thought. All but him, perhaps.

'But you did it,' she said.

'I don't know what I did. I hope no one ever knows what I did.'

The features of the canyon began to emerge in the morning light. The different coloured sandstone walls were all charred black. Cliffs, gutted, hollow-eyed, disjointed, wore a mask of black. Black smoke rode over the morning wind without moving.

'I hope I never know.'

The flame lights looked like the stars of a universe that had died and collapsed upon itself. As the sun rose at Youngman's back the stars faded and, one by one, disappeared.